THE WORLD'S CLASSICS

THE MACDERMOTS OF BALLYCLORAN

ANTHONY TROLLOPE (1815–82), the son of a failing London barrister, was brought up an awkward and unhappy youth amidst debt and privation. His mother maintained the family by writing, but Anthony's own first novel did not appear until 1847, when he had at length established a successful Civil Service career in the Post Office, from which he retired in 1867. After a slow start, he achieved fame, with 47 novels and some 16 other books, and sales sometimes topping 100,000. He was acclaimed an unsurpassed portraitist of the lives of the professional and landed classes, especially in his perennially popular *Chronicles of Barsetshire* (1855–67), and his six brilliant Palliser novels (1864–80). His fascinating *Autobiography* (1883) recounts his successes with an enthusiasm with stems from memories of a miserable youth. Throughout the 1870s he developed new styles of fiction, but was losing critical favour by the time of his death.

ROBERT TRACY is Professor of English at the University of California, Berkeley. He is the author of *Trollope's Later Novels* (1978), the translator of *Kamen'* (1913, 1916), poems by the Russian poet Osip Mandelstam, as *Stone* (1981), and has edited *The Aran Islands and other writings* by John Millington Synge (1962) and Trollope's *The Way We Live Now* (1974).

THE WORLD'S CLASSICS

ANTHONY TROLLOPE

The Macdermots of Ballycloran

Edited with an Introduction by
ROBERT TRACY

Oxford   New York
OXFORD UNIVERSITY PRESS

Oxford University Press, Walton Street, Oxford OX2 6DP

Oxford New York Toronto
Delhi Bombay Calcutta Madras Karachi
Kuala Lumpur Singapore Hong Kong Tokyo
Nairobi Dar es Salaam Cape Town
Melbourne Auckland Madrid

and associated companies in
Berlin Ibadan

Oxford is a trade mark of Oxford University Press

First published 1847
First issued as a World's Classics paperback 1989

British Library Cataloguing in Publication Data
Data available

Library of Congress Cataloging in Publication Data
Trollope, Anthony, 1815 1882.
The Macdermots of Ballycloran / Anthony Trollope ; edited with an
introduction by Robert Tracy.
p. cm.—(The World's classics) Bibliography: p.
I. Tracy, Robert, 1928- . II. Title. III. Series.
PR5684.M3 1989 88 38383
823'.8 —dc19

ISBN 0 19-282181-4

3 5 7 9 10 8 6 4 2

Printed in Great Britain by
BPCC Hazells Ltd
Aylesbury, Bucks.

CONTENTS

County Leitrim: the Macdermot Country

INTRODUCTION

Trollope begins *The Macdermots of Ballycloran* by describing his visit to the Irish village of Drumsna, the walk which led him to the ruins of a pretentious house, where he read 'The usual story' of folly and extravagance, and his subsequent opportunity to hear the unusual story of the Macdermots from 'the guard of the Boyle coach'. The novel we are about to read is a poor substitute, he declares, for the guard's racy narrative, the novelist himself merely an imperfect transcriber.

Pretending to be no more than the transmitter of another's story is a common narrative device, especially for a beginning novelist: Dickens claims only to be editing and arranging the records of the Pickwick Club. For Trollope, the son of a well-known writer, it was perhaps a necessary device, a shield against inevitable comparisons. It also allowed him to offer, then withhold, a narrative in Irish–English, enhanced with the drolleries expected of Irish narrators. This is to be a different kind of Irish story.

In *An Autobiography*, Trollope tells us a little more about the genesis of *The Macdermots*, and makes it clear that the tale was of his own invention. As a lonely child, he had developed a habit of telling himself stories—his 'castles in the air'—which he could sustain and develop in his mind 'for weeks, for months, if I remember rightly, from year to year'. After joining the Post Office, he resolved to supplement his income by writing novels, and began to search for a subject. Post Office business brought him to Drumsna in August 1843—'the postmaster had come to some sorrow about his money'—and there his friend John Merivale joined him for a brief stay. Among those ruins near Drumsna, Trollope's habit of narration, his resolve, and the spirit of the place fused, and he knew that he was ready to begin his first novel:

As we were taking a walk . . . we turned up through a deserted gateway, along a weedy, grass-grown avenue, till we came to the

modern ruins of a country house. It was one of the most melancholy
spots I ever visited . . . We wandered about the place, suggesting
to each other causes for the misery we saw there, and while I was
still among the ruined walls and decayed beams I fabricated the
plot of *The Macdermots of Ballycloran*. As to the plot itself, I do not
know that I ever made one so good,—or, at any rate, one so susceptible of pathos. I am aware that I broke down in the telling, not
having yet studied the art. Nevertheless, *The Macdermots* is a good
novel, and worth reading by anyone who wishes to understand
what Irish life was before the potato disease, the famine, and the
Encumbered Estates Bill.
    When my friend left me, I set to work and wrote the first chapter
or two. Up to this time I had continued that practice of castle-
building . . . but now the castle I built was among the ruins of that
old house.[1]

The would-be novelist had recently, at the age of 26,
taken stock—and taken charge—of his life. In *An
Autobiography* he describes his loneliness as a child, his misery
as a day-boy at Harrow and Winchester, scorned by the fee-
paying pupils as 'a wretched farmer's boy, reeking from a
dunghill' (*Autobiography*, 12). He describes his father's
retreat, first from his profession as barrister, then from any
active life; his attempts to live as a landed gentleman; his
failures, his near arrest for debt—events that helped to
create the shabby, confused, reclusive, irascible figure of old
Larry Macdermot, incapable of business or of any effort on
his own behalf, convinced of his own gentility, threatened,
like Thomas Trollope, with arrest for debt. Larry is the first
of Trollope's haggard solitaries—Mr Crawley, Mr Kennedy, Louis Trevelyan, Cousin Henry. The type was to
haunt him throughout his career as a novelist. If Trollope
built his castle of fiction among the ruins of 'Ballycloran', its
materials came from the gloomy and 'wretched tumbledown farmhouse' (*Autobiography*, 11) of his childhood.
Trollope's schooldays at Harrow and Winchester were
followed by a series of false starts: a few weeks teaching, a
scheme for a career in the Austrian cavalry. In November

    [1] Anthony Trollope, *An Autobiography* (London: Oxford University
Press, 1950), 42–3, 70–1. All subsequent references to *An Autobiography* will
be to this edition.

1834 a family friend arranged his appointment as a clerk in the Secretary's Office at the General Post Office in London, the administrative centre of the British postal system. His duties were to record, copy, and file official correspondence.

Trollope spent the next seven years at the General Post Office. In *An Autobiography* he makes much of his own idleness and inefficiency, and of his superiors' dissatisfaction with his work. Nevertheless, he did advance both in salary —£90 per year in 1834, £140 by 1841—and in responsibility. But he describes his first twenty-six years as 'years of suffering, disgrace, and inward remorse . . . I was wretched' (*Autobiography*, 60). Then, in July 1841, convinced 'that my life was taking me downwards to the lowest pits' (*Autobiography*, 58), Trollope learned of a vacancy in the Irish branch of the postal service, as Surveyor's Clerk—a Surveyor was responsible for the general superintendence of postal services, postmasters, and postal routes—for the Central District of Ireland, to be stationed at Banagher, in King's County (now County Offaly), a busy river port on the River Shannon.

'There was . . . a conviction that nothing could be worse than the berth of a surveyor's clerk in Ireland.' But Trollope approaches his superior 'boldly, and volunteered for Ireland if he would send me. He was glad to be so rid of me, and I went . . . This was the first good fortune of my life . . . from the day on which I set my foot in Ireland all . . . evils went away from me. Since that time who has had a happier life than mine?' (*Autobiography*, 58–60). Though his salary was reduced to £100, Ireland was cheaper than London, and Trollope found that travel allowances raised his income to about £300 (the Drumsna postmaster's yearly salary was £25 in 1841, while a mail coach guard earned £100).

Trollope enjoyed the work, he enjoyed Banagher, and he liked the Irish. 'It was altogether a very jolly life that I led in Ireland', he declares. He found the people 'good-humoured, clever—the working classes very much more intelligent than those of England—economical, and hospitable', though he added, 'they are perverse, irrational and but little bound by the love of truth' (*Autobiography*, 65). He quickly learned his

new tasks, partly by making a defaulting postmaster explain
how accounts were to be kept, then dismissing the man. He
even managed to get along with his Surveyor, the notoriously
difficult James Drought.[2]

Trollope's willingness to curb his own temper and work
successfully with Drought suggests how determined he was
to change his life. Not 'many months passed before I found
that my services were valued', he writes proudly. 'Before a
year was over, I had acquired the character of a thoroughly
good public servant' (*Autobiography*, 63). Until his retirement
in 1867, Trollope's Post Office career was a distinguished
one. In Ireland he rose to be Surveyor of the Northern
District, then Surveyor for the Eastern District of England,
and negotiated postal treaties with Egypt and the United
States.

The Ireland that Trollope came to know in the early 1840s
was about to vanish forever in the overwhelming catastrophe
of the Great Famine of 1845–9, when the potato, the staple
diet of the people, succumbed to blight for five successive
years. The population shrank from about eight to six-and-a-
half million by 1851. Many died of starvation or of the
'famine fever'. Many others emigrated to Britain, Canada,
or the United States. The Famine hit hardest in the west and
south-west, areas Trollope knew well. There, roads and services were least developed, and land was poor. Population
pressures had allowed landlords to raise rents until tenants
were pauperized. Some could not pay their rents, and so
their landlords were unable to pay their own debts. The
destruction or displacement of the peasantry was soon
followed by the disappearance of marginal landlords like the
Macdermots. Trollope's description of their poverty, and
the threat of eviction that hangs over them, was at once
accurate and prophetic. It indicates how thoroughly he had

---

[2] 'I have frequently reported him for systematic obstruction to my
orders, and for insubordination . . . I consider Mr Drought unfitted to be
retained in the public service', declared the Secretary of the Irish Post Office
in 1854, during an angry and extensive correspondence about Drought's
activities, which culminated in Drought's dismissal after thirty-seven years
of service. See *House of Commons Parliamentary Papers* 1860, LXII 129.

come to understand his new country and its problems. A few years later, writing on the condition of Ireland in the *Examiner*, he described the debt-encumbered landlord of the post-Famine years in terms that remind us of his novel: 'The landlord . . . holds on to the wreck of the ship . . . his acres lie on his hands, and he has not capital to farm them . . . his coat and hat become worn and shabby; he takes to his house and locks his door, fearing unfriendly visitors; here, within doors, the lack of luxuries is quickly followed by the want of necessaries . . .' (*Examiner*, 1 June 1850).[3]

If Trollope anticipated some of the Famine's effects in his novel—the awful rapacious hunger of Andy McEvoy is uncannily prophetic—the Famine also seems to have affected the novel's reception. He finished *The Macdermots* in July 1845. On 9 September the *Dublin Evening Post* reported the first signs of potato blight. Six days later, Trollope signed an agreement granting him half the book's future profits, if any, with his London publisher, Thomas Newby. When *The Macdermots* appeared, in mid-March 1847, the Famine had been raging for two years. British newspapers regularly printed graphic accounts of Irish poverty, starvation, and disease. The government, still unable or unwilling to grasp the extent of the disaster, could not settle on a policy. Were the Irish simply to be fed, or should they be made to work on relief projects to earn their food? Would public charity sap initiative, independence, and industrious habits? Should recipients of charity be forced to abandon their cabins and enter the workhouse? Who was to pay? There were constant appeals to private charity. Novel readers perhaps felt that they were hearing too much about Irish misery, and that a novel about Ireland would be depressing.

The leading critical journals of the day praised *The Macdermots*, but the novel did not sell. Neither did its two successors, another Irish novel, *The Kellys and the O'Kellys* (1848), and *La Vendée* (1850), a novel about the French Revolution. Trollope failed with a play, an Irish guidebook,

---

[3] 'The Real Condition of Ireland', *Examiner*, 1 June 1850, reprinted in Helen Garlinghouse King, 'Trollope's Letters to the *Examiner*', *Princeton University Library Chronicle* 26 (Winter 1965), 71–101.

and *The New Zealander*, a 'condition of England' declamation, before he began his successful career with the first of the Barchester novels, *The Warden* (1855).

In *An Autobiography*, Trollope insists on the utter failure of *The Macdermots*. 'I was sure that the book would fail, and it did fail most absolutely', he boasts.

I never heard of a person reading it in those days. If there was any notice taken of it by any critic of the day, I did not see it . . . after the publication I never said a word about the book, even to my wife . . . In Ireland, I think that no one knew that I had written a novel. But I went on writing. (75)

It is hard to believe that a beginning novelist, a member of a writing family, really did not know that the *Athenaeum* and *John Bull* had reviewed *The Macdermots* favourably, and that other journals had praised aspects of the book. Trollope also fails to mention that Chapman and Hall, his usual publishers after 1858, reissued the novel in 1860, and several times thereafter; it was apparently at this time that Trollope made revisions and shortened it by three chapters. His description of *The Macdermots* as a failure, indeed as a kind of shameful secret, is intended to serve the theme of *An Autobiography*: Trollope's rise from poverty, scorn, and obscurity to success through perseverance, hard work, and the exercise of underestimated powers. The *Athenaeum* reviewer responded to the novel accurately: 'Twenty years ago 'The Macdermots' would have made a reputation for its author. Now, those who read it will join, we have little doubt, in our verdict: but their number will be fewer'.[4]

Nor did *The Macdermots* lack appreciative Irish readers. William Gregory of Coole Park, County Galway, Trollope's friend and schoolfellow, believed that Trollope had written the best Irish novel in fifty years—that is, since Maria Edgeworth's *Castle Rackrent* (1800). So did Sir Patrick O'Brien, who represented King's County in Parliament.[5]

---

[4] *Athenaeum*, 15 May 1847, reprinted in *Trollope: the Critical Heritage*, ed. Donald Smalley (London: Routledge and Kegan Paul, 1969), 548.

[5] T. H. S. Escott, *Anthony Trollope: his Public Services, Private Friends, and Literary Originals* (1913; repr. Port Washington, N.Y.: Kennikat Press, 1967), 61.

INTRODUCTION xiii

In 1849 Isaac Butt, later the founder of the Home Rule movement, showed how well he knew the trial scenes in the novel.
Cross-examining Trollope at the trial of a postmistress for
theft—Trollope had ingeniously caught her by tracking a
marked coin through a series of post offices—Butt asked,

Mr. Butt: Do you know *The Macdermots of Ballycloran* [laughter]?
Mr. Trollope: I know of a book by that name.
Mr. Butt: Do you remember the barrister of the name of Allwind
  [laughter]?
Mr. Trollope: I do.
Mr. Butt: And another named O'Napper.
Mr. Trollope: Yes.
Mr. Butt: I believe in drawing that character, it was your intention
  to favour the world with the beau ideal of a good cross-examiner?
Mr. Trollope: Yes. I dreamed of you [loud laughter].[6]

Trollope earned the attention of his readers, Irish and
English, by his novel's merits. Thirty years later he listed
them as 'truth, freshness, and a certain tragic
earnestness'.[7] He was accurate about Irish speech, attitudes, and customs, and he had begun to observe the Irish
mind. Like Gerald Griffin, whose *The Collegians* (1829) he
admired, Trollope 'had not written a novel *about* Ireland; he
had written an Irish novel'.[8]

Trollope's unusual daring and commitment are implicit
in the opening paragraph of *The Macdermots*, when he turns
away from the Anglo-Irish attractions of Sir Gilbert King's
demesne—recommended to the traveller by contemporary
gazetteers and road-books—and instead seeks out the ruins
that become a metaphor for the ruined Irish family he is to
portray. This novel is not to be about the Anglo-Irish gentry
and their Irish retainers, who people the works of Maria
Edgeworth, Charles Lever, and Somerville and Ross, but
about the obscure survivors of the old Irish Catholic gentry,

[6] *Trollope: Interviews and Recollections*, ed. R. C. Terry (London: Macmillan, 1987), 44.
[7] *The Letters of Anthony Trollope*, ed. N. John Hall (2 vols.; Stanford:
Stanford University Press, 1983), II, 613.
[8] Thomas Flanagan, *The Irish Novelists 1800–1850* (New York: Colum-
bia University Press, 1959), 230.

trapped in the ironies and anomalies of their position. Their ancestors once ruled Connaught. Now the Macdermots cling precariously to a few impoverished acres, a tumbledown house, and what remains of traditional deference to 'the ould blood'. They are doubly marginal, excluded from the society of their fellow landlords by religion and poverty, and from the peasantry by their still-remembered rank.

Trollope's brief sketch of the Macdermot genealogy is a little condescending. He seems uncomfortable with claims to rank not recognized by British usage. But, after blaming their present poverty on a foolish determination to marry for blood rather than money—and Irish blood at that—Trollope develops the characters of Larry, Thady, and Feemy in such a way as to recognize the tragic potential in their position, and to show how Irish history, Irish conditions, and Irish enmities shape their destinies. If their immediate poverty is caused by the unpaid and unpayable debt to Flannelly, who holds the mortgage on Ballycloran, it is also more remotely due to the long years of confiscations and penal laws which stripped the Irish Catholic gentry of their lands. Flannelly holds the mortgage because he built the Macdermots' expensive and pretentious house, their effort to assert their unrecognized dignity with a house like those of their Anglo-Irish neighbours.

Old Larry Macdermot, brooding alone over his misfortunes, suspects that even his own son is plotting against him. His isolation recalls the cautious reclusive life of the Catholic gentry under the Penal Laws. Thady struggles hopelessly to make the estate earn enough to pay interest on the debt. He is trapped in his obligations, half eager for some violent act. As for Feemy, she anticipates many later Trollope heroines: she has gentle blood but no money. Her options are extremely limited. The Anglo-Irish will have nothing to do with her. Catholic gentry are few and often as poor as herself. She cannot descend into the peasantry or the world of small tradesmen. Not surprisingly, she spends her time reading romantic novels, Gothic thrillers which often feature isolated and threatened young women of noble lineage, rescued at last and restored to their rightful eminence. Only

Captain Ussher, an outsider in County Leitrim, illegitimate, a man without lineage, shows any interest in her, and
even he has no thought of marrying so disadvantageously.
Her isolation and romantic dreams make her all too
vulnerable.

Trollope lived and wrote in Ireland at the time of Daniel
O'Connell's second great crusade. O'Connell had led the
successful fight for Catholic Emancipation in 1829. In 1840
he began his campaign for Repeal of the Union—that union
of the British and Irish parliaments accomplished in
1800—and the restoration of an Irish Parliament. Trollope
could not have been unaware of countless songs, poems, car-
toons, and patriotic orations portraying Ireland as a lovely
young woman, helpless, poor, and victimized by a
masculine England: Kathleen ni Houlihan, Banba, Dark
Rosaleen. Like the seventeenth- and eighteenth-century
Gaelic poems which invented the image of Ireland as
woman-victim, these depictions artfully made sexual ex-
ploitation a political metaphor. Kathleen ni Houlihan has
lost her land and her rights. She has been violated, raped,
by England. Some day her destined husband will come and
restore her. By making Feemy's seducer a uniformed police
officer in the service of Britain, particularly zealous in pursu-
ing illicit distillers who consider themselves rebels, Trollope
adds a political dimension to Feemy's seduction and
Ussher's death.

This double aspect of Feemy's seduction becomes crucial
when Trollope makes Thady's fate turn on the blurred
distinction between Ussher as sexual exploiter and Ussher as
zealous British official. Thady kills Ussher when he comes
upon him at night, in the grounds of Ballycloran, 'half dragging, half carrying' the senseless Feemy, and hears him 'say
loudly, and somewhat angrily, "This is d—d nonsense,
Feemy! you know you must come now." ' Thady does not
know that Feemy has agreed to run off with Ussher, even
though she suspects she is to be his mistress, not his wife.
Already pregnant with his child, she has fainted under the
stress of the moment. Thady strikes at Ussher to defend his
sister, as he thinks, from abduction. The blow is fatal.

Thady is executed because most of the local Anglo-Irish gentry and the authorities consider the murder of Ussher a political crime, an act of rebellion against British rule. Thady has been seen earlier drinking with the local 'Ribbonmen'—allegedly political conspirators—who are known to resent Ussher's police activities. A combination of misleading appearances, perjured testimony, Anglo-Irish hostility, and official belief in a widespread conspiracy destroys Thady. He is a victim of Irish history and English politics. Counsellor O'Malley, who defends Thady in court, correctly predicts that an appeal for mercy to the Lord Lieutenant, the representative of the Crown in Ireland, will not succeed, out of fear that the Tory opposition in Parliament will portray leniency as weakness in the face of rebellion. Thady dies because he can be made to look like an Irish political assassin rather than a man defending his sister's honour.

Ussher's death may echo the killing of one Captain M'Leod, a very active magistrate at Ballinamore, who was shot from ambush on the night of 29 January 1845, as he stood in a gentleman's drive waiting for the gates to be opened. M'Leod had recently refused bail to 'Molly Maguire's Sons', the local group of nocturnal rebels. The shooting provoked initial outrage, but a month later a Dublin paper hinted that M'Leod's murderer was not a peasant, and had killed him for personal rather than political reasons (*Times* 5 Feb., 3 Mar. 1845).

Ribbonism—or Ribandism, as the *Times* called it—was already an obsolete term in the 1830s, the period of the story. The existence of Ribbonism as a national, or as a truly political movement at any time is doubtful, though it figured as such in the nightmares of Anglo-Ireland. In various localities, at various times, tenants and landless men burned houses, barns, and ricks, broke fences, and attacked bailiffs or landlords, or sometimes those who leased land from which a previous tenant had been evicted. These individual and local acts of anger or revenge were represented, sometimes by letters or proclamations from the agitators themselves, as the acts of a vast national conspiracy against

private property and British rule. Trollope makes it clear
that Joe Reynolds and his gang are not political conspirators
but petty criminals. 'Ribbonism, about 183–, was again
becoming very prevalent in parts of Ireland', he comments,
a little skeptically:

> at any rate so said the stipendiary magistrates and the inspectors
> of police; and if they said true, County Leitrim was full of ribbon-
> men . . . Joe was aware that he was a marked man, and con-
> sequently, if not actually a ribbonman, was very well inclined to
> that or anything else, which might be inimical to gaols, police-
> men, inspectors, gaugers, or any other recognised authority; in
> fact, he was a reckless man, originally rendered so by inability to
> pay high rent for miserably bad land, and afterwards becoming
> doubly so from having recourse to illegal means to ease him of his
> difficulties. (37)

Joe Reynolds and his gang want Ussher out of the way
because he has seriously interfered with their distilling
activities. They half believe that these activities are a kind
of political conspiracy, and dignify them with oaths and
rituals. Not for the last time, ordinary criminal acts are
disguised as acts of rebellion.

Trollope's recognition that his characters, like nineteenth-
century Ireland, are trapped in history, binds the story
closely to its locale. He is careful to depict that locale
accurately, in physical details and in attitudes. The towns of
Mohill and Carrick-on-Shannon were much as he describes
them. Thady's flight from Ballycloran to Aughacashel can
be traced on a map, and Trollope—who made a practice of
accompanying rural postmen on their rounds—knows how
long it would take. The Ordnance Survey calls the mountain
where Thady took refuge Slieve Anierin (Iron Mountain),
but Trollope calls it Aughacashel, the name used by those
who lived on its southern slopes, where there is a townland,
a house, and a small river of that name. Loch Driney is
officially Lough Scur, but Driney House, beside the lake in
Driney townland, may have supplied an alternate locally
used name.

Contemporary travellers authenticate Trollope's descriptions of the one-room peasant cabins where Thady finds

refuge: Corney Dolan's, furnished only with a single bed and 'two rude stools' (401), its hearth an open fire in the middle of the floor, and Andy McEvoy's, which boasts a second bed, 'if a filthy, ragged cotton tick filled with straw, and lying on the ground, could be called a bed' (414). McEvoy's cabin is high on the mountain, on land too poor to farm, but farmed anyway in the crowded years before the Famine. 'Below these ridges the economist-historian draws a line, and calls it the starvation-line', Sean O'Faolain observes. 'That century could not afford to make such a distinction'.[9]

Trollope knew that there was a bridewell at Ballinamore, and that the Carrick jail had solitary cells. He knew that Catholic churches in Ireland were called chapels, and that there was no chapel in Drumsna at the time of his story. He knew that two Catholic priests served the parish in which Drumsna is located. He knew what tunes an Irish piper would play at a wedding, and that pipers were often blind. He knew that Andy McEvoy's daughter would sleep naked, and dress before strangers 'with no feeling of conventional modesty' (415). He knew how Feemy would dress when at home, and noted the dirty undergarment beneath that 'dreadful gap' (104) in her shabby gown. He knew how McKeon and his cronies would behave on the eve of the Carrick races, and does not omit the drunken officer vomiting over Keegan's shoes (316).

Irish names indicate descent from a common ancestor, and were highly localized until the Famine. To some degree they are localized still. With or without the prefixes O or Mac, Donovan, Keefe, and Sullivan are County Cork names, Doherty is Donegal, Tracy is Fermanagh or Limerick, Fitzgerald is Kerry. Trollope's secondary characters bear names indigenous to County Leitrim, or the counties immediately adjacent: Reynolds, Keegan, McKeon, Dolan, Brady. Anglo-Irish names are not so localized, but Trollope may have known, or half remembered, that a Brown family

[9] Sean O'Faolain, *King of the Beggars: a Life of Daniel O'Connell* (1938; repr. Dublin; Poolbeg Press, 1980), 144.

was settled at Mount Brown in County Roscommon, about
fifteen miles south of Carrick. When he described the
squalor of Mohill, and anticipated Dickens's attack on
'telescopic philanthropy' in *Bleak House* (1852–3) by describing the absentee Lord Birmingham, indifferent to his
tenants' misery but busy helping Polish refugees and West
Indian slaves, Trollope would have known that the town
belonged to the Earl of Leitrim. But did he know that the
Earl's son and heir, Viscount Clements, bore the Christian
names Robert Bermingham?

Even the Macdermots have their origin in reality. The
Macdermots did once rule much of Connaught. The chief
of the family was able to preserve a tiny fragment of the
ancestral lands after the Cromwellian and Williamite confiscations, and settled at Coolavin in County Sligo. The head
of the family, The Macdermot—always spelled with a single
't'—was and is called the Prince of Coolavin. Touring Ireland
in 1776, Arthur Young described the chieftain of that time,
who, 'though he has not above £100 a year, will not admit his
children to sit down in his presence'. Young adds a brief anec-
dote about The Macdermot's indifference to British notions of
rank and prestige: 'Lord Kingsborough, Mr. Ponsonby, Mr.
O'Hara, Mr. Sandford, &c. came to see him, and his address
was curious: "*O'Hara! you are welcome; Sandford, I am glad to see
your mother's son*: (his mother was an O'Brien) *as to the rest of ye,
come in as ye can*" '.[10] Trollope makes his fictional characters
members of this real family.

Trollope's accuracy is not limited to topography, social
customs, and historical detail. He can imagine a gesture or
an action that fully reveals a character: Larry Macdermot
raising an empty glass to his lips when disturbed by a loud
noise (382), Mr. O'Malley half concealing himself in the
darkened courtroom to hear the verdict, sympathetic to his
client but embarrassed at failing to maintain the professional
indifference expected of him (606). This psychological
accuracy can combine with social and historical accuracy. In

[10] Arthur Young, *A Tour in Ireland (1776–1779)*, ed. Arthur Woolaston
Hutton (London: George Bell, 1892), i. 219.

his portrait of Andy McEvoy, that silent, idle, apathetic old man in the mountain cabin, Trollope shows us the hopeless torpor of the peasantry. Sean O'Faolain has defined the 'horror' of eighteenth- and nineteenth-century peasant Ireland as a 'mental horror—the murder of the mind . . . spiritual chloroform . . . creeping paralysis of the soul'[11]. For the fugitive Thady, McEvoy in his 'apathy and look of idle contentment' becomes 'that horrid man' (427–8). McEvoy's company, as he sits 'there so quiet, doing nothing—saying nothing—looking at nothing—and apparently thinking of nothing' is like 'sitting with a dead body or a ghost' (418). Thady's own mind has been busy with problems and expedients to keep Ballycloran going. Now it is busy with the memory of his crime, plans for escape, fears of capture, imprisonment, execution. He finds McEvoy's blank presence more horrifying than his own thoughts, a grim version of that paralysis Joyce would portray in *Dubliners*.

Writing about Ireland, Trollope also needed to achieve linguistic accuracy in representing Irish people speaking English. Earlier Irish novelists had frequently used Irish-English primarily for comic effect. By not making the guard of the Boyle coach his narrator, Trollope deliberately avoids any temptation to let an Irish narrator tell long droll stories in Irish-English, as Mickey Free does in Charles Lever's *Charles O'Malley* (1840–1), or Andy in Samuel Lover's *Handy Andy* (1842). Father John teases Denis McGovery to provoke some comic dialogue, but generally Trollope uses Irish-English for accuracy rather than to make his characters seem quaint or ridiculous. They are not stage-Irish, but men and women who talk after the manner of their time and place and have important subjects to discuss with one another. Trollope's use of forms and spelling usually associated with the grotesque and the facetious makes his tragic tale even more sombre.

Trollope solves his problems of language with considerable skill. His own standard English, analytic in tone

[11] O'Faolain, 140.

and slightly detached, controls the narrative. Within the story, certain characters—the upstart Keegan, the sportsmen celebrating the Carrick races, Counsellor O'Malley, Father John—speak standard English, with an occasional Hibernicism, though the priest sometimes adopts the idiom of his parishioners, especially with Denis McGovery.

Writing at a time of linguistic displacement in Ireland, Trollope implicitly reminds us how English is advancing. English had begun to invade Irish-speaking areas even before the Famine, and O'Connell had urged his followers to abandon the native language if they wished to succeed. The Catholic Church was also promoting English, as were the new state-schools. Thady is defended and condemned by speakers of standard English, in a British court where the Irish-English usages of Pat Brady are sharply questioned. Thady and Feemy are imprisoned in their Irish-English. Ussher seduces and evades Feemy in standard English. After his death, she is essentially incapable of speech, and her silence dooms Thady. When Thady takes refuge at Aughacashel, he finds that old Andy McEvoy cannot speak English. Thady shifts to Irish, only to find that Andy has nothing to say.

Between Andy's silenced Irish and standard English lies Irish-English, which often preserves words or pronunciations abandoned by standard-English speakers, and also borrows Irish words and syntax. Douglas Hyde, Lady Gregory, and John Synge would shape Irish-English into a powerful and distinctive literary instrument at the end of the nineteenth century. Trollope had no such ambition, but he recognized and accurately transcribed its peculiarities, even recording differences in usage between speakers of different social status. Thady is poorly educated, but his Irish-English is closer to standard English than Pat Brady's, and Brady's is closer than the speech of Joe Reynolds and Corney Dolan. In his brief time in Ireland, Trollope had clearly studied Irish discourse, as he heard it all around him and as he found it recorded in the Irish novels he read.

Trollope's dialogue accurately reproduces features of Irish-English that have been noted by linguists: the substitu-

tion of short -i for e (rints/rents, niver/never, thim/them);
the lengthened -o (ould/old, cowld/cold); the softening of
initial d (dhrink/drink) and of hard t (gutther/gutter). The
most frequent of these is the shift of the dipthong -ea to a
broad -a: mane/mean, plaze/please, tay/tea, aisy/easy,
which preserves the standard English pronunciation of the
early eighteenth century. 'Here Thou, Great *Anna*! whom
three realms obey,' writes Pope, 'Dost sometimes Counsel
take—and sometimes *Tea*' (*The Rape of the Lock*, III. 7–8).

Trollope had met Charles Lever, the author of *Charles
O'Malley*, at Coole Park, and he twice refers to Lever's novel
in *The Macdermots*. *Charles O'Malley* was probably Trollope's
manual of instruction in the literary use of Irish-English,
supplementing his own observations. Most of the Irish-
English forms and Irish words Trollope uses appear there,
though his two different versions of the Irish *Seamus an
píobaire*, Seamus the Piper—Shamus na Pe'bria, Shamuth
na Pibu'a (107, 190)—suggest that he was trying to
reproduce phonetically a phrase he had heard and
remembered.

Ballycloran seems to be Trollope's deliberate—and
correct—invention of an Irish place name. Nowhere in
Ireland is there a townland, parish, village, or barony of
Ballycloran, though there are many places named Cloran, or
some variant thereof. Trollope invented a name that suggests stony ground, a profitless estate, with little chance for
material or spiritual sustenance: *Baile cloichráin*, the place of
stones, stonestead.

We can only speculate about Trollope's knowledge of
Irish, but there is no doubt about his knowledge of Irish fiction. He learned about his new country chiefly by living and
working in it, but also by reading the Irish novelists,[12]
whose works became his partial models, and in one case his
foil. Trollope specifically refers to three of these novelists in
The Macdermots. As Father John travels to Dublin to engage
a lawyer for Thady, in a chapter deleted from the 1860 text,
the coach passes 'the residence of the authoress of whom

[12] Escott, 53–4.

Ireland may well be so proud; I doubt,' Trollope adds, 'if
any travel that road, however poor or uneducated they may
be, without looking with some degree of interest to the house
where Maria Edgeworth is still living, and where she has
passed the greatest part of so long and valuable a life' (642).
In the same chapter he compares two of the coach passengers
to Frank Webber, a rambunctious student in *Charles
O'Malley*, a novel that has its place in Father John's library.
Chapter XVII, 'Sports of the West', pays tribute, in title
and action, to William Maxwell's *Wild Sports of the West*
(1832), an early celebration of the hard-riding, hard-
drinking country gentlemen of the West of Ireland.

Trollope's Joe Reynolds and the other gang members
probably owe something to William Carleton's novels and
stories, especially *Fardorougha the Miser* (1839), in which the
innocent hero is made to seem part of a criminal conspiracy.
The attack on Keegan recalls the savagery of Carleton's
'Wildgoose Lodge' (1833). So does Trollope's comparison of
the decayed house to 'the skeleton of a felon left to rot on an
open gibbet' (4); Carleton's tale had its origin in an encounter with a hanged and rotting corpse, as Trollope's
originated in his visit to a ruined house. Other aspects of the
story recall Griffin's *The Collegians*, the most popular Irish
novel of the nineteenth century. There too we feel a sense of
doom, especially for those poised between the gentry and the
violent peasantry. Griffin's characters, like Trollope's, are
captives of their social and economic dilemmas. His seducer,
Hardress Cregan, is, like Ussher, unwilling to marry the
penniless Irish girl he has seduced; later he is tried for her
murder and transported for life. Eily O'Connor's exile to an
isolated mountain cabin may have supplied Trollope with a
few touches for Aughacashel. There is a trial with evasive
witnesses, a racing meet, and scenes of boisterous and
bibulous squireen revelry, contrasted, as in Trollope's
novel, with grim tragedy.

Trollope's most important use of Irish fiction is the way
his own novel echoes, responds to, and to some extent
parodies Lady Morgan's *The Wild Irish Girl* (1806), like *The
Macdermots* a novel about the Irish Catholic gentry, proud,

poor, ignored by and isolated from the Anglo-Irish. Lady Morgan's heroine, Glorvina (*glor*, voice; *binn*, sweet), inhabits a half-ruined castle, where we see her at sunset in a long white robe, her hair unbound, playing the harp and singing. She lives with her reclusive invalid father, the Prince, modelled on The Macdermot, Prince of Coolavin. There is a chaplain, Father John educated at St Omer like Trollope's Father John. In both stories, the daughter of the house falls in love with a man of English or Anglo-Irish ancestry who is a newcomer to the neighbourhood. But Trollope's characters are without the glamour of Lady Morgan's. He replaces her dignified old Prince in his ruined castle with the shambling, senile figure of old Larry Macdermot, drunk and dishevelled, hiding from his creditors in his tumbledown house. Instead of the learned and accomplished Glorvina at her harp, Trollope shows us Feemy in her dirty gown, her hair untidy, reading a well-thumbed Gothic thriller with her feet on the fender. Glorvina is wooed by an incognito nobleman, and regains the lands of her ancestors through marriage; Feemy lets herself be seduced by an illegitimate scion of Anglo-Ireland, and dies in disgrace. Trollope deliberately turns Lady Morgan's romantic novel inside-out, to show us a bleak reality of poverty, disgrace, and death. Though he believed that 'the Irish character is peculiarly well fitted for romance' (*Autobiography* 156), *The Macdermots* is his first experiment in that anti-romantic mode he was later to employ so often. In a sense, Trollope rewrites *The Wild Irish Girl* as a realistic novel, though in doing so he relies on melodrama in a way he would soon abandon.

In *The Macdermots* Trollope also adapts the form of the nineteenth-century Irish novel, a form partly determined by Irish social conditions. The English novel developed in a middle-class culture. It traditionally celebrated that culture, and its role as mediator between high and low in a gradated society. Trollope's English novels frequently stress the need to conform to the general expectations of society, and assume that these are generally understood. But Irish society lacked this stabilizing middle class, and could not be seen as

gradated and cohesive. It consisted of two mutually exclusive and often mutually hostile nations. Like Disraeli's two
nations, they can be described as the rich and the poor, but
these categories were not only economic. The rich were Protestant, land-owning, and usually of British ancestry. The
poor were Catholic, tenants, and represented the dispossessed
native race. It was a society of colonizers and colonized,
unable to cohere.

The English novel assumes the possibility of social
coherence, maintained by the mediating role of the middle
class. It appeals continually to social coherence as a goal,
even when depicting injustice or agitation. Its form reflects
this coherence, with characters and situations subordinated
to and integrated into the total work. The Irish novel,
depicting a divided society, rarely achieves such formal
coherence. It tends to be episodic, a series of encounters or
activities not wholly integrated into a plot—a tendency that
persists even in *Ulysses*. In this, as in its insights, *The Macdermots* is an Irish novel. Trollope regularly interrupts his tragic
story with comic episodes, most of them sketches or genre
pictures illustrating Irish customs or 'humours': Denis
McGovery's wedding, the squireens' party on the eve of the
Carrick races, the races themselves, Father John's coach
journey to Dublin, the Carrick-on-Shannon assizes. In these
episodes, Trollope virtually abandons the forward progress
of his story to present comic scenes allegedly typical of Irish
life. They are rich in comic observation, but irrelevant to his
plot.

But it is precisely in these episodes that Trollope is able
to suggest the vitality of Irish life, and to reinforce the sense
that Ireland is two countries, not one. The episodes contrast
the isolation and inaction of the Macdermots with the
reckless energy all around them, an energy that brings about
their downfall. Because the excitement of the wedding brief-
ly alters Thady's mood, his participation in the Ribbonmen's wild talk becomes important evidence against him.
When the Ribbonmen assault Keegan and cut off his foot
with an axe, or when Counsellor Webb and Mr Brown fight
their duel, the anarchic brutality of these encounters

highlight for us the nature of Thady's world, despite his personal isolation from both groups. Only the police—Captain Ussher—have access to all of the novel's mutually exclusive groups.

In 1860 *The Macdermots* was revised, almost certainly by Trollope himself, although he has left no record of the fact. That revised text is printed here. The revisions are extensive, appearing on almost every page, but most of them are of minor importance, changing sentence structure or punctuation. He assigned titles to the chapters, and toned down some of the language: he left plenty of d—ns in his account of the pre-race festivities, but there are not as many as there were in 1847.

The major changes are the dropping of an important sentence and of three chapters. The sentence emphasizes what a reader of the 1860 text assumes, that Feemy dies in abortive childbirth, just before she is called to testify at Thady's trial and possibly save him by her evidence. When Father John enters an ante-room where she has been waiting, to bring her into court, he finds she has collapsed:

Father John was soon made to understand that medical skill could avail but little, and that all the aid which Feemy could now receive from her fellow-creatures was to come from him. *Her many griefs and inward struggles had brought on premature parturition, and she was now dying from its effects*. (590–1; italicized sentence omitted in 1860).

The three omitted chapters belong near the end of the novel. Two of them describe Father John's coach journey from Drumsna to Dublin, and his activities there. They were placed between chapters XXV and XXVI of the present text, and helped to suggest the passage of time between Thady's surrender to the authorities and his trial, an interlude of five months. In the first of these chapters, Trollope records the scenery and humorous incidents of an Irish journey, and the behaviour of Father John's fellow passengers. In the second, he shows us how well he knew the city of Dublin. The journey, and the tour of Dublin, are interesting but not very important to the story's development, except in creating atmosphere. But the Dublin chapter also contains Father John's long interview with Counsellor O'Malley, who is to defend Thady. The interview is important because it establishes more clearly than the revised text the precise legal reasons why Feemy's testimony is crucial to Thady's defence. The absence of that testimony dooms him. With O'Malley's sympathetic but relentless probings, Trollope begins his gallery of lawyers. For the first time he depicts a kind of encounter he will return to again and again, between a lay person convinced of a truth and the lawyer who must explain how truth is established in a courtroom, the difference between belief and evidence.

Trollope also dropped his final chapter, describing the subsequent fates of the surviving characters, from the 1860 version. This chapter centred around Father John. Trollope emphasizes his devastation at Thady's death, making the priest even more sympathetic and important to the story. But the final chapter dilutes the effect of Thady's death on the reader, and Trollope was right to drop it.

The modern visitor to Drumsna will find that Trollope and his story have their place in local memory. Near the river, a wooden plaque records his stay at the former mail-coach inn, now Taylor's pub, with topographical if not chronological accuracy: 'Anthony Trollope, 1815–1882, celebrated nineteenth century novelist, stayed at this house, then an inn, and commenced his first novel *The Macdermots of Ballycloran* here in 1848.' Local tradition mingles Trollope's account of his visit to Ballycloran in the first pages of the novel, where he describes himself as alone, with the *Autobiography* account, where he is accompanied by John Merivale: he was alone 'because he was waiting for his friend who was delayed', then later showed Merivale the ruin.

In Drumsna, Trollope's coinage *Ballycloran* has displaced the official name of the town-land and the ruined house it contains. Feemy Macdermot is said to be buried in the Protestant churchyard—a circumstance locally explained by noting that, though of course she was Catholic, 'in those days they buried them all in together'. Thady is remembered as 'the last man hanged at Carrick gaol—after him,

they hung them only at Galway gaol'. The non-denomina-
tional character of Irish country graveyards, and the sinister
reputation of Galway gaol, are indeed accurate. Trollope's
imaginary characters have come to inhabit the real land-
scape he described so carefully.

Nowadays the road away from the river is neither dusty
nor disagreeable. The little bridge has been rebuilt. The
woods are gone, but a short walk up a low hill brings you
to Ballycloran. The hill is as boggy as it is stony, a 'weeping
hillside' in Irish phrasing, rich with iris in summer. Only
fragments remain of the house that Trollope saw already
ruined. Roof, floors, front and back walls are gone, but both
end walls still stand, about fifty feet apart. Twisted vines
spring from the ground and climb—probably sustain—one
wall. The partly ruined stables and outbuildings are still
used to store hay and farm implements. Ballycloran is no
longer a symbol of foolish grandeur, as Trollope saw it. It
has become another stark Irish ruin, one with Cashel and
Clonmacnoise. But in Trollope's novel it remains for us an
image of pre-Famine Ireland, peopled and doomed.

Robert Tracy

Berkeley, California
St Patrick's Day, 1988

A NOTE ON THE TEXT

The Macdermots of Ballycloran was originally published in March 1847 by Thomas Cautley Newby, a London publisher. This first edition was in three volumes, of twelve chapters each; Volume III (437 pages) was considerably longer than Volume I (345) or II (382). Newby reissued the novel in 1848, with a new title-page and the misleading subtitle, 'A Historical Romance'.

Trollope's agreement with Newby, signed in September 1845, stipulated that he would receive 'half profits', a common arrangement for beginning writers: Newby would first deduct from any proceeds his costs for printing, binding, advertising, and overheads, then share remaining proceeds equally with Trollope. Newby printed only 400 copies, and was sparing with advertisements. He was also unwilling to persevere if a novel did not 'take' immediately. Since nearly 200 copies would have had to be sold quickly before Trollope could expect to receive anything, it is not surprising that *An Autobiography* describes *The Macdermots* as a failure. Newby was also slow in bringing the book out; he had originally promised that it would appear by February 1846. Newby's contract with Trollope, his inadequacies as a publisher, and his generally unsavory reputation are described in J. A. Sutherland, *Victorian Novelists and Publishers*.

It is unclear how or when Trollope regained the copyright for *The Macdermots*, but in March 1860 he persuaded Chapman and Hall, then his regular publishers, to accept a half share in it for a half share in his popular *Doctor Thorne*; five years later he offered another (?) half share to George Smith. Late in 1860, Chapman and Hall published *The Macdermots* in a revised, and drastically shortened version, which they reissued later in the 1860s. Ward Lock brought out the same text about 1880, as did John Lane in 1906. This revised version is printed here. Three chapters omitted from the 1860 and all subsequent editions are included in an appendix (pp. 625–75).

Trollope nowhere refers to the revising of *The Macdermots*, but it is unthinkable that he would have let anyone else alter his text. Since he was unusually busy, even for him, between August 1859 and June 1860, when he worked simultaneously on *Castle Richmond* and *Framley Parsonage*, carried on Post Office business, and moved his family from Dublin to Waltham Cross in Hertfordshire, the revision was probably done soon after 1 July 1860. R. C. Terry discusses the revision in 'Three Lost Chapters of Trollope's First Novel', *Nineteenth-Century Fiction*, 27:1 (June 1972), 71–80.

SELECT BIBLIOGRAPHY

There is no complete edition of Trollope's works. Thirty-six titles (in 62 volumes) appear in *Selected Works of Anthony Trollope* (1981), under the general editorship of N. John Hall; Hall himself edited *The Macdermots of Ballycloran* (the original 1847 text) for this series, with a valuable introduction. Many of Trollope's novels are available in the Oxford World's Classics series. The standard bibliography is by Michael Sadleir: *Trollope: a Bibliography* (1928; repr. 1977).

Trollope's *An Autobiography* (1883) is an important work of literature in its own right, apart from the information it contains. It is best supplemented by *The Letters of Anthony Trollope* (1983), ed. N. John Hall. Hall is also at work on a biography, which will supersede those by T. H. S. Escott (1913; repr. 1967), Michael Sadleir (1927), and James Pope Hennessy (1971); Pope Hennessy is especially well informed on Trollope's Irish years. R. H. Super, *Trollope in the Post Office* (1981), explains Trollope's postal duties and the circumstances of his visit to Drumsna. J. A. Sutherland, *Victorian Novelists and Publishers* (1976), discusses Trollope's arrangements for publishing *The Macdermots*. R. C. Terry, *Trollope: Interviews and Recollections* (1987), offers many glimpses of Trollope in action.

There are two bibliographies of Trollope criticism: Rafael Holling, *A Century of Trollope Criticism* (1956), and *The Reputation of Trollope: an Annotated Bibliography 1925–1975* (1978), ed. John Charles Olmsted and Jeffrey Welch. *Trollope: the Critical Heritage* (1969), ed. Donald Smalley, reprints contemporary reviews and criticism. There are three useful collections of more recent criticism: *Anthony Trollope* (1980), ed. T. E. Bareham; *The Trollope Critics* (1980), ed. N. John Hall; *Trollope Centenary Essays* (1982), ed. John Halperin.

There are many general critical studies: Ruth ap Roberts, *Trollope: Artist and Moralist* (1971; published in the United States as *The Moral Trollope*); Bradford A. Booth, *Anthony Trollope: Aspects of his Life and Work* (1958); A. O. J.

Cockshut, *Anthony Trollope: a Critical Study* (1955); John Halperin, *Trollope and Politics* (1977); James R. Kincaid, *The Novels of Anthony Trollope* (1977); Robert M. Polhemus, *The Changing World of Anthony Trollope* (1968); R. C. Terry, *Anthony Trollope: the Artist in Hiding* (1977); Robert Tracy, *Trollope's Later Novels* (1978); and Andrew Wright, *Anthony Trollope: Dream and Art* (1983). The studies by Polhemus and Terry give particular attention to *The Macdermots*.

Several brief studies of aspects of *The Macdermots* have appeared in periodicals: Doris Asmundsson, 'Trollope's First Novel: a Re-examination', *Éire-Ireland* 6 (Fall 1971), 83–91; Sarah Gilead, 'Trollope's Ground of Meaning: *The Macdermots of Ballycloran*', *Victorian Newsletter* 69 (Spring 1986), 23–9; John Hynes, 'Anthony Trollope's "Creative Shock": Banagher, 1841', *Éire-Ireland* 21 (Fall 1986), 124–131; Robert Tracy, ' "The Unnatural Ruin": Trollope and Nineteenth-Century Irish Fiction', *Nineteenth-Century Fiction* 37 (December 1982), 358–82; and E. W. Wittig, 'Trollope's Irish Fiction', *Éire-Ireland* 9 (Autumn 1974), 97–118.

J. W. Clark, *The Language and Style of Anthony Trollope* (1975), discusses Trollope's use of Irish and Irish-English. The Irish-English idiom and intonation is more generally examined in P. L. Henry, *An Anglo-Irish Dialect of North Roscommon* (1957), J. Taniguchi, *A Grammatical Analysis of Artistic Representation of Irish English* (1972), and especially P. W. Joyce, *English as We Speak it in Ireland* (1910; repr. 1979).

There are many contemporary accounts of Trollope's Ireland, among them Alexis de Tocqueville, *Journeys to England and Ireland* (1958), tr. George Lawrence and K. P. Mayer; S. C. Hall and Anna Hall, *Ireland: its Scenery, Character, Etc.* (1841); Henry D. Inglis, *A Journey Throughout Ireland during the Spring, Summer, and Autumn of 1834* (1838); and William Makepeace Thackeray, *The Irish Sketch Book* (1843). These are best supplemented by M. O'C. Bianconi and S. J. Watson, *Bianconi: King of the Irish Roads* (1962) and Sean O'Faolain, *King of the Beggars: a Life of Daniel O'Connell* (1938; repr. 1980). The Irish novelists Trollope read are studied in Thomas Flanagan, *The Irish Novelists 1800–1850* (1959).

A CHRONOLOGY OF
ANTHONY TROLLOPE

Virtually all Trollope's fiction after *Framley Parsonage* (1860–1) appeared first in serial form, with book publication usually coming just prior to the final instalment of the serial.

1815   (24 Apr.) Born at 16 Keppel Street, Bloomsbury, the fourth son of Thomas and Frances Trollope.
(Summer ?) Family moves to Harrow-on-the-Hill.

1823   To Harrow School as a day-boy.

1825   To a private school at Sunbury.

1827   To school at Winchester College.

1830   Removed from Winchester and returned to Harrow.

1834   (Apr.) The family flees to Bruges to escape creditors.
(Nov.) Accepts a junior clerkship in the General Post Office, London.

1841   (Sept.) Made Postal Surveyor's Clerk at Banagher, King's County, Ireland.

1843   (mid-Sept.) Begins work on his first novel, *The Macdermots of Ballycloran*.

1844   (11 June) Marries Rose Heseltine.
(Aug.) Transferred to Clonmel, County Tipperary.

1846   (13 Mar.) Son, Henry Merivale Trollope, born.

1847   *The Macdermots of Ballycloran*, published in 3 vols. (Newby).
(27 Sept.) Son, Frederic James Anthony Trollope, born.

1848   *The Kellys and the O'Kellys; or Landlords and Tenants* 3 vols. (Colburn).
(Autumn) Moves to Mallow, County Cork.

1850   *La Vendée; An Historical Romance* 3 vols. (Colburn).
Writes *The Noble Jilt* (A play, published 1923).

1851   (1 Aug.) Sent to south-west of England on special postal mission.

1853   (29 July) Begins *The Warden* (the first of the Barsetshire novels).
(29 Aug.) Moves to Belfast as Acting Surveyor.

1854   (9 Oct.) Appointed Surveyor of Northern District of Ireland.

1855   *The Warden* 1 vol. (Longman).
        Writes *The New Zealander*.
        (June) Moves to Donnybrook, Dublin.

1857   *Barchester Towers* 3 vols. (Longman).

1858   *The Three Clerks* 3 vols. (Bentley).
        Doctor Thorne 3 vols. (Chapman & Hall).
        (Jan.) Departs for Egypt on Post Office business.
        (Mar.) Visits Holy Land.
        (Apr.–May) Returns via Malta, Gibraltar and Spain.
        (May–Sept.) Visits Scotland and north of England on postal business.
        (16 Nov.) Leaves for the West Indies on postal mission.

1859   *The Bertrams* 3 vols. (Chapman & Hall).
        The West Indies and the Spanish Main 1 vol. (Chapman & Hall).
        (3 July) Arrives home.
        (Nov.) Leaves Ireland; settles at Waltham Cross, Hertfordshire, after being appointed Surveyor of the Eastern District of England.

1860   *Castle Richmond* 3 vols. (Chapman & Hall).
        First serialized fiction, *Framley Parsonage*, published in the *Cornhill Magazine*.
        (Oct.) Visits, with his wife, his mother and brother in Florence; makes the acquaintance of Kate Field, a 22-year-old American for whom he forms a romantic attachment.

1861   *Framley Parsonage* 3 vols. (Smith, Elder).
        Tales of All Countries 1 vol. (Chapman & Hall).
        (24 Aug.) Leaves for America to write a travel book.

1862   *Orley Farm* 2 vols. (Chapman & Hall).
        North America 2 vols. (Chapman & Hall).
        The Struggles of Brown, Jones and Robinson: By One of the Firm 1 vol. (New York, Harper—an American piracy; first English edition 1870, Smith, Elder).
        (25 Mar.) Arrives home from America.
        (5 Apr.) Elected to the Garrick Club.

1863   *Tales of All Countries*, Second Series, 1 vol. (Chapman & Hall).
        Rachel Ray 2 vols. (Chapman & Hall).
        (6 Oct.) Death of his mother, Mrs Frances Trollope.

1864   *The Small House at Allington* 2 vols. (Smith, Elder).
         (12 Apr.) Elected a member of the Athenaeum Club.

1865   *Can You Forgive Her?* 2 vols. (Chapman & Hall).
         Miss Mackenzie 1 vol. (Chapman & Hall).
         Hunting Sketches 1 vol. (Chapman & Hall).

1866   *The Belton Estate* 3 vols. (Chapman & Hall).
         Travelling Sketches 1 vol. (Chapman & Hall).
         Clergymen of the Church of England 1 vol. (Chapman & Hall).

1867   *Nina Balatka* 2 vols. (Blackwood).
         The Claverings 2 vols. (Smith, Elder).
         The Last Chronicle of Barset 2 vols. (Smith, Elder).
         Lotta Schmidt and Other Stories 1 vol. (Strahan).
         (1 Sept.) Resigns from the Post Office.
         Assumes editorship of *Saint Pauls Magazine*.

1868   *Linda Tressel* 2 vols. (Blackwood).
         (11 Apr.) Leaves London for the United States on postal
         mission.
         (26 July) Returns from America.
         (Nov.) Stands unsuccessfully as Liberal candidate for
         Beverley, Yorkshire.

1869   *Phineas Finn; the Irish Member* 2 vols. (Virtue & Co).
         He Knew He Was Right 2 vols. (Strahan).
         Did He Steal It? A Comedy in Three Acts (a version of *The Last
         Chronicle of Barset*, privately printed by Virtue & Co).

1870   *The Vicar of Bullhampton* 1 vol. (Bradbury, Evans).
         An Editor's Tales 1 vol. (Strahan).
         The Commentaries of Caesar 1 vol. (Blackwood).
         (Jan.–July) Eased out of *Saint Pauls Magazine*.

1871   *Sir Harry Hotspur of Humblethwaite* 1 vol. (Hurst &
         Blackett).
         Ralph the Heir 3 vols. (Hurst & Blackett).
         (Apr.) Gives up house at Waltham Cross.
         (24 May) Sails to Australia to visit his son.
         (27 July) Arrives at Melbourne.

1872   *The Golden Lion of Granpere* 1 vol. (Tinsley).
         (Jan.–Oct.) Travelling in Australia and New Zealand.
         (Dec.) Returns via the United states.

1873   *The Eustace Diamonds* 3 vols. (Chapman & Hall).
         Australia and New Zealand 2 vols. (Chapman & Hall).
         (Apr.) Settles in Montagu Square, London.

1874   *Phineas Redux* 2 vols. (Chapman & Hall).

Lady Anna 2 vols. (Chapman & Hall).
Harry Heathcote of Gangoil. A Tale of Australian Bush Life 1 vol. (Sampson Low).

1875   *The Way We Live Now* 2 vols. (Chapman & Hall).
(1 Mar.) Leaves for Australia via Brindisi, the Suez Canal, and Ceylon.
(4 May) Arrives in Australia.
(Aug.–Oct.) Sailing homewards.
(Oct.) Begins *An Autobiography*.

1876   *The Prime Minister* 4 vols. (Chapman & Hall).

1877   *The American Senator* 3 vols. (Chapman & Hall).
(29 June) Leaves for South Africa.
(11 Dec.) Sails for home.

1878   *South Africa* 2 vols. (Chapman & Hall).
Is He Popenjoy? 3 vols. (Chapman & Hall).
(June–July) Travels to Iceland in the yacht 'Mastiff'.
How the 'Mastiffs' Went to Ireland 1 vol. (privately printed, Virtue & Co).

1879   *An Eye for an Eye* 2 vols. (Chapman & Hall).
Thackeray 1 vol. (Macmillan).
John Candigate 3 vols. (Chapman & Hall).
Cousin Henry 2 vols. (Chapman & Hall).

1880   *The Duke's Children* 3 vols. (Chapman & Hall).
The Life of Cicero 2 vols. (Chapman & Hall).
(July) Settles at South Harting, Sussex, near Petersfield.

1881   *Dr Wortle's School* 2 vols. (Chapman & Hall).
Ayala's Angel 3 vols. (Chapman & Hall).

1882   *Why Frau Frohmann Raised Her Prices; and Other Stories* 1 vol. (Isbister).
The Fixed Period 2 vols. (Blackwood).
Marion Fay 3 vols. (Chapman & Hall).
Lord Palmerston 1 vol. (Isbister).
Kept in the Dark 2 vols. (Chatto & Windus).
(May) Visits Ireland to collect material for a new Irish novel.
(Aug.) Returns to Ireland a second time.
(2 Oct.) Takes rooms for the winter at Garlant's Hotel, Suffolk St., London.
(3 Nov.) Suffers paralytic stroke.
(6 Dec.) Dies in nursing home, 34 Welbeck St., London.

1883   *Mr. Scarborough's Family* 3 vols. (Chatto & Windus).
        The Landleaguers (unfinished) 3 vols. (Chatto &
        Windus).
        An Autobiography 2 vols. (Blackwood).

1884   *An Old Man's Love* 2 vols. (Blackwood).

1923   *The Noble Jilt* 1 vol. (Constable).

1927   *London Tradesmen* 1 vol. (Elkin Mathews and Marrat).

1972   *The New Zealander* 1 vol. (Oxford University Press).

THE MACDERMOTS
OF BALLYCLORAN

CONTENTS

Contents

THE MACDERMOTS
OF BALLYCLORAN

CHAPTER I

BALLYCLORAN HOUSE AS FIRST SEEN BY THE
AUTHOR

In the autumn, 184—, business took me into
the West of Ireland, and, amongst other places,
to the quiet little village of Drumsna, which is
in the province of Connaught, County Leitrim,
about 72 miles w.n.w. of Dublin, on the mail-
coach road* to Sligo. I reached the little inn
there in the morning by the said mail, my
purpose being to leave it late in the evening by
the day coach; and as my business was but of
short duration, I was left, after an early dinner,
to amuse myself. Now, in such a situation, to
take a walk is all the brightest man can do, and
the dullest always does the same. There is a
kind of gratification in seeing what one has
never seen before, be it ever so little worth
seeing; and the gratification is the greater if
the chances be that one will never see it again.
Now Drumsna stands on a bend in the Shannon;

the street leads down to a bridge, passing over
which one finds oneself in the County Roscommon ; and the road runs by the well-wooded
demesne of Sir G— K— ;* moreover there is a
beautiful little hill, from which the demesne,
river, bridge, and village can all be seen ; and
what farther *agremens** than these could be
wanted to make a pretty walk ? But, alas ! I
knew not of their existence then. One cannot
ask the maid at an inn to show one where to
find the beauties of nature. So, trusting to
myself, I went directly away from river, woods,
and all,—along as dusty, ugly, and disagreeable
a road as is to be found in any county in
Ireland.

After proceeding a mile or so, taking two
or three turns to look for improvement, I
began to perceive evident signs on the part of
the road of retrograding into lane-ism ; the
county had evidently deserted it, and though
made for cars and coaches, its traffic appeared
to be now confined to donkeys carrying turf
home from the bog, in double kishes* on their
back. Presently the fragments of a bridge
presented themselves, but they too were utterly
fallen away from their palmy days, and in their
present state afforded but indifferent stepping-
stones over a bog stream which ran, or rather
crept, across the road. These, however, I
luckily traversed, and was rewarded by finding
a broken down entrance to a kind of wood on
the right hand. In Ireland, particularly in the
poorer parts—to rank among which, County
Leitrim has a right which will not be disputed
—a few trees together are always the recognised

sign of a demesne, of a gentleman's seat, or the place where a gentleman's seat has been; and I directly knew that this must be a demesne. But ah! how impoverished, if one might judge from outward appearances. Two brick pillars, from which the outside plaster had peeled off and the coping fallen, gave evidence of former gates; the space was closed up with a loose-built wall, but on the outer side of each post was a little well-worn footpath, made of soft bog mould. I of course could not resist such temptation, and entered the demesne. The road was nearly covered with that short dry grass which stones seem to throw up, when no longer polished by the wealthier portion of man or brute kind.

About thirty feet from the gap a tall fir had half fallen, and lay across the road, so that a man should stoop to walk under it; it was a perfect barrier to any equipage, however humble, and the roots had nearly refixed themselves in their reversed position, showing that the tree had evidently been in that fallen state for years.

The usual story, thought I, of Connaught gentlemen; an extravagant landlord, reckless tenants, debt, embarrassment, despair, and ruin. Well, I walked up the deserted avenue, and very shortly found myself in front of the house. Oh, what a picture of misery, of useless expenditure, unfinished pretence, and premature decay!

The house was two stories high, with large stone steps up to the front door, with four

windows in the lower, and six in the upper
story, and an area with kitchens, etc., below.
The entire roof was off; one could see the
rotting joists and beams, some fallen, some
falling, the rest ready to fall, like the skeleton
of a felon left to rot on an open gibbet. The
stone steps had nearly dropped through into the
area, the rails of which had been wrenched up.
The knocker was still on the door,—a large
modern lion-headed knocker; but half the door
was gone; on creeping to the door-sill, I found
about six feet of the floor of the hall gone also
—stolen for fire-wood. But the joists of the
flooring were there, and the whitewash of the
walls showed that but a few, a very few years
back, the house had been inhabited. I leaped
across the gulf, at great risk of falling into the
cellar, and reached the bottom of the stairs;
here my courage failed me; all that was left
was so damp and so rotten, so much had been
gradually taken away, that I did not dare to go
up: the doors on the ground floor would not
open; the ceiling above me was all gone, and
I could see the threatening timbers of the roof,
which seemed only hanging till they had an
opportunity of injuring some one by their fall.
I crept out of the demi-door again, and down
the ruined steps, and walked round the mansion;
not only was there not a pane of glass in the
whole, but the window frames were all gone;
everything that wanted keeping was gone;
everything that required care to preserve it had
perished. Time had not touched it. Time had
evidently not yet had leisure to do his work.
He is sure, but slow. Ruin works fast enough

unaided, where once he puts his foot. Time
would have pulled down the chimneys—Ruin
had taken off the slates; Time would have
bulged the walls—Ruin brought in the rain,
rotted the timbers, and assisted the thieves.
Poor old Time will have but little left him at
Ballycloran! The gardens had been large;
half were now covered by rubbish heaps, and
the other half consisted of potato patches; and
round the out-houses I saw clustering a lot of
those wretched cabins which the poor Irish
build against a deserted wall, when they can
find one, as jackdaws do their nests in a super-
annuated chimney. In the front there had
been, I presume a tolerably spacious lawn, with
a drive through it, surrounded on all sides,
except towards the house, by thick trees. The
trees remained, but the lawn, the drive, and the
flower patches, which of course once existed
there, were now all alike, equally prolific in
large brown dock weeds and sorrels. There
were two or three narrow footpaths through and
across the space, up to the cabins behind the
house, but other marks of humanity were there
none.

A large ash, apparently cut down years ago,
with the branches still on it, was stretched
somewhat out of the wood: on this I sat,
lighted a cigar, and meditated on this cha-
racteristic specimen of Irish life. The sun was
setting beautifully behind the trees, and its imperfect light through the foliage gave the unnatural ruin a still stronger appearance of death
and decay, and brought into my mind thoughts
of the wrong, oppression, misery, and despair,

to which some one had been subjected by what I saw before me.

I had not been long seated, when four or five ragged boys and girls came through the wood, driving a lot of geese along one of the paths. When they saw me, they all came up and stood round me, as if wondering what I could be. I could learn nothing from them—the very poor Irish children will never speak to you; but a middle-aged man soon followed them. He told me the place was called Ballycloran: "he did not know who it belonged to; a gintleman in Dublin recaved the rints, and a very stiff gintleman he was too; and hard it was upon them to pay two pounds tin* an acre for the garden there, and that half covered with the ould house and the bricks and rubbish, only on behalf of the bog that was convaynient, and plinty of the timber, tho' that was rotten, and illigant out-houses for the pigs and the geese, and the ould bricks of the wall wor good manure for the praties "*(this, in all my farming, I had never dreamt of); "but times was very hard on the poor, the praties being ninepence a stone in Carrick* all last summer; God help the poor, the crayturs! for the gintlemin, their raal frinds, that should be, couldn't help thimselves now, let alone others"—and so on, now speaking of his sorrow and poverty, and again descanting on the "illigance" of his abode. I could only learn that a family called the Macdermots had lived there some six or seven years back, that they were an unfortunate people, he had heard tell, but he had not been in the country then, and it was a bloody story, etc. etc. etc. The

evening was drawing on, and the time for my
coach to come was fast approaching; so I was
obliged to leave Ballycloran, unsatisfied as to
its history, and to return to Drumsna.

Here I had no time to make further inquiries,
as Mr. Hartley's servants* always keep their
time; and very shortly the four horses clattered
down the hill into the village. I got up behind,
for McC—, the guard,* was an old friend of
mine; and after the usual salutations and
strapping of portmanteaus, and shifting down
into places, as McC— knows everything, I
began to ask him if he knew anything of a place
called Ballycloran.

"'Deed then, Sir, and I do," said he, "and
good reason have I to know; and well I knew
those that lived in it, ruined, and black, and
desolate, as Ballycloran is now:" and between
Drumsna and Boyle, he gave me the heads of
the following story. And, reader, if I thought
it would ever be your good fortune to hear the
history of Ballycloran from the guard of the
Boyle coach, I would recommend you to get it
from him, and shut my book forthwith.

CHAPTER II

THE MACDERMOT FAMILY

McC—'s story runs thus. About sixty years ago,
a something Macdermot, true Milesian,* pious
Catholic, and descendant of king somebody,*

died somewhere, having managed, through all
the troubles of his poor country, to keep a
comfortable little portion of his ancestors' royal-
ties to console him for the loss of their sceptre.
He having two sons, and disdaining to make
anything but estated gentlemen of them, made
over in some fictitious manner (for in those
righteous days a Roman Catholic could make
no legal will)*to his eldest, the estate on which
he lived, and to the youngest, that of Ballycloran
—about six hundred as bad acres as a gentleman might wish to call his own. But Thaddeus,
otherwise Thady Macdermot, being an estated
gentleman, must have a gentleman's residence
on his estate, and the house of Ballycloran was
accordingly built. Had Thady Macdermot had
ready money, it might have been well built;
but though an estated gentleman, he had none.
He had debts even when his father died; and
though he planned, ordered, and agreed for a
house, such as he thought the descendant of a
Connaught Prince might inhabit without disgrace, it was ill-built, half finished, and paid for
by long bills.* This, however, is so customary
in poor Ireland that it but little harassed
Thady. He had a fine, showy house, with
stables, etc., gardens, an avenue, and a walk
round his demesne; and his neighbours had no
more. It was little he cared for comfort, but
he would not be the first of the Macdermots
that would not be respectable. When his house
was finished, Thady went into County Galway,
and got himself a wife with two thousand pounds
fortune, for which he had to go to law with
his brother-in-law. The lawsuit, the continual

necessity of renewing the bills with which the builder in Carrick-on-Shannon every quarter attacked him, the fruitless endeavour to make his tenants pay thirty shillings an acre* for half-reclaimed bog, and a somewhat strongly developed aptitude for potheen,* sent poor Thady to another world rather prematurely, and his son and heir, Lawrence, came to the throne at the tender age of twelve. The Galway brother-in-law compromised the lawsuit; the builder took a mortgage on the property from the boy's guardian; the mother gave new leases to the tenants; Larry went to school at Longford*; and Mrs. Mac kept up the glory of Ballycloran.

At the age of twenty, Lawrence, or Larry, married a Milesian damsel, portionless, but of true descent. The builder from Carrick had made overtures about a daughter he had at home, and offered poor Larry his own house, as her fortune. But the blood of the Macdermots could not mix with the lime and water that flowed in a builder's veins; he therefore made an enemy where he most wanted a friend, and brought his wife home to live with his mother. In order that we may quickly rid ourselves of encumbrances, it may be as well to say that during the next twenty-five years his mother and wife died; he had christened his only son Thaddeus, after his grandfather, and his only daughter had been christened Euphemia, after her grandmother. He had never got over that deadly builder, with his horrid percentage coming out of the precarious rents; twice, indeed, had writs* been out against him for his arrears, and once he had received notice from

Mr. Hyacinth Keegan, the oily attorney of Carrick, that Mr. Flannelly meant to foreclose. Rents were greatly in arrear, his credit was very bad among the dealers in Mohill,* with Carrick he had no other dealings than those to which necessity compelled him with Mr. Flannelly the builder, and Larry Macdermot was anything but an easy man.

Thady was at this time about twenty-four. As had been the case with his father, he had been educated at a country school; he could read and write, but could do little more: he was brought up to no profession or business; he acted as his father's agent over the property —by which I mean to signify that he occupied himself in harrowing the tenantry for money which they had no means of paying; he was occasionally head driver and ejector*; and he considered, as Irish landlords are apt to do, that he had an absolute right over the tenants, as feudal vassals. Still, they respected and to a certain extent loved him; "for why? wasn't he the masther's son, and wouldn't he be the masther hisself?" And he had a regard, perhaps an affection, for the poor creatures; against any one else he would defend them; and would they but coin their bones into pounds, shillings, and pence, he would have been as tender to them as a man so nurtured could be. With all his faults, Thady was perhaps a better man than his father; he was not so indomitably idle; had he been brought up to anything, he would have done it; he was more energetic, and felt the degradation of his position; he felt that his family was sinking lower and lower

daily; but as he knew not what to do, he only
became more gloomy and more tyrannical.
Beyond this, he had acquired a strong taste for
tobacco, which he incessantly smoked out of a
dhudheen*; and was content to pass his dull
life without excitement or pleasure.

Euphemia, or Feemy, was about twenty; she
was a tall, dark girl, with that bold, upright,
well-poised figure, which is so peculiarly Irish.
She walked as if all the blood of the old Irish
Princes was in her veins : her step, at any rate,
was princely. Feemy, also, had large, bright
brown eyes, and long, soft, shining dark hair,
which was divided behind, and fell over her
shoulders, or was tied with ribands; and she
had a well-formed nose, as all coming of old
families have; and a bright olive complexion,
only the olive was a little too brown, the skin a
little too coarse; and then Feemy's mouth was,
oh! half an inch too long; but her teeth were
white and good, and her chin was well turned
and short, with a dimple on it large enough for
any finger Venus might put there. In all,
Feemy was a fine girl in the eyes of a man
not too much accustomed to refinement. Her
hands were too large and too red, but if Feemy
got gloves sufficient to go to mass with, it was
all she could do in that way; and though
Feemy had as fine a leg as ever bore a pretty
girl, she was never well shod,—her shoes were
seldom clean, often slipshod, usually in holes;
and her stockings—but no! I will not further
violate the mysteries of Feemy's wardrobe. But
if the beautiful girls of this poor country knew
but half the charms which neatness has, they

would not so often appear as poor Feemy too usually appeared.

Like her brother, she was ardent and energetic, if she had aught to be ardent about ; she was addicted to novels, when she could get them from the dirty little circulating library at Mohill ; she was passionately fond of dancing, which was her chief accomplishment ; she played on an old spinnet which had belonged to her mother ; and controlled the motions and actions of the two barefooted damsels who officiated as domestics at Ballycloran.

Such was the family at Ballycloran in the summer of 183—,* and though not perfect, I hope they have charms enough to make a further acquaintance not unacceptable.

CHAPTER III

THE TENANTRY OF BALLYCLORAN

"Thady," said old Macdermot, as he sat eating stirabout* and thick milk, over a great turf fire, one morning about the beginning of October, " Thady, will you be getting the money out of them born divils this turn, and they owing it, some two, some three years this November, bad cess* to them for tenants ? Thady, I say," shouted, or rather screamed, the old man, as his son continued silently eating his breakfast, " Thady, I say ; have they the money, at all at all, any of them ; or is it stubborn they are ?

There's Flannelly and Keegan with their d——d
papers and bills and costs ; will you be making
out the £142 7s. 6d. before Christmas for the
hell-hounds ; or it's them 'll be masters in
Ballycloran ? Then let the boys see the landlord they'll have over them, that time !"

"Well, Larry," said the son (unless in a
passion, he always called his father by his
baptismal name, or rather by its abbreviation),
"what's the use going on that way before the girls
there, and Feemy too." Feemy, however, was
reading the " Mysterious Assassin,"*and paying
little heed to her father's lamentations. "When
we're done, and the things is out, we'll have a
look at the rent-book, and send for the boys to
come in ; and if they haven't it, why, Pat Brady
must go round agin, and see what he can do*
with the potatoes and oats, and the pigs ; but
the times, Larry, is very hard on them ; too
hard entirely, so it is, poor things—— "

" Poor things !" said the father, " and aint I
a poor thing ? and won't you and Feemy be
poor things ? Hard times, too ! who is the
times hardest on ? See that sneaking ould
robber, Flannelly, that cozened* my father—
good father for him—with such a house as this,
that's falling this day over his son's head, and
it not hardly fifty years built, bad luck to it for
a house ! See that ould robber, Flannelly, who
has been living and thriving on it for all them
years, and a stone or stick not as good as paid
for yet ; and he getting two hundred a year off
the land from the crayturs*of tenants."

True enough it was, that Mr. Joe Flannelly,
of Carrick-on-Shannon, whatever might have

been the original charge of building the Ballycloran mansion, now claimed £200 a-year from
that estate, to which his ingenious friend and
legal adviser, Mr. Hyacinth Keegan, usually
managed to add certain mysterious costs and
ceremonious expenses, which made each half-
year's rent of Larry Macdermot's own house
about £140, before the poor man had managed
to scrape it together. To add to this annoyance, Mr. Macdermot had continually before
his eyes the time, which he could not but
foresee was not distant, when this hated Flannelly would come down on the property itself,
insist on being paid his principal, and probably
not only sell, but buy, Ballycloran itself. And
whither, then, would the Macdermots betake
themselves?

Often and often did Larry, in his misfortunes,
regret the slighted offers of Sally Flannelly's
charms and cash. Oh, had he but then
condescended to have married the builder's
daughter, he would not now have been the
builder's slave. But Sally Flannelly was now
Sally Keegan, the wife of Hyacinth Keegan,
Esq., Attorney; who, if he had not the same
advantages as Larry in birth and blood, had
compensation for his inferiority in cash and
comforts. When the poor man thought of
these things—and he did little else now but
think of them—bitterly, though generally in
silence, he cursed him whom he looked upon
as his oppressor and incubus.* It never occurred
to him that if Mr. Flannelly built the house he
lived in, he should be paid for it. He never
reflected that he had lived to the extent of, and

above his precarious income, as if his house had been paid for; that, instead of passing his existence in hating the Carrick tradesman, he should have used his industry in finding the means to pay him. He sometimes blamed his father, having an indefinite feeling that he ought not to have permitted Flannelly to have anything to do with Ballycloran, after building it; but himself he never blamed; people never do; it is so much easier to blame others,—and so much more comfortable. Mr. Macdermot thus regarded his creditor as a vulgar, low-born blood-sucker, who, having by chicanery obtained an unwarrantable hold over him, was determined, if possible, to crush him. The builder, on the other hand, who had spent a long life of constant industry, but doubtful honesty, in scraping up a decent fortune, looked on his debtor as one who gave himself airs to which his poverty did not entitle him; and was determined to make him feel that though he could not be the father, he could be the master of a "rale gintleman."

After the short conversation between father and son the breakfast passed over in silence. The father finished his stirabout, and turned round to the blazing turf, to find consolation there. Feemy descended into the kitchen, to scold the girls, give out the dinner,—if there was any to give out; and to do those offices, whatever they be, in performing which all Irish ladies, bred, born, and living in moderate country-houses, pass the first two hours after breakfast in the kitchen. Thady took his rent-book and went into an outhouse, which he complimented by the name of his office, at the door of which he was joined by Pat Brady. Now Pat was an appendage, unfortunately very necessary in Ireland to such an estate as Macdermot's; and his business was not only to assist in collecting the rents, by taking possession of the little crops, and driving the cows, or the pig; but he was, moreover, expected to know who could, and who could not, make out the money; to have obtained, and always have ready, that secret knowledge of the affairs of the estate, which is thought to be, and is so, necessary to the managing of the Irish peasantry in the way they are managed. Pat Brady was all this; moreover, he had as little compunction in driving the cow or the only pig from his neighbour or cousin, and in selling off the oats or potatoes of his uncle or brother-in-law, as if he was doing that which would be quite agreeable to them. But still he was liked on the estate; he had a manner with him which had its charms to them; he was a kind of leader to them in their agrarian feelings and troubles; and though the tenants of Ballycloran half feared, they all liked and courted Pat Brady.

The most remarkable feature in his personal appearance was a broken nose; not a common, ordinary broken nose, such as would give it an apparent partiality to the right or left cheek, nor such as would, by indenting it, give the face that good-natured look which Irish broken noses usually possess. Pat Brady's broken nose was all but flattened on to his face, as if it had never lifted its head after the fatal blow which had laid it low. He was strong-built, round-

16-12-92

1   *6.99

1   *6.99 TL
       *10.00 CA ←
       *3.01 CA →

500 № 0395A
   20-34

shouldered, bow-legged, about five feet six in height, and he had that kind of external respectability about him, which a tolerably decent hat, strong brogues, and worsted stockings give to a man, when those among whom he lives are without such luxuries. When I add to the above particulars that Pat was chief minister, adviser, and confidential manager in young Macdermot's affairs, I have said all that need be said. The development of his character must be left to disclose itself.

"Well, Pat," began his master, seating himself on the solitary old chair, which, with a still older looking desk on four shaking legs, comprised the furniture of Macdermot's rent-office, "what news from Mohill to-day? was there much in the fair*at all?"

"Well, yer honor, then, for them as had money to buy, the fair was good enough; but for them as had money to get, it was as bad as them that wor afore it, and as them as is likely to come afther it."

"Were the boys in it,*Pat?"

"They wor, yer honor, the most of 'em."

"Well, Pat?"

"Oh, they wor just there, that's all."

"Tim Brady should have got the top price for that oats of his, Pat."

"Maybe he might, Masther Thady."

"What did he get? there should be twelve barrels there."

"Eleven, or thereabouts, yer honor."

"Did he sell it all, yesterday?"

"Divil a grain, then, at all at all, he took to the fair yesterday."

"Bad manners to him, and why didn't he? why he owes" (and Thady turned over the old book) "five half years this gale,* and there's no use gammoning*; father must get the money off the land, or Flannelly will help himself."

"I knows, Masther Thady; I knows all about it. Tim has between five and six acres, and he owes twenty-two pound tin; his oats is worth, maybe, five pound fifteen,—from that to six pound, and his cow about six pound more; that's all Tim has, barring the brats and the mother of them. An' he knows right well, yer honor, if he brings you the price of the oats, you wouldn't let him off that way; for the cow should folly the oats, as is nathural; the cabin would be saized next; so Tim ses, if you choose to take the corn yourself, you can do so;—well an' good, and save him the throuble of bringin' it to Mohill."

"Did the widow Reynolds sell her pig?"

"She did, yer honor, for two pound tin."

"And she owes seven pound. And Dan Coulahan—"

"Dan didn't cut the oats, good or bad."

"I'll cut it for him, then. Was ould Tierney there?"

"He war, yer honor; and I was tellin' him yer honor 'id be wantin' the money this week, an' I axed him to stip up o' Friday mornin'; an', sis I, 'Misthur Tierney'—for since he made out the mare and the ould car,* it's Misthur Tierney he goes by—' it's a fine saison any way for the corn,' sis I, 'the Lord be praised; an' the hay all saved on thim illigant bottoms* of yours, Misthur Tierney. The masther was glad to hear the cocks was all up afore the heavy rain was come.' 'Well, Pat,' sis he, ' I'll be at Ballycloran o' Friday, plase God, but it's little I'll have with me but myself; an' if the masthur likes the corn an' the hay, he may just take them av' it's plazin' to him, for the divil a cock or grain will I sell, an' the prices so bad.'"

"Obstinate ould fool! why, Pat, he must have the money."

"Money, to be shure he has the money, Misthur Thady; but maybe he'd be the bigger fool if he gave it to your father."

" Do the boys mane to say they won't pay the rent at all?"

"They mane to say they can't; an' it's nearly thrue for them."

"Was Joe Reynolds at the fair, Pat?"

" He wor not; that's to say, he wor not at the fair, but I seen him in the evening, with the other boys from Drumleesh,* at Mrs. Mulready's."

"Them boys has always the money when they want a drop of whiskey. By dad, if they go to Mulready's with the money in their pockets on a Tuesday, where's the wonder they come here with them empty on a Friday? Fetch me a coal for the pipe, Pat."

Whilst Pat walked into the kitchen for a lighted piece of turf (*Hibernice,* coal) to kindle his patron's pipe, Thady stuck the said pipe in his jaw, and continued poring over the unsatisfactory figures of the Ballycloran rent-book.

" I tell you what it is, Pat," said he, after finishing the process of blowing, and drawing, and throwing the coal on the earthen floor, and pressing down the hot burning tobacco with the top of his forefinger repeatedly, " Misthur Joe Reynolds will out of that.* I told him so last April, and divil a penny of his we've seen since ; he don't do the best he can for us ; and my belief is, he hinders the others ; eh, Brady ? " and he looked up into Brady's face for confirmation or refutation of this opinion. But that gentleman, contrary to his usual wont, seemed to have no opinion on the matter ; he continued scratching his head, and swinging one leg, while he stood on the other. Thady, finding that his counsellor said nothing, continued,

" Joe Reynolds will out of that this time, d'you hear ? what has he on that bit of land of his ? "

" Praties mostly, Misthur Thady. He had half an acre of whate ; he parted that on the ground to ould Tierney ; he owed Tierney money."

" An' so the tenants buy the crops from one another, and yet won't pay their own rents. Well, my father's to blame himself ; av he'd put a man like Keegan over them, or have let the land to some rough hand as would make them pay, divil a much he need care for Flannelly this day."

" An' you'd be for puttin' a stranger over thim, Misthur Thady ; an' they that would stand between you an' all harum, or the masthur, or the old masthur afore him ; becaze of the dirthy money, and becaze a blagguard and a black ruffian like Flannelly has an ould paper signed by the masthur, or the like ? An' as for Mr. Hyacinth Keegan,—I'm thinking, the first time he goes collectin' on the lands of Drumleesh, it's a warm welcome he'll be gettin'; at any rate, he'd have more recates*in his carcass than in his pocket, that day."

"That's very fine talk, Pat; but if Keegan had them, he'd tame them, as he has others before; not but I'd be sorry they should be in his hands, the robber, bad as they are. But it'll come to that, whether or no. How's my father to get this money for Flannelly?"

"D—n Flannelly!" was Brady's easy solution of the family difficulties. "Let him take the house he built, and be d—d to him; and if we can't build a betther one for the masthur and Miss Feemy and you, without his help, may praties choke me!"

"By dad, if he'd take the house, and leave the ground, he's my welcome, and ceade mille faltha,* Pat. But the land will stick to the house; and mark me, when ould Flannelly dies (an' the divil die along with him), Mr. Keegan of Carrick will write himself, Hyacinth Keegan, Esquire, of Ballycloran."

"May I nivir see that day, an' he an' I alive, amen," said Brady, as he crossed himself in sign of the sacred truth of his wish; "but I think, Misthur Thady, when you come to consider of it, you'll find plenty of manes of keepin' Mr. Keegan and Mrs. Keegan out of the parlour of Ballycloran. But about Joe Reynolds, yer honor was sayin'—— "

"I was saying that divil another potato he should dig in Drumleesh, nor another grain of corn shall he sow or rape; that's what I was saying."

"Well, Misthur Thady, you're the masthur, thank God, an' if you say so, it must be done. But Joe Reynolds is not that bad either : he was sayin' tho' at Mrs. Mulready's that he expected little from yer honor, but just leave to go where he liked, and lave the cow and the praties behind him."

"What wor they saying at Mulready's, Pat ?"

"They were only jist passin' their remarks, yer honor, about how thick you war this time back with Captain Ussher; an' Miss Feemy too, an' the masthur ; an' that when the likes of him wor as one of the family, it's little the likes of them would be gettin' now from Ballycloran, only hard words, and maybe a help to Carrick Gaol."

"Because Captain Ussher visits at Ballycloran, is that any reason why he should interfere between my father and his tenants ?"

"Sorra a one av me knows then, Misthur Thady ; only that the tenants is no good frinds to the Captain ; nor why should they, an' he going through the counthry with a lot of idle blagguards,* with arms, an' guns, sazin' the poor divils for nothin' at all, only for thryin' to make out the rint for yer honor, with a thrifle of potheen ? That's quare friendship ; ay, an' it's the truth I'm tellin' you, Misthur Thady, for he's no frind to you or yours. Shure isn't Pat Reynolds in Ballinamore Bridewell* on his account, an' two other boys from the mountains behind Drumleesh, becaze they found a thrifle of half malted barley up there among them ? an' be the same token, Joe was sayin', if the frind of the family war parsecuting them that way, an' puttin' his brother in gaol, whilst the masthur wouldn't rise a finger, barrin' for the rint, the sooner he an' his were off the estate, the betther he'd like it; for Joe sed he'd not be fightin' agin his own masthur, but whin you war not his masthur any more,—then let every one look to hisself."

Whilst Brady was giving this short *exposé* of the feelings displayed at the little whiskey shop in Mohill on the previous fair day, young Macdermot was pulling hard at the dhudheen, as if trying to hide his embarrassment in smoke. Brady paused for some time, and then added,

"Joe mostly leads those boys up at Drumleesh, an' hard to lead they are; I'm thinking Captain Ussher, with all his revenue of peelers* an' his guns, may meet his match there yit. They'll hole him,* av he goes on much farthur, as shure as my name's Pat."

"They'll get the worst of that, Brady—not that I care a thrawneen* for him and his company. It's true for you; he is persecuting them too far; what with revenue police, constabulary police, and magistrates' warrants, they won't let them walk to mass quietly next. I didn't care what they did to Master Myles,* but they'd have the worst of it in the end."

"And it's little you ought to care for the same Captain, Misthur Thady, av you heard all. It's little he's making of Miss Feemy's name with the police captain, and the young gauger,* and young James Fitzsimon, when they're over there at Ballinamore together—and great nights they have of it too; though they all have it in Mohill he's to marry Miss Feemy.

If so, indeed! but then isn't he a black Protestant,*sorrow take them for Protestants! There's Hyacinth Keegan calls himself a Protestant now; his father warn't ashamed of the ould religion, when he sarved processes away to Drumshambo."

"And what wor the gentlemen saying about Feemy, Pat?"

"Oh, yer honor, how could I know what gentlemin is saying over their punch, together? only they do be sayin' in Ballinamore, that the Captain doesn't spake that dacently of Miss Feemy, as if they wor to be man and wife: sorrow blister his tongue the day he'd say a bad word of her!"

"Faith he'd better take care of himself, if it's my sister he's playing his game with; he'll find out, though there aint much to be got worth having at Ballycloran now, as long as there's a Macdermot in it, he may still get the traitment a blackguard desarves, if he plays his tricks with Feemy!"

Pat saw that his object had been gained; he suspected that no warm feelings of friendship existed in his master towards the aforesaid Captain, and he was determined there should be none if he could help it. He was not wrong in his surmises; for, from the constant visits of Myles Ussher to Ballycloran, people had for some time been saying that he meant to marry Feemy. They now began to say that he ought to do so.

While her brother and his minister are discussing that subject, and others—settling who could pay, or who should pay, at the convocation of the tenants to be held on the coming Friday, and who couldn't, and who should be ejected, and who not—we will obtain a little insight into Captain Ussher's affairs, and account for the residence of so gallant a gentleman in the little town of Mohill.

CHAPTER IV

MYLES USSHER

EVERY one knows that Ireland, for her sins, maintains two distinct, regularly organised bodies of police; the duties of the one being to prevent the distillation of potheen or illicit whiskey, those of the other to check the riots created by its consumption. These forces, for they are in fact military forces, have each their officers, sub-officers, and privates, as the army has; their dress, full dress, and half dress; their arms, field arms, and house arms; their barracks, stations, and military regulations; their captains, colonels, and commander-in-chief, but called by other names; and, in fact, each body is a regularly disciplined force, only differing from the standing army by being carried on in a more expensive manner.

The first of these—that for preventing the distillation of potheen, commonly called the revenue police—was, at the time of our story, honoured by the services of Myles Ussher. He held the office of one of the sub-inspectors in

the county of Leitrim, and he resided in the
town of Mohill; he had a body of about five-
and-twenty men under him, with a sergeant;
and his duty was, as I have before said, to
prevent the distillation of potheen. This was
only to be done by seizing it when made, or in
the process of making; and, as a considerable
portion of the fine levied in all cases possible
from the dealers in the trade, became the per-
quisite of the sub-inspector or officer effecting
the seizure, the situation in a wild lawless district was one of considerable emolument; consequently gentlemen of repute and good family
were glad to get their sons into the service, and
at the present time, a commission in the revenue
police is considered, if not a more fashionable,
at any rate a more lucrative appointment than
a commission in the army. Among these officers
some of course would be more active than others,
and would consequently make more money;
but it will be easily imagined, that however
much the activity of a sub-inspector of revenue
police might add to his character and standing
at headquarters, it would not be likely to make
him popular in the neighbourhood in which he
resided.

Myles Ussher was most active in the situation
which he filled; whether an impartial judge
would have said that he was too much so,
would be a question difficult to settle, as I have
no impartial judge on the subject to whom I
can refer; but the persons among whom he
lived thought that he was. At the time I allude
to, about ten years ago, a great deal of whiskey
was distilled in the mountains running between

the counties of Leitrim and Cavan, and in different parts of the County Leitrim. Father Mathew's pledge*was then unknown ; the district is a wild country, not much favoured by gentlemen's residences, and very poor; and though it may seem to be an anomaly, it will always be found to be the case that the poorer the people are the more they drink ; and, consequently, Captain Ussher, as he was usually called in the neighbourhood, found sufficient occupation for himself and his men.

Now the case is different ; the revenue police remain, but their duties have, in most districts, gone ; and they may be seen patrolling the roads with their officers accompanying them, being bound to walk so many miles a day. It is very seldom one hears of their effecting a seizure, and their inactivity is no doubt owing to the prevalence of Father Mathew's pledge of total abstinence.

Myles Ussher was a Protestant, from the County Antrim in the north of Ireland, the illegitimate son of a gentleman of large property, who had procured him the situation which he held ; he had been tolerably well educated ; that is, he could read and write sufficiently, understood somewhat of the nature of figures, and had learnt, and since utterly forgotten, the Latin grammar. He had natural abilities somewhat above par ; was good-looking, strongly made, and possessed that kind of courage, which arises more from animal spirits, and from not having yet experienced the evil effects of danger, than from real capabilities of enduring its consequences. Myles Ussher had never yet been

hit in a duel, and would therefore have no
hesitation in fighting one; he had never yet
been seriously injured in riding, and would
therefore ride any horse boldly; he had never
had his head broken in a row, and therefore
would readily go into one; he cared little for
bodily pain if it did not incapacitate him,—little
at least for any pain he had as yet endured, and
his imagination was not strong enough to suggest
any worse evil. And this kind of courage,
which is the species by far most generally met
with, was sufficient for the life he had to lead.

But the quality in which Ussher chiefly excelled, and which was most conducive to give
him the character which he certainly held in the
country for courage, talent, and gallantry, was
his self-confidence and assurance. He believed
himself inferior to none in powers of body and
mind, and that he could accomplish whatever
he perseveringly attempted. He had, moreover,
an overwhelming contempt for the poor, amongst
whom his duties so constantly brought him, and
it is not therefore wonderful that he was equally
feared and execrated by them. I should also
state that Myles Ussher had had sagacity
enough to keep some of the money which he
had received, and this added not a little both
to his reputation and standing in the country,
and also to the real power which he possessed;
for in Connaught ready money is scarce, and its
scarcity creates its importance.

This, then, was Feemy's lover, and she
certainly did love him dearly; he had all the
chief ornaments of her novel heroes—he was
handsome, he carried arms, was a man of

danger, and talked of deeds of courage ; he
wore a uniform ; he rode more gracefully, talked
more fluently, and seemed a more mighty
personage, than any other one whom Feemy
usually met. Besides, he gloried in the title of
Captain, and would not that be sufficient to
engage the heart of any girl in Feemy's position ?
let alone any Irish girl, to whom the ornaments
of arms are always dear. But whether he loved
her as truly, might, I fear, be considered doubtful ; if so, why were they not married ?

Larry Macdermot was too broken-hearted a
man, and too low-spirited, to have objected to
Myles on the ground of his being a Protestant :
it was not that he was indifferent about his
religion, but he had not heart enough left to be
energetic on any subject. In other respects,
Myles was more than a match for his daughter,
in the present fallen condition of the family.
But the matter had not even been mentioned
to him by his daughter or her lover. Ussher
was constantly at Ballycloran,—was in the habit
of riding over from Mohill, only three miles,
almost daily, when disengaged, giving his horse
to Patsy,*the only male attendant at Ballycloran,
and staying the whole morning, or the evening,
there, without invitation ; and Larry, if he never
seemed particularly glad, at any rate never
evinced any dislike to his visits.

Whatever war the sub-inspector might wage
against run spirits in the mountains and bogs,
he always appeared on good terms with it at
Ballycloran, and as the Macdermots had but
little else to give in the way of hospitality, this
was well.

Young Thady could not but see that his sister was attached to Ussher; but he knew that she could not do better than marry him, and if he considered much about it, he thought that she was only taking her fun out of it, as other girls did, and that it would all come right. Thady was warmly attached to his sister; he had had no one else really to love; he was too sullen at his prospects, too gloomy from his situation, to have chosen for himself any loved one on whom to expend his heart; he was of a disposition too saturnine, though an Irishman, to go and look for love when it did not fall in his way, and all that he had to give he gave to his sister. But it must be remembered that poor Thady had no refinement; how should he? And though he would let no one injure Feemy if he could help it, he hardly knew how effectually to protect her. His suspicions were now aroused by his counsellor Pat Brady; but the effect was rather to create increased dislike in him against Ussher, than to give rise to any properly concerted scheme for his sister's welfare.

On the evening previous to the fair at Mohill mentioned in the last chapter, Captain Ussher with a party of his men had succeeded in making a seizure of some half-malted barley in a cabin on the margin of a little lake on the low mountains, which lay between Mohill and Cashcarrigan.* He had, as in these cases was always his practice, received information from a spy in his pay, who accompanied him, dressed as one of his own men, to prevent any chance of his being recognised; this man's name was Cogan, and he had been in the habit of buying illicit whiskey from the makers at a very cheap rate, and carrying it round to the farmers' houses and towns for sale, whereby he obtained considerable profit, but at considerable risk. With this employment Captain Ussher had made himself acquainted, and instead of seizing the man whilst in possession of the whiskey, he had sounded him, and finding him sufficiently a villain, had taken him into his pay as a spy; this trade Cogan found more lucrative even than the former, but also more dangerous; as if detected he might reckon on his death as certain. He still continued to buy the spirits from the people, but in smaller quantities; he offered lower prices; and though he nominally kept up the trade, it was more for the purpose of knowing where the potheen was, than of buying and selling it.

It was not wonderful therefore that more seizures than ever had been lately made, and that the men were getting more cautious, and at the same time more irate and violent in their language. In the present instance the party had come on the cabin in question unawares; not that they might not have been noticed, but that the people were confident of not being suspected. No whiskey had been run there; and the barley had only lately been brought in turf kishes from another cabin where it was not thought to be safe.

Three men and an old woman were found in the cabin when Captain Ussher entered with three of his own men. On being questioned they denied the existence of either whiskey, malt, or barley; but on searching, the illicit article was found in the very kishes in which it had been brought; they were easily discovered shoved into the dark chimney corner farthest from the door.

" Dat*I may never see the light," began the old woman, " if I thought it wor anything but the turf, and jist the kishes that Barney Smith left there, the morn; and he to say nothing of the barley, and bring all these throubles on me and yer honer,—the like of him, the spalpeen*! "

" Never mind my trouble, my dear," said Ussher; " it is little we think of the trouble of easing you; and who's Barney Smith, ma'am ? "

" Oh, then, Barney's jist my daughter's own son; and he coming down from the mountains with turf, and said he must lave the kishes here, till he just went back round Loch Sheen with the ass he'd borrowed from Paddy Byrne, and he'd be— "

" And very good natured it was of him to leave you the malt instead of the turf; and who are you, my good men ? "

The men had continued smoking their pipes quietly at the fire without stirring.

" We be sthrangers here, yer honer," said one; " that is, not sthrangers jist, but we don't live here, yer honer."

" Where do you live, and what's your names ? "

" I and Joe Smith live down away jist on the road to Cash, about half a mile out of this; and Tim Reynolds, he lives away at Drumleesh, on Mr. Macdermot's land; and my name's Paddy Byrne."

" Oh, oh; so one of you is father of the lad

νᴀo brought the donkey, and the other the owner of it ; and you neither of you knew what was in the kishes."

"Sorrow a know, yer honer ; ye see Barney brought them down here from the mountains when we warn't in it ; and it war some of the boys up there was getting him to get away the malt unknownst, hearing of yer honer, maybe."

"Ah, yes, I see—whose land is this on?"

"Counseller Webb's, yer honer."

"Who holds the cabin and potato garden?"

"I do, your honer, jist for my wife's mother, ye see ; but I live down towards Cash."*

"Ah, very good-natured of you to your wife's mother. I hope the three of you have no objection to take a walk to Mohill this evening."

"Ochone, ochone,* and it's ruined we'll be, yer honer ; and that I may never see the light if the boys knew it ; and yer honer wouldn't have the death of an ould woman on ye!" the old woman was exclaiming, while the police began seizing the malt and making prisoners of the men.

"Carol, see and get an ass to put these kishes on," said Ussher. "Killeen, pass a rope across these fellows' arms ; I suppose they'll go quiet."

It was now full time for the men to arise when they found that the rope was to be fastened across their arms ; which meant that a rope was to be fastened on the right arm of one, passed behind his back, fastened to the arm of the second, and so behind his back to the third. Smith and Byrne, the former of whom in spite of his protestations to the contrary was the inhabitant of the cabin, had given the matter up as lost; but as the other, Tim Reynolds, did in fact reside at Drumleesh, he thought he might still show some cause why he should not be arrested for visiting his friend Joe Smith.

"Yer honer won't be afther taking an innocent boy like me," began Tim, "that knows nothing at all at all about it. Shure yer honer knows the masther, Mr. Thady down at Ballycloran; he will tell yer honer I'd nothing in life to do in it. Then don't you know yourself I live with Joe Reynolds down at Drumleesh, and war only up here jist gagging with the ould woman and the boys, and knew nothing in life—how could I?—about the malt, Captain Ussher."

"Oh no, Mr. Reynolds, of course you could not; how could you, as you justly observe,—particularly being the brother of that inoffensive character Mr. Joe Reynolds, and you living too on Mr. Macdermot's property. You and your brother never ran whiskey at Drumleesh, I suppose. Why should a tenant of the Macdermots escape any more than one of Counsellor Webb's?"

"No, yer honer, in course not; only you being so thick with the masther, and that like; and av he'd spake a good word for me—as why shouldn't he?—and I knowing nothing at all at all about it, perhaps yer honer—"

"I'm sorry, Mr. Reynolds, I cannot oblige you in this little matter, but that's not the way I do business. Come along, Killeen; hurry, it's getting d—d cold here by the water."

With this Captain Ussher walked out of the cabin, and the two men followed, each having an end of the rope. Smith and Byrne followed doggedly, but silently; but poor Reynolds, though no lawyer, could not but feel that he was unjustly treated.

"And will I go to gaol then, jist for coming up to see ould widow Byrne, Captain?"

"Yes, Mr. Reynolds, as far as I can foresee, you will."

"Then, Captain Ussher, it's you'll be sorry for the day you were trating that way an innocent boy that knows nothing at all at all about it."

"Do you mean to be threatening me, you ruffian?"

"No, Captain Ussher, I doesn't threaten you, but there is them as does; and it's this day's work, or this night's that's all the same, will be the black night work to you. It's the like of you that makes ruffians of the boys about; they isn't left the manes of living, not even of getting the dhry pratees; and when they tries to make out the rint with the whiskey, which is not for themselves but for them as is your own friends, you hunts them through the mountains and bogs like worried foxes; and not that only; but for them as does it, and them as does not be doing it, is all the same; and it's little the masther, or, for the like of that, the masther's daughter either, will be getting from being so thick with sich as you,—harrowing and sazing his tenants jist for your own fun and divarsion. Mind I am not threatening you, Captain Ussher, but it's little good you or them as is in Bally-cloran will be getting for the work you're now doing—What are you pulling at, misther?

D'ye think I can't walk av myself, without your hauling and pulling like a gossoon*at a pig's hind leg."

The last part of 'Tim's eloquence was addressed to the man who held the foremost end of the rope, and who was following his officer at a rapid pace.

Captain Ussher made no further answer to his remonstrating prisoner, but marched on rapidly towards Carrick after the advanced party, with whom was Cogan the informer. He, after having pointed out the cabin, of course did not wait to be recognised by its occupiers. This capture was the subject of the discussion held on the fair-day at Mulready's whiskey-shop in Mohill, at which Joe Reynolds the prisoner's brother had presided, as Brady informed Thady Macdermot,—or at any rate had taken the most noisy part. To tell the truth, our friend Pat himself had been present all the evening at Mulready's, and if he did not talk so loud, he had said full as much as Joe. The latter was naturally indignant at the capture of his brother, who, in fact, at the time was living in his cabin, though he did hold an acre or two of ground in the same town-land*as Joe Smith and the widow Byrne. He was not, however, engaged in the potheen making there; and though at the moment of the entrance of the police, the party were all talking of the malt, which had, in fact, been brought from Byrne's cabin to that of his mother and brother-in-law, Reynolds had really nothing to do with the concern.

His known innocence made the party more

indignant, and they consequently swore that among them they'd put an end to our poor friend Ussher, or as Joe Reynolds expressed it, " we'll hole him till there ar'nt a bit left in him to hole." Now, for the benefit of the ignorant, I may say that, " holing a man," means putting a bullet through him.

The injuries done by the police were not, however, the only subject discussed at Mulready's that night.

Ribbonism,*about 183–, was again becoming very prevalent in parts of Ireland, at any rate so said the stipendiary magistrates and the inspectors of police; and if they said true, County Leitrim was full of ribbonmen, and no town so full as Mohill. Consequently the police sub-inspector at Ballinamore, Captain Greenough, had his spies as well as Captain Ussher, and Joe Reynolds was a man against whom secret information had been given. Joe was aware that he was a marked man, and consequently, if not actually a ribbonman, was very well inclined to that or anything else, which might be inimical to gaols, policemen, inspectors, gaugers, or any other recognised authority; in fact, he was a reckless man, originally rendered so by inability to pay high rent for miserably bad land, and afterwards becoming doubly so from having recourse to illegal means to ease him of his difficulties.

He, and many others in the neighbourhood of Mohill somewhat similarly situated, had joined together, bound themselves by oaths, and had determined to become ribbonmen; their chief objects, however, at present, were to free themselves from the terrors of Captains Ussher and Greenough, and to prevent their landlords ejecting them for non-payment of rent. It would be supposed a man of Pat Brady's discernment, station, and character, would not have wished to belong to, or have been admitted by, so desperate a society; but he, nevertheless, was not only of them, but one of their leaders, and it can only be supposed that "he had his rasons."

All these things were fully talked over at Mulready's that night. The indignities offered to humanity by police of every kind, the iniquities of all Protestants, the benefits likely to accrue to mankind from an unlimited manufacture of potheen, and the injustice of rents, were fully discussed; on the latter head certainly Brady fought the battle of his master, and not unsuccessfully; but not on the head that he had a right to his own rents, but what he was to do about Flannelly, if he did not get them.

"And shure, boys, what would the ould masther do, and what would Mr. Thady do without the rint among ye,—an' ould Flannelly dunning about him with his bonds, and his bills and morgidges? How'd ye like to see the good ould blood that's in it now, driven out by the likes of Flannelly and Keegan, and them to be masthers in Ballycloran?"

"That's all very well, Pat, and we'd be sorry to see harum come to Mr. Larry and the young masther along of such born robbers as them; but is them dearer to us than our own flesh and blood? As long as they and the like of them'd stand between us and want, the divil a Keegan

of them all'd dare put a foot in Ballycloran.
But who is it now rules all at Ballycloran?
Who, but that bloody robber, Ussher? They'd
go through the country for him, the born ruffian,
—may food choke him!—and he making little
of them all the time. Bad manners to the like
of him! they say he never called an honest
woman his mother. Will I, Mr. Brady, be
giving my blood for them, and he putting my
brother in gaol, and all for sitting up warming
his shins at Loch Sheen? No; may this be
my curse if I do!" and Joe Reynolds swallowed
a glass of whiskey; "and you may tell Mr.
Thady, Pat, if he wants the boys to stick to
him, let him stick to them, and not be helping
a d—d ruffian to be dhriving the lives out of
them he should befriend. And maybe he will
want us, and that soon; and if he'll stick to us
now, as his fathers always did, sure it's little he
need be fearing Flannelly and Keegan. By
G—, the first foot they set in Ballycloran they
shall leave there for ever, if Thady Macdermot
will help rid his father's land of that bloody
ruffian."

"It's little Mr. Thady loves the Captain, Joe,
and it's little he ever will, I think; however,
you can come up, you know, on Friday, and
say your own say about your brother, and the
rint and all."

"And so I will come, Pat; but there's all the
rint I have, and Mrs. Mulready, I think, 'll have
the best part of that," and he jingled a few halfpence in his pocket. So ended the meeting
previous to the conversation in Macdermot's
rent-office.

CHAPTER V

FATHER JOHN

THE Rev. John McGrath was priest of the parish
of Drumsna at the time of which we write. This
parish contains the post town of Drumsna and
the country adjacent, including the town-land
and demesne*of Ballycloran. At this time the
spacious chapel* which now stands on the hill
about two miles out of Drumsna had not been
built, and Father John's chapel was situated on
the road from Drumsna to Ballycloran. Near
this he had built himself a small cottage in the
quasi-Gothic style, for Father John was a man
of taste ; he rented also about twenty acres of
land, half of this being on the Macdermots'
estate.

The Rev. Mr. McGrath is destined to appear
somewhat prominently in this history, and I
must therefore be excused in giving a somewhat
elaborate description of him.

He had been, like many of the present parish
priests in Ireland, educated in France ; he had
been at college at St. Omer,* and afterwards at
Paris, and had officiated as a curé*there ; he
had consequently seen more of French manners
and society than usually falls to the lot of Irish
theological students in that capital. He was,
also, which is equally unusual, a man of good
family, and from his early avocations was more
fitted than is generally the case with those of

his order, to mix in society. He possessed also
very considerable talents, and much more than
ordinary acquirements, great natural *bonhomie*,
and perpetual good temper. He was a thorough
French scholar, and had read the better portion
of their modern literature. On leaving Paris
he had gone to Rome on a begging expedition,
to raise funds for building chapels in his own
country, and there too he had been well received;
and from thence he had returned to take possession of a populous parish in one of the very
poorest parts of Ireland.

With all his acquirements, however, in many
things Father John was little better than a child.
Though his zeal had enabled him to raise
money for the church, he could never keep any
of his own; he had always his little difficulties,
and though he sedulously strove to live within
his income, and never really much outstripped
it, he was always in want of money. He had
built his house, and, unlike his neighbour, had
managed to pay for it; but he was always in
trouble about it; the rats were in the roof, and
his flooring was all warped, and his windows
would neither open nor shut, and the damp
would get to his books. Therefore, though his
cottage was, exteriorly, the prettiest house in his
parish, interiorly, it was discomfort personified.

A more hospitable man than Father McGrath
never lived even in Connaught; he took a look
in at dinner time as a personal favour; and
whatever might be the state of his larder, his
heart was always full, and the emptiness of the
former never troubled him. He had not the
slightest shame at asking any one to eat potatoes

and cold mutton. They all knew him, and what they were likely to get at his house, and if they did not choose, they need not come. Whoever did come had as good as he had himself. A more temperate man never lived; but he had as much pleasure in seeing another man drink a tumbler of punch, as any one else would in drinking it himself. He kept under his own bed a great stone jar, always, partly at least, full of whiskey of native manufacture; and though, were he alone, the jar would long have remained untouched, as it was, it very often had to be refilled. Tumblers he had only two; when his guests exceeded that, the tea-cups made their appearance, and he would naïvely tell his friends that he meant to buy tumblers when he got any money; but, heaven help them! if he got in debt, the people would never be paid.

His whole domestic arrangements were on a par: his crockery was of a most heterogeneous and scanty description; his furniture of the most common kind, put in bit by bit, as it was found indispensable. In two things only did Father John show his extravagance; in the first, too, his expenditure was only so to be called, in comparison with that of others round him, of the same profession. It was this—he was always dressed like a gentleman; Father John's black coat was always black, never rusty brown; his waistcoat, his trowsers, his garters, even shoes, the same; and not only did his clothes always look new, but they were always well made, as far as his figure would allow; his hat was neat, and his linen clean; his hands, too, were always clean, and, when he was from

home, always gloved; even his steady cob,*
whom he called Paul (it was rumoured that
he had called him St. Paul, but the bishop
objected), together with his saddle and bridle,
was always neat; this particular was nearly all
that the polish of French society had left him,
and those who are accustomed to see Irish
priests will know that this peculiarity would be
striking. His other expensive taste was that
of books; he could not resist the temptation
to buy books, books of every sort, from volumi-
nous editions of St. Chrysostom to Nicholas
Nicklebys and Charles O'Malleys*; and consequently he had a great many. But alas! he
had no book-shelves, not one; some few
volumes, those of every day use, were piled
on the top of one another in his little sitting-
room; the others were closely packed in great
boxes in different parts of the cottage—his bed-
room, his little offertory, his parlour, and many
in a little drawing-room, as he called it, but in
which was neither chair nor table, nor ever
appeared the sign of fire! No wonder the poor
man complained the damp got to his books.

In all other respects Father John was a fair
specimen of the Irish priesthood. He must
have been an eloquent man, for he had been
sent on different foreign missions to obtain
money for building chapels by preaching ser-
mons. But his appearance was anything but
dignified; he was very short, and very fat, and
had little or no appearance of neck; his face,
however, was intelligent; he had bright, small
black eyes, a fine, high forehead, very white
teeth, and short thick, curling, dark hair.

As I am on the subject of the church, I might as well say now that his curate, Father Cullen, was unlike him in everything but his zeal for the church. He was educated at Maynooth,* was the son of a little farmer in the neighbourhood, was perfectly illiterate,—but chiefly showed his dissimilarity to the parish priest by his dirt and untidiness. He was a violent politician; the Catholic Emancipation had become law,* and he therefore had no longer that grievance to complain of; but he still had national grievances, respecting which he zealously declaimed, when he could find a hearer. Repeal of the Union* was not, at that time, the common topic, morning and night, at work and at rest, at table and even at the altar, as it afterwards became; but there were, even then, some who maintained that Ireland would never be herself, till the Union was repealed; and among these was Father Cullen. He was as zealous for his religion as for his politics; and he could become tolerably intimate with no Protestant, without thinking he was specially called on to convert him. A disciple less likely to make converts than Father Cullen it would be difficult to imagine, seeing that in language he was most violent and ungrammatical—in appearance most uncouth—in argument most unfair. He was impatient if any one spoke but himself. He relied in all such arguments on his power of proving logically that his own church was the true church, and as his education had been logical, he put all his arguments into syllogisms. If you could not answer him in syllogisms, he conceived that you must be, evidently to yourself, in the wrong, and that obstinacy alone prevented you from owning it. Father Cullen's redeeming point was his earnestness,—his reality; he had no humbug about him; whatever was there, was real; he had no possible appreciation for a joke, and he understood no ridicule. You might gull him, and dupe him for ever, he would never find you out; his heart and mind were full of the Roman Catholic church and of his country's wrongs; he could neither think nor speak of aught beside.

Ussher was the only Protestant whom this poor man was in the habit of meeting, and he was continually attempting to convert him; in which pursuit Ussher rather encouraged him with the purpose of turning him into ridicule.

Such were the spiritual guides of the inmates of Ballycloran and its neighbourhood.

On the Wednesday morning after the fair, Father John was sitting eating his breakfast in his little parlour, attending much more to a book on the table before him than to the large lumps of bread and butter which he unconsciously swallowed, when the old woman servant, Judy McCan, opened the door and said,

"Father John, plase, there's Denis McGovery wanting to see yer riverence, below then."

People in Connaught always call the hall, door, and passage "below," the parlour, or sitting-room, "above," though, in nine cases out of ten, they are on the same floor.

"Why, then, Judy," said Father John, with his mouth full, "bad manners to them; mayn't I eat a bit of breakfast in peace and quiet?

There was I at the widow Byrne's all night, destroyed with the cold, and nothing the matter with her at last, and now I must lose my breakfast, as well as my sleep."

"It's nothing of that sort, I'm thinking, Father John, but Denis McGovery is afther going to get married, I hear."

"Oh," exclaimed Father John, "that's a horse of another colour; going to get married, is he? and why shouldn't he, and he able to support a wife? let him come in, Judy."

It will be remembered that the "above" and "below" in the priest's house were only terms of compliment, and, as Denis McGovery was standing in the hall,—that is, at the open door of the very room in which Judy McCan had been announcing his attendance,—he, of course, had heard what had passed; therefore, when Father John said "let him come in," he wanted no further introduction, but, thrusting himself just through the door, and taking hold of a scanty lock of hair on his forehead, by way of reverential salutation, he said, "Iss, yer honor."

Now, laconic as this was, it was intended to convey, and did convey, a full assent not only to Judy's assertion that he was "afther going to get married," but also to the priest's remark, that there was no good reason on earth why he shouldn't, seeing that he was able to support a family.

"Iss, yer honor," said Denis McGovery.

"Well, Denis—that'll do, Judy," meaning that Judy need not listen any longer, at any rate within the room—"so you are going to get married, are you?"

"Didn't Father Cullen say anything to your riverence about it, then?"

"Oh, yes, he did then; I didn't remember it just at first, when Judy mentioned your name."

"Iss, yer riverence; if ye plaze, I am going to be married."

The bridegroom in this case was a man about forty years of age, who seemed, certainly, never to have eaten the bread of idleness, for he was all gristle and muscle; nor had he; he was a smith living in Drumsna, and the reputed best shoer of horses in the neighbourhood; and consequently was, as the priest had said, able to maintain a family: in fact, Denis had the reputation of hoarded wealth, for it was said he had thirty or forty pounds in the Loan Fund Office at Carrick-on-Shannon. He was a hard-working, ill-favoured, saving man; but, as he was able to keep a comfortable home over a wife, he had no difficulty in getting one.

"Oh then it pleases me entirely, because you are the boy that's both able and willing to pay your clergyman respectably as you should——"

"In course, your riverence, though the likes of a poor boy like me hasn't much, I wouldn't not be married dacently, Father John; and in course I couldn't expect yer riverence to be doing it for nothing."

"For nothing indeed! Where would I be getting the coat on my back, and the roof over my head?—no, the poor themselves always make out something for me; and you, Denis, that are comfortable, would of course be sorry to set a bad example to those that are not so."

"Oh then, yer riverence is poking yer fun at me."

"No fun at all, Denis. If you that have the money don't pay your priest, who is to, I'd like to know. Fun indeed! no, but it's good earnest I'm talking; and if you have a character that you wish to support, and to give your children after you, it's now you should be looking to it."

Denis McGovery began twirling his hat round in his hand, and bending his knees, as if nonplussed. He had known well enough, beforehand, what the priest would say to him, and the priest too, what answer he would get. The question in these cases is, which would cajole the other the best, and of course the priest would have the best of it. This may seem odd to those who do not know the country; but did he not do so, the Roman Catholic clergyman could not get even the moderate remuneration which he does receive for his laborious services.

"Oh, yer riverence," continued Denis, attempting a grim smile, "you know it's the young woman, or her friends, as always pays the priest mostly."

"And who is the young woman, Denis; Betsy Cane, isn't it?"

"No, Father John," said Denis, blushing almost black through his dark skin; "it ain't Betsy."

"Not Betsy Cane! why she told me three weeks ago you were to be married to her."

"And so I was, yer riverence, only ye see for a mistake as happened."

"A mistake! Was it she made the mistake or you?"

"Why, it warn't exactly herself thin as did it; it war her mother."

"Her mother made a mistake! What mistake did her mother make?"

"Along of the cow, yer riverence." Denis seemed very slow of explaining, and Father John began to be impatient.

"What cow, Denis? How did the mother's making a mistake about the cow prevent your marrying her daughter?"

"Why, yer riverence, then, if you'll let me, I'll jist explain the matter. Ould Betsy Cane —that's her mother, you know—promised me the brown cow, yer riverence may know, as is in the little garden behint the cabin, for her dater's fortin; and says I to her, 'Well, may be she may be worth four pound tin, Mrs. Cane.' 'Four pound tin,' says she, 'Mr. McGovery; and you to know no better than that, and she to calve before Christmas! well then, four pound tin indeed,'—jist in that manner, yer riverence. Well then I looks at the cow, and she seemed a purty sort of a cow, and I agreed to the bargain, yer honer, purviding the cow turned out to be with calf. Well, yer honer, now it's no such thing, but it's sticking me she was entirely about the cow: so now she got the cow and her daughter both at home; and likely to for me."

"And so, Denis, you broke your promise, and refused to marry the girl you were engaged to, because a cow was not in calf?"

"No I didn't, yer honer; that is, I did refuse

to marry the girl; why wouldn't I? But I didn't break my promise, becase I only promised, purviding—; and you see, Father John, they was only decaving me."

"Well, Denis; and who is it after all that you are going to have?"

"Well, then, it's jist Mary Brady."

"What! Pat Brady's sister is it?"

"Iss, yer honer."

"And is her cow really in the family way?"

"Now yer riverence 'll make a handle of that agin me!"

"Never mind, Denis, how I handle the cow, so long as you handle the calf; but has Mary a cow?"

"No, Father John, she aint got a cow then, as I knows on."

"Well, Denis, and what fortune are you to get? You are not the man would take a wife unless she brought something with her."

"Well then, it's only jist a pair of young pigs and a small thrifle of change."

"A trifle of change, eh! Then, Mr. McGovery, I take it, it wasn't only along of the mistake about a cow that you left poor Betsy Cane, but you found you could do better, I suppose."

"Well then, it might be jist a little of both; but you see, Father John, they war the first to decave me."

"Well, Denis, and when's the wedding to be?"

"Oh—then, to-morrow evening, if yer riverence plazes."

"What! so soon, Denis? Take care; perhaps after all Betsy Cane's cow may calve; see;

would you be too much in a hurry after the pigs?"

"Sorrow to the tongue of me then that I tould yer riverence a word about it!"

"But what are you in such a hurry about? Won't the pigs do as well at Pat Brady's as they will down at Drumsna?"

"Why you see, Father John, after to-morrow is Friday, which wouldn't do for the two legs of mutton Pat brought from Carrick with him yesterday, and the fine ham, yer riverence, Mrs. McKeon, long life to her, has sent us up from Drumsna; and Saturday wouldn't shute at all, seeing the boys will mostly be dhrunk, which may be yer honer wouldn't like on the morning of the blessed Sabbath."

"Nor on any other morning. Can't they take their fun without getting drunk, like beasts? But drunk they'll be, of course. And why would not Monday do?"

"Why that's next week, yer riverence!"

"You've remained single all this time, and only jilted poor Betsy Cane last week; and are you so hot after Mary Brady that you can't wait till next Monday to be married? Or is it the pigs, Denis? Are you afraid Pat may change his mind about the pigs, as you did about the cow?"

"Oh, drat the cow now, Father McGrath! and will ye never be aisy with yer joke agin a poor boy? It was not about the pigs then, nor nothing of the kind, but jist that I heard as how, but—" and Denis began scratching his head—"yer honer 'll be after twisting what I'll be tellin' yer, and poking your fun at me."

"Not I, my boy; out with it. You know nothing goes farther with me."

"Then it war just this, yer riverence, as makes me so hurried about getting the thing done. I heard tell that Tom Ginty, the pig-jobber, has comed home to Dromod from where he was away tiv' Athlone; and they do be telling me, he brought a thrifle of money with him; and yer honer knows Mary had half given a promise to Ginty afore he went; and so, yer riverence, lest there be any scrimmage* betwixt Ginty and I, ye see it's as well to get the marriage done off hand."

"Oh yes, I see; you were afraid Tom Ginty would be taking Mary Brady's pigs to Athlone. That was it, was it?"

"No, yer honer, I war not afraid of that; but it might be as well there should be no scrimmage betwixt us, as in course there would not be, and we oncet man and wife. But as in course Mary has promised me now, she could not go and act like that."

"Why no, Denis, not well; unless, you know, she was to find your cow would not have any calf, eh?"

"Oh, bother it for a calf then!"

"No; for not being a calf, Denis."

"Well then, yer honer, I'll jist go and spake to Father Cullen. Though he is not so good-humoured like,—at least, he don't be always laughing at a boy."

"Come back, McGovery, and don't be a fool. Father Cullen's gone to Dromod. I think I heard him say Tom Ginty wanted him."

"Is it Tom Ginty? but shure what would

Tom be doing with Father Cullen? wouldn't
he be going to his own priest? Well, what
time will yer riverence come up to Pat Brady's
to-morrow?"

"Well, get the mutton done about seven to-
morrow evening, and I'll be with you. But
you'll ask Tom Ginty, eh?"

"Sorrow a foot,*then!"

"Nor Betsy Cane, Denis?"

"It ar'nt for me to ax the company, Father
John, but if Betsy likes to come up and shake
her feet*and take her sup, she's welcome for
me."

"That's kind of you; and you know you
could be asking after the——"

"Well then, Father John, may it be long
before I spake another word to you, barring my
sins!"

"Well, Denis, I've done. But, look ye now
you've a good supper for the boys, and lots of
the stuff,*I'll go bail. Let there be plenty of
them in it, and don't let them come with their
pockets empty. By dad, they think their priest
can live on the point*without the potatoes."

"Oh, Father John, Pat says there'll be plenty
of them in it, and a great wedding he says he'll
make it: there's a lot of the boys over from
Mohill is to be there."

"From Mohill, eh? then they've my leave to
stay away; I don't care how little I see of the
boys from Mohill. Why can't he get his company from Drumsna and the parish?"

"Oh shure, yer riverence, an' he'll do that
too; won't there be all the Ballycloran tenants,
and the boys and girls from Drumleesh?"

"Oh yes, Drumleesh; Drumleesh is as bad as Mohill; I'm thinking it's those fellows in Drumleesh that make Mohill what it is; but I suppose Pat Brady would tell me he has a right to choose his own company."

Oh, Pat would not tell your riverence the like of that."

"And he's the boy that would do it, directly. And mind this, McGovery, you've the name of a prudent fellow—when you're once married, the less you see of your brother-in-law the better, and stick to your work in Drumsna."

"And so I manes. Oh, yer riverence, they won't be making me be wasting my hard arned wages at Mrs. Mulready's. Pat wanted me to be there last night of all, as I was coming out of the fair; but, no, says I; if ye'd like to see yer sister respectable, don't be axing me to go there; if ye'd like her to be on the roads, and me in Carrick Gaol, why that's the way, I take it."

"Stick to that, Denis, and you'll be the better of it. Well, I'll be down with you to-morrow evening; but mind now, two thirties* is the very least; and you should make it more, if you want any luck in your marriage."

"I'll spake to Pat, Father John; you know that's his business; but your riverence, Father John, you'll not be saying anything up there before the boys and girls about you know— Betsy Cane, you know."

"Oh! the cow!—only, you see, if you don't come down with the money as you should, it might be an excuse for your poverty. But, Denis, I'll take care; and if any one should say anything about the price of cows or the like, I'll tell them all it isn't Betsy Cane's cow, who wouldn't have the calf, though she was engaged."

Denis McGovery now hurried off. Father John called for Judy to take away the cold tea, and prepared to sally forth to some of his numerous parochial duties.

But Father McGrath was doomed to still further interruptions. He had not walked above a mile on his road,—he was going by Ballycloran,—when, coming down the avenue, he saw Pat Brady with his master, Mr. Thady, and of course he didn't pass without waiting to speak to them.

"Well, Thady," and "Well, Father John," as they shook hands; and, "Well, Pat Brady," and "Well, yer riverence," as the latter made a motion with his hand towards his hat, was the first salutation.

It will be remembered that Thady and the other had just been talking over affairs in the rent-office, and Thady did not seem as though he were exactly in a good humour.

"So, Pat, your sister is getting married to Denis McGovery. I'll tell you what—she might do a deal worse."

"She might do what she plased for me, Father John. But, faix, I was tired enough of her myself; so, you see, Denis is welcome to his bargain."

"What! are you going to bring a wife of your own home then?"

"Devil a wife, then, axing your riverence's pardon. What'd I be doing with a wife?"

"Who'll keep the house over you now, Pat, your sister's as good as gone?"

"I won't be axing a woman to keep the house over me; so Mary's welcome to go; or, she wor welcome to stay, too, for me. I didn't ax her to have him, and, by the 'postles, when Denis is tired of his bargain, he'll be recollecting I wasn't axing him to have her."

"Well, Thady, I suppose you and Feemy 'll be at the wedding, eh? and, Pat, you must make them bring Captain Ussher. Mrs. McGovery, as is to be, must have the Captain at her wedding; you'll be there, Thady?"

"Oh, Pat's been telling me about it, and I suppose I and Feemy must go down. If Brady chooses to ask the Captain, I've nothing to say; it's not for me to ask him, and, as he'd only be quizzing*at all he saw, I think he might as well be away."

"Ah! Thady, but you never think of your priest; think of the half-crown* it would be to me. Never mind, Pat, you ask him; he'll come anywhere, where Miss Feemy is likely to be; eh, Thady?"

"Then I wish Feemy had never set eyes on him, Father John; and can't you be doing better than coupling her name with that of his, that way? and he a black ruffian and a Protestant, and filling her head up with nonsense: I thought you had more respect for the family. Well, Pat, jist go down to them boys, and do as I was telling you:"—and Pat walked off.

"And what more respect for the family could I have, Thady, than to wish to see your sister decently married?" and Father John turned

round to walk back with young Macdermot the
way he was going, " what better respect could
I have ? If Captain Ussher were not a proper
young man in general, your father and you,
Thady, wouldn't be letting him be so much with
Feemy; and, now we're on it, if you did not
mean it to be a match, and if you did not mean
they should marry, why have you let him be so
much at Ballycloran, seeing your father doesn't
meddle much in anything now ? "

"That's just the reason, Father John, I couldn't
be seeing all day who was in it and who was
not; besides, Feemy's grown now; she's no
mother,* and must learn to care for herself."

" No, Thady, she's no mother; and no father,
poor girl, that can do much for her; and isn't
that the reason you should care the more for
her ? Mind, I'm not blaming you, Thady, for
I know you do care for her; and you only want
to know how to be a better brother to her; and
what could she do better than marry Captain
Ussher ? "

" But isn't he a black Protestant, Father John ;
and don't the country hate him for the way he's
riding down the poor ? "

" He may be Protestant, Thady, and yet not
'black.' Mind, I'm not saying I wouldn't rather
see Feemy marry a good Catholic; but if she's
set her heart on a Protestant, I wouldn't have
you be against him for that : that's not the way
to show your religion; it's only nursing your
pride ; and sure, mightn't she make a Catholic
of him too ? "

" Oh, Father Cullen has tried that."

" Well, I wouldn't tell him so, but I think

your sister would show more power in convert-
ing a young fellow like Ussher than poor Cullen.
And then, as to his riding down the poor; you
know every one must do his duty, and if the
boys will be acting against the laws, why, of
course, they must bear the consequences. Not
but that I think Captain Ussher is too hard
upon them. But, Thady, are you telling me
the truth in this? Is it not that you fear the
young man won't marry Feemy, rather than that
he will?"

"Why, Father John?"

"I'll tell you why, Thady: this Captain
Ussher has been the intimate friend in your
house now for more than six months back; he
has been received there willingly by your father,
and willingly by yourself, but still more willingly
by Feemy; all the country knows this; of course
they all said Feemy was to be married to him;
and who could say why she shouldn't, if her
father and brother agreed? I always thought
it would be a match; and though, as I said
before, I would sooner have married Feemy to
a good Catholic, I should have thought myself
much exceeding my duty as her priest, had I
said a word to persuade her against it. Now
people begin to say—and you know what they
say in the parish always comes to my ears—that
Captain Ussher thinks too much of himself to
take a wife from Ballycloran, and that he has
only been amusing himself with your sister; and
I must tell you, Thady, if you didn't know more
of Captain Ussher and his intentions than you
seem to do, it isn't to-day you should be thinking what you ought to do."

Thady walked on with his head down, and the priest went on.

" I've been meaning to speak to you of this some days back, for your poor father is hardly capable to manage these things now; and it's the respect I have for the family, and the love I have for Feemy,—and, for the matter of that, for you too,—that makes me be mentioning it. You aint angry with your priest, are you, Thady, for speaking of the welfare of your sister ? If you are, I'll say no more."

" Oh no ! angry, Father John ! in course I aint angry. But what can I do then ? Bad luck to the day that Ussher darkened the door of Ballycloran ! By dad, if he plays Feemy foul he'll shortly enter no door, barring that of hell fire ! "

" Whisht, Thady, whisht !*it's not cursing 'll do you any good in life, or Feemy either ; "— and then continued the priest, seeing that poor Macdermot still appeared miserably doubtful what to say or do, " come in here awhile," they had just got to the gate of Father John's Gothic cottage, "just come in here awhile, and we'll talk over what will be best to do."

They entered the little parlour in which McGovery had shortly before been discussing his matrimonial engagements, and having closed the door, and, this time, taking care that Judy McCan was not just on the other side of it, and making Macdermot sit down opposite to him, the priest began, in the least disagreeable manner he could, to advise him on the very delicate subject in question.

" You see, Thady, there's not the least doubt in life poor Feemy's very fond of him ; and how could she not be, poor thing, and she seeing no one else, and mewed up there all day with your father?—no blame to her—and in course she thinks he means all right; only she doesn't like to be asking him to be naming the day, or talking to you or Larry, or the like, and that's natural too; but what I fear is, that he's taking advantage of her ignorance and quietness, you see; and, though I don't think she would do anything really wrong, nor would he lead her astray altogether—"

"And av he did, Father John, I'd knock the brains out of the scoundrel, though they hung me in Carrick Gaol for it; I would, by G—!"

"Whisht, now, Thady; I don't mean that at all—but you get so hot—but what I really mean is this; though no actual harm might come of it, it doesn't give a girl a good name through the country, for her to be carrying on with a young man too long, and that all for nothing; and Feemy's too pretty and too good, to have a bad word about her. And so, to make a long story short, I think you'd better just speak to her, and tell her, if you like, what I say; and then, you know, if you find things not just as they should be, ask her not to be seeing the Captain any more, except just as she can't help; and do you tell him that he's not so welcome at Ballycloran as he was, or ask him at once what he means about your sister. It's making too little of any girl to be asking a man to marry her, but better that than let her break her heart, and get ill spoken of through the country too."

"I don't think they dare do that yet, poor as the Macdermots now are, or, by heaven——"

"There's your pride, — bad pride, again, Thady. Poor or rich, high or low, don't let your sister leave it to any one to speak bad of her, or put it in any man's power to hurt her character. At any rate, by following my advice, you'll find how the land lies."

"But you see, Father John, she mightn't exactly mind what I say. Feemy has had so much of her own way, and up to this I haven't looked after her ways,—not so much as I should, perhaps; though, for the matter of that, there's been little need, I believe; but she's been left to herself, and if she got cross upon me when I spoke of Ussher, it would only be making ill blood between us. I'd sooner a deal be speaking to Captain Ussher."

"Nonsense, Thady; do you mean to say you are afraid to speak to your sister when you see the necessity? By speaking to Captain Ussher you mean quarrelling with him, and that's not what'll do Feemy any good."

"Well, then, I'm sure, I'll do anything you tell me, Father John; but if she don't mind me, will you speak to her?"

"Of course I will, Thady, if you wish it; but go and see her now at once, while it's on your mind, and though Feemy may be a little headstrong, I think you'll find her honest with you."

"I'll tell you another thing, Father John; father is so taken up with Ussher, and—to out with it at once—he's trying to borrow a thrifle of money from him; not that that should stand in my way, but the ould man gets obstinate, you know."

"Oh, then, that'd be very bad, Thady; why

doesn't he go to his natural friends for money, and not to be borrowing it of a false friend and a stranger?"

"Nathural friends! and who is his nathural friends! Is it Flannelly, and Hyacinth Keegan? I tell you what it is, Father John, Feemy and her father and I won't have the roof over our heads shortly, with such nathural friends as we have. God knows where I'm to make out the money by next November, even let alone what's to come after."

"Anything better than borrowing from Ussher, my boy; but sure, bad as the time is, the rints more than pay Flannelly's interest money, any how."

"I wish you had to collect them then, Father John, and then you'd see how plentiful they are; besides, little as is spent, or as there is to spend up above there, we can't live altogether for nothing."

"No, Thady, the Lord knows we can none of us do that—and, tell the truth now, only I stopped the words in your throat about poor Feemy's business, weren't you just going to be dunning me for the bit of rent? out with it now."

"It's little heart I have now to be saying to you what I was going to do, for my soul's sick within me, with all the throubles that are on me. An' av it warn't for Feemy then, Father John, bad as I know I've been to her, laving her all alone there at Ballycloran, with her novels and her trash,*—av it warn't for her, it's little I'd mind about Ballycloran. There is them still as wouldn't let the ould man want his stirabout, and his tumbler of punch, bad as they all are to us; and for me, I'd sthrike one blow for the counthry, and then, if I war hung or shot, or murthered any way, devil a care. But I couldn't bear to see the house taken off her, and she to lose the rispect of the counthry entirely, and the name of Macdermot still on her!"

"Oh, nonsense, Thady, about blows for your country, and getting hung and murthered. You're very fond of being hung in theory, but wait till you've tried it in practice, my boy."

"May be I may! there be many things to try me."

"Oh, bother Thady; stop with your nonsense now. Go up to your sister, and have your talk well out with her, and then come down to me. Judy McCan has got the best half of a goose, and there's as fine a bit of cold ham—or any way there ought to be—as ever frightened a Jew; and when you get a tumbler of punch in you, and have told me all you've said to Feemy, and all Feemy s said to you, why, then you can begin to dun in earnest, and we'll tall over how we'll make out the rint."

"No, Father John, I'd rather not coming down."

"But it's yes, Father John, and I'm not saying what you'd rather do, but showing you your duty; so at five, Thady, you'll be down, and see what sort of a mess Judy makes of the goose."

There was no gainsaying this, so Thady started off for Ballycloran, and Father John once more set about performing his parochial duties.

CHAPTER VI

THE BROTHER AND SISTER

AT the time that the priest and young Macdermot were talking over Feemy's affairs at the
cottage, she and her lover were together at
Ballycloran.

Nothing that her brother or Father John had
said about her, either for her or against, would
give a fair idea of her character.

She was not naturally what is called strong-
minded; but her feelings and courage were
strong, and they stood to her in the place of
mind.

She would have been a fine creature had she
been educated, but she had not been educated,
and consequently her ideas were ill-formed, and
her abilities were exercised in a wrong direction.

She was by far the most talented of her
family, but she did not know how to use what
God had given her, and therefore, abused it.
Her mother had died before she had grown up,
and her grandmother had soon followed her
mother. Whatever her feelings were,—and for
her mother they were strong,—the real effect of
this was, that she was freed from the restraint
and constant scolding of two stupid women at
a very early age; consequently she was left
alone with her father and her brother, neither
of whom were at all fitting guides for so way-
ward a pupil. By both she was loved more

than any other living creature; but their very
love prevented them taking that care of her
they should have taken. Her father had
become almost like the tables and chairs in
the parlour, only much less useful and more
difficult to move. What little natural power he
had ever had, could not be said to have been
impaired by age, for Lawrence Macdermot was
not in years an old man—he was not above
fifty; but a total want of energy, joined to a
despairing apathy, had rendered him by this
time little better than an idiot.

Very soon after his coming to his property
Flannelly had become a daily and intolerant
burthen to him. He had in his prime made
some ineffectual fight against this man,—he had
made some faint attempts rather to parry blows,
than overcome his foe; but from the time that
Keegan's cunning had been added to Flannelly's
weight, poor Lawrence Macdermot had, as it
were, owned himself thoroughly vanquished for
this world. Since that time he had done nothing
but complain.

Joined to all this—and no wonder—he had
taken to drink,—not drinking in the would-be-
jolly, rollicking, old Irish style, as his father
had done before him; but a slow, desperate,
solitary, continual melancholy kind of suction,
which left him never drunk and never sober.
It had come to that, that if he were left throughout the morning without his whiskey and water,
he would cry like a child; whatever power he
had of endurance would leave him, and he
would sit over the fire whining the names of
Flannelly and Keegan, and slobbering over his

wrongs and persecutions, till he had again drank himself into silence and passive tolerance.

Not only his hair and his whiskers, but his very face had become grey from the effect of the miserable, torpid life he led. He looked as if he were degenerating into the grub even before he died.

The only visible feeling left to him was a kind of stupid family pride, which solely, or chiefly, showed itself in continual complaints that the descendants and the present family of the Macdermots should be harrowed and brought to the ground by such low-born ruffians as Flannelly and Keegan.

It is odd that though Feemy often thwarted him and Thady rarely did,—and though Thady was making the best fight he could, poor fellow, for the Macdermots and Ballycloran,—the old man always seemed cross to him, and never was so to her. May be he spent more of his time with her, and was more afraid of her; but so it was; and though he certainly loved her better than anything, excepting Ballycloran and his own name, it will be owned that he was no guide for a girl like Feemy, possessed of strong natural powers, stronger passions, and but very indifferent education.

And from circumstances her brother was not much better. He had been called on at a very early age to bear the weight of the family. From the time of his leaving school he had been subjected to constant vexation; on the contrary, his pleasures were very few and far between; his constant occupation for many years had been hunting for money, which was not to be got. If his heart could have been seen, the word "Rent" would have been found engraved on it. Collecting the rent, and managing the few acres of land which the Macdermots kept in their own hands, were his employments, and hard he laboured at them. He was therefore constantly out of the house; and of an evening after his punch, he spent his hours in totting and calculating, adding and subtracting at his old greasy book, till he would turn into bed, to forget another day's woes, and dream of punctual tenants and unembarrassed properties. Alas! it was only in his dreams he was destined to meet such halcyon things. What could such a man have to say to a young girl that would attract or amuse her? Poor Thady had little to say to any one, except in the way of business, and on that subject Feemy would not listen to him. She constantly heard her father growling about his Carrick foes, and her brother cursing the tenants; but she had so long been used to it, that now she did not think much of it. She knew they were very poor, and that it was with difficulty she now and again got the price of a new dress from her brother; and when she did, it was usually somewhat in this fashion: Pat Kelly owed two years' rent or so, may be five pounds. Mrs. Brennan, the Mohill haberdasher, took Pat's pig or his oats in liquidation of the small bill then due to her from Ballycloran, and Feemy's credit at the shop was good again about to the amount of another pig. It was very rarely ready money found its way to Ballycloran.

On the whole, therefore, she paid little or no

attention to the family misfortunes. She had
used to confine her desires to occasional visits
to Carrick or Mohill; for they still possessed
an old car, and sometimes she could take the
old mare destined to perform the whole farming
work of Ballycloran; and sometimes she coaxed
the loan of Paul for a day from Father John;
and if she could do that, could always have a
novel from Mohill, and see her friends the Miss
McKeons at Drumsna two or three times a
week, she was tolerably contented and good-
humoured. But of late things were altered.
Feemy had got a lover. Her novels ceased to
interest her; she did not care about going to
Carrick, and the Miss McKeons were neglected.
It was only quite lately, however, that Feemy
had begun to show signs of petulance and ill
temper. When her father grumbled she left
him to grumble alone, and if her brother asked
her to do any ordinary little thing about the
house, she would show her displeasure. She
did not attend either so closely as she used to
do to Biddy and Katty, the two kitchen girls,
and consequently the fare at Ballycloran grew
worse than ever.

Larry always grumbled, but no one marked
his grumbling more than heretofore. Thady
had too many causes of real suffering to grumble
much at trifles, and usually passed over his
sister's petulance in silence : but the truth was,
her lover was sometimes cross to her.

Soon after Father John and young Macdermot
had turned their backs on Ballycloran, Pat
Brady, who stood smoking his pipe, and idly
leaning against the gate-post from which, even

then, the gate was half wrenched, heard the sounds of Captain Ussher's horse on the road from Mohill. As soon as he came up, Brady very civilly touched his hat: "Well then long life to you, Captain Ussher, and it's you enjoys a fine horse, and it'd be a pity you shouldn't have one. You war with the Carrick harriers* last Monday, I'll go bail."

"No doubt, Mr. Brady, you would go bail for that or anything else; but I was not there."

"You war not! faix but you war in the wrong then, Captain, for they had fine sport, right away behind Lord Lorton's new farms*—right to Boyle. I wonder yer honer warn't in it."

"Seeing you know very well I was arresting prisoners up at Loch Sheen, Mr. Brady, your wonder is wonderful."

"Sorrow a taste I knew then, Captain. I did hear at the fair poor Paddy Smith was in throuble about a thrifle of sperits, or the like. But I didn't know yer honer'd been at it yerself. If the boys, ye know, will be going agin the laws, why in course they'd be the worse of it, when they is took."

"A very true and moral reflection. Was it a note you were taking to Mr. Keegan's at Carrick from the master, about the money perhaps, on Monday evening?"

"Me in Carrick Monday evening!" said Pat, a little confused; "so I war shure enough, yer honer, jist to buy the mate for the supper as is to be for McGovery's marriage. You've heard in course, Captain, that Mary—that's my sister—is to be married to Denis McGovery to-morrow night?"

"Why I didn't see it in the Dublin news-papers."

"Oh, yer honer; the newspapers indeed! Perhaps, Captain, you'd not think it too much throuble to come down; Miss Feemy of course has promised Mary to be there,"—and Pat attempted a facetious grin.

"I shall be most proud, Mr. Brady," and the Captain made a mock bow; "but do they sell mutton at Mr. Keegan's little office door?"

Here Brady again seemed confused, and muttered something about Keegan's boy and messages*: but he was evidently annoyed.

"Shall I take yer honer's horse round then?" said he; and Ussher dismounted without saying anything further, and ran up the stone steps, at the top of which Feemy opened the hall door for him.

There were two sitting-rooms at Ballycloran, one at each side of the hall; in that on the right as you entered the family breakfasted, dined, and in fact lived; and here also Larry sat throughout the day sipping his grog, and warming his shins over the fire from morning to night. He would every now and again walk to the hall door; and if it were warm, he would slowly creep down the steps, and stand looking at the trees and the lawn till he was cold, when he would creep back again.

The other room seemed to be the exclusive property of Feemy; here she made and mended her clothes, and sometimes even washed and ironed them too; here she read her novels, received the two Miss McKeons, and thought of Captain Ussher; and here also it was, that he would tell her all the soft things which had filled her young heart, and made her dislike Ballycloran.

"Well, Myles," she said as soon as he was in the room, and before the door was shut, "where were you all this time, since Sunday?" and she stood on tiptoe to give him the kiss which she rather offered than he asked. "Who have you got in Mohill then that keeps you away from Feemy? It's Mary Cassidy now; what business had you shopping with Mary Cassidy?"

"And was I shopping with Mary Cassidy, Feemy? 'deed then I forget it. Oh yes, it was fair-day yesterday, and I saw them all in at Brennan's."

"And what did you want at Brennan's, Myles?" said she, playfully shaking his shoulder with her hand; "it's talking to that pretty girl in the shop you're after."

"Oh, of course, Feemy; I was making love to the three Miss Cassidys, and Jane Thompson, and old widow Brennan at once. But why was I there, you say? why then, I was just buying this for Mary Cassidy, and I wanted your opinion, my pet;" and he took from his pocket some article of finery he had bought for his mistress.

"Oh, Myles, how good of you! but why do you be squandering your money; but it is very pretty," and Feemy put the collar over her shoulders.

"Don't toss it now, or Mary Cassidy won't take it from me, and then it would be left on my hands, for Mrs. Brennan wouldn't take it back anyhow," and he put out his hand for the article.

"No fear, Myles; no fear," said the laughing girl, running round the table. "It won't be left on your hands; I'll wear it to-morrow at Mary Brady's wedding."

"But you won't keep it from me without paying me, Feemy?"

"Oh, paying you, Captain Ussher; oh, I'll pay you; bring in your bill;"—and she came round to him, and he took her in his arms and kissed her. Then at least he seemed fondly attached to her.

Her lover was evidently in one of his best humours, and Feemy was quite happy. I won't further violate their conversation, as it is not essential to the tale, and was much such as those conversations usually are.

Feemy told her lover of the wedding, and he told her that he had already been invited, and had promised to go; and then she was more happy, for Feemy dearly loved a dance, though it was only a jig at a country wedding; but a dance with her lover would be delightful; she had only danced with him twice. On the first of these occasions she had met him at a grand gala party, at Mrs. Cassidy's, the wife of Lord Birmingham's agent in Mohill, where first Captain Ussher had made up his mind that Feemy Macdermot was a finer girl than pretty little Mary Cassidy, though perhaps not so well educated; and once again at a little tea-party at Mrs. McKeon's, which had been got up on purpose by Feemy's friends, to ask her husband as was to be—when first people said it was a

settled thing. Oh! that was a happy night to
Feemy, for her friends then all thought that
her intimacy with Ussher was as good a thing
as could be wished for; and when Feemy
danced the whole night with him, the Miss
McKeons all thought what a happy girl she
was;—and that night she was happy. Then
he first told her she should be his wife, and
swore that he never had loved, and never would
love any but her; and oh, how truly she believed
him! Why should she not? was not she happy
to love him, and why should not he be as much
so to love her? If any one had whispered a
word of caution to her, how she would have
hated the whisperer! But there was no one
to whisper caution to Feemy, and she had
given all she had—her heart, her love, her obedience, her very soul—to him without having
any guarantee that she really had aught in
return.

It was not because she began to doubt her
lover that she was now occasionally fretful and
uneasy. No; the idea to doubt him never
reached her, but nevertheless she felt that
things were not quite as they should be.

He seldom talked of marriage though he
said enough of love; and when he did, it was
with vague promises, saying how happy they
would be when she was his wife, how much
more comfortable her home would be, how
nicely she would receive her friends in Mohill.
These, and little jokes about their future *ménage*
in a married state, were all he had ever said.
She never asked him—indeed, she did not dare
to ask; she did not like to press him; and

Captain Ussher had a frown about him, which, somehow, Feemy had already learnt to fear.

He treated her too a little cavalierly, and her father and brother not a little. He ridiculed openly all that with her, hitherto, had been most sacred—her priest and her religion. She was not angry at this; she was hardly aware of it; and, in fact, was gradually falling into his way of thinking; but the effect upon her was the same—it made her uncomfortable. A girl should never obey her lover till she is married to him; she may comply with his wishes, but she should not allow herself to be told with authority that this or that should be her line of conduct.

Now Feemy had so given herself up to her lover, that she was obedient to him in all things; to him, even in opposition to her brother or her priest, and consequently she was to a degree humiliated even in his eyes. She did not feel the degradation herself, but there was still a feeling within, which she could not define, which usually destroyed her comfort.

Now, however, Myles was in so good a temper, and seemed so kind to her, that that, and her little prospect of pleasure, did make her happy.

She was sitting in this humour on the old sofa close to him, leaning on his arm, which was round her waist, when she heard her brother's footstep at the hall door.

"Here's Thady, Myles; sit off a bit."

Myles got up and walked to the window, and Thady entered with anything but a gay look; he had just left Father John.

"Well, Thady?" said Feemy.

"How are you, Thady, this morning?" said the Captain, offering his hand, which the other reluctantly took.

"Good morning, Captain Ussher."

"Did you hear, Thady, I caught another of your boys with malt up at Loch Sheen last Monday,—Joe Reynolds, or Tim Reynolds, or something? He's safe in Carrick."

"I did hear you got a poor boy up there, who was in it by chance, and took him off just for nothing. But he's no tenant of ours, so I have nothing to do with it; his brother Joe lives on our land."

"Do you mean to tell me, Thady, you believe all that d—d nonsense about knowing nothing about it; and he sitting there in the cabin, and the malt hadn't been in it half an hour?"

"I don't know what you call d—d nonsense, Captain Ussher; but I suppose I may believe what I please without going to Carrick Gaol too for it."

"Believe what you please for me, Master Thady. Why you seem to have got out of bed the wrong side this morning; or have you and Keegan been striking up some new tiff about the 'rints?'"

"Mr. Keegan's affairs with me arn't any affairs of yours, Captain Ussher. When I ask you to set them right, then you can talk to me about them."

"Hoity toity, Mr. Macdermot; your affairs, and Mr. Keegan's affairs, and my affairs! Why I suppose you'll be calling me out next for taking up a d—d whining thief of a fellow because his brother is a tenant of your father's, and send me the challenge by Mr. Brady, who invited me to a party at his house just now."

Thady said nothing to this, but stood with his back to the fire, looking as grim as death.

" Oh, Captain Ussher!" said Feemy, " you wouldn't be quarrelling with Thady about nothing? You know he has so much to bother him with the rents and things. Will you come to Mary's wedding to-morrow, Thady?"

" Quarrelling with him! 'Deed then and I will not, but it seems he wants to quarrel with me."

" When I do want to quarrel with you, Captain Ussher,—that is, should I ever want,— you may be quite certain it's not in a round about way I'll be telling you of it."

" No, don't, my boy, for ten to one I shouldn't understand what you'd be after. Didn't you say you'd walk up to Aughermore, Miss Macdermot?"

" I'm sorry to baulk Feemy of her walk, Captain Ussher, if she did say so. It's not very often I ask her to put herself out for me; but this afternoon, I shall feel obliged to her not to go.

Captain Ussher stared, and Feemy opened wide her large bright eyes; for what reason could her brother desire her to stay indoors?

" What can you want me in the house for, Thady, this time of day?"

" Well, never mind, Feemy; I do want you, and you'll oblige me by staying."

Feemy still had on the new collar, and she pulled it off and threw it on the table; she

evidently imagined that it had something to do
with her brother's unusual request. She certainly would not have put it on in that loose
way, had she thought he would have seen it ;
but then he so seldom came in there.

"Well, Captain Ussher," she at last said
slowly, "I suppose then I can't go to Aughermore to-day."

Captain Ussher had turned to the window as
if not to notice Thady's request, and now came
back into the middle of the room, as if Feemy's
last sentence had been the first he had heard
on the subject.

"Oh! you have changed your mind, then,"
said he ; and his face acquired the look that
Feemy dreaded. "Ladies, you know, are at
liberty to think twice."

"But, Thady, I did wish to go to Aughermore particularly to-day ; wouldn't this evening
or to-morrow do ? "

"No, Feemy," and Thady looked still blacker
than Myles ; "this evening won't do, nor to-
morrow."

"Well, Captain Ussher, you see we must put
it off," and she looked deprecatingly at her
lover.

His answering look gave her no comfort ; far
from it, but he said, "I see no must about it,
but that's for you to judge ; perhaps you should
ask your father's leave to go so far from home."

This was a cruel cut at all the fallen family,
the father's incapacity, the sister's helplessness,
and the brother's weak authority. Feemy did not
feel it so, she felt nothing to be cruel that came
from Ussher ; but Thady felt it strongly, he was

as indignant as if he had lived all his life among those who thought and felt nobly, but, poor fellow, he could not express his indignation as well.

"My sister, Captain Ussher, has long been left her own misthress to go in and out as she plazes, without lave from father, mother, or brother; better perhaps for her that she had not! God knows I have seldom stopped her wishes, though may be not often able to forward them. If she likes she may go now to Aughermore, but if a brother's love is anything to her, she'll stay this day with me."

Feemy looked from one to the other; she knew well by Myles' look, that he still expected her to go, and strange as it may be, she hardly dared to disobey him; but then her brother looked determined and sadly resolute, and it was so unusual in him to speak in that way.

"Well, Miss Macdermot," said Ussher, seeing he could not prevail without causing an absolute break with Thady, "your brother wants you to count the rent for him. I'm glad he has received so much; it must be that, I presume, for he seldom troubles himself on much else, I believe."

"I do what I have to do, and must do; God knows it's throuble enough. Do you go and do the same; even that, bad as it is, is better than amusing my sister by laughing at me."

"Oh, Thady, how can you be saying such things! you see I am staying for you, and why can't you be quiet?"

Thady made no reply; the Captain twirled his hat, and ceremoniously bowing to the lady, took his leave.

Thady had screwed his courage to the sticking point while the Captain was the foe with
whom he had to contend, and he had carried on
the battle manfully while he spoke to Feemy in
the Captain's presence; but to tell the truth,
when he heard the clatter of his horse's feet he
almost wished him back again, or that Feemy
was away with him to Aughermore. He was
puzzled how to begin; he could not think what
he was to say; was he to quarrel with his sister
for having a lover without telling him? was he
to put it on the ground that her lover was a
Protestant? That would have been the easiest
line, but then Father John had especially barred
that! Was he to scold her because her lover
would not marry her at once? That seemed
unreasonable. It had never occurred to him,
in his indignation, to think of these difficulties,
and he now stood with his back to the fire,
looking awfully black, but saying nothing.

"Well, Thady, what is it I'll be doing for
you, instead of going to Aughermore this morning?" at last said Feemy, the first to begin the
disagreeable conversation.

When Thady looked up, thir ..ing what to
answer to this plain speech, his eye, luckily for
him, fell on the new Mohill collar.

"Where were you getting that collar, Feemy?"

"And are you afther making me stay at home
all the blessed day, and sending Captain Ussher
all the way back to Mohill, and he having come
over here by engagement to walk with me,"—
this was a fib of Feemy's—"and all to ask me
where I got a new collar?"

"May be I was, Feemy, and may be I wasn't;

but I suppose there isn't any harum in my asking the question, or in you answering it?"

"Oh no, not the laist; only it ain't usual in
you to be asking such questions."

"But if there's no harum, I ask it now; where
were you getting the collar?"

"Well, you're very queer; but if you must
know, Captain Ussher brought it with him from
Mohill."

"And if you wanted a parcel from Mohill,
why couldn't you let Brady bring it, who is in it
constantly, instead of that upstart policeman,
who'd think it more condescension to bring that
from Mohill, than I would to be carrying a sack
of potatoes so far."

"There then you're wrong; the policeman, as
you're pleased to call him, thinks no such thing."

"Well, Feemy, but did you bid him bring it,
or did he bring it of his own accord?"

Feemy could now shuffle no longer, so blushing slightly, she said, "Well, if you must know
then, it was a present; and there's no such great
harm in that, I suppose."

Here Thady was again bothered; he really
did not know whether there was any harm in
it or not; a week ago he certainly would have
thought not, but he was now inclined to think
that there was; but he was not sure, and he
sadly wished for Father John to tell him what
to do.

"Well, Thady, now what was it you were
wanting of me?"—and then after a pause,
she added, her courage rising as she saw her
brother's falling: "Was it anything about
Captain Ussher?"

"Yes, it was."

"Well?"

"Is there anything between you and he, Feemy?"

"What do you mean by between us, Thady?" and Feemy made a little fruitless attempt to laugh.

"Well then; you're in love with him, ain't you? there now, that's the long and the short."

"Supposing I was, why shouldn't I?"

"Only this, Feemy, he's not in love with you."

This put Feemy's back up, "'Deed then, it's little you know about it, for he just is; and I love him too with all my heart, and that's all about it; and you might have found that out without sending him back to Mohill."

"I wish then he'd stay at Mohill, and that I might never see him over the door at Bally-cloran again!"

"That's kind of you, Thady, after what I just told you; but don't tell him so, that's all."

"But it's just what I mane to tell him, and what I shall go over to Mohill on purpose to tell him, to-morrow."

"Good gracious, Thady! and for why?"

"For why, Feemy! becase I still want to see my father's daughter an honest woman, though she may be soon a beggar; becase I don't want to see my sister crouching under a blackguard's foot; becase I don't want the worst disgrace that can happen a family to blacken the name of Macdermot!"

Feemy was now really surprised; fear at her brother's strange words brought out at once what was ever most present in her mind.

"Oh, heavens, Thady! sure we're to be married."

It must be remembered that this was not an interview between a fashionable brother and an elegant sister, both highly educated, in which the former had considered himself called upon to remonstrate with the latter for having waltzed too often with the same gentleman, and in which any expression of actual blame would highly offend the delicacy of the lady. Thady and his sister had not been accustomed to delicacy; and though she was much shocked at his violence, she hardly felt the strong imputation against herself, as she had so good an answer for it. She therefore exclaimed,

"Oh heavens, Thady! sure we're to be married."

"Well, now, Feemy, jist listen to me. If Captain Ussher manes to marry you, under all circumstances, I don't know you could do better. I don't like him, as how should I, for isn't he a Protestant, and a low-born, impudent ruffian? but you do like him, and I suppose, if he marries you, it's becase he likes you; if not, why should he do it? And when once married, you'll have to fight your own battles, and no joke it'll be for either of you. But if, as I'm thinking, he has no idea on arth of marrying you, no more than he has of Mary Brady, I'll be d——d if I let him come here fooling*you, though you haven't sperit enough to prevent it yourself. We're low enough

already, Feemy, but for heaven's sake don't be
making us lower yet !"

"Well, now, Thady, is that all? and you're
wrong then, as you always are, for Captain
Ussher has asked me to have him, just as plain
as I'm telling you now ; and he's no ruffian.
It is you're the ruffian to him, snubbing him
when he speaks good-naturedly to you. And
as for being a Protestant, I suppose he's none
the worse for that, if he's none the better. I
don't know why you do be hating him so, unless
it's because I love him."

"I'm not talking about my hating him, or
loving him. If he's honest to you, I'll neither
say nor do anything to cross him. But if he
does mane to marry you, it's time he did it ;
that's all. Did he say anything to father
about it ?"

"What should he be saying to him? Of
course, dada would have no objection."

"And would you then be letting him come
here as he likes, and settling nothing, and just
maning to marry you or not, as he likes, and
you and he talked of over the counthry these
four months back, and he talking about you,
jist as his misthress, through the counthry?"

Feemy was now regularly roused.

"That's a lie for you, Thady! and a black
lie—about your own sister too, to say he ever
spoke a bad word against me! Pat Brady was
telling you that perhaps. It's what he never
did, or would do; for he's as true as you are
false ; and it's from jealousy, and just from your
hate, because everybody else likes him, makes
you say it. And now we are on it, Thady, I'll

just tell you one thing : I'm not to do what you tell me, nor will I, for I'm much more able to manage myself than you are for me. And for all you say about him, I'd attend more to one word from Myles, than to all you say, if you stood talking till night ; and talk you may, but I'll not stand and hear you ! " And she bounced out of the room, slamming the door in a manner which made Mr. Flannelly's building shake to the foundation.

Poor Thady was signally defeated. There he stood with his back to the fire, his old and dirty hat pulled low over his brow, his hands stuck into the pockets of his much-worn shooting coat, his strong brogues and the bottoms of his corduroy trowsers covered with dirt and dry mould, with the same heavy discontented look about his face which he always now wore. He certainly appeared but a sorry Mentor for a young lady in a love affair ! He felt that his sister despised him, the more from her being accustomed to the comparatively gentleman-like appearance and refined manners of her lover.

There he stood a long time without stirring, and so he stood in absolute silence. He had put his pipe down when first Captain Ussher left the room, and he had not resumed it, now even that he was alone. With Thady this was a sign that his heart was very full indeed ; and so it was, full almost to breaking.

He had come there eager with two high feelings, love for his sister, real fond brotherly affection, and love and respect for his family name ; he had wished to protect the former from insult and unhappiness, and to sustain the fallen respectability of the latter; and he had only been scoffed at and upbraided by the sister he loved. For he did love her, though little real communication had ever passed between them; he had always supposed that she loved him; he had taken it for granted, and had asked for no demonstrative affection; but her manner and her words now cut him very deep. He was not aware how very uncouth his own manner had been; that instead of reasoning with her gently he had began by sneering at her lover, that he had taken the very course to offend her self-love, and that therefore Feemy was quite as convinced at the end of the meeting that she had a right to be angry, as he was that he was the injured party.

At any rate, there he stood perfectly baffled. His object had been to advise her, if Captain Ussher did not at once declare his purpose to her family, to put a stop to his further visits; and if she refused to comply with his advice, to tell her that he should himself ask Captain Ussher his intentions, and that if they were not such as he approved, he should inform him that he was no longer welcome at Ballycloran.

This had seemed, though disagreeable, straightforward and easy enough before the meeting; and now that it was over he could not think why he had not said exactly what he had come there to say. To give him his due, he blamed himself as much as he did his sister; he was very unhappy about it all, but he could not think how he had been so very stupid.

Had he lived more in the world, he would have had recourse to the common resort in

cases where speech is difficult; he would have
written a letter to his sister. But this never
occurred to him; even had it done so, Thady's
epistolary powers were very small, and his
practice very limited; a memento to the better
sort of tenants, as to their "thrifle of rint," or a
few written directions to Pat Brady, about seizing
crops and driving pigs, was its extent; and these
were written on pieces of coarse paper, which
had been ruled for accounts, and were smeared
rather than fastened with very much salivated
wafers. His writing too was very slow, and his
choice of language not extensive; a letter on
such a subject from a brother to a sister should
be well turned, impressive, terse, sententious:
that scheme would never have done for Thady.

What then should he do? if he were to go to
Captain Ussher now, and tell him to discontinue
his visits, he would only be asked if he had his
sister's authority for doing so, or his father's.
Should he get, or try to get, his father's
authority? The old man he knew was moping
over the parlour fire, half drunk, half stupid, and
half asleep.

After thinking over it alone there in Feemy's
sitting-room for an hour, he determined that all
he could do was to go back again to his only
friend, Father John.

When Feemy slammed the door, as she did
at the end of her violent oration above given,
she betook herself to her bedroom, and began
to cry.

Though she had so well assumed the air of
an injured person, and had to the best of her
abilities vindicated her absent lover, still she

was very unhappy at what her brother had said
to her. Nor, in truth, was it only because
Thady had expressed himself unkindly about
Myles, but she also could not but feel that there
was something wrong. She never for a moment
believed that her lover spoke loosely of her
behind her back, for she never for a moment
doubted his love; but she did feel that it would
be more comfortable if Myles would speak, or
let her speak to some of her family, if it were
only to her father. Though she knew so little
of what was usual in the world, still she felt that
even his sanction, stupid, tipsy, unconscious as
he was, would give to her attachment a respectability which it wanted now; and if a day for
her marriage were fixed, though circumstances
might require that it should be ever so distant,
she would be able to talk much more satisfactorily of her prospects to Mary Cassidy, and
the Miss McKeons. Besides, if she could bring
matters to this state, she could so triumphantly
prove that Thady was wrong in his unhandsome
conjectures, and she determined before she had
done thinking on the subject, to give Myles a
few hints as to her wishes. The next day he
would be sure to come to Ballycloran on his
way to McGovery's wedding, and he would
probably ask why Thady had prevented their
walk to Aughermore; and then she would have
a good opportunity of saying what she wanted.

CHAPTER VII

THE PRIEST'S DINNER PARTY

THADY, as I said, walked off to the priest's cottage, to partake of the relics of a goose, and seek counsel of his friend; but it was not Father John's dinner hour yet, and he found no one in but Judy McCan. He walked into the priest's little parlour, and sat down to wait for him, again meditating on all the evils which hung over his devoted family, and sitting thus he at length fell fast asleep.

Here he slept for above an hour, when he was awakened by the door opening behind him, and in jumping up to meet Father John, as he thought, he encountered the lank and yellow features, much-worn dress, and dirty, moist hand of Father Cullen.

"Were you sleeping, then, Mr. Thady, before Father McGrath's fire? 'deed, then, I dare say you've been walking a great sight, for you look jaded. I'm not that fresh myself, for I've been away to Loch Sheen, to widow Byrne's. Bad luck to the cratures, there's nothing but sick calls now, and my heart's broken with them, so it is."

Thady's only answer to this was, "How are you, Father Cullen?" He wished him back at Maynooth.

"Well, I hope Father McGrath isn't far off, thin," and he looked at a watch nearly as big as

a church clock, " for I'm very hungry, and, my !
it's only twenty minutes to six——"

This gave Thady the very unwelcome intelligence that Father Cullen meant to dine at the
cottage.

"And now the pony's lamed undher me, I
had to walk all the way to Loch Sheen, in the
dirt and gutther."*

Thady's mind was full of one object, and he
could not interest himself about the curate's
misfortunes in the lameness of his pony and the
dirt of his walk.

"And bad manners to them Commissioners
and people they sent over bothering and altering
the people ! Couldn't we have our own parishes
as we like, and fix them ourselves, but they
must be sending English people to give us
English parishes, altering the meerings*just to
be doing something ? You know, Thady, the
far end of Loch Sheen up there ? "

"Yes, Father Cullen, I know where Loch
Sheen is."

"Well, that used to be Cashcarrigan parish ;
and Father Comyns——that's the parish priest in
Cash——don't live not two miles all out from
there ; and the widow Byrne's is six miles from
where I live out yonder, if it's a step, and yet
they must go and put Loch Sheen into this
parish."

Father Cullen's misfortunes still did not
come home to Macdermot; he sat looking at
the fire.

"There's that poor ould woman, too, up
there, left to starve by herself, the crature, now
they've gone and put her two sons into gaol.

I wonder what the counthry'll be the better for
all them boys being crammed into gaol. I wish
they'd kept that Ussher down in the north when
he was there; he's fitter for that place than
County Leitrim, any how."

"What's that about Captain Ussher, Father
Cullen?"

"Shure didn't you hear he put three more of
the boys into gaol Tuesday evening, and one of
them off Drumleesh?"

"Heard it! of course I heard it; and more
than I'll be hearing it too. Oh, Father Cullen,
wherever that Ussher came from, I wish they'd
kept him there."

Thady's earnestness in this surprised the
young priest.

"Why, I thought you and he were so thick;
but I'm glad it's not so much so. Why would
the like of you be making so free with a Protestant like him? Did you break with him,
then, Mr. Thady?"

Macdermot by no means desired to admit
Father Cullen into the conference about his
sister; the strong expression of his dislike had
fallen from him as it were involuntarily: he
therefore turned off the question.

"Oh no; break with him! why would I
break with him? But you can't think I like
to see him dhriving the boys into the gaol like
sheep to the shambles. What business had
they sending Tim Reynolds into gaol? There'll
be noise enough in the counthry about that yet,
Father Cullen."

"There'll never be noise enough about that,
and such-like cruelties, till he and all of the

sort is put down intirely in the counthry; and
that'll only be when the counthry rights herself
as she should do, and, by God's blessing, will
still; and that you and I, Mr. Thady, may live
to see it——"

The further expression of Father Cullen's
favourite political opinions was here interrupted
by Father John's quick, heavy step on the little
gravel walk.

"Well, boys," said he, sitting down and pulling off his dirty gaiters and shoes before the
fire, "waiting for the goose, eh? Egad, when
I found what time it was, I thought you'd be
bribing Judy to divide it between you. Cullen,
you look awfully hungry; I'd better set you at
the ham first, or you'll make terrible work at
the half bird—for a half is all there is for the
three of us. Well, Judy, let's have the stew."

The dinner was now brought in, and Father
John talked joyously, as though nothing was
on his mind; and yet we know the sad conversation he had had with young Macdermot
that very morning, and that Thady was there
chiefly to tell the upshot of his mission,—and
Thady's face was certainly no emblem of good
news. He had also had a sad morning's work
with his curate, his parishioners were in great
troubles, the times were very bad on them;
many of them were in gaol for illegal distillation; more were engaged in the business, and
were determined so to continue in open defiance
of the police; many of them were becoming
ribbonmen, or, at any rate, were joining secret
and illegal societies. Driven from their cabins
and little holdings, their crops and cattle taken

from them, they were everywhere around desperate with poverty, and discontented equally with their own landlords and the restraints put upon them by government. All this weighed heavily on Father John's mind, and he strongly felt the difficulty of his own situation; but he was not the man to allow his spirits to master him when entertaining others in his own house. Had only Cullen or only Thady been there, he would have tuned his own mind to that of his guest; but as their cases were so different, he tried to cheer them both.

"Egad, Thady, here's another leg—come, my boy, we've still a leg to stand upon—Cullen has just finished one, and I could have sworn I ate the other yesterday. See, did Judy put one of her own in the hash—'*ex pede Herculem*'*—you'd know it so any way by the toughness. Lend me your fork, Thady, or excuse my own. Well, when I get the cash from Denis's marriage, I'll get a carving-knife and fork from Garley's; not but what I ought to have one. Judy, where's the big fork?"

"Why, didn't yer riverence smash it entirely drawing the cork from the bottle of sherry wine ye got for Doctor Blake the day he was here about the dispinsary business?"

This little explanation Judy bawled from the kitchen.

"It is true for you, Judy; so I did, and bad luck to the day and Doctor Blake, too. That same day, Thady, cost me three good shillings for a bottle of bad wine, my old fork, and a leg of mutton and all; for I thought I'd be able to come round the doctor about his coming down to Drumsna here once a week* regular; and when he'd ate my mutton and drank the sherry, he just told me it was not possible."

"He'd sooner be making may be twenty or thirty poor sick craturs be walking five or six miles, than he'd ride over to see them; though it's little he'd think of the distance av he'd a fee to touch."

"For the matter of that, Cullen, I think yourself would go quicker to a wedding than you would to a sick call. 'Deed, and I know myself I like the part of the business where the cash is."

"In course, Mr. McGrath, I'd go with more sperit, but not a foot quicker, nor so quick. May be I'd grumble at the one and not at the other; but what the church tells me, I'll do, if it plazes God to let me."

"Oh, Cullen, you'd make one think I was admonishing you. A fine martyr he'd make, wouldn't he, Thady?"

Cullen, who took everything in downright earnest, clasped his dirty hands, and exclaimed,

"If the church required it, and it was God's will, I hope I would."

"Well, well, but it'll be just at present much more comfortable for all parties you should square round a little, and take your punch. Come, Thady, are you going to be a martyr, too? it's a heathenish kind of penance, though, to be holding your tongue so long. Come, my boy, you were to bring the ticket about the rent with you."

Thady opened his ears at the word rent, but before he'd time to make any suitable reply,

Judy was moving the things, Father John was pulling back the table, and pushing Cullen into a corner by the fire.

"Now, Judy, the fire under the pump, you know; out with the groceries,—see, but have I any sugar, then?"

"Sorrow a bit of lump, but moist and plenty, Father John."

"Well, my boys, you must make your punch with brown sugar for once in your life; and what's the harm? what we want in sugar, we'll make up in the whiskey, I'll be bound. Judy, bring the tumblers."

Out came the tumblers—that is, two tumblers, one with a stand, the other with a flat bottom, and a tea-cup with a spoon in it. The tea-cup was put opposite Father John's chair, and the reverend father himself proceeded to pour a tolerable modicum of spirits out of the stone jar into a good-sized milk jug, and placed it on the table.

"Isn't it queer, then, Thady, I can't get a bottle, or a decanter, or anything of glass to remain in the house at all? I'm sure I had a decanter, though I didn't see it these six months."

"And wouldn't it be odd if you did, Father John? wasn't it smashed last February?"

"Smashed! why, I think everything gets smashed."

"Well now, Mr. Thady, to hear his riverence going on the like of that," said the old woman, appealing to Macdermot; "and wasn't it himself sent the broth down in it to Widow Green the latter end of last winter, and didn't the foolish slip of a girl, her grand-dater, go to hait it over the hot coals for the ould woman, jist as it was, and in course the hait smashed the glass, and why wouldn't it, and the broth was all spilt? But isn't the jug just as good for the sperits, yer honers?"

"Well, well; boiling mutton broth over a turf fire, in my cut decanter! '*optat ephippia bos piger.*'* That'll do, Judy, that'll do."

And the old woman retreated with a look of injured innocence.

Father John sniffed the whiskey. '*Fumum bibere institutæ ;*'* it's the right smell of the smoke. Come, Cullen, make your punch; come, Thady, don't be sitting there that way;" —and he proceeded to make a most unpalatable-looking decoction of punch in his tea-cup, to which the moist sugar gave a peculiarly nasty appearance.

But all Father John's attempted jovialities and preparations for enjoyment could not dispel the sadness from Thady's face, or the settled solemnity from Father Cullen's visage; he never joked, and rarely conversed; when he did speak, it was usually to argue or declaim; and Thady, even in his best times, was but a sorry companion for such a man as Father John. There the three of them sat, with their eyes fixed on the fire, all drinking their punch, it is true, but with very little signs of enjoying it.

How long they remained thus, I am unable to say; but Father John was getting very tired of his company, when they were all three startled by a sharp rap at the hall door, and before they had had time to surmise who it was, Captain Ussher walked in.

Now, though neither Father John nor his curate were very fond of Ussher, they both were tolerably intimate with him; indeed, till lately, when the priest began to think the gallant Captain was playing his fair parishioner false, and the opinion was becoming general that he was acting the tyrant among the people, Father John had rather liked Ussher than not. He was lively;—and if not well educated, he had some little general comprehension of which no others of those the priest knew around him could boast. He had met him first very frequently at Ballycloran, had since dined with him at Mohill, and had more than once induced him to join the unpretending festivities of the cottage. There was nothing, therefore, very singular in Captain Ussher's visit; and yet, from what was uppermost in the mind of each of the party, it did surprise them all.

Father John, however, was never taken aback. "Ah, my darling, and how are you? come to see we are drinking parliament* and not cheating the king."

Although they were drinking potheen, and though Ussher might, doubtless, have put a fine of from five to fifty pounds on the priest for doing so, Father John knew that he was safe. It was at that time considered that no revenue officer would notice potheen if he met it, as a guest. People are rather more careful now on the matter.

"Oh, Father John, I never bring my government taster with me when I am not on service;

but if you've any charity, give me an air of the fire and a drop of what's going forward, all for love. How are you, Father Cullen?" and he shook hands with the curate. " How are you, Thady, old boy?" and he slapped Macdermot on the back as though they were the best friends in the world.

" How are you, Captain Ussher?" said the former, sitting down again as though the Captain's salutation were a signal for him to do so, and as if he did not dare do it before. Nor would he. Father Cullen had been told that he should stand up when strangers came into a room,—that it was a point of etiquette; and there he would have stood, though it had been ten minutes, if Ussher had not addressed him.

Thady did not get up at all; in fact, he did not know what to do or to say. He had been waiting anxiously, hoping that Father Cullen would go, and now the difficulties in his way were more than doubled.

Captain Ussher, however, took no notice of his silence; but, sitting down by Father John, began rubbing and warming his hands at the fire.

"Well, may I be d—d—begging your reverence's pardon—if this isn't as cold a night as I'd wish to be out in, and as dark as my hat. I say, Thady, this'll be the night for the boys to be running a drop of the stuff; there'd be no seeing the smoke now, anyhow. I was dining early at Carrick, and was getting away home as quick as I could, and my mare threw a shoe, luckily just opposite the forge down there; so I walked up here, Father John, and I told them to bring the mare up when she's shod."

"I'm glad the mare made herself so agreeable. Come, Judy, another tumbler here. By the by, then, Cullen, you must takę to a tea-cup like myself—you're used to it; and Captain Ussher, you must take brown sugar in your punch, though you are not used to it. If I could make lump sugar for you, I'd do it myself directly."

"Oh, what's the odds! I'm so cold I shan't feel it;" and without any apology, he took poor Father Cullen's tumbler, who emptied the rest of his punch into a tea-cup.

"Well, Thady, and who do you think there was at Hewson's, but Keegan, your friend, you know? and a very pleasant fellow he is in his way: but how he does abuse you Catholics!"

"Well, Captain, and it's little good you'll hear any of us say of him, so that's all fair," said Father John.

"Take it that way, so it is; but I thought I heard some of you at Ballycloran say he was once a Catholic," said Ussher, turning to Thady; "your father was telling me so, I think."

He seemed determined to make Thady say something, but he only muttered an affirmative.

"Whoever said so, said wrong," began Father Cullen, rising up and putting his hands on the table, as if he was going to make a speech, "Whoever said so, said wrong. His father was a Catholic, and his mother was a Catholic, but he never was a Catholic; and how could he, for he never was a Christian,"—and as he sat down he turned round his large obtruding eyes for approval.

"Oh, if you go on that high ground, you'll lose half your flock. We are glad to get them whether they are Christians or not, so long as they are good Protestants; so you see Keegan's good enough for us; and what could he do, poor fellow? if you wouldn't have him, he must come to us."

"Oh then, Father John, he's satisfied to say men become Protestants when they are no longer fit to be Catholics; was that the way yourself become a Protestant, Captain Ussher?"

"If I'm to be d—d for that, you know, it's my father's and mother's fault. I ain't like Keegan. I didn't choose the bad road myself."

"Oh, but isn't it for yourself to choose the good road? didn't you say you knew ours was the ould church as it stood always down from Christ? If you do go wrong, you don't do it from ignorance, but you do it wilfully, and your sowl will howl in hell for it."

Captain Ussher only burst out laughing at this little outbreak, but Father John exclaimed, "Whist! whist! Cullen, none of that here: if you can take any steps towards sending Captain Ussher to heaven, well and good; but don't be sending him the other way while the poor fellow is over his punch."

"Never mind, Father John; I and Father Cullen are very good friends, and I think he'll hear me read my recantation yet; but he can't do it to-night, as here's my mare. I must go by Ballycloran, Thady; will you walk as far as the avenue with me?"

"Thank you, Captain Ussher, I'll not be going out of this just yet."

"Ah, well; I see you're out with me for the tiff we had this morning. He's angry now, Father John, just through my telling him he couldn't count all the money he'd received this week."

Father John observed the different manners of the young men towards each other, and from Thady's silence, was quite sure that matters had gone amiss between them.

"I didn't know it before then, Captain Ussher," said Thady; "but if you must know, I've business to spake to Father John about."

"Oh, well; open confession's good for the soul; I hope he'll absolve you for your bad temper."

"It's I am to get the absolution, if I can, this time; it's the old story, Captain, 'a trifle of rint that's owing, nothing more.'"

"Well, it's all one to me: good night to you all," and Captain Ussher rode away home to Mohill.

Father Cullen reseated himself by the fire, and again assumed his gaze at the hot turf, just as he was before Ussher came in, and looked hopelessly immovable. Thady shifted about uneasily in his chair, then got up and walked round the room, and then sat down again; but the curate wouldn't move. At last Father John ended the affair by saying,

"Any more punch, Cullen?"

"Thank you, no, Sir."

"Then just go home, there's a good fellow."

Cullen rose up, not the least offended—nothing would offend him—took his hat, and did as he was bid. At last Thady and Father John were left alone.

"Now, my boy," said the priest, as he put on more turf, "we'll be alone for half an hour, or it is odd. Well, you spoke to Feemy?"

"I did spake to her, Father John; but I'd better have left it alone; for when I began she only snubbed me, and she told me she'd manage her own business; but, oh, Father John, I fear it will be a bad business! She told me she loved him, and that he had gone so far as asking her to marry him, and all that; but as far as I could learn, it was only just talk, that. But I could say nothing to her, for she got the better of me, and then flew out of the room, saying, it did not matter what I said."

And then Macdermot told the priest exactly what had passed; how headstrong Feemy was, how infatuated she was with her lover, and how regardless of what any one could say to her on the subject; "and now, Father John, what on 'arth shall I do at all, for the heart's broken in me, with all the throubles that's on me."

"I'll tell you what, Thady: don't be falling out with Captain Ussher—any way, not yet— for he may mean honestly, you know, though I own my heart doubts him; but take my advice, and don't be falling out with him yet. I'll see Feemy to-morrow, and if she won't hear or won't heed what her priest says to her, I'll tell you what we'll do. One woman will always listen to another, and I'll ask Mrs. McKeon to speak to Feemy, and tell her the character she'll be giving herself. Mrs. McKeon has daughters of her own, and when I remind her that Feemy has neither mother, nor sister, nor female friend of any kind, she'll not be refusing me this, disagreeable though it may be to her. And now, Thady, do you go home to bed, and pray to God to protect your sister; and, remember, my boy, that though you may have reason to be displeased with her, as I said, she has neither mother nor sister; she has no one to look to but yourself, and if there is much in her to forgive, there are many causes for forgiveness."

Thady silently shook hands with his friend, and went home; and whether or no he obeyed the priest's injunctions to pray for protection for his sister, that good man himself did not go to sleep till he had long been on his knees, imploring aid for her, and the numerous unfortunates of his flock.

CHAPTER VIII

MISS MACDERMOT AT HOME

At any rate, the priest's admonitions had this effect on Thady, that when he came in to breakfast after his morning avocations, he spoke to Feemy, whom he had not seen since their stormy interview of yesterday, with kindness, and, for him, gentleness. But she seemed only half inclined to accept the proffered olive branch. Thady's morning salutations couldn't go far towards putting a young girl in good

humour, for even now that he meant to be
gracious it was only—" Well, Feemy, how's
yourself this morning; and will you be ready
for Mary Brady's wedding?" But her answer—
"Oh, in course; will you take your breakfast
there?" showed him that she had not forgiven
his aspersions against her lover, and the breakfast passed over in silence, with the exception
of Larry's usual growls. Thady, therefore,
when he had swallowed his potatoes and milk,
betook himself again to Pat Brady and the
fields. Larry was left alone to sleep, if he
could, over the fire, and Feemy betook herself
to her own parlour, and proceeded to penetrate
farther into the mysteries of the " Mysterious
Assassin."

There she sat—a striking contradiction of
that proverb which we so often quote with
reference to young ladies, and which so seldom
can be quoted with truth, " Beauty unadorned,
adorned the most."

Ussher would not come till the evening, and
her hair was therefore in papers—and the very
papers themselves looked soiled and often used.
Her back hair had been hastily fastened up with
a bit of old black ribbon and a comb boasting
only two teeth, and the short hairs round the
bottom of her well-turned head were jagged
and uneven, as though bristling with anger at
the want of that attention which they required.
She had no collar on, but a tippet* of different
material and colour from her frock was thrown
over her shoulders. Her dress itself was the
very picture of untidiness; it looked as though
it had never seen a mangle;* the sleeves drooped

down, hanging despondingly below her elbows; and the tuck of her frock was all ripped and torn—she had trod on it, or some one else had done it for her, and she had not been at the trouble of mending it. It was also too tight, or else Feemy had not fastened it properly, for a dreadful gap appeared in the back, showing some article beneath which was by no means as white as it should be;—"but then, wasn't it only her morning frock?" In front of it, too, was a streaked mark of grease, the long since deposited remains of some of her culinary labours. Her feet were stuffed into slippers—truth compels me to say they would more properly be called shoes down at heel—her stockings were wofully dirty, and, horror of all horrors, out at the heels! There she sat, with her feet on the fender, her face on her hands, and her elbows on her knees, with her thumb-worn novel lying in her lap between them.

There she sat; how little like the girl that had eclipsed Mary Cassidy at the ball at Mohill! Poor though Feemy was, she could make out a dress, and a handsome dress, for such an occasion as that. Then every hair on her fine head had been in its place; the curls of her rich brown hair were enough to win the heart of any man; the collar round her fair neck had been beautifully washed and ironed, for her own hands had been at work on it half the morning; her white long gloves had been new and well fitting, and her only pair of silk stockings had been scrupulously neat; her dress fitted her fine person as though made by Carson, and she had walked as though she knew she need

not be ashamed of herself. But now how great
was the contrast!

No girls know better how to dress themselves
than Irish girls, or can do it with less assistance
or less expense; but they are too much given
to morning dishevelment. If they would only
remember that the change in a man's opinion
and mind respecting a girl will often take place
as quick as the change in her appearance, and
that the contrast will be quite as striking, they
would be more particular. And they never can
be sure of themselves, take what precautions
they will. Lovers will drop in at most un-
seasonable hours; they have messages to deliver,
plans to propose, or leave to take. They can
never be kept out with certainty, and all the
good done by a series of brilliant evenings—
satin dresses, new flowers for the hair, expensive patterns, and tediously finished toilets
—may be, and often is, suddenly counter-
acted by one untidy head, soiled dress, or dirty
stocking.

I will, however, return to my story. There
sat Feemy, apparently perfectly contented with
her appearance and occupation, till a tap at the
door disturbed her, and in walked Mary Brady,
the bride elect.

"Well, Miss Feemy, and how's your beautiful
self this morning?"

"And how are you, Mary, now the time is
coming so near?"

Mary Brady was a very tall woman, being
about the same height as her brother, thirty or
thirty-three years of age, with a plain, though
good-humoured looking face, over which her

coarse hair was divided on the left temple. She had long ungainly limbs, and was very awkward in the use of them, and though not absolutely disagreeable in her appearance, she was so nearly so, that she would hardly have got married without the assistance of the "two small pigs, and thrifle of change," which had given her charms in the eyes both of Ginty and Denis McGovery.

"Oh! Miss Feemy, and I'm fretting so these two days, that is, ever since Denis said it was to be this blessed day,—the Lord help me!—and I with it all on my shoulders, and the divil a one to lend a hand the laste taste*in life."

"Why, Mary, what can there be so much to do at all?"

"Och! then, hadn't I my white dress to get made, and the pair of sheets to get hemmed, for Denis said his'n warn't large enough for him and I,"—and here the Amazon gave a grin of modesty,—"and you know it was part of the bargain, I was to have a pair of new sheets" (Denis had kept this back from Father John in his inventory of his bride's fortune); "and isn't there the supper to get ready, and the things, and the house to ready and all!—and then when I'd done that, it war all for nothing, for the wedding isn't to be at Pat's at all."

"The wedding not to be at Brady's! where is it to be then?"

"Oh, jist at Mrs. Mehan's shop below, at the loch."

"Oh, that's better still, Mary; we won't have so far to go in the mud."

"That's jist what the boys war saying, Miss;
and there be so much more room, and there be
so many to be in it, they couldn't all be in it,
at all at all, at home. So you see we is to be
married in the room inside, where the two beds
is, and they is to come out of it, and the supper
is to be there, Miss, you see, and the most
of the dhrinking, and then we'll have the big
kitchen comfortable to oursells for the music
and the dancing. And what do you think!
Pat has got Shamus na Pe'bria,* all the ways
out of County Mayo, him that makes all the
pipes through the counthry, Miss; and did the
music about O'Connell* all out of his own head,
Miss. Oh, it 'll be the most illigant wedding
intirely, Miss, anywhere through the counthry,
this long time back! When one is to be married,
it's as well to do it dacently as not; arn't it,
Miss?"

"Oh! that it is, Mary, and yours 'll be quite
a dash."

"Yours 'll be the next, you know, Miss
Feemy, and that will be the wedding! But
there's one thing that bothers me intirely."

"Well, out with it at once, Mary; I suppose
you want to borrow the plates, and knives, and
forks, and things?"

"Oh, that's in course, Miss Feemy; and it's
very good in you to be offering them that way
before I axed the loan of them at all; but that
ain't all. You see, I'm so bothered intirely with
them big sheets, and they not half finished, and
not a taste in life done to the cap of me yet,
and the pratees and vegetables to get ready,
and the things to dress, and not a sowl to lend

me a hand at all, unless jist Mrs. Mehan's bit
of a girl, and she's busy readying the rooms;
and so, Miss Feemy, if you'd jist let Biddy slip
up for the afthernoon,—you know Katty could
be doing for you down here,—and then, Miss,
I'd be made intirely."

"Well, Mary, I suppose she must go up then;
one thing's certain, you can't be getting married
every day."

"Why no, Miss, that is sartain; for even if
Denis were to die away like,—as in course he
must one day, for he ain't quite so young now,—
I would have to be waiting a little, Miss, before
I got my second."

Mary Brady had been above thirty years
getting one husband; she was, therefore, probably right as to the delay she might experience
in obtaining a second.

"Well, Mary, Biddy may go with you."

"Long life to you, Miss; and about the
things then you know—the plates, and the
knives, and the glasses?"

"Oh! Mary, I'll not have you bringing the
glasses down there at all; sure Mrs. Mehan's
glasses enough of her own, and she selling
whiskey. You may take the knives, and the
forks, and the plates; though you must leave
us enough for ourselves—and there an't so
many of them in it after all."

"Well, Miss Feemy, that's very good of you
now. And you'll be bringing your own sweetheart with you, won't you, dear?—and it's I'd
be sorry you'd be at my wedding, and no one
fit to dance with your father's daughter."

"Oh! if you mean Captain Ussher, he told

me Pat asked him himself, and he'd sure be there."

"And who else should I main, alanna*; sure isn't he your own beau, and ain't you to be married to him, Miss Feemy?"

"Nonsense, Mary."

"Well, now, but sure you wouldn't be ashamed of telling me—isn't you going to have him, Miss?"

"But musn't I wait to be asked, like another?—Sure, Mary, you didn't go asking Denis McGovery, did you?"

"No, then, indeed, I didn't, darling; and glad enough he was to be axing me."

"Well, and musn't I be the same?"

"Oh! in course; but, Miss Feemy, the Captain's been up here coorting at Ballycloran now these six months; sure he axed you before this, Miss Feemy?"

Feemy was rather puzzled; she didn't like to say she was not engaged; she had a presentiment Mary Brady was fishing to find out if the report about the Captain's inconstancy was true, and as matters stood she did not exactly like to say that the affair was arranged.

"Well, Mary, then I'll tell you exactly how it is—but mind, I don't want it talked about yet for rasons; so you won't say anything about it if I tell you?"

"Och then! is it I? Sorrow a word in life shall any one be the better av me, and you know, Miss Feemy, I wouldn't tell you a lie for worlds."

"Well, then, it's jist this way—I and the Captain is engaged, but there's rasons for him why we couldn't be married just immediately; so you see that's why I don't want it talked about."

"Ah! well, dear, I knew there was something av that in it, and a nice handsome gentleman like the Captain wouldn't be trating the likes of you that way."

"What way, Mary?"

"Why, they do be saying—"

"Who do be saying?"

"Why, jist through the counthry,—people you know, Miss, who must always have their gag*; they do be saying—that's only some of them, you know, Miss, who don't be quite frindly to Ballycloran—that the Captain don't main to be married at all, and is only playing his tricks with you, and that he's a schamer. But I knew you wouldn't be letting him go on that way, and so I said to Pat."

Feemy didn't quite like all this—it was a corroboration of what her brother had said; for though the Captain had certainly promised to marry her, he had never thought it necessary to ask her. She knew the matter did not rest on a proper footing; and though she was hardly aware of it, she felt the indignity of the probability of being jilted being talked over by such persons as Pat Brady.

"Your brother, Mary, might have saved himself the throuble of telling lies about either the Captain or me; not of course that I care."

"Oh! it warn't Pat, Miss, said it, only he heard it, you know, Miss, through the counthry."

"Well, it don't signify who said it, but don't you be repeating what I told you."

"Is it I, Miss? Sorrow a word, Miss, will any one hear from me av it. Would I tell a lie about it? But I'll be glad to see the day you're married, for that'll be the great wedding through the counthry.——Oh laws!"

This exclamation was not a part of the last speech, but was a kind of long-drawn, melancholy sigh, which did not take place for some minute or two after she had done speaking, during which time Feemy had been thinking of her own affairs, quite forgetful of Mary Brady and her wedding.

"My! Mary, what are you sighing about?"

"Well then, Miss Feemy, and isn't it a dreadful thing to be laving one's home, and one's frinds like, and to be going right away into another house intirely, Miss; and altogether the thoughts of what is the married life at all frets me greatly."

"Why, you needn't be married unless you like it, Mary."

"Oh! Miss Feemy, that's in course too; but then a young woman is behove to do something for her family."

"But you haven't a family, you know, Mary, now."

"No, but Miss Feemy alanna, you know the chances is I shall have now I'm to be married; and it's for them, the little innocents, I does it."

The strength of this argument did not exactly strike Feemy, but she thought it was all right, and said nothing.

"And then the throubles of a married life, darling,—supposing them is too many for me, what'll I do at all? I wonder, Miss Feemy, will I get any sleep at all?"

"Indeed, Mary, I was never married; but why shouldn't you sleep?"

"'Deed then, Miss, I don't jist know, but they do be saying that Denis is so noisy at nights, a-shoeing all the cattle over again as he shod in the day, and counting the money; and you see, av he was hammering away the blessed live-long night that way, maybe I'd be hurted."

"It's too late for you to think of that now; but he'll be quieter than that, I should think, when you're with him."

"Maybe he will, Miss; and as you say, I couldn't dacently be off it now. But thin— oh laws!—I'm thinking what will poor Pat be doing without me, and no one in it at all to bile the pratees and feed the pigs—the craturs!"

"That's nonsense, Mary—you and he was always fighting; he'll have more peace in it when you're gone."

"That's thrue for you, Miss, sartanly, and that's what breaks the heart of me intirely. Too much pace isn't good for Pat, no how; he'll never do no good, you'll see, when he comes to have so much of his own way. 'Deed then, the heart's low within me, to be laving Pat this way!" And Miss Brady put the tail of her gown into the corner of her eye.

"But, Mary, you'll have to be caring more for your husband now. I suppose you love Denis McGovery, don't you? I'd never marry a man unless I loved him."

"Oh! that's in course—I do love him; why wouldn't I? for he has a nice little room all dacently furnished for any young woman to go into—besides the shop; and he never has the horses at all into the one we sleeps in, as is to be. And he's a handful of money, and can make any woman comfortable; and in course I love him—so I do. But what's the use of loving a man, if he's to be hammering away at a horseshoe all night?"

"Oh, they're making game of you—they are, Mary; depend upon it, when he's tired working all day, he'll sleep sound enough."

"Well, I s'poses he will; but now, Miss Feemy, I wonder is he a quiet sort of man? will he be fighting at all, do you think?"

"Really then, I can't tell; but even if he does, they say you can take your own part pretty well, when it's necessary."

"For the matter of that, so I can; and I don't mind a scrimmage jist now and again— sich as I and Pat have—av it's only to show I won't be put under; but they do say Denis is very sthrong. I don't think I'd ever have had him, av' I'd known afore he'd been so mortial sthrong."

"Well, that's all too late now for you to be talking of; and take my advice, Mary, don't be fighting with him at all if you can help it; for from what people say of him I think your husband, as will be, sticks mostly to his own way, and I don't think he'll let his wife interfere. But he's a hard-working man, and it'll be a great comfort to you that you'll never see your children wanting."

"Oh, the childhren, the little dears! it's of them I'm thinking. God he knows, it's chiefly along of them as makes me do it; but—oh laws! Miss it's a dreadful thing to come over one all at once. But it's a great comfort anyway your letting Biddy come down to ready the mutton and pratees, and things; and so, Miss, as I've so much to do, you'll excuse my waiting any longer; and you and Mr. Thady and the Captain,—for I'm thinking the Masther won't be coming,—'ll not be down later than sivin, for Father John's to be in it at sivin exact."

"And who's to get the kiss, Mary?"

"Oh, Miss!"

"The Captain says he'll have a try for it anyway."

"Oh, that'd be too much honor intirely, Miss. But av here isn't Father John coming up the avenue!"

And Mary hurried off into the realms under ground to secure the willing assistance of Biddy, and Father John's ponderous foot up the hall steps gave Feemy anything but a pleasant sensation. She was very fond of Father John too, but somehow, just at present she did not feel quite pleased to see him.

The doors were all open, and Father John walked into Feemy's boudoir. However, he was only Father John, and it wasn't her dress therefore that annoyed her; any dress would do for a priest.

After the common greetings were over, and Father John had asked after the family, and Feemy had surmised that it was either her father or her brother that he wished to see, the priest began his task.

"No, Feemy, my dear, it's not your father or your brother I want to see this turn, but just your own self." And Father John sat himself down by the fire. "I'm come just to have a little chat with you, and you musn't be angry with me for meddling with what, perhaps, you'll say was no business of mine."

This exordium made Feemy's heart palpitate, for she knew it must be about Captain Ussher, but she only said,

"Oh! no, Father John, I won't be angry with you."

"That's my darling, for you know it's only out of love for you and Thady that I'm speaking, and a real friend to you can't do you any harm, if after all you shouldn't take his advice."

"Oh! no, Father John, and I'm sure I'm very much obliged to you."

Father John himself hardly knew how to take the sting from the rebuke, which he was aware his mission could not but convey; and he was no less aware, that unless the dose had a little sugar in it, at any rate to hide its unprepossessing appearance even if it did not render it palatable, his patient would never take it.

"Thady, you know, was dining with me yesterday, and we were talking over Ballycloran and old Flannelly's money matters; and I was, you see, just making a bad tenant's excuses to him, and so on from one thing to another, till we got talking about you, Feemy;—in short, he didn't seem quite happy about you."

"I don't know I ever did anything to make him unhappy."

"No, it wasn't anything you had done to make him unhappy, but he is afraid you ain't happy in yourself; and Feemy, my dear, you should always remember, that though Thady is rough in his manners, and perhaps not at all times so gentle in his words as he should be, his heart is in the right place,—at any rate where you are concerned. Though maybe he doesn't say so as often as others might, he's a very fond brother to you."

"And I'm sure I'm always very fond of him— but then he's so queer; but, Father John, if I've offended Thady, I'll beg his pardon, for I'm sure I don't want to be out with him."

"I'm sure you don't, Feemy; but that's not exactly it either. Thady's not the least in life offended with you; he's not at all easy to take offence, at least not with you; but he doesn't think you are just at ease with yourself; and to come to the truth at once, he was telling me what passed between you yesterday."

Feemy blushed up to her paper curls, but she said nothing.

"Now, I'm thinking Thady didn't go about saying what he wanted to say yesterday, quite the way he should have done, and I am not sure I shall do it any better myself. But I thought it as well to step up, as I was certain you'd hear whatever your priest had to say to you."

"I don't think the better of Thady, though, for going and talking about me. If he'd only let me alone by myself I'd do well enough;

it's all that talking does the harm, Father John."

Father John didn't exactly like to tell Feemy that girls in her situation were just the people that ought not to be left alone by themselves,—which probably means being left alone with some one of their own choosing; and that he was of opinion that she would not do very well if left alone in that way. That, however, was what he wished to convey to her.

"Oh, but, my dear, you must think better of Thady for wishing to protect you as well as he can, and you left alone so much yourself here. So you know,"—and Father John even blushed a little as he said it,—"it's about this fine lover of yours we are speaking. Now, my dear, I've nothing whatever to say against Captain Ussher, for you know he and I are great cronies; indeed, it's only last night he was taking his punch with your brother and Cullen down at the cottage——"

"You weren't saying anything to Captain Ussher about me, Father John?"

"You may take your oath of that, my dear. I respect a lady's secret a great deal too much for that. No; I was only saying that he was down at the cottage last night, to prove that he and I are friends, and it's not out of any prejudice I'm speaking—about his being a Protestant, and all that; not but that I'd sooner be marrying you to a good Catholic, Feemy—but that's neither here nor there. But you've known him now a long time; it's now four months since we all heard for certain it was to be a match; and, to tell you the truth,

my dear, people are saying that Captain Ussher
doesn't mean anything serious."

"I think they'll dhrive me mad with their
talk! And what good will it do for you and
Thady to be coming telling me what they
say?"

"This good, Feemy; if what they say is
false and unfounded, as I am sure I hope it
is,—and if you're so fond of Captain Ussher,—
don't you think it would be as well to put an
end to the report by telling your father and
brother of your being engaged, and settling
something about your marriage, and all that?"

"I did tell my brother I was engaged, Father
John; what would you have?"

"I'll tell you what I'd have. I'd have Captain Ussher ask your father or brother's consent:
there's no doubt, we all know, but he'd get it;
but it's customary, and, in my mind, it would
only be decent."

"So he will, I dare say; but mayn't there
be rasons why he don't wish to have it talked
about yet?"

"Then, Feemy, in your situation, do you
think a long clandestine engagement is quite
the thing for you; is quite prudent?"

"And how can it be clandestine, Father
John, when you and Thady, and every one
else almost, knows all about it?"

Feemy's sharpness was too much for Father
John, so he had to put it on another tack.

"Well, Feemy, now just look at the matter
this way, one moment: supposing now—only
just for supposition—this lover of yours was
not the sort of man we all take him to be, and

that he was to turn out false, or inconstant; suppose now it turned out he had another wife somewhere else——"

"Oh, that's nonsense, you know, Father John."

"Yes, but just supposing it,—or that he took some vagary into his head, and changed his mind! You must have heard of men doing such things, and why shouldn't your lover as well as another girl's? We're all likely to be deceived in people, and why mayn't we be as well deceived in Captain Ussher, as others have been in those they loved as well? We'll all hope, and think, and believe it's not so; but isn't it as well to be on the safe side, particularly in so important a thing as your happiness, Feemy? You wouldn't like it to be said through the country that you'd been jilted by the handsome captain, and that you'd been thrown off by your lover as soon as he was tired of you?"

"And that's thrue for you, Father John; but Myles isn't tired of me, else why should he be coming up here to see me oftener than ever?"

"But it's that he never may be tired of you, Feemy; take my word for it, he'll respect you a great deal more if you'll show more respect to yourself."

"Well, Father John, and what is it you'd have me be doing?"

"Why, then, I'd just ask him to speak a word to Thady—just to propose himself in the regular way."

"But Thady hates him so."

"No; Thady don't hate him: he's only

jealous lest Captain Ussher isn't treating you quite as he ought to do."

"But Thady is so queer in his manners; and I know Myles wouldn't like to be asking leave and permission to be courting me."

"But, Feemy, he must like it; and you shouldn't like your lover the more for thinking so little of your brother, or, for the matter of that, of yourself either."

"You know, Father John, I can't help what he thinks of Thady. As to his thinking of me, I'm quite satisfied with that, and I suppose that's enough."

Father John was beginning to wax wroth, partly because he was displeased with Feemy himself, and partly because Feemy answered him too knowingly.

"Well, then, Feemy, it'll be one of the two: either Captain Ussher will have to speak to Thady, and settle something about the marriage in a proper and decent way; or else Thady will be speaking to him. And now, which do you think will be the best?"

"It's not like you, Father John, to be making Thady quarrel with Captain Ussher. You know it'd come to a quarrel if Thady was to be spaking to Myles that way; and he would never think of doing so av you didn't be putting him up to it."

"And that's little like you, Feemy, to be saying that to your priest; telling me I put the young men up to be quarrelling: it's to save you many a heart-ache, and many a sting of sorrow and remorse; it's to prevent all the evil of unlawful love—bad blood, and false looks—that I've come here on a most disagreeable and thankless errand; and now you tell me I'd be putting the young men up to fight!"

Feemy had, by this time, become sullen, but she didn't dare go farther with her priest.

"I didn't say you'd be making them fight, Father John. I only said, if you told Thady not to be meddling with Myles, why, in course, they wouldn't be quarrelling."

"And how could I tell a brother not to meddle with his sister's honour, and reputation, and happiness? But now, Feemy, I'll propose another plan to you. If you don't think my advice on such a subject likely to be good—and very likely it isn't, for you see I never had a lover of my own—what do you say to your speaking to your friend, Mrs. McKeon, about it? Or, if you like, I'll speak to her; and then, perhaps, you won't be against taking her advice on the subject. Supposing, now, she was to speak to Captain Ussher—from herself, you know, as your friend—do you think he'd love the girl that's to be his wife worse for having a friend that was willing to stand in the place of a mother to her, when she'd none of her own?"

"Why, I do think it would look odd, Mrs. McKeon meddling with it."

"Well, then, Feemy, what in the blessed name do you mean to do, if you won't let any of your friends act for you? I think you must be very much afraid of this lover of yours, when you won't allow any one to speak to him about you. Are you afraid of him, Feemy?"

"Afraid of him?—no, of course I'm not afraid

of him; but men don't like to be bothered about such things."

"That's very true; men, when they're false, and try to deceive young girls, and are playing their own wicked game with them, do not like to be bothered about such things. But I never heard of an honest man, who really wanted to marry a young woman, being bothered by getting her friends' consent. And you think, then, things should go on just as they are?"

"Now, Father John, only you've been scolding me so much, I'd have told you before. I mane to spake to Myles myself to-night, just to arrange things; and then I won't have Mrs. McKeon cocking* over me that she made up the match."

"There's little danger of that kind, I fear, Feemy, nor would she be doing so; but if you are actually going to speak to Captain Ussher yourself to-night, I'll say no more about it now; but I hope you'll tell Thady to-morrow what passes."

"Oh, Father John, I won't promise that."

"Will you tell me, then, or Mrs. McKeon?"

"Oh, perhaps I'll be telling you, you know, when I come down to confession at Christmas; but indeed I shan't be telling Mrs. McKeon anything about it, to go talking over the counthry."

"Then, Feemy, I may as well tell you at once—if you will not trust to me, to your brother, or any friend who may be able to protect you from insult—nor prevail on your lover to come forward in a decent and respectable way, and avow his purpose—it will become your brother's duty to tell him that his visits can no longer be allowed at Ballycloran."

"Ballycloran doesn't belong to Thady, and he can't tell him not to come."

"That's not well said of you, Feemy; for you know your father is not capable of interfering in this business; but if, as under those circumstances he will do, Thady quietly and firmly desires Captain Ussher to stay away from Ballycloran, I think he'll not venture to come here. If he does, there are those who will still interfere to prevent him."

"And if among you all, that are so set up against him because he's not one of your own set, you dhrive him out of Ballycloran, I can tell you, I'll not remain in it!"

"Then your sins and your sorrows must be on your own head!"

And without saying anything further, Father John took his hat, and walked off. Feemy snatched her novel into her lap, to show how little what was said impressed her, and resumed her attitude over the fire. But she didn't read; her spirit was stubborn and wouldn't bend, but her reason and her conscience were touched by what the priest had said to her, and the bitter thought for the first time came over her, that her lover, perhaps, was not so true to her, as she to him. There she sat, sorrowfully musing; and though she did not repent of what she thought her own firmness, she was bitterly tormented by the doubts with which her brother, Mary Brady, and the priest, had gradually disturbed her happiness.

She loved Ussher as well as ever—yes, almost

more than ever, as the idea that she might perhaps lose him came across her—but she began to be discontented with herself, and to think that she had not played her part as well as she might. In fact, she felt herself to be miserable, and, for the time, hated her brother and Father John for having made her so.

Father John walked sorrowfully back to his cottage, thinking Miss Feemy Macdermot the most stiff-necked young lady it had ever been his hard lot to meet.

CHAPTER IX

MOHILL

WE must now request our reader to accompany us to the little town of Mohill; not that there is anything attractive in the place to repay him for the trouble of going there.

Mohill is a small country town, standing on no high road, nor on any thoroughfare from the metropolis; and therefore it owes to itself whatever importance it may possess—and, in truth, that is not much. It is, or, at any rate, was, at the time of which we are writing, the picture of an impoverished town—the property of a non-resident landlord—destitute of anything to give it interest or prosperity—without business, without trade, and without society. The idea that would strike one on entering it was chiefly this: "Why was it a town at all?—why

were there, on that spot, so many houses congregated, called Mohill?—what was the inducement to people to come and live there?—Why
didn't they go to Longford, to Cavan, to Carrick,
to Dublin,—anywhere rather than there, when
they were going to settle themselves?" This
is a question which proposes itself at the sight
of many Irish towns; they look so poor, so
destitute of advantage, so unfriended. Mohill
is by no means the only town in the west of
Ireland, that strikes one as being there without
a cause.

It is built on the side of a steep hill, and one
part of the town seems constantly threatening
the destruction of the other. Every now and
again, down each side of the hill, there is a
slated house, but they are few and far between;
and the long spaces intervening are filled with
the most miserable descriptions of cabins—
hovels without chimneys, windows, door, or
signs of humanity, except the children playing
on the collected filth in front of them. The
very scraughs* of which the roofs are composed
are germinating afresh, and, sickly green with a
new growth, look more like the tops of long-
neglected dungheaps, than the only protection
over Christian beings from the winds of heaven.

Look at that mud hovel on the left, which
seems as if it had thrust itself between its
neighbours, so narrow is its front! The door-
way, all insufficient as it is, takes nearly the
whole facing to the street. The roof, looking
as if it were only the dirty eaves hanging from
its more aspiring neighbour on the right, supports
itself against the cabin on the left, about three

feet above the ground. Can that be the habitation of any of the human race? Few but such as those whose lot has fallen on such barren places would venture in; but for a moment let us see what is there.

But the dark misery within hides itself in thick obscurity. The unaccustomed eye is at first unable to distinguish any object, and only feels the painful effect of the confined smoke; but when, at length, a faint struggling light makes its way through the entrance, how wretched is all around!

A sickly woman, the entangled nature of whose insufficient garments would defy description, is sitting on a low stool before the fire, suckling a miserably dirty infant; a boy, whose only covering is a tattered shirt, is putting fresh, but, alas, damp turf beneath the pot in which are put to boil the potatoes—their only food. Two or three dim children—their number is lost in their obscurity—are cowering round the dull, dark fire, atop of one another; and on a miserable pallet beyond—a few rotten boards, propped upon equally infirm supports, and covered over with only one thin black quilt—is sitting the master of the mansion; his grizzly, unshorn beard, his lantern jaws and shaggy hair, are such as his home and family would lead one to expect. And now you have counted all that this man possesses; other furniture has he none —neither table nor chair, except that low stool on which his wife is sitting. Squatting on the ground—from off the ground, like pigs, only much more poorly fed—his children eat the scanty earnings of his continual labour.

And yet for this abode the man pays rent.

The miserable appearance of Irish peasants, when in the very lowest poverty, strikes one more forcibly in the towns than in the open country. The dirt and filth around them seems so much more oppressive on them; they have no escape from it. There is much also in ideas and associations. On a road-side, or on the borders of a bog, the dusty colour of the cabin walls, the potato patch around it, the green scraughs or damp brown straw which form its roof, all the appurtenances, in fact, of the cabin, seem suited to the things around it. But in a town this is not so. It evidently should not be there—its squalidness and filth are all that strike you. Poverty, to be picturesque, should be rural. Suburban misery is as hideous as it is pitiable.

Again, see that big house, with such pretensions to comfort, and even elegance,—with its neat slated roof, brass knocker on the door, verandahs to the large sashed windows, and iron railing before the front. Its very grandeur is much more striking, that from each gable-end hangs another cabin, the same as those we have above described. It is true that an entrance for horses, cars, and carriages has been constructed, as it were through one end of the house itself; otherwise the mansion is but one house in the continuous street.

Here lives Mr. Cassidy, the agent; a fat, good-natured, easy man, with an active grown-up son. Every one says that Mr. Cassidy is a good man, as good to the poor as he can be. But he is not the landlord, he is only the agent.

What can he do more than he does? Is the landlord then so hard a man? so regardless of those who depend on him in all their wants and miseries? No, indeed; Lord Birmingham* is also a kind, good man, a most charitable man! Look at his name on all the lists of gifts for unfortunates of every description. Is he not the presiding genius of the company for relieving the Poles? a vice-presiding genius for relieving destitute authors, destitute actors, destitute clergy-men's widows, destitute half-pay officers' widows? Is he not patron of the Mendicity Society, patron of the Lying-in, Small Pox, Lock, and Fever Hospitals? Is his name not down for large amounts in aid of funds of every description for lessening human wants and pangs? How con-spicuous and eager a part too he took in giving the poor Blacks their liberty*! was not his aid strongly and gratefully felt by the friends of Catholic emancipation? In short, is not every one aware that Lord Birmingham has spent a long and brilliant life in acts of public and private philanthropy? 'Tis true he lives in England, was rarely in his life in Ireland, never in Mohill. Could he be blamed for this? Could he live in two countries at once? or would the world have been benefited had he left the Parlia-ment and the Cabinet, to whitewash Irish cabins, and assist in the distribution of meal?*

This would be his own excuse, and does it not seem a valid one? Yet shall no one be blamed for the misery which belonged to him; for the squalid sources of the wealth with which Poles were fed, and literary paupers clothed? was no one answerable for the grim despair of

that half-starved wretch, whom but now we saw,
looking down so sadly on the young sufferers to
whom he had given life and poverty? That can
hardly be. And if we feel the difficulty which,
among his numerous philanthropic works, Lord
Birmingham must experience in attending to the
state of his numerous dependents, it only makes
us reflect more often, that from him to whom
much is given, much indeed will be required!

But we are getting far from our story. Going
a little further down the hill, there is a lane to
the right. This always was a dirty, ill-con-
ditioned lane, of bad repute and habits. Father
Mathew and the rigour of the police have of
late somewhat mended its manners and morals.
Here too one now sees, but a short way from
the main street, the grand new stirring poor-
house,* which ten years ago was not in being.

In this lane at the time to which we allude
the widow Mulready kept the shebeen* shop, of
which mention has before been made.

In her business Mrs. Mulready acquired much
more profit than respectability, for, whether well
or ill-deserved, she had but a bad name in the
country; in spite of this, however, to the
company assembled here on Wednesday evening,—the same evening that Thady dined with
Father John,—we must introduce our readers.

The house, or rather cabin, consisted only of
two rooms, both on the ground, and both without flooring or ceiling; the black rafters on
which the thatch was lying was above, and the
uneven soil below; still this place of entertainment was not like the cabins of the very poor:
the rooms were both long, and as they ran length-

ways down the street, each was the full breadth
of the house : in the first sat the widow Mulready,
a strong, red-faced, indomitable-looking woman
about fifty. She sat on a large wooden seat
with a back, capable of containing two persons ;
there was an immense blazing fire of turf, on
which water was boiling in a great potato pot,
should any of her guests be able to treat themselves to the expensive luxury of punch. A
remarkably dirty small deal table was beside her,
on which were placed a large jar, containing a
quantity of the only merchandize in which she
dealt, and an old battered pewter measure, in
which she gave it out ; in a corner of the table
away from the fire was cut a hole through
the board, in which was stuck a small flickering candle. No further implements appeared
necessary to Mrs. Mulready in the business
which she conducted. A barefooted girl, with
unwashed hands and face, and unbrushed head,
crouched in the corner of the fire, ready to obey
the behests of Mrs. Mulready, and attend to
the numerous calls of her customers. This
Hebe* rejoiced in the musical name of Kathleen.

The Mohill resort of the wicked, the desperate,
and the drunken, was not certainly so grand, nor
so conspicuous, as the gas-lighted, mahogany
fitted, pilastered gin palaces of London ; but the
freedom from decent restraint, and the power
of inebriety at a cheap rate, were the same in
each.

There was a door at the further end of the
room, which opened into the one where Mrs.
Mulready's more known and regular visitors

were accustomed to sit and drink, and here rumour said a Ribon lodge was held; there was a fire also here, at the further end, and a long narrow table ran nearly the whole length of the room under the two windows, with a form on each side of it. Opposite this was Mrs. Mulready's own bed, which proved that whatever improprieties might be perpetrated in the house, the careful widow herself never retired to rest till they were all over.

The assembly on the night in question was not very numerous; there might be about twelve in it, and they all were of the poorer kind; some even had neither shoes nor stockings, and there was one poor fellow had neither hat nor coat,—nothing but a tattered shirt and trousers.

The most decent among them all was Pat Brady, who occupied a comfortable seat near the fire, drinking his tumbler of punch and smoking like a gentleman; Joe Reynolds was sitting on the widow's bed, with a spade in his hand; he had only just come in. They were all from Drumleesh, with one or two exceptions; the man without the coat was Jack Byrne, the brother of the man whom Captain Ussher had taken when the malt was found in his brother-in-law's house.

"Kathleen, agra,*" hallooed Joe Reynolds, "bring me a glass of sperrits, will you?"

"Send out the rint, Joe," hallooed out the wary widow, and Kathleen came in for the money.

"Sorrow to your sowl then, mother Mulready; d'ye think I'm so bad already then, that they haven't left me the price of a glass?" and he put three halfpence into the girl's hand.

"Oh, Joe," said Brady, "don't be taking your sperrits that way; come over here, like a dacent fellow, and we'll be talking over this."

"Oh, that's all right for you, Pat; you've nothing to be dhriving the life out of yer very heart. I am cowld within me, and divil a word I'll spake, till I dhriv it out of me with the sperrits," and he poured the glass of whiskey down his throat, as though he was pouring it into a pitcher. "And now, my boys, you'll see Joe Reynolds 'll talk may be as well as any of you. Give us a draw of the pipe, Pat."

He took the pipe from Pat's hand, and stuck it in his mouth.

"Well, Jack, I see'd your brother in Carrick; and I towld him how you'd done all you could for him, and pawned the clothes off your back to scrape the few shillings together for him; and what d'ye think he'd have me do then? why he towld me to take the money to Hyacinth Keegan, Esq., jist to stand to him and get him off. Why he couldn't do it, not av he was to give his sowl—and that's not his own to give, for the divil has it; and av he could, he wouldn't walk across Carrick to do them a good turn—though, by Jasus, he'd be quick enough pocketing the brads.* Begad, Jack, and it's cowld you're looking without the frieze*; come and warm your shins, my boy, and take a draw out of Pat's pipe."

"And, Joe," said Pat, "what magisthrates war there in it?"

"Why, there war Sir Michael, and Counsellor Webb, and there war that black ruffian Jonas Brown."

"And they jist sent him back to gaol agin, Joe?"

"No, they didn't! Counsellor Webb stuck to the boys hard and fast, while he could; both his own boys and poor Tim; and that he may never sup sorrow; for he proved hisself this day the raal friend to the poor man——"

"But it war all no good in the end?"

"Divil a good. That thief of the world,* old Brown, after axing Ussher a sight of questions, was sthrong for sending 'em back; and then Counsellor Webb axed Ussher how he could prove that the boys knew the stuff was in it; and he, the black-hearted viper, said, that warn't necessary, so long as they war in the same house; and then they jawed it out* ever so long, and Ussher said as how the whole counthry through war worse than ever with the stills; and Counsellor Webb said that war the fault of the landlords; and Brown said, he hoped they'd take every mother's son of 'em as they could lay hands on in the counthry, and bring 'em there; and so they jawed it out a long while; and then, Sir Michael, who'd niver said a word at all, good, bad, or indifferent, said, as how Paddy Byrne and Smith war to pay each twenty pounds, and Tim ten, or else to go to gaol as long as the bloody owld barrister chose to keep 'em there."

"Jack," said one of the others, "did Paddy, d'y remimber, happen to have an odd twenty pound in his breeches pocket? becase av so, he might jist put it down genteel, and walk out afore thim all."

"Well, then, Corney," answered Jack, with Pat Brady's pipe in his mouth, " av Paddy had sich a thrifle about then, I disremember it entirely ; but shure, why wouldn't he? He'd hardly be so far as Carrick, in sich good company too, without a little change in his pocket."

"But to go and put twenty pound on them boys !" observed the more earnest Joe ; " the like of them to be getting twenty pounds ! mightn't he as well have said twenty thousand? and tin pounds on Tim too ! More power to you, Jonas Brown ; tin pounds for a poor boy's warming his shins, and gagging over an owld hag's bit of turf !"

"But, Joe," said Brady, " is it in Carrick they're to stop?"

" Not at all ; they're to go over to the Bridewell in Ballinamore. Captain Greenough was there. A lot of his men is to take them to Ballinamore to-morrow ; unless indeed, they all has the thrifle of change in their pockets, Corney was axing about."

"And supposing now, Joe," said Jack, " the boys paid the money, or some of the gentlemen put it down for 'em ; who'd be getting it?"

"Sorrow a one of me rightly knows. Who would be getting the brads, Pat, av they war paid ?"

"Who'd be getting 'em? why, who would have 'em but Masther Ussher? D'ye think he'd be so keen afther the stills, av he war not to make something by it? where d'ye think he'd be making out the hunters, and living there better nor the gentlemen themselves, av he didn't be getting the fines, and rewards, and things, for sazing the whiskey?"

"Choke him for fines!" said Jack; "that the gay horse he rides might break the wicked neck of him!"

"Sorrow a good is there in cursing, boys," continued Joe. "Av there war any of you really'd have the heart to be doing anything!"

"What'd we be doing, Joe? kicking our toes agin Carrick Gaol, till the police comed and spiked us? The boys is now in gaol, and there they're like to be, for anything we'll do to get 'em out again."

Joe Reynolds was now puzzled a little, so he fumbled in his pockets, and bringing out another three halfpence, hallooed to Kathleen.

"Kathleen, d'ye hear, ye young divil's imp! bring me another half noggin of speerits," and he gave her the halfpence; "and here, bring a glass for Jack too."

"Sind out the rint, Joe, my darling," again bawled the widow, proving that very little said in the inner room was lost upon her.

"Oh, sink you and your rint, you owld hag!" but he paid for the glass for his friend; "and may I be d——d if they ain't the very last coppers I've got."

"Long life to you, Joe," said the other, as he swallowed the raw whiskey; "may be I'll be able to stand to you, the same way, some of these days, bad as things is yet. You is all to be up at Ballycloran afther to-morrow, with the rints, eh, Brady? What'll you be saying to the young Masther, Joe?"

Joe was now somewhat elated by the second glass of whiskey.

"What 'll I be saying to him, is it? well, I'll tell you what I'll be saying. I'll just say this— 'I owes two years' rint, Misther Macdermot, for the thrifle of bog, and the cabin I holds up at Drumleesh, and there's what I got to pay it!' And I'll show him what he may put in his eye and see none the worse: and I'll go on, and I'll say, 'Now, Misther Macdermot, there is the bit of oats up there, as I and poor Tim broke the back of us dhrying the land for last winter; and there is the bit of pratees; and I didn't yet be cutting of the one, nor digging of the other; and if ye likes, ye may go and do both; and take them with yer for me; and ye may take the roof off the bit of a cabin I built myself over the ould mother; and ye may turn out the ould hag to die in the cowld and the bog; and ye may send me off, to get myself into the first gaol as is open to me. That's what you can do, Misther Macdermot: and when you've done all that, there'll be one, as would have stood betwixt you and all harum, will then go far enough to give you back your own in the hardships you've druv him to.' And then I'll go on, and I'll say, 'And you can do this—you can tell me to go and be d—d, as ye did many a day, and give me what bad language ye like; and you can send Pat to me next day or so, jist to tell me to sell the oats, and bring in what thrifle I can; and then, Mr. Thady, there'll be one who'll not let a foot or finger of that hell-hound Keegan go on Ballycloran: there'll be one '— and when there's me, my boys, there'll be lots more—'as 'll keep you safe and snug in yer own father's house, though all the Keegans and Flannellys in County Leitrim come to turn you out!' And that's what I'll say to the Masther; and now, Pat—for he tells you pretty much all—what'll the Masther be saying to that?"

"What'll he be saying to it, Joe! Faix then I don't know what he'll be saying to it; it's little mind, I think, he'll have to be saying much comfort to any of you; for he'll be vexed and out with everything, jist at present. He doesn't like the way that Captain Ussher is schaming with his sister."

"Like it! no, I wonder av he did; a black-hearted Protestant like him. What business is it a Macdermot would have taking up with the likes of him?"

"That's not it neither, Joe; but he thinks the Captain don't mane fair by Miss Feemy! and by the blessed Virgin, he ain't far wrong."

"Then why don't he knock the life out of the traitor? or av there is rasons why he shouldn't do it hisself, why don't he get one of the boys as'd be glad of the job to help him. Look here, Pat——" and Reynolds went over to the fire-place, and with his arm against the back wall and leaning down over the seat where Brady was sitting, began whispering earnestly in his ear; and then Brady muttered something dissenting, in a low voice; and Reynolds went on whispering again, with gesticulations, and many signs. This continued for a long time, till Corney exclaimed,

"What the divil, boys, are ye colloquing

about there; arn't we all sworn frinds, and what need ye be whispering about? Why can't ye spake what ye've got to say out like a man, instead of huggery muggering there in the corner with Brady, as though any one here wasn't thrue to ye all."

"Whist, Corney, ye born idiot, ye don't know I s'pose what long ears the old hag there has? and ye'd be wanting her to hang two or three of us, I s'pose?"

"Divil a hang, Joe; av no one towld of any but her, we'd be safe enough that way; but what is it ye're saying?"

But instead of answering him Reynolds continued urging something to Pat Brady; at last he exclaimed,

"Tear and ages!*and why wouldn't he side with the boys as lives on his own land? av he don't make frinds of them, where will he find frinds? Is it among the great gintlemen of the counthry? By dad, they don't think no more of him nor they do of us. And is it the likes of Captain Ussher as'll be good frinds to him? He's thinking of his own schames, and taking the honest name from his sister. Is that his frind, Pat?"

"Didn't I tell ye, Joe, he hates Ussher a d—d sight worse nor you or I; there's little need to say anything to him about that."

"Why wouldn't he join us then? Who else is there to help him at all? won't he be as bad as we are, if Flannelly dhrives him and the ould man out of Ballycloran; but av he'll stick to us, divil a lawyer of 'em all shall put a keeper on the lands; and I said before, and I say it agin,

—and av I prove a liar, may I never see the blessed glory,—av young Macdermot 'll help the boys to right themselves, the first foot Keegan puts on Ballycloran, he shall leave there, by G——d!"

"But, Joe, s'pose now Mr. Thady agreed to join you here, what'd you have him be doing at all?"

"I'd have him lend a hand to punish the murthering ruffian as have got half the counthry dhruv into gaols, and as is playing his tricks now with his own sisther."

"But what could any of you do? You wouldn't dare knock the chap on the head?"

"Who wouldn't dare? by the 'tarnal, I'd dare it myself! Isn't there two of us here, whose brothers is now in gaol along of him? Wouldn't you dare, Jack, av he was up there again in the counthry, to tache him how to be sazing your people?"

"By dad, I'd do anything, Joe; but I don't know jist as to murthering. I'd do as bad to him as he did to Paddy: av they hung him, then I'd murther him, and wilcome; but Paddy'll be out of that some of these days—and I think therefore, Joe, av we stripped his ears, it'd do this go."

Jack Byrne's equal justice pleased the majority of his hearers; but it did not satisfy Joe. As for Pat, he continued smoking, and said nothing.

"Oh, my boys, that's nonsense," said Joe; "either do the job, or let it alone. Av you've a mind to let Captain Ussher walk into your cabins and take any of you off to Carrick, jist as he plazes—why you can; but I'm d——d if I does! I've had enough of him now; and by the 'tarnal powers, though I swing for it, putting Tim in gaol shall cost him his life!"

Joe was very much excited and half tipsy; but he only said what most of them were waiting to hear said, and what each of them expected; not one voice was raised in dissent. Pat said nothing, but smoked and gazed on the fire.

"Masther Thady 'll be in at the wedding to-morrow, Pat?"

"Oh in course he will."

"Will you be axing him, thin?"

"Axing him what? is it to murther Ussher?"

"No, in course not that; but will you be thrying him, will he join wid us to rid the counthry of him?"

"I tell ye, Joe, he's willing enough to be shut of him entirely, av he knew how."

"Oh yes, Pat, I dare say he'd be willing any poor boy'd knock him on the head, and so be rid of him; and av that he who did do it, did be hung for it, what matther in life to him? That may do very well for Masther Thady, but by the powers, it'll not do for me!"

"Well, you can be spaking to him yourself to-morrow."

"Yes, but you must be getting him jist to come out, and spake to us; jist dhraw him out a bit, you know."

"Well then, boys, I've said as much to the Masther already, and he expects to meet you up there."

"That's the sort, Pat! and av he'll but join us, divil a fear at all for Captain Ussher. Come, my boys, we'll dhrink the gentleman's health,

as would be only dacent and proper of us, seeing the great throuble he's at with us."

"But where'll ye get the whiskey, Joe?"
said Corney; "I don't think mother Mulready
'll be too quick giving you thrust."

"That's thrue any way; which of ye's got the
rint among yer? come, Pat, fork out for once."

"Is it for all of ye? I'll stand a glass for
myself, and one for Joe."

"Well, Jack," said Corney, "you and I'll
have a dhrop together; you shan't say I let you
go away dhry."

The rest made it up among them; and Kathleen, having duly received the price in advance,
brought in a glass of spirits for each. The
widow Mulready had only two glasses, and
they therefore had to drink one after the other.
Joe took his first, saying, "And there's more
power and success to you, Captain Ussher;
and it's a fine gentleman is the only name for
ye; but av you're above the sod this day three
months, may none of us that is in it this night
ever see the blessed glory!"

And they all drank the toast which their
leader gave them.

They now prepared to leave; but not so
quickly but that Mrs. Mulready had to give
them very forcible hints that she wanted quiet
possession of her bed-room; and much animated
conversation passed on the occasion.

"And now, an't ye a pretty set of boys, the
whole of ye, blackguards that ye are! that ye
can't dhrink yer sperrits quietly, in a lone
woman's house, but you must be bringing the
town on her, by yer d—d ructions; and av I

niver saw the foot of any of ye agin, it's little I'd be grieving for ye."

"Quit that, you ould hag of the divil ! or I'll give you more to talk about than'll plaze you."

"Is it you, Joe ? by the mortial then, if ye don't quit that, you'll soon be having a stone roof over yer head. By the blessed Virgin, I'll be the hanging of you av you don't be keeping yerself to yerself."

"Is it hanging yer talking of ? And where'll you be yerself ? Not but hanging's twice too good for you. Come, Corney, is you coming up to Loch Sheen ?"

After a few more exchanges of similar civilities between the landlady and her guests, the latter at length took their departure ; and the widow having duly put away the apparatus of her trade, that is, having drank what whiskey there remained in the jug, betook herself to her couch in her usual state of intoxication.

Joe Reynolds and Pat Brady had each about three miles to go home, and the greater part of the way they walked together—talking over their plans, and discussing the probability of their success.

The two men were very different. The former was impoverished, desperate, all but houseless ; he had been continually at war with the world, and the world with him. Whether, had he been more fortunate, he might have been an honest man is a question difficult to solve ; most certainly he had been a hard working man, but his work had never come to good ; he had long been a maker of potheen, and from the different rows in which he had been

connected, had got a bad name through the
country. The effect of all this was, that he was
now desperate; ready not only to take part
against any form of restrictive authority, but
anxious to be a leader in doing so; he had
somehow conceived the idea that it would be
a grand thing to make a figure through the
country; and, as he would have said himself,
"av he were hanged, what harum?"

Pat Brady was a very different character. In
a very poor country he enjoyed comparative
comfort; he had never been rendered desperate
by want and oppression. Poor as was the
Ballycloran property, he had always, by his
driving and ejecting, and by one or another art
of rural law which is always sure to be paid for,
managed to live decently, and certainly above
want: it was difficult to conceive why he should
be leagued with so desperate a set of men, sworn
together to murder a government officer.

Yet in the conversation they had going home
he was by far the most eager of the two; he
spoke of the certainty they had of getting young
Macdermot to join them the next evening; told
Reynolds how he would get him, if possible, to
drink, and, when excited, would bring him out
to talk to the boys; in short, planned and
arranged all those things about which Reynolds
had been so anxious—but as to which he could
get so little done at the widow's. When there,
Pat had been almost silent; at any rate, he had
himself proposed nothing. It had never occurred
to the other, poor fellow, that Brady was making
a tool of him; that though the rent-collector
was now so eager in proving how easily young

Macdermot might be induced to join their party, he would commit himself to nothing when they were congregated at the widow Mulready's. Had Reynolds not been so completely duped, he would have seen that Brady made him take the part of leader when others were present, who might possibly be called upon as witnesses; but that when they were alone together, he, Brady, was always the most eager to press the necessity of some desperate measure. On the present occasion, too, Reynolds was half drunk, whereas Brady was quite sober.

"So," said the latter on their way home, "thim boys is fixed in gaol for the next twelve months any way. Tim warn't thinking he'd get lodgings for nothing so long, when he went up to widow Smith's there at Loch Sheen."

"Well, Pat, a year is a dreary long time for a poor boy to be locked up all for nothing; and poor Tim won't bear up well as most might; but he that put him there will soon be sent where he'll be treated even worser than Tim at Ballinamore;—and he won't get out of it that soon. By G—d, I'd sooner be in Tim's shoes this night than in Captain Ussher's, fine gentleman as he thinks hisself!"

"But, Joe, will them boys from Loch Sheen let Tim and the others be taken quietly to Ballinamore? Won't they try a reskey* on the road?"

"There arn't that sperrit left in 'em, Pat;— and how should it? what is the like of them with their shilelahs, and may be a few stones, agin them b—— pailers* in the daylight? Av it had been at night, we might have tried a

reskey; but the sperrit ain't in 'em at all. I
axed 'em to go snacks with me in doing the
job, but they was afeard—and no wonder."

"Well, you'll be up at Mary's wedding to-
morrow, and see what the young masther 'll be
saying."

And so the two friends parted to their
different homes.

CHAPTER X

MR. KEEGAN

IT will be remembered that the priest left
Feemy after his stormy interview in a somewhat
irritable mood; she was still chewing the cud
of the bitter thoughts to which the events of the
last few hours had given rise, and was trying
to make herself believe that her brother and
Father John and Pat Brady, and all the rest of
them, were wrong in their detestable surmises,
and that her own Myles was true to her, when
another stranger called at Ballycloran; and a
perfect stranger he must have been, for he
absolutely raised the lion-headed, rusty knocker,
and knocked at the door—a ceremony to which
the customary visitors of the house never
dreamed of having recourse. So unusual was
this proceeding, that it frightened the sole
remaining domestic, Katty, out of all her
decorum. It will be remembered that Mary
Brady had absconded with Biddy. Poor Katty

did not well know how to act under the trying emergencies of the case; she could not get to the door of Miss Feemy's parlour, as a strange gentleman was standing in the hall, so she ran round the house, and ascertaining that the intruder was well in the hall, and could not see her, she clambered up to her mistress's window, and exclaimed,

"Hist! Miss Feemy, there's a sthranger gintleman a rapping at the big knocker, and I think it's the fat lawyer from Carrick; what'll I do thin, Miss?"

"Why, you fool!" whispered Feemy through one of the broken panes of glass, "go and ask him who he wants, and tell him Thady an't at home."

So Katty dropped from the window-sill again, and went to receive the gentleman into the house by following him in at the hall door. By the time, however, that she had entered herself, old Larry Macdermot had been aroused out of his lethargy by a third knocking of the stranger; and on opening his own parlour door, was startled to see Mr. Hyacinth Keegan, the attorney from Carrick-on-Shannon, standing before him.

Mr. Hyacinth Keegan requires some little introduction, as he is one of the principal personages of my tale. As Father Cullen before remarked, his father was a process-server living at a small town called Drumshambo;—that is, he obtained his bread by performing the legal acts to which Irish landlords are so often obliged to have resort in obtaining their rent from their tenants. This process-server was a poor man, and a Roman Catholic, but he had managed to give his son a decent education; he had gotten him a place as an errand boy in an attorney's office, from whence he had risen to the dignity of clerk, and he was now, not only an attorney himself, but a flourishing one, and a Protestant to boot. His great step in the world had been his marriage with Sally Flannelly,—that Sally whom Macdermot had rejected, —for from the time of his wedding he had much prospered in all worldly things. He was a hard-working man, and in that consisted his only good quality; he was plausible, a good flatterer, not deficient in that sort of sharpness which made him a successful attorney in a small provincial town, and he could be a jovial companion, when called on to take that part. Principle had never stood much in his way, and he had completely taught himself to believe that what was legal was right; and he knew how to stretch legal ties to the utmost. As a convert, Mr. Keegan was very enthusiastically attached to the Protestant religion and the Tory party, for which he had fought tooth and nail at the last county election.

Mr. Keegan boasted a useful kind of courage; he cared but little for the ill name he had acquired by his practice in the country among the poorer classes, and to do him justice, had shown pluck enough in the dangerous duties which he sometimes had to perform; for he acted as agent to the small properties of some absentee landlords, and for a man of his character such duties in County Leitrim were not at that time without risk. He had been shot at, had once been knocked off his horse, and had received various threatening letters; but it always turned out that he discovered the aggressor, and prosecuted and convicted him. One man he had transported for life; in the last case, the man who had shot at him was hung; and consequently the people began to be afraid of Mr. Keegan.

Our friend was fond of popularity, and was consequently a bit of a sportsman, as most Connaught attorneys are. He had the shooting of two or three bogs, kept a good horse or two, went to all the country races, and made a small book on the events of the Curragh. These accomplishments all had their effect, and as I said before, Mr. Keegan was successful. In appearance he was a large, burly man, gradually growing corpulent, with a soft oily face, on which there was generally a smile; and well for him that there was, for though his smile was not prepossessing, and carried the genuine stamp of deceit, it concealed the malice, treachery, and selfishness which his face so plainly bore without it. His eyes were light, large, and bright, but it was that kind of brightness which belongs to an opaque, and not to a transparent body—they never sparkled; his mouth was very large, and his lip heavy, and he carried a huge pair of brick-coloured whiskers. His dress was somewhat dandified, but it usually had not a few of the characteristics of a horse jockey; in age he was about forty-five. His wife was some years his senior; he had married her when she was rather falling into the yellow leaf; and though Mr. Hyacinth Keegan was always on perfectly good and confidential terms with his respected father-in-law, report in Carrick-on-Shannon declared, that great battles took place beside the attorney's fireside, as to who was to have dominion in the house. The lady's temper also might be a little roused by the ill-natured reports which reached her ears, that her handsome Hyacinth lavished more of his attentions and gallantry abroad than at home. Such was the visitor who now came to call at Ballycloran.

Mr. Macdermot was very much surprised, for Mr. Keegan's business with Ballycloran was never done by personal visits. If money was received, Thady used to call and pay it at Keegan's office; if other steps were to be taken, he employed one of those messengers, so frequently unwelcome at the houses of the Connaught gentry, and this usually ended in Thady calling at Mr. Keegan's for a fresh bill for his father to sign. Old Macdermot was therefore so surprised that he knew not how to address his visitor. This, together with his hatred of the man, and his customary inability to do or say anything, made him so perplexed that he could not comprehend Mr. Keegan's first words, which were not only conciliatory and civil, but almost affectionate.

"Ah! Mr. Macdermot, how do you do— how d'ye do? I'm glad to see you—very glad to see you—looking so well, too. Why, what a time it is since I last had the pleasure—but then I'm so tied by the leg—so much business, Mr. Macdermot; indeed, though I was determined to drop in this morning as a friend, still even now I've just a word to say on business. You see I must join business and pleasure; so if you are not very much engaged, and could spare a minute or two, why I have a little proposal to make to you—acting for Mr. Flannelly, you know—which I think you'll not be sorry to hear."

The attorney had been obliged to begin his story thus far in the hall—as the old man had shown no inclination to ask him into the parlour: nor did Larry even now move from the door; and, indeed, he did not look as though he was a fit subject to enter on business with an attorney. He had not shaved, or rather been shaved, since Sunday last; his eyes, though wide open, looked as if they had very lately been asleep, and were not quite awake; his clothes were huddled on him, and hung about him almost in tatters; the slaver was running down from his half-open mouth, and his breath smelt very strongly of whiskey.

Keegan, finding that his host did not seem bent on hospitality, was edging himself into the room, when Feemy, who had heard his address to her father, came out to the old man's relief, and told the visitor that he was not just himself that morning—that Thady was out, but that she would desire him to call at Mr. Keegan's office the next day.

"Ah! Miss Feemy, and how's your pretty self this morning?—and is it the fact what we hear down at Carrick, that we are to have a wedding soon at Ballycloran? Ah! well, of course you wouldn't be after telling me, but I was very glad to hear it; that I was, Miss Feemy. But, Mr. Macdermot—it was your

father, Miss Feemy, I was wishing to see this
morning, not Mr. Thady—if you could allow
me ten minutes or so—just a message from our
old friend, Flannelly:"—and by this time
Keegan had wedged his way into the room, out
of which any one who knew him would be very
sure he would not stir, until he had said what
he had come to say.

Larry, hobbling back after him, sat himself
down in his accustomed chair, and Feemy, as
if to protect her father in her brother's absence,
followed him.

"It's very hard, then, Mr. Keegan, that you
should come up here ; as if sending your processes, and latitats, and distraining,* weren't
enough, but now you must——"

"Ah ! my dear Sir, it's not about such disagreeable business at all—we're done with all
that. It's not about such business at all. When
I've disagreeable jobs to do—of course we must
have disagreeable jobs sometimes—why, I
always send some of my disagreeable fellows to
do it ; but when I've good news, why I like to
bring it myself, and that's why I rode down
this morning."

Larry, stupid as he was, couldn't be talked
round by the attorney so easily.

"If it's good news you have, why shouldn't
Thady hear it then ? I am sure, poor fellow,
he hears enough of bad news from you one way
or another. And I tell you I can't understand
business to-day, and Flannelly's bill, doesn't
come round till next month—I know that ; and
so, if you plaze, Thady can hear what you have
to say, at Carrick, on Saturday or Monday, or

any day you plaze. Feemy, my darling, get something for Mr. Keegan to eat. I'll be glad to see you eat a bit, but I can't talk any more." And the old man turned himself away, and began groaning over the fire.

"You see, Mr. Keegan, my father can't go to business this morning. When shall I tell Thady to call down?—But wouldn't you take a glass of——"

Wine, Feemy was going to say, but she knew she had none to offer.

"Not a taste in life of anything, thank you, Miss Feemy; not a drop, I'm very much obliged to you: but I'm sorry to find your good father so bent on not hearing me, as I have something to propose which he couldn't but be glad to hear."

"Well, father, will you listen to what Mr. Keegan has to say?"

"Don't I tell you, Feemy, that the bill doesn't come round before November? and it's very hard he won't lave me in pace till that time comes."

"You see," continued Feemy, "that he won't hear anything; don't you think you'd better wait and see Thady down at Carrick?"

Now this was what Mr. Keegan did not want; in fact, his wish was to talk over Larry Macdermot to agree to something to which he feared Thady would object; but he had had no idea the old man would be so obstinate. He, however, was at a loss how to proceed, when Feemy declared that Thady was seen approaching.

"Well, then, Miss Feemy, as your brother is

here, and as your father isn't just himself this morning, I might as well do my business with him; but as it is of some importance, and as Mr. Flannelly wishes to have your father's answer as soon as possible, he will not object, I hope, to giving his opinion, when he shall have heard what I have to say."

By this time Thady was before the door, and on Feemy's calling to him, informing him that Mr. Keegan was in the house, waiting to speak to him, he came up into the parlour.

"How do you do this morning?" said the lawyer, shaking Thady by the hand, "how d'ye do? I've just ridden up here to bring a message to your father from Mr. Flannelly about this mortgage he holds; but your father doesn't seem quite the thing this morning, and therefore it's as well you came in. Of course what I have to say concerns you as well as him."

"Of course, Mr. Keegan; I look after the affairs at Ballycloran mostly, now. Don't you know it's me you look to for the money?— and I'm sorry you should have to bother my father about it. Just step out of the room, Feemy."

And the young lady retreated to her own possessions.

"Why, now, Mr. Thady, how you all put your backs up because an unfortunate attorney comes to call on you. What I'm come to say is what I hope and think you'll both be glad to hear; and I trust you've too much good sense to put your father against it merely because it comes from me."

"You may be sure I shall not put my father

against anything which would be good for him or Feemy—"

"Well, Mr. Thady, so far so good; and I'm sure you wouldn't; besides, what I've got to say is greatly to your advantage."

"Well, Mr. Keegan, out with it."

"Why, you see, Mr. Macdermot,"—and the attorney turned to the father, who sat poring over the fire, as if he was determined not to hear a word that passed,—"you see, Mr. Macdermot, Mr. Flannelly is thinking how much better it would be to settle the affair of this mortgage out and out. He's getting very old, Mr. Macdermot. Why, Thady, he's more than thirty years older than your father; and you see he wants to arrange all his money matters. Between us and the bedpost, by-the-by, I wish he didn't think so much of those nephews of his. However, he wishes the matter settled, and I explained to him that after knowing one another so long, it wouldn't be fair—though, for the matter of that, of course it would be fair, but, in fact, the old man doesn't exactly wish it himself—that is, you know, to foreclose at once, and sell the estate———"

Here he paused; while Larry merely fidgeted in his chair, and Thady said, "Well, Mr. Keegan?"

"So, you see, he just wishes the affair to be settled amicably. I fear, Mr. Thady, your father hasn't just got the amount of the principal debt."

"Oh! you know that of yourself, Mr. Keegan; you know he hasn't the interest itself, till I screw it out of them poor devils of tenants."

"Well, Mr. Macdermot, as you haven't the money to pay the principal debt, of course you can't clear the estate. Why, you see, the interest amounts to £198 odd shillings a-year; and before that's paid—times is so bad, you see—Mr. Flannelly is obliged—obliged, in his own defence, you see—to run you to great expense. Well, now, perhaps you'd say, if Flannelly wants his money at once, you'd borrow it on another mortgage—that is, sell the mortgage, Mr. Thady; but money's so scarce these days, and the property is so little improved, and the tenants so bad, that you couldn't raise the money on it—you couldn't possibly raise the money on it."

"Why, Mr. Keegan, father pays Mr. Flannelly £5 per cent., and the property is near to £400 a-year, even now."

"Well, of course, if you think so, I wouldn't advise you to the contrary; only, if so, Mr. Flannelly must foreclose at once, in which case the property would be sold out and out; but perhaps you could effect a loan in time——"

"Well, Mr. Keegan, what was it you said you had to propose?"

"What Mr. Flannelly proposes, you mean;—of course I'm only his messenger now. What he proposes is this. You see, the property is so unimproved, and bad—why, the house is tumbling down—it's enough to kill your father, now he's getting a little infirm."

"Well, well, Mr. Keegan; what is it Mr. Flannelly wishes to do with us?"

"Wishes to do?—oh, he doesn't wish anything, of course; the law is open to him to get

his own; in fact, the law would give him much
more than he wishes to take: but he proposes
to buy Ballycloran himself."

" Buy Ballycloran ! " screamed Larry.

" Well, well, father; let's hear what Mr.
Keegan has to say.—Well, Mr. Keegan, does
he propose giving anything but what he has got
himself already?—or does he propose to take
the estate for the mortgage, and cry quits; so
that father, and Feemy, and I, can walk out
just where we plaze ? "

" Of course not, of course not. It's to make
your father what he thinks a fair offer that I'm
come up; and it's what I'm sure you must think
is a generous offer."

" Well, out with it."

" Well then; what he proposes to do is, to
settle an annuity on your father for his life;
and give you a sum of money down for yourself and your sister."

" Let's hear what he offers," said Thady.

Larry, whose back was nearly turned to
the chair where the attorney was sitting, said
nothing; but he gave an ominous look round,
which showed that he had heard what had
passed. But it did not show that he by any
means approved of the proposition.

" I'm coming to that. You see the rent is
mostly all swallowed up by this mortgage. Now
can you say you've £50 a-year coming into the
house? I'm afraid not, Mr. Thady—I'm afraid
not; and then all your time is occupied in
collecting it, and scraping it; and if it's true
what I hear—to be plain, I fear you'll hardly
have the interest money this November; and

if you like Mr. Flannelly's proposal, he'll give
in that half year; so that you'd have something in hand to begin. And how comfortable
Mr. Macdermot would be in lodgings down at
Carrick; you've no idea how reasonable he
might board there; say at Dargan's, for instance,
for about ten shillings a-week. And I'm very
glad, I can assure you, to hear of the very respectable match your sister is making. Ussher is
a very steady nice fellow, knows what's what, and
won't be less ready to come to the scratch when
he knows he'll have to touch a little ready cash."

"You'd better let us know what your offer
is, and lave my sisther alone. It doesn't do to
bring every old woman's story in, when we're
talking business; so, if you plaze, we won't
calculate on Feemy's marriage."

"Well, well, I didn't mean anything more
than that I just heard that a match was made
between them. So, Mr. Macdermot, Mr. Flannelly will settle £50 a-year on you, paid as
you like; or come, say a pound a week, as
you would probably like to pay your lodgings
weekly; and he would give £100 each to your
son and daughter, ready money down, you know,
Mr. Thady. What do you say, Mr. Macdermot?" And he got up and walked round so as
to stand over the side of Larry's chair.

"Didn't I tell you, then, I wouldn't be
bothered with your business? If you must
come up here jawing and talking, can't you
have it out with Thady there?"

"Well, Thady, what do you say? You see
how much your father's comfort would be improved; and as I suppose, after all, your sister

is to be married, you couldn't well keep the
house up; and I'll tell you what more Mr.
Flannelly proposes for yourself."

"I don't want what Mr. Flannelly will do
for me; but I'm thinking of the old man, and
Feemy there."

"Well, don't you see how much more comfortable he must be?—nothing to bother him,
you know; no bills coming due; and as for
yourself, you should have a lease, say for five
years, of any land you liked; say forty acres or
so, and with your ready money, you know."

"Sure isn't the land crowded with tenants
already?" said Thady.

"Ah yes; those wretched cabin holders with
their half acres. Mr. Flannelly would soon get
shut of them: he means to have no whiskey
making on the land! Let me alone to eject
those fellows. By dad! I'll soon clear off most
of them."

"What! strip their roofs?"*

"Yes, if they wouldn't go quietly; but they
most of them know me now; and I give you
my word of honour—indeed, Flannelly said as
much—you should have any forty acres you
please, at a fair rent. Say what the poor devils
are paying now, without any capital, you know."

"No, Mr. Keegan; I wouldn't have act or
part in dhriving off the poor craturs that know
me so well; nor would I be safe if I did; nor,
for the matter of that, could I well bring myself
to be one of Mr. Flannelly's tenants at Ballycloran. But I won't say I won't be advising
the owld man to take the offer, if you only
make it a little fairer. Consider, Mr. Keegan;

the whole property—nigh £400 a-year, besides
the house—and Mr. Flannelly's debt on it
only £200."

"Ah! £400 a-year and the house is very
well," said Keegan; "but did you ever see the
£400—and isn't the house half falling down
already?"

"Whose fault is that—who built it then, Mr.
Keegan?—bad luck to it for a house!"

"Well, I don't know it's much use going into
that now; but you can't say but what the
proposal is a fair one."

"Ah! Mr. Keegan, £1 a-week is too little
for the owld man; make it £100 a-year for
his life, and give Feemy £300, so that she,
poor girl, may have some chance of neither
begging or starving, if she shouldn't get married,
and I'll not go against the bargain. I'd get a
bit of land somewhere, though I couldn't be a
tenant on Ballycloran. 'Deed for the matter
of that, if we must part it, I don't care how
long it is before I see a sod of it again."

"Nonsense, Mr. Thady; £100 a-year is out
of the question; why, your father's hardly to be
called an elderly man yet. I couldn't think of
advising Mr. Flannelly to give more than he
has already proposed.—Don't you think, Mr.
Macdermot,"—and he began speaking loudly to
the old man;—"£1 a-week, regularly paid, you
know, would be a nice thing for you, now that
your daughter is going to get married, and that
Thady here thinks of taking a farm for himself?"

"I towld you before I'd nothing to say about
it—and I will say nothing about it; the bill
don't come round till November, and it's very

hard you should be bothering the life out of me this way."

Keegan turned away, and taking Thady by the collar of his coat, led him to the window; he began to find he could do nothing with Larry.

"You see, Macdermot," he said in a half whisper, "it is impossible to get your father to listen to me; and therefore the responsibility must rest upon you as to advising him what he'd better do. And now let me put it to you this way: you know that you have not the means of raising the money to pay off this debt, and that Flannelly can sell the estate any day he pleases; well,—suppose you drive us to this, and suppose the thing fetches a little over what his claim is, don't you know there are great expenses attached to such a sale? All would have to come out of the property; and your father's other creditors would come on the little remainder, and where would you be then? You see, my boy, it's quite impossible the estate should ever come to you. Now, by what I propose, your father would sell the estate while still he had the power; he would get comfortably settled—and I'd take care to manage the annuity so that the other creditors couldn't touch it; and you'd get a handful of money to set you up something more decently than the way you're going on here with your tenants."

"But my sisther, Mr. Keegan; when the home came to be taken from over her head, what would become of Feemy? She and the owld man could hardly live on a pound a-week. And when the owld man should die—— "

"Why, nonsense, man! Isn't your sister as

good as married? or if not, a strapping girl like
her is sure of a husband. Besides, when she's
a hundred pounds in her pocket, she won't have
to go far to look for a lover. There's plenty in
Carrick would be glad to take her."

"Take her, Mr. Keegan! Do you think I'd
be offering her that way to any huckster in
Carrick that wanted a hundred pound;—or that
she would put up with the like of that?—Bad
as we are, we an't come to that yet."

"There you go with your family pride, Thady;
but family pride won't feed you, and the offer
I've made will; so you'd better bring the old
man round to accept it."

"Make it £80 a-year for my father, and
£250 for Feemy, and I'll do the best I can."

"Not a penny more than I offered. Indeed,
Mr. Flannelly would get the property cheaper if
he sold it the regular way under the mortgage, so
that he doesn't care about it: only he'd sooner
you got the difference than strangers.—Well, you
won't get the old man to take the offer—eh?"

"I can't advise him to sell his property, and
his house, and everything, so for nothing."

"Then you know we must sell it for him."

"Will you give me till Monday," said Thady,
"till I ask some friend what I ought to do?"

"Some friend;—what friend do you want to
be asking—some attorney? Dolan, I suppose,
who of course would tell you not to part with
the property, that he might make a penny of it.
No, Master Thady, that won't do; either yes or
no—no or yes; I don't care which; but an
answer, if you please, as Flannelly is determined
he will do something."

"It's no lawyer I want to spake to, Mr. Keegan; I've had too much of lawyers; but it's my friend, Father John."

"What, the priest! thank ye for nothing; I'll have no d—d priest meddling; and to tell you the truth at once, it's either now or never. And think where your father 'll be if the house is sold over his head, before he has a place to stretch himself in."

"Oh! you know, and I know, you can't sell it out of hand, in that way,—all at once."

"'Deed but we can though; and, by G—d, if you mean to be stiff about it, you shall be out of the place before the May rents become due."

"Would you want me to go and sell all that's left in the family, without giving me a day to consider?—without asking my friends what's best to do for the old man, and for poor Feemy? Surely, Mr. Keegan——"

"Surely, nonsense. You see how it is; I want to give Flannelly an answer; he's not asking anything of you—he's offering a provision to you all, which you might go far to look for if the law takes its course,—as of course it will do if you oppose his offer. But perhaps you're thinking we can't sell the estate; and from the old man's state, because he's not *compos*,* you can get Ballycloran into your own hands. If that's the game you're playing, you'll soon find yourself in the wrong box, my lad."

"It's not of myself I'm thinking; and it's only you, and such as you, would be saying so of me. But supposing now, the owld man consinted to this bargain,—how would he be sure of his money?"

"Sure of his money! why, wouldn't it be settled on him?—wouldn't it be named as one of the conditions of the sale? He'd be a deal surer of that, than he is now of his daily dinner; for that I believe he's not very sure of as things are going at Ballycloran."

Thady looked at the attorney as though he longed to answer him in the same strain; but he said nothing of the sort; he remained looking out of the window for a short time, considering what he should do.

"Well, Macdermot, I can't be waiting here all day, you know; what do you say to it?"

"I'll spake to my father; it's he must decide, you know, at last, and not me. Larry, you heard what Mr. Keegan said, didn't you?" and he explained to his father the nature of the offer; and tried to make him understand that at any rate Ballycloran must go; and that it would be better to go at once, with some provision to look to, than to stay there, and be driven out, without any; and that Mr. Flannelly would not be content any longer with getting the interest for his money, but that he was determined to get the principal, either by having the property sold, or by taking possession of it himself. It was long before he could make the old man precisely understand what it was that was required of him; during which time Keegan remained at the window, as if he was not hearing a word that passed between the father and son.

"And does he want us to go clane out of it, Thady?"

"Root and branch, father, for iver and iver;

and there'll be the finish of the Macdermots of
Ballycloran; but, Larry,"—and he put his hand,
with more tenderness than seemed to belong to
his rough nature, on his father's arm;—" but,
Larry, you know you'll never want for anything
then; you'll be snug enough jist wherever you
plaze; and your money coming due and paid
every week—you'd be better than in this
wretched place; eh, Larry?"

" And what's to become of Feemy?"

"Why, we must get Feemy a husband; till
then she'll stay with you; she'll have a thrifle
of money herself, you know; she'll be poor
enough, though, God knows!—It's the thought
of her that throubles me most."

" And yourself, Thady, where would you go,
till you got Ballycloran again?"

"Got Ballycloran again! why, Larry, you're
to sell it outright; clane away altogether. As
for me, I must get a bit of land, I suppose,
or 'list,* or do something; go to America,
perhaps."

" And was it Keegan wanted to buy Ballycloran?"

"Oh, it's between them, I suppose; but what
does it matter—Keegan or Flannelly?"

" And what did you say, Thady?"

"What did I say! Oh, I could say nothing,
you know? it's for you to do it. But, Larry, I
think it's the best for you, and you may be sure
I'll not be complaining afther; or saying ill of
you for what you did, when you could do no
other."

" And you didn't tell the blackguard ruffian
robber to be gone out of that, when he asked

you to dhrive your own family out of your own house?"

"Whist, father, whist!"

When Keegan heard old Macdermot break out in this way, he was obliged to turn round; so he walked up to the fire, and said—

"Mr. Macdermot, may I ask who you are speaking of?"

Larry was again commencing, when Thady held him down gently, and said—

"It's not so asy, Mr. Keegan, for an old man to hear for the first time, that he's to lave his house and his home for iver; where he and his father and his grandfather have lived. You'd better let me talk to him a while."

"Oh! for the matter of that, I don't care for his passion; but if he means to come to reason, let him do so at once, for as I said before, I won't wait here all day."

"Nobody wants you to wait—nobody wants you to wait!" said the father.

"Whist, Larry, whist! be asy a while."

"I won't whist, and I won't be asy: so, Mr. Keegan, if you want to have my answer, take it, and carry it down to that old bricklayer in Carrick, whose daughter has the divil's bargain in you; and for the like of that you're not bad matched. Tell him from me, Larry Macdermot —tell him from me, that I'm not so old yet, nor so poor, nor so silly, that he can swindle me out of my lands and house that way. So clever as you think yourself, Mr. Keegan, you may walk back to Carrick again, and don't think to call yourself masther of Ballycloran yet awhile."

"Very well, Mr. Macdermot; very well, my

fine fellow; look to yourself, and mind, I tell you, I'll have a cheaper bargain of the place by this day six months, than I should have now by the terms I'm offering myself."

"You dirthy mane ruffian—if it was only myself you was wanting to turn out of it—but to be robbing the boy there of his property, that has been working his sowl out these six years for that dirthy owld bricklayer!—And you want the place all to yourself, do you, Mr. Keegan? Faix, and a fine estated gintleman you'd make, any how!"

"Well, now; you'll repent the day you made yourself such a fool. However, good morning, Mr. Macdermot—good morning; I'll tell them down at Carrick, to keep a warm corner for you in the lane there, where them old beggars sleep at night!"

"Kick him out, Thady; kick him out, will ye?—Have ye none of the owld blood left round your heart, that you'll not kick him out of the house, for a pettifogging schaming blackguard!" and Larry got up as though he meant to have a kick at the attorney himself.

"Be asy, father, and let him go of himself; he'll go fast enough now. Sit down awhile; sit down till I come back," and Thady followed the attorney down the steps on to the gravel road.

"You'll see, my boy," said Keegan—and now the benevolent attorney had altogether lost his smile,—"you'll see, my boy, whether I won't make the two of you pay for this; ay! and the whole family too, for a set of proud, beggarly, starved-out paupers. By G——, I'll sell every rotten stick of old furniture left in the house, on the 6th of next month; and the three of you shall be tramping in the roads before the winter's over!"

"You're worse than the old man with your passion, Mr. Keegan," said Thady; "ten times worse; you know I did what I could to advise him; and even now, if you'll lave him to me, I'll bring him round."

"Be d——d to you with your bringing round! I'll have no more to do with the pack of you."

"Would you go to remember the passionate words of an owld man that's lost his senses, Mr. Keegan? for shame on you. If you'll stick to the offer you made before, I'll bring the old man round yet."

"I tell you I'll do no such thing, Master Thady; but root and branch I'll have you out of that, and that right soon; a pack of beggars like you! What right have you to be keeping a respectable man out of his money?"

"Respictable indeed! very respictable!—Look at the house, Mr. Keegan, for which you want to take the whole property,—tumbling down already; and you call that respictable! And to be threatening to be dhriving an owld man, past his senses, out of his house for a few foolish words; and a poor innocent defenceless girl too!" Thady himself was beginning to get in a passion now,—"And since you will have it, the owld man was not far wrong, for it is robbers you are, both of you, and that's your respictability!"

"Robbers are we? and what are you and your innocent sister? You know, Thady, she can go to Ussher; he says he'll keep her. She won't be a huckster's wife, you say? better that than a captain's misthress, as all agree she is now."

As Keegan said this, he seemed to expect that he would be answered by some personal violence. The two were together, standing at the end of the avenue, all but on the public road. Keegan had a stout walking-stick in his hand, and he walked out into the road as he said the last words, turning round as he did so, so as to face Thady.

The young man stood still for a second or two, as if the meaning of the words had hardly reached him, and then rushed at the attorney with his clenched fist; but the man of law was too quick for him, for striking out with his stick, he cried—

"By the Lord of heaven, if you come nearer I'll brain you!" and, as the young man endeavoured to get within the sweep of the stick, he received a blow on the arm and elbow, which, for the moment, disabled him; and the pain was so sharp, as to prevent him from any further immediate attack.

"Mr. Keegan, by the living Lord, this day's work shall cost you dear!" and then, indulging that ready profuseness of threats in which the less educated of his countrymen are so prone to indulge, he returned within the gateway of the avenue, and proceeded a short way towards the house. Here he reached a felled tree, lying somewhat across the path, on which he sat down; for he felt that he could not go to the house before he had considered, in his sad heart, what he would say there, and how he would say it.

Keegan, when he found that his antagonist, like a dog cowed by a blow, was not inclined to come again to the fight, turned on his heel, and walked back to the place where he had left his horse.

For some time Thady did not recover from the immediate sharp pain arising from the blow, and during these minutes firm determinations of signal vengeance filled his imagination, damped by no thought of the punishment to which he might thereby be subjecting himself. But the luxury of these resolves—for they had a certain luxury—was soon banished by the thoughts that crowded on his mind, when pain gave him liberty to think. Firstly, his own impotence with regard to retaliating on Keegan; secondly, the horrid charge brought against Feemy, and the conviction that the scurrility of it would not have occurred to Keegan had it not previously been rumoured or suggested by others; and the dreadful doubt—for it was dreadful to Thady—whether there could be any grounds for it: then the recollection of their defenceless state—the certainty that Flannelly would take every legal step against them, and that Keegan's threat, that they should be turned out to wander through the roads, would be realized:—all these things forced themselves on his recollection, and he could not go up to the house. He could not meet his father, and tell him that, between them, they had destroyed all hopes of conciliation; that they must wander forth as beggars, to starve. He could not ask counsel from Feemy; his inability to protect her made him averse to see her.

In his misery, and half broken-hearted as he was, he all but made up his mind to join the boys, who, he knew, were meeting with some secret plans for proposed deliverance from their superiors. Better, at any rate, join them now, thought he, than be driven to do it when he was no better than them—as would soon be the case; and, if he was to perish, better first strike a blow at those who had pressed him so low! And then it occurred to him that, at any rate, he would first go to his only good counsellor; and he accordingly retraced his steps to the bottom of the avenue, resolved, if he could find him, to tell all his new sorrow to Father John.

CHAPTER XI

PAT BRADY

WHEN Thady reached the end of the avenue, where the fracas had taken place between himself and Keegan, he met Pat Brady.

As I fear that this talented young man must by this time be subject to heavy suspicions; that his faith and honesty must be greatly doubted; and as, even with those who may still look upon him as a trusty servant, it would be impossible to keep up the delusion much longer, I may as well now make his character no longer doubtful, by explaining some passages which had occurred in his life during the last few months.

In the first place, however, we must return for a short time to Mr. Keegan.

It will be remembered that this gentleman was the son-in-law of Larry Macdermot's creditor, Mr. Flannelly; and it had been arranged between the two worthy relations that if, by some lawcraft or other means, Keegan could obtain possession of the estate of Ballycloran in payment of the debt due by the proprietor, it should become his, Keegan's, property.

Now, this gentleman had long looked forward to the day when he should be able to describe himself as Hyacinth Keegan, Esq., of Ballycloran—having been aware that, after his father-in-law's death, all right in the property would become his own; but since he had induced the old man to make a gift instead of a legacy of the debt, his passion to become an estated gentleman had hourly increased. An ambitious man in his own way was Hyacinth Keegan: he had first longed to obtain admission into the more decent society of Carrick-on-Shannon —that he had some time since achieved; he then sought to mix among the second-rate country gentlemen; and by making himself useful to them, by plausibility, by some degree of talent, and by great effrontery, he had become sufficiently intimate with many of them to shake hands with them at race-courses and ordinaries, and to talk of them to others as " Blake," " Brown," and " Jones." To some few, who now usually called him " Hyacinth," and occasionally invited him to drinking parties at their houses, he had lent small sums of money on good security; and now he was looking to obtain the sub-shrievalty*of the county, and to be Hyacinth Keegan, Esq., of Ballycloran.

Since the immediate probability of realizing this brilliant vision had occurred to him, he had left nothing undone which could, as he thought, lead to its completion. From the constant business which he had with Thady, he pretty well knew all the difficulties of the Macdermots, and the great poverty of their house; and he had observed how completely Pat Brady was in young Macdermot's confidence. He also knew that if any direct legal steps were necessary in selling the estate under the mortgage, or if any underhand scheming should be required to drive the Macdermots into further difficulties, Pat Brady could, and probably would—for a consideration—give him his zealous co-operation. There were also other reasons why he desired the assistance of our friend Pat. It was a part of Mr. Keegan's daily practice to obtain what information he could of the habits of those with whom he was likely to form any connection; and it was generally believed through the county, that he could usually tell those who were, and who were not, guilty of the common crimes of the times— illicit distillation, and secret conspiracies among the poor to injure their superiors, or to redress their fancied wrongs. It was from his accurate information on these points that he was usually employed in their defence when they were brought to trial, and that he had been able to detect and punish those by whom he had himself been attacked. This, moreover, as his character became known, had materially led to his own safety; for the boys knew that he knew everything through the county, and thus had learnt to become afraid of him.

He felt, therefore, that as it was probable that Ballycloran would become his own, Pat Brady's assured services might be of great utility; and he found but little difficulty in obtaining them. Pat was clever enough to foresee that the days of the Macdermots were over, and that it was necessary for him to ingratiate himself with the probable future "masther;" and though he, of course, made a sufficiently good market of his treachery, he felt that in all ways he consulted his own interest best in making himself useful to Keegan. He had dim prospects, too, of great worldly advantages which might accrue from being chief informer*to so conspicuous a man as Mr. Keegan was likely to prove himself, and, with no false self-vanity, he felt himself qualified for such a situation. There was considerable danger in being always among people of a wild and savage nature, to entrap and ensnare whom would be his duty, and he felt that he had the requisite courage. Moreover, there was a certain cunning and prudence necessary, and in that also he, with some truth, fancied himself not deficient; and as Mr. Keegan's scheme opened upon him, the idea of entrapping his young master into the difficulties which lay around, offered not a bad opportunity for the display of his talents.

That such a man as Brady is described to be, should exist and find employment in a country,

is a fact which must shock and disgust; but that
it is a fact in great parts of Ireland, those who
are most conversant with the country will not
pretend to deny. It is true, that by paid spies
and informers, real criminals may not unfrequently be brought to justice; but those who
have observed the working of the system must
admit that the treachery which it creates—the
feeling of suspicion which it generates—but,
above all, the villanies to which it gives and has
given rise, in allowing informers, by the prospect
of blood-money, to give false informations, and
to entrap the unwary into crimes—are by no
means atoned for by the occasional detection
and punishment of a criminal.

Let the police use such open means as they
have—and, God knows, in Ireland they should
be effective enough; but I cannot but think the
system of secret informers—to which those in
positions of inferior authority too often have
recourse—has greatly increased crime in many
districts of Ireland. I by no means intend to
assert that this system is patronised or even
recognised by Government. I believe the
contrary most fully; but those to whom the
execution of the criminal laws in detail are
committed, and who look to obtain advance-
ment and character by their activity, do very
frequently employ what I must call a most
iniquitous system of espionage.

A very few years since I was walking down
the street of a small town with a gentleman who
was at that time in the immediate employment
of the Government. It was a fair day, and we
were strolling through the crowd, which was

moving slowly hither and thither, as though in
absolute idleness. The dusk was fast commencing, and he pointed out to me two or three men,
who had come in from the country like the
others, telling me that they were waiting till it
was dark to speak to him; that they did not
dare to speak to him during the light; that they
were in his pay; and that they had information
to give him respecting illegal societies, and
hidden arms. He ridiculed me when I questioned the propriety of his system; in fact, he was
so accustomed to it that he could not conceive
the possibility of going on without it. In the
same way I have had men pointed out to me
by the officer leading a party of revenue police
in quest of illicit stills, who were dressed as
policemen though not belonging to the force,
and who were brought in that disguise that they
might not be known by their neighbours whose
haunts they were going to disclose.

The momentary success no doubt reconciles
this usage to the officer employing it; but the
result must be to create suspicion of each other
among the poor, and fearfully to increase instead
of diminishing crime.

Now that our friend Brady's character is
perfectly understood, we will return to our
story; first, however, explaining that he had
witnessed the scene between the attorney and
his master, and had determined to make the
most of it.

Thady had turned on the road towards the
priest's house without taking any notice of his
dependant, but this Pat could not allow.

"Well, Mr. Thady, you'll live to be even

with him yet——the born ruffian! faix*and a good
sight more nor even; else it'll be no one's fault
but yer own."

"Even with who?"

"With who now? why didn't I see it with my
own eyes?——the born thief of the world! Didn't
he knock flashes out of yer shoulther with the
shilaleh he had——Mr. Keegan, I main? And if
it worn't that you hadn't——bad cess to the luck
of it!——your own bit of a stick in your hand,
wouldn't you have knocked the life out of him
for the name he put on your sisther, Miss
Feemy?——the blackguard!"

"And did you hear him, Pat?"

"Shure I did, yer honer."

"And did you see him?"

"See him, yes, shure; I seed him riz his big
stick, and I thought it was nigh kilt you were."

"And you heard him call your misthress the
name he called; and you saw him sthrike at me
the way he did, and I having nothing but my
fist to help me; and were you so afraid of a
man like Keegan, you wouldn't step forward to
strike a blow for me?"

"Afraid of Keegan! No, Masther Thady, I
arn't afraid of him; but you wouldn't have had
me come up, jist to witness that you war the
first to strike at him."

"Nonsense! wasn't he the first to call my
sisther the name he did?"

"Ah! but that warn't a braich of the pace.*
You see, Mr. Thady, thim divils of lawyers is
so cute; and av I had come to help you, or
sthrike a blow, or riz my stick, he'd have had
both before old Jonas Brown to-morrow morning;

and where'd we've been then? But, Mr. Thady,
as I said before, you'll be more nor even with
Mr. Keegan yet, any way."

"How'll I be even with him, Pat?"

"But where are you going, Mr. Thady?
shure an't it your dinner time at the house? and
remimber you've to be at the wedding to-
night."

"Oh! d—n the wedding. Do you think I'd
be playing the fool at weddings to-night, afther
what just took place? I want to see Father
John; and I'll go and catch him before he goes
down to your sisther."

"What, Mr. Thady! to tell about the blow,
and the dishonour the ruffian put on you and
Miss Feemy?—shurely you wouldn't be doing
that."

"And why not?—won't all Carrick have it
before long?"

"That's no rule why you should be going and
telling Father John about it yourself. And
won't he be putting you against revenging yourself; and you wouldn't, Mr. Thady, with the
owld blood in your veins, and in Miss Feemy's
—may the divil's curse blacken him for the
name he give her!—you wouldn't be putting
up quiet and aisy with what he's done?—and
the like of him too!"

By this time Thady had stopped, and was
beginning to waver in his determination of
going to the priest. He felt that what Brady
said was true—that the priest would implore
him not to avenge himself, in the manner in
which his heart strongly prompted him to do.
He felt he could not forego the impulse to

inflict personal punishment on Keegan. And after all, what could Father John do for him?

"Besides, Mr. Thady, now I think of it, Father John an't in it at all, for he was to be at Drumsna before the wedding; and I know he's to dine with Mrs. McKeon; he does mostly when he's in Drumsna this time of day, so I'm sure he arn't in it."

Satisfied by this, Thady allowed himself to be led back again; and they walked together in silence a little way.

"You've only to say the word," continued Pat, in a low voice, "you've only to say the word to them boys as'll be there to-night, and they'll see you righted with Keegan."

"What boys—and how righted?"

"How righted! why, how should you be righted afther what he's afther doing?—and I tell you them's the boys as will not see your father's son put upon that way."

"Which them d'ye main, Pat?"

"Oh! there's a lot of them up to anything. There's Jack Byrne and Joe Reynolds is mad to be having a fling at Ussher; you know their brothers is in gaol about the malt they found away at Loch Sheen; and there's Corney Dolan, and McKeon, and a lot more of them; I knows them all, and it'll be jist as good to them to be making a job of Keegan, as the other."

"I wouldn't have the ruffian murthered, Pat; you don't think I want to have him murthered?"

"Whist, Mr. Thady; may be the children about in the trees there would hear you. Who says anything of murdher? No, but just give him a bating that would go nigh taching him the taste of being murdhered,—and the same for Master Ussher; for I tell ye—may the tongue of the cowardly ruffian be blisthered for putting the name he did on your sisther !— but he was only repating what Ussher has said hisself, and that more nor once nor twice."

Thady made no reply, but walked on slowly; he gave no assent, but he showed no indignation at the kind of revenge which was proposed to him.

"And what was he saying about the estate,— Keegan, I main, Mr. Thady,—before you came to be quarrelling that way?"

"He was saying what'll be thrue enough,— that Ballycloran 'll be sold, right away, before next May; and that he himself will be the purchaser—and that we'll be wandering the road like any other set of beggars."

"And did he say he'd buy Ballycloran?"

"He did."

"And turn you all out, Mr. Thady?"

"And he'll do it too," said Thady.

"Tunder and ages !*man, and would you be letting him come over ye that way? If any blackguard of a lawyer could be selling an estate that way, because money may be a little scarce or so, would there be so many gintlemen in the counthry, enjoying themselves in their own houses, just keeping the right side of the door?* Only take care the owld man don't be showing hisself that way he does be doing on the big steps there; and take care the door is kept shut, instead of right open; and make Biddy understand she an't to open it for any one at all, at all—except yerself jist, and Father John, or the like, who wouldn't mind going round to the back door. I tell ye that all the Flannellys and Keegans in Ireland can't sell Ballycloran, unless they first get hould of the owld man."

"But can't they put resavers* on every acre of the land, and wouldn't that be all one as selling it?"

"Oh! let the boys alone for that; stick to them, and they'll not let a resaver do much among them; faix, I'm thinking I for one wouldn't like to go resaving rents up to Drumleesh for any one but the Masther hisself. But any way you'll be coming down to the boys and spaking to them yerself this night—you wouldn't go, Mr. Thady, not to be at Mary's wedding?"

"You know that ruffian Ussher 'll be there; and I don't want to be meeting him."

"But that's jist it; don't let him be there playing what tricks he plazes with Miss Feemy, and you not there to purtect her—and there's all them boys expect you. You won't let Keegan run off with land and house, and all without a blow sthrick?"*

"They'll all be up at Ballycloran to-morrow, and I'll hear what they have to say then."

"But I tell you, they won't be there at all to-morrow, unless you come down to them to-night," answered Pat.

"Do they main to say they refuse out and out to pay the rint?"

"Not at all; but they'll be getting stiff if they think you're so thick with him as is their inimy*—and isn't that natural too? It's only to come down and say a kind word or so to 'em yourself, and you'll find them all right—and ready to stand by you and yours to the last, Mr. Thady."

"Well, Pat, I'll be down there. Father John would think it odd if I weren't there."

By this time they had got round to the back of the house, where the outhouse stood; and the young man told Brady to go into the kitchen and get him a coal for his pipe, and to tell the girl to say he wouldn't be in to dinner.

"And won't you be wanting your dinner, Mr. Thady?"

"No, Pat; I'll jist sit and have a smoke in the stable, till it's time to go down to you. I couldn't face the owld man and Feemy, afther what jist happened."

So we will for the present leave him smoking in the stable, and return to the inmates of the house.

It will be remembered that when Father John left Feemy after his morning visit, she remained alone till Mr. Keegan came: and that she was dismissed from the dining-room when they began to talk on business. She then betook herself to dress for the evening amusement; that is, to make herself something decent before she met Ussher; to brush her hair, and to dismiss all the traces of that disenchanting dishabille which I have attempted to describe. Whilst at her toilet Feemy turned over in her mind all that her brother and Father John had said, and firmly resolved not to let the evening pass without telling her lover the comfort it would be to have some decided steps taken as to their engagement: and yet she almost shuddered at the thoughts of doing so; there was a frown which occasionally came over Ussher's face, which made her dread him; and she couldn't but feel that if he wished to take any such steps, he would do so without her asking him; in fact, that it would be much better that he should do so unasked. And then, if he got angry,—if he should tell her that as she could not wait and trust him, they must part; how could she bear the idea of losing him? What could she say or do, if he answered her sternly?—if he scolded her, or perhaps worse, absolutely quarrelled with her? Poor Feemy began to wish the evening over to which she had looked forward as the source of so much pleasure; she feared to neglect the warnings she had received, and she felt that things could not go on always as they were; but she trembled at the idea of telling this to Ussher.

Her silent dinner was soon over; she made her father's punch, and sat down to wait for her lover. Larry kept up a continual growl about Thady's absence, suggesting that Keegan had cozened him off to Carrick, to sign the estate away; accusing him of conspiracy with the attorney, to rob him, his father; wondering why he wouldn't come to dinner, etc.: to all which Feemy made no reply; she never noticed his grumblings; she sat absorbed in her own thoughts, meditating what she would say to Ussher, till she heard his horse's feet at the head of the avenue, and then she jumped up to meet him at the hall door.

"How are you, Myles?" and "Well, Feemy, how's yourself?" and then, having reached the hall door, he took the fond girl in his arms and kissed her. "Ah; don't then, Myles; there's Katty on the stairs; come in then, and take your punch;" and they entered the room where Larry was sitting over the fire.

"How are you this evening, Sir?" said Ussher, "this fine night."

The old man always brightened up a little when Ussher came in.

"How d'ye do, Captain?—I'm glad to see you. Did the Captain get his dinner then, Feemy?—you don't ask Captain Ussher whether he got his dinner."

"Feemy knows she needn't ask about that; that's one of the things I always take care of. But where's Thady, Mr. Macdermot? I wanted to speak to him about Keegan, that sworn friend of his:" and Ussher began to make himself comfortable with the hot water, sugar, etc.

"Thady is it you're axing* afther? 'Deed then, I don't know where he is. And as for Keegan — but you don't make your punch, Captain—as for Keegan, the ruffian, he was here this blessed morning,—wanting me, and Feemy, and Thady too, to walk clane out of the place! but I walked him off.* The like of him to be buying Ballycloran; and his father a process-server, and his wife's father that d—d bricklayer Flannelly!"

"Holloa! Mr. Macdermot; so you've had a breeze with the attorney, have you? And was Thady here at the time?"

"He was in it all the time; and divil a word he'd say for himself, or Feemy, or his father, or the owld place either; but just wanted me, Captain, to give it all up to them at once, the ruffians ! and when I wouldn't, he went off with Keegan to Carrick. There's my own son joined with 'em agin me ; and he'll help to dhrive me out, he will,—and Feemy too, poor girl ! "

In vain Ussher endeavoured to make him believe that his son had not conspired against him, to deprive him of his property. The old man had taken it into his head that Thady had gone off to Carrick with Keegan, and was determined to make the most of this new grievance, and would not be comforted. He seemed cunning enough in his determination to thwart the attorney in his plan of buying the estate, and explained to Ussher that he had made up his mind not to be taken*personally ; assuring him, that from that time nothing should induce him to leave his own fireside, or so much as show himself at the hall door; that he would have the hall door barricadoed ; and, in short, that he would himself take all those precautions which Brady had enumerated to his son, as proper to be put in practice on such an occasion. And from that time, with one sad exception, it was many months before Larry Macdermot was seen to cross his threshold; he strictly adhered to his resolution ; and although during that time many attempts to arrest him were made, he eluded them all. He could not, however, be brought to understand that, for the present, this was useless—that no one could arrest him till after Christmas. The dread of losing his property had come upon him, and he would not allow himself even to be seen by any one but those of his own household, and by Ussher.

After listening to his grievances as long as he

thought necessary, Ussher followed Feemy into her own room, and here we will leave them, till we meet them again at Denis McGovery's wedding; merely remarking, that poor Feemy, though more than once she prepared to make her dreaded speech to her lover, each time hesitated and stopped, and at last made up her mind that it would be just as well to put off the evil hour till her pleasure was over; and finally determined to have the conversation on the return home, for she well knew that Ussher would walk back with her to Ballycloran, where his horse would be left.

CHAPTER XII

THE WEDDING

WHEN Ussher first came into the parlour at Ballycloran, he asked after Thady, and it will be necessary to explain why he did so; the terms on which the two men stood towards each other not being such as to render it probable that either should be very anxious for the presence of the other.

It had come to the knowledge of Denis McGovery that Brady had asked to the wedding a lot of men from Drumleesh, and some also from Mohill—characters with whom Denis was not apt to consort himself, and whom he looked on as paupers and rapparees.* He had also made out, it is presumed with the aid of his affianced, that some other motive was probably ensuring their attendance than merely that of doing honour to his, Denis's, nuptials. Pat Brady was not likely to have made a confidant of his sister or of Denis on the occasion; but nevertheless, the bridegroom had discovered that the meeting was, to some extent, to be a political one, and moreover, that Thady Macdermot was expected to be there.

Now McGovery, although it must be presumed that, in common with all Irishmen of the lower order, he conceived that he was to a certain degree injured and oppressed by the operation of the existing laws, nevertheless had always thought it the wiser course to be with the laws, bad as they might be, than against them. When, therefore, he learnt that the brothers of the men whom Ussher had put into prison were to be of the party, and that many of their more immediate neighbours would be there, and remembered also that Captain Ussher himself had promised to come to the "divarsion," mighty fears suggested themselves to him, and he began to dread that the occasion would be taken for offering some personal injury to the latter! In which case, might not all be implicated? — and among the number that dear person for whom Denis felt the tenderest regard—viz. himself?

Actuated by these apprehensions, Denis, on the morning of the wedding, had gone to Ussher to unfold his budget of dreadful news,—to assure the Captain that his only object "was to get himself married," and to see that the "pigs and the thrifle of change were all right,"—and strongly to advise the Captain to stay away; "not that it wouldn't be a great honer for a poor boy like him to see his honer down there, for he had the greatest rispect in life for him, and all that wore the King's sword; but there war no knowing what them boys might be afther when they got the dhrink in them."

Ussher thanked Denis for his communication, but at the same time begged him not to disquiet himself—told him that there was no danger in life; and declared that he felt so confident of the good feeling of the men through the country towards him, particularly those at Drumleesh and Mohill, that he should always feel perfectly safe in their company—in fact, that he looked on their presence as a protection. Poor Denis stared hard at him; but as he soon perceived that the Captain was laughing at him for his solicitude, he retreated with a grin on his face, remarking that he had meant all for the best.

Though Captain Ussher affected to set no value on McGovery's tale, he nevertheless thought that there might be something in it. He determined, however, not to be deterred from going to the wedding. Though in many respects a bad man, Ussher was very vigilant in the performance of his official duties, and, as has been before said, was possessed of sufficient courage. It had been part of McGovery's disclosure that Thady Macdermot was to be at the wedding, and it occurred to Ussher, that at any rate no personal violence would be offered as long as young Macdermot was with him; he therefore determined to see him first, and tell

him what he had heard. It is true he had no
great love for the poor fellow; still he would
have been sorry to see him, from any cause of
uneasiness or distress, throw himself into the
hands of men who might probably induce him
to join in acts which would render him subject
to the severest penalties of the law. Ussher
understood Thady's character tolerably well; and
though he had no real sympathy for his sufferings, still he had manly feeling enough to wish
to save him, as Feemy's brother, from the
danger into which he believed him so likely
to fall.

It was for the purpose of talking on this
subject that he asked for Thady; but when he
found he was not in the house, nor expected
home to dinner, he was obliged to postpone
what he had to say till he met him at Mary
Brady's wedding.

About seven o'clock, Feemy and her lover
arrived at Mrs. Mehan's little whiskey shop,
where the marriage was to take place. The
whole party were already there: Father John
was standing with his back to a huge turf fire,
in the outer room—the usual drinking room of
the establishment—amusing the bystanders with
jokes, apparently at the expense of the bridegroom. Mary Brady was dressed in a white
muslin gown, which, though it was quite clean,
seemed to have been neither mangled nor
ironed, so multitudinous had been the efforts to
make it fit her ungainly person. She had a large
white cap on her head, extending widely over
her ears; and her hair, parted on her left brow,
was smeared flat over her forehead with oil: her

arms were bare, and quite red, and her hands
were thrust into huge white cotton gloves, which
seemed to make them so ashamed of themselves
as utterly to unfit them for their ordinary uses.
Every one that entered, said, " Well, Mary," or,
" Well, alanna, how's yourself?" or some greet-
ing of the kind, to which she answered only with
a grin. She and her future husband seemed
totally unacquainted with each other, for since
he came in he hadn't spoken to her. In fact,
poor Mary, as she expressed herself to Feemy,
" couldn't get her sperrits up at all, and felt
quite cowed like."

Biddy, from Ballycloran, was her bridesmaid,
and she, though she did not emulate the bride in
her white dress, had also thrust her head into a
huge cap, which, if it did not much add to her
beauty, at any rate made her sufficiently remarkable to show that she was one of the principal
characters of the evening.

Denis had procured himself a second-hand
light-brown coat, with metal buttons; this was
the only attempt at wedding finery which he
had made; but even this seemed to make him
somewhat beside himself, and gave him a strong
resemblance to that well-known martyr to unaccustomed grandeur—a hog in armour. Pat
seemed to scorn the party altogether, though he
was to officiate in giving away the bride; he was
talking apart to Reynolds and one or two others,
and seeing to the proper arrangement and distribution of the good things which were to follow
the wedding. Thady was not in the place; he
had not yet arrived.

" Ah! Feemy," began Father John, as she

walked in, followed by Ussher, "how are you? and this is kind of you, Captain."

"Long life to you, Miss Feemy! and you, too, Captain dear," said Mary, at last excited to speak by the greatness of the occasion.

"Your honers are welcome, Miss; your honers are welcome, Captain Ussher," said Denis, forgetting that, for the present, he was only a guest himself; and then Brady, and then Shamuth na Pibu'a, the blind piper from County Mayo, "who had made the music out of his own head, all about O'Connell"—and then Biddy, and Mrs. Mehan, and all the boys and girls one after another, got up, and ducked their heads down in token of kindly welcome to the "young misthress and her lover;" and though most of those present, at other times, would have said that it was a pity their own Miss Feemy should be marrying "a born inimey of the counthry, like a Revenue officer, and a black Prothestant too," it wasn't now, when she had come to honour the wedding of one of themselves, that they would be remembering anything against her or her lover.

"Well, Mary, so the time's nearly come," said Feemy, as she sat down on the bench by the fire, that Mary, regardless of all bridal propriety, wiped down for her with the tail of her white dress; saying, as she did so, "What harum? sure won't the dust make it worse, when the dancing comes on, and——"

"Whisper, Mary."

"What is it, Miss?"

"Whisper, then."

"Ah, now! you'll be at me like the rest of

'em;" and she put her big face down over Feemy's.

"Are the sheets done, Mary?"

"Ah now! Miss, you're worse than 'em all!" and Mary put her big hand with the big cotton glove, with the fingers widely extended, before her face to hide the virgin blush.

"What's that, Feemy?" said Father John; "what's that I heard?"

"Go asy, now, Father John, do;" and Mary gave the priest a playful push, which nearly put him into the fire; "for God's sake, Miss, don't be telling him, now; you won't, darlint?"

"What was it, Feemy? all's fair now, you know."

"Only just something Mary was to get ready for her husband, then, Father John—nothing particular. You'll never be married yourself, you know, so you needn't ask."

"Oh! part of the fortune, was it? Trust Denis, he'll look to that; is it the pigs, eh, Denis?"

"No, Father John, it jist an't the pigs," said Mary.

"Come, what is it?—out with it, Denis."

"Sorrow a one of me knows what you're talking about," said Denis.

"It an't the calf at last, Denis, is it?"

"Bad luck to it for a calf!" exclaimed McGovery; and then, sidling up to the priest, "you wouldn't be setting all the boys laughing at me, Father John, and thim sthrangers, too."

"Well, well, Denis, but why didn't you tell me the whole?"

When Ussher had first entered, Brady had come up, expressly to welcome him; and there was something in his extreme servility which made Ussher fear all was not quite right. But Ussher had become habituated to treat the servility of the poor as the only means they had of deprecating the injuries so frequently in his power to inflict; he had, too, from his necessity of not attending to their supplications, acquired a habit of treating them with constant derision, which they well understood and appreciated; and the contempt which he always showed for them was one of the reasons why he was so particularly hated through the country. Though now a guest of Brady's, he could not help showing the same feeling. Moreover, Ussher, who as far as the conduct of man to man is concerned had nothing of treachery about him, strongly suspected Pat's true character, and was therefore less likely to treat him with respect.

"Thank you, Brady, I'll do very well; don't you expect Mr. Thady here?"

"Is it the young masthur, Captain? In course we do. Mary wouldn't be married av he warn't to the fore."

"Indeed! I didn't know you'd so much respect for Mr. Macdermot as that."

"Is it for the masthur, Captain?"

"For the matter of that, Brady, you wouldn't much mind how many masters you had if they all paid you, I'm thinking."

"And that's thrue for you, Captain," said Pat, grinning in his perplexity, for he didn't know whether to take what Ussher said for a joke or not.

"Keegan, now, wouldn't be a bad master," said Ussher.

"And what puts him in your head, Captain Ussher?"

"Only they say he pays well to a sharp fellow like you."

" 'Deed I don't know who he pays. They do be saying you pay a few of the boys too an odd time or two yourself."

"Is it I? What should I be paying them for?"

"Jist for a sight of a whiskey still, or a little white smoke in the mountains on a fine night or so. They say that same would be worth a brace of guineas to a boy I could name."

"You're very sharp, Mr. Brady; but should I want such assistance, I don't know any I'd sooner ask than yourself."

"Don't go for to throuble yourself, for I don't want to be holed of a night yet; and that's what'll happen them that's at that work, I'm thinking; and that afore long—not that I'm blaming you, for, in course, every one knows it's only your dooty."

"You're very kind; but when will Mr. Thady be here?"

" 'Deed I wonder he an't here, Captain; but war you wanting him?"

"Not in particular. Is it true the brothers of those poor fellows I took up at Loch Sheen are here to-night?"

"They is, both of 'em; there's Joe Reynolds, sitting behind there—in the corner where I was when you and Miss Feemy come in."

"It's lucky he wasn't with his brother, that's all: and he'd better look sharp himself, or he'll go next."

"Oh, he's a poor harmless boy, Captain. He never does nothing that way : though, in course, I knows nothing of what they do be doing; how should I ? "

"How should you, indeed ! though you seem to be ready enough to answer for your friend Reynolds. However, I don't want to be taking any more of the boys at Drumleesh ; so if he is a friend of yours, you'd better warn him, that's all : " and he walked away.

"And it's warning you want yourself, Captain dear," said Pat to himself; "how clever you think yourself, with your Mr. Keegan and your spies, and your fine lady Miss, there ; but if you an't quiet enough before Christmas, it's odd, that's all."

They were called into the inner room now, as Father John was going to perform the ceremony ; and such marshalling and arranging as he had ! —trying to put people into their proper places who would be somewhere else—shoving down the forms out of the way—moving the tables— removing the dishes and plates ; for the supper was to be eaten off the table at which the couple were to be married. And though all the company had probably been at weddings before, and that often, they seemed new to the proceedings.

"Denis, you born fool, will you come here, where I told you ? and don't keep the mutton spoiling all night ; " and he shoved McGovery round the table.

"Mary Brady, if you wish to change the ugly name that's on you this night, will you come here ? " and he seized hold of the young woman's arm and dragged her round ; "and who's wanting you, Biddy?" as the girl followed close behind her principal.

"Shure, Father John, an't I to be bridesmaid, then?"

"You bridesmaid, and Miss Feemy to the fore! stay where you are. Come, Feemy."

"Oh! Father John, I an't bridesmaid."

"Oh! but you will be; and, as Thady an't here, Captain Ussher 'll be best man; come round, Captain,"—and Ussher came round. "And mind, Captain," he added, whispering, "when I come to 'salute nostrâ'—those are the last words—you're to kiss the bride;* you are to kiss her first, and then you'll be married yourself before the year's out."

"But I am not at all ambitious that way."

"Never mind, do as I tell you; and don't forget to have a half-crown in your hand, or so, when I bring the plate round. Come, Pat, where are you? you've to give her away."

"She'll jist give herself away, then, Father John; by dad, she's ready and willing enough!"

"Do as I tell you, and don't stand bothering. You want to keep those shiners*in your pocket —I know you;" and Brady, shamed into compliance, also went into his place.

"Now, Denis, the other side of her, boy; why, you're as awkward to marry as shoeing a colt."

"Why then, Father John, that's thrue; for I shod many a colt, and never was married."

"You'll not be so long, avick;* and may be you'll know more about it this time next week. But here's the plate; what do you mean to give the bride? you must put something handsome here for Mary."

"Faix then I forgot about that;" and he put his hand into his pocket and forked out half a crown, which, with a sheepish look, he put in the plate.

"Half a crown, indeed, for a tradesman like you! There's Corney Dolan there, who don't seem to have a coat that fits him too well, would do more for his wife, if it was God's pleasure he was to have one this night."

"Well, there;" and Denis put down another half-crown. This money, which is always put down just before the marriage, is a bridal present to the bride, and becomes her exclusive property.

"Well, Mary, you must be getting the rest of it from him another time."

"Let her alone for that, yer riverence," said Corney Dolan—who considered that Father John's allusion to his coat privileged him to put in his joke—"let her alone for that; she knows how to be getting the halfpence, and to hoult them too."

"It's a great deal you're knowing about it, I'm thinking, Mr. Dolan," retorted Denis; "it's a pity you couldn't keep the hoult of any yerself."

"Wisht, boys! how am I to marry you at all, if you go on this way? Come, Mary, off with that glove of yours; now for the ring, Denis:" and Mary hauled away at the glove, which the heat of her hand prevented her from pulling off.

"Drat it for a glove, then!"

"Ah, alanna, gloves come so nathural to your purty hand, they don't like to lave it at all."

At last, however, Mary got her hands ready for action; the ring was in the plate with the two half-crowns; Father John was standing between the two matrimonial aspirants; Ussher and Feemy were close behind Mary, and Brady was sitting down on the right hand of Denis; and the priest opened his book and began.

The marriage ceremony took about five minutes; but during this time Father John found occasion to whisper Ussher to come up close to the bride; and then, after hurrying over a great part of the service almost under his breath, he pronounced the final words—*salute nostrâ*—in a loud voice, adding at the same time to Ussher, "Now, my boy!"

Ussher, in obedience to the priest's injunction, seized hold of the bride at one side, to kiss her; while McGovery, determined to vindicate his own right, pounced on her on the other; justly thinking that the first kiss she should have after her wedding ought to be given to her by her lawful married husband.

But, alas! both aspirants were foiled, and Mary got no kiss at all. She, in her dismay at the energy of the two aspirants, ducked her head down nearly to the level of the table, and Denis, in his zeal and his hurry, struck Ussher in the face with his own forehead with no slight force. The Captain retreated, half-stunned, and not very well pleased with the salute he had received; and Denis was so shocked at what he had done, that he forgot his wife—and, apparently even the pigs and the money—in his regrets and apologies.

"Egad, Captain," said Father John, "that's

more of a kiss than I meant to get you; why, you're as awkward, McGovery, as a bullcalf. Who'd have thought to see you butting at the Captain, like an old goat on his hind legs!"

"Faix then, yer riverence, I didn't intend to be trating the Captain in that way; but any way the Captain's head is 'most as hard as my own, for the flashes isn't out of my eyes yet."

"Never mind," said Ussher; "and if you always take care of your wife the same way, my good fellow, you'll be sure she'll not come to any harm, for want of looking after."

In the mean time Mary had escaped from the salute intended for her, and was, with the aid of Biddy, Mrs. Mehan, and sundry others of her visitors, engaged in extricating two legs of mutton, a ham, and large quantities of green cabbages from the pots in which they had been boiling in the outer room.

"God bless you, Sally dear, and will you drain them pratees? they'll be biled to starch. And, Mrs. Mehan, darling, my heart's broke with the big pot here, will you lend me a hand? good luck to you then. There's Denis and Pat, bad manners to them, they'd see me kilt with all the bother, and stand there doing nothing under the sun."

And poor Mary McGovery, as we must now call her, toiled and groaned under the labours of her wedding day till the perspiration ran from under her wedding cap; and her wedding-dress gave manifold signs of her zeal in preparing the wedding-supper.

Whilst Mary was dishing the mutton, etc.,

Father John was employed in the not less important business of collecting his dues.

Between McGovery and Pat Brady he had succeeded in getting two thirty-shilling notes, which lay in the bottom of the plate, and formed a respectable base for the little heap of silver which he would collect; and if he did not get as much as the occasion would seem to warrant, the deficiency arose from no delicacy in asking, or want of perseverance in urging.

"Now, Captain, you're the only Protestant among us; show these Catholics of mine a liberal example—show them what they ought to do for their priest,"—here Captain Ussher put a couple of half-crowns in the plate. "There, boys, see what a Protestant does for me. Well, Feemy, I never ask the ladies, you know, but I shan't let Thady off; though he ain't here, I shall settle that in the rent."

"Oh yes, Father John; make Thady pay for himself and me; Mrs. Brennan has got all my money."

"But where's Thady, Feemy dear? I hope you and he are good friends now."

"Oh yes, Father John; that is, I didn't see him since morning."

"But will he be here to-night?"

"He said he would; but you'd best ask Pat, he knows most about him."

This conversation took place in an under tone, and the priest walked on with his plate.

"Come, Mr. Tierney, how's yourself? I see you're waiting there, quite impatient, with your hands in your pocket. It's nothing less than a crown piece, I'll go bail."

"'Deed then, crown pieces an't that plenty in the counthry, these days, Father John; the likes of them"—and he put half a crown in the plate—"are scarce enough."

The speaker was an old man, rather decently dressed in knee-breeches and gaiters; he was one of those who, even in bad times, manage by thrift and industry to get, among the poor, the reputation of comparative wealth.

"And that's true for you, Mr. Tierney, and thank you kindly; they do however say, that however scarce they are in the country, you've your share of them."

"Go on, Father John, go on, you do be saying* more than you know."

And by degrees the priest went through them all. From most of them he got something; from some a shilling, from some only sixpence; some few gave nothing at all: these in general endeavoured to escape observation behind the backs of the donors, but Father John let none of them off; and those who were unprepared, and who alleged their poverty, and their inability, he reproved for their idleness, and hinted rather strongly that their visits to Mrs. Mulready's, or similar establishments, were the cause of their not being able to do what he called their duty by their priest.

Standing in a corner, at the further end of the room, and resting against a wall, was Joe Reynolds: as Father John had a bad opinion of this man, and as he was not a parishioner of his, he was returning without speaking to him, when Joe said—

"You're in the right of it, Father John, not

to be axing such a poor divil as me ; you know,
betwixt them all, they've not left me the sign of
a copper harp."*

" I know, Reynolds, you're too fond of Mrs.
Mulready's to have much for your own priest,
let alone another."

" Faix then, Father John, you shouldn't spake
agin mother Mulready, for she's something like
your riverence ; and a poor boy with an empty
pocket will get neither comfort nor good words
from either of ye."

Father John did not think it to be consistent
with his dignity to answer this sally ; so he
returned to the other end of the room, carefully
counting as he went, and pocketing the money
which he had collected.   In the mean time the
bride, with such assistance as she could get, had
succeeded in putting the supper on the table : a
leg of mutton at the top, reclining on a vast bed
of cabbage ; a similar dish at the bottom ; and
a ham, with the same garniture, in the middle.
The rest of the table was elegantly sprinkled
with plates of smoking potatoes ; and what
knives and forks and spoons and plates could
be spared from the head of the table, where a
few were laid out with some little order for the
more aristocratic of the guests, were collected
together in a heap.   At first, no one seemed
inclined to sit down ; every one was struck with
a sudden bashfulness, till Father John, taking
up the knife and fork at the top of the
table, called McGovery to bring his wife to
supper.

" Now, Denis, my man, don't be thinking of
those two pigs, but bring your better half with

you, and let's see how you can behave as a married man."

"Come, Miss Feemy," said Mary, "if you and the Captain now would jist sit down, and begin—there's a dear, Miss, do."

"Oh, Mary, nobody must sit down before you, to-night."

"Never mind me, Miss,—if I could only get you and the Captain seated; yer honer," and she turned round with a curtsey to Ussher, "there's Denis and Pat there will do nothing in life to help me!" and the poor woman seemed at her wit's end to know how to arrange her guests.

At last, however, Ussher and Feemy sat down at one side of the priest, Denis and his wife at the other, and by degrees the table got quite full; so much so, that when the boys saw one another taking their seats, they were as eager as before they had been slow; and they hustled each other at the bottom of the table, till they were so crowded that they hadn't room to use their arms. Pat sat at the bottom, and he and the priest emulated each other in the zeal and celerity with which they cut up and distributed the joints before them.

At Pat's end of the table plates were scarce, and the boys round him took the huge lumps of blood-red mutton in their fists, and seemed perfectly independent of such conventional wants as knives and forks, in the ease and enjoyment with which they dispatched their repast. At last Brady had done all to the joint that carving could do, and having kept a tolerably sufficient lion's share for himself, he passed

the bone down the table, which was speedily
divided into as many portions as nature had
intended that it should be.

Matters were conducted in a rather more
decorous manner among the aristocrats at
Father John's end of the table—though even
here they were carried on in a somewhat rapid
and voracious fashion. The priest helped
Feemy and Ussher, Mary and her husband;
and then remarking that he had done all the
hard work of the evening, and that he thought
it was time to get a bit himself, he filled a
moderate plate for his own consumption, and
passed the joint down to be treated after the
same manner as its fellow.

As long as the eating continued there was
not much said; but when the viands had disappeared, and the various bottles came into requisition, the clatter of tongues became loud
and joyous; and though the first part of the
entertainment had to all appearance come to
a rather too speedy termination for want of
material to carry it on, there seemed, from the
quantity of whiskey produced, little chance of
any similar disappointment in what the greater
portion of the guests considered the more agreeable part of the entertainment.

"Well, Denis," said Father John, "I believe
I've done all I can this time; and as I know
you'll want to be looking after the cow that's
in calf—no, not the cow, but the pigs—I'll
be off."

"Folly on, Father John, folly on; it's always
the way with yer riverence—to be making yer
game of a poor boy like me! But you're not

going out of this till you've dhrunk Mary's health here, and heard a tune on the pipes, any way."

"Not a drop, Denis, thank ye," and Father John got up; "and now, boys and girls, good night, and God bless you—and behave yourselves."

"Faix, then, yer riverence," said Joe Reynolds from the bottom of the table, "you may tell by the way the boys take to the bottle, that they'll behave themselves dacently and discreatly, like Christians."

"Indeed, then, Reynolds, where you are, and the whiskey with you, I believe there's likely to be little discretion but the discretion of drunkenness,—and not much of that."

"Thank ye, Father John, and it's you have always the kind word for me."

"But, Father John," began Mary, "you're not really going to go without so much as a tumbler of punch?"

"Not a drop, Mary, my dear; I took my punch after dinner—and I can't stand too much. Good night, Feemy—you'll stay and have a dance, I suppose; good night, Captain Ussher."

And Father John got up from table, and went out of the room. As soon, however, as Denis saw that he was really going, he rose and followed him out of the door.

"Sit down, Denis, sit down—don't be laving your company such a night as this."

"But I want to have jist a word with yer riverence."

"Well, what is it?"

"Jist step outside then, Father John."

"Well, Denis; is it anything about Betsy
Cane? or has Ginty come home, and is he
wanting the pigs?"

"No, but would you just step outside here,
Mr. McGrath; where those long-eared ruffians
won't be hearing me?" and he and the priest
walked a little distance from the door of Mrs.
Mehan's house.

"I'm afeard, Father John, them born divils
from Drumleesh and Mohill, as Pat brought here
to-night, are maning more than good to Captain
Ussher."

"And what makes you think that, Denis?"

"Why, Father John, Mary was saying that
Pat towld her a lot of his own frinds would be
up with him, and that if they war talking together,
she and those as are with her dancing and the
like, warn't to be disturbing them; and then I
knows them boys is very mad with the Captain
about that whiskey business up at Loch Sheen;
and then Joe Reynolds and Jack Byrne are in
it, and their brothers are two of them as war
sazed and are now in Ballinamore Bridewell;—
and I know there is something of the sort going
on through the counthry; and faix, Father
John, I wouldn't for money that anything
happened, and I in it the while; for a poor
boy is always made to be mixed up in them
affairs, if by bad luck he is anywhere near at
the time."

"But what do you think they'd do to the
Captain to-night, Denis?"

"Faix then, yer riverence, I don't know what
they'd be doing,—murther him, maybe."

"God forbid! But, Denis, those men from Drumleesh could hardly know Captain Ussher was going to be at the wedding to-night."

"Oh! yer riverence, they'd know it well enough from Pat Brady."

"But you don't think your wife's brother would join a party to murder Ussher?"

"Why then, Father John—I think it's just he that would be putting the others up to it."

"Good gracious, Denis! and what would he get by such deeds as that? Isn't he comfortable enough."

"It isn't them as is poorest, is always the worst. But any how, Father John, if you'd come back, and yer riverence wouldn't mind for the onst jist sitting it out—jist dhrinking a dhrop at an odd time, or colloguing a bit with owld Mr. Tierney, till we get the Captain out of that, shure they'd never be doing anything out of the way as long as yer riverence is in it."

"It isn't here—in the house, where there are so many together—they'd attack him, even if they meant to do so; and I don't think they mean it to-night; but it's on his way home—and my going back would not in any way prevent that. But why don't you at once tell Captain Ussher, and warn him that you fear he is not safe among those fellows at night."

"That's jist what I did then; but he's so foolish, and so bowld, there's no making him mind what one would say. I did tell him, Father John, that I was afeared that there would be some lads in it wouldn't be his well-wishers. But he laughed at me, and towld me there were

none of the boys through the counthry war so
fond of him as those Reynoldses and Byrnes,
and all them others down at Drumleesh."

"Well, Denis, and what can I do more; if
he laughs at you, why wouldn't he also laugh
at me?"

"Why, yer riverence, you and he are frinds
like; besides, he wouldn't trate the like of you
as he would such a one as I; why, I believe he
don't think the poor are Christians at all."

"It's true enough for some of them; but
what would you have me do? I couldn't walk
back to Mohill by his horse's side;—and I tell
you if they attack him at all, it will not be at
the house there, but on his way home."

"'Deed then, Father John, any way I wish
he was well out of that."

"It seems, Denis, it's yourself you're thinking of, more than the Captain."

"Shure, and why wouldn't I—and I just
married? A purty thing for me just now, to
be took up among a lot of blackguard ruffians
for murthering a king's officer."

"Well, Denis, I won't go back now,—it would
look odd and do no good; so do you go back
and drink a tumbler of punch with the men,
and dance a turn or two with the girls, as you
should on your wedding night; and by and by
I'll come down again as if to see what was
going on—and to walk home with Miss Feemy.
The Captain must go back to Ballycloran for
his horse; and if he can be persuaded that there
is any danger, he can go up and sleep at the
cottage; for I tell you, if they mean to hurt him
at all, it's on the road home to Mohill they'd

make the attempt. Do you go in and say nothing about it, and I'll be down by and by."

Father John walked away towards his house, and Denis McGovery went back with a heavy heart to dance at his own wedding; for though his solicitude for the "king's officer" would not have been of the most intense kind, had he thought that he was to be murdered anywhere else, he had a great horror at the idea of any evil happening to that important personage, when it could in any way affect his own comfort.

When Denis returned into Mrs. Mehan's big kitchen, the amusements of the evening— dancing and drinking—were on the point of commencing. Shamuth of the pipes, the celebrated composer and musician, was sitting in the corner of the huge fireplace, with a tumbler of punch within reach of his hand, preparing his instrument,—squeaking, and puffing, and blowing in the most approved preparatory style. Mary was working and toiling again for the benefit of her guests—carrying kettles of boiling water into the inner room—emptying pounds of brown sugar into slop-basins and mugs— telling the boys to take their punch—taking a drop herself now and again, with some one who was wishing her health and happiness, and comfort with the man she'd got—inciting the girls to go and dance—and scolding her brother and husband, because, "bad manners to them, divil a hand they'd lend to help her, and she with so much to do, and so many to mind."

"And now, Miss Feemy, if you'd only get up and begin, dear, the others would soon folly;

come, Captain Ussher—would yer honer jist stand up with Miss Feemy?"

"Oh no, Mary,—you're the bride, you know; Captain Ussher must dance with you first."

"Oh! laws, Miss, but that'd be too much honour intirely."

"No, Mrs. McGovery, but it's I that'll be honoured; so if you will be good enough to stand up with me, I shall be glad to shake a foot with you:" and the gallant Captain led Mary into the middle of the floor.

"But, Captain dear, sorrow a sup of dhrink did I see you take this blessed evening; shure then you'll let me get you a glass of wine before we all begin, jist to prevent your being smothered with the dust like; shure yer honour hasn't taken a dhrop yet."

"I won't be so long, Mary; but I won't have the wine yet, I'll wash the dust out with a tumbler of punch just now. Here's your husband, you must make him dance with the bridesmaid."

"I'm afraid then he ain't much good at dancing."

"Oh! but he must try.—Come, McGovery, there's Biddy waiting for you to take her out; and here's Shamuth waiting—you don't think, man, he'd begin till you're ready."

"Come, Denis," said his gentle spouse, "I never see sich a man; can't ye stand up and be dancing, and not keeping every one waiting that way?"

"Mind yourself, Mary, and you'll have enough to mind. Come, Biddy, alanna, let us have a shake together, all for luck;" and the

happy husband led forth Biddy of Ballycloran
—she with the big cap—who was only now
beginning to regain the serene looks, which
had been dispelled by Father John's not per-
mitting her to act as bridesmaid.

And now Shamuth — his preparatory puffs
having been accomplished—struck up "Paddy
Carey"* with full force and energy. As this
was the first dance, no one stood up but the
two couple above named; there were therefore
the more left to admire the performance, and
better room left for the performers to show their
activity.

"Faix then, Mary," said one, "it's yerself that
dances illigant—the Lord be praised!—only
look to her feet."

"Well, dear—Denis, shure no one thought
you were that good at a jig; give him a turn,
Biddy—don't spare him—he's able for you and
more."

"Ah! but see the Captain, Kathleen; it's he
that could give the time to the music; an't he
and Mary well met?—you must put more wind
into the pipes, Shamuth, before they're down."*

"But if you want to see the dancing, wait
till Miss Feemy stands up—it's she that can
dance; you'll stand up with the Captain, Miss
Feemy, won't you?"

"Indeed I will, Corney, if he asks me."

"Axes you! ah, there's little doubt of that;
it's he that's ready and willing to ax you, now
and always."

"Ah! Mr. McGovery, shure man, you're not
bait*yet! you wouldn't give in to Biddy that
soon?"

Poor Denis was giving signs of having had enough of the amusement. There was a tolerably large fire on the hearth, near which he had been destined to perform his gyrations— which, if not very graceful, had, at any rate, been sufficiently active; and the exertion, heat, and dust were showing plainly on his shining countenance.

"Ah! Mr. McGovery," panted Biddy, "shure you're not down yet, and I only jist begun!"

"Indeed, then, Biddy, I am, and quite enough I've had, too, for one while. Here, Corney, come and take my place;" and Denis deposited a penny in a little wooden dish by the piper's side.

"By dad, Denis," said Corney, "you'll sleep to-night, any ways—to look at you."

"That's jist what he won't, then; for it'll be morning before he's in bed, and Mary'll have too much to say to him, when he is there, to let him sleep."

"Never mind, boys; do you dance, and I'll get myself a dhrink, for I'm choked with the dust;—and here's Mr. Thady. Why, Mr. Thady, why didn't you come in time for the supper, then?"

Just as Denis McGovery gave over dancing, Thady entered the house, having anything but a wedding countenance. He had been, since the time we parted from him after his interview with Keegan, lying in the stable, smoking. He had eaten nothing, but had remained meditating over the different things which conspired to make his heart sad.

His father's state — the impossibility of

carrying on the war any longer against the enmity of Flannelly and Keegan—his own forlorn prospects—the insult and blow he had just received from the overbearing, heartless lawyer —but, above all, Feemy's condition, and his fears respecting her, were too much for him to bear. After his sister and Captain Ussher had left Ballycloran, he had gone up to the house and had swallowed a couple of glasses of raw whiskey, to drive, as he said to himself, the sorrow out of his heart; and he had now come down to seek the friends whom Brady had recommended to him, and determined, at whatever cost, to revenge himself, by their aid, against Keegan, for the insults he had heaped upon him, and against Ussher for the name which, he believed, he had put upon his sister.

It was with these feelings and determinations that Thady had come down to McGovery's wedding; and, as he entered the room, Ussher and Feemy were just standing up to dance.

CHAPTER XIII

HOW THE WEDDING PARTY WAS CONCLUDED

WHEN Thady entered the room where the party was dancing, the welcomes with which he was greeted by McGovery and his wife prevented him from immediately seeking Pat Brady, as he had intended; for he was obliged to stop to refuse the invitations and offers which he received, that supper should be got for him. And it was well for those that made the offers that he did refuse them; for every vestige of what was eatable in the house had been devoured, and had he acceded to Mary's reiterated wishes that he would "take jist the laste bit in the world," it would have puzzled her to make good her offer in the most literal sense of the words.

Luckily, however, Thady declined her hospitality, and was passing through to the inner room when he was stopped by Ussher, who, as we have before said, was standing up to dance with Feemy. The last time the two young men had met was at the priest's house, when, it will be remembered, Thady had shown a resolution not to be on good terms with the Captain, and subsequent events had not at all mollified his temper; so when Ussher good-humouredly asked him how he was, and told him he wanted to speak to him a word or two as soon as he should have tired Feemy dancing, or, what was more probable, Feemy should have tired him, Thady answered him surlily enough, saying that if Captain Ussher had anything to say to him, he should be within, but that he didn't mean to stay there all night, and that perhaps Captain Ussher had better say it at once.

"Well, Macdermot, perhaps I had; so, if your sister'll excuse me, I won't be a minute.— Just step to the door a moment, will you?" and Thady followed him out.

"Well, Captain Ussher, what is it?"

"I don't know why it is, Macdermot, but for the last two or three days you seem to want to quarrel with me; if it is so, why don't you speak out like a man?"

" Is that what you were wanting to say to me ? "

" Indeed it was not; for it's little I care whether you choose to quarrel or let it alone; but I heard something to-night, which, though I don't wholly believe it, may like enough be partly true; and if you choose to listen, I will tell you what it was; perhaps you can tell me whether it was all false; and if you cannot, what I tell you may keep yourself out of a scrape."

" Well."

" McGovery tells me that he thinks some of the boys that are here to-night are come to hold some secret meeting; and that, from the brothers of the two men I arrested the other day being in it, he thinks their purpose is to revenge themselves on me."

" And if it war so, Captain Ussher, what have I to do with it ? "

Ussher looked very hard at Thady's face, but it was much too dark for him to see anything that was there.

" Probably not much yourself; but I thought that as these men were your father's tenants, you might feel unwilling that they should turn murderers; and as I am your father's friend, you might, for his sake, wish to prevent them murdering me."

" And is it from what such a gaping fool as McGovery says, you have become afraid that men would murder you, who never so much as raised their hand agin any of those who are from day to day crushing and ruining them ? "

" If I had been afraid, I should not have come here. Indeed, it was to show them that

I am not afraid of coming among them without my own men at my back that I came here. But though I am not afraid, and though it is not what McGovery says I mind—and he is not such a fool as some others—nevertheless I do think, in fact, from different sources, I know, that there is something going on through the country, which will bring the poor into worse troubles than they've suffered yet; and if, as I much think, they've come here to talk of their plans to-night, and if you know that it is so, you're foolish to be among them."

"Is that all you've to say to me, Captain Ussher?"

"Not quite; I wanted to ask you, on your honour, as a man and an Irishman, do you know whether there is any conspiracy among them to murder or do any injury to me?" Ussher paused for a moment; and as Thady did not answer him, he went on—"and I wanted to warn you against one who is, I know, trying his best to ruin you and your father."

"Who is that, Captain Ussher? I believe I know my own friends and my own inimies," said Thady, who thought the revenue officer alluded to Keegan.

"Answer my question first."

"And suppose I don't choose to answer it?"

"Why, if you won't answer it, I cannot but think you are aware of such a conspiracy, and that you approve of it."

"Do you mean to say, Captain Ussher, that I have conspired to murdher you?"

"No, I say no such thing; but surely, if you heard of such a scheme, or thought there was such an intention in the country, wouldn't you tell me, or any one else that was so doomed, that they might be on their guard?"

"You're very much frightened on a sudden, Captain."

"That's not true, Macdermot; you know I'm not frightened; but will you answer the question?"

Thady was puzzled; he did not know what to say exactly. He had not absolutely heard that the men whom he was going to meet that night, and whom he knew he meant to join, intended to murder Ussher; but Brady had told him that they were determined to have a fling at him, and it was by their promise to treat the attorney in the same way, that Thady had been induced to come down to them. It had never struck him that he was going to join a body of men pledged to commit murder—that he was to become a murderer, and that he was to become so that very night. His feeling had been confined to the desire of revenging himself for the gross and palpable injuries with which he had been afflicted, whilst endeavouring to do the best he could for his father, his sister, and his house. But now—confronted with Ussher—asked by him as to the plots of the men whom he was on the point of joining, and directly questioned as to their intentions by the very man he knew they were determined to destroy. Thady felt awed, abashed, and confused.

Then it occurred to him that he had not, at any rate as yet, pledged himself to any such deed, or even in his mind conceived the idea of

such a deed; that there was no cause why he
should give his surmises respecting what he
believed might be the intentions of others to
the man whom, of all others—perhaps, not
excepting the lawyer—he disliked and hated;
and that there could be no reason why he should
warn Captain Ussher against danger. Though
these things passed through Thady's mind very
quickly, still he paused some time, leaning
against the corner of an outhouse, till Ussher
said—

"Well, Macdermot, surely you'll not refuse to
answer me such a question as that. Though—
God knows why—we mayn't be friends, you
would not wish to have such ill as that happen
to me."

"I don't know why you should come to me,
Captain Ussher, to ask such questions. If you
were to ask your own frinds that you consort with,
in course they would feel more concerned in
answering you than I can. Not that I want to
have art or part in your blood, or to have you
murdhered—or any one else. But to tell you
God's holy truth, if you were out of the counthry
intirely,* I would be better pleased, as would be
many others. And since you are axing me, I'll
tell you, Captain Ussher, that I do think the
way you do be going on with the poor in
the counthry—dhriving and sazing them, and
having spies over them—isn't such as is likely
to make you frinds in the counthry, except with
such as Jonas Brown and the like. And though,
mind you, I know nothing of plots and conspiracies among the boys, I don't think you're
over safe whilst staying among thim you have

been trating that way; and if they were to shoot you some night, it's no more than many would expect. To tell you the truth, then, Captain Ussher, I think you'd be safer anywhere than at Mohill."

Thady considered that he thus made a just compromise between the faith he thought he owed to the men with whom he was going to league himself, and the duty, which he could not but feel he ought to perform, of warning Ussher of the danger in which he was placed.

Ussher felt quite satisfied with what Thady had said. He was not at all surprised at his expressions of personal dislike, and he felt confident, from the manner in which young Macdermot had spoken of his perilous situation, that even if any conspiracy had been formed, of which he was the object, there was no intention to put it into immediate operation, and that, at any rate in Macdermot's opinion, no concerted plan had yet been made to attack him. A good many reasons also induced Ussher to think that he stood in no danger of any personal assault. In the first place, though the country was in a lawless state—though illicit distillation was carried to a great extent—though many of the tenants refused to pay either rent, tithes, or county cesses*till compelled to do so—the disturbances arising from these causes had not lately led to murder or bloodshed. He had carried on his official duties in the same manner for a considerable time without molestation, and custom had begotten the feeling of security. Moreover, he thought the poor were cowed and frightened. He despised them too much to think they would have the spirit to rise up against him. In fact, he made up his mind that Thady's intention was to frighten him out of the country, if possible, and he resolved that he would not allow anything he had heard on the subject either to disturb his comfort, or actuate his conduct.

"Well, Macdermot, that's fair and above board—and what I expected, though it's neither friendly nor flattering; and I am not vexed with you for that; for if you don't feel friendly to me you shouldn't speak as if you did, and therefore I'm obliged to you. And I will say that if I am to be shot down, like a dog, whilst performing my duty to the best of my ability, at any rate, I won't let the fear of such a thing frighten me out of my comfort before it happens. And now if you'll let me say a word or two to you about yourself———"

"I'm much obliged to you, Captain Ussher, but if you can take care of yourself, so can I of myself."

"Why, how cranky you are, man! If you hate me, hate me in God's name, but don't be so absurd as to forget you're a man, and to act like a child. I listened to you—and why can't you listen to me?"

"Well, spake on, I'll listen."

"Mind, I don't pretend to know more of your affairs than you would wish me; but, as I am intimate with your father, I cannot but see that you, in managing your father's concerns, put great confidence in the man within there."

"What! Pat Brady?"

"Yes, Brady! Now, if you only employed

him as any other farm servant, he would not, probably, have much power to injure you ; but I believe he does more than that—that he collects your rents, and knows the affairs of all your tenants."

" Well ? "

" I have very strong reason to think that he is also in the employment, or at any rate in the pay, of Mr. Keegan, the attorney at Carrick."

" What makes you think that, Captain Ussher ? "

" I could hardly explain the different things which make me think so; but I'm sure of it ; and it is for you to judge whether, if such be the case, your confidence will not enable him, under the present state of affairs at Ballycloran, to do you and your father much injury. He is also, to my certain knowledge, joined in whatever societies—all of them illegal—are being formed in the country ; and he is a man, therefore, not to be trusted. I may add also that if you listen too much to his advice and counsels, you will be likely to find yourself in worse troubles than even those which your father's property brings on you."

" Don't alarm yourself about me ; I don't be in the habit of taking a servant's advice about things, Captain Ussher."

" There's your back up again ; I don't mean to offend you, I tell you; however, if you remember what I have said to you, it may prevent much trouble to you :"—and Ussher walked into the house.

" Prevent throubles," soliloquised Thady ; " there is no way with me to prevent all manner of throuble—I believe I'll go in and get a tumbler of punch;"—and determined to adopt this mode of quieting troubles, if he could not prevent them, he followed Ussher.

Ussher was now dancing with Feemy, and the fun had become universal and incessant; there were ten or twelve couple dancing on the earthen floor of Mrs. Mehan's shop. The piper was playing those provocative Irish tunes, which, like the fiddle in the German tale, compel the hearers to dance whether they wish it or no; and they did dance with a rapidity and energy which showed itself in the streams of perspiration running down from the performers' faces. Not much to their immediate comfort a huge fire was kept up on the hearth; but the unnecessary heat thus produced was atoned for by the numerous glasses of punch with which they were thereby enabled to regale themselves, when for a moment they relaxed their labours.

This pleasant recreation began also to show its agreeable effects in the increased intimacy of the partners and the spirit of the party. All diffidence in standing up had ceased—and now the only difficulty was for the aspirants to get room on which to make their complicated steps; and oh, the precision, regularity, and energy of those motions! Although the piper played with a rapidity which would have convinced the uninitiated of the impossibility of dancing to the time, every foot in the room fell to the notes of the music as surely as though the movements of the whole set had been regulated by a steam machine. And such movements as they were! Not only did the feet keep time, but every limb and every muscle had each its own work, and twisted, shook, and twirled itself in perfect unison and measure, the arms performed their figure with as much accuracy as the legs.

"Take a sup of punch now, Miss Tierney; shure you're fainting away entirely for the want of a dhrop." The lady addressed was wiping, with the tail of her gown, a face which showed the labour that had been necessary to perform the feat of dancing down the whole company to the tune of the "wind that shakes the barley,"* and was now leaning against the wall, whilst her last partner was offering her punch made on the half and half system: "Take a sup, Miss Tierney, then; shure you're wanting it."

"Thank ye, Mr. Kelly, but I am afther taking a little jist now, and the head's not sthrong with me afther dancing;" she took the tumbler, however. "Faix, Mr. Kelly, but it's yourself can make a tumbler of punch with any man."

"'Deed then there's no sperrits in it at all— only a thrifle to take the wakeness off the water. Come, Miss Tierney, you didn't take what'd baptize a babby."

"It'd be a big babby then; one like yerself may be."

"Here's long life to the first you have yerself, any way, Miss Tierney!" and he finished the glass, of which the blushing beauty had drunk half. "Might a boy make a guess who'd be the father of it?"

"Go asy now, masther Morty,"—the swain

rejoiced in the name of Mortimer Kelley. "It'll be some quiet, dacent fellow, that an't given to chaffing nor too fond of sperrits."

"By dad, my darling, and an't that me to a hair's breadth?"

"Is it you a dacent, asy*boy?"

"Sure if it an't me, where's sich a one in the counthry at all? And it's I'd be fond of the child—and the child's mother more especial," and he gave her a loving squeeze, which in a less energetic society might have formed good ground for an action for violent assault.

"Ah don't! Go asy I tell you, Morty. But come, an't you going to dance instead of wasting your time here all night?" and the pair, re-invigorated by their intellectual and animal refreshment, again commenced their dancing.

Whilst the fun was going on fast and furious among the dancers, those in the inner room were not less busily engaged. Brady was still sitting in the chair which he had occupied during the supper, at the bottom of the table, though he had turned round a little towards the fire. At the further end of it Thady was seated, with a lighted pipe in his mouth, and a tumbler of punch on the shelf over the fire-place. Joe Reynolds was seated a little behind, but between Thady and Pat Brady; and a lot of others were standing around, or squatting on the end of the table—leaning against the fireplace, or sitting two on a chair, wherever two had been lucky enough to secure one between them. They were all drinking, most of them raw spirits—and all of them smoking. At the other end of the room, three or four boys and girls were standing in the door-way, looking at the dancing, and getting cool after their own performances ; and Denis McGovery was sitting in the chair which Father John had occupied, with his head on the table, apparently asleep, but more probably intent on listening to what was going on among them at the other end of the room, whom he so strongly suspected of some proposed iniquity. The noise, how-ever, of the music and the dancing, the low tones in which the suspected parties spoke, and the distance at which they sat, must have made Denis's occupation of eaves-dropping difficult, if not impracticable.

Thady had just been speaking, and it was evident from the thickness of his voice that the whiskey he had drunk was beginning to have its effects on him. Instead of eating his dinner, he had been drinking raw spirits in the morning, to which he was not accustomed ; for though when cold, or when pressed by others, he could swallow a glass of raw whiskey with that facility which seems to indicate an iron throttle,*he had been too little accustomed to give way to any temptation to become habitually a drunkard. Now, however, he was certainly becoming tipsy, and, therefore, more likely to agree to whatever those around him might propose."

"Asy, Mr. Thady !" said Pat ; "there's that long-eared ruffian, McGovery, listening to every word he can catch. Be spaking now as if you war axing the boys about the rint."

"And isn't it about that he is axing ? " said Joe. "But how can he get the rint, or we be

paying it, unless he gives us his hand to rid the
counthry of thim as robs us of our names, and
desthroys him and us, and all thim as should
be frinds to him and the owld Masther, and
to Ballycloran?"

"You know, all of ye, that I never was hard
on you," continued Thady, "when, God knows,
the money was wanted bad enough at Ballycloran. You know I've waited longer for what
was owed than many a one has done who has
never felt what it was to want a pound. Did I
ever pull the roof off any of you? And though
queer tenants you've most of you been, an't the
same set on the land now mostly that there was
four years ago? There's none of you can call
me a hard man, I think; and when I've stuck
to you so long, it isn't now I'll break away from
you."

"Long life to you, Mr. Thady!" "Long life
to yer honer—and may ye live to see the esthate
your own yet, and not owe a shilling!" "It's
thrue for the masther what he says; why should
he turn agin his own now? God bless him!"
Such were the exclamations with which Thady's
last speech was received.

"And I'll tell you what it is," and he now
spoke in a low thick whisper, "I'll tell you
what's on my mind. Those that you hate, I
don't love a bit too well. You all know
Hyacinth Keegan, I think?"

"'Deed we do—may the big devil fetch him
home!"

"Well, then, would you like him for your
landlord, out and out? such a fine gentleman
as he is!"

"Blast him for a gintleman!" said Joe; "I'd sooner have his father; he war an honest man, more by token he war no Protestant; he sarved processes for Richard Peyton, up by Loch Allen."

"Well, then," continued Thady, "if you don't like him, boys, I can tell you he don't like you a bit better; and if he can contrive to call himself masther at Ballycloran, as I can tell you he manes to try, it's not one of you he'll have on the land."

"Did he tell you that himself, Mr. Thady?" whispered Brady. Now, though young Macdermot was nearly drunk—quite drunk enough to have lost what little good sense was left to him, after being fool enough to come at all among those with whom he was at present drinking—still, what Ussher had said about his follower was not forgotten, and though he did not absolutely believe that Brady was a creature of Keegan's, what he had heard prevented his having the same inclination to listen to Pat, or the same confidence in what he said.

"Faith then, he told me so with his own mouth; and it isn't only the others 'd be going, but you'd have to walk yourself, masther Pat."

"And why wouldn't I? D'ye think I'd be staying at Ballycloran afther you war gone, Mr. Thady?"

"Don't be making any vows, Pat; maybe you wouldn't be axed, and maybe, av you war, you wouldn't refuse to ate yer bread, though it war Keegan paid for it."

"That the first mouthful may choke me that I ever ate of his paying for!"

" Well, however, boys, Hyacinth Keegan will sthrip the roof off every mother's son of you if he ever conthrives to put his foot in Ballycloran ; but, by God, he never shall ! Mind, boys, he can never do that till he can lay his hands on the owld man ; and where'll you all be, I wonder, to let him or any one he sends do that, or take a sod of turf, or a grain of oats off the land either ? "

" By dad, you're right, Mr. Thady," said one of them. " Shure wouldn't we have him in a bog-hole, or as many as he'd send ; and then they might take away what they could carry in their mouths."

" I'll tell you what, Sir," said Joe Reynolds, and he laid his hand on Thady's knee, and leant forward till his mouth was near the young man's ear—so near, that not only could not McGovery overhear his words, but of the whole party round the fire, only Brady and Byrne, besides Thady himself, could catch what he said ; " I'll tell you what, Sir, Keegan shall never harum you or yours, if you'll be one of us—one of us heart and sowl ; and I know you will, and I know it's not in you to put up with what they're putting on you ; an' dearly he'll pay for the blow he strik you, an' the word he said—surely, Mr. Thady ! " And he whispered still lower into his ear, " Let alone the esthate, an' the house, an' all that, you'd niver put up with what he has been about this day, paceable an' in quiet ? "

" You're thrue in that, Joe, by G—d ! "

" Well, then, won't we see you righted ? Let the bloody ruffian come to Ballycloran, an' then see the way he'll go back again to Carrick. Will you say the word, Mr. Thady? Will you join us agin thim that is as much, an' a deal more, agin you than they are agin us?"

"But what is it you main to do?"

"That's what you'll know when you've joined us; but you know it isn't now or here we'd be telling you that which, maybe, would put our necks in your hand. But when you've taken the oath*we've all taken, we'll be ready then not only to tell you all, but follow you anywhere."

The young man paused.

"Isn't it enough for you to know that our inimies is your inimies—that thim you wishes ill to, we wishes ill to? Isn't Keegan the man you've most cause to hate, an' won't we right you with him? Don't we hate that bloody Captain that is this moment playing his villain's tricks with your own sisther in the next room there? and shure you can't feel very frindly to him. By the holy Virgin, when you're one of us, it's not much longer he shall throuble you. If you can put up with what the likes of them is doing to you—if you can bear all that—why, Mr. Thady, you're not the man I took you for. But mind, divil a penny of rint 'll ever go to Ballycloran agin from Drumleesh; for the matter's up now;—you're either our frind or our inimy. But if, Mr. Thady, you've the pluck they all says you have—an' which I iver see in you, God bless you!—it's not only one of us you'll be, but the head of us all; for there isn't one but 'll go to hell's gate for your word; an' then the first tinant on the place that pays as much as a tinpenny to Keegan, or to any but jist yourself—by the cross! he may dig his own grave."

What Thady immediately said does not much signify; before long he had promised to come over to Mrs. Mulready's at Mohill with Pat Brady, on an appointed night, there to take the oath of the party to whom he now belonged.

Though it was agreed that the secret determinations of the party were not to be divulged to him until he had joined them there, it nevertheless was pretty clearly declared that their immediate and chief object was the destruction of Ussher, and, if possible, the liberation of the three men who had lately been confined in Ballinamore Bridewell, for the malt that had been seized in the cabin by Loch Sheen. However, to prevent the evil arising from this carelessness in the performance of their duties as conspirators, Thady was requested to swear on a cross made with the handles of two knives, that he would not divulge anything that had occurred or been said in that room that night —with which request he complied.

By the time this was done most of them were drunk, but none were so drunk as poor Macdermot. His intoxication, moreover, was unfortunately not of that sort which was likely to end in quiescence and incapability. It was a sign of the great degradation to which Macdermot had submitted, in joining these men, that in talking over the injuries which Ussher had inflicted on them all, he had quietly heard them canvass Ussher's conduct to his sister, and that in no measured terms. This had gone much against the grain with him at first, because he could not but strongly feel that, in abusing Ussher, they were equally reproaching Feemy. But the fall of high and fine feelings, when once commenced, is soon accomplished, even when the fall is from a higher dignity than those of Thady's had ever reached; and though, a few hours since, he would have allowed no one but Father John, even to connect his sister's name with Ussher, he had soon accustomed himself to hear the poorest tenant on his father's property speak familiarly on the subject, when urging him to join them in common cause against his enemy. But though he had so far sacrificed his sister's dignity in his drunken conversation with these men, he was not the less indignant with the man whose name they had so unceremoniously joined with hers; and he got up with the resolution to inform Ussher that the intercourse between him and Feemy must immediately cease. The spirits he had taken gave him a false feeling of confidence that he should find means to carry his resolution into effect without delay.

When he got into the outer room, Ussher and Feemy were not there. The dancing and drinking were going on as fast as ever; Shamuth, the piper, was in the same seat, with probably not the same tumbler of punch beside him, and was fingering away at his pipes as if the feeling of fatigue was unknown to him; and Mary, the bride, was still dancing as though her heart had not been broken all the morning with the work she had had to do. Biddy also, the Ballycloran housemaid, was in the seventh heaven of happiness—for hadn't she music and punch galore? and though the glory of her once well-starched cap was dimmed, if not totally extinguished by the dust and heat, her heart was now too warm with the fun to grieve for that, especially when such a neat-made boy as Barney Egan was dancing foranenst her.* It did not, however, add to her happiness, when, after being addressed once or twice in vain, she heard her young master's voice.

"Biddy—d'ye hear, and be d—d to you!—is your misthress gone home?"

"'Deed, Mr. Thady, I think she be."

"And why the divil, then, an't you gone with her? d'you mane to be dancing here all night?"

Now Thady was in general so very unobservant—so little inclined to interfere with, if he could not promote, the amusements of his dependants—moreover, so unaccustomed to scold—that Biddy and the others round her soon saw that something was the matter.

"What are you staring at, you born fool? If Miss Feemy's gone up to Ballycloran, do you follow her."

Thady's thick voice, red face, and sparkling eyes showed that he was intoxicated, and Biddy, if not preparing to obey him—for the temptation to stay was too strong—was preparing to pretend to do so, when Mary McGovery, by way of allaying Macdermot's wrath, said—

"I don't believe, then, Mr. Thady, that Miss Feemy's gone home, at all at all.* I think she and the Captain is only walked down the lane a bit, jist to cool themselves, for sure it's hot work dancing——"

Thady did not stop to ask any more questions,

but hurried out of the door, and turning away
from Ballycloran, walked as fast as his unsteady
legs would carry him towards Mohill; and, unfortunately, Ussher and Feemy were strolling
down the lane in that direction.

When Pat Brady saw Macdermot hurry out
of the house, he said to his sister, "Begad!
Mary, you'd better hurry down the lane—if
Captain Ussher and Miss Feemy is in it—jist
to take care of her; for he and the masther'll
have a great fight of it this night. The masther's
blood's up, and the two'll be slating*one another
afore they're parted."

"Goodness gracious!" exclaimed Mary, "why
don't you go yourself, Pat? Mr. Thady's taken
a dhrop, and maybe he'll be hurting Miss Feemy
or the Captain. Denis, dear,"—her husband
came in the room just then,—"there's a ruction*
between the Captain and Mr. Thady; in God's
name go and bring away Miss Feemy!"

Ussher and Feemy had not been out of the
house many minutes; it was a beautiful mild
moonlight night in October, and as the girl had
said, they had come out to cool themselves
after the heat and noise and dirt of the room
in which they had been dancing. Myles was
in one of his best humours; he had persuaded
himself that he had no real danger to fear from
the men who, as he was told, were so hostile
to him. Feemy, too, had looked very pretty
and nice, and had not contradicted him; and
whereas what Thady had drunk had made him
cross, Ussher had only just had enough to
make him good-humoured. Feemy too was
very happy; she had contrived to forget her

brother's croaking and Father John's warning, or at least the misery which they had occasioned her, and was very happy in Ussher's good-humour. It were bootless to repeat their conversation, or to tell how often it was interrupted by some unchided caress on the part of Ussher. Feemy, however, had not forgotten her resolution, and was bringing up all her courage to make some gentle hint to Myles on the subject on which she had promised Father John to speak to him, when her heart sunk within her, on hearing her brother's voice calling to her from behind.

"Good heaven, Myles, there's Thady! what can he be wanting here?"

Ussher's arm fell from the fair girl's waist as he answered, "Never fear, dear, don't you speak to him; leave him to me." By this time, Thady had nearly joined them.

"Is that you, Feemy, here at this hour? What the d— are you doing there, this time of night? Here, take my arm, and come home; it's time you had some one to mind you, I'm thinking."

Feemy saw that her brother was intoxicated, and was frightened; she turned, though she did not take his arm, and Ussher turned too.

"Your sister's not alone, Macdermot; as I'm with her, I don't think you have much cause to fear, because she is about a mile from Ballycloran."

"May be, Captain Ussher, you're being with her mayn't make her much safer; at any rate, you'll let me manage my own affairs. I suppose I can take my sisther to her own home

without your interference," and he took hold
of his sister's arm, as if to drag it within his
own.

"Good heavens, Thady, what are you afther?
shure an't I walking with you; don't be dragging
me!"

"It appears to me, Macdermot," said Ussher,
"that though your sister was in want of no
protector before you came, she is in great want
of one now."

"She wanted it thin, and she wants it
now, and will do as long as she's fool enough
to put herself in the way of such as you;
but, by G—d, as long as I'm with her, she
shall have it!" and he dragged her along by
the arm.

"But, Thady," said the poor girl, afraid both
of her brother and her lover, and hardly knowing to which to address herself; "but, Thady,
you're hurting me, and I'll walk with you quiet
enough. I was only getting a little cool afther
the dancing, and what's the great harm in
that?"

"Well—there," and he let her go, "I'm not
hurting you now; it's very tender you've got of
a sudden, when I touch you. Captain Ussher,
if you'll plaze to go on, or stay behind, I'll be
obliged, for I want to spake to Feemy; and
there's no occasion in life for my throubling you
to hear what I've to say."

"You can say what you like, Macdermot, but
I shan't leave you; for though Feemy's your
sister, you're not fit to guide her, or yourself
either, for you're drunk."

"And there you lie, Captain Ussher! you

lie—that's what you're used to! but it's the last of your lies she'll hear."

"Ah! you're drunk," replied Ussher, "besides, you know I'd not notice what you'd say before your sister; if, however, you're not so very drunk as to forget what you've called me to-morrow morning, and would then like to repeat it, I'll thrash you as you deserve."

"Then, by Jasus, you'll have your wish! you asked me to-night if I had a mind to quarrel with you, and now I'll tell you, if I find you at Ballycloran schaming agin, you'll find me ready and willing enough."

"That's where you'll find me to-morrow morning, then, for I'll certainly come to ask your sister how she is, after the brutal manner you've frightened her this night; and then perhaps you'll have the goodness to tell me what you mean by what you call ' schaming.'"

"I'll tell you now, then; it's schaming to be coming with your lies and your blarney*afther a girl like Feemy, only maning to desave her—it's schaming to go about humbugging a poor silly owld man like my father,—and it's the higth of schaming and blackguardness to pretend to be so frindly to a family, when you know you're maning them all the harum in your power to do. But you'll find, my fine Captain, it an't quite so asy to play your thricks at Ballycloran as you think, though we are so poor."

Feemy, when the young men had begun to use hard words to one another, had commenced crying, and was now sobbing away at a desperate rate.

"Don't distress yourself, Feemy," said Ussher,

"your brother 'll be more himself to-morrow morning; he'll be sorry for what he has said then—and if he is so, I am not the man to remember what any one says when they've taken a little too much punch."

They had now come near enough to Mrs. Mehan's to see that there were a number of people outside the door. As soon after Thady's departure as Denis McGovery and the rest had been able to make up their minds what it would be the best to do in the emergency of the case, Denis and his wife sallied forth; the former to carry home whichever of the combatants might be slaughtered in the battle, and Mary to give to Feemy what comfort and assistance might be in her power. Pat Brady prudently thought that under all circumstances it would be safest for himself to remain where he was. The married pair, however, bent on peace if possible, and if not, on assuaging the horrors of war, had barely got into the road, when they encountered Father John returning to the wedding party.

"Oh, and it's yer riverence is welcome agin this blessed evening. God be praised that sent you, for it's yerself 'll be wanted, I'm afeard, and that immediately."

It was some time before the priest could learn what was the matter. At last he discovered that Ussher and Feemy had gone out walking, —that Thady had got drunk, and had gone after them; and he was inquiring whether he had gone towards Mohill, or towards Ballycloran, which none of them knew, when the three came in sight.

Father John instantly walked up to them, and

if he had learnt it from nothing else, soon discovered from Feemy's tears, that something was the matter.

"How are you, Thady?" he said, putting out his hand to take the young man's, which was given with apparent reluctance; "how are you? is there anything wrong, that Feemy is crying so?"

"Oh, you know, Father John, there is a d—d deal wrong, and I've jist told the Captain what it is, that's all. I'll not have the girl humbugged any longer, that's all."

"There must be a great deal wrong, Thady, when you'd curse that way before me."

"I can't be picking my words now, for priest or parson."

They were now surrounded by the whole crowd out of the house, who were staring and gaping, and absolutely shocked at Thady's impudence to his friend and priest. Feemy was sobbing, and on Ussher offering her his arm to take her from the crowd, took it.

"By G—d!" exclaimed Thady, "if you touch that ruffian's arm again, I'll niver call you sisther, or shall you iver call me brother; so now choose betwixt us."

Feemy dropped her hand from Ussher's arm, but turning to the priest, she said, "For heaven's sake take him away, Father John, he's drunk!"

"Drunk or sober, you may choose now; it's either me or him; but if you disgrace yourself, you shall not disgrace me!"

Father John took Feemy's arm on his, and telling the people to go back to their dancing, laid his hand on Thady's shoulder, and said—

"At any rate, Thady, come a little out of this; if you must speak to your sister in that way, you don't wish all the parish to hear what you're saying."

"What matthers, Father John; what matthers? Shure they've all heard too much already;—don't they all say she's the blackguard's misthress?"

"Oh, Thady, how can you repeat that word of me?" sobbed the poor girl.

"Why did you let them say it? Why don't you tell the man that's blackening your name while he's desaving you, to be laving you now, and not following you through the country like a curse?"

By this time the whole party, consisting of Father John, the two young men, and Feemy, were walking on rapidly towards Ballycloran. Feemy was crying, but saying nothing. Ussher was silent, although Thady was heaping on him every term of abuse he could think of;—and Father John was in vain attempting to moderate his wrath. Thus they continued until they came to the avenue leading up to the house, and on Ussher's proceeding with them through the gate, Thady put himself in the way, stopping him.

"You'll not come a step in here, Captain, if I know it; you might follow us along the road, for I couldn't help it,—but, by G—d, you don't come in here!"

"Nonsense, man; do you think I'll stop out for a drunken man's riot? let me pass."

"Set a foot in here, you blackguard, and I'll stretch you!"*

Thady had an alpine* in his hand, and was preparing to strike a blow at the Captain, exactly on the spot where Keegan had struck him, when the priest pushed his burly body in between them. " I'll have no blows, boys, at any rate while I'm with you; put your stick down, Thady," and he forced the young man's stick down; " run up to the house, Feemy, and get to bed; I'll see you in the morning." Feemy, however, did not move. " Now, Captain Ussher, I am not saying a word on the matter, one way or other, for I don't well know how the quarrel began,—but do you think it's well to be forcing your way in here, when the master desires you not ? "

" But, Mr. McGrath, I've yet to learn that this drunken fellow is master here; besides, I suppose it is not a part of his project to rob me of my horse, which is in his father's stable."

Thady was at length persuaded to allow Ussher to go to the stables for his horse, and the Captain, after what had passed, did not now wish to go into the house. He was, however, going up to Feemy to shake hands with her, when the priest caught him by the arm, saying—

" Why would you anger a drunken man, and that, too, when the feeling in his heart is right ? I'll tell you what, Captain, if what that young man fears is true, you're almost as much worse than him as vice is than virtue."

" Spare me your sermon now, Father John ; if I see you to-morrow I'll hear it in patience," and he galloped down the avenue.

Thady and Feemy went into the house, and we hope each got to bed without further words ;

and Father John walked slowly home, thinking of all the misery he saw in store for his parishioners at Ballycloran.

CHAPTER XIV

DENIS M'GOVERY'S TIDINGS

As soon as he had finished his breakfast on the morning after the night's events just recorded, Father John took his hat and stick, and walked down to Drumsna, still charitably intent on finding some means to soften, if he could not avert, the storm which he saw must follow the scenes he had witnessed on the previous evening. Ussher would have considered it want of pluck to stay away because Thady had told him to do so; Feemy also would encourage his visits, and would lean more to her lover than her brother—especially as her father, if it were attempted to make him aware of the state of the case, would be sure to take Feemy's part. Father John felt it would be impossible to induce the old man to desire Ussher to discontinue his visits, and he was confident that unless he did so, the Captain would take advantage of the unfortunate state of affairs at Ballycloran, and consider himself as an invited guest, in spite of the efforts Thady might make to induce him to leave it. But what the priest most feared was, that the unfortunate girl would be induced to go off with her lover, who he knew under such circumstances would never marry her; and his present object was to take her out of the way of such temptation. Father John gave Feemy credit for principles and feelings sufficiently high to prevent her from falling immediately into vice, but he at the same time feared, that with the strong influence Ussher had over her, he might easily persuade her to leave her home, partly by promising at some early time to marry her, and partly by threatening her with desertion. He thought that if she were at present domiciled at Mrs. McKeon's, Ussher might then be brought to hear reason, and be made to understand that if he was not contented to propose for and marry Feemy, in a proper decent manner, he must altogether drop her acquaintance.

He was not far wrong in the estimate he formed of both their characters. Though Ussher loved Feemy, perhaps as well as he was ever likely to love any woman, circumstances might easily have induced him to give her up. It was the impediments in the way, and the opposition he now met with, which would give the affair a fresh interest in his eyes. He certainly did not intend to marry the poor girl; had she had sufficient tact, she might, perhaps, have persuaded him to do so ; but her fervent love and perfect confidence, though very gratifying to his vanity, did not inspire him with that feeling of respect which any man would wish to have for the girl he was going to marry. I do not say that his premeditated object had been to persuade her to leave her home, but Father John was not far wrong in fearing, that unless steps were taken to prevent it, it would be the most probable termination of the whole affair.

With regard to Feemy, he was quite right in thinking that her love of Ussher was strong enough to induce her to take almost any step that he might desire ; and that that love, joined to her own obstinacy and determined resistance to the advice of those to whom she should have listened, was such as to render it most unlikely that she should be induced to give him up ; but though he so well understood the weakness of her character, he was not aware of, for he had had no opportunity of trying, its strength.

As long as Feemy had her own way, as at the present time she had, she would, as we have seen, yield entirely to her strong love ; but this was not all ; had circumstances enabled her friends to remove her entirely out of Ussher's way, and had they done so, her love would have remained the same ; her passion was so strong, that it could not be weakened or strengthened by absence or opposition. When Father John calculated that by good management Ussher might be brought to relinquish Feemy, he was right, but he was far from right, when he thought that Feemy could be taught to forget him. She literally cared for no one but him ; her life had been so dull before she knew him, and so full of interest since—he so nearly came up to her *beau ideal* of what a man should be, for she had seen, or at any rate had known, no better —he so greatly excelled her brother and father, and was so much better looking than young Cassidy, and so much more spirited than Frank McKeon, that to her young heart he was all perfection.

She had lately been vexed, tormented, and

even frightened; but her fear was merely that Ussher did not love her as she did him—that he might be made to leave her; and she was learning to hate her brother for opposing, as she would have said, the only source of her happiness. As to being induced by prudence or propriety to be cool to her lover—as to taking the first step herself towards making a breach between them—nothing that her brother or the priest had said, nothing that they could ever say, could either make her think of doing so, or think that it could be advisable, or in any way proper, that she should do so. For this strong feeling Father John did not give our heroine credit; but he still felt that she was headstrong enough to make it a very difficult task for him to manage her in any way. But as his charity was unbounded, so were his zeal and courage great.

His present plan was to induce his friend, Mrs. McKeon, to ask Feemy to come over and spend some time with her and her daughters at Drumsna. There were difficulties in this; for, in the first place, although Feemy and the Miss McKeons had been very good friends, still the reports which had lately been afloat, both about her and the affairs of her family, might make Mrs. McKeon, a prudent woman, unwilling to comply with the priest's wishes— though indeed it was not often that she contradicted him in anything; then, after he had talked Mrs. McKeon over, when he had aroused her charitable feelings and excited the good nature, which, to tell the truth, was never very dormant in her bosom, he had the more difficult task of persuading Feemy to accept the invitation. Not that under ordinary circumstances she would not be willing enough to go to Mrs. McKeon's, but at present she would be likely to suspect a double meaning in everything. Father John had already mentioned Mrs. McKeon's name to her, in reference to her attachment to Ussher; and it was more than probable that if he now brought her an invitation from that lady, she would perceive that the object was to separate her from her lover, and that she would obstinately persist in remaining at Ballycloran.

As Father John was entering Drumsna, he met his curate, Cullen, and McGovery, who, considering that he had only been married the evening before, and that if he had not been dancing himself, he had been kept up by his guests doing so till four or five in the morning, had left his bride rather early; for, according to custom, he had slept the first night after his wedding at his wife's house, and, though it was only ten o'clock, he had been on a visit to Father Cullen, with whom he was now eagerly talking.

On the previous evening, when feigning to be asleep, he had managed to overhear a small portion of what had passed between Thady, Joe Reynolds, and the rest; but what he had overheard had reference solely to Keegan; for when they began to speak of Ussher, everything had been said in so low a voice, that he had been unable to comprehend a word. He had contrived, however, to pick up something, in which Ballycloran, rents, Keegan, and a bog-hole were

introduced in marvellous close connection, and
he was not slow in coming to the determination
that he had been wrong when he fancied that
Ussher was the object against whom plots were
being formed, and that Keegan was the doomed
man; but what was worse still, he was led to
imagine that the perpetrators of Mr. Keegan's
future watery grave were instigated by young
Macdermot! He was well aware that Flannelly
and Keegan, for they were all one, had the
greater portion of the rents out of Ballycloran,
and he now plainly saw that the more active
of this firm was to be made away with, while
collecting, or attempting to collect, the rent.

Denis was puzzled as to what he should do;
his conscience would not allow the man to be
murdered without his interference; he had no
great love for Mr. Keegan, and his sympathies
were not more strongly excited than they had
been when he thought Ussher was to be the
victim. Should he tell Mr. Keegan? that would
be setting the devil in arms against his wife's
brother—against his wife's brother's master—
and against his wife's brother's master's tenants;
this was too near cutting his own throat, to be
a line of action agreeable to Denis. Then it
occurred to him to have recourse again to
Father John: but Father John had made light
of his former warning. Besides, the fact of his
having been wrong in his last surmises, would
have thrown stronger doubts on those he now
entertained. Father John too was always
quizzing him, and Denis did not like to be
quizzed. After much consideration, McGovery
resolved to go to Father Cullen, and disclose

his secret to him; Father Cullen was a modest, steady man, who would neither make light of, or ridicule what he heard; and if after that Keegan was drowned in a bog-hole, it would be entirely off Denis's conscience.

When Father John met the pair, they had just been discussing the subject; Cullen was far from making light of it; for, in the first place, he believed every word McGovery told him, and in the next, he was shocked, and greatly grieved, that one of his own parishioners, and one also of the most respectable of them, should be concerned in such a business: he felt towards Keegan all the abhorrence which a very bigoted and ignorant Roman Catholic could feel towards a Protestant convert, but he would have done anything to prevent his meeting his death by the hands, or with the connivance, of Thady Macdermot.

As soon as Cullen had heard McGovery's statement—which, by-the-by, had been made without any reference to his previous statement to Father John, or his warning to Captain Ussher—he determined to tell it all to the parish priest, and to take McGovery with him. This plan did not, however, suit Denis at all, and he used all his eloquence to persuade Father Cullen, that if he told Mr. McGrath at all, he, Denis, had better not make one of the party; and he was at the moment considering what excuse he could give for refusing to go into the priest's cottage, when they met Father John on the road coming into Drumsna.

Denis was greatly disconcerted,—but Cullen, full of his news, and as eager to communicate it as if it had been arranged definitely that Keegan was to be put into the bog-hole at noon precisely, was very glad to see him, and instantly opened his budget.

" I'm very glad to meet you this morning, Mr. McGrath," he began, " and it's well since you're out so early, that it's not the other way you went,—for I'd been greatly bothered if I hadn't found you."

" But here I am, you see,—and if it was only after me you were going, I suppose you can turn, for I'm going to Drumsna."

" Oh, to be sure I can ; don't you be going, Denis McGovery." Denis had taken off his hat, and muttering something about his wife, and "good morning, yer riverence," was decamping towards Ballycloran.

" Why, man," said Father John, " what business have you so far from your wife at this hour of the morning, after your wedding ? Have you been to take the two pigs home ? "

" He, he, Father John, you'll niver have done with them pigs !—But the wife'll be waiting for me, and, as yer riverence says, I mustn't be baulking*her the first morning. "

" Stay a while,—as you've come so far without her, you can stop a moment."

" Oh yes," said Cullen, " wait till you've told Mr. McGrath what you told me."

Denis was unwillingly obliged to remain, and repeat to Father John the whole story he had told Cullen. Though he could hardly tell why himself, he softened down a little the strong assurance he had given Cullen that Thady himself had been urging the boys to make away with Keegan. Father John listened to all in silence, till Denis ended by wishing "that the two young men got home safe last night, and that there war nothing worse nor harder than words betwixt them."

"Get home safe, you fool!" answered Father John, "and why wouldn't they?—don't you know the difference yet, between a few foolish words, said half in fun, and a quarrel? To be sure they got home safe;—and let me tell you, Denis, for a sensible fellow as you pretend to be, you'd be a deal better employed minding your business, than thinking of other people's quarrels, or trying to pick up stories of murders, and heaven knows what—filling your own mind and other people's too with foolish fears, for which there are no grounds. And now, if you'd take my advice, you'll go home, and leave your betters to take care of themselves, for you'll find it quite enough to take care of yourself;—and mind, McGovery, if I find this cock and bull story of yours gets through the country, so as to reach Mr. Keegan's ears, or to annoy Mr. Macdermot, I shall know where it came from; and perhaps you're not aware, that a person inventing such a story as you've been telling Mr. Cullen, might soon find himself in Carrick Gaol."

It would be impossible to say whether Cullen was most astonished, or McGovery disconcerted, by Father John's address.

"But," began Cullen, "if the man really heard the plan proposed, Mr. McGrath, and if Mr. Thady was one of them——"

"Ah, nonsense, Cullen."

"But I haven't invented a word, Father John," said McGovery; "I heard it every word; and shure, afther hearing it all with my own ears, was I to let the man be shot into a bog-hole, without saying a word to no one about it, Father John?"

"Ah, you're a nice boy, Denis,—and why did you pass my gate to come all the way down to Father Cullen, to tell him the dreadful tale? why didn't you come to me, eh—when you knew, not only that I was nearer you than Mr. Cullen, but also nearer to the place where all this was to happen?"

"Why then, Father John, not to tell you a lie, it is because you do be going on with your gagging at me so."

"Nonsense, man;—how can you say you are not going to lie, when you know you've a lie in your mouth at the moment."

"Sorrow a lie is there in it at all, Father John,—I wish the tongue of me had been blistered this morning, before I said a word of it."

"I wish it had been. Why, Cullen, it was only last night that he wanted to persuade me that a lot of boys were to meet at the place where he was married, to agree to murder Ussher; and to hear the man, you'd think it was all arranged, who was to strike the blow and all; and now here he is with you, with a similar story about Keegan! He was afraid to come to me, because he knew he'd half humbugged me with his other story last night."

"But I tell you, Father John, I heard it all with my own ears this time."

"And I tell you, you were dreaming. Do you think you'd make me believe that such a young gentleman as Mr. Thady would turn murderer all of a sudden? Now go home, and take my advice; if you don't want to find yourself in a worse scrape than Captain Ussher, or Mr. Keegan, don't repeat such a tale as that to any one."

McGovery sneaked off with his tail, allegorically speaking, between his legs. He didn't exactly know what to make of it; for though, as has been before said, he did not wish on this occasion to make Father John the depositary of his fears, he did not expect even from him to meet with such total discomfiture. He consoled himself, however, with the recollection that if anything did happen now, either to the revenue officer or the attorney,—and he almost hoped there would,—he could fairly say that he had given warning and premonitory tidings of it to the parish priests, which, if attended to, might have prevented all harm. With this comfortable feeling, to atone for Father John's displeasure, and now not quite sure whether he had overheard any allusion last night to Keegan and a bog-hole or not, he returned to his wife.

As soon as he was gone, Cullen, as much surprised as McGovery at the manner in which Father John had received the story, asked him if he thought it was all a lie.

"Perhaps not all a lie," answered the priest; "perhaps he heard something about Keegan— not very flattering to the attorney; no doubt Thady was asking the boys about the rent, and

threatening them with Keegan as a receiver
over the property, or something of that sort;
and very likely one of those boys from Drumleesh said something about a bog-hole, which
may be Thady didn't reprove as he ought to
have done. I've no doubt it all came about in
that way,—but that fellow with his tales and
his stories, will get his ears cut off*some of
these days, and serve him right. Why, he
wanted yesterday to make me believe that
these fellows who are to drown Keegan this
morning were to shoot Ussher last night! He's
just the fellow to do more harm in the country
than all the stills, if he were listened to.—Well,
Cullen, good day, I'm going into Mr. McKeon's
here;"—and Cullen went away quite satisfied
with Father John's view of the affair.

Not so Father John. For Thady's sake—to
screen his character, and because he did not
think there was any immediate danger—he had
given the affair the turn which it had just taken;
but he himself feared—more than feared—felt
sure that there was too much truth in what the
man had said. Thady's unusual intoxication
last night—his brutal conduct to his sister—to
Ussher, and to himself—the men with whom
he had been drinking—his own knowledge of
the feeling the young man entertained towards
Keegan, and the hatred the tenants felt for the
attorney—all these things conspired to convince
Father John that McGovery had too surely
overheard a conversation, which, if repeated to
Keegan, might probably, considering how many
had been present at it, give him a desperate
hold over young Macdermot, which he would

not fail to use, either by frightening him into measures destructive to the property, or by proceeding criminally against him. Father John was not only greatly grieved that such a meeting should have been held, with reference to its immediate consequences, but he was shocked that Thady should so far have forgotten himself and his duty as to have attended it. But with the unceasing charity which made the great beauty of Father John's character, he, in his heart, instantly made allowances for him; he remembered all his distress and misery—his want of friends—his grief for his sister—his continued attempts and continued inability to relieve his father from his difficulties; and he determined to endeavour to screen him.

His success with McGovery, whom he had made to disbelieve his own senses, and with Cullen, who was ready enough to take his superior's views in any secular affair, had been complete; and he did not think that either would now be likely to repeat the story in a manner that would do any injury. We shall, in a short time, see what steps he took in the matter with Thady himself. In the mean while, we will follow him into Mrs. McKeon's house, at whose door he had now arrived.

CHAPTER XV

THE M'KEONS

WHEN Father John opened the wicket gate
leading into the small garden which separated
Mrs. McKeon's house from the street, he saw
her husband standing in the open door-way,
ruminating. Mr. McKeon was said to be a
comfortable man, and he looked to be so; he
was something between forty-five and fifty,
about six feet two high, with a good-humoured
red face. He was inclined to be corpulent,
and would no doubt have followed his inclination had he not accustomed himself to continual
bodily activity. He was a great eater, and a
very great drinker; it is said he could put any
man in Connaught under the table, and carry
himself to bed sober. At any rate, he was never
seen drunk, and it was known that he had often
taken fifteen tumblers of punch after dinner,
and rumour told of certain times when he had
made up and exceeded the score.

He was comfortable in means as well as in
appearance. Though Mr. McKeon had no
property of his own, he was much better off
than many around him that had. He had a
large farm on a profitable lease; he underlet a
good deal of land by con-acre, or corn-acre;*—
few of my English readers will understand the
complicated misery to the poorest of the Irish
which this accursed word embraces;—he took
contracts for making and repairing roads and
bridges; and, altogether, he contrived to live

very well on his ways and means. Although a very hard-working man he was a bit of a sportsman, and usually kept one or two well-trained horses, which, as he was too heavy to ride them himself, he was always willing, and usually able, to sell at remunerating prices. He was considered a very good hand at a handicap, and understood well—no one better—the dangerous mysteries of "knocking."* He was sure to have some animal to run at the different steeple-chases in the neighbourhood, and it was generally supposed, that even when not winning his race, Tony McKeon seldom lost much by attending the meeting. There was now going to be a steeple-chase at Carrick-on-Shannon in a few days, and McKeon was much intent on bringing his mare, Playful,—a wicked devil, within twenty yards of whom no one but himself and groom could come,—into the field in fine order and condition. In addition to this, Mr. McKeon was a very hospitable man, his only failing in that respect being his firm determination and usual practice to make every man that dined with him drunk. He was honest in everything, barring horse-flesh; was a good Catholic, and very fond of his daughters—Louey and Lydia. His wife was a kind, good, easy creature, fond of the world and the world's goods, and yet not selfish or niggardly with those with which she was blessed. She was sufficiently contented with her husband, whose friends never came out of the dining-room after dinner, and therefore did not annoy her; she looked on his foibles with a lenient eye, for she had been accustomed to such all her life; and when she heard he had parted with her car in a handicap, or had lost her two fat pigs in a knock, she bore it with great good-humour. She was always willing to procure amusement for her daughters, and was beginning to feel anxious to get them husbands; she was a good neighbour, and if she had a strong feeling at all, it was her partiality for Father John. Her daughters had nothing very remarkable about them to recommend them to our attention: they were both rather pretty, tolerably well educated, to the extent of a two years' sojourn in a convent in Sligo; were both very fond of novels, dancing, ribbons and potato cakes; and both thought that to dance at a race-ball with an officer in his regimentals was the most supreme terrestrial blessing of which their lot was susceptible.

We have, however, kept the father too long standing at his own door, while we have been describing his family.

"Well, Father John," said McKeon, "how are you this morning?"

"Why, then, as luckily I didn't dine with you, Mr. McKeon, I'm pretty much as I usually am,—and, thank God, that's well. I'm told you had those poor fellows that were with you last night, laid on a mattress, and that you sent them home that way to Carrick on a country car, and that they couldn't move, leaving this at six this morning."

"Oh, nonsense, Father John! who was telling you them lies?"

"But wasn't it true? Didn't they go home on one of the cars off the farm, and young Michael driving them, and they on a mattress?"

"And sure, Father John, you wouldn't have had me let them walk home to Carrick after dinner?"

"They were little fit for walking, I believe; why, they couldn't so much as sit up in the car. Will you never have done, Mr. McKeon; don't you know the sin of drunkenness?"

"The sin of drunkenness! me know it! Indeed I don't then. When did you ever see me drunk? Come, which was a case last, Father John—you or I?"

"God forgive me, but I believe some boys did make me rather tipsy the first day I ever was in France; and my head should have been full of other things; and I believe if you were to swim in punch it wouldn't hurt you; but you know as well as I can tell you, it's worse for you to be making others drink so much who can't bear it as you can, than if you were hurting yourself."

"And you know, as well as I can tell you, that yourself would be the last man to take the whiskey off the table, as long as the lads that were with you chose to be drinking it; and I think when I sent them boys off to Carrick as comfortably asleep as if they were in bed, so that they wouldn't be too late at business this morning, I acted by them as I'd wish anybody to act by me if I had an accident; and if that an't being a good Christian, I don't know what is. So lave off preaching, Father John, and come round to the stables, till I show you the mare that'll win at Carrick; at least, it'll be a very good nag that'll take the shine out of her."

"I hope you'll win, Mr. McKeon, in spite of your villany in making those young fellows drunk. But I'll not look at the mare just at present; more by token I'm told she's not very civil to morning visitors."

"Arrah, nonsense, man! she's as quiet a mare as ever went over a fence, when she's well handled."

"But you see I can't handle her well; and as I want to see the good woman that owns you, if you please, I'll go into the house instead of into the stable."

"Well, every man to his choice; and I'll see Playful get her gallop. But I tell you what, Father John, if you don't mind what you're after with Mrs. McKeon, I'll treat you a deal worse than I did those two fellows I sent home to Carrick on a mattress."

So Mr. McKeon walked off to superintend the training of his mare; and the priest, in spite of the marital caution he had received, walked into the dining-room, where he knew that at that hour he should probably find the mother and daughters surrounded by their household cares.

When the usual greetings were over, and the two girls had asked all the particulars of Mary Brady's wedding, and Mrs. McKeon had got through her usual gossip, Father John warily began the subject respecting which he was so anxious to rouse his friend's soft sympathies.

Mrs. McKeon had gone so far herself as to ask him whether anything had been settled yet at Ballycloran, about Ussher, and whether he thought that the young man really intended to marry the girl.

The way this question was asked, was a great

damper to Father John's hopes. If there had been any kindly feelings towards poor Feemy at the moment in her breast, she would have called her by her name, and not spoken of her as "the girl;" it showed that Mrs. McKeon was losing, or had lost, whatever good opinion she might ever have had of Feemy: and when Louey ill-naturedly added, "Oh laws!—not he —the man never thought of her," Father John felt sure that there was a slight feeling of triumph among the female McKeons at the idea of Feemy's losing the lover of whom, perhaps, she had been somewhat too proud.

Still, however, he did not despair; he knew that if they spoke with ill-nature, it arose from thoughtlessness—and that it was, at any rate with the mother, only necessary to point out to her the benefit she could confer, to arouse a kindly feeling within her.

"I think you're wrong there, Miss Louey," said Father John; "I think he not only did think of her—but does think of her; and I'll tell you what I know, that if Feemy Macdermot had the great blessing which you have, and that is a kind, good, careful mother to the fore, she'd have been married to him before this."

"But, Father John," said the kind, good, careful mother, "what is there to prevent them marrying, if he's ready? I always pitied Feemy being left alone there with her father and brother; but if Captain Ussher is in earnest, I don't see how twenty mothers would make it a bit easier for her."

"Don't you, Mrs. McKeon!—then it's little you know the advantage your own girls have in

yourself. Don't you think a man would prefer
taking a girl from a house where a good mother
gave signs that the daughter would make a good
wife, than from one where there was no one to
mind her but a silly old man, and a young one
like Thady?—a very good young man in his
way, but not very fit, Mrs. McKeon, to act a
mother's part to a girl like Feemy."

"That's true enough; but then why did she
make all the world believe he was engaged to
her, if he wasn't?—And if he wasn't, why did
she let him go on as though he was, being at all
hours,* I'm told, with her at Ballycloran?—and
if they are not to be married, why does her
brother let him be coming there at all? I know
you're fond of them, Father John, and I'd be
sorry to think ill of your friends; but I must
say it begins to look odd."

"You're right any how, in saying I'm very
fond of them; indeed I am, and so is yourself,
Mrs. McKeon; and I know, though you speak
in that way to me, you wouldn't say anything
that could hurt the poor girl, any where but
just among ourselves. If it wasn't in a kind
mother, with such a heart as your own,—
especially in one she'd known so long,—in
whom could a poor motherless, friendless girl,
like Feemy, expect to find a friend?"

"God forbid I should hurt her, Father John!
And, indeed, I'd befriend her if I knew how;
but don't you think, yourself now, she's played
a foolish game with that young man?"

"Why, as I never was a young lady in love,
I can't exactly say how a young lady in love
should behave; but, my dear woman, look at it

this way ; I suppose there's no harm in Feemy wishing to get herself married, more than any other young lady ? "

" Oh ! dear no, Father John ; quite right she should."

" And every one seems to think this Captain Ussher would be a proper match for her."

" Why, barring that he's a Protestant, of course he's a very good match for her."

" Oh ! as to his being a Protestant, we won't mind that now. Well, then, Mrs. McKeon, under these circumstances, what could Feemy do better than encourage this Captain ? "

" I never blamed her for encouraging him ; only she should not have gone the length she has, unless he downright proposed for her."

" But he has downright proposed for her."

" No ! Father John," said Louey.

" Has he though, really ! " exclaimed Lyddy.

" Then, why, in the name of the blessed Virgin, don't he marry her ? " said the mother.

" That's poor Feemy's difficulty, you see, Mrs. McKeon. Now, if any man you approved of were to make off with Miss Lyddy's heart—and I'm sure she'll never give it to any one you don't approve of—why, of course he'd naturally come to you or her father, and the matter would be settled ; but Feemy has no mother for him to go to, and her father, you know, can't mind such things now."

" But she has a brother ; in short, if he meant to marry her, it would soon be done. Where there's a will, there's a way."

" But that's where it is ; you know young men, and what they are, a deal better than I do ; and you can understand that a young man may propose to a girl, and be accepted, and afterwards shilly shally about it, and perhaps at last change his mind altogether—merely because the girl's friends don't take care that the affair is regularly and properly carried on ; now isn't that so, Mrs. McKeon ? "

" Indeed, Father John, it's all true."

" Well, that's just Feemy's case ; may be, after, as you say, having given the young man so much encouragement, she'll lose him because she has no mother to keep him steady, as it were, and fix him*; and no blame to her in the matter either, is there, Mrs. McKeon ? "

" Why, if you look at it in that way, of course, she's not so much to blame."

" Of course not," said Father John, obliged to be satisfied with this modicum of applause ; " of course not ; but it's a pity for the poor girl."

" You think he'll jilt her altogether, then ? "

" I don't think he means it yet ; but I think he will mean it soon,—unless, indeed, Mrs. McKeon, you'd befriend her now."

" Me, Father John ! "

" If you'd take a mother's part with her for a week or so, it would all be right; and I don't know a greater charity one Christian could do another this side the grave, than you could do her."

" What could I do, Father John ? " said the good woman,—rather frightened, for she would now be called on to take some active part in the matter, which perhaps she might not altogether relish ;—" what could I do ? You see, Ballycloran is three miles out of this, and I couldn't always be up there when Ussher was coming. And though I believe I'd be bold enough where one of my own girls was concerned, I'd be shy of speaking to a man like Captain Ussher, when it was no business of my own."

"As for that, I believe you'd never want wit or spirit either, to say what you'd wish to say to any man, and that in the very best manner. It's true enough, though, you couldn't be always up at Ballycloran; but why couldn't Feemy be down at Drumsna?"——Father John paused a minute, and Mrs. McKeon said nothing, but looked very grave.——"Now be a good woman, Mrs. McKeon, and ask the poor girl down here for a fortnight or so; I know Lyddy and Louey are very fond of their friend, and Feemy 'd be nice company for them; and then as you are acquainted with Captain Ussher, of course he'd be coming after his sweetheart; and then, when Feemy is under your protection, of course you'd speak to him in your own quiet lady-like way; and then, take my word for it, I'd be marrying them in this very room before Christmas. Wouldn't we have dancing upstairs, eh, Miss Louey?"——Mrs. McKeon still said nothing.—— "And even supposing Ussher did not come down here, and nothing was done, why it would be evident the match was not to take place, and that Ussher was a blackguard; then of course Feemy must give up all thoughts of him. And though, maybe, she'd grieve awhile, it would be better so than going on as she is now up at the old place, with no one to give her any advice, or tell her what she ought to do or say to the man. Anyway, you see, it

would be doing her a kind service. Come,
Mrs. McKeon, make up your mind to be a
kind, good neighbour to the poor girl; and
do you and the two young ladies go up to
Ballycloran, and ask her to come down and
spend a week or two with you here."

"But perhaps," said Louey, "Feemy won't
like to leave Ballycloran, and come so far from
her beau; because she couldn't see him here
as she does there, you know, Father John."

"Why, Miss Louey, I don't think you know
how she sees him. I believe he goes and calls
there, much as you'd like your beau to come
and call here, if you had one."

"Indeed, Father John, when I do have one,
I hope I shall manage better than to be talked
about as much as she is, any way. I hardly
think it would do to ask her at present, mother.
You know Mr. Gayner is to be here the night
of the race-ball, and we've only the one bed."

"Come, come, Miss Louey, I didn't expect
to hear you say a word against your old friend;
why should you be less good-natured than your
mother? You see, she's thinking how she can
best do what I'm asking."

"As for old friends," said Louey, "I and
Miss Macdermot were never so very intimate;
and as for being ill-natured, I never was told
before that I was more ill-natured than mother.
But of course mamma will do as she likes, only
she can't very well turn Mr. Gayner out of the
house after having asked him to come for the
races, that's all:" and Miss Louey flounced
out of the room.

"Come, Mrs. McKeon," continued Father

John, "think of the benefit this would be to Feemy; and you can't have any real objection; the race-ball is only for one night, and the girls will be too tired after that to think very much of sleeping together."

"But you seem to forget—very likely Mr. McKeon wouldn't like my asking her; you know I couldn't think of doing it without asking him."

"Oh! Mrs. McKeon, that's a good joke! You'll make me believe, won't you, that you're not as much mistress of your own house as any woman in Ireland? As if Mr. McKeon would interfere with your asking any one you pleased to your own house."

"But you see the girls are against it."

"I hope they are not against anything that would be charitable and kind in their mother; but if they were, I'm quite sure their mother shouldn't give way to them. Wouldn't you be glad to have Miss Feemy here a short time, Miss Lyddy?"

"Indeed, I'd have no objection, if mamma pleases, Father John."

"There, you see, Mrs. McKeon—I am afraid I said something rude which set Miss Louey's back up, but I am sure in her heart she'd be glad of anything that would be of service to Feemy. Come, Mrs. McKeon, will you drive over to Ballycloran this fine morning, and ask her?"

"But suppose she won't come?"

"Then it won't be your fault;—you can tell her it's just for the races and the ball you're asking her—that she may see Mr. McKeon's horse win the race, and dance with Ussher at the ball afterwards. Oh! if you mean her to come, she'll come fast enough;—let you alone for carrying your point when you're in earnest. I know your way of asking, when you don't mean to take a refusal;—and to give you your due this day, I never heard you give an invitation you didn't mean to be accepted."

"Well, Father John, as you think it will be of so much service to Feemy, and as, as you say, she has no mother, poor girl, of her own, and no female friend that she can look to, I'll ask her over here. But it mustn't be for a week or a fortnight, but till the affair of Captain Ussher is finally settled. And if the girl behaves herself as she ought, when once she is here, Tony won't see her wronged by any man."

"That's my own friend!" said Father John, with tears in his eyes. "What could any poor priest like me do in a parish, if it wasn't that there were such women as yourself to help him?"

"But, Father John—whisper here," and she took him aside into the window, and spoke in a low voice; "you can't have helped hearing the stories people have been talking about Feemy. As I have heard them, of course you must."

"Heard them! of course I have—but you know what lies get talked abroad."

"But they say she walks with him after dark; and goes in and out there at Ballycloran, at all hours, just as she pleases. Of course I can have none of those doings here."

"Of course not; it is because she has no one there to tell her what is right or wrong that I wish her to be here. Of course you have regular hours here, and you'll find you'll have no difficulty with her that way."

"Well, Father John, I've only one more thing to say, and you'll answer me that as a priest and a Christian. God knows, I wouldn't believe any ill-natured story against any poor girl situated as Feemy is; but you know, such things will get about:—people say Ussher speaks of her as his mistress, instead of as his wife. Now, Father John, if this unfortunate girl, whom I'm ready and willing to help, has done anything really wrong, you would not be the means of bringing her into the house with my own dear girls! Have you, Father John, told me all you know about her attachment to this man?"

"Indeed then if she was unfit to associate with your girls, Mrs. McKeon, I'd be the last man on earth to ask you to invite her here. If Feemy has been imprudent in going out too much alone with Ussher, it's the most that with truth can be said against her; and as you ask me to tell you all, I'll tell you one thing I didn't wish to mention before the girls." And Father John told her how Thady had got drunk, and insulted Ussher, telling him not to come to Ballycloran again, and all that: but he did not tell her how strongly he suspected that Thady was right in his fears for his sister, and that his chief object in getting Feemy away from Ballycloran was to remove her as far as possible from Ussher's influence.

"Well, Father John, I'll go to Ballycloran, and ask her here; I suppose she'll hardly be

ready to come to-day, but if she pleases, I'll
drive over again for her after to-morrow. I'll
go now and talk Louey over, for you and she
seem to have quarrelled somehow."

"And God bless you, Mrs. McKeon; it's
yourself is a good woman; and you never did
a kinder action than the one you're going to
do this morning!" and Father John took his
leave.

The breakfast party at Ballycloran the morning
after the wedding was not a very lively one;
indeed the meals at Ballycloran seldom were
very gay, but this was more than usually sombre.

Larry was brooding over Keegan's threats,
his fears that Thady meant to betray him into
the attorney's hands, and his determination
never from that day forth to stir from his
fireside, lest the horrid myrmidons of the law
should pounce upon him.

Feemy was intent on the insults which had
been offered to her lover, and her temper was
somewhat soured by the remembrance that she
had not effected her purpose of questioning
Ussher about his intentions. Thady, however,
was the blackest looking of the family. Everything was dark within his breast. He thought
of the ruffians with whom he had leagued himself; and though previously he had only considered them as poor, hard used, somewhat
lawless characters, they now appeared to him
everything that was iniquitous and bad. Secret
murder was their object—black, foul, midnight
murder—and he was sworn, or soon would be
sworn, not only to help them, but to lead them
on. What he had already done might hang

him. He felt his life to be in the power of each of those blackguards, with whom, in wretched equality, he had been drinking on the previous evening. And what had led him to this? If he had been wronged and injured, why could not he redress himself like other injured men? If revenge were necessary to him, why could he not avenge himself like a man, instead of leaguing with others to commit murder in the dark, like a coward and a felon? And then he thought of his position with Keegan and Ussher. There was something manly in his original disposition; he would have given anything for a stand-up fight with the attorney with equal weapons; if it had been sure death to both, he would have fought him to the death; but he had no such opportunity; the dastardly brute had trampled on him when he could not turn against him. And then with rancorous hatred he thought of the blow that Keegan had struck him,—of the manner in which he had insulted his father, and worse than all, of the name he had applied to his sister; and, remembering all this, he almost reconciled himself to the only means he had of punishing the wretch that had inflicted all these injuries on him. Then he thought of Ussher, and the scene which had passed between them last night; he knew he had been drunk, and had but a very confused recollection of what he had done or said. He remembered, however, that he had insulted Ussher; this did not annoy him; but he had a faint recollection of having committed his sister's name, by talking of her in his drunken brawl, and of having done, or

said something, he knew not what, to Father
John.

Though Thady had never known the refine-
ments of a gentleman, or the comforts of good
society, still he felt that the fall, even from his
present station to that in which he was going to
place himself, would be dreadful. But it was
not the privations which he might suffer, but
the disgrace, the additional disgrace which he
would bring on his family, which afflicted him.
How could he now presume to prescribe to
Feemy what her conduct should be, or to his
father in what way he should act respecting the
property? He already felt as though he was
unworthy of either of them, and was afraid to
look them in the face. After breakfast he
wandered forth, striving to attend to his usual
work, but the incentives to industry were all
gone; he had no longer any hope that industry
would be of service to him; he walked along
the hedges and ditches, unconsciously planning
in his mind the different ways of committing the
crimes which he really so abhorred, but in which
he was about to pledge himself to join. He
thought, if it should be his lot to murder
Keegan, how he would accomplish it. Should
it be at night?—or in the day?—would he shoot
him?—and if he did, would not the powder or
the gun be traced home to him?—would not
his footsteps in the bog be tracked and known?
—if he struck him down on the road, would
not the blood be found on his coat, or his shirt
be torn in the struggle?—and, above all, would
not his own comrades betray him? He had,
some short time since, heard the whole of a trial

for murder at Carrick assizes, and though he had not then paid particular attention to it, all the horrid detail and circumstances of the case now came vividly before his mind's eye. He planned and plotted how, had he in that case been the murderer, he would have foreseen and provided against the different things, the untoward accidents, which then came in evidence against the prisoner; he thought how much more wary he would be than the poor wretch who was then tried, and of what benefit the experience he had gained would be to him. Then he remembered that the principal witness in the case was an ill-featured, sullen-looking fellow, who had been called king's evidence—one who, in answering the tormenting questions put to him, had appeared almost more miserable than the prisoner himself;—that this man had been the friend and assistant of the murderer—the sharer and promoter of all his plans—the man who had led him on to the murder—his sworn friend. He remembered how it had come out on the trial, that the two had for months shared the same bed—tilled in the same field—eat from the same mess—and had sinned together in the same great sin. Yet this man had come forward to hang his friend!—and Thady shuddered coldly as he thought how likely it might be that his associates would betray him. He had not slept, eat, and worked with them—he was not leagued to them by equal rank, equal wants, and equal sufferings. If that wretched witness had been induced to give evidence against the man so strongly bound to him, how much more likely that Byrne

or Reynolds should hang him! or Pat Brady!
And as Brady's name occurred to him, he
remembered Ussher's caution respecting that
man, and his assurance that he was in Keegan's
pay. If this were true, he had already committed the oversight to guard against which he
had calculated that his superior cunning would
be sufficient; and then the cold perspiration
trickled from his brow, and he abruptly stopped,
leaning against a bank, to meditate again on the
position in which he stood.

It was not that during this time Thády had
been absolutely planning murder. He had not
been making any definite scheme, to be carried
into immediate execution against any individual.
He was not a murderer, even in mind or wish;
he would have given anything to have driven
the idea from his mind, but he could not; he
could not avoid thinking what he would do, if
he had resolved to do the deed—how the crime
would be most safely perpetrated—how the laws
most cunningly evaded. Then he half resolved
to have nothing more to do with Reynolds and
his followers, and to quiet his conscience while
yet he possibly could; but the insolence of
Keegan, the injuries of Ussher, and the sure
enmity of those whom he had sworn to join,
and now scarcely dared to desert, stifled his
remorse, and destroyed the resolution before it
was half made. He thought of enlisting—but
he could not desert his sister; of going to Father
John, and confessing all; but would Father
John befriend him after his late conduct to
him? Thus he wandered on, through the
whole long morning. Twice he returned to

the house, and creeping in through the back door, got himself a glass of spirits, which he swallowed, and again sallied forth, to find if movement would give him comfort, or his thoughts suggest anything to him in mitigation of his sorrows.

As he was returning, the third time, for the same bad purpose,—for the short stimulus of the dram was the only relief he could find to the depression which seemed to weigh him down and make his heart feel like a cold lump within him,—and just as he was turning from the avenue to the back of the house, he met Ussher walking down. He did not know what to do; he remembered that the evening before he had defied this man; he even recollected that he had arrogantly declared that he should not again set his foot on Ballycloran; he had forbad him the house, as if he had been the master; and at the present moment he felt as though he did not dare address him, for it seemed to him as if every one now would look down on him, as he looked down on himself,—as if every one could see what was in his breast, as plainly as he saw it himself.

This annoyance, however, was of short duration, for Ussher passed him with a slight unembarrassed nod, as if nothing had passed between them on the previous evening—as if they were still good friends, and had met and been talking together but a short time before. Ussher had walked by quickly, and there was a look of satisfaction or rather gratified vanity in his face; he seemed, also, absorbed with the subject of his thoughts; Thady, however, as

soon as he had passed, took but little notice of
him, but walked on into the kitchen, at the rear
of the house.

Here, on a small settle by the fireside, where
he had been placed out of the way by Biddy or
Katty, sat a ragged bare-legged little boy, known
as Patsy, the priest's gossoon; he was the only
assistant Judy had in the management of Father
John's *ménage*. He ran on errands to Drumsna,
and occasionally to Carrick-on-Shannon—
fetched the priest's letters—dug his potatoes
—planted his cabbages, and cleaned his horse
Paul. He had now come up to Ballycloran
with a message to Thady, and having been
desired to stay there till he could see him himself, he had been quietly sitting in the kitchen
since a little after Thady had first left the house;
he now jumped up to give his message.

" Misther Thady, yer honer, Father John
says as how he'll be glad av yer honer'll come
down to dinner with him at six; and he says
as how you must come, Mr. Thady, because
divil a bit he'll ate himself, he says, till you're
in it."

" For shame, Patsy!" interposed Biddy,
" putting those words into his riverence's mouth.
I'm sure thin Father John wasn't cursing that
way."

" Faix thin, ma'am, thim wor his very words
—' Tell Mr. Thady, av he don't come down to
the cottage to his dinner this day, divil a bit
will I ate till he does.'"

" Well, to hear the brat!" continued Biddy,
shocked at the indecorous language which was
put into her priest's mouth.

"And who's to be at Father John's else?" said Thady.

"Sorrow a one av me rightly knows thin, for I wasn't hearing; all I wor told wor, I warn't to come out of this widout yer honer."

"But I can't go to-night, Patsy."

"But Father John says you must, Mr. Thady."

"Tell Father John, Patsy, that I'm very much obliged to him, but that I'm not just well enough to come out to-night. I couldn't go to-night, do you hear; go down and tell him so, or he'll be waiting dinner."

"But, Mr. Thady," said the boy, half sobbing, "Father John said as how I warn't to come at all widout you."

"Do as I tell you, you fool; but mind you tell Father John I'm very much obliged to him, only I'm ill."

"Well," muttered the boy, at length taking his departure, "I know Father John'll be very mad,* but any way it ain't my fault."

Thady was gratified with the priest's invitation, for it showed that he at least had forgiven him; but he did not dare to face him by accepting it.

He got himself another glass of whiskey, and lighting his pipe, sat down to smoke by the kitchen fire; after he had been some time sitting there, Pat Brady came into the kitchen. Thady, however, took no notice, except muttering something in answer to Pat's usual salutation. They remained both some time silent, till at last Brady observed that, "They'd all of them had ilegant divarsion last night—most

of them stayed a power later nor you, Mr.
Thady."

This allusion to last night was not at present
the subject most likely to make Thady talk
freely, so he still continued silent. At last Pat
said—

"Could I spake to you a moment, Mr.
Thady?"

"Spake out—what is it?"

"Oh, it's business, yer honer; it's something
about money—wouldn't you step out to the
rint-office?"

"Don't you see I'm just going to dinner;
besides, I ain't well—it'll keep till to-morrow, I
suppose?"

"But it won't keep, Mr. Thady."

At this moment, Biddy, who had been taking
some smoking viands out of a big black pot
and transferring them to a dish, went out of
the kitchen with them on her road to the
dining-room, and Pat took the opportunity of
whispering to his master that, "the boys
wor to meet at Mulready's on the next
evening."

"What of that?" answered Thady; "I suppose some of them meet there mostly every
night?"

"But to-morrow's the night, Mr. Thady, when
yer honer's to be inisheated* among us sworn
brothers."

"I shan't be in it at all to-morrow, then."

"Not be in it! why, you promised; and the
boys is all noticed* now. Didn't you take the
oath, Mr. Thady?" and he whispered down
close to his ear.

" I took no oath about any day. I suppose I needn't come before I choose ? "

Biddy now returned, and Thady got up to go to his dinner ; Pat followed him, and renewed the conversation in the passage. Thady, however, would give no definite promise to come to-morrow, or the next day, but said he meant to come some day. Pat observed that the boys would be furious—that they would think themselves deceived and betrayed—then urged the necessity of taking steps to prevent their paying the rent to Keegan—hinted that Ussher had been with Miss Feemy that morning—and at last departed when he found that his master was not in a proper mood to be persuaded, remarking that " he would come up again in the morning, when perhaps his honer would be thinking better of it, and not break his promised word to the boys, as there would be a great ruction among them, av he didn't go down jist to spake a word to them afther what had passed ; besides, Mr. Thady," he added, " av you wor to go back now, some of thim boys as wor in it last night, would be going to Jonas Brown's, thinking to get the first word agin you*—thinking, you know, as how you would 'peach*agin thim, may be."

After this threat, Pat took his leave, and Thady, with a sad heart, and low spirits, which even three glasses of whiskey had not raised, went in to dinner. After swallowing a few hasty morsels, without speaking either to his father or his sister, he returned to the kitchen and again sat there smoking, till one of the girls came in, telling him that Father John was on the steps of the hall door waiting for him—that

he couldn't come in, but that he said he had
important business to speak of, and must see
Mr. Thady.

"Confound you," muttered Thady, in a low
voice, " why didn't you say I was out ? "

"Shure, you niver told me, Mr. Thady."

Thady considered a moment, whether he
should escape through the back door ; at last,
however, he plucked up his courage, and went
out to meet the priest.

CHAPTER XVI

PROMOTION

As soon as Father John had gone, Mrs. McKeon
prepared to persuade her refractory daughter to
agree to the propriety of what she was going to
do with respect to Feemy, and to inform her
husband of the visitor she intended to ask
to her house ; she had not much difficulty with
either, for though Louey was indignant when
Father John hinted at her want of a beau, she
was not really ill-natured, and when her mother
told her that Father John had said that this
invitation would be the performance of a
Christian duty, she soon reconciled herself to
the prospect of Feemy's company, in spite of
Mr. Gayner and his bed. And as for Mr.
McKeon, he seldom interfered with the internal
management of his house, and when his spouse
informed him that Feemy was coming to

Drumsna, he merely remarked that "no wonder the poor girl was dull at that old ramshackle place up there, and that though Drumsna was dull enough itself, it was a little better than Ballycloran, especially now the Carrick races were coming on;" and so the three ladies put on their best bonnets and set off on their journey of charity.

Feemy was in her own sitting-room, and was somewhat more neat in her appearance than the last time we saw her there, for Ussher had said he would call early in the morning; but she was employed in the same manner as then—sitting over the fire with a novel in her hand, when she heard the sound of the car wheels, and on going to the window, saw Mrs. McKeon and her daughters.

That lady managed her business with all the tact and sincerity for which Father John had given her credit; she made no particular allusion to Ussher, but merely said that they should have a party to the race-course, as Mr. McKeon had a horse to run, and that afterwards they should all go to the ball at Carrick; and Mrs. McKeon added, "You know Feemy, you'll meet your old friend Captain Ussher there."

She then assured Feemy how glad she would be if she would stay a short time at Drumsna, after the races were over, as her two daughters were now at home, and that if she would, she would try to make the house as pleasant as possible for her.

This was all said and done so pleasantly, that Feemy did not detect any other motive in her friend's civility than the one which was apparent, and after a little pressing, agreed to accept the invitation. It was agreed that Mrs. McKeon was to call for her on the Monday following, when, if her father made no objection, she would accompany her home to Drumsna.

As soon as they were gone, Feemy made her father understand who had been there, and obtained his consent to her proposed visit, which he gave, saying at the time, " God knows, my dear, whether you'll ever come back, for your brother's determined to part with the owld place if he can, in spite of all your poor father can say to the contrary."

She then returned to her room, resuming her novel, and waiting with what patience she could for Ussher's coming. About two o'clock he made his appearance, and she was beginning gently to upbraid him for being so late, when he stopped her, by saying—

" Well, Feemy, I have strange news for you this morning."

" Strange news, Myles! what is it? I hope it's good news."

Ussher had not quite his usual confidence and ease about him; he seemed as if he had something to say which he almost feared to disclose at once, and he did not give Feemy a direct answer.

" Why, as to that, it is, and it isn't. I suppose it's good news to me,—at least I ought to think so; but I don't know what you'll think of it."

Poor Feemy's face fell, and she sat down on the chair from which she had risen, as if she had not strength to stand. Myles stood still, with his back to the fire, trying to look as if he were not disconcerted.

"Well, Myles, what is it? won't you tell me?" And then, when he smiled, she said, "Why did you try and frighten me?"

"Frighten you! why you frightened yourself."

"But what is it, Myles?" and she walked up to him, and put her two hands on his shoulders, and looked up in his face—"what is your strange news?"

"In the first place, I am promoted to the next rank. I'm in the highest now, next to a County Inspector."

"Oh! Myles, I'm so glad! but you couldn't but know that would be good news to me;—but what else?"

"Why, they've sent me a letter from Dublin, with a lot of blarney about praiseworthy energy and activity, and all that——"

"That's why they've promoted you : but you don't tell me all."

"No, that's not all : then they say they think there's reason why I'd better not stay in this immediate neighbourhood."

"Ah! I thought so!" exclaimed the poor girl; "you're to go away out of this!"

"And they say I'm to commence in the new rank at Cashel,* in County Tipperary."

Feemy for a time remained quiet. She was endeavouring to realize to herself the idea that her lover was going away, and then trying in her mind to comprehend whether it must follow naturally, as a consequence from this, that he was going away from her, as well as from Bally-cloran. Ussher still stood up by the fireplace, with the same smile on his face. What he had told Feemy was all true; he had unexpectedly received an official letter that morning from the Dublin office, complimenting him on his services, informing him that he was to be moved to a higher grade, and that on his promotion he was to leave Mohill, and take charge of the men stationed at Cashel. All this in itself was very agreeable; promotion and increased pay were of course desirable; Mohill was by no means a residence which it would cause such a man as Ussher much regret to leave; and though he had made up his mind not to fear any injury from those among whom he was situated, he could not but feel that he should be more assured of safety at any other place than that at which he now resided. All this was so far gratifying, but still he was perplexed to think what he should do about Feemy. It was true he could leave her, and let her, if she chose, break her heart; or he might promise to come back and marry her, when he was settled, with the intention of taking no further notice of her after he had left the place;—and so let her break her heart that way. But he was too fond of her for this; he could not decide what he would do; and when he came up to see her at the present time, the only conclusion to which he could bring himself with certainty was this— that nothing should induce him to marry her; but still he did not like to leave her.

He was, however, rather perplexed to know what to say to her, and therefore preferred waiting to see what turn she herself would give to the conversation. At length Feemy said—

" And when do you leave this ? "

" Oh ! they've given me a month's leave of absence. I'm to be in Cashel in a month."

Even this seemed a reprieve to Feemy, who at first thought that he would have to start immediately, — perhaps that evening ; a good deal might be done in a month ; now, however, she regretted that she had promised to go to Mrs. McKeon's.

" Then, Myles, you'll not leave this for a month? "

" I don't know about that ; that depends on circumstances. I've to run up to Dublin, and a deal to do."

" But when do you mean to be out of this? "

" Why, I tell you, I haven't settled yet— perhaps immediately after the races."

Again they were silent for some time ; Feemy longed for Ussher to say something that might sound at any rate kind ; he had never met her before without an affectionate word—and now, on the eve of his departure, he stood at the fire and merely answered her questions coldly and harshly. At length she felt that this must be the time, if ever, for saying to him what she had made up her mind to say on the previous evening, when her courage failed her. So, plucking up all the heart she could, and blushing at the time to the top of her forehead, she said—

" An't I to go with you, Myles, when you go ? "

Ussher still remained silent ; he did not know how to answer to this question. " Come, Myles, speak to me. I know you came down to tell me your plans. What am I to do? You know you must settle now, if you're going so soon. What are your plans?"

"Why, Feemy, it's not two hours or more since I've received the letter; of course I couldn't think of everything at once. Tell me; what do you think best yourself?"

"Me! what do I think?—you know I'd do anything you bid me. Won't you step in and tell father about it?"

"Oh, you can tell him. I couldn't make him understand it at all, he's so foolish."

Feemy bore the slur on her father without indignation.

"But, Myles, if you go so soon, am I to go with you?" and when after a few minutes he did not answer,—"Speak, Myles, an't we to be married before you go?" When she said this, she sat down on the old sofa, looking up into his face, as if she would read there what was passing in his mind. That which was passing in his mind must be the arbitrament of her fate.

"Why, Feemy, how can you be so foolish? —How can we be married in eight days' time? I must go, I tell you, in eight days from this."

"But you won't go to this new place then. You'll be back here, won't you, before you go to Cashel?"

"How can I be back again?—No, I could not be back again then; besides, Feemy, I wouldn't be married in this place after what your brother and Father John said to me last night. If we are to be married at all, it can't be here."

"If we are to be married!" exclaimed Feemy, rising up—"if we are! Why, Myles, what do you mean?" and rushing to him she threw her arms round his neck, and hiding her face on his bosom, she continued, "Oh, Myles! you don't mean to desert me! Myles—dear Myles —my own Myles—don't you love me?—you won't leave me now—say you won't leave me!" and she sobbed and cried as though her heart was breaking.

Ussher put his arm round her waist and kissed her; he seated her on the sofa—sat down by her—and tried to comfort her by caresses: but he still said nothing.

"Why don't you speak, Myles? I shall die if you don't speak! Only tell me what you mean to do; I'll do anything you bid me, if you'll only say you don't mean to desert me."

"Desert you, Feemy! who spoke of deserting you, dearest?"

"Then you won't leave me, my own Myles? You won't leave me here with those I hate! I love no one—I care for no one but you; only say you won't leave me here when you're gone!" and again she clung to him as though she could have detained him there for ever by holding him.

"But, Feemy, what can I do?—you see I've told you after what passed I couldn't be married here."

"Why not, Myles? why not?—never mind what Thady said—or Father John. What does it signify?—you'll be soon away from them. I'll never treat you that way, my own Myles —I'd put up with more than that for you—I

wouldn't mind what the world might say to me
—I'd bear anything for you!"

"I tell you, Feemy, there are reasons why
I couldn't be married before I get to Cashel.
There,—to tell you the whole, they wouldn't let
a man take his rise from one rank to another
if he's married. They can't prevent the officers
in the force marrying, but they don't like it;
and it's a rule that they won't promote a married
man. You see, I couldn't marry till after I was
settled at Cashel."

Feemy received the lie with which Ussher's
brain had at the moment furnished him, without
a doubt; she believed it all, and then went on—

"But when you've got your rank, you'll come
back, Myles, won't you?"

"Why, that's the difficulty—I couldn't well
again get leave of absence."

"Then, Myles, what will you do?"

And by degrees he proposed to her to leave
her home and her friends, and trust herself to
him, and go off with him unmarried, without
her father's blessing, or the priest's—to go with
him in a manner which she knew would disgrace herself, her name, and her family, and
to trust to him afterwards to give her what
reparation a tardy marriage could afford. She,
poor girl, at first received the offer with sobs
and tears. She proposed a clandestine marriage, but he swore that when afterwards detected,
it would cause his dismissal;—then that she
would come to him at Cashel, when he was
settled; but no,—he told her other lies equally
false, to prove that this could not be done.
She prayed and begged, and lay upon his

bosom imploring him to spare her this utter degradation; but now that the proposal had been fairly made, that he had got her to discuss the plan, his usual sternness returned; and at last he told her, somewhat roughly, that if she would not come with him in the manner he proposed, he would leave her now and for ever.

Poor Feemy fell with her knees on the ground and her face on the sofa, and there she lay sobbing for many minutes, while he again stood silent with his back against the fireplace. During this time, old feelings, principles, religious scruples, the love of honour and fair fame, and the fear of the world's harsh word, were sorely fighting in her bosom; they were striving to enable her to conquer the strong love she felt for Ussher, and make her reject the disgrace to which he was alluring her. Then he stooped to lift her up, and as he kissed the tears from her face, passion prevailed, and she whispered in his ear that she would go.

He stayed there for a considerable time after that; at first Feemy was so agitated and so miserable, that she was unable to converse with him, or listen to his plans for her removal. She sat there sobbing and crying, and all he could say—all his protestations of love—all his declarations that it was his firm intention to marry her at Cashel—all his promises of kind and good treatment, were unable to console her. He tried to animate her by describing to her the pleasure she would have in seeing Dublin—the delight it would be to her to leave so dull a place as Ballycloran, and see something

of the world, from which she had hitherto
been excluded. But for a long time it was
in vain; she was thinking—though she rarely
thought of them—of her father and her brother;
of what the old man would feel, when she, his
only joy, had gone from him in such a manner;
of what Thady would do and say, when he
found that the suspicions, which she knew he
already entertained, were too true. She could
not bring her heart to give up Ussher; but the
struggles within her breast at length made her
hysterical, and Ussher was greatly frightened
lest he should have to call in assistance to
bring her to herself. She did not, however,
lose her senses, and after a time she became
more tranquil, and was able to listen to his
plans. She first of all told him that she had
promised Mrs. McKeon to go to her house for
a short time, during the races, and suggested
that she should now send some excuse for
declining the visit; but this he negatived. He
desired her to go there—to go to the races and
the ball—and, above all, to keep up her spirits,
and at any rate seem to enjoy herself there as
if nothing particular had happened. This she
promised to do, but with a voice and face which
gave but little sign of her being able to keep
her promise.

He told her that he would occasionally call
at Mrs. McKeon's, so that no remark might
be made about his not coming to see her; he
desired her to tell no one that he was going
permanently to leave the country, and that he
should not himself let it be known at Mohill
till the day or so before he went; and he added

that even when it was known that he was going, there would be less suspicion arising respecting her, if she was at Drumsna, than if she remained at Ballycloran.

To all this she quietly submitted. He was to meet her at the ball at Carrick-on-Shannon, and then tell her what his definite plan of carrying her off would be; but he added that the ball night would be the last she would spend in the country, for that they would leave the next evening.

About five o'clock Ussher took his leave; she begged of him to come and see her the next day—every day till they went; but this he refused; she said that unless she saw him every day to comfort her, she would not be able to keep up her strength—that she was sure she would fall ill. It was now Friday, and she was to go to Mrs. McKeon's on Monday; on Tuesday he said he would call on her there; the races and ball were to be on the Tuesday week. In vain she asked him how she was to bear the long days till she saw him again; Ussher had no true sympathy for such feelings as were racking Feemy's heart and brain; he merely bid her keep up her spirits, and not be foolish; —that he would see her on Tuesday, and that after Tuesday week she would have nothing more to make her unhappy. And then, kissing her, he went away,—and as we have seen, Thady met him in the avenue, so satisfied in appearance, so contented, so triumphant, that he was able to forget the words which had been applied to him on the previous evening, and to nod to Feemy's brother with as pleasant an

air as though there were no grounds for ill-feeling
between them.

Poor Feemy! those vain words that " after
Tuesday week she would have nothing more to
make her unhappy," sounded strangely in her
ears. Nothing more to make her unhappy!
Could she have anything more, then or ever,
to make her happy? Could she ever be happy
again? All that had happened during the last
few days passed through her mind, and added
to her torment. How indignant had she been
when her brother had hinted to her that Ussher
did not intend honestly by her; into what a
passion had she flown with Father John, when
he had cautioned her that she should be circum-
spect in her conduct with her lover; what an
insult she had felt it when Mary Brady alluded
to the chance of Ussher's deserting her! And
now so soon after all this—but a few hours
after this strong feeling—after the indignation
she had then shown, she had herself submitted
to worse than they had even dared to suspect;
she had herself agreed to leave her father's
house as the mistress of the man, of whom she
had then confidently boasted as her future
husband! And it was not only for her own
degradation, dreadful as that was, that she
grieved, but Ussher himself—he of whom she
had felt so fond—whom she had so loved—
was this his truth, his love?—was this the protection he had sworn to give her against her
father's folly, and her brother's violence?—and,
as he had basely added, against Father John's
bigotry? Was this the protection—roughly to
swear he'd leave her, desert her for ever, unless

she agreed to give up her family, her home, her principles, and follow him, a base low creature, without a name? And was it likely that after she had agreed to this—after she had so debased herself, that he who· had already deceived her so grossly would at last keep his word by marrying her?

She was lying down with her face buried in her hands, tormenting herself with such thoughts, when Biddy came to tell her that dinner was on the table. Feemy did not dare to refuse to go in lest something should be suspected; so she rubbed her red eyes till they were still redder, and went into the parlour, where she alleged that she had a racking headache, which would give her no peace; and having sat there for a miserable half hour till her father and Thady had finished their dinner, she went upstairs to her bed-room, and after laying awake half the night, at last succeeded in crying herself to sleep.

When Thady came from the kitchen, on being told that Father John was waiting for him at the hall door, he left his pipe behind him, swallowed a draught of water to take off the smell of the spirits, and prepared to listen to the priest's lecture, as he expected, with sullenness and patience; but he was surprised out of his determined demeanour by the kindness of the priest's address. He came forward, and taking his hand, said,

"What, Thady, are you ill? What ails you?"

"Not much, then, Father John; only a headache."

"Are you too bad, my boy, to take a turn with me? I've a word or two I want to say;

but if you're really sick, Thady, and are going to bed, I'll come down early to-morrow morning. Would you sooner I did so?"

Father John said this because he thought that Thady really looked ill. And so he did; his face was yellow, his hair unbrushed, his eyes sunken, and the expression of his countenance sad and painful; but he was overcome by the kindness of the priest's manner, and replied—

"Oh no! I'm not going to bed. I believe, Father John, I did not come up to you because I was ashamed to see you afther last night."

"So I thought, my boy; and that's why I came down. I'm not sorry for your shame, though there was not much cause for it. If it was a usual thing with you to be drinking too much, you wouldn't be thinking so much of it yourself the next day."

"But I believe I said something to yourself, Father John."

"Something to me! Egad, I forget what you said to me, or whether you said anything. Oh no! you weren't so bad as that; but you were going to eat Ussher about something. But never mind that now; don't get tipsy again, if you can help it, and that's all about it. It's not the drinking I'm come to talk to you about; for you're no drunkard, Thady; and indeed it's not as your priest I want to talk to you at all, but as one friend to another. And now, my dear boy, will you take what I've to say in good part?"

These gentle words were the first comfort that had reached Thady's heart that day, and tears were in his eyes as he answered—

" Indeed I will, Father John, for you're the only friend I have now."

It was a fine moonlight evening, and they were on the road leading to the Cottage.

" Walk up this way, Thady; we'll be less likely to be interrupted in the little parlour than here;" and they walked on to the priest's house, Father John discoursing the while on the brightness of the moon and the beauty of the night, and Thady alternately thinking with pleasure of his kindness, and with dread of the questions he was about to be called upon to answer.

When they were in the parlour, and Thady had refused his host's offers of punch, tea, or supper, and the door was close shut, Father John at once struck into the subject at his heart.

" I told you, Thady, that I thought but little of your having been drinking yesterday evening; not but that I think it very foolish for a man to make himself a beast; but what I did think of was the company you were drinking in. Now I heard—and I know you won't contradict me unless it's untrue—that the party consisted of you, and Brady, and Joe Reynolds, and Byrne, and Corney Dolan, and one or two others from Drumleesh, your own or your father's tenants, and the very lowest of them—all of them infamous characters—men never, or seldom, seen at mass—makers of potheen—fellows who are known to be meeting nightly at that house of Mrs. Mulready, at Mohill, and who are strongly suspected to be Ribbonmen, or Terryalts,* or to call themselves by some infernal name and sect,

by belonging to which they have all become
liable to death or transportation."*

The priest paused; but Thady sat quite still,
listening, with his eyes fixed on the fender.

"Now, Thady, if this is so, what could you
gain by mixing with them? You weren't drunk
when you went among them, or I should think
nothing about it—for a drunken man doesn't
know what he does; and it wasn't from chance
—for a man never seeks society so much beneath himself from chance; and it wasn't from
habit—for I know your habits well enough, and
that's not one of them; but I fear you were
there by agreement. If so, what could you get
by a secret meeting with such men as those?
You know their characters and vices; are you
fool enough to think that you will find comfort in their society, or assistance in their
advice?"

"I didn't think so, Father John."

"Then why were you with them? I know
the most of your sorrows, Thady, and the most
of your cares; and I also know and appreciate
the courage with which you have tried to bear
them; and if you would make me your friend,
your assistant, and your counsellor, though I
mightn't do much for you, I think I could do
more, or show you how to do more, than you
are likely to learn from the men you were with
yesterday; and at any rate, I shall not lead you
into the danger which will beset you if you
listen to them, and which, you may be sure,
would soon end in your disgrace and destruction. Can you tell me, Thady, why you were
with them, or they were with you?"

" I was only just talking to them about—"
Thady began ; but he felt that he was going to
tell his friend a falsehood, and again held his
tongue.

" If you'll not tell me why you were there,
I'll tell you ; at least, I'll tell you what my fears
are. You went to them to talk over your father's
affairs respecting Keegan and Flannelly ; you
went to induce those poor misguided men not
to pay their rent to him ; and oh ! Thady, if
what I've heard is true, you went there to
consult with them respecting a greater crime
than I'll now name, and to instigate them to
do that which would lead to their and your
eternal shame and punishment."

Thady now shook in his chair, as though he
could hardly keep his seat ; he felt the perspiration stand upon his brow, and he wiped it off
with his sleeve ; he did not dare to deny that
he had done this, of which Father John was
accusing him, though he felt that he had been
far from instigating them to any crime like
murder. Father John continued—

" If you have joined these men,—if you have
bound yourself to these men by any oath,—if
there is any league between you and them, let
me implore you to disregard it ; nothing can be
binding, that is only to bind you to greater
wickedness. I do not ask you to tell me any
of their secrets or plans, though, God knows,
what you tell me now would be as sacred as if
I heard it in the confessional ; but if you have
such secrets, if you know their signs,* whatever
may be the consequence, at once renounce
them."

"I know no secrets or signs, Father John, and I don't belong to any society."

"Then, if you don't, you can have nothing to bind you. Is it true that you were rash enough, mad enough, to speak to these men about murdering Keegan? Tell me; have you a plan made to murder Keegan? Have you had such a crime in your thoughts?"

It had been in his thoughts all day: what answer should he make? should he lie, and deny it all? or should he confess it all, just as it was?

"If you'll not tell me, I must, for Mr. Keegan's sake, take some step to secure his safety. Come, Thady, come; you know it's not by threats I wish to guide you; you know I love you. I know well enough your patient industry—your want of selfishness. I know, if you have for a moment thought of this crime, you have now repented it: tell me how far you have gone, and if you are in danger;—if you have done that which was very, very wicked. I will still try and screen you from the effects of a sin, which I am sure was not premeditated. Is there any plot to murder Keegan?"

"There is not."

"As you are a living man, there's none?"

"There is not."

"What were you saying about Keegan, then, to those men yesterday?"

"I don't know what I said—I don't know I said anything; they were threatening him, if he came on Drumleesh for rent; if they have a plot I don't know it."

"But, Thady, are you to join them again?

do you mean again to renew your revellings of last night? have you agreed to see them again?"

"I have."

"And where?"

"At Mulready's in Mohill."

"And when?"

"They sent to-day to say it was to-morrow night, but I have refused to go."

"You have refused?"

"Yes, Father John. I got the message from them just before dinner, and I said I'd not go to-morrow."

"But have you said you'd never join them again? have you sent to them to say you'd never put your foot in that hole of sin? did you say you were mad when you promised it, and that you would never keep that promise? did you say, Thady, that you would not come? or are you still, in their opinion, one of their accursed set?"

"I'll niver go there, Father John. I've not had one moment's ase since I said I would; it's been on my heart like lead all the morning; indeed, indeed, Father John, I'll niver go there."

"I will not doubt you, Thady; but still, that you may feel how solemnly you are bound not to peril your life and soul by joining them who can only wish to lead you into crime, give me your honour, on the sacred word of God, that you will never go to that place;—or join those men in any lawless plans or secret meetings."

And Thady swore most solemnly, on the sacred volume, that he would do as the priest directed him respecting these men.

Father John then gradually drew from him
in conversation what had really taken place.
He told him what he had heard from McGovery
—how he had quieted that man and Cullen—
and advised him by his own demeanour to his
tenants, to pass over what had been said, as
though it had been a drunken frolic. He asked
him, however, whether he considered that Mr.
Keegan or Ussher were in any real danger;
and Thady assured him that he did not think
they were—that there was no plot laid—that
the men were angry and violent, but that,
unless further instigated, he did not think they
would commit any act of absolute violence.
These opinions were not given spontaneously,
but in answer to various questions from the
priest, who at last satisfied himself that in con-
firming the horror with which Thady evidently
regarded what he had already done, and in
preventing him from following any further the
course he was about to pursue, he had done
all that was possible in the case to prevent
crime.

Whether he thought that either of those who
had been named as the object of hatred to these
unruly men might ultimately fall a victim to the
feeling to which their actions had given rise in
the country, is another question. If he did, he
could not prevent it—nor was it his especial
business to attend to it; but he felt tolerably
sure that to whatever bad feelings hardships
and cruelty might have given rise in Thady's
breast, he would not now gratify them by such
atrocious means as those which McGovery's
statement had induced him to apprehend.

Under this impression he bade him good night, with another kind shake of the hand; telling him that though, at present, there might be much to sadden and distress him, if he confronted his difficulties with manly courage and honest purposes, he would be sure sooner or later to overcome them.

Thady returned home more comfortable than he had been in the morning, but he could not bring himself to that state of mind in which Father John had hoped to dismiss him. He felt, that though he was determined not to go to Mrs. Mulready's, the affair could not rest there. He felt himself to be, in some horrible manner, in the power of Brady and Joe Reynolds—as though he could not escape from them. A general despondency respecting all his prospects weighed him down, and when he reached Ballycloran, he was nearly as unhappy as he had been in leaving it.

CHAPTER XVII

SPORT IN THE WEST

CARRICK-ON-SHANNON, the assize town of County Leitrim, though an assize town, is a very poor place. It consists of one long narrow, irregular street, lying along the Shannon, in which slated houses and thatched cabins delightfully relieve each other, and prevent the eye from being annoyed with sameness or monotony. The

houses are mostly all shops, and even the
cabins profess to afford "lodging and enther-
thainment;" so that it is to be presumed that
the poverty of the place is attributable to
circumstances and misfortune, and not to the
idleness of the inhabitants. The prevailing
feeling, however, arising in any human mind,
on entering the place, would be that of compassion for the judges, barristers, attorneys,
crown clerks, grand jury, long panel,* witnesses,
etc., who have to be crammed into this little
place, and lodged and fed for five or six days,
twice a year during the assizes.

There is, however, a tolerably good hotel in
the place, and we at present beg to take our
reader with us into the largest room therein,
which was usually dignified by the name of
the Ball Room. It was not, however, by any
means dedicated solely to the worship of Terpsichore :* all the public dinners eaten in Carrick
were eaten here; all the public meetings held
in Carrick were held here; all the public
speeches were spoken here. Here committees
harangued; Gallagher ventriloquised; itinerant
actors acted; itinerant concert-givers held their
concerts; itinerant Lancashire bell-ringers rang
their bells. Here also were carried on the
mysteries of the Carrick-on-Shannon masonic
lodge, with all due zeal and secrecy.

On the present occasion the room was, or
rather had been, devoted to the purpose of
feeding; an ordinary* had been held here
previous to the races; and most of those who
were in any way interested in the coming event
were there. The cloth had been just taken

away, decanters of whiskey and jugs of boiling water alternated each other down the table, and large basins of white sugar were scattered about unsparingly. The party were evidently about to enjoy themselves. There were about thirty of them there, some of them owners of horses, some of them riders, some of them backers; the rest were eaters, drinkers, and spectators.

The chair was filled by Major McDonnell, one of the stewards—a little man, who had probably never crossed a horse* himself, and had nothing of the sportsman about him. He had, however, lately inherited an estate in the neighbourhood, and having some idea of stand- ing for the county on the Tory interest at the next election, was desirous of obtaining popularity, and had consequently given forty pounds to be run for—had agreed to wear a red coat at the races, and call himself a steward —sit at the top of the table and carve for thirty hungry sportsmen to-day, with each of whom he had to drink wine—and get partners for all the ugly girls, if there be any in County Leitrim, on the morrow. This was certainly hard work; in reward for which he was probably destined to have his head broken at the next election, if he should have sufficient courage to show himself as a Tory candidate for the county.

There, however, he sat on this day, very unfit to take the chief part among the spirits by whom he was surrounded.

Opposite to him, at the other end of the room, sat our big and burly friend, McKeon, a very different character. Whenever six or

eight were talking aloud together, his voice
might always be heard the loudest. Whenever
a shout of laughter arose—and that was incessantly—his shout was always the longest. It
seemed that every bet that was offered was
taken by him, and that every bet taken by any
one else had been offered by him. He was
always scribbling something in that well-worn
book of his, and yet he never had his hand
away from his tumbler—except when it was
on the decanter. All the waiters came to him
for orders, and he seemed perfectly competent
to attend to them. If any man finished his
punch and did not fill again, McKeon reminded
him of his duty—and that not only by preaching,
but by continual practice. In fact, he was just
in his element, and enjoying himself.

There was an empty chair next Mr. McKeon,
where his friend Mr. Gayner had been sitting—
I won't say during his dinner, for he had not
swallowed a mouthful. He was now standing
up against the fireplace, sucking a lemon. He
had a large great coat on, buttoned up to the
neck, and a huge choker round his throat. He
was McKeon's jockey, and was to ride Playful
for the forty pounds on the morrow.

Bob Gayner, as he was usually called, was
one of the best gentlemen riders*in the country.
He came from County Roscommon,—the county,
by-the-by, which can probably boast the best
riders in Ireland,—where he had a small
property of his own, near Athlone ; but the
chief part of his time was spent in riding races
and training for them. He had been at it all
his life—and certainly, if there be any merit in

the perfection of such an art, Bob was entitled
to it, for he rode beautifully. It was not only
that he could put his horse at a fence without
fear, and sit him whilst he was going over it—
any man with practice could do that; but Bob
had a sympathy with the animal he was riding
which enabled him not only to know what he
could do himself, but also what the horse could
do. He knew exactly where a horse wanted
assistance from his rider. And he had another
knack too, not unfrequently made use of in
steeple-chases—Bob seldom let his own horse
baulk, but he very generally made those that
others were riding do so. And then, at a
finish, how admirable was Bob! In leap races
the finish is seldom so near a thing as in flat
races; but when it did come to be neck and
neck at the post, there was no man in Ireland
could give a horse a stretch and land him in a
winner like Bob. He had also an exquisite
genius for tumbling. Horses will occasionally
fall, and when they do, riders must follow them;
but no one fell so safely, recovered so actively,
and was again so instantly in the saddle as our
friend; and, consequently, wherever there was
a steeple-chase to be run, where pluck, science,
and practice were wanting, there Bob was in
requisition, and there he usually was found.
It was a great thing to secure his services;
and knowing this, Tony McKeon had, in his
own way, long since, made Gayner his fast
friend; how, I cannot say, for Bob was much
above being bought, and though, no doubt,
he made money by his races, he would have
thought little of shooting any one who was bold

enough to offer to pay him for riding. When
in his cap, jacket, boots, and breeches, he
would, if he thought occasion required or his
interests demanded it, wrangle like a devil.
Though its back were turned to him, he could
see a horse go on the wrong side of a post;
and woe betide the man who came to the
scales as a winner an ounce below the weight.
Bob, from long practice, knew all these dodges,
and he made the most of them. But when
once his cap was off, and his coat was on, he
was a quiet, easy, unassuming fellow—liked
and petted by all he knew; for he never spoke
little of others nor bragged of himself.

He was now talking to another member of
the same confraternity, but of a very different
character. He also had been sitting dinnerless,
—for both these gentlemen, in the pursuit of their
amusement, were obliged to starve and sweat
themselves down to a certain standard, about
twenty pounds below their ordinary weight,—
and he was now also sucking a lemon. George
Brown was the second son of Jonas Brown, of
Brown Hall, the magistrate by whom Tim
Reynolds and the others had been committed
to Ballinamore, and, like his father, was most
unpopular in his own country. He was arrogant,
overbearing, conceited, and passionate—without
any rank which could excuse pride, or any
acquirement that could justify conceit. It is,
however, as a gentleman jockey that we are at
present to make his acquaintance, and in that
capacity he was about as much inferior to the
grooms by whom the horses were trained as Bob
was superior to them. He had courage enough,

however, and would ride at anything; and as
his own relations and friends, for whom he rode,
were tolerably wealthy, and he was therefore
generally well mounted, he sometimes won; but
he had killed more horses under him than any
man in Ireland—and no wonder, for he had a
coarse hand and a loose seat; and it was no
uncommon thing to see George coming the first
of the two over a fence headlong into the next
field as if he had been flung there by a petard,*
leaving the unfortunate brute he had been riding
panting behind him, with his breast cut open,
or his knees destroyed by the fence, over which
his rider had had neither skill nor patience to
land him. He was now going to ride his own
horse, Conqueror, and had talked himself, and
had been talked, into the belief that it was
impossible that anything could beat him.

These two were standing talking at the fire-
place, and as they also had their little books in
their hands, it is to be presumed that they were
mixing business with amusement.

There were others there, sitting at the table,
who were to ride to-morrow, but whose usual
weight allowed them to do so, without the
annoyance to which Gayner and Brown had to
subject themselves. There was little Larry
Kelly, from Roscommon, who could ride something under eight stone; Nicholas Blake, from
the land of the Blakes, Burkes, and Bodkins;*
Pat Conner, with one eye, from Strokestown,
who had brought his garron* over under the
speculation that if the weather should come wet,
and the horses should fall at the heavy banks,
she would be sure to crawl over,—knowing, too,

that as the priest was his second cousin, he could not refuse him the loan of a stable gratis.

There was Ussher there also, sitting next to George Brown, who was a friend of his—much more intent, however, on his own business than that which had brought the others here; and Greenough, the sub-inspector of police, from Ballinamore; and young Fitzpatrick, of Streamstown, who kept the subscription pack of harriers; and a couple of officers from Boyle, one of whom owned a horse, for which he was endeavouring to get a rider, but which none of those present seemed to fancy; and there was Peter Dillon, from beyond Castlebar, who had brought up a strong-looking, long-legged colt, which he had bred in County Mayo, with the hope that he might part with it advantageously in a handicap, to some of those Roscommon lads, who were said to have money in their pockets; and there were many others apparently happy, joyous fellows, who seemed not to have a care in the world; and last, but not least, there was Hyacinth Keegan, attorney at law, and gent.

There he was, smiling and chatting, oily and amiable; getting a word in with any one he could; creeping into intimacy with those who were not sharp enough to see what he was after; jabbering of horses,—of which he considered himself a complete judge,—and of shooting, hunting, and racing, as if the sports of a gentleman had been his occupation from his youth upwards.

"Well, boys!" said McKeon; "I suppose we're to have an auction. What's it to be? the owld thing—half a crown each, I suppose?"

"An auction, Mr. McKeon!" said the chairman. "What's an auction?"

"We'll show you, Major. All you've to do is to give me half a crown."

Now, as many may be as ignorant as Major McDonnell respecting an auction in sporting phraseology, I will, if I can, explain what it is.

It has but little reference or similitude to those auctions from which Sir Robert Peel has removed the duty.

Supposing there may be twenty members, each having half a crown; and six horses to run. Twenty bits of paper are placed in a hat, on six of which are written the names of the running horses—the others are blanks—and they are then drawn, as lots, out of the hat. The tickets bearing the horses' names are sold by the auctioneer; the last bidder has to pay twice the sum he bids—one moiety to the man who drew the horse, the other is added to the fund composed of the twenty half-crowns. After the race, the happy man holding the ticket bearing the name of the winning horse receives the whole. There are, therefore, different winners in this transaction; the man drawing the name of the favourite horse of course wins what is bid for the ticket; any one drawing the name of any horse would probably win something, as his chance, if the beast have more than three legs, must be worth at least five shillings. Such, however, is an auction, and on the present occasion it was a very animated one.

The thirty half-crowns were now collected and handed over to McKeon; the names of the eight horses expected to start scrawled in pencil

on the backs of fragments of race-bills; and
those, together with the blanks, deposited in
the hat, which was carried round by one of the
party.

"Ah! now, Pat, come to me last," said
Gayner; "I've never any luck with the first
haul; never mind, I'll take it," and he drew a
lot, "and, by the Virgin, Tony, I've got my
own mare!"

"Have you got Playful, Gayner?" said a
dozen at once. This made their chance less,
for Playful was second favourite.

Brown was next, and he got a blank; and the
next, and the next.

"I've drawn Brickbat," said Fitzpatrick, "a
d—d good horse; he won the hunters' plate at
Tuam last year."

"Oh! I wish you joy," said Gayner, "for he
won't start to-morrow, my boy: he's at Tuam
now."

"Begad! he'll start as soon as yourself, Bob,"
said little Larry; "he came to Castleknock last
night, and he's at Frenchpark now: Murphy
from Frenchpark is to ride him."

These details brought Brickbat up in the
market.

"They might have left him at Tuam then,
and saved themselves money," said Gayner.
"Why, he hadn't had a gallop last Tuesday
week; I was in his stable myself. If Burke's
cattle had been as fat at Ballinasloe, he'd have
got better prices."

"I say, McKeon," said Fitzpatrick, "what
odds will you bet Bob doesn't buy Brickbat
himself?"

The hat went round, and others got blanks. Ussher got Miss Fidget, Larry Kelly's mare, and was advised in a whisper by that cunning little gentleman—who meant to buy Conqueror by way of a hedge,* and who therefore wanted to swell the stakes—to be sure and buy the mare himself, for she didn't know how to fall ; "and," he added, "you know she's no weight on her ;" and when Ussher looked at Larry Kelly, who was to ride her himself, he couldn't but think the latter part was true.

Then Nicholas Blake drew Kickie-wickie, the officer's mare, whereupon the gallant Captain, who knew Blake was a sporting fellow, thought this was a good opportunity to sound that gentleman about getting him a rider, and began whispering to him all the qualities of the mare ; how she could do everything a mare should do ; how high she was bred and how well she was trained, and how she was like the poacher, and could "leap on anywhere ;" for all which, and Kickie-wickie herself, with her owner into the bargain, Blake did not care a straw ;—for he was confident of winning himself with the Galway horse, Thunderer.

Then some one else drew Thunderer ; and Peter Dillon got Conqueror, greatly to his joy, for he reckoned that his expenses from Castlebar would thus be mostly paid, even if he couldn't sell the long-legged colt. The Major drew Crom-a-boo,* a Carrick horse, who had once been a decent hunter, and whose owner had entered it at the instigation of his fellow townsmen, and by the assurance that these sort of races were often won by your steady old horses; and Mr. Stark, the owner, since he had first made up his mind to pay the £5 stake, had gradually deceived himself into the idea that he should probably win; and having never before even owned a horse—for this was a late purchase, or rather the beast had been taken in lieu of a debt—had now, for the last three weeks, talked of nothing but sweats, gallops, physics, training, running, and leaping: and having secured the services of a groom for the day, who was capable of riding his horse, had entirely given himself up to the delights of horse-racing. Lucky was it for Mr. Stark that Crom-a-boo was sure to lose; for had he won, Stark would have been a ruined man; nothing would have kept him from the Curragh and a conviction that the turf was his proper vocation.

The Major was delighted at his prize; he had not drawn a blank, and that was sufficient for him.

Then, at last, Keegan got Pat Conner's mare from Strokestown. She was called Diana, and his was the last paper drawn.

"Faith, Keegan, you're in luck," said McKeon, "for the mare can't but run well. Pat's been training her since May last. I was over there going to Castlereagh, and I saw Pat at her then."

"'Deed, then, Mr. McKeon," said Conner, "maybe she'll beat your own mare, much as you think of her."

"Oh! I'm sure she will; there's so much running about her. Was she at plough after last winter, Pat?"

"She had other work to do, then, for she had

310 The Macdermots of Ballycloran

to carry me twice a-week through the season; and that she did—and that's not light work, I think."

"Carry you, Pat!" said Gayner; "why, you don't mean to say you hunt that old garron you call Diana? Faith, man, you're too bold; your friends ought to look to you; what would the country do if you broke your neck?"

"It's your own is in most danger, I'm thinking," replied Pat; "faith, I wouldn't take all the pick up*to-morrow, to ride that devil you're to ride over the course."

"And I'll take devilish good care you're not asked," said McKeon: "but now, boys, as I fear the Major's hardly up to it, I'll dispose of the prizes. Come, which shall I put up first? which was drawn first?"

"Your own mare, Tony; Gayner got Playful at the first start."

"Well, gentlemen, here's the mare Playful. I believe I'm to say all the good I can about her, and upon my word she doesn't want spirit." Here he whispered Gayner, whom he told to bid for themselves conjointly. "Come, gentlemen, what do you offer? people say she's wicked, but she'll not kick you if you don't come in her reach. She can go if she likes, and she can, I suppose, if she likes, stand still; but upon my soul, I never saw her to do so in the field."

"I'll say thirty shillings, Tony," said Bob.

"Five and thirty," said young Brown.

"Two pounds," said Bob.

"I'll not go beyond that," said Brown.

"Two pounds—who'll give more than two pounds for Playful? Gentlemen, the horses are all favourites, and the pool will consequently be a large one. Who'll give more than two pounds? Bob, you've got the mare; hand me two pounds, and hand yourself two more."

Then Brickbat and Miss Fidget were sold, both at good prices; for the horse had won the last race at Tuam, and that put him up in the market, in spite of Bob's vile comparison between him and his owner's bullocks; and the mare was a favourite among the Roscommon gentry, who knew little Larry could ride when he meant it.

Kickie-wickie was the next put up, but in spite of all that had been said about her by her gallant owner, she was in very little request, and was purchased cheap.

Thunderer fetched a good price; Galway horses always do; and it was easy to see that Nicholas Blake was in earnest, and Nick was a man that wouldn't come from Loughrea to Carrick-on-Shannon, and lose a day with the Galway dogs*for nothing; George Brown made the purchase, for if anything could beat Conqueror it was Thunderer.

Then came Conqueror, and bidding began in earnest. George offered two pounds to frighten the field; but both Larry Kelly and McKeon wanted to hedge, and they raised the price against each other by half-crowns, till at last little Larry Kelly got the winner, that was to be, for three pounds ten, much to Gayner's satisfaction, who felt no such confidence in George Brown's invincibility, and was very glad to see the pool increased by those who did.

When Crom-a-boo was put up—his owner

rashly offered five shillings—for which sum he was allowed to retain him. He could not, however, comprehend that, because he had bid five, he was to pay ten—however, he had to do it, and began to find that the pleasures of the turf were not entirely unalloyed.

The Strokestown garron did not create much emulation, but Peter Dillon, knowing that though Pat had only one eye, that one was a good one, and that he wouldn't lose the race for want of hard work and patience, and having little Larry's three pounds ten in his pocket to back him, at length doubled Keegan's offer of half a crown which he made to keep his own ticket, and Diana was knocked down to him at the same price that Crom-a-boo had fetched.

Then the fun grew fast and furious, and calls for hot water and spirits were loud and incessant.

"By the holy poker, boys, I'm thirsty after that," said McKeon; "you should stand me a bottle of champagne among ye, no less—just to take the dryness out of my throat, before I begin drinking."

"Champagne, indeed, Tony; wouldn't a bucket of brandy and water serve you?"

"Indeed, Fitz, if you're to pay for it yourself, a mouthful of brandy and water wouldn't be a bad thing—for I want something more than ordinary afther that work. Ah! Conner, it was the bidding afther that mare of yours that broke my heart entirely—why, man, you see, every one wanted her."

"Niver mind, Mr. McKeon, niver mind!" said Pat, with his one eye fixed on his punch.

"She's a nice, good, easy creature, anyway. I don't have to be sending a boy down through the rack to be cleaning her,* as they say you do with the one you're going to start to-morrow—pray God she don't kill any of us, that's all."

"Pray God she don't, Pat, and especially you. Well, Fitz, where's this brandy and water you're talking about?"

"To hear Tony talking," said little Larry, "one would think he didn't drink this week; when he got a sup at every bid that was made, and finished a tumbler as every horse was knocked down; why, that was eight tumblers of punch!"

"Water, Larry, all water to clear my throat—ask the waiter else."

"It's little of that cure you take, I'm thinking—waiter, bring some tobacco here."

And now the party began smoking as well as drinking; and an atmosphere was formed which soon drove the Major out of the room—not, however, before McKeon implored him to stay just for one handicap, as he wanted to challenge the bay gelding he drove under his gig*; and as the Major was waiting for his hat, Tony threw a shilling on the table.

"Come, Major, cover that, just for luck; I must have a shy at that gig horse; I want him for Mrs. McKeon's car. Come, I'll tell you every beast I've got, and you may choose from them all, from the mare that's to win to-morrow, down to the flock of turkeys that's in the yard at Drumsna."

But the Major was inexorable; he thought the £40 and the red coat which he had had to buy for to-morrow's use, together with the hard work he had to do, was enough for popularity; and may be he had heard of Tony's celebrity in a knock, and he did not wish to sacrifice his own nag, for a chance selection out of those in McKeon's yard, nor yet for a flock of turkeys.

However, though the Major wouldn't join in a handicap, others would—and McKeon wasn't baulked of his amusement. Men soon had their hands in their pockets, waiting the awards of the arbiter, which were speedily pronounced; and various and detailed were the descriptions given of the brutes which were intended to change hands; but not in general such as made those who got them satisfied with their bargains, when they afterwards became acquainted with their real merits.

Peter Dillon threw away sundry shillings in endeavouring to part with the Mayo colt, but either he had been there before with the same kind of cattle, or he priced him too high; he couldn't get his money for him, either from little Larry Kelly, or his elder brother who was there.

Tony, before the evening was over, gave the Boyle officers two or three most desperate bargains. First, he got the celebrated mare Kickie-wickie for a pair of broken-down gig horses, to run tandem: engaged to go quiet and not kick in harness. They couldn't be warranted sound: but then, as Tony said, what horse could? and he was so particular—he would never say a horse was sound, unless he knew it; in fact, he never warranted a horse sound; which was true enough, for Tony knew no one

would take his warrant; and then when the
Captain was in the first fit of grief for Kickie-
wickie, some good-natured friend having told
him that the two gig horses weren't worth a feed
of oats, Tony gave her back again for a good
hack hunter, and a sum of money to boot, about
the real value of the mare. Again, late in the
evening—when the punch had made further in-
roads upon the poor warrior's brain—he gave
him back his own hunter for the two gig horses
and a further sum of money : from all which it
will be seen by those who understand the art,
that the officer from Boyle could not have made
a great deal, and that Tony McKeon could not
be much out of pocket.

This fun continued till about two, when half
the party were too drunk to care about winning
and losing—and the other half, mostly consisting of the married men, too wary to attempt
business with those as knowing as themselves.
Gayner and Brown had gone home to bed, as
they had to be up and walk ten miles before
breakfast, with their great coats on ; after which,
as Gayner had told Mrs. McKeon, he would
trouble her for the loan of two feather beds, and
three or four buckets of turf ; as he thought that
after laying between them for an hour or so
before a roaring fire, and then being rubbed
down with flannels by Tony and his two men,
there was little doubt but he'd be able to ride
11 stone 4 ; and he was to be up at that weight
on the next day.

Keegan had become very drunk and talkative,
had offered to sing two or three songs, to make
two or three speeches, and had ultimately fallen

backwards, on his chair being drawn away, from which position he was unable to get up, and little Larry's brother was now amiably engaged painting his face with lampblack. Mrs. Keegan the while was sitting in her cold, dark, little back parlour, meditating the awful punishment to be visited on the delinquent when he did return home.

Vain woman, there she sat till four, while Hyacinth lay happy beneath the table ; nor did he return home, till brought on the waiter's back, at eight the next morning.

Pat was winking with his one eye, and nodding on his chair, with his pipe still stuck in his mouth. Little Larry was laughing till he cried at his brother's performance. Peter Dillon and young Fitzpatrick, each with a whiskey bottle in his hand, were guarding the door, at which Stark, the unfortunate owner of Crom-a-boo, was vainly endeavouring to make his exit, which he was assured he should not be allowed to do till he had sung a song standing on the sideboard. And the younger son of Mars, conquered by tobacco and whiskey, was leaning his unfortunate head on the table, and deluging Keegan's feet with the shower which he was unable to restrain.

Ussher was detailing in half drunken glee to his friend Fred Brown, George's brother, his plan for carrying off poor Feemy ; and Brown, always, as he said, ready to help a friend in necessity, was offering him the loan of his gig to take her as far as Longford, at which place he could arrive in time to catch the mail, if he could manage to take Feemy away from

Ballycloran immediately after sunset. "And I'll send a boy to bring the gig back from Longford," added Fred, "so you'll have no trouble at all; and I'll tell you what it is, you're taking the prettiest girl out of County Leitrim with you —so here's her health."

Tony, Nicholas Blake, and Greenough were the only three left who were still able to drink steadily, and they kept at it till about four, when they all agreed, that if they meant to do any good at all to-morrow, they'd better be getting to bed; they consequently took one tumbler more, because it was to be the last, and made towards the door, out of which Stark had at length escaped, after having a bottle of whiskey poured over his head. As they passed the Captain, who was snoring against the wall, McKeon slightly touched his foot with his toe, and said to Blake, "Well; if I was as soft as that fellow, I'd have my head boiled in a pudding-bag. By gad, the Colonel oughtn't to let him out without his nurse."

"You oughtn't to talk then, Tony, for you didn't make a bad thing of him to-night."

"Oh, d—n his money," said McKeon; "I'd much sooner be without such a fellow. I'd sooner by half have a bargain with a man that knew how to take care of himself, than a greenhorn, who'd let you rob him of his eyes without seeing you."

By this time they'd got to the front door, at which was now standing Tony's buggy and servant; Greenough was going to walk to his lodgings, and Blake had come to the door to see his friend off; when they heard a loud

shrieking down the street, and they saw the unfortunate Stark running towards the hotel, still
followed by Fitzpatrick and Dillon, each with
an empty bottle in his hand.

When he had escaped from the inn, his per-
secutors had followed him, still swearing that he
should sing. Stark had run towards his home,
but before he got there his pursuers headed him
in the street and turned him back, and now
as he rushed along, half blinded by the spirits
in his eyes, they followed him, whooping and
yelling like two insane devils, and were just
catching him near the door of the hotel, when
poor Stark, striking his foot against the curb
stone, fell violently on his face, and Dillon,
who was just behind him, stumbled and fell
upon him.

"Halloo, Fitzpatrick, is that you?" said
Tony; "what in G—d's name are you doing
with that poor devil? I believe you and Dillon
have killed him."

By this time Dillon had got up; and McKeon
and Blake together helped the other man to his
feet; his wrath was by this time thoroughly
kindled, and he was swearing all manner of vengeance against Fitzpatrick — the other man's
name he did not know. They, contented with
their sport, carried the decanters, wonderful to
relate, unbroken in triumph into the hotel,—and
McKeon, bidding the boy to bring the gig after
him, helped Stark, whose face was dreadfully
bleeding, to his home, trying to console him,
and assuring him that the mischief was all owing
to Dillon, and that Fitzpatrick, who was a
neighbour and friend of Tony's, had had little

or nothing to do with it; and having left him at his hall door, he drove quietly home to his own house, and went soberly to bed.

CHAPTER XVIII

HOW PAT BRADY AND JOE REYNOLDS WERE ELOQUENT IN VAIN

THE day after Ussher had obtained Feemy's consent to go off with him, she passed in the same manner as she had that afternoon—sometimes sitting quiet with her eyes fixed on vacancy—sometimes sobbing and crying, as though she must have fallen into an hysterical fit. Once or twice she attempted to make some slight preparation for her visit to Mrs. McKeon's, such as looking through her clothes, mending them, etc., but in fact she did nothing. The next day, Sunday, she spent in the same manner; she omitted going to mass, a thing she had not done for years, unless kept at home by very bad weather, or real illness; she never took up a book, nor spoke a word, except such as she could not possibly avoid, to the servant or her father. Of Thady she saw nothing, except at her meals, and then they took no notice of each other. They had not spoken since the night when Thady had upbraided her whilst walking in the lane with Ussher.

On the Monday morning she was obliged to exert herself, for she had to pack the little trunk that was to carry her ball-room finery to Mrs.

McKeon's, and prepare everything that was necessary for her visit.

Biddy, the favourite of the two girls, had once or twice asked her mistress what ailed her, and whether she was ill; but Feemy only answered her crossly that she was bothered with that horrid headache, and the girl could only believe that either this was actually the case, or else that she had quarrelled with her lover; and as it was now three days since he had been at Ballycloran, she at last determined that this was the case.

During these three days, Feemy had frequently made up her mind, or rather she fancied she had made up her mind to give Ussher up,— to go and confess it all to Father John, or to tell it to Mrs. McKeon; and if it had not been for the false pride within her, which would not allow her to own that she had been deceived, and that her lover was unworthy, she would have done so. His present coolness, and his cruelty in not coming to see her, though they did not destroy her love, greatly shook it; and had she had one kind word to assist her in the struggle within herself, she might still have prevented much of the misery which her folly was fated to produce.

When Mrs. McKeon and her daughters came for her about one o'clock on Monday, the small exertion necessary for putting up her clothes, had made her somewhat better—something more able to talk than she had been before, and they did not then observe anything particular about her; but she had been but a very short time at Drumsna before it was evident to Mrs.

McKeon, that something was the matter with
her. When she questioned her, Feemy gave
the same answer—that she had a racking headache; and though this did very well for a time,
before the evening was over, the good lady was
certain that something more than a headache
afflicted her guest.

The next day, according to his promise,
Ussher called, but of course at Mrs. McKeon's
house he could not see her alone; that lady
and her daughters were present all the time.
When he came in, Ussher shook hands with
Feemy as he would with anybody else, and
began talking gaily to the two other girls. He
had regained his presence of mind completely,
and however deficient Feemy might be in that
respect, he now proved himself a perfect master
of hypocrisy. He did not stay long, and as he
got up to go away, he merely remarked that he
hoped he should meet the ladies that day week
on the race-course, and at the ball; and the
only thing he said especially to Feemy was, that
he should call at Ballycloran on his way to the
races, and that when he saw her on the course,
he would tell her how her father and brother
were; and he remarked that he should not go
home that night, as he had been asked to dine
and sleep at Brown Hall.

The week passed on, and Feemy remained in
the same melancholy desponding way; saying
nothing to Mrs. McKeon, and little to the two
girls, who, in spite of Feemy's sin in having a
lover, did everything in their power to cheer
and enliven her.

Father John usually dined at Mrs. McKeon's

on Sunday, and she came to the determination of having another talk with him about Feemy. So before dinner on that day, she opened her mind to him, telling him the state in which Feemy had been the whole of the week, and that she thought the sooner she could be made to understand that she must give up all thoughts of Ussher, the better.

Feemy had been at mass with the family, and when she met Father John afterwards, she exerted herself to appear before him as she usually did, and to a certain extent she succeeded. Father John was himself usually cheerful, and he spoke to her good humouredly, and she made an effort to answer him in the same strain ; this deceived the priest, and when Mrs. McKeon spoke to him about Feemy's deep melancholy, and suggested the propriety of speaking to her on the subject which they supposed was nearest her heart, he said—

"Better let her alone, Mrs. McKeon ; I think you'd better let her alone, and time will cure her. You see, Feemy is proud, and perhaps a little too headstrong, and I don't think she'd bear just as quietly as she ought any one speaking to her about the man now. It isn't only the losing him that vexes her ; it isn't only that she has been deceived : but that everyone knows that she has lost him, and has been deceived. It's this that hurts her pride, and talking to her about it will only make her more fretful. If you'll take my advice, you'll just leave her to herself, take no especial notice of her, and let her go to this ball ; and when she sees the man paying attention to others,—

dancing and philandering with them, and neg-
lecting her—her pride will make her feel that she
must at any rate appear to be indifferent ; and
when she has once enabled herself to appear so,
she will soon become really so. Just let her go
to the races, and the ball ; and your kindness
and the girls' society will soon bring her round."

All Monday Feemy spent in bed, but Mrs.
McKeon and her girls took no notice of it,
except carefully tending her—offering to read to
her, and bring her what she wanted. They soon,
however, found that she preferred being left
alone ; and they consequently allowed her to
think over her own gloomy prospects in solitude
and silence.

Feemy had, however, declared her intention
of going both to the races and to the ball.
Ussher had desired her to do so, and she feared
to disobey him ; besides, at one of these places
he had to give her final instructions as to their
departure. She was, therefore, dressed for starting on the Tuesday morning, when the other
girls were ready ; and though her eyes and nose
were somewhat red, and her cheeks somewhat
pale, and though she did not now deserve the
compliment that Fred Brown had paid her,
when he told Ussher that he was going to carry
off the prettiest girl in County Leitrim, still she
did not look unwell, and Mrs. McKeon kindly
comforted herself by the reflection, that as she
was both able and willing to dress herself for
amusement, there could not be much really the
matter with her.

In the mean time Thady had been honestly
firm to the promise he had made to Father

John, not to join the Mulreadyites. His sister's absence from Ballycloran at the present time had been a relief to him; and on the morning after his visit to the priest he had returned to his work, not certainly with much happiness or satisfaction, but still with his mind made up to struggle on in the best way he could—to do nothing which he knew to be wrong, and come what come might, to leave Reynolds and his associates to their own schemes and villanies. He felt determined, if he could not protect himself and his family from his enemies by honest means, to leave it to circumstances to protect him; and though he could not shake off a deep desponding as to the future, still there was a kind of contentment in the feeling that he knew he had to suffer, and that he had made up his mind to do so firmly and bravely.

On the Saturday morning, Pat Brady had again come to his master, informing him that all the boys were to be on that evening at the whiskey shop, and using all his powers of oratory to induce him to come down; but Thady was firm, and he not only refused to come then, but plainly told Pat that he had entirely altered his mind, and that he did not intend to go down to them at all. He advised Pat also to give them up, hinting that if he did not, they two, viz. Pat Brady and Thady Macdermot, would probably soon have to part company.

This was a threat, however, for which Pat did not much care; for he knew that there was little more to be made by his old master; and, like a wise man, he had already provided himself with a new one, and a more prosperous and wealthy one than him he was going to leave. Rats always leave a falling house, and Brady was a real rat.

Still, however, though he did not expect to get much more from his service with Thady, he was, for his own reasons, anxious that his present master should not be quit of the companions with whom he had been so anxious to join him : and therefore when he found that he could no longer work on his master's mind by the arguments he had hitherto used, he began to threaten him—telling him of the different perils from the law which he would have to encounter by having joined the party, and various dangers to which he would subject himself by deserting it. But in vain—Thady was firm ; and when Pat got violent and inclined to be impertinent on the subject, he told him that he would knock him down with the alpine in his hand if he said another word about it.

On Sunday, Thady went to mass, and afterwards took a walk with his friend the priest, who said everything he could to raise his spirits, and to a certain degree he did so. On the next morning, as he was going to his work, a messenger brought a letter from Keegan to his father. This was a legal notice on Flannelly's part, that on some day in November, which was named, he—Flannelly—would require not only the payment of the interest money which would then be due, but also the principal ; and in this notice was set forth the exact sum to be paid for principal, for interest, for costs ; and it further stated that if the sum was not paid on or before that day, writs would be issued for his body—that is, the body of poor Larry Macdermot—and latitats, and sheriff's warrants, and Heaven knows what besides, for selling the property at Ballycloran; and that the mortgage would be immediately foreclosed, and the property itself disposed of for the final settlement of the debt.

This agreeable document was very legibly addressed to Lawrence Macdermot, Esq., etc. etc. etc., Ballycloran; and its unusual dimensions and appearance made Thady at once feel that it was some infernal missile come still further to harass him, and leave him, if possible, more miserable than it found him. However, such as it was, it was necessary that it should be read; so he took it to his father, and having broken the seal, said—

"Here's a letter from Keegan, Larry; shall I read it you?"

"D—n Keegan," was the father's consolatory reply, "I don't want his letters. I tell you he can't call for his money before November, and this is October yet."

"That's thrue," said Thady, when he had spelt through the epistle; "that's thrue, father; but this is to say that he manes to come in 'arnest, when that time comes."

"And don't he always come in 'arnest? is it in joke he comes, when he axes for a hundred pound every half year? come in 'arnest! why, d—n him, he's always in 'arnest!"

"But, father, it's not only the hundred pound now, but the whole debt he demands;" and, at last, Thady succeeded in reading the letter to his father.

Larry at first got into a violent passion, swearing fearfully at Keegan, and hinting that he, Larry, knew well enough how to take care of his own body; and that he, Keegan, might get more than he bargained for, if he came to meddle with it. After that he began to whimper piteously and cry, complaining that it was a most grievous thing that his own son should bring such a letter to him; and he ended by accusing Thady of leaguing with the attorney to turn him out of his own house, and even asked him whether, when they had effected their purpose, he and Keegan intended to live at Ballycloran together.

All this was not comfortable. Thady, however, quietly folded up the letter, put it in the old bureau, left his father to his pipe and his fireside, and went out again to his occupations.

Nothing new occurred at Ballycloran for a few days, and he began to flatter himself that Mrs. Mulready's boys and their threats would annoy him no more, and he was even thinking of sending Pat down to Drumleesh to notice the tenants again to come up with the rents, if it were only to see what steps they would then take. As he was returning home, however, on Friday evening, across the fields, a little after dusk, he saw the figure of a man standing in a gap through which he had to pass, and when he came close to him, he perceived it was Joe Reynolds.

Thady had been rather surprised that he had not seen Joe before, and had been inclined to think that that worthy gentleman had been intimidated, when he heard of his own defection ; but Joe was not a character so easily frightened. The truth was that he had for the last few days left his own cabin at Drumleesh, and had been engaged with others in the mountains which lay between Loch Sheen and Ballinamore, in making potheen in large quantities, and drinking no small portion of what they made. The morning after the wedding, he had been boasting to his comrades there of the success he had had in bringing over his landlord to their ranks ; and he had brought down a large party of them from that quarter, all sworn friends, to be present at his proposed initiation—and great was their wrath and loud were their threatenings when they found that Thady would not come. Joe had, however, been obliged to join them again at their business, and though he had heard the ill success of Brady's second attempt, he had not been able till now to try the effects of his own eloquence.

He had now come down for that purpose, and had been for the greater portion of the evening watching Thady, till he could get a good opportunity of talking to him undisturbed ; and he was now determined not to leave him, till he had used every means in his power of inducing him to change the resolution to which he had so suddenly come.

When Thady came close to him he respectfully raised his old battered hat, and said—

" Long life to ye, Mr. Thady ; I hope yer honer is finding yerself well this evening."

" Quite well, thank you, Joe," and Joe walked on with him a few steps.

"Have you the rint ready for me yet?" continued Thady.

"Rint is it? faix then I have not—not a penny; but it wasn't rint I was wanting to talk to your honer about just now; not but what the rint 'll be coming, and that right soon, Mr. Thady, and plenty too—if you'll only listen to me."

"Those 'd be glorious times, Joe, when the rint came that way," and Thady walked on faster, for he didn't want to prolong the conversation beyond what he could help.

"Stop, Mr. Thady; what are ye in sich a hurry for? I've come a long way to spake to you—and we'll both talk pleasanter av' you'd go a little aisier."

"Well, Joe, what is it, then? I'm in a hurry."

"In a hurry is it? but why wor ye in sich a hurry to break the promise you made us all, at Mrs. Mehan's, Thursday night week past? Ah! Mr. Thady, you worn't in a hurry when you said you'd come down and be one of us at Mohill—ay! and swore it too on the blessed cross; you worn't in sich a hurry then, and what hurries you now so fast?"

"Now, Reynolds, it's no use you're saying more of that. I sent you word by Pat that I wouldn't come, and I won't—so there's an end of it."

"But that an't an end of it; no, nor nigh the end of it; I suppose, Mr. Thady,"—and he paused, and, resuming his respectful tone, said, "and didn't you say you niver had deserted us and niver would, and that you'd always stick to us that you've known so long? Shure,

Mr. Thady, you'll not change your mind now."
And Reynolds paused in the little path they
were walking in, and Thady was obliged to
stand too, for Reynolds had got before him,
and he couldn't pass unless he pushed the
man aside. "And shure—do you mane to let
Keegan off, and Ussher, the black ruffian, that
way? do you intend to put up with everything
from the likes of them? Come, Mr. Thady,
say the word—only say the word you swore
before, and by the holy cross you swore on,
before next week is over Keegan shall be put
where he'll never spake another bad word, or
do another bad deed."

"Come, Reynolds, out of this, and let me
pass," said Thady, perceiving that he must now
absolutely make the man understand that he
was not to be talked over, "out of that, and
let me pass. And I'll tell you what, I'll not
have my neck in danger; and if I hear you
threatening murdher, I'll have you before the
magisthrates," and he pushed by the man, who,
however, still walked close behind him.

"And is that the way with you now? Have
me before the magisthrates will you? and
where'd you be all the time? Why, there's not
one of them that was in it, at Mrs. Mehan's
that night, but could have you before the magisthrates, and I'm thinking thim folk would make
a deal more of you than they would of me. Av
you talk of magisthrates, Mr. Thady, may be
you'll find there's too many of them in the
counthry for yerself."

Thady walked on fast, but did not answer
him, and Reynolds continued—"Come, Mr.

Thady, I don't intend to anger you, or affront you; and av I've said anything that way, I axes your pardon; but just answer me—will you come down there only for once, av it wor only becase you swore it afore them all on the holy cross?"

"No, Joe, I will not; av I took any oath at all, I was dhrunk: besides, I said I wouldn't, and I won't; so now good night."

"But, Mr. Thady, av you'd only come there to tell the boys so themselves, it would be all right. Shure you're not afeard to trust yerself among them."

"Not a foot, Joe."

"Well, then, I tell you, you'll be sorry; not that I'd say a word agin you myself, becase though you've ill-trated me now, you wor always a kind landlord, and becase it's not in your heart to hurt a poor man; but I tell you, and you'll find it comes thrue enough, there were them there that night at Mrs. Mehan's as will turn agin you, unless you do as I'm axing you now."

"Well, Joe, I can't help it if they do, so good night."

They had now come to a lane, and as Thady was going to jump on the bank to get over, Joe put his hand on his coat.

"One more word, yer honer, may be yet you'll change your mind."

"Indeed, I shall not, then."

"May be you will, and I'm thinking when you find Keegan too hard on you it'll come to that. Well, av you do, let me know, and I'll make it all right for you. Just tell Corney Dolan, and he's still at Drumleesh, that you're wanting me, and I won't be far off."

Thady did not answer him, but merely saying, " Good night, Joe," jumped into the road, and Joe by some devious path, through bogs and bottoms, betook himself to Mrs. Mulready's, and drowned the feeling of his ill success in whiskey.

Thady went home to his dinner or supper—rather glad that he had had the interview, for the man's manner was not so insolent as he had expected it would be ; and he now felt tolerably confident that he should not again be solicited to keep the unfortunate promise which he had made.

His father, however, was still muttering over the misfortunes which he was doomed to bear from the hands of his own son. Thady took all the pains he could, and all the patience he could muster, to prove to the old man that he was only desirous to do the best he could for him and Feemy. He had even told him that he had absolutely quarrelled and come to blows with the attorney, on the day of his visit ; but it was all in vain, and when he got himself to bed he was puzzled to think whether Keegan and Ussher, or his father and Feemy, caused him most trouble and unhappiness.

CHAPTER XIX

THE RACES

ALTHOUGH we have hitherto only seen Ussher as a guest at Ballycloran, or figuring as a lion at Mary Brady's wedding, he was, nevertheless, in the habit of frequenting much better society, and was not unfrequently a guest at the houses of certain gentlemen in the neighbourhood of Carrick-on-Shannon.

For Ussher could assume the manners of a gentleman when he chose, and moreover, be a lively and agreeable companion; and this, perhaps, quite as much as the attribute, made him somewhat of a favourite among many of the surrounding gentry. He was, however, more intimate at Brown Hall than at any other house; and he had now been asked over there, to spend the few days previous to his final departure from County Leitrim.

The establishment at Brown Hall consisted of Jonas Brown, the father—an irritable, overbearing magistrate, a greedy landlord, and an unprincipled father—and his two sons, who had both been brought up to consider sport their only business; horses and dogs their only care; grooms and trainers the only persons worthy of attention, and the mysteries of the field and the stable the only pursuits which were fit to be cultivated with industry or learnt with precision. They could read, as was sufficiently testified by their intimate knowledge of the information

contained in " Nimrod upon Horses,"*and the
Veterinary Magazine ; and the Clerk of the
Course at the Curragh could prove that they
could write, by the many scrawls he had received from them—entering horses, and giving
their particulars as to age, colour, breeding,
qualifications, etc., but beyond this they had
no acquirements. For the elder son, who was
only intended to be a landlord and a magistrate,
and to spend about a thousand a-year, this did
not signify ; but for the younger it afforded but
a melancholy prospect, had his eyes been open
to see it.

For the estate, which was all set at a rack
rent,* was strictly entailed*; and as Jonas had
always lived beyond his income, there would be
little to leave to a younger son. When their
mother died the two young men, together with
a sister, had been left to the father's care. She
also had learnt to ride, and ride hard—to go to
the stable and see that her own horse was made
up—and to rate her groom in no gentle terms,
if things in that department were not as they
should be. She also could be eloquent on
thrush, sandcracks, and overreaches — could
detect a splint or a spavin* at a glance—knew
all the parts and portions and joints of a
horse much more accurately than she did of a
sheep, and was a thorough judge of condition.
Rumour also not unfrequently hinted, among
the tabbies* of Carrick-on-Shannon, that Miss
Julia could not only ride with her brothers in the
morning, but that she was also occasionally not
ill inclined to drink with them of an evening.

Things were in this state, when it occurred

to Jonas and his favourite son Fred, that it were well for all parties if they could get Miss Julia off from Brown Hall, as there was reason to fear she was coming out a little too fast; and that if they did not get rid of her now, she might in a short time become a card somewhat hard to play. They consequently invited a squireen*of three or four hundred a-year to the house, who had rather unequivocally expressed his admiration for Di Vernon*; and under the fostering auspices of father and brother, the two soon made up matters together, though the lady was unable to follow her prototype's example, by wooing her lover over the pages of Dante. However, though Dante was wanting, opportunity was not, which for one so well inclined as Miss Julia was sufficient; and before the young gentleman had been three weeks in the house, Fred was enabled to hint to him one day, as he was pulling off his boots before dinner, that of course he presumed his intentions to his sister were honourable and explicit, now that things had gone so far. Toby Armstrong—for such was the name of Di Vernon's admirer—not relishing pistols and coffee, made no objection to the young lady; but he absolutely refused to take her empty handed, and, in consequence, Jonas and Fred had to hand him over their joint bond for two thousand pounds, before he would be induced to make her mistress of Castle Armstrong. There she now reigned supreme, and it is to be hoped, for the sake of the future generation, that she had by this time learnt to transfer her attention from the stable to the nursery.

The Browns were at any rate quit of the young lady, and had Brown Hall now wholly to themselves; and this was a satisfaction. Still, the hundred a-year which they had to pay their dear brother-in-law, Toby, was a great loss to them, and made it more improbable that when the old man should be gathered to his fathers, George should have anything to subsist on except his brother's affection and bounty.

As Fred inherited all his father's love of money, joined to an irresistible passion for everything that he called pleasure; and as he was already continually quarrelling with his younger brother, who was as continually impertinent to him, George's prospect in life was not particularly bright. As to turning his mind to any useful pursuit—studying for any profession, or endeavouring in any way to earn his own bread honestly—he would have been as angered and felt as insulted by such a proposition, as though any one had asked him to turn cobbler, and sit cross-legged at the window of one of the little shops at Carrick-on-Shannon.

As, however, he at present had food to eat, wine to drink, horses to ride, and usually cash to bet with, he concerned himself but little for the future; and we, therefore, may fairly be equally apathetic respecting it. It would not, however, be difficult to foretell his fate. Should he not break his neck before his father's death, he will quarrel with and slander his brother; he will ride for those who are young and green enough to trust their horses to him, and pay him for mounting them; he will spunge upon

all his acquaintance till he is turned out of their
houses; he will be a hanger on at the Curragh
and all race-courses; he will finally become
a blackleg and swindler; and will die in the
Marshalsea,* if he does not, as he most probably
will, break his neck by a fall from the saddle;
for, to the last, George will preserve his pluck—
the only quality on which he could ever pride
himself.

On the morning of the races the two brothers
and Ussher were sitting over a very late breakfast at Brown Hall. The father had long since
been out; careful to see that he got the full
twelve hours' work from the unfortunate men
whom he hired at five pence a-day, and who
had out of that to feed themselves and families,
and pay their rent; we will not talk about
clothing them, it would be a mockery to
call the rags with which the labouring poor
in that part of the country are partially covered,
clothes, or to attach value to them, though
I suppose they must once have cost something.

"Why, what nonsense, Ussher," said Fred,
"to be sending that mare of yours down to
Munster; she'd never be fast enough for that
country—not the thing at all for 'Tipperary
fences—all gaps and breaks; besides the expense of sending her, and the chances that she's
lamed on the road. You'd better let me have
her; she's only fit for this country. I'll tell you
what I'll do: I'll give you the horse and gig
you're to take that girl of yours to Longford in
to-morrow for her."

" Hush, man, for G—d's sake ! If the servants

hear you talking that way, I'm dished. If it once got abroad about my taking her off, I'd have the devil to pay before I got out of the country."

"I believe Ussher thinks," said George, "no one ran away with a girl before himself. Why, if you were going to seize a dozen stills, you couldn't make more row about it."

"I shouldn't make any about that, for it would come natural to me; and I'd a deal sooner be doing that, than what I have to do to-morrow night. I'm d—d, but I'd sooner take a score of frieze-coats, with only five or six of my own men to back me, than drive twenty miles in a gig with a squalling girl."

"If you're sick of the job, I'll take her off your hands," said the good-natured Fred.

"Thank ye, no; as I've got so far with it, I believe I'll go on now."

"Well, if you won't take a kind offer about the girl, will you take the one I made about the mare? To tell the truth, I'd sooner have the mare than the girl myself."

"Thank ye, no; I believe I'll keep both."

"I'll tell you what I'll do," said Fred, getting anxious in his hankering after the mare, "I'll throw the harness into the bargain—spick and span new from Hamilton's. I paid eight pound ten for it not a month since. All the new fashion—brass fittings and brass haines. You could have the crests taken out, and new ones put in, for a few shillings; only send me down the old ones."

"What would I do with a gig and horse? Besides, the gig's shook, the shafts are all loose, and the boxes are battered; and the horse was saying his prayers lately, by the look of his knees."

"Never down in his life, by G—d," said George, willing to help his brother in a matter of horseflesh; "it's only a knock he got when I was trying to put him over the little wall beyond the lawn there; but I couldn't make the brute jump, though he's the sweetest horse in harness I ever sat behind." ·

Ussher was not to be done; and Fred consoled himself by assuring him that he'd be sorry for it, when he found the mare was not the least use in life down in Munster, and that no one would give him a twenty-pound note for her.

A drag now came round to the door. George was making his toilet before the fire, having eaten about half an ounce of dry toast after his morning exercise under the three great-coats. He was adjusting his boots and breeches—and George was not a little proud of his appearance in his riding costume; the jacket and cap were carried loose; and after many exclamations from Fred, that they would be late, and that as he had backed Conqueror, it was a shame for his brother to give the stewards the chance of starting the horses without him, which were answered by rejoinders from George that they wouldn't dare to do so—showing that he didn't care how much all the rest might be inconvenienced by his delay, so long as he didn't suffer himself, the three got into the conveyance at the door, about an hour after the time at which the horses were advertised to start punctually; and Fred drove them to the course, which was not above a mile distant.

I cannot say that the ground displayed much that was elegant in the way of equipages, or anything very refined in the countenances belonging to the race-course.

The weighing stand consisted of the scales in which potatoes and oats were usually weighed in the market-place in Carrick, and were borrowed from the municipality for the occasion. The judge's chair was formed of a somewhat more than ordinary high stool, with a kind of handle sticking up at one corner, by holding on to which he was barely able to keep his place, so constantly were the mob pressing round him.

There was a stand, from which a tolerable view of the race could be obtained, admission one shilling; but few ascended it, and long before the start, the price had fallen to sixpence.

There were two or three carriages; one containing Counsellor Webb's family. He himself was one of the stewards, and, consequently, appeared on horseback in a red coat. Another belonged to Sir Michael Gipson, who owned the greater part of the town, and who drawing about six thousand a-year from this county and the next, had given ten pounds, to be run for by farmers' horses, contriving thereby to show them that he thought they ought to indulge in expensive amusements, and to stimulate them to idleness and gambling. As, however, the land in the country was chiefly let in patches under twenty acres each, and to men who were unable to feed the sorry beast necessary to keep them in tillage, Sir Michael's generosity had not the effect which it might be presumed to cause; and his ten pound was annually won by some large tenant, who might call himself a farmer, but who would make a desperate noise if another man presumed to call him anything but a gentleman. Of cars there were plenty, crowded with pretty faces, all evidently intending to be pleased; not invariably, however, for there was Mrs. Keegan in one of those altogether abominable affairs called inside cars, not because you had any of the comforts of an inside place in case of rain, for they have no covering, but because the inmates, sitting on each side, have full power to kick each other's shins, and no liberty to stretch their legs. There she sat alone, as sour as at the moment when she had first seen her Hyacinth as he was deposited by the hotel waiter on the mat inside her hall door.

She looked little as if she was there for amusement, and, in truth, she was not. After a time, Hyacinth had come to himself; and by dint of continual scolding, much soda-water, and various lavations, he had enabled himself to make a very sickly appearance on horseback; but the wife of his bosom was determined that he should not escape from thence to another ordinary, or even to any hospitable table where he might get drunk for nothing; and, consequently, she was there to watch him.

There was but one other there that did not seem bent on enjoyment, and this was poor Feemy. There she was, sitting on the same side of the car with Lyddy McKeon; and the good-natured mother had taken care that this should be the side facing the horses; but Feemy took no interest in them. She had given over crying and sobbing; but she was silent, and apparently sullen, and would much have preferred her own little room at Ballycloran.

There were to be three races. Had there been a prospect of thirty, and among them a trial of speed between all the favourites of the Derby, there could not have been a greater crowd, or more anxiety; every ragged, bare-footed boy there knew the names of each horse, and to whom he belonged, and believed in the invincibility of some favourite beast,—probably from attachment to its owner,—and were as anxious as if the animals were their own. Among this set, McKeon or little Larry Kelly were booked to win;—they were kind, friendly masters, and these judges thought that kind men ought to have winning horses.

"Shure thin," said one half-naked urchin, stuck up in a small tree, growing just out of one of the banks over which the horses were to pass; "shure thin, Playful's an illigant swate baste entirely. I'll go bail there's nothin'll come nigh her this day!"

"That Tony may win the day thin!" said another. "It's he is the fine sportsman."

"Bedad, ye're both out," said a third, squatting as close on the bank as the men would let him; "it's Mr. Larry'll win, God bless him!—and none but him—and he the weight all wid him, and why not? There's none of 'em in the counthry so good as the Kellys. Hoorroo for the Kellys! them's the boys."

"They do say," said the second speaker, who was only halfway up the tree, "that Conqueror 'll win. By Jasus, av he do, won't young Brown be going it!"

"Is it Conqueror?" said the higher, and more sanguine votary of McKeon. "Is it the Brown Hall horse? He can't win, I tell ye! I saw him as Paddy Cane was leading him down, and he didn't look like winning; he hasn't got it in him. That he may fall at the first lep, and never stir again! Tony'll win, boys! Hurroo for Tony McKeon."

The weighing was now accomplished, and jockeys mounted. Major McDonnell had to look after this part of the business, of which he knew as much as he did of Arabic. However, he was shoved about unmercifully for half an hour—had his toes awfully trodden on, for he was told he should dismount to see the weighing—narrowly escaped a half-hundred-weight, which was dropped within three inches of his foot, and did, I dare say, as much good as stewards usually do on such occasions.

Counsellor Webb was to start them, and, though a counsellor, he was an old hand at the work. He always started the horses at the Carrick races, and usually one of his own among the lot. The Counsellor, by-the-by, was a great favourite with all parties, and what was more, he was a good man and a gentleman.

Major Longsword from Boyle was the third steward, and he, like his military colleague, was rather out of his element. He was desired to keep the populace back and preserve the course; but it seemed to Major Longsword

that the populace didn't care a button for him
and his red coat, and though he valiantly
attempted to ride in among men, women, and
children, he couldn't move them; they merely
pushed the horse back with their hands, and
the brute, frightened by their numbers, wouldn't
go on. They screamed, "Arrah, sir! go asy;
shure you're on my foot; musha*thin, can't you
be quiet*with the big horse? faix I'm murdhered
with you, sir,—is you going to ride over us?
shure, yer honer, won't you go over there?
look how the boys is pressing in there." The
Major soon saw he could do no good, so he
rode out of the crowd, mentally determining
that the jockeys might, if they could, clear the
course for themselves.

And now they were off—at least seven of
them; for when the important morning came,
the Captain had in vain used every exertion
to get a rider for Kickie-wickie. His ambition
had at first soared so high that he had determined
to let no one but a gentleman jockey mount
her; but gradually his hopes declined, and at
the ordinary he was making fruitless inquiries
respecting some proper person; but in vain,
and now he had been from twelve to one
searching for any groom in possession of the
necessary toggery. He would have let the
veriest tailor in Carrick get on his mare if he
had merely been legitimately dressed. Really,
his exertions and his misery were distressing,
for at last he was obliged to send her back to
Boyle, after having paid the stakes and the
stable charges for her, and console himself
by telling his friends that the gentleman from

Galway, who was to ride for him, had deceived him, and that he could not possibly have put any one he did not know upon Kickie-wickie.

But the seven are off. There they go, gently cantering, looking so pretty, and so clean—the riders so steady—the horses so eager. How different they will look when three or four, or more probably only two, are returning to the post! The horses jaded, the men heated, with whip speedily raised, and sharply falling—spurs bloody—and jackets soiled, by perhaps more than one violent fall; and yet in ten minutes this will be their appearance.

"There they go—Hurroo! they're off. Faix, there's Playful at her tricks already—by dad she'll be over the ropes! steady, Bob—steady, or she'll back on you—give it her, Gayner, my boy, give it her, never spare her—laws! did you see that? Well, if he gets her over the course, he'd ride the very divil. Well done, Bob, now you've got her—Hurroo, Tony, my boy, you're all right now:"—and the mare, after a dozen preliminary plunges, joined the other horses. "Faix, they're all over that—did you see that big brown horse? He's Thunderer—he's a good horse intirely; did you see the lep he took at the wall?"—and now they had come to a big drain; all the horses being well together as far as this, excepting Crom-a-boo, who having been forced through a breach made by some other of the horses in the first wall, had baulked at a bank which came next, and never went any further. Some one told poor Stark on the course that the horse didn't run to-day nearly so well as his owner did last night; and it was true enough.

"There goes Conqueror—he's over! Faith then, George is leading.—Brown Hall against the field!"

"Never mind," said some knowing fellow, "he's a deal too fond of leading—he's a deal oftener seen leading than winning."

"There's little Larry—my! how sweet the mare went over the water. There's Brickbat in it;—no, he's out. He's an awkward beast. That's Thunderer—Holy Virgin, what a leap! He goes at everything as if there were twenty foot to cross, and a six-foot wall in the middle."

"There's Playful at it again—he'll never get her round. Bad cess to you, you vixen—what made me bet on you? There, she's over—no, she's not;—there's Diana—did you see Pat walk her through? Faith, she'd crawl up a steeple, and down the other side. There's Playful over—no, she's not;—right in the middle, by heavens!"

"And Bob under her—come away. My God, he'll be drowned!"

"Gracious glory! did you see that? He's up again;—d—n it but he dived under her; well, I never saw the like of that; she's out."

"And look, look! Bob's in the seat—you'll win your money now. Well, Bob Gayner, afther that you'll never live till you're drowned! Come away to the double ditch; that's where they'll show what they're made of—the mare'll be cooled now, and she'll run as easy as a coach-horse."

And the two rode away to the big fence mentioned, which consisted of a broad flat-topped bank between two wide dry ditches ; while the horses went the round of the course over four or five intermediate banks.

" Here they come ! there's Blake leading. What a stride that horse has ! but you'll see he'll die away now. Larry's second—no, George is second, but Larry's well up."

" Faith, and he's been down too—he and the mare. There's Playful, how she pulls—where's Brickbat ? now then ! "

And the Galway horse came at the big fence —Blake pulling him off a little as he came to it, then stuck his spurs into his horse's flank—gave a lift at his head, and threw his left hand to the tree of the saddle. The horse gave a terrific leap on the bank—paused for a moment—and clearing the second ditch, came down safe on his legs with a shock that seemed to shake the field.

" Hurroo ! well done ! beat that, George— now for Brown Hall ; no, by Jasus, little Larry's next,—now, Larry, the Virgin send you safe over ! " The mare with the light weight on her back made nothing of what seemed in the horse so tremendous a jump, and without losing her running, skimmed on to the bank and off it, and collared the horse before he had regained his stride.

" Good luck to you, Masther Larry, it's you that can ride. Hurroo for the Kellys !—Oh, by the holy, they're both dead ! " This last exclamation referred to Conqueror, who had come up to the fence much heated, but at a great pace. George, never attempting to pull him off, or give him a moment of breath, using his whip and riding forward over his horse's neck, hurried him on. The gallant brute leapt with all his force, but not being able to master the height, breasted it violently, sending his rider a dozen feet into the next field, and falling himself into the ditch, his head on to the field, with a broken heart, and dead! George, however, was soon on his feet, for his head was hard and he was used to tumbling.

Before he was on his legs, however, up came Playful, awfully rushing, her neck out—her nose forward—her nostrils open—her eye eager—covered with foam, but showing no sign of fatigue, nor any further inclination to baulk. Gayner was sitting her beautifully, not attempting to hold her, for he knew that if he stopped her, whipcord wouldn't make her run again; but with a firm, steady pull on her mouth—his hands low, and both on the reins, and his legs well tucked in. There she came, on at the leap without easing her pace for a moment, and going over the carcass of the dying animal, cleared it all, bank and ditches, at one leap—two and thirty feet at one stride! There are the marks to this day, for Tony McKeon, in his pride, measured the ground, and put in stakes to point out the spot where his mare showed herself so worthy of all his trouble.

Brickbat had quarrelled with some of his namesakes at a wall, and was now nowhere; Diana still persevered, and got well over the big fence, but her chance was out, unless some unaccountable accident happened to the three other horses that were still running. On they went; there were only three more fences, two

small banks, and a five-foot wall. Thunderer
and Miss Fidget neck and neck took the two
banks, the big horse making awfully high leaps
at them, Playful nearing them at every stride,
galloping over the banks as though they were
but a part of the level field. Now for the wall.
"Now, Nicholas Blake, now, show them how
little they think of a five-foot wall in Galway.
Faith though, Larry's first—bravo, Roscommon!" He's over, and a couple of bricks only
falling show how lightly Miss Fidget touched it
with her hind feet; not so Thunderer; again
the horse made an awful leap, but the pace had
been too much for him, he struck the wall
violently with his knees, and, bursting through,
gave Blake a fall over his shoulders. Galway,
however, was soon in his saddle again, but
not before Bob was over, and had long passed
him.

And now there was a beautiful race in between
the two mares; and oh! how charmingly both
were ridden! But though Miss Fidget was
so favoured in weight, and had begun with the
lead, her elder rival collared her, and beat her
at the post by a head. "And why shouldn't
she win?" as Tony said in triumph to his
friends, "for hadn't she the dhrop in her?
wasn't she by Coriander, out of Pink, by High-
flyer? Of course she'd win—hadn't he known
it all the time?"

"That's all very well," said Larry, as he stood
with his saddle in his hand, waiting till Bob got
out of the scales, "it was only her d—d long
nose and neck that won after all, for I'll swear
my head was past the post before Bob's."

"Well, then, Larry, we'll make a case for the stewards, whether it's your head or the horse's the judge should go by."

"There's two of 'em," whispered Gayner, "wouldn't know if you were to ask 'em."

Thunderer came in third, and a couple of minutes afterwards, Diana ;—and Pat Conner, when he was laughed at as to his place, truly boasted that at any rate he was the only one that had been able to ride round the course without a fall.

The chief and most exciting race of the day being over, the more aristocratic of the multitude seemed with one accord to turn their attention to luncheon. The ladies began to unpack the treasures with which the wells of their cars had been loaded—cold hams—shoulders of mutton —pigeon pies—bottles of sherry—and dozens of porter soon made their appearance ; and pretty girls putting cork-screws and carving knives into the hands of their admirers, bid them work for their food before they ate. Woe betide the young man there who had no female friends on the course—no one to relieve the pangs of his hunger, or to alleviate that intolerable delay which seems always necessary between races.

Then were made engagements for the ball ; quadrilles and waltzes were given in exchange for sandwiches and ale—Lieutenants were to be had for sherry—a glass of champagne would secure a Captain.

Great was the crowd round Mrs. McKeon's car, and plentiful the partners who solicited the honour of dancing with Lyddy, Louey, and

Feemy. McKeon was there in all his glory,
shaking hands with every one—praising his
mare with his mouth full of ham, and uttering
vehement eulogiums on Gayner between the
different tumblers of porter, which in his joy he
seemed to swallow unconsciously. Then Bob
came up himself, glowing with triumph, for he
knew that he had acquitted himself more than
ordinarily well. He had changed all his clothes,
for he had been completely drenched by his fall
in the brook; and now, having nearly altogether
fasted for the last forty-eight hours, was not at all
disinclined to assist at Mrs. McKeon's banquet.

He shook hands with her, and all the three
girls round, and with Tony—although he had
already done that three times before; and he
began a full history of the race, which we needn't
repeat.

"I knew Brickbat was as fat as a bullock; he
couldn't keep the pace up; but I'll tell you
what, Tony, if any horse there could beat
Playful, it was Conqueror. But George can't
wait—I win fifteen pound from him—he's made
a bad thing of it—lost his horse and all."

"Did you see the horse, Bob, when you came
to the big ditch?"

"By my honour, then, I didn't see anything
from the time I got out of the brook. I'd
enough to do to sit where I was, and keep
the mare's head straight. When she made the
great leap, I hardly felt her feet come to the
ground, she came down so lightly."

While he was speaking, Ussher came up to
the car, and began congratulating them. He
had now openly stated that he was to leave

the country altogether, and that he had been ordered to Cashel. Mrs. McKeon was therefore no longer at a loss to account for Feemy's melancholy; and whilst she felt a cordial dislike to the man, who she thought had so basely deceived Feemy and was now going to desert her, she was heartily glad for her sake he was going, and reflected that as he was to be off to-morrow, it was useless for her now to begin to be uncivil to him.

"I'm glad to congratulate you, Mr. McKeon —I'm glad you won, as my friend Brown didn't; a bad thing his losing his horse, isn't it?"

"Thank ye, Captain; and I'm to congratulate you too. I hear you're promoted, and going away from us—very glad for one, sorry for t'other. Take a bit of cold pie; d—n it, I forgot—the pie's all gone, but there's cold mutton and plenty of sherry. Lyddy, give Captain Ussher a glass of sherry."

And Ussher went round to the side of the car where Feemy was sitting, and shook hands with her and the other girls. It was the first time through the whole long morning he had come near her; indeed, it was the first time he had seen her since his short visit at Mrs. McKeon's, and very cruel poor Feemy had thought such conduct. Yet now, when he merely came to speak a few words, it was a relief to her, and she took it actually for a kindness. She felt herself so fallen in the world— so utterly degraded—she was so sure that soon every one else would shun her, that she shuddered at the idea of his ill-treating or deserting her. He soon left her, having got an

opportunity of desiring her in a whisper to
dance the first quadrille with him, as he didn't
think he should remain late at the ball.

As for Ussher himself, he would now have
been glad if he had been able to have got rid of
Feemy altogether. As I said before, when he
started for Ballycloran on the day that he heard
he had to remove his quarters, he had by no
means made up his mind as to what he would
do : it was not at that time at all his purpose to
induce Feemy to leave her home, or go with him
in the scandalous manner he had at last proposed. It was the warmth of her own affection,
and the vanity which this had inspired, or rather
strengthened in his breast, that had at the
moment induced him to do so ; and now he
could not avoid it. He had told his sporting
friends of his intention, and if even he could
have brought himself to endure their ridicule by
leaving her behind him, he had gone so far that
he could not well break off with Feemy herself.

He was considerably bothered, however, by
his position ; he felt that she would be a dreadful chain round his neck at the place he was
going to, and he began already to dislike her.
Poor Feemy! she had already lost that for
which she had agreed to sacrifice her pride, her
family, her happiness, and herself.

Ussher now returned to his two friends,
whose tempers were by no means improved
by the calamity which had occurred. Fred
declared it was all George's fault—that he had
ridden his horse too fast or too slow—that he
had been too forward, or not forward enough.
His temper was by far too much soured by the

loss of his own bets, to allow him to console his brother for the more serious injury he had suffered.

At length, however, the three got into the drag, and returned to Brown Hall. After dinner, each endeavoured to solace himself by no stinted application to the bottle. George declared, that as he had been able to drink nothing for the last three days, he'd make up for it now, and that he wouldn't allow himself to be disturbed to dress for the best ball that could be given in Ireland. Fred, however, was not so insatiable, and at about eleven he and Ussher dressed and again drove into Carrick.

The ball at Carrick passed off as such balls always do. There was but little brilliancy, but a great deal of good humour. The dresses were not the most costly, nor possibly the most fashionable, but the faces were as pretty, and the figures as good, as any that could be adorned for Almack's* by a Parisian head-dresser or milliner. The band was neither numerous nor artistic, but it played in good time, and never got tired. The tallow candles,* fixed in sconces round the walls of the room, in which a short time since we saw some of our friends celebrating the orgies of Bacchus, gave quite sufficient light for the votaries of the nimblefooted muse to see their partners, mind their steps, and not come in too rude collision with one another. Quadrilles succeeded waltzes, and waltzes quadrilles, with most unceasing energy; and no one dreamt of giving way to fatigue, or supposed that it was at all desirable to sit down for a single dance. From ten to two they kept it up

without five minutes' pause, and then went joy-
fully to supper—not to drink half a glass of
wine, and eat a mouthful of jelly or *blanc-manger*
standing—but to sit down with well-prepared
appetite to hot joints—ham and chicken, veal
pies, potatoes, and bottled porter. And then
the songs that were sung ! It would have done
your heart good to hear young Fitzpatrick sing
the "Widow Machree;"* and then all the
punch that was mixed ! and the eloquence that
was used, not in vain, to induce the fairer
portion of the company to taste it !

This state of things was not, however, allowed
to remain long. It was not at all the thing that
men—at any rate unmarried men—should waste
their time in drinking when they had come
there to dance ; and after the ladies had left
them about ten minutes, messages came hot
and thick from the ball-room, desiring their
immediate presence ; nor were they so bold as
to neglect these summonses, excepting some
few inveterate sinners, who, having whiskey and
hot water in their possession, and looking
forward to a game at loo,* neglected the commands which were brought to them.

Soon again the fiddles sounded, and quick
feet flew round the floor with more rapidity than
before. The tedium of the quadrille was found
to be too slow, and from three till six a succes-
sion of waltzes, reels, and country dances, kept
the room in one whirl of confusion, and at last
sent the performers home, not from a feeling
of satiety at the amusement, but because, from
very weariness, they were no longer able to use
their feet.

Feemy, early in the evening, had danced with Ussher, and received his final instructions respecting their departure on the morrow. He was to leave Brown Hall early for Mohill, and Fred's gig and horse were to be sent over to him there. He was to send his heavy luggage on by the car, and leaving Mohill about seven, when it would be dusk, drive by the avenue at Ballycloran and pick Feemy up as he passed, and they would then reach Longford in time for the mail-coach during the night.

Ussher calculated that Feemy would not be missed till he had had two hours' start, and that then it would be impossible to catch him before he reached Dublin.

"But, Myles," said Feemy, "how am I to get home? You know I am at Mrs. McKeon's now."

"Why, how helpless you are," replied he; "can't you easily make some excuse to get home? say you are ill—and sick—and want to be at home. Or if it must come to that, say you will go home; who's to stop you?"

"But I wouldn't like to quarrel with them, Myles; just now, too, when they've been so kind to me."

"Well, dearest, you needn't quarrel with them; say you're ill, and wish to be at home; but don't make difficulties, love; don't look so unhappy; you'll be as happy as the day is long, when we're once away—that is, if you still love me, Feemy. I hope, after all I'm doing for you, you'll not be sullen and cold to me because you're leaving such a hole as Ballycloran. If you don't love me, Feemy, say so, and you may stay where you are."

"Oh! Myles, how can you say such words now! you know I love you—how much I love you—else I wouldn't be leaving my home for you this way! And though Ballycloran is——"

Here the poor girl could say no more; for she was using all her energies to prevent herself from sobbing in the ball-room.

"Good G—d! you're not going to cry here; come out of the room, Feemy;" and he led her into the passage, where, under the pretence of looking at the moon, they could turn their faces to the window. "What are you crying for now?"

"Don't you know I love you? why else would I be going with you?"

"Well, don't cry then; but mind, I shan't see you again before the time, for I'm going out of this at once now. I shall be at the avenue at a quarter before eight; don't keep me waiting. If you are there first, as you will be, walk a few steps along the Mohill road, so as to meet me; no one will know you, if you should meet any one, for it will be nearly if not quite dark; the moon won't rise till past ten; do you understand, Feemy?"

"Oh, yes, I understand!"

"Well, good night then, my own love, for I must be off."

"But, Myles, I want to say one thing."

"Hurry then, dear, what is it?"

"What 'll I do about my things?"

"What things?"

"Why, Myles, I must bring some things with me; clothes, you know, and things of that sort."

This puzzled Ussher rather; he had considered that he should have enough trouble with Feemy herself; he had quite forgotten the concomitant evils of the bandboxes, bundles, and draperies which it would be necessary for Feemy to take with her.

"Ah! you can get clothes in Dublin; you can't want to take much with you; you can bring a bundle in your hand just that distance. Can't you, eh, Feemy?"

Feemy could not but think that a week since he would not have asked her to carry all her travelling wardrobe in a bundle, in her hand. However, she only said—

"Why, not well, Myles; I shall have so many things to think of; but I shan't have much, and if you'll let me, I'll send Biddy to meet you with what I must take. She'll meet you on the road, and put it into the gig."

"Good heavens! what do you mean? would you tell the girl what you're going to do? Why, she'll tell your father, and Thady, and raise the whole country on me."

"No, she wouldn't, Myles; she wouldn't tell anybody a word, when I told her not. You don't know those sort of people; she'd not say a word; so if you'll let me, I'll send her on to meet you with my things."

With a good deal of reluctance Ussher agreed to this; and then, again enjoining Feemy not to keep him and the gig waiting in the road, he took his leave, and departed, with his friend Fred, for Brown Hall; first of all taking Feemy into the refreshment-room, and making her drink a glass of sherry. This did her much

good, and when she got back into the ball-
room, she was able to dance with tolerable
spirit; and Mrs. McKeon, who had been
watching her, and had seen her dance with
Ussher, was glad to think that her *protegée* had
made up her mind to part with her lover in
good spirits, and before the evening was over
she assured Louey, with great glee, that, in
spite of all that had been said, she foresaw that
as soon as that horrid man had been gone
three or four days, Feemy would be as well and
as cheerful as ever.

Feemy was, nevertheless, very glad when she
was told to get her cloak on, and found herself
on the car going to Drumsna. She then told
her friend that she wanted to be home with her
father on the morrow,—that she had promised
to be home the day after the ball. She even
pretended that she had received a message that
evening from her father, begging her return.
Mrs. McKeon did not think much about it,
supposing that Feemy's presence might be
necessary for household purposes at Ballycloran, and she readily promised her the loan
of the car, at four in the afternoon, on condition
that she would return to Drumsna at least in
a day or two. This Feemy promised, rejoicing
that her expected difficulties as to getting to
Ballycloran were so easily overcome, and going
to bed, she slept more soundly than she had
yet done since she had given her fatal consent
to Ussher's proposal.

CHAPTER XX

HOW CAPTAIN USSHER SUCCEEDED

LATE the next morning, Feemy and the other girls got up; they had slept together to make room in the house for the victorious Bob, but, as Father John had prophesied, they were all too tired to be much inconvenienced by this. Immediately after breakfast the car came round, and Feemy, afraid to wish her friends good-bye too affectionately lest suspicion should be raised, and promising to come back again in a day or two, returned to Ballycloran.

Thady was out when she got there, but he was expected in to dinner. Her father was glad to see her, and began assuring her that he would do all in his power to protect her from the evil machinations of her brother, and then again took his grog and his pipe. She went into the kitchen, and summoning Biddy, desired her to follow her up to her bedroom. When there, she carefully closed the door, and sitting down on the bed, looked in her attendant's face and said—

"Biddy, if I told you a secret, you'd never betray me, would you?"

"Is it I, Miss Feemy, that's known you so long? in course I wouldn't," and the girl pricked up her ears, and looked all anxiety. "What is it, Miss?—Shure you know av you tould me to hould my tongue, never a word I'd spake to any mortial about anything."

"I know you wouldn't, Biddy; that's why I'm going to tell you; but you mustn't whisper it to Katty, for I think she'd be telling Thady."

"Niver fear, Miss; sorrow a word I'll whisper it to any one, at all at all."

"Well, Biddy, did you hear Captain Ussher's going away from this intirely?"

"What! away from Ballycloran?"

"No, but from Mohill, and from County Leitrim altogether. He's going a long way off, to a place called Cashel."

"And what for is he going there, and you living here, Miss Feemy?"

"That's the secret, Biddy; I'm going with him."

"My! and is you married in sacret, Miss?" said the girl, coming nearer to her mistress, and opening her eyes as wide as she could.

Feemy blushed up to the roots of her hair, and said, "No, we're not married yet; we're to be married in Dublin; we couldn't be married here, you know, because Captain Ussher is a Protestant."

"Holy Mary! Miss, you're not a going to lave the ould religion; you're not a going to turn Prothesthant, is you, Miss Feemy?"

"No, Biddy; why should I turn Protestant? but you see there's rasons why we couldn't be married here; we're to be married in Dublin, to-morrow."

"To-morrow!" ejaculated Biddy; "what, is you going to-night?"

"This very evening; and now I want you to help me, and when we're settled, Biddy, if you like to lave this ould place, I mane you to come and live with us."

"To be shure, Miss; and wouldn't I go the world round wid you? and why not? for it's you was always the kind misthress to me. But what'll I be doing to help you?"

And then Feemy explained to her her plans, and began to pack up the few treasures she could take with her, in a box small enough for Biddy to carry; and the two kneeled down together to the work.

Feemy's tears dropped quickly on the little things she was packing, and the poor girl soon followed the example her mistress gave her.

"Ochone! ochone! Miss Feemy, alanna, what'll we be doing widout you?" and she came round and began kissing her mistress's dress, and hands, and face, "What shall we do widout you at all then? what will the ould man be doing, when you're not to the fore to mix his punch?"

"Don't talk that way," said Feemy. "Shure, won't I be coming back to see him when I'm married?"

"In course you will; but it'll be a great miss, when he and Mr. Thady finds you're gone. What'll I say at all, when I come back from seeing you off—and they finds that you are gone?"

"But you mustn't stay to see me off at all. When you've put the box in the gig you must go on to Mrs. Mehan's, and when you come back you can say you'd been down to look for something that was left the day of Mary's wedding; but mind, Biddy, don't say a word about it at Mrs. Mehan's, and above all, don't mention it to Katty."

"Not a word, Miss; niver fear: but what'll I be doing when you're gone? But I suppose it's all for the best; may sorrow seize him thin av he don't make you the good husband."

It was then settled that Feemy's bonnet and shawl were to be brought down into the sitting-room opposite the dining-room—that dinner was to be put off as late as possible—that when Larry and Thady were at their punch, Feemy was to escape unobserved. Biddy was enjoined, when she slipped out with the box, to leave the front door ajar, so that her mistress could follow her without making any noise. The girl was also to carry down her mistress's cloak—so that she might the easier run down the avenue.

When these things were all settled, Biddy returned to the kitchen, big with the secret; but she was too prudent to say or hint anything which could create a suspicion in her colleague's breast.

Thady came in about the usual dinner-hour, and Feemy spoke good-humouredly to her brother—more so than she had done since the day he had desired her not to walk with Captain Ussher. Thady himself was less gloomy than usual, for he had been rejoiced by hearing that the revenue officer was immediately going to leave the country. He had only been told it that morning at Mohill, as a secret, and he therefore presumed that Feemy did not know it. He thought that he would not distress her by telling her of it now—that he had better leave her to find it out herself after he was gone; but the reflection of the misery it would occasion her when she did know it, gave rise to a feeling of pity for her in his heart, which made him more inclined to be gentle and tender to her than he had felt for a long time.

After sitting over the fire with their father for some time, Thady said—

"Well, Feemy, these are fashionable hours you've brought with you from Drumsna. Does Mrs. McKeon always dine as late as this? Why, it's half-past six !"

"The stupid girl forgot the potatoes, Thady. You could have them now; but you know, you wouldn't eat them as hard as stones. I'll go and hurry her."

"'Deed and I'm starving," said the father. "Why can't we have dinner then, Feemy dear? Why won't they bring dinner in ?"

And Feemy went out, not to hurry them, but to cause grounds for fresh delay. At last, a little after seven, she allowed dinner to go in, and following it herself, she sat down and made as good a meal as she could, and endeavoured to answer Thady's questions about the races and the ball with some appearance of having taken interest, at any rate in the latter. If she did not altogether succeed, the attempt was not so futile as to betray her; and the dinner passed over, and the hot water came in, without anything arising especially to excite her alarm. At last she heard the front door open, and she listened with apprehension to every creak the rusty hinges made as Biddy vainly endeavoured to close it without a noise; but the sounds, which, in her fear, seemed so loud and remarkable

to her, attracted no notice from her father or
brother. Then she mixed their punch. Had
Thady been looking at her he might have seen
a tear drop into the tumbler as she handed it
to him; but his eyes were on the fireplace, and
she slipped out of the room without her tell-tale
face having been observed.

It was now, as she calculated, about the time
that she should start; and with trembling hands
she tied on her bonnet. Having thrown her
shawl over her shivering shoulders, she opened
her book upon the table with a handkerchief
upon it—placed her chair by the fire, and leaving
the candle alight, slowly crept through the hall
door, down the front steps, and into the avenue
leading to the road. She shuddered when she
found herself alone in the cold dark air; but
soon plucking up her courage, she ran down as
quickly as she could to the spot where the old
gate always stood open, and leaning against the
post, listened intently for the sound of the gig
wheels. She stood there, listening for three or
four minutes, which seemed to her to be an
hour, and then getting cold, she thought she'd
walk on to meet Ussher as he had directed her;
but before she had gone a dozen yards the
darkness frightened her, and she returned. As
soon as she had again reached the gateway she
heard a man's footstep on the road a little
above; and still more frightened at this, she
ran back the avenue towards the house till the
footsteps had passed the gate. She did not,
however, dare again to stand in sight of the
road, though it was so dark that no one passing
could have seen her if she were a few yards up

the avenue; so she sat down on the stump of a
tree that had been lately felled, and determined
to wait till she heard the sound of the gig.

There she remained for what seemed to her
a cruelly long time; she became so cold that
she could hardly feel the ground beneath her
feet; and her teeth shook in her head as she
sat there alone in the cold night air of an
October night, with no warmer wrapping than
a slight shawl thrown over her shoulders. There
she sat, listening for every sound—longing to
catch the rattle of the wheels that were to carry
her away—fancying every moment that she
heard footsteps approaching, and dreading lest
the awful creak of the house-door opening
should reach her ears.

She could not conceive why Ussher did not
come—she had absolutely been there half an
hour, and she thought it must be past ten—she
had long been crying, and was now really suffering with bodily pain from cold and fright; and
then the whole of Ussher's conduct to her since
that horrid morning passed through her mind—
she saw things now in their true light, which
had never struck her so before. What would
she not have given to have been safe again at
Mrs. McKeon's; to have been in her own room,
of which she could still see the light through
the window; in fact, to be anywhere but where
she was? She did not dare, however, to return
to the house, or even again to walk down the
road. Poor, unhappy Feemy! she already felt
the wretched fruits of her obstinacy and her
pride.

At last she absolutely heard the front-door

pushed open, and could plainly see a man's figure standing on the threshold. It must be Thady! They had discovered her departure, and he was already coming to drag her back! She heard his feet descending the hall steps; but they were as slow and as deliberate as usual; and she could perceive that, instead of coming down the avenue, he turned towards the stables. This was a slight relief to her—it was evident she was not yet missed; but she was dreadfully cold, and what was she to do if Thady heard the noise of the gig, and perceived that it had stopped at their gate?

Ussher had driven over to Mohill early in the morning, and had gotten everything ready for his departure in the manner he had proposed; but when the time for starting came, he had been detained by business connected with his official duties, and it was eight o'clock before he was able to bid adieu to the interesting town of Mohill. He had then, at the risk of his own neck, driven off as fast as Fred Brown's broken-knee'd horse could take him, and was proceeding at a gallop towards Ballycloran, when he was stopped near Mrs. Mehan's well-known shop by Biddy, who was standing by the road-side opposite.

He stopped the horse as quick as he could, and Biddy came running to him with Feemy's bundle.

"Is that yer honer, at last? Glory be to God! but I thought you wor niver coming. The misthress'll be perished with the could."

"Never mind—hurry—give me what you've got!"

And Biddy handed in the bundle and cloak, and Ussher again drove on.

"Musha then, but he's a niggardly baste!" soliloquised Biddy, "not to give me the sign of a bit of money, after waiting there for him these two hours by the roadside, and me with his sacret and all, that could ruin him if I chose to spake the word, only I wouldn't for Miss Feemy's sake. But maybe it was the hurry and all that made him be forgitting, for he was niver the man for a mane action. I wish he may trate her well, that's all; for he's a hard man, and it's bad for her to be leaving the ould place without the priest's blessing."

Ussher was at the gateway; but when he got there, he could not see Feemy. He waited about a minute, and then whistled—a minute more, and he whistled again. What should he do? It would be so foolish now for him to go without her! He knew the horse was steady and would stand; so he got out and walked up the avenue till he saw the figure of Feemy, still sitting on the root of the tree where we left her. There was a light colour in her shawl, and the little white collar round her neck enabled him to see her at some distance; and she saw, or at any rate heard him, but she neither moved to or from him.

She had caught, some time since, the sound of the gig wheels; but just as she did so, she again saw the figure of Thady as he came round from the stables; and he evidently had heard it also, for he stood still on the open space before the house. He was smoking, for she caught the smell of the tobacco, and she plainly heard

the stones on the pathway rattle as he now
and then struck them with the stick in his
hand. He didn't move towards her ; but
there he stood, as if determined to ascertain whether the vehicle which he must have
heard would pass along the road by the
gate.

Then the sound ceased. It was when Biddy
was putting in it the cloak and bundle, and
again it continued closer and closer. The road
came round the little shrubbery through which
the avenue passed ; the gig was therefore at one
time even nearer to Feemy than it would be
when it stopped at the avenue gate ; and when
it passed this place, she fancied she could hear
Ussher moving in his seat. She did not dare
to stir, however, for there still stood Thady,
listening like herself to the sounds within forty
yards of her ; and had she risen he must have
seen her.

And now the gig stopped at the avenue gate.
Feemy was all but fainting ; what with the cold
and her former fear, and the dreadful position
in which she found herself, she could not have
moved if she had tried ; she just preserved her
senses sufficiently to torture her, and that was
all. Plainly she heard her lover whistle ; and
plainly Thady heard it too, for he kept his
stick completely still, and took the pipe from
his mouth : then the second whistle—then she
heard Ussher's foot on the ground—heard him
approaching, and saw his figure draw nearer ;
in vain she endeavoured to make signs to him,
in vain she thought she whispered, "keep back;"
for when she tried to speak, the words would

not come. On he came till he was close to her, and in a low voice he said—

"Feemy, is that you? why don't you come? what are you here for?" and he put down his hand to raise her. Feemy tried to rise and whisper something, but she was unable, and when Ussher stooped and absolutely lifted her from her seat, she had really fainted. "Come, Feemy," said he, still unaware of Thady being near, "come; this is nonsense—hurry, there's a love. Come, Feemy, stand, can't you?"

When Thady had first come out of the house, it had merely been for the purpose of going into the stable, as was his practice, to see the two farm horses fed; as he returned, he caught the sound of Ussher's gig; but it was more for the purpose of smoking his pipe in the open air than from any curiosity that he lingered out of doors. When, however, the vehicle stopped at Ballycloran gate, and he heard the whistle twice repeated, his interest was excited, and he thought that something was not right. He then heard Ussher's footsteps up the avenue, and he fancied he could hear him speak; but he had no idea who he was; nor had he the slightest suspicion that his sister was so near him.

But when Ussher stopped, Thady gently came down the avenue unperceived; he saw him stoop, and lift something in his arms, but still up to this time he had not recognised the voice. It was Thady's idea that something had been stolen from the yard, which the thief was now removing, under cover of the darkness. By degrees, as he got nearer, he perceived it was a woman's form that the man was half dragging, half carrying, and then he heard Ussher's voice say loudly, and somewhat angrily, "This is d—d nonsense, Feemy! you know you must come now."

These were the last words he ever uttered. Thady was soon close to him, and with the heavy stick he always carried in his hand, he struck him violently upon the head. Ussher, when he had heard the footsteps immediately behind him, dropped Feemy, who was still insensible, upon the path; but he could not do so quick enough to prevent the stunning blow which brought him on his knees. His hat partially saved him, and he was on the point of rising, when Thady again struck him with all his power; this time the heavy bludgeon came down on his bare temple, and the young man fell, never to rise again. He neither moved nor groaned; the force of the blow, and the great weight of the stick falling on his uncovered head as he was rising, had shattered his brains, and he lay as dead as though he had been struck down by a thunder-bolt from heaven.

Though it was so dark that Thady could not see the blood he had shed, or watch how immovable was the body of the man he had attacked, still he knew that Ussher was no more. He had felt the skull give way beneath the stroke; he had heard the body fall heavily on the earth, and he was sure his enemy was dead.

At first he felt completely paralysed, and unable to do anything; but he was soon aroused by a long sigh from poor Feemy. The cold had revived her, and she now regained her senses. Thady threw his stick upon the ground, and stooping to lift her up, said—

"Oh! Feemy, Feemy, what have you brought upon me!"

When she recognised her brother's voice, and found that she was in his arms, she said—

"Where am I, Thady? What have you done with him? Where is he?"

"Never mind now. He's gone—come to the house."

"Gone!—he's not gone; don't I know he would not go without me?" and then escaping from her brother's arms, she screamed, "Myles, Myles!—what have you done with him? I'll not stir with you till you tell me where he is!" and then the poor girl shuddered, and added, "Oh! I'm cold, so miserably cold!"

"Come to the house with me, Feemy;—this is no place for you now."

"I'll not go with you, Thady. It's no use, for you shan't make me; tell me what you've done with him—I'll go nowhere without him."

Thady paused a minute, thinking what he'd say, and then replied: "You'll never go with him now, Feemy, for Captain Ussher is dead!"

Feemy only repeated the last word after her brother, and again fell insensible on the ground.

Thady at length succeeded in getting her to the house; and pushing open the front door, which was still unlatched, with his foot, took her into her own room on the left-hand side of the passage, and deposited her still insensible on the sofa. He then went into the kitchen, and sent Katty to her assistance.

Pat Brady was sitting over the kitchen fire,

smoking. Though this man was still hanging about the place, and had not come to an actual rupture with his master, still there had been no cordiality or confidence between them since Brady had failed to induce Thady to keep his appointment at the widow Mulready's; and for the last two days not even a single word had passed between them. Now, however, there was no one else but Pat about the place, and Thady felt that he must tell some one of the deed that he had done. It would be useless to consult his father; his sister was already insensible; the two girls would be worse than useless; besides, he could not now conceal the deed; he could not leave the body to lie there on the road.

"Brady," said he, "come out; I want to spake to you. Is there a lanthern in the place at all?"

"No, Mr. Thady, there is not," said he, without moving; "what is it you want to-night?"

"Come out, and bring a lighted candle, if you can."

Brady now saw from his master's pale face, and fear-struck expression, that something extraordinary had happened, and he followed him with a candle under his hat; but the precaution was useless, the wind blew it out at once.

"Pat," said Thady, as soon as the two were out before the front door; "Pat," and he didn't know how to pronounce the thing he wished to tell.

"Good God! Mr. Thady, what's the matther? has anything happened the owld man?"

"What owld man?"

" Your father."

" No, nothing's happened him; but—but
Captain Ussher is dead ! "

" Gracious glory—no ! why, he was laving
this for good and all this night.   And how did
he die ? "—and he whispered in his master's
ear—" did the boys do for him ? "

" I killed him by myself," answered Thady,
in a whisper.

" You killed him, Mr. Thady ! ah ! now,
you're joking."

" Stop ! " said Thady—for they were now in
the avenue—" joking or not, his body is somewhere here ;—and he had Feemy here, dragging
her along the road, and I struck him with my
stick across the head, and now they'll say I've
murdhered him."

Brady soon touched the body with his foot ;
and the two raised it together, and put it off the
path on the grass, and then held a council
together, as to what steps had better be taken.

Brady, after his first surprise and awe at
hearing of Ussher's death was over, spoke of it
very unconcernedly, and rather as a good thing
done than otherwise.   He recommended his
master to get out of the way; he advised him
at once to go down to Drumleesh and find out
Joe Reynolds ; he assured Thady that the man
would even now be willing to befriend him and
get him out of harm's way.   He told him that
Reynolds and others had places up in the
mountains where he might lie concealed, and
where the police would never be able to find
him ; and that if he only got out of the way for
a time, it might probably not be found murder

by the Coroner, and that in that case he could return quietly to Ballycloran.

Thady listened sadly to Brady's advice, but he did not know what better to propose himself. He remembered the last words which Reynolds had said to him, and he made up his mind to go down at once to Corney Dolan's, who was a tenant of his own, and from him find out where Reynolds was.

"But, Pat," said Thady, when he had made up his mind to the line of conduct he meant to pursue, "what shall we do with the man's body? We can't let it lie here. As I trust in God, I had no thoughts to kill him! and I would not run away, and lave the body here, as though I'd murdhered him."

"Jist lay him asy among the trees, Mr. Thady, till you're out of the counthry; and then I'll find it,—by accident in course, and get the police to carry it off. Thim fellows is paid for sich work."

"No, Pat; that wouldn't do at all. I won't have them say I hid the body; every one 'll know 'twas I did it; mind, I don't ask you to tell a lie about it; and I'll not have it left here, as though I'd run away the moment afther I struck him. We must take him into the house, Brady."

"Into the house, yer honer! not a foot of it! Why, you'd have Miss Feemy in fits; and the owld man'd be worse still, wid all thim fellows coming from Carrick and sitting on the body, discoursing whether it wor to be murdher or not."

"Well, then; we'll take it to Mrs. Mehan's."

" Av you do, Mr. Thady, the country 'll have it all in no time. Howsomever, they must take it there if you choose, as it's a public ;* but you'd better lave it where it is, and let me send it down by-and-by—jist to give you an hour's start or so."

This Thady absolutely refused, stating that he would not leave the body till he had seen it deposited in some decent and proper place ; and the two men took it up between them and carried it away, meaning to take it to Mrs. Mehan's. But at the avenue gate they found Fred Brown's horse and gig, exactly where Ussher had left it, excepting that the horse was leisurely employed in browsing the grass from the ditch side.

Brady soon recognised both the horse and gig as belonging to Brown Hall ; and he then proposed putting the body of its former occupant in it, and driving it to the station of the police at Carrick-on-Shannon, and restoring at the same time the horse and gig to its proper owner at Brown Hall. To this scheme Thady at last agreed ; but he made the man promise him, that when he got to the police at Carrick he would tell them that he, Thady, had desired him to do so ; and that, instead of running away, he had not left the body till he had seen it put into the vehicle, to be carried into Carrick-on-Shannon. And with these injunctions Brady departed with his charge.

CHAPTER XXI

THE CORONER'S INQUEST

DURING the short time that elapsed between
the heavy blow which had occasioned Ussher's
death, and the departure of Pat Brady with the
gig, a great many thoughts had passed through
Thady's mind, although he had been in action
the whole time. His first idea had certainly
been that Ussher was carrying off Feemy against
her will; the last words which Ussher had
spoken before his death, and which were the
only words of his that Thady had heard,—
" This is d—d nonsense; you know you must
come now,"—certainly were calculated to make
him think so. But he soon reflected that had
this been so, Feemy could not have been sitting
alone in the place where Ussher found her;
besides, her own conduct when she came to
herself disproved it. Feemy had therefore
evidently been a consenting party. Still, however, he thought that he could not but be justified in doing what he had done in his sister's
defence, even though his interference was in
opposition to her wishes. Then he thought of
the man himself, whom he had known so long,
seen so frequently, and hated so bitterly. There
he was now—dead—a cold corpse—entirely
harmless, and unable to injure him or his more.
But Thady already felt his enemy's blood heavy
on his conscience, and he would have died

himself to see him rise on his feet. Thoughts
as to his own safety crowded on his mind; he
felt that if he intended boldly to justify the
deed, he should himself declare what he had
done—see that the body was properly taken
care of—and give himself up at once to the
police. As to the fact of his having killed the
man, that he had declared to his sister before
he had at all thought what his conduct ought to
be, and he had done the same to Brady; it was
useless for him therefore to attempt to conceal
it, even if he had wished to do so. But he felt
afraid to give himself up to the police; he
abhorred the idea of what he thought would
be the disgrace of being in confinement; and
instead of going, as he at first thought to have
done, at once to Father John, and telling him
all that had happened, he listened to Brady's
traitorous advice, and determined to take himself, at any rate for a time, to the fancied
security of Joe Reynolds and his haunts.

After Brady had departed he stood on the
road, till he could hear no longer the sound of
the retreating wheels, and while standing there
determined he would not leave the place, for
the last time perhaps, till he had told his father
what had happened, and ascertained whether
Feemy had recovered. He reflected that it
would be a dreadful thing for her to tell her
father and the servants, and to be called on to
explain why her brother was away; having made
this resolution he walked again up to the house.

He pushed the door open, and at once went
into his sister's room. Here she was still lying
on the sofa, and Katty was sitting beside her—

begging her mistress to tell her what was the matter. But Feemy had not spoken since she had been there; she had recovered her senses, for she held her hands before her eyes, and the tears were falling fast beneath them : but she had not spoken a word to Katty since her brother had placed her on the sofa.

When he entered the room she uncovered her eyes for a moment ; but as soon as she saw him she buried her face in the pillow, and it was plain from her sobbing that she was crying more violently than before.

Thady walked up to the sofa, and as he did so the girl got up.

"Go out, Katty," said he, "I want to spake a word to your misthress, but be in the kitchen ; I'll call you when I've done."

She retreated,—not, however, farther than the door, which she closed, and left the brother and sister together. The last time they had been so in that room—the last time the two had conversed alone together before, was when Thady cautioned his sister against the man he just now killed ; he thought of this, but he was too generous to let the reflection dwell on his mind at such a moment.

"Feemy," he said, as he attempted to take his sister's hand—which, however, she violently drew back from him—"Feemy, I'm going to lave you a long time, and I must spake to you first,—perhaps the last words I'll ever be able to say to you at all. Feemy darling, won't you listen to me, then ?—eh, Feemy ?"

Feemy, however, only buried her head further in the sofa, and did not answer him a word.

"I must spake a word to you," continued Thady, "about him that is now—him that was with you on the avenue. I told you, Feemy, he was dead, and what I told you then was only too true. God knows when I struck him I did not wish for that; but how was I to see him with you in his arms—carrying you off through the dark night, and from your own house, without raising my stick to strike him? I don't say this to be blaming you now, and I don't ask you to tell me why you were there; but you must know, dearest, that it was for your sake I raised my hand; and though the blow I struck has killed him you loved, you shouldn't now at such a moment turn from your brother, who has brought all this upon himself only to protect your honer and your name."

Still Feemy did not turn her face towards him, or answer him.

"Well! I know what's on your heart, and may be it's as heavy as that which is weighing on my own. I must say a word or two to the owld man, that he may not larn from sthrangers what it is his son has done; and then I must wish good-bye to Ballycloran—I trust for iver! But there's one thing I'll ask you, Feemy, before I go. There'll be men from Carrick here before the night is over, looking for me; and when they come, they'll be asking you all manner of questions about this deed; tell them it was I that did it—but tell them how and why I did it; tell them that it was not my purpose to kill the man, but that I could not see him dragging my sister from her house before my eyes, without raising my stick against the man that was

doing it; that, Feemy, is all I want of you,"—
and he turned to go, but when he reached the
door he returned, and putting his hand on his
sister's shoulder, said—"Sister, my own sister,
will you kiss me before I lave you for so long?"

Feemy shuddered horribly as she felt his
hand upon her. Thady quickly withdrew it,
for he saw it was all covered with blood;
Feemy, however, had seen it, for she screamed
loudly—she had raised her head to answer, and
at last she said—"Kiss you! no; I hate you—
you're a murdherer; you've murdhered him
because you knew I loved him; go away—go
out of that; you'll kill me too if you stand there
with his blood upon your hand!"

Thady, who had fallen on his knees to kiss
his sister, now hastily jumped upon his feet,
and a dark frown came upon his brow. It was
just upon his lips to tell his sister to whose
folly it was owing that Myles Ussher was now a
corpse; but before the words had left his mouth
he checked himself. Even then, at that saddest
moment of all, when the horrid word he so
dreaded had been applied to him by the only
person whom he really loved, he was able to
restrain his passion, and was too high-minded
to add to the suffering of his sister, though she
was so unjust and cruel to him.

"God forgive you, Feemy," he said; "but
that's a cruel word to come from you!"—and
he left the room. He met the two girls in
the passage, for Biddy had returned from Mrs.
Mehan's, whither she had gone after Ussher had
passed, and she was now horrified to find that
her mistress's plans had been, as she thought,

defeated by her brother, and her departure prevented.

"Good God! Mr. Thady," said she, with pretended astonishment, "what ails the misthress, then?"

"Go in to her, Biddy, she'll want you; Captain Ussher is dead," and he went into his father's room.

Here a still more distressing scene awaited him. He felt that if he meant to escape he should not lose much time, but he could not leave his father in ignorance of what had taken place. Larry was sitting, as usual, over the fire with his pipe in his mouth, and was nearly asleep, when Thady came in. The noise of the closing door roused him, however; but he only put his empty glass to his lips, and when he found there was nothing in it he turned round again dissatisfied to the fire.

"Larry," said his son, "I've bad news for you."

"You've always bad news. I niver knew you have anything else."

"I'm going to lave you, father, altogether."

"Faix, then, that's no such bad news," said the cross old man. "The door's open, and you've my lave; may be we'll do as well without you, as we're like to do with you."

Thady made no answer to this piece of silly ill-nature, but continued — "Larry, you'll be sorry to hear what I've to tell you, but I'd sooner you should hear it from me than from another. Myles Ussher is dead; it was I, father, that killed him."

At the first declaration the old man had

turned round in his chair, and he sat staring at his son ; but when he heard the second and more dreadful part of the story, his jaw dropped, and he sat for some time the picture of an idiot.

" He was bringing disgrace on you Larry, and on your name ; he was disgracing your family, and your daughter, and myself; he was dragging Feemy away with him by night. I saw him with her, speechless and fainting in his arms, and I struck him down as he was doing it with my stick. I didn't think, father, to strike so hard, but his skull was broken, and he died without a struggle."—The old man still stared at him, and Thady continued—

" And now, father, I am going to lave you ; for av I'm found here, when they come to look for me, they'll take me to prison, and may be when they come to hear the truth of it all,—and I suppose they will,—they'll see I didn't mane to kill him ; but if they call it murdher, why then I trust you'll niver see me agin."

" Murdher," at last said the old man, laughing ; " who doubts but that it was murdher ? in course they'll call it murdher. Well, he was the only frind you'd left me, and now that you've murdhered him, you may go now ; you may go now—but mind I tell you, they'll be sure to hang you."

This was old Macdermot's last address to his son. It was very evident that the poor old man had gradually become more and more imbecile during the last few days, and the suddenness of the melancholy news he now heard utterly destroyed his mind. Each, however, of the dreadful words he uttered fell with an awful appearance of intention and sane purpose on the ears of his son. He had hitherto restrained his feeling powerfully, and had shown no outward signs of strong emotion; but when his father said that there was no doubt the deed he'd done was murder, he burst into a flood of tears, and left the room without being able to articulate a word.

When the police came, which they did before the night was over, in search of Thady, they were unable to make anything of the old man; at first he took them for emissaries of Keegan's, and swore that they should not have admittance into the house, and when they were in it he endeavoured to hide himself, declaring at the same time, that he understood the law; that the money was not due till November, and that Keegan had no right to send the men there, harassing him, yet. When, however, he was made to understand that it was not about Keegan and the rents, but about the death of Ussher that they had come, he whimpered and whined, declaring that he had not murdered him; that he loved Ussher better than any one in the world—yes, better than his own children —and that for the world he would not hurt him. When at length the men explained to him that they were only there to look for Thady, he was worse than ever; for he began cursing his son dreadfully, swearing that if he had committed the murder, he would neither hide nor screen him, and finally declaring that he hoped they might catch him and hang him.

The next morning he was taken away to give evidence before the Coroner at Carrick-on-

Shannon. It was the first day since the summer that he had been above a few yards from his own hall door, and though the day was fine, he suffered much from the cold. When he got to his destination he could hardly speak ; the room was greatly crowded, for the whole neighbourhood had by that time heard of the event ; and when the poor old man had warmed himself by the fire, near which a seat had been procured for him, he smiled and nodded to those around, perfectly unconscious of the cause which had brought him there, but evidently thinking it must be holiday occasion.

Brady had stated to the Coroner pretty accurately what he knew, for there was nothing which it could have benefited him to falsify. The two girls proved that after Brady had started with the body, Thady had had interviews with his sister and his father, and it was necessary that both of them should be examined.

When the book, on which he was to be sworn, was handed to Larry Macdermot, he at first refused it, and when it was again tendered to him, he put it in his pocket, and made the man who gave it to him a bow. The Coroner, seeing he was in such a state of mind as rendered him unable to give evidence and unfit to be sworn, asked him some questions on the subject, but Larry instantly began to cry, and protest his own innocence, swearing, as he had done before, that he had loved Ussher better even than his own family.

It was a most melancholy sight—that poor, weak old man, whom so many of those now present had known so long, and who so very few years before had been in the full strength of manhood and health, for even now he was hardly more than fifty.

But sad as all this was, the examination of Feemy was still worse. As she had been actually present at the moment when Ussher had been killed, it was absolutely necessary that her evidence should be taken by the Coroner; and the sergeant of police, who came with a car from Carrick for them in the morning, insisted, in spite of all that she and the maids could say to the contrary, that she must accompany him back. She had got on the same car with her father; Biddy and the other girl were on the same seat with her, one on each side; but before they reached Drumsna she was in such a state that they could hardly keep her on the seat.

When they reached that village, the car was stopped by Father John. He had heard of the sad occurrence late on the previous evening, for Pat Brady had spared no exertions in disseminating the news of the catastrophe far and wide as he returned from Carrick. He had stopped at the priest's gate, and finding Father John absent on a sick visit, had nearly frightened Judy out of her life by telling her what had happened. Father John had not returned home till two in the morning, and he then heard some garbled version of the story, from which he was led to believe that Thady was in custody at Carrick, for the murder of Ussher.

Early on the morning of the inquest, he went into Carrick, and there learnt from the police the truth, and ascertained the fact that an inquest was to be held on the body that day, and that both old Macdermot and his daughter were to be examined at it.

Up to this time Father John did not know that Feemy had left Drumsna; and though the police informed him that she had been absolutely present when the fatal blow was struck, he could not believe it, and hurried off to Mrs. McKeon's, to tell her all that he knew, and learn from her all that she could tell him.

The kind-hearted man hardly knew what he was doing, so shocked was he, and surprised by what he had heard. He could hardly believe that after what Thady had said to him, after the promises he had made, he would deliberately, and with premeditation, plan and execute Ussher's murder. Such an idea was incompatible with the knowledge that he had of Thady's disposition, and he concluded that there must have been some quarrel between the two men, in which Ussher had fallen the victim. He little dreamt when he started for Mrs. McKeon's, how much more justly the blood which had been shed was to be attributed to the sister than to the brother, or he would hardly dared again to solicit her kind offices for his *protégée*.

When he got to Drumsna, the McKeons were only just rising from breakfast, but Father John saw, on entering the room, from their grave and anxious faces, that they had all heard the news. Tony had been out to his fields before breakfast, and had there been told by one of the men that Ussher's body had on the previous night been taken through Drumsna to the police station at Carrick, and that it was said that Thady Macdermot, the murderer, had already escaped out of the country.

This tale Tony had communicated in a whisper to his wife, and she had afterwards told the girls. What was the good of keeping it secret? before the evening it would be known to the whole country. When Father John came in, they all crowded round him, to learn what really might be relied on as the truth of the case; but he could only tell them that it was too sure that Ussher had died by Thady's hand,—that that young man was not in custody, —and that he had been informed that Feemy herself was present when the blow had been struck.

"Feemy and their poor father," added Father John, "are to be examined to-day before the Coroner; it will be a dreadful thing for her, poor girl! to be forced to tell all her secrets, to declare all that she would most wish to conceal before the mob that will be in the room at Carrick."

"Yes," added Tony, "and to stand there without any one to support her, and to be asked questions, which if they're answered correctly, may be will hang her brother."

"I'll never believe," said Father John, "that he killed him in cold blood. Yourself, Mrs. McKeon, hasn't a kinder heart within you than that young man; he never would have committed a wilful, premeditated murder; I don't think yet it will come to be so bad as what McKeon says. But when did Feemy leave this? I thought she was here, and was to stay here for some time to come."

Mrs. McKeon then explained how Feemy had insisted on returning home the morning after the ball, with the promise of returning again. After talking over the various unaccountable circumstances of the case, without once suspecting that Feemy had consented to and had actually been in the act of going off with Ussher, Mrs. McKeon agreed, at the instigation of her husband and the priest, to accompany Feemy to the inquest, and after it was over to bring her to her own house, and to allow her to remain there till something should be definitely arranged as to her future residence.

"For," said Tony, "Ballycloran will be no place for her again, nor the county either for the matter of that; but now that she's unhappy she shan't want a roof over her head; we were glad enough to see her when she held her head high, and I wouldn't advise any one to say much against her now she's in throuble—unless he wished to quarrel with me." And Tony McKeon closed his fist as much as to show that if any one did entertain so preposterous a wish he could be little better than a born idiot.

Tony then sent a message into Carrick for a postchaise, that Feemy might not be exposed to the curiosity of every one in the street by sitting on an outside vehicle*; and when she arrived in Drumsna from Ballycloran, she was taken off the car on which her father was sitting, and brought into Mrs. McKeon's house. She would not, however, speak to any one, and could hardly sit on a chair without being supported. She squeezed, however, her kind friend's hand, when she promised to go to the inquest with her, and seemed grateful when she was told that she should not return to Ballycloran, but should again occupy her old quarters at Drumsna.

At length they got into the hack chaise,* and were driven into the yard of the hotel where the inquest was to be held. This was the same house in which McKeon and his party had dined on the evening before the races, and there the cold stiff body of the man was lying on the same table round which he and so many others were carousing but a few hours since. There he lay, at least all that mortal remained of him, who was then so joyous, so reckless, and so triumphant, in the very room in which he had boasted, in his wilful wickedness, of the sad tragedy he was intending to inflict on those who had been so friendly to him at Ballycloran, and of which he was now himself the first victim.

The table on which he was laid out had been hastily removed for the dance, and it had now been as hastily replaced for its present purpose. The laurel wreaths with which the walls had been decorated were yet remaining, and when the Coroner entered the room his foot slipped on a faded flower, which some wearied beauty had dropped when leaving it on the previous morning. Little more than four and twenty hours had elapsed since the fiddles were playing there, and some of those who were now summoned upon their oaths to decide in what manner Ussher had met his death, had on that morning been nearly the last to leave the room in which they were now to exercise so different a vocation.

Biddy and Katty were first examined, and it was from the evidence of the former that Father John first heard that Feemy had agreed to elope with Ussher; and it appeared from what the girl said that her mistress was to have left the house some time previous to the time at which the other girl proved that she had been brought back by her brother. This added greatly to his sorrow; but at the same time, he now instantly perceived under what provocation Thady had struck the fatal blow. Brady proved that his master had confessed to him that it was he who had killed Ussher, and that he had said that when he did so his sister was in Ussher's arms. The stick was then brought forward, which was proved to be the one usually carried by Thady; and the blood upon the stick, and the nature of the wound upon the dead man's head, left no doubt that this was the weapon with which he had been killed.

The father was then brought in, and we have already seen the manner in which he conducted himself. It was now necessary to examine Feemy, and at last she came in, almost carried in Mrs. McKeon's arms, with a thick veil over her face, which, however well it hid her countenance, by no means rendered her sobs inaudible. Two chairs were placed for them by the table, and when they were both seated the book was handed to Feemy; then she had to take her glove from her right hand, and this was so wetted with her tears, and she herself was so weak, that it was long before she could get it off; and when she had taken the oath,—when she had sworn to tell not only the truth, but the whole truth,—she found it impossible to speak a word, and the Coroner was obliged to ask her questions, to which Mrs. McKeon was allowed to get the answers, spoken below her breath, and in whispers.

"Did she know Captain Ussher was dead?"

"She did."

"Did she know that it was her brother who had killed him? Was it her brother Thady?"

"Yes, it was."

"How did she know it was he who had done it? Did she see him do it?"

"No, she didn't see him."

"How then did she know it?"

"He had told her so afterwards."

"Could she say how he killed him?"

"No, she could not."

"Or why?"

To this question even Mrs. McKeon could get no answer.

"Where was she when Captain Ussher was killed?"

No answer.

"Was she with Captain Ussher?"

"She believed she was."

"Why, or for what purpose, was she with him?"

To this question, although pressed for some time, she would not answer; and Mrs. McKeon, who was up to this time totally ignorant of the locality in which Ussher had been killed, and was really unaware how it had come to pass that Feemy was present at the time, was quite unable

to suggest to her what answer she ought to
make; and finding that it was with difficulty
she could keep Feemy from falling from her
chair, she told the Coroner she was really afraid
Miss Macdermot was so ill, that she would be
quite incapable of answering any more questions;
and she added, that considering all the circumstances of the case,—that the young lady had
been engaged to the unfortunate man who was
dead, and was the sister of the man who had
killed him, it was not to be wondered at, if she
found her dreadful position too much for her.

The Coroner answered that he was quite
prepared to give Miss Macdermot every indulgence in his power, as he felt as strongly as any
one could do the distressing situation in which
the young lady was placed, but that it was
absolutely imperative that the last question he
had asked should be answered. And that he
was sure when he stated that the result of the
inquest very probably depended on what the
answer to the question might be,—as from that
the jurors would probably have to decide
whether her brother was to be accused of
murder, or merely homicide,—he was quite
sure, he said, under these circumstances, Miss
Macdermot would make an effort to answer it
fully and firmly. He was willing, he added, to
put the question in a form which might render
it more simple for her to answer, though it
would oblige him to say that which he feared
would be still further distressing to her feelings.

He then told her and Mrs. McKeon, that
from the evidence of the servants it had appeared
that she, Feemy, had agreed to elope with

Captain Ussher; and that, as far as could be judged from circumstantial evidence, she was, in fact, eloping with him when Thady had killed him; now, it was necessary for her to state whether she was there of her own good will, going away with him; or if not, what she was doing at the moment of the tragical occurrence.

After many fruitless attempts made by Mrs. McKeon to get an answer to this, Feemy said, through her friend, that she was sitting down.

"Does she mean that she was sitting down when the blow was struck?"

"She doesn't know where she was."

"When was she sitting down?"

"She was sitting down till Captain Ussher lifted her up."

"When Captain Ussher lifted her up, was she going away willingly with him?"

"Yes, she was."

"Did she struggle with him at all?"

"No."

"Did any of her friends know she was going with him?"

Before, however, the poor girl could be got to answer this question, she had fainted, and it was found impossible to restore her for a long time; and when she had recovered, it was only to give way to the most distressing cries and hysterical shrieks; she threw herself on the floor of the bedroom to which she had been taken, and Mrs. McKeon was afraid that she would have broken a blood-vessel in the violence of her emotions. As it was, she was for a long time spitting blood, and fell from one fit into another, until the medical man who was now with her was afraid that she would become entirely delirious.

It had long been found impossible to proceed with her examination any further. She had, however, unwittingly, and hardly knowing at the time what she was saying, given evidence against her brother which the facts of the case did not warrant.

For when Thady had first seen her, she was not going willingly with Ussher; she had then fainted, and Ussher was dragging her, apparently with violence, along the road.

When it was found in the inquest room that Feemy Macdermot could not possibly attend again, the coroner gave the jury the substance of the evidence on the case. He pointed out to them that though there could be no doubt that young Macdermot was the man by whom Captain Ussher had been killed, still if they thought there was sufficient ground for them to believe that Ussher was ill-treating his sister, and that the brother had interfered on her behalf, they should not come to the decision that murder had been committed.

The jury, after consulting for a short time, brought in a verdict of wilful murder against Thaddeus Macdermot; and, accordingly, a coroner's warrant was issued for his apprehension and trial, and was handed over to the police, that they might lose no time in endeavouring to take him prisoner.

CHAPTER XXII

THE ESCAPE

THADY left the house immediately after the last cruel speech his father made to him, with the tears running fast down his face. He leapt down the steps, hurried across the lawn, through the little shrubbery, and over the wall into the road. He did not dare to go alone down the avenue, and by the spot where Ussher's body had lain, and where the ground would still be moist with his blood.

His father's words still rang dreadfully in his ears—"Murdered! of course they'll call it murder! of course they'll be sure to hang you!" And then he thought of all the bearings of the case, and it seemed to him that his father must be right; that there could be no doubt but that all men would call it by that horrid name which sounded so hideously in his ears. If that which he had done was not murder, what manner in which one man could kill another would be thought so? It was now evident to him that Feemy had been with Ussher willingly—that she was there of her own consent and by appointment; and merely because she had fainted in his arms, he had struck him down and killed him. Of course his father was right; of course they would call it murder. And then again, even if he could justify the deed to himself—even if he could make himself believe that the man was at the time using violence to

his sister—how could he get that proved?
whereas proofs of her having consented to go
off with him would no doubt not be wanting.
And then again, Thady remembered—and as
he did so the cold sweat stood upon his brow—
how lately he had sat in company where the
murder of this very man whom now he had
killed had been coolly canvassed and decided
on, and he had been one of those who were to
be banded together for its execution. Would
all this be forgotten at his trial? Would there
not certainly be some one to come forward at
that horrid hour, and swear these things against
him—ay, and truly swear them? And then he
fancied the precision with which he knew
each damning word he had lightly uttered
would be brought against him. Would not these
things surely condemn him? Would they
not surely hang him? It would be useless for
him, then, to open his bosom and to declare to
them how hateful—even during the feverish
hours of that detested evening—the idea of
murder had been to his soul. It would be
useless for him to tell them that even then, at
that same time, he had cautioned Ussher to
avoid the danger with which he was threatened.
It would be vain for him to declare how soon
and how entirely he had since repented of the
folly of which he had on that occasion been
guilty. The stern faces by whom he would be
surrounded at his trial—when he should stand
in that disgraceful spot, with his head leaning
on that bar so often pressed by murderers,
miscreants, and thieves—would receive his protestations very differently from that benign

friend who had previously comforted him in his
misery. They would neither listen to nor
believe his assurances; and he said involuntarily
to himself—" Murder! of course they'll call it
murder! of course they'll hang me!"

The oftener he thought of this, the more he
hurried, for he felt that the police would be
soon in search of him, and that at most he had
but that night to escape from them. As these
ideas crossed his mind he hastened along the
lane leading to Drumleesh, sometimes running
and sometimes walking, till the perspiration
stood upon his brow. If it was murder that
he had done—if the world should consider it as
murder—then he would most probably soon be
in the same condition as that criminal whose
trial had so vividly occurred to his recollection
a few days ago. At that time the idea had only
haunted him; he had only then dreamt of the
possibility of his situation being the same as
that man's, and the very horror he had then
felt at the bare thought had made him determined to avoid those who could even talk of
the crime which would lead to that situation.
But now he had of his own accord committed
that crime; and how had he done it? In such
a manner that he could by no possibility escape
detection. Then again he tried to comfort
himself by reflecting that it was not murder—
that his intention had not been to murder the
man; but his father's horrid words again rang
through his ears, and he felt that there was no
hope for him but in flight.

The moon got up when he was about halfway
to his destination, and he left the road lest by

chance there might be any one out at that hour
who would recognise him. He crept on by the
hedges and ditches, sometimes running along
the bits of grass between the tillage and fences
—sometimes having almost to wade through the
wet bottoms which he crossed, often falling, in
his hurry and in the imperfect light of the cloudy
moon, till at last, tired, hot, and covered with
dirt, pale with fear, and nearly overcome by the
misery of his own reflections, he reached Corney Dolan's cabin. It was now about eleven
o'clock; it had been past ten when he left
Ballycloran, and in the interval he had traversed
above five Irish miles.* There was no light in
the cabin, which was a solitary one, standing on
the edge of a bog. Now he was there he feared
to knock, as he did not know what to say to
Corney when he should come to the door.
Besides, he was aware that his hands and coat
were soiled with blood, and he was unwilling
that the inmates of the cabin should see him in
that plight.

He had, however, no time to spare, and as
it was necessary that he should do something,
after pausing a few minutes, he knocked at the
door. No one answered, and he had to knock
two or three times before he was asked in a
woman's voice who he was, and what he wanted
there at that hour of the night. He stated
that he wanted to see Corney Dolan. The
woman told him that Corney Dolan wasn't at
home, and that he couldn't see him. Thady
knew that he lived alone with his mother, an
aged woman, nearly eighty years old, and that
it was she who was speaking to him now.

"Nonsense, mother," said he; "he's at home I know, and I must see him. Don't you know me?"

"Faix, then, I don't—and I don't want," said the old hag. "At any rate, Corney's not here; so you may jist go back agin, whoever you call yerself."

"But where is he, then? Can you tell me where I'll find him?"

"I can't tell you thin. What should I know myself? So now you know as much about it as I do."

"Well, then, get up and let me in. Don't you know me? I'm Corney's landlord, Thady Macdermot. I'll wait here till he comes; so get up and let me in."

There was a silence for some time; then he heard the old woman say to some one else—

"The Lord be praised! It can't be him—it can't be Mr. Thady coming here at this time of night. Don't stir, I tell ye—don't stir, avick!"

"Oh! but it wor him, mother. Shure, don't I know his voice?" answered the child that the old woman had spoken to.

"I tell you it is me," shouted Thady. "Open the door, will you! and not keep me here all night!"

The child now got up and opened the door, and let him into the single room which the cabin contained. There were still a few embers of turf alight on the hearth, but not sufficient to have enabled Thady to see anything had not the moon shone brightly in through the door. There was but one bed in the place,—at the end of the cabin farthest from the door, standing between the hearth and the wall,* and in this the old woman was lying. The child, about eight years, had jumped out of bed, stark naked, and now in this condition was endeavouring with a bit of stick to poke the hot embers together, so as to give out a better heat and light. But Thady was in want of neither, and he therefore desired the boy to get into bed, and upsetting with his foot the little heap which the urchin had so industriously collected together for his benefit, so as to extinguish the few flickering flames which it afforded, he sat down to try and think what it would now be best for him to do.

"Where's Corney, then," he said, "at this hour? Will he be long before he's here?"

"Not a one of me rightly knows, yer honer; maybe it'll not be long afore he's here, and maybe it'll not be afore the morning," said the child.

"And, maybe, not then," added his grandmother. "There's no knowing when he'll be here; maybe not for days. I don't know what's come to them at all now—being out night skirring* through the counthry; it can't come to no good, any ways."

"When Corney's at home, where does he sleep?" said Thady, looking round the cabin for a second bed, but seeing none.

"He mostly takes a stretch then down there afore the fire; but Corney's not over partickler where he sleeps. For the matter of that, I b'lieve he sleeps most out in the bog at day time."

Thady now sat down on one of the two rude stools with which the place was furnished, either to wait for Corney, or to make up his mind what other steps he would take. He had closed and bolted the door, and was just in the act of asking the old woman whether Joe Reynolds was at present living on his bit of land, or if not, where he was, when he heard footsteps coming up to the little path to the door, and the woman, sitting up in bed, said—

"There's both on 'em thin; get up, Terry, and open the door."

One of the men outside rattled the latch quietly, to let the inmates know who it was that desired admittance; and the naked boy again jumped out of bed, and opening the door, ran back and jumped in again.

Two men now entered, whom Thady, as they appeared in the moonlight through the open door, at once recognised as Joe Reynolds and Corney Dolan. He was seated close to the fire, and in the darkness and obscurity of the cabin, they did not at first perceive him.

A few moments since he had been longing for these two men who now stood before him, as the only persons on whom he could depend for security and concealment, and now that they were there he almost wished them back again, so difficult did he find it to tell them what he had to say, and to beg of them the assistance he required.

"Who the divil are you?" said Corney; "who's this you've got here, mother?—and what made you let him in here this time of night?"

"Shure it's the young masther, Corney, and he axing afther you; you wouldn't have me keeping him out in the cowld, and he waiting there to see you that ought to have been at home and asleep two hours since."

"Faix, Mr. Thady, and is that yerself?" said Corney; "well, anyway you're welcome here."

"I'm glad to see you here, Mr. Thady," said Joe; "didn't I tell you you'd be coming? though it's a quare time you've chosen. Didn't I tell you you'd be changing yourmind?"

"But was yer honer wanting me, Mr. Thady?" said Corney; "'deed but this is a bad place for you to come to; sorrow a light for ye or the laste thing in life; what for did you not get a light, you ould hag, when the masther came in?"

"A light is it, Corney; and how was I to be getting a light, when there's not been a sighth of a bit of candle in the place since last winter, nor likely to be the way you're going on now."

"Whisht there now," said Joe; "we'll be doing very well without a light; but why wasn't you down here earlier, Mr. Thady?—We two have just come from mother Mulready's, an' by rights, as you've come round agin, you should have been there with us."

"Never mind that, Joe, but come out; I want to spake to you."

"Did you hear the news about Ussher?" continued Joe without moving, and in a whisper which the old woman could not hear. "That blackguard Ussher has escaped out of the counthry afther all, without paying any of us the debt that he owed us, for all the evils he's done. He went away out of Mohill this night, an' he's not to be back agin; av I'd known it afore he started I'd have stopped him in the road, an' by G—d he should niver have got alive out of the barony."*

"But did you hear he was gone?" said Corney.

"I did," replied Thady: "but, Joe, I want to spake to you, and there's no time to spare; come here," and Joe followed him to the door. "Come further; I don't want him to hear what I've to say to you;" and he walked on some little way before he continued,—"you were wishing just now that you had shed Ussher's blood?"

"Well—I wor; I suppose, Mr. Thady, you're not going to threaten me with the magisthrate again. I wor wishing it—an' I do wish it; he was the hardest man on the poor—an' the cruelest ruffian I iver knew. Isn't there my brother, that niver even acted agin the laws in the laste thing in life,—the quietest boy, as you know, Mr. Thady, anywhere in the counthry, an' who knew no more about stilling than the babe that's unborn; isn't he lying in gaol this night all along of him? an' it an't only him; isn't there more? many more in the same way, in gaol all through the counthry; an' who but him put 'em there? I do wish he was for-a-nens't me this moment, an' that I might lave him here as cowld a corpse as iver wor stretched upon the ground!"

"I tell you, Joe, av you had your wish—av* you struck the blow, and the man you so hate was dead beneath your feet, you'd give all you had—you'd give your own life to see him agin, standing alive upon the ground, and to feel for one moment that you'd not his blood to answer for."

"By G—d! no, Mr. Thady; I'm not so

wake; and as for answering for his blood, by the blessed Virgin, but I'd think it war a good deed to rid the counthry of such a tyrant."

"He'll niver act the tyrant again, Joe, for he is dead. I struck him down with my stick in the avenue at Ballycloran, this night, and he niver moved agin afther I hit him."

"The holy Virgin save us! But are you in arnest, Mr. Thady? D'ye main to say he's dead—that you killed him?" And after walking on a little, he said,—"By the holy Virgin, I'd sooner it had been myself; for I could have borne the thoughts of having done it better than you are like to do. An' what did you do with the body?"

"Brady took it into Carrick."

"And does Brady know it war you did it?"

"Yes, they all know it—father and all; what was the use of telling a lie about? Feemy was with him when I struck him."

"And war she going off with him? Niver mind, Mr. Thady, niver mind; it's a comfort to think you've saved your sisther from him, an' you know what a ruffian he was. By all the powers of glory, there's a weight off my mind now I know he's not escaped from the counthry, where he caused so much misery, and did so much ill. But I'd a deal sooner it had been I that done it than yourself."

"I wish it war not done at all—I wish he were alive this day. What will I do now, Joe?"

"Faix, that's the question; any way, this is not the place for you any longer; they'd have you in Carrick Gaol before to-morrow night, av you were not out of this, an' far out of this too."

"Where is it you have the stills, Joe? Av I were there, couldn't I be safe, for a little time at laste, till I got some plan of getting entirely out of the counthry? Or may be when they hear the case, and how it all happened, they mightn't think it murder at all,—the Coroner I main; and then I could go home agin, or at any rate go away where I choose without hindrance; it's little I care where I was, so long as it's not in prison."

"I'm afraid, Mr. Thady, there's no hopes for you in that way. The magisthrates, with Jonas Brown at the head of them, will be a dail too willing to make a bad case of it, the divil mend them, to let you off; an' the only thing for you is, to keep out of their hands."

"Would they find me there, Joe, up in the mountains, where you have the stills?"

"They might, and they mightn't; but if you war there, an' they did find you, they'd be finding the stills too, an' the boys wouldn't like that."

"Where shall I go, then? I thought you'd be able to help me. In heaven's name, what shall I do? the night's half over now; can't you think of any place where I might be, for to-morrow at any rate? I depended on you, Joe, and now you won't help me."

"There you're wrong. I'm thinking now, where is the best place for you: and by G—d as long as I can stick to you, I will; both becase you were always a kind masther to the poor, an' becase the man you killed war him I hated worse than all the world besides; but it's no asy thing to say where you'd be safest. D'you know Aughacashel,* Mr. Thady?"

"I niver was there, but I know that's the name of the big mountain over Loch Allen,* to the north of Cash."*

"Well, that's where the stills are mostly at work now, an' that's where I was to be myself, to-morrow evening; but now we must both be there before the sun's up, for no one must see us on the road. But, Mr. Thady, how'll I do about taking you there, when you wouldn't come to Mulready's to take the oath, which all must do afore they'll be allowed among the boys that is together, or as will be together there to-morrow evening?"

Thady then promised him, that when he reached their destination, he would take any or every oath that might be proposed to him; that he would join their society in every respect, whatever might be its laws, and that if they would assist him in his present condition by affording him whatever security might be in their power, he would faithfully conform to all their rules and regulations. So far did his fears and the agitated state of his mind overcome the great repugnance which still he felt to break the solemn promise he had given Father John, and which he had so faithfully intended to keep.

Reynolds reflected that though it was contrary to their regulations to bring a stranger to the haunts where his companions carried on their illegal trade, they could hardly be unwilling to give shelter to the man who had killed the enemy whom they all so cordially hated, and to murder whom they were all sworn; particularly when his present necessity of concealment arose from the fact of his having done so. Reynolds had an idea of justice in his composition: he knew that had he murdered Ussher, his companions would have used every effort to conceal him, and to baffle his pursuers; and he was determined that they should do as much for Thady.

He went back to the cabin for Corney Dolan, and told him the story which he had just heard; and at about midnight the party started for the mountains.

Aughacashel is a mountain on the eastern side of Loch Allen, near the borders of the County Cavan—uncultivated and rocky at the top, but nevertheless inhabited, and studded with many miserably poor cabins, till within about a quarter of a mile of the summit. The owners of these cabins, with great labour, have contrived to obtain wretchedly poor crops of potatoes from the barren soil immediately round their cabins. To their agricultural pursuits many joined the more profitable but hazardous business of making potheen, and they were, generally speaking, a lawless, reckless set of people—paying, some little, and others no rent, and living without the common blessings or restraints of civilization: no road, or sign of a road, came within some miles of them; Drumshambo, the nearest village, was seven or eight miles distant from them; and although they knew that neither the barrenness of their locality, nor the want of means of approach would altogether secure them from the unwelcome visits of the Revenue police or the Constabulary, still they felt sure that neither

of these inimical forces could come into their
immediate neighbourhood, without their making
themselves aware of their approach, in time to
guard against any injury which they might do
them, either by removing all vestiges of their
trade, or by sending those who were in fear
of being taken up, into the more inaccessible
portions of the mountain. On the western side
of Aughacashel, immediately over Loch Allen,
and about halfway between the lowlands and
the summit, a kind of rude limekiln had been
made, apparently for the purpose of burning
lime for the neighbouring land; but the very
poor state of the rocky ground about, which
gave signs of but little industry, afforded
evidence that the limekiln had not added
much to the agricultural wealth of the country.
It was now at any rate made use of for other
purposes, for it was in here that Joe Reynolds
at present usually worked his still. There were
only two cabins immediately close to it; one
of which was occupied by a very old man and
his daughter, but in which Corney Dolan and
Reynolds resided, when they were away from
Drumleesh; and the other belonged to another
partner in the business, who considered himself
the owner of the limekiln, and the head of the
party concerned in it. This man's name was
Daniel Kennedy, and to the reckless, desperate
contempt of authority and hatred of those who
exercised it, which characterized Reynolds, he
added a cruelty of disposition, and a love of
wickedness, from which the other was much
more free.

This was the place to which his two guides

were now conducting Thady, and where it was proposed that he should, at any rate for some time, conceal himself from those, who, it was presumed, would soon be scouring the country in search of him. It was now a bright moonlight night, and the three men hurried across the country with all the haste they could make. Little was said between them as they went, excepting observations made between Joe and his comrade, as to the characters and occupations of the residents in the various cabins by which they passed. After going for some considerable way across fields and bogs and bottom lands, they came out on a lane, running close round a small lake lying in the bed of the low hills which rose on the other side of it. The water was beautifully calm, and the moon shining immediately down upon it, gave it the appearance of a large surface of polished silver. At this spot the fields came close down to the road, and also to the water, and in the corner thus formed stood a very small poor cabin.

This lake was Loch Sheen, and it was in that cabin that Ussher had apprehended Tim Reynolds and the two other men, little more than a fortnight ago.

Joe stopped a moment when he reached the spot, till Thady, who was following the other man, had come up, and then, pointing to the low door, close to which he stood, said—

"The last deed as that ruffian did as now lies so low was in that cabin. It war there he sazed Tim, an' dragged him off with ropes round his arms, an' sent him to Ballinamore Bridewell, an' all for spaking a few words of comfort to

an owld woman he'd known since he war a
little child. I swore, Mr. Thady, that that man
should be put beneath the sod*before the time
came round that Tim should be out agin; an'
this very night I war a grieving in my heart
to think that he war out of the country safe
an' merry—ready agin to play the same bloody
game with them among he war going; an' that
I should let him go without so much as making
one effort to keep my word with him! By
G—d, Mr. Thady, quare as you may think it,
who are now so low within yerself with what
you've done, that thought was heavy on my
heart this night. Had I known what way he
war to travel, I'd followed him, had it been
for days an' nights, till I had got one fair blow.
By dad, he would niver have wanted a second.
Corney, what's the owld hag doing since her two
sons is in gaol along with Tim?"

"Ah! thin, she's doing badly enough; she
war niver from her bed since. Faix, Joe, they'll
niver be out in time to bury her."

"Is it starving she is?"

"Well, thin, I b'lieve that's the worst of it;
that an' the aguy,* an' no one to mind her at all,
is enough to kill an owld woman like her."

"Niver mind," replied Joe, "it will be a
comfort to her any way to hear that Ussher's
gone before her; not but what they'll go to
different places, though." And then, after a
time, he added, "Ussher's black soul has gone
its long journey this night with more curses on
it than there are stones on these shingles.* But
come on, lads, we mustn't be standing here; we
must be in Aughacashel before sunrise, or else

they'll be stopping us as we pass through the counthry."

And again they went through the clear bright moonlight. They passed Loch Sheen, and soon afterwards another little lake, lying also to the left of the road, and then they found themselves in the small village of Cashcarrigan. This they passed through silently and quickly and without speaking a word, and having proceeded about half a mile on the road towards Ballinamore, they again left it and took to the fields. They went along the northern margin of Loch Dieney, running where the ground was hard enough, at other times stepping from one dry sod to another, through gaps and fences, which seemed as well known to Thady's guides as the cabins in which they had passed their lives. They left Drumshambo to their left, and at about four in the morning they came to Loch Allen. Here they got upon a road which for some way skirts the eastern side of the lake, along which they ran for about a mile and a half, and then turned into a small boreen*or path, and began to ascend the mountains.

" Asy, boys, now," said Corney; " we're all right when we're here ; an', by the powers ! I'm hot," and the man began wiping his brow with his sleeve.

"What, Corney, you're not blown yet !" said the other, "an' here's Mr. Thady as fresh as a four year old. Come along, man ; the sooner he's got a snug room over his head the better he'll be. You forget he's not accustomed to be out all night, and take his supper of moonshine, as you are. Come along, Mr. Thady; you'll soon be where you'll get as good a dhrop as iver man tasted, an' you'll feel a deal better when you've got a glass or two of that stuff in you."

Thady, who, in spite of Joe's compliment as to his freshness, was so weary that he could hardly drag his legs along, and who had seated himself for a moment upon one of the big loose stones which were scattered over the side of the hill, again rose, and they all resumed their journey. They soon lost the track of the boreen, but they still continued to ascend, keeping by the sides of the loose-built walls with which the land was subdivided. It was astonishing what labour had seemingly been wasted in piling wall after wall in that barren place, and that even in spots where no attempt had been made at tillage, and where the only produce the land afforded was the food of a few miserable sheep and goats, which it might be thought could have grazed in safety without the necessity for all those numerous fences. These, however, after a time, ceased too; but just at the spot where the open mountain no longer showed any signs of man's handiwork, Dan Kennedy's lime-kiln was built, and immediately behind it were the two cabins of which we have before spoken.

It was at the door of the furthest of these two that Joe—did not knock—but raised the latch and rattled it. The old man within well knew the sign, and, getting out of bed, drew the wooden bolt, and admitted the three into the cabin. Though he did not expect Joe or Corney, and had not an idea who Thady was; and though Thady's dress, which was somewhat better than those worn by his usual associates, must have struck him as uncommon, he made no remark, but hobbled into bed again, merely saying, in Irish, " God save ye kindly, boys! it's a fine night ye've had, the Lord be praised!" There was a second bed in the place—if a filthy, ragged cotton tick* filled with straw, and lying on the ground, could be called a bed—in which the old man's daughter was lying. It was nearly dark now out of doors, for the moon had disappeared, and it was hardly yet six o'clock; but one of the men lighted a candle, of which there were two or three hanging against the wall. The girl was not asleep, for her eyes were wide open, looking at the party, but she seemed not at all surprised by their entrance, or at the addition to their usual numbers, for she lay quite quiet where she was, as if such morning guests in her bed-chamber were no unusual thing.

Joe now got a stool for Thady; and he and Corney sat down opposite the fire, while Reynolds drew a stone jar out from beneath the old man's bed—he seemed well to know the place where it was to be found—and reaching a cracked cup down from a shelf which was fixed into the wall over the fire-place, filled it with spirits and handed it to Thady. He swallowed a considerable portion of it and returned it, when Joe filled it again, finished the contents himself, and gave it again full to Corney, who in a very short time did the same.

" By gor," said the latter, " I wanted that; an' I tell you that's not bad work. Why, Mr. Thady——"

"Have done with your Misthers, Corney," said Joe, in a whisper, "let them find out who he is theyselves. They'll know soon enough, divil doubt them! there's no good telling them yet, any how."

"That's thrue, Joe; but as I was saying, that's not bad work; why, Mr. Thady——"

"Sorrow saze yer tongue, thin, ye born idiot!"

"Well, by dad, it comes so natural to me, Joe, to call him by his own name, that one can't help it; but it war only four o'clock when we left this, this blessed afthernoon—that is, yesterday afthernoon—an' since that we wor down at Mulready's, an' then at Drumleesh, an' now we're here agin; why, how many miles is that?"

"Niver mind the miles; he"—and Joe pointed to Thady—"he has done a deal more than that in the same time—an' whatever comes of it, he did a good deed. Howsomever, if you'll take my advice, you'll take a stretch now. Meg!—I say, Meg,"—and he turned round to the girl who was lying in the corner—"get out of that, an' make room for this man to lie down. You've been asleep all night; make room for yer betthers now."

The girl, without grumbling, turned out of bed, and burthened with no feeling of conventional modesty, commenced and finished her toilet, by getting into an old ragged calico gown, and tying up, with a bit of antique tape, her long rough locks which had escaped from their bondage during her sleep. Thady for a long time resisted, but Joe at last was successful

in persuading him to take advantage of the bed
which Meg had so good-humouredly relinquished.

"I an' Corney have still-work to do afore
daylight, an' we won't be back afore it's night,"
said Joe, "but do you bide here, an' you'll be
safe. You must put up with the pratees this
day, for there's nothing better in it at all; but
I'll be getting something fitter for you by night;
an' av' you feel low, which you'll be doing when
you wakes, mind, there's the sperrits in the jar
there undher the bed; a sup of it won't hurt
you now an' agin, for indeed you'll be wanting
it, by yerself here all day. An' look you,"—and
he led him to the door as he spoke, and pointed
to the two within—"they'll soon know who you
are, an' all about it; but you needn't be talking to
them, you know; an' you may be quite certain,
that even should any one be axing about you,
they'll niver 'peach, or give the word to the
police, or any one else. Av you like to go out
of this during the day, don't go further than the
kiln; an' av you lie there, you could easily see
them miles afore they war nigh you, even av
anything should put it into their heads to think
of coming afther you to Aughacashel."

The two guides then took their leave of him,
and Thady laid himself down on Meg's bed, and,
after a time, from sheer fatigue and exhaustion,
he fell asleep.

CHAPTER XXIII

AUGHACASHEL

AT what hour he woke Thady did not know, but it was broad day, and the sun was high in the heavens; he would have slept again if he could, that he might again forget the dreadful deed which had made the last night so horrible, but he could not; he was obliged therefore to get up, and when he did so he felt himself weak for want of food. Meg, it appears, had gone out. The old man could not speak a word of English; but Thady could talk Irish, and he had no difficulty in getting plenty of potatoes from him, and as he was eating them the old man pulled out the jar of whiskey. Thady took part of another cup full, and then felt less sad than he had done before. After his breakfast he sat for a long time over the fire, smoked his pipe till he had no tobacco left in it, got up and sat down again, walked to the door and then again returned to his seat. At last he became dreadfully fatigued; he felt all the misery which a man, usually active, always feels when condemned for a time to idleness; he sat watching the turf, as though he could employ his mind, or interest himself in observing the different forms which the sods took, or how soon they would reduce themselves to ashes; then he counted the smutty rafters on which the crazy roof was supported, and then the different scraughs of which it was composed; he next endeavoured

to think how the old man got through the
tedium of his miserable existence. There he
sat on the bed, quite imperturbable ; he had not
spoken ten words since Thady had got up, and
seemed quite satisfied in sitting there enjoying
the warmth of the fire, and having nothing to
do. How Thady envied his quiescence ! Then
he began to reflect what had been this man's
life ; had he always been content to sit thus
tranquil, and find his comfort in idleness ? At
last he got almost alarmed at this old man ; why
did not he speak to him ? why did he sit there so
quiet, doing nothing—saying nothing—looking
at nothing—and apparently thinking of nothing ?
it was as sitting with a dead body or a ghost—
that sitting there with that lifeless but yet breath-
ing creature. Every now and again, as he
endeavoured to fill his mind with some idea
that was not distressing to him, the thoughts of
the horrors of his own position would come
across him—the almost certainty of detection—
the ignominy of his future punishment—the
disgrace to his father and his sister ; and even
if not detected, if left in his present concealment, the horrors of such a life as he was now
leading, a few hours of which had already
nearly made him frantic, nearly overwhelmed
him.

He got up, and leaving his companion to
himself, he went to the lime-kiln and laid himself on the top of it, looking down the mountain
towards Loch Allen and Drumshambo, that he
might see if any of the police were coming in
search of him. The open air was for a time
pleasanter than the close heat of the burning

turf, and solitude by far preferable to the
company of that silent old man,—but it was
only for a short time that he felt the relief. The
horrid inactivity of the day, joined to the weight
that was on his mind, nearly drove him mad;
as long as he had work to do,—while he had to
dispose of the dead man's body,—while he had
his father and his sister near him,—as long as
he was hurrying through the country with
Reynolds,—the energy of whose character had
for a time relieved him,—as long as the sweat
was pouring down his face, and his legs had
been weary under him,—he had borne much
better the misery, which he felt now he was
always doomed to bear; for he had then thought
less of the past and the future; but now he
could occupy his mind with nothing but the
remembrance of the death he had inflicted, and
the anticipation of the death he was to suffer.
He tried to sleep, but it was in vain; he tried
to imitate that old man, and let his mind sleep,
but no, he could only think—he could not but
think. Oh! he said to himself, that it were all
over—if it were only done—if he could only
swallow up the next six months and be dead
and forgotten! If he had got past that dreadful trial—that cold unfeeling prison, with the
harsh noise of the large key and the fetters, the
stern judge, and the twelve stern men sworn to
hang him if he deserved it! If he could escape
the eyes of the whole country which would then
be on him; the harsh, cold, solemn words
which would then be addressed to him—the
sorrow of his father—the shame of his sister—
and, last and worst, the horrid touch of that

dread man with the fatal rope! It was not death he feared—it was the disgrace of death, and the misery of the ignominious preparations. He knew in his heart that heaven could not call it murder that he had done; but he felt equally sure that man would do so.

He lay there on the lime-kiln till the sun had already set, and then he was again driven into the cabin by the cold.

There sat that silent, still old man. He had not moved from his former position, his bare feet thrust into old ragged shoes, which in some former generation had been made for some strong man double his size, and hanging down so that his toes just reached the floor—his hands resting on the quilt on each side of him, and his head dropping on his chest. Oh, what an easy, quiet mind, thought Thady, must that man have—how devoid of care and fear must he be, to be able to sit there motionless all the live-long day, and not feel it dreary, long, endless, insupportable, as he did.

The girl was still absent, and Thady again sat himself down by the fire, the blazing turf on which gave the only signs that the old man had moved. Again he counted the rafters, counted the miserable scraps of furniture, counted the sods of turf, speculated where the turf was cut —who cut it? who was the landlord of the cabin? what rent was paid? who collected it? But a minute—half a minute sufficed for the full consideration of all these things, and again he began to reflect how long it would be before the police would find him, and drag him forth from that dreary place; how long it would be before he should feel the handcuffs on his wrist; and before the first day of his concealment had passed over, he had become almost impatient for that time; and looked forward to the excitement of his capture, which he knew must sooner or later take place, with something like a wish that it might soon occur, to relieve him from the weight of his present condition.

At last he determined to speak to his companion, and after considering for some time what he should say to him, he asked him what his name was; but Thady had spoken in his usual language, and the old man, looking up, answered that he had no English.

"What's your name?" asked Thady, in Irish.

"Andy McEvoy."

"And is this cabin your own?"

"Yes."

"And who's your landlord?"

"The mountain belongs mostly to Sir Michael."

"But don't you pay any rent?"

"No."

"And what is it you do all day long?"

"Why then mostly nothing; I'm very old."

"And what does your daughter be doing?"

"Why then I don't rightly know; she's mostly out for Dan Kennedy."

"And where do you be getting the pratees?"

"'Deed I b'lieve Meg gets them mostly from Dan's garden."

"Who does Dan pay his rent to?"

"Why then I can't be saying."

It was useless carrying on a conversation any longer with such a man. He neither interested

himself about his house, his food, his landlord,
nor his family, and Thady again held his tongue.

Soon after dusk Meg returned; she had in
the folds of her gown a loaf of bread and a very
small piece of bacon, and it was evident to
Thady that whatever had become of Joe and
the other, they had not forgotten him or their
promise to provide him with some better food
than the lumpers* which sufficed for Andy
McEvoy and his daughter.

When the old man saw the provisions his
eyes glistened a little, and he clutched the dirty
quilt somewhat faster, and by the eagerness he
evinced for the food it was a relief to see that
he had some human feeling left. Meg boiled
the bacon and some potatoes together, and
when they were ready, put them on the dirty
deal table before Thady; she did not seem
much more communicative than her father, but
she asked him civilly if he would eat, and
evidently knew he was of a higher rank than
those with whom she was accustomed to associate, for she went through the ceremony of
wiping the top of the table with the tail of her
gown. Thady ate a portion of what was given
him; and as he did so he saw the old man's
greedy eyes glare on him, as he still sat in his
accustomed seat; it was quite horrible to see
how greedy and ravenous he appeared. Thady,
however, left much more than he consumed,
and the girl carefully putting the bit of bread
away, for his breakfast in the morning, divided
the remnant of the bacon with her father.

Then the man's apathy and tranquillity
vanished, and the voracity with which he

devoured the unaccustomed dainty showed that
though he might have no demon thoughts to
rack his brain, the vulture in his stomach
tortured him as violently.

Joe Reynolds and Corney returned about an
hour after dark, and requested Thady to come
out with them, which he did. They then told
him that it was necessary that he should now
take the oath, which they before warned him
that he would have to take if he accompanied
them to their haunts at Aughacashel. He at
first felt inclined to declare that he had again
changed his mind, and that instead of taking
this oath and joining himself in any league with
them, he was prepared to return home to Ballycloran, and give himself up to the police; but
his courage failed him now that he was, as it
were, in their own country, and particularly
after the kindness and attention that Reynolds
had showed him. He therefore followed them,
and they entered together the other cabin
belonging to Dan Kennedy. Dan and his wife,
and another man, his brother, were there. Dan
was a sullen, surly, brutal looking ruffian, about
fifty years old, and his wife was a fitting mate
for such a man; she was dirty, squalid, and
meagre; but there was a determined look of
passion and self-will about her, which plainly
declared that whoever Dan bullied, he did not,
and could not, bully his wife.

His brother Abraham was a cripple, having
no use in either of his legs; but he had an
appearance of intelligence and wit in his face,
which his brother in no degree shared, and he
was very powerful with his arms. It was he

who chiefly made the spirits, while Dan and the others procured the barley—brought it up to Aughacashel, malted it, and afterwards disposed of the whiskey.

"Well, my hearty," said Dan, as Thady followed his guides into the cabin, where his family party were engaged drinking raw spirits round the fire, "so you've done for that bloody thief of the world, have you? Joe tells me you riz agin him quick enough when you found him at his tricks with yer sisther. Divil a toe though you stirred to come to mother Mulready's when we axed you, in spite of the oath you took on the holy cross; but you're quick enough coming among us now you're in the wrong box yourself."

"Asy, Dan," said Joe; "what's the use of all that bother now; an't he here? and hasn't he rid us of him that would have got clane off from us, but for Mr. Thady here, that struck the blow we ought to have struck?"

"Thrue for you, Joe," said Abraham; "so hould yer jaw, Dan, and give me hoult of the blessed book till I give him the oath."

"All's right," said Dan; "and I'm glad to see you here, my lad of wax,* seeing what sent you; but business first and play after. I s'pose if you're maning to stay here wid us—an' by G—d you're wilcome—you'll not be saying anything agin giving me or Corney there, a bit of a line to some of your frinds at Ballycloran, to be sending you up a thrifle of money or so, or a few odd bits of duds, or may be a lump of mate or bacon, or a pound or two of sugar to swaiten the punch."

Thady looked very blank at this, for he by

no means wished to be writing to his friends at
Ballycloran, nor were the articles mentioned in
Dan's catalogue at all too plentiful in that place;
however, before he could answer, Joe indignantly scoffed at his friend's shabbiness.

"D—n it, Dan, I didn't think you war that
main, to be charging a boy for the morsel he'd
be ating, an' the sup he' be taking, an' him
undher a cloud, an' he afther doing us sich a
sarvice."

"Av he wor one of ourselves," replied Dan;
"but a gintleman the likes of him, may be,
would be plased not to be beholden to the likes
of us."

"Nonsense, Dan," said Joe; "don't think of
giving such a line at all, Mr. Thady. I'm not
so bad off, but I'll not see you wanting; you're
as wilcome to everything here as daylight."

"Spake for yerself; you're mighty ready, I'm
thinking, to spake for others," said Dan's helpmate; "av the gintleman's willing to help a
poor man like Dan for putting a house over his
head in his throubles, who's to hinder him?"

Thady, however, made them understand that
he would give them no such letter to his father
or his sister as they proposed, and Abraham
then proceeded to administer the oath to him.
By this he bound himself, first of all, never
to divulge to any one, particularly not to any
magistrate or policeman, or in any court of law,
anything that should be done or said in that
place where he now was, that might be prejudicial
to any of the party. Secondly, to give all aid
and assistance in his power to all those now
present, and to any which might be in possession

of a certain pass-word, and who might be able
to answer certain questions with the fit and
appointed answers, and to help in the escape
or concealment of any such, when they might
be either in confinement, or in dread of being
arrested. And thirdly, that he would aid and
assist in all schemes of vengeance and punishment which would be entered into by those
with whom he was now bound, against any who
attempted to molest them, but especially against
all Revenue officers and their men.

To all these conditions Thady bound himself, and as he finished repeating each article
after Abraham, he kissed the dirty prayer-book
which that man presented to him ; and having
done this, he made one of the party round the
fire, whilst Corney, Dan, and Joe took it by
turns to go out and watch that no unexpected
visitor was at hand.

When the night was tolerably advanced the
three left the family of the Kennedys to themselves, and returned to Andy's cabin ; and
Thady having refused to allow that Meg should
be again disturbed for his accommodation, they
all stretched themselves upon the earthen floor
before the fire, and were soon asleep.

The next morning Joe and Corney again
went away early, and Thady found himself
doomed to pass just such another day as the
preceding one.

After giving him his breakfast Meg again also
went out, and left Thady alone with her father.

By way of propitiating the old man he gave
him half the bit of bread which he was eating.
Andy devoured it as he had done the bacon,

and then resumed the same apathy and look of
idle contentment which had so harassed Thady
on the previous day. This second day was more
grievous, more intolerable even than the first.
He walked from the cabin to the lime-kiln, and
from the lime-kiln to the cabin twenty times.
He went to Kennedy's cabin, to try if he could
kill time by subjecting himself to the brutality
of the man or his wife; but the door was locked
or bolted, and there was apparently no one in
it; he clambered up the hill and then down
again—and again threw himself upon the
walls of the lime-kiln, and looked upon the
silver lake that lay beneath him. But the day
would not pass—it was not even yet noon—he
could see that the sun had yet a heavy space
to cover before it would reach the middle of
the skies. Oh heavens! what should he do?
Should he sit there from day to day, when
every hour seemed like an age of misery, waiting
till he should be dragged out like a badger from
its hole. He looked towards the village, and
to different bits of road which his eye could
reach, thinking that he should see the dark
uniform of a policeman; but no, nothing ever
was stirring—it seemed as if nothing ever stirred
—as if nothing had life by day, in that lifeless,
desolate spot. At length he thought to himself
that he would bear it no longer; that he would
not remain for a short time indebted for his
food to such a man as Dan Kennedy, and then
at length be taken away to the fate which he
knew awaited him, and be dragged along the
roads by a policeman, with handcuffs on his
wrists—a show, to be gaped at by the country!

No; he would return at once, and give himself up; he would boldly go to the magistrates at Carrick—declare that he had done the deed, and under what provocation he had done it, and then let them do the worst they chose with him.

After much considering, and many changes in his resolutions, he at length determined that he would do this—that as soon as it began to be dusk, he would leave the horrid mountain where he had passed the saddest hours that he had yet known, and go at once from thence to Father John, and implicitly follow the advice which he might give him.

When once he had definitely resolved on this line of conduct he was much easier in his mind; he had at any rate once more something to do— some occupation. He had freed himself from the prospect of long, weary, unending days, to be passed with that horrid man; and he was comparatively comfortable.

He determined to wait till it was nearly or quite dusk, which would be about five or half-past five o'clock, and then to leave the cabin, and making what haste he could to Drum-shambo, go from thence by the road to Cash-carrigan and Ballycloran; and he calculated that he would be able to reach Father John's cottage between ten and eleven, before the priest had gone to bed; and having finally settled this in his mind, he returned to the cabin for the last time, determined manfully to sit out the remainder of the afternoon in the same apathetic tranquillity, which his enemy Andy displayed.

CHAPTER XXIV

.

THE SECOND ESCAPE

FOR four long hours there he remained, seated on the same stool, without moving or speaking; and for the same time there sat Andy on his bed, looking at the fire, and from time to time dragging a few sods from under the bed to throw them upon the ashes and keep up the warmth which seemed to be his only comfort. At length Thady thought it was dark enough, and without saying a word to the old man, he left the cabin and again descended the hill. He would not return by the same path by which he had come for fear he should meet Joe or Corney, or Meg—for he was unwilling that even she should see him escaping from his hiding-place. By the time that he reached Drumshambo it was dark, and it continued so till he got to Cashcarrigan, which he did without meeting any one who either recognised him or spoke to him. From thence he passed back by the two small lakes and the cabin of the poor widow who owed her misery to Ussher's energy, and across the bog of Drumleesh to the lane which would take him by Ballycloran to Father John's cottage. But before he reached Ballycloran the moon again rose bright and clear, and as he passed the spot where he more particularly wished to be shrouded by the darkness, it was so light that any one passing could not but recognise him.

He pulled his hat far over his forehead, and passed on quickly; but just as he got to the gateway he met Mary McGovery, who was on the very point of turning up the avenue to the house. The turn in the road, exactly at the spot, had prevented him from seeing her before, and she immediately recognised him.

"Holy Virgin! Mr. Thady," she said; "and is that yerself?"

"Hist, Mary, don't spake so loud—not that I care who spakes now; you see it's me; and I'm going to the Cottage. Is Father John at home?"

"And what would you do with Father John, now? Don't you know the police is afther you?"

"What matther? it's not much throuble I'll be giving thim, looking for me. I'm going to thim myself now."

"An' what for would you do that, Mr. Thady? Don't you know they found it murdher agin you? We all hoped you were out of the counthry afore this. What for would you go to the police? Time enough when they catches you."

This was the first time that Thady had heard that a verdict of murder had been found against him before the Coroner, and though it was only what he expected, nevertheless the certainty, now that it reached him, almost made him change his mind and return to Aughacashel. The remembrance, however, of that weary day, and the feeling that even though he were there, he would assuredly be ultimately taken, strengthened his resolution, and he said—

"No, Mary, I've had enough of running away already. But tell me; how's Feemy?"

"Why, thin, Mr. Thady, she's nothing much to boast of; since she was in Carrick, yesterday, she's been very bad intirely."

"What is it ails her? It's—it's that man's death, isn't it, Mary?"

"'Deed, Mr. Thady, I s'pose that war the first on it. Poor young lady! in course she feels it.—Wouldn't I feel it, av any one was to knock poor Denis on the head?—not that it's the same thing, altogether, for the Captain wasn't her lawful wedded husband.—Not that I'm saying agin you, Mr. Thady, for what ye did."

"Never mind about that, Mary; what I've done is my own look out. But would Feemy see me, do you think?"

"See you, Mr. Thady! How could she see you, an' she in a raging fever in bed at Mrs. McKeon's? in course she couldn't see you."

"Good God! and is she so bad as that?"

"Faith, then, she is, very bad intirely; at laste, Docther Blake says so."

"It's very well, any way, that she's at Drumsna, instead of here at Ballycloran. Mrs. McKeon must be a kind woman to take her at such a time as this. And what's the owld man doing here by himself?"

"He's very quare in his ways, they do be saying; but I didn't see him meself yet; I'm going down to mind him, meself, this blessed moment."

"Why, isn't the two girls in it still?"

"Yes, they is, Mr. Thady; but they got

frighted with the quare ways the owld man brought back with him from Carrick. He's wake in the head, they say, Mr. Thady, since he war up afore the gintlemen at the inquest; an' as the two girls wor frighted with 'im, an' as I am, maybe, a bit sthronger, an' a thrifle owlder nor they, Father John said I'd better step down an' mind him a bit; an' when all was settled, that he would see my expinses war paid."

"Well, Mary, good night! Be kind and gentle with the owld man, for he's enough on him jist now to unsettle his mind, av it were sthronger than it iver was; and don't tell him you see me here, for it would only be making him more onasy."

"Good night, thin, an' God bless you, Mr. Thady," said Mary. "You've a peck of throubles on yer head, this night," she added to herself, as she walked up the avenue, "an' it's little you did to desarve 'em, onless working hard night an' day war a sin. Well, God forgive us! shure you're betther off still, than the gay man* you stretched the other night;" and she went on to commence her new business— that of watching and consoling Larry Macdermot in his idiotcy.

Thady pursued his road to the Cottage, without meeting any one else, and with some hesitation knocked at the priest's door. His heart palpitated violently within him as he waited some little time for an answer. It was about eleven, and he knew that at that hour Father John would still be up, if he were at home, though Judy would probably have retired to her slumbers. He was right in his calculation;

for in a short time he heard the heavy step
of Father John in the hall, and then the
rusty door-key grated in the lock. Thady's
knees shook beneath him as he listened to
the rising latch. How should he meet Father
John's eyes after what he had done? How
should he find words to tell him that he had
broken the solemn vow that he had taken on
the holy scriptures, and had, in his first difficulty,
flown to the disreputable security to be found
in the haunts of such men as Joe Reynolds and
Dan Kennedy. However, this he would have
to tell him; for the door was now open, and
there stood the priest, with his eyes fixed on
Thady's sad face and soiled appearance.

Thady had not had his clothes off for the
last two nights, and they now bore all the soil
and stains of his two midnight walks; his
countenance was pale in the extreme, and,
never full or healthy, now seemed more thin
and wan, than forty-eight hours' sorrow could
possibly have made it. He was much fatigued,
for his shoes had become soaked with water in
the moist grounds through which he had passed
and repassed, and his feet were blistered with
his long and unaccustomed walks.

When Father John saw him, his heart melted
within him at the sight of the young man's sad
and melancholy figure. We already know that
from the moment he had first heard of the
catastrophe, he had made excuses in his own
heart for Thady; and when he had heard, as
he did at the inquest, that his sister had been
with Ussher when he lifted his stick against
him, he had not only acquitted him in his own

estimation, from anything like the crime of
murder, but he also felt certain that had he
been in the same situation, he would most
assuredly have done the same as Thady had
done. He had been much surprised at the
Coroner's verdict ; he could not think how
twelve men on their oath could call Ussher's
death murder, when it so evidently appeared to
him that the man stigmatised by that verdict
as a murderer, had only been actuated by the
praiseworthy purpose of defending his sister
from disgrace and violence ; and when, moreover, it was so plain that Thady's presence on
the scene at the moment was accidental,
and that the attack could not have been premeditated.

The jurors, however, had not been Thady's
friends, as Father John was, nor were they
inclined to look upon such a deed with the
same lenient eyes. It appeared to them that
Ussher was not using any violence to the young
lady, who had herself admitted in her evidence,
that she was a willing party to Ussher's proceedings. Doubtless, there might be circumstances, which at the prisoner's trial would be
properly put forward in palliation of the murder,
by his counsel ; but with that the jury before
the Coroner could have nothing to do ; and on
these considerations, the jurors with very little
delay had come to the conclusion which had so
surprised and grieved Father John. Still, however, he looked forward with almost absolute
certainty to Thady's acquittal at his trial, and
was by far more angry with the young man himself, at his folly in attempting to fly from justice,

than he was at the deed which had put him
under its power. Now, however, when he saw
him pale, fatigued, harassed, and in sorrow at
his door, his anger all turned to pity, and the
only feeling left in his bosom led him to think
how he could assuage his sufferings and comfort
him in his afflictions.

Thady was the first to speak, — " Father
John," he said, " I've come to give myself up;
I thought I'd tell you, as I passed the door."

" Oh, my son, my son!" said Father John.
" Come in though, Thady, come in—till we
think what's best to do in this sad time ;" and
they went again into the little parlour, where so
short a time ago Thady had made the promise
which he now had to confess he had broken.

He then gave the priest, by degrees, the whole
history of the affair ; he told how the different
events had happened ; he explained how
Feemy's appearance as she lay fainting in
Ussher's arms, and that man's words to her,
when he declared that she must come with him,
had at the moment made him think that she
was being dragged away by violence; and that
he had had this conviction on his mind when
he raised his stick to strike. He then told
Father John exactly what he had done since
the occurrence, the precautions which he took
respecting the body—the visit which he paid to
his father and his sister, and lastly, how he
had fled for the sake of security, and passed
two miserable days among the mountains in
Aughacashel.

" Ah ! my poor boy," said Father John,
" that's what I have to blame you for. What

made you fly there? what made you fly anywhere? why did you not with an honest face at
once place yourself in the hands of the police,
from whom you must know you couldn't have
remained concealed?"

"Oh, Father John, av you could feel all I
felt when I first knew the man was dead—when
my own sisther spurned me—and when my
father told me I was a murdherer, you wouldn't
wonder at my flying, av it were only for an
hour."

"That's true, my boy—that's very true; and
I won't ask you now where you were, or who
were with you—or what folly you may have
done whilst there; for I haven't the heart to
blame you for what you've done in the extremity
of your misery. But now, Thady, we must
think of the future; of course you know, that
having come to my house, and having seen me,
you must at once place yourself in the hands of
the police."

"In course, Father John; I was only on my
way to Carrick when I called here. In truth,
I wanted a kind word from you before they put
me in that horrid place."

"My poor, dear boy, it's little comfort I can
give you, except to tell you that we all think,—
that is, McKeon and I, and the rest of us,—
that when the trial comes on they must acquit
you—any jury must acquit you; and that till
that time comes, you may be sure whatever can
be done for you by the warmest friends, shall
be done by us. But you know, Thady, till that
time does come—till the trial is over, you must
remain in prison."

"But, Father John, do you think they'll acquit me? do you think—does Mr. McKeon think, they'll not find it murder?"

"Indeed he does, Thady, and so do I; and so I'm sure does the Coroner, by what he said to the jury. I'm sure he didn't expect them to find it murder at the inquest."

"That's great comfort, Father John; but you always had comfort for me. But tell me, what's this I hear about Feemy and my father; is it thrue they're both ill?"

"I've little comfort for you in that quarter, I'm afraid; but though Feemy's ill, I don't think she's dangerously so. She will want time to bring her round; but I've no doubt time will bring her round. She has had a great deal to try her too; she was very fond of that man, though he was so unworthy of her; and it isn't easy for a girl like Feemy to get over at once the loss of him she loved so dearly."

"God send she may recover! I did it all for the best. Larry was long ailing; I fear this has knocked him up intirely; what'll the tinants do now at all? they'll have no one over thim but Keegan, I suppose: he'll be resaving the rints now, Father John; won't he?"

"Don't mind that now, my boy; you've enough on your heart now without troubling yourself about that."

"Well, then, I'll be wishing you good-bye; I'll go on to Carrick."

"No, Thady, not to-night; stay here to-night. I would not have you go in and give yourself up under cover of the dark. Early to-morrow —as soon as Counsellor Webb will be up, you

shall go with me to him. He'll no doubt
commit you; indeed he must do so; but that
will be better for you than lying all night in the
guard-room at the police-station, and being
dragged out in the morning, cold, comfortless,
and hungry."

Father John then got him supper and had
a bed prepared for him, and early in the morning he sent down to Ballycloran for his linen
and clothes that he might appear in a more
respectable manner before the magistrate; he
had his horse and car ready for them after
breakfast, and at about ten they started for
Counsellor Webb's.

They found the magistrate at home, and
Father John sent in word to him that Mr.
Macdermot having heard the verdict which had
been returned at the Coroner's inquest, had
come to surrender himself. Mr. Webb received
the two into his study, and having explained to
Thady that it was of course his duty immediately
to commit him, sent to Carrick for police, in
whose charge it would be necessary that the
prisoner should be sent from thence.

"I'm very sorry," said Webb, "that this
should be my principal duty, and that I should
be obliged to hand you over to the constables;
but you must have been aware that I should do
so, when you came to me."

Father John then took Mr. Webb aside, and
explained to him all the particulars of the case,
which had not come out at the inquest; and at
last it was agreed that he, Mr. Webb, should go
with them into Carrick—that they would call at
the police-office to inform the sergeant there

that the prisoner was in custody, and that they should go direct to the gaol, and that Thady should be immediately handed over to the custody of the gaoler. This was accordingly done, and he avoided the disgrace, which he so feared, of being led through the town with handcuffs on his wrists.

Father John did not leave him until he had seen him settled with whatever comfort a prison could afford; but of these things, now that he was there, he seemed to think much less than the priest himself.

When Father John was kindly petitioning with the Governor to allow the prisoner a light in his cell, he said, "What matters? a light won't make the time pass over quicker."

The next assizes* would not take place till April, six months after the present time; and it was finally agreed that Father John should take on himself all the cares connected with his defence, and should from time to time visit him in his confinement, and give him such news respecting his father, his sister, and the affairs at Ballycloran, as he might have to bring;— and then he took his leave.

When he was gone Thady was once more alone and in solitude; moreover, he felt strongly the gloom of the big cold walls around him—of the huge locks which kept him—the austerity and discomforts of prison discipline, and all the miseries of confinement; but yet even there, in gaol and committed to take his trial for life— though doomed to the monotony of that dull cell for six months—still he felt infinitely less wretched than he had done whilst sitting in

Andy McEvoy's cabin, wondering at the torpidity of its owner. The feeling of suspense, of inactivity, the dread of being found and dragged away, joined to the horror he felt at remaining in so desolate a place, would have driven him mad. Now he knew that he had no daily accident to fear—no new misfortune to dread—and he nerved himself to bear the six long coming months with fortitude and patience. Though the time was long, and his weary days generally unbroken by anything that could interest or enliven them, still, from the hour when Father John first spoke to him at his hall door, to that in which he was led into the Court-house dock as a prisoner to take his trial for his life, he never once repented that he had quitted Aughacashel and his mountain security, to give himself up as a prisoner to the authorities of Carrick.

CHAPTER XXV

RETROSPECTIVE

As story-tellers of every description have, from time immemorial, been considered free from those niceties by which all attempts in the nobler classes of literature are or should be restrained, we consider no apology necessary for requesting the reader to leap over with us the space of four months; but still, before we continue our tale from that date, it will be as well that we should give a short outline of the

principal events which produced the state in
which the circumstances of the Macdermots
will then be found, and we are sorry to say that
they were not such as could offer much consolation to them.

It will be remembered that Pat Brady was com-
missioned by his master to take Ussher's body
to the police-station at Carrick, in Fred Brown's
gig. This commission he promptly performed,
and also that of restoring the gig to its owner;
and after having thus completed his master's
behests like a good servant, he paid a visit on
his own account to Mr. Keegan.

Although it was late, he still found that active
gentleman up, and gave him a tolerably accurate
account of what had happened at Ballycloran,
adding that "the young masther had gone off
to join the boys, at laste that's what he supposed he'd be afther now." As soon as Keegan's surprise was a little abated, he perceived
that the affair would probably act as a stepping-
stone, on which he might walk into Ballycloran
even sooner than he had hitherto thought to do;
and when, as one of the jurors at the coroner's
inquest, on the next morning, he saw that
poor Larry had evidently fallen into absolute
idiotcy, and heard that Thady had, in fact,
escaped, he instantly determined to take such
legal steps on behalf of his father-in-law as
would put the property under his management.
And this, accordingly, he did. The proper
steps for proving the old man to be of unsound
mind would have been attended with very great
expense; instead of doing this, he got himself made receiver over the property, and

determined to arrest Larry, which, in his existing
state, he conceived he should have no difficulty
in doing. Here, however, he found himself
very much mistaken, for nothing could induce
the old man to leave his own room, or so much
as allow the front door to be unlocked. Mary
Brady still continued to attend him every day,
returning home to her husband after sunset, and
she found him very easy to manage in every
other particular, so long as he was allowed to
have his own way in this.

He had quite lost the triumphant feeling
which led him to boast in the streets of Carrick,
after leaving the inquest, that he had escaped
from Flannelly's power, and that he would
never have to pay him another farthing; for
now if he heard a strange step, he fancied it to
be a bailiff's, and if there was the slightest noise
in the house, he thought that an attempt was
being made to drag him off by violence. It
was a miserable sight to see the old man,
thin, wan, and worn out, sitting during that
cold winter, by a few sods of turf, with the door
of his own room ajar, watching the front door
from morning till night, to see that no one
opened it. Before Christmas he had his bed
brought down into the same room, in order
that he might not be betrayed into the hands of
his enemies in the morning before he was up,
and from that time no inducement could prevail on him to leave the room for a moment.

During this time his poverty was very great;
the tenants had been served with legal notices
to pay neither to him nor to Thady any portion
of their rents, and consequently provisions were

very low and very scarce at Ballycloran; in fact,
had it not been for the kindness of Father John,
Mr. McKeon, and Counsellor Webb, whose property was adjoining to Ballycloran, Larry would
have been starved into a surrender. Mr. Webb
went so far as to interfere with Mr. Keegan,
and to point out to him that in all humanity he
should stay his proceedings till after Thady's
trial, but Keegan replied that he was only acting
for Mr. Flannelly, who was determined ·to have
the matter settled at once; that all he wanted
was his own, and that he had already waited
too long.

When Keegan found that Larry Macdermot,
in spite of his infirmities, was too wary to be
caught, he endeavoured to bribe Mary to open
the door to his emissaries, and to betray the
old man; but though Mary was very fond of
money, she was too honest for this, and she
replied to the attorney by telling him, "that for
all the money in the bank of Carrick, she
wouldn't be the one to trate the ould blood*
that way." Larry consequently still held out at
Ballycloran, living on the chance presents of
his friends, who sent him at one time a few
stone of potatoes, at another a pound of tea,
then a bit of bacon or a few bottles of whiskey;
this last, however, was confided to Mary, with
injunctions not to allow him too frequently
to have recourse to the only comforter that was
left to him.

Though Keegan failed to gain admission into
the house, and could not therefore put himself
into absolute possession of the estate, still he
could do what he pleased with the lands, and

he was not long in availing himself of the power. In January he served notices on all the tenants that unless the whole arrears were paid on or before the end of the next month, they would be ejected; and to many of those who held portions of the better part of the land, he sent summary notices to quit on the first of May next following. These notices were all served by Pat, who assured the tenants that he only performed the duties which he had now undertaken that he might look after Mr. Thady's interests, and as, as he said, " there could be no use in life in his refusing to do it, for av he didn't, another would, and the tenants would be no betther, and he a dale the worse."

These things by no means tended to make Keegan's name popular on the estate, particularly at Drumleesh, where the tenants were but ill prepared to pay their rent by small portions at a time, and were utterly confounded at the idea of having to pay up the arrears in a lump; but Pat assured him that although they were surly and sullen, they gave no signs or showed any determination of having recourse to violence, or of openly rebelling against the authority of their new landlord.

Pat, however, knew but little of what was going on amongst them now. Although they found no absolute fault with the arguments which he used for acting on Mr. Keegan's behalf, still he soon discovered that the tenants had withdrawn their confidence from him, and that they looked upon him rather as the servant of their new tyrant, than as the friend to whom they had been accustomed to turn, when they wanted any little favour from their old master. He had, moreover, discontinued his visits to Mrs. Mulready's, and had for a long time seen nothing of Joe Reynolds and his set, who spent most of their time in Aughacashel, or at any rate away from Drumleesh.

Joe Reynolds had been altogether unable to account for Thady's sudden disappearance from Aughacashel. At first he thought he must have been taken prisoner by some of the police, whilst roaming about in the neighbourhood; and although he ultimately heard that Father John and he had gone together to Counsellor Webb's, still he never could learn how Thady had fallen into the priest's hands. Joe, however, did not forget that Thady had done what he considered the good service of ridding the country of Ussher, and he swore that he would repay it by punishing the man, who in his estimation was robbing Thady of his right and his property; he had long since declared at Mrs. Mulready's, as we are aware, that if Thady would come over and join his party, Keegan should not come upon the estate with impunity, and he was now determined to keep his word.

Keegan, trusting to the assurance of Pat, that the tenants were all quiet and peaceable, at length began to go among them himself, and had, about the beginning of February, once or twice ridden over portions of the property. About five o'clock one evening in that month, he was riding towards home along the little lane that skirts Drumleesh bog, after having seen as much of that delectable neighbourhood as a man could do on horseback, when his horse was stopped by a man wrapped in a very large frieze coat, but whose face was not concealed, who asked him, "could he spake to his honer about a bit of land that he was thinking of axing afther, when the man that was on it was put off, as he heard war to be done." As the man said this he laid his hands on the bridle, and Keegan fearing from this that something was not right, put his hand into his coat pocket, where his pistols were, and told the man to come to him at Carrick, if he wanted to say anything. The man, however, continued, "av his honer wouldn't think it too much throuble jist to come down for one moment, he'd point out the cabin which he meant." Keegan was now sure from the man's continuing to keep his hand on the bridle, that some injury to him was intended, and was in the act of drawing his pistol from his pocket, when he was knocked altogether from off his horse by a blow which he received on the head with a large stone, thrown from the other side of one of the banks which ran along the road. The blow and the fall completely stunned him, and when he came to himself he was lying on the road; the man who had stopped his horse was kneeling on his chest; a man, whose face was blackened, was holding down his two feet, and a third, whose face had also been blackened, was kneeling on the road beside him with a small axe in his hand. Keegan's courage utterly failed him when he saw the sharp instrument in the ruffian's grasp; he began to promise largely if they would let him escape—forgiveness—money—land—anything—everything for his life. Neither of them, however, answered

him, and before the first sentence he uttered
was well out of his mouth, the instrument fell
on his leg, just above the ankle, with all the
man's force ; the first blow only cut his trousers
and his boot, and bruised him sorely,—for his
boots protected him ; the second cut the flesh,
and grated against the bone ; in vain he struggled
violently, and with all the force of a man
struggling for his life ; a third, and a fourth, and
a fifth descended, crushing the bone, dividing
the marrow, and ultimately severing the foot
from the leg. When they had done their work,
they left him on the road, till some passer by
should have compassion on him, and obtain for
him the means of conveyance to his home.

In a short time Keegan fainted from loss
of blood, but the cold frost soon brought him
to his senses ; he got up and hobbled to the
nearest cabin, dragging after him the mutilated
foot, which still attached itself to his body by
the cartilages and by the fragments of his boot
and trousers ; and from thence reached his
home on a country car, racked by pain, which
the jolting of the car and the sharp frost did not
tend to assuage.

At the time of which we are writing—about
the first week in March—he had been entirely
unable to ascertain any of the party by whom
he had been attacked. The men were Dan
Kennedy, Joe Reynolds, and Corney Dolan ;
of these, Joe alone was personally known to
Keegan, and it was he who used the axe with
such fell cruelty ; but he had been so completely disguised at the time, that Keegan had
not in the least recognised him. Dan was the

man who had at first stopped the horse, and he being confident that Keegan had not even heard his name, and that he was very unlikely to be in any place where his victim could again see him so as to know him, had not feared to stop the horse, and address its rider without any disguise.

This act, which was originally proposed and finally executed more with the intent of avenging Thady, than with any other purpose, was the most unfortunate thing for him that could have happened ; for in the first place it made the magistrates and the government imagine that the country was in a disorderly state generally, and that it was therefore necessary to follow up the prosecutions at the Assizes with more than ordinary vigour ; and in the next place, it made Keegan determined to do all that he could to secure Thady's conviction, for he attributed his horrible mutilation to the influence of the Macdermots.

Other things had also occurred during the four months since Thady had given himself up to the authorities, which had determined the law officers of the government to follow up Ussher's murderer with all severity, and obtain if possible a conviction.

The man who had been sent to Mohill in Ussher's place was by no means his equal either in courage, determination, or perseverance ; still, it had been necessary for him to follow to a certain degree in his predecessor's steps, especially as at the time illicit distillation had become more general in the country than it had ever been known to be before. A man named

Cogan, who had acted very successfully as a spy to Ussher, also offered his services to the new officer, by whom they were accepted. This man had learnt that potheen was being made at Aughacashel, and, dressed in the uniform of one of the Revenue police, had led the men to Dan Kennedy's cabin. Here they merely found Abraham, the cripple, harmlessly employed in superintending the boiling of some lumpers, and Andy McEvoy in the other cabin, sitting on his bed ; not a drop of potheen—not a grain of malt—not a utensil used in distillation was found, and they had to return foiled and beaten.

The new officer, whose name was Foster, also received various threatening letters, and among them the following :—

" This is to giv' notis, Captin Furster, av you'll live and let live, and be quite an' pacable —divil a rason is there, why you need be afeard—but av you go on among the Leatrim boys—as that bloody thundhering ruffin Ussher, by the etarnal blessed Glory, you wul soon be streatched as he war—for the Leatrim boys isn't thim as wul put up with it."

This was only one of many that he received —and these, together with the futility of his first attempt—a tremendous stoning which he and his men received in the neighbourhood of Drumshambo—the burning of Cogan's cabin, and the fate of his predecessor, totally frightened him ; and he represented to the head office in Dublin that the country was in such a state, that he was unable, with the small body of men at his command, to carry on his business with anything approaching to security.

These things all operated much against the chance of Thady's acquittal, and his warmest friends could not but feel that they did so. People in the country began to say that some severe example was necessary—that the country was in a dreadful state—and that the government must be upheld ; and these fears became ten times greater, when it was generally known that Thady, a day or two before the catastrophe, had absolutely associated with some of the most desperate characters in the country.

Brady, at first, had been unwilling to divulge all that he knew to Mr. Keegan ; for, though he felt no hesitation in betraying his old master, he was not desirous to hang him ; but Keegan, by degrees, got it all out of him, and bribed so high that Pat, at last, consented to come forward at the trial and swear to all the circumstances of the meeting at Mrs. Mehan's, and the attorney lost no time in informing the solicitor, who was to conduct the prosecution on behalf of the crown, what this witness was able to prove.

All this was sad news for Father John, and his friend McKeon, but still they would not despair. They talked the matter over and over again in McKeon's parlour, and Tony occasionally almost forgot his punch in his anxiety to put forward and make the most of all those points, which he considered to be in Thady's favour. It was not only the love of justice, his regard for the family of the Macdermots, and Father John's eloquence which had enlisted McKeon so thoroughly in Thady's interest,

—though, no doubt, these three things had great weight with him,—but his own personal predilections had also a considerable share in doing so.

The three leading resident gentlemen in the neighbourhood were Sir Michael Gibson, Mr. Jonas Brown, and Counsellor Webb ; they were the three magistrates who regularly attended the petty sessions at Carrick ; and as they usually held different opinions on all important subjects relative to the locality in which they resided, so all their neighbours swore by one of them, condemning the other two as little better than fools or knaves.

Sir Michael was by far the richest, and would, therefore, naturally have had the greatest number of followers, had it not been that it was usually extremely difficult to find out what his opinion was. He was neither a bad nor a good landlord—that is to say, his land was seldom let for more than double its value ; and his agent did not eject his tenants as long as they contrived not to increase the arrears which they owed when he undertook the management of the property ; but Sir Michael himself neither looked after their welfare, nor took the slightest care to see that they were comfortable.

On the bench, by attempting to agree with both his colleagues, he very generally managed to express an opinion different from either of them ; and as he was, of course, the chairman, the decisions of the bench were in consequence frequently of a rather singular nature ; however, on the whole, Sir Michael was popular, for if he benefited none, he harmed none ; and he was

considered by many a safe constitutional man,
with no flighty ideas on any side.

Jonas Brown was hated by the poor. In
every case he would, if he had the power, visit
every fault committed by them with the severest
penalty awarded by the law. He was a stern,
hard, cruel man, with no sympathy for any one,
and was actuated by the most superlative contempt for the poor, from whom he drew his
whole income. He was a clever, clear-headed,
avaricious man ; and he knew that the only
means of keeping the peasantry in their present
utterly helpless and dependent state, was to
deny them education, and to oppose every
scheme for their improvement and welfare. He
dreaded every movement which tended to teach
them anything, and when he heard of landlords
reducing their rents, improving cabins, and
building schools, he would prophesy to his
neighbour, Sir Michael, that the gentry would
soon begin to repent of their folly, when the
rents they had reduced were not paid, the
cabins which they had made comfortable were
filled with ribbonmen, and when the poor had
learnt in the schools to disobey their masters
and landlords. Sir Michael never contradicted
all this, and he would probably have become a
second Jonas Brown, and much more injurious,
because so much more extensive in his interests, were it not for the counteracting influence
of Counsellor Webb, who was in all his opinions
diametrically opposed to Mr. Brown.

Mr. Webb was a clear-headed and a much
more talented man than his brother magistrate.
He was, moreover, a kind-hearted landlord—

ever anxious to ameliorate the condition of the poor—and by no means greedy after money, though he was neither very opulent nor very economical. But, nevertheless, with all these high qualities he was hardly the man most fit to do real good in a very poor and ignorant neighbourhood. He was, in the first place, by far too fond of popularity, and of being the favourite among the peasantry; and, in the next, he had become so habituated to oppose Jonas Brown in all his sayings and doings, that he now did so whether he was right or wrong.

Thady's case had been much talked of in the country, and the rival magistrates, of course, held diametrically opposite opinions respecting it.

Jonas Brown had declared at his own table, that "unless that young man were hanged, there would be an end to anything like law in the country; his being the son of a landlord made it ten times worse; if the landlords themselves turned ribbonmen, and taught the tenants all manner of iniquity, and the law didn't then interfere, it would be impossible to live in the country; he, for one, should leave it. Here had a most praiseworthy servant of the crown—a man who had merited the thanks of the whole country by the fearless manner in which he had performed his duties, here," he said, "had this man been murdered in cold blood by a known ribbonman, by one, who, as he understood, had, a few days before the murder, conspired with others to commit it; and yet he was told there were a pack of people through the country— priests, and popularity hunters, who were not

only using their best endeavours to screen the
murderer, but who absolutely justified the deed.
By G—d, he couldn't understand how a man,
holding the position of a gentleman, could so
far forget what he owed to his country and himself as to dirty his hands with such a filthy
business as this, however absurd his general
opinions on politics might be. As for the man's
sister, that was all a got up story since the business. Every one knew that the family had been
trying to catch the young man for the girl; she
had been allowed to walk with Captain Ussher
at all hours, night and day; and he was doing
no more than walking with her when he was
basely murdered by her brother. As for him
(Jonas Brown), he hoped and trusted the murderer would be hung as he deserved."

The purport of this piece of after-dinner
eloquence was duly conveyed to Counsellor
Webb, who fully appreciated the remarks about
the popularity-hunting gentleman who was dirty-
ing his hands. Up to this time these two men,
though differing so widely from each other, had
still kept up a show of courtesy between them; but
Mr. Brown's remarks altogether put an end to it.

Counsellor Webb never again addressed him
in friendly terms.

He did not, however, in the least relax his
efforts on Thady's behalf, or express less strongly
his opinion on the case. He told Sir Michael
one morning in Carrick, after some public meeting at which all the gentry of the neighbourhood
had been present, and while many of them, and
among them Mr. Brown, were standing by, that
" he had lately been giving a great deal of very

close attention to that very distressing case of
young Mr. Macdermot; he thought it was the
most melancholy and heartrending case he had
ever known. It was proved beyond possibility
of doubt that Ussher was eloping with the young
man's sister; it seemed now to be pretty certain
that the girl was herself absolutely senseless at
the time the occurrence took place; he believed she had changed her mind, or got frightened, or what not; it was now a known fact,
that she was being dragged senseless in the
man's arms, when Macdermot attacked him.
And was a brother to stand by and look on at
such a sight as that, and not protect his sister,
and punish the miscreant who was endeavouring
to dishonour her? Was Mr. Macdermot to
turn his back upon the affair, and leave his
sister to her fate because, forsooth, the man who
did it was a Revenue officer? Let us bring the
matter home to ourselves, Sir Michael," he continued. "Suppose you saw that gay young
Captain Jem Boyle hurrying through the demesne at Knockadrum with one of your own
fair flock in his arms, violently carrying her off,
wouldn't you not only knock him down yourself, if you could catch him, but also set all
your people after him, begging them to do the
same? Of course, you would; and what more
has this young man done? Unfortunately he
struck too hard; but that, although we may
deplore the circumstance, shows no criminality
on his part; but only the strong indignation
which he very properly felt. As to the cock
and bull story of his being a ribbonman, no
man of sense could entertain it. It appears

that a few nights before the occurrence he went
to a tenant's wedding, and unfortunately took
a drop too much punch. That had been many
a good man's case* before his. And then he
got among a lot of men who were uttering vague,
nonsensical threats against different persons,
whom they disliked. One, I hear, says that
Ussher was threatened ; and another—and, I
am told, by far the more creditable witness—
that it was Keegan, the attorney, whose name
was mentioned ; it appears, that when drunk,
he promised to join these men in another
drinking party, which promise he, of course,
never thought of keeping after he was sober ;
and yet there are some who are cruel enough to
say—I won't say harsh enough to believe, for
they can't believe it—that when he attacked
Ussher in his sister's defence, Macdermot was
only carrying into execution a premeditated
plan of murdering him ! Premeditated indeed,
when it was plain to every one, that it was by
the merest accident that he happened to be in
the avenue at the time. People might just as
well say that it was he who cut off the attorney's
foot the other day, though he was in gaol at the
time. I must say," continued the Counsellor,
" that should the poor young man fall a victim
to the false evidence which I am aware private
malice and wretchedly vindictive feeling will
supply, then the basest murder will really have
been committed which ever disgraced this
county. I don't envy the state of mind of any
gentleman who can look forward with a feeling
of satisfaction to the prospect of that poor
youth's being hanged for protecting his sister,

merely because the seducer was in habits of intimacy with himself or his family."

Mr. Brown left the meeting, taking no immediate notice of the Counsellor's philippic.* It was not, however, because he did not comprehend the latter part of it, or that he meant to overlook it.

Sir Michael was much distressed in making up his mind finally on the subject. It was reported, however, soon after the meeting above alluded to, that he had stated to some of his more immediate friends and admirers, that " he considered it highly discreditable, he might say disgraceful, for any of the more respectable classes to give any countenance to the illegal meetings, which he was afraid were too general through the country, and that there was too much reason to fear that the unfortunate man in prison had been guilty in doing so ; but that there could be no doubt that every one was justified — he might add, only performed his bounden duty—in protecting the females of his family from injury or violence."

Now, Tony McKeon was a tenant both of Sir Michael and of the Counsellor ; he also held land from other landlords, but he had no connexion whatever with Mr. Brown : he was not at all the sort of tenant that Jonas liked; for though he always punctually paid his rent to the day, he usually chose to have everything his own way, and would take no land except at a fair rent and on a long lease.

Mr. Webb, however, was his chief friend and principal ally in the country. Sir Michael was altogether too grand for him, seeing that Tony

had no idea of being a humble dependent; but
Mr. Webb would occasionally come and dine
with him—and often asked him in return. Mrs.
Webb too was civil to his wife and the girls—
always lent them the Dublin pattern for their
frills, frocks, and other frippery—and seldom
drove into Drumsna without calling. The consequence was, that the Counsellor was a man
after Tony's own heart. Though they were of
different religions, they had, generally speaking,
the same political feelings and opinions—the
same philanthropical principles—and the same
popular prejudices; and after a few years' intimacy in each other's neighbourhood, Mr. Webb
well knew where to find a powerful recruit for
any service in which he might wish to enlist one.

Tony declared that if any one spoke ill of
Feemy's character, he should make it personal
with himself; that he was ready, willing, and
moreover determined to quarrel with any one
who dared to apply the opprobrious name of
murderer to Thady; and he had even been
heard, on one or two occasions, to stand up for
Larry himself, and to declare that although he
might be a little light-headed or so, he was still
a deal better than those muddy-minded blackguards at Carrick who had driven him to his
present state.

For a long time Feemy had been very ill,
but after Christmas she had apparently got a
little stronger; she would sit up in her bed-room
for a few hours in the day; but still she would
talk to no one. Mrs. McKeon endeavoured
more than once to lead her to the subject which
she knew must be nearest her heart, thinking

that if she could be got to speak of it, she would be relieved; but in vain. In vain she tried to interest her in her brother's fate—in vain she tried to make her understand that Thady's safety—that his acquittal would, in a great degree, depend on her being able to prove, at the trial, that at the time when the occurrence took place, she was herself insensible. She shuddered violently at the idea of being again questioned, and declared with sobs that she should die if she were again dragged to that horrid place. When Mrs. McKeon asked her if she would not make a struggle to save her brother's life, she remained mute. It was evident that it was for her lover that she was still grieving, and that it was not the danger or ignominy of Thady's position that afflicted her.

Mrs. McKeon, however, conceived it to be her duty to persevere with her—and, at last, told her how wrong it was of her to give way to a grief, which was in its first stage respected. Feemy answered her only with tears; and on the next morning told her that she had determined to return to Ballycloran, as she thought she would be better there, at home with her father.

To this, however, Mrs. McKeon would not consent, and Feemy was told that the doctor had forbidden her to be moved. She was, therefore, obliged to remain satisfied for the present, as she had no means of escaping from Drumsna; but she soon became more sullen than ever—and, at last, almost refused to speak to any one.

Things went on in this way till about the middle of March. Feemy constantly requested

to be allowed to go home, which request was as
constantly refused ; when different circumstances
acting together gave rise to a dreadful suspicion
in Mrs. McKeon's mind. She began to fear
that Ussher, before his death, had accomplished
the poor girl's ruin, and that she was now in the
family way. For some few days she was determined to reject the idea, and endeavoured to
make herself believe that she was mistaken ;
but the more close her observations were, the
more certain she became that her suspicions
were well founded. She was much distressed
as to what she should do. Her first and most
natural feelings were those of anger against
Feemy, and of dismay at the situation into
which her own and her husband's good nature
had brought herself and her daughters ; and
she made up her mind that Feemy should at
once have her wish and return to Ballycloran.
But then, she might be mistaken—or even, if it
were too true—how could she turn the poor
girl, weak, ill, and miserable, out of her house,
and send her to an empty unprovided barrack,*
inhabited by an infirm, idiotical old man, where
she could receive none of that attention which
her situation so much required ?

She communicated her suspicions to the
doctor, and after a few days' observations, he
told her that there was too much reason to fear
that the case was as she supposed. He, however, strongly advised her to speak to Miss
Macdermot herself on the subject. This she
did, at last, most tenderly, and with the greatest
gentleness—but still imploring Feemy to tell her
the truth. Feemy, at first, could not speak in

reply; she threw herself on her bed sobbing
most violently, and fell from one fit into another,
till Mrs. McKeon was afraid that she would
choke herself with the violence of her emotion.
At last, however, she declared that the accusation brought against her was untrue—protested
on her most solemn word and honour that it
was not the case—and ended by saying how
thankful she was to Mrs. McKeon for her kindness and protection, but that she must now beg
her to allow her to return to Ballycloran.

Feemy's denial of the charge against her was
so firm, and so positively made, that it very
much shook her friend's suspicions. When
Feemy begged to be sent home, she told her
not to agitate herself at present—that they
would all see how she was in a day or two—
and then speaking a few kind words to her, left
her to herself.*

CHAPTER XXVI

THE DUEL

MR. JONAS BROWN was in a towering passion,
when he left the meeting at which he had
listened to, but had not ventured to answer,
Counsellor Webb's remarks respecting Thady
Macdermot and the supposed intimacy between
Ussher and the inmates of Brown Hall. He
had so openly expressed his wish that the young
man might be capitally punished—and this

joined to the fact that Ussher had not been as intimate at any other house as he had been at Brown Hall, could leave no doubt on the mind of any one who had been present, that Webb's allusion had been intended for him. His first impulse was to challenge his foe at once ; but his ardour on that point soon cooled a little, and he came to the conclusion of sleeping on the matter, or, at any rate, of drinking a bottle or two of wine over it with his sons.

As soon as the servant had withdrawn after dinner he began his grievance.

"By G—d, Fred, that ruffian Webb is passing all bounds. He's not only forgotten the opinions and notions of a gentleman, but he has lain down the manners of one too."

"Why, what has he done now ? With all his queer ideas, Webb can be a gentleman if he pleases," said Fred.

"I must say," said George, "the Counsellor is a good fellow on the course. I don't care how seldom I see him anywhere else."

"I don't know what you may call being a good fellow or a gentleman," replied the father ; "but I know he has insulted me publicly, and that in the most gross way, and before half the country. I don't know whether that's your idea of acting like a gentleman or a good fellow."

"It's what many a gentleman and many a good fellow has done before him," said George ; "but if he has insulted you, of course he must apologize—or do the other thing."

"What—let it alone ? " rejoined Fred.

"No ; fight—and that's what he's a deal the most likely to do," said George.

"Be d—d," said old Brown, "but I think both of you seem glad to hear that your father has been insulted! you've neither of you a grain of proper feeling."

"It's with a grain or two of gunpowder, I'd take it," said George, "and I'd advise you, father, to do the same; a precious deal better thing than good feeling to settle an insult with."

"But you've not told us what it's all about?" said Fred; "what was the quarrel about?"

"Quarrel! there was no quarrel at all in the matter—I couldn't quarrel with him, for I wouldn't speak to him. It was about that infernal friend of yours, Fred, that Ussher; I wish he'd never darkened this door."

"Poor devil!" answered Fred; "there's no use abusing him now he's dead. I suppose the row wasn't his fault."

"It was about him, though, and the low blackguard that murdered him. Webb was talking about him, making a speech in the public-room, taking the fellow's part, as I'm told he's always doing, and going on with all the clap-trap story about protecting his sister;—as if every one in the country didn't know that she'd been Ussher's mistress for months back. Well, that was all nothing to me—only he'll be rightly served when he finds every man on his estate has become a ribbonman, and every other tenant ready to turn murderer. But this wasn't enough for him, but at the end of the whole he must declare—I forget what it was he said—but something about Ussher's intimacy here—that it was a shameful thing of me to be wishing on

464 The Macdermots of Ballycloran

that account that this Macdermot should be hanged, as he deserves."

"Did he actually mention Brown Hall?" asked Fred.

"No; but he put it so that there could be no mistake about it; he said he didn't envy my state of mind."

"Well, tell him you don't envy his. I don't think you could call him out for that," said George.

"By heavens, you're enough to provoke a saint!" continued the father. "Can't you believe me, when I tell you, he made as direct a cut at Brown Hall as he could, because I can't repeat all his words like a newspaper? By G——d, the pluck's gone out of the country entirely! If as much had been said to my father, when I was your age, I'd have had the fellow who said it out, if he'd been the best shot in Connaught."

"Don't say another word, father," said George, "if that's what you're after. I thought, may be, you'd like the fun yourself, or I'd have offered. I'd call him out with a heart and a half; there's nothing I'd like better. May be I'd be able to make up a match between Diamond and the Counsellor's brown mare, when it's done. He'd be a little soft, would Webb, after such a job as that, and wouldn't stand for a few pounds difference."

"That's nonsense, George," said the father, a little mollified by the son's dutiful offer. "I don't want any one to take the thing off my hands. I don't want to be shelved that way— but I wish you to see the matter in the right

light. I tell you the man was cursedly insolent,
Fred; in fact, he said what I don't mean to put
up with; and the question is, what had I better
do?"

"He didn't say anything, did he," asked Fred,
"with your name, or Brown Hall in it?"

"No, he didn't name them exactly."

"Then I don't think you can call for an
apology; write him a civil note, and beg him to
say that he intended no allusion to you or your
family in what he said."

"Fred's right for once," said George, "that's
all you can do as the matter stands now. If
he won't say that, call him out and have done
with it."

"I've no wish to be fighting," said the father;
"in fact, at my time of life I'd rather not. I
was ready enough once, but I'd sooner settle it
quietly."

"Why, there's no contenting you," answered
Fred; "just now nothing but pistols and coffee
would do for you; and then you were in a
passion because one of us wouldn't take a
challenge for you at once, without knowing anything about it; and now you're just the other
way; if you don't like the business, there's
George will take it off your hands, he says."

After a considerable quantity of squabbling
among this family party it was at last decided
that a civil note should be sent to Ardrum, in
which Mr. Webb should be desired to state
that he had made no allusion to Brown Hall;
accordingly a servant on horseback was dispatched on the Monday morning with the
following missive :—

"Brown Hall, Sunday Evening.

"Mr. Brown presents his compliments to Mr. Webb, and begs to inform him that certain expressions which fell from him at the meeting at Carrick on Saturday respecting the murder of Captain Ussher, have been thought by many to have had reference to the family at Brown Hall. Mr. Brown feels himself assured that Mr. Webb would not so far forget himself, as to make any such allusion in public to a neighbouring gentleman and magistrate; but as Mr. Webb's words were certainly singular in their reference to Captain Ussher's intimacy with some family in the neighbourhood, and as many conceive that they were directly pointed at Brown Hall, Mr. Brown must beg Mr. Webb to give him his direct assurance in writing that nothing which fell from him was intended to apply either to Mr. Brown or his family.

"To W. Webb, Esq., Ardrum."

Mr. Webb was at home when the servant arrived, and, only detaining him two minutes, sent him back with the following answer:—

"Ardrum, Monday Morning.

"Mr. Webb presents his compliments to Mr. Brown. Mr. Webb regrets that he cannot comply with the request made in Mr. Brown's letter of yesterday's date.

"To Jonas Brown, Esq., Brown Hall."

The conclave at Brown Hall, on receipt of this laconic epistle, unanimously declared that it was tantamount to a declaration of war, and that desperate measures must at once be adopted.

"The sod's the only place now, father," said George; "by heavens, I like him the better for not recanting."

"He's a cursed good shot," said Fred. "Would you like to send for Keegan before you go out?"

"Keegan be d—d!" said George; "but have Blake by, for he'll wing you as sure as Moses."

"May be not," said Fred. "Webb's a d—d good shot in a gallery; but may be he won't allow for the wind on the sod; but it'll be as well to have the sawbones."

"No fear of your legs, governor, for he'll fire high. The shoulder's his spot; you may always tell from a man's eye where he'll fix the sight of a pistol. Webb always looks up. If his tool lifts a little, he'll fire over you."

"Yes, he might," said Fred; "or take you on the head—which wouldn't be so pleasant. I'm not particular—but I'd better run my chance myself with a chap that fired low."

"There you're out," answered the brother. "The low shot's the death-shot. Why, man, if you did catch a ball in the head, you'd get over it—if it was in the mouth, or cheek, or neck, or anywhere but the temple; but your body's all over tender bits. May heaven always keep lead out of my bowels—I'd sooner have it in my brains."

The father fidgeted about very uneasily whilst enduring these pleasant remarks from his affectionate children, which, it is needless to say, they made for his particular comfort and amusement at the present moment. At last he lost his temper, and exclaimed—

"D—n your brains, you fool—I don't believe you've got any! what's the use of the two of you. going on that way—you that were never out in your life? I tell you when a man's standing to be fired at, he doesn't know, nine times in ten, whether he fires high or low. Who'll I get to go out with me?"

"Yes, and take your message," said Fred; "you've a deal to do yet before you're snug home again."

"Well, who'll I get to go to him?"

"Why wouldn't I do?" suggested George. George, at any rate, had the merit of being a good son.

"Nonsense," said Fred; "if the governor got shot you'd be considered a brute if you were cool; and a man should be cool then."

"Cool," said George; "I'd be as cool as a cucumber."

"Nonsense," said the father; "of course I couldn't go out with my own son*; there's Theobald French; I went out with his cousin just after Waterloo."

"He can't show—he's on his keeping.* He'd be nabbed before he was on the ground."

"Then I'll have Larkin; I've known him since I was a boy."

"Larkin's too old for that game now; he'd be letting them have Webb up with his back to the sun."*

"Murphy, of Mullough; he's used to these things—I'll send over to him."

"Murphy's up to snuff; but since the affair of the bill he forged Dan Connolly's name to, he's queerly thought of. It wouldn't do at all,

governor, to send any one that Webb's friend
could refuse to meet."

"I'll tell you, father, who'd be proud of the
job—and he's quite a gentleman now, since he
got an estate of his own—and that's Cynthy
Keegan. It'd be great fun to see him stepping
the ground,* and he only with one foot."

"By heavens, George, you're a born fool;
must you have your d—d joke, when I'm talking
so seriously?"

"Upon my soul, then, if it were myself, I'd
send for Keegan. He'd think the compliment
so great, he wouldn't refuse, and it'd be such a
joke to see him on the ground with his crutches.
But if you don't like the attorney, send to Fitzpatrick."

"He's so young," said the father; "he'd do
very well for either of you; but I'd want some
one steadier."

"Besides," said Fred, "Webb and Fitz are
bosom friends. I wouldn't wonder if Fitz were
Webb's friend himself."

"I tell you, father — Major Longsword's
exactly the boy," said George; "send to Boyle
for him; he wants to get a name in the country,
and the job'll just suit him."

"You're right for once, George," said Jonas,
"Longsword's just the man that will answer."
And accordingly it was at last decided that
Major Longsword was to be the honoured individual. He had dined once or twice at
Brown Hall, and therefore there was some
excuse for calling upon him; and a note was
accordingly written to him, with a great deal of
blarney about his station and experience, and

the inexpediency of entrusting affairs of honour to inexperienced country gentlemen. This had the effect of immediately bringing him over to Brown Hall, and on the Tuesday morning he was dispatched to Ardrum, to make what arrangements he pleased with Mr. Webb.

To give Major Longsword his due, Mr. Brown could not have made a much better choice; for though he was a disciple of that school, which thoroughly entertained the now anti-quated notion that the world—that is, the world of men in broad cloth*—could not go on with-out duels, or a pretence of duels; still he was one who, as a second, would do all in his power to prevent an absolute effusion of lead. He was a great hand at an apology, and could regulate its proper degree of indifference or abjectness to the exact state of the case; he could make it almost satisfactory to the receiver, without being very disagreeable to the giver; he could twaddle about honour for ever without causing bloodshed; and would, if possible, protect a man's reputation and body at the same time.

He started on his mission of peace with the determined intention of returning with some document in his pocket which would appease Mr. Brown's irritated feelings, and add another laurel to the wreath which he considered his due as a peace-maker.

He was shown into Mr. Webb's parlour, where that gentleman soon joined him, and he was not long in making known his business. Major Longsword plumed himself on his man-ners in such embassies, and to-day he was perfect.

"Now, Mr. Webb," he continued after a long

preamble, " of course I am not to judge of the propriety of any words you may think fit to use ; but, I am afraid I must admit in this case, a somewhat—I must say a somewhat unwarranted allusion was made to my friend. Such, I can assure you, is the general opinion. Now, if you will allow me to say as much, I think—I cannot but think, you were right—perfectly right—in not disclaiming such an allusion, having once made it ; but I trust, indeed I feel confident, that a man of your acknowledged sense, and general character as a man of the world, will not object to give me a line—a mere line will suffice — addressed to myself ; I wouldn't ask you in such a matter to write to Mr. Brown—a mere line, just stating that you regret having said anything in your fervour which should hurt any one's feelings. The matter, you know, is now in my hands, and I pledge myself that shall suffice ; I really think such a bagatelle as that cannot be objectionable to you. Were I in your place, I can assure you, Mr. Webb, as a man of honour, I should be delighted to do the same."

"Were you in my place, Major Longsword," replied the Counsellor, "you would, no doubt, act with more judgment than I shall do ; but without wishing to say anything offensive to you, I may as well assure you at once that I will give no letter to any one on the subject."

" But, Mr. Webb, you cannot deny or justify the allusion—the very pointed allusion ? "

" I certainly shall not deny it ; indeed to you, Major Longsword, I have no objection to acknowledge it."

"And yet you'll not just state your regret—in a note to myself, mind! Why, Mr. Webb, you can't but regret it; you can't desire bloodshed."

"Indeed, Major, I do not regret it. Your friend considered himself at liberty to accuse me in private—not by name, but by allusion, as you say—of certain feelings and opinions derogatory to me. I have retaliated in public. I believe now you will own that I consult your convenience best by telling you that Major Macdonnel, of Tramore, is my friend in this matter. He will make all arrangements with you for the immediate termination of this affair."

"I shall be proud to see the Major; but still let me hope, Mr. Webb, that this little affair may be arranged. As a magistrate, and as a man, I may say, not exactly in your *première jeunesse*——" *

"As a magistrate, and as a man not exactly, as you say, in my *première jeunesse*, for I was fifty yesterday, let me assure you that if Mr. Brown intends to call me out, I shall go out. If he intends to let me alone, I shall be better pleased to be let alone ; as for a word, or a line of retractation or apology, I will not give it."

"But, Mr. Webb——"

"Forgive me for interrupting you, but allow me to suggest that any further remarks you may have to make on the subject had better be made to my friend, Major Macdonnel."

"Would you allow me to put it to you in another light? Suppose, now——"

"Major Longsword, the idea of being uncourteous to any man in my own house is particularly grievous to me ; but with your pardon I must say that I cannot continue this conversation with you. If you will allow me the honour of considering the remainder of your visit one of compliment, I shall be proud to increase my acquaintance with a gentleman for whom I entertain so profound a respect."

The baffled Major was obliged to take the hint, to move himself off, and have recourse to his brother major. Major Macdonnel received his visitor with a very long face, assured him that his principal had left him nothing to do but to arrange the meeting, and that however willing he might be to agree to pacific measures himself, he had no power to do so. The Boyle Major, however, found a more willing listener in his colleague than in the Counsellor, and made many eloquent dissertations ; but it was all to no purpose ; he was obliged to return to Brown Hall, signally defeated as he felt himself, and with the tidings that a place had been agreed to, and that the meeting was to take place at eight A.M. the next morning.

"I had really hoped, Mr. Brown, to have been able to settle this little matter amicably ; indeed I had no doubt about it ; but I must say a more impracticable gentleman to deal with than Mr. Webb it was never my lot to meet upon such an occasion."

The Major dined at Brown Hall, and could not but admire the solicitude which the two sons expressed for their father's safety, and the filial manner in which they comforted him. During dinner he was somewhat silent and moody ; but when he got to his wine he recovered his spirits, and seemed tolerably happy. Indeed he conducted himself wonderfully well, considering that during the whole evening Fred and George would talk of nothing but trepanned skulls, false knee-caps—cork legs—bullets that had come out of men's backs ten years after they had entered men's bellies—surgeon's knives —pincers and tourniquets—wills—attorneys— leaden coffins, and the family vault. George expressed a great desire to go and see his parent shot. Fred said that eight o'clock was so damnation early, or else he'd be happy. George was so warm in his solicitude, that in spite of his father's declining this mark of his affection, he insisted on attending him to the ground ; and it was only when Major Longsword gravely assured him that if he, George, was there, he, Major Longsword, would not be there too, that the anxious son was prevailed on to give up his project.

The affair was to come off in the County Roscommon, about a mile and a half from Carrick, at the edge of a small copse, about a mile on the left-hand side of the Boyle road. A message had been conveyed to Doctor Blake to be near the spot with the different instruments that had been so freely named on the previous evening. At the hour appointed, the military Major and his friend arrived in the Brown Hall chariot, and a few minutes after wards the ex-military Major and his man appeared on the Counsellor's car. Had any one walked about the ground with very scrutinising eyes, he might have espied Doctor Blake snugly ensconced under a bank with a cigar in his mouth, and a small mahogany box lying at his feet.

The carriages had been left a few hundred yards distant, and the two servants, well knowing what was going to happen, discussed cosily and leisurely the chance they either of them had of carrying home a dead master.

"Faix, Barney," said the Brown Hall whip, "I believe we stand a baddish chance; they do be saying the Counsellor's mighty handy with the powdher; would you plaze to try a blast* this cowld morning?" and he handed him his pipe.

"And thank ye kindly too, Dan; it's a mighty cowld place. Why, thin, it's thrue for you,—the masther is handy with the powdher; more power to his elbow this morning."

"But whisper now,* Barney, did he iver shoot many now to your knowing? did he shoot 'em dead? I wonder whether Mr. Fred will be keeping on the chariot; he's more taste in the gig way, I'm fearing."

"Why, thin, the Counsellor mayn't shoot him dead; that is, av he behaves himself, and don't have no blusthering. Was old Jonas much afeard, now, Dan?"

"Afeard, is it! the divil wouldn't fright him. Maybe, after all, it's the Counsellor 'll be shot first."

"Oh, in course he may," said Barney; "oh musha, musha, wirrasthrue,* how'd I ever be looking the misthress and the young ladies in the face, av I was taking him home dead and buried as he's likely to be, av he don't hit that owld masther of yours in the very first go off;"

and then the man's air of triumph at the idea of
his master's shooting Jonas Brown, turned to
despondency as the thought struck him that the
Counsellor might be shot himself. But he soon
cheered up again at a brighter reflection,

" But that'd be the wake, Dan ! My ; there'd
have been nothing like that in the counthry,
since old Peyton was waked up at Castleboy ;
not a man in the county but would be there,
nor a woman neither ; and signs on, there's not
another in the counthry at all like the masther
for a poor man."

At this moment two shots were heard.

"Virgin Mary !—there they are at it," said
Dan ; " now they're oncet began in arnest,
they'll not lave it till they're both dead, or
there's not a grain of powdher left. Bad cess
to them Majors for bringing thim together ;
couldn't they be fighting theyselles av they
plazed, and not be setting the real gentry of the
counthry at each other like game cocks ? "

" Had they much powdher, I wonder, Dan ?
Was there a dail* of ammunition in the carriage ? "

" Faix there war so ; that Major, bad luck to
him, had his own and Master George's horns
crammed with powdher, and as many bullets in
a bag under his coat-tail as he could well-nigh
carry."

" Then they're one or both as good as dead ;
they're loading again now, I'll go bail. Och !
that I'd thrown the owld horse down coming
over the bridge, and pitched the masther into
the wather. I'd be a dail readier getting him
out of that, than putting the life into him when

he's had three or four of them bullets through
his skin."

"It's thrue for you, Barney," said the good-
natured Dan; "and as Mr. Fred couldn't well
be turning an owld servant like me off the place
av he didn't keep up the chariot, I wish it mayn't
be the Counsellor's luck to be first kilt, for he's
as good a man as iver trod."

In the mean time the two Majors had paced
the ground with a good deal of official propriety, loaded the pistols, and exchanged a
quantity of courtesies.

"Not so agreeable an occasion as when we
last acted together in the field, Major Macdonnel; I'd sooner be clearing the course for
my friend's horse, than measuring the ground
for his fire."

"True, indeed, Major Longsword; true, indeed. Don't you think you're putting your
friend a leetle too much under the shade? I
don't know—perhaps not—but a foot or two
off the trees gives a more equal light; that's it."

"I believe we're ready now—eh, Major?"

"Quite ready, Major. We'll have it over in
two minutes."

"I say, Major," and the other Major whispered; "Blake's just under the small bush
there, I hope you won't want him."

"Thank ye, Major, thank ye—I hope not."

"And, Major, there can be no necessity for
a second shot, I think—eh? Brown won't want
a second shot, will he?"

"Not at all, Major, not at all; a trifling thing
like this—we'll have it over now in a double
crack, eh?"

" True, Major, true; put your man up, and
I'll give the word."

And the Majors put up their men with great
dexterity, and the word was given. They both
fired, each at his adversary, but each without
attempting to cover the other. Brown's ball
whistled harmlessly away without approaching
within any dangerous proximity of the Counsellor's body; but not so Webb's; it was very
evident Jonas was hit, for his body gave a spas-
modic jerk forwards, his knees bent under him,
and his head became thrown back somewhat
over his shoulders. He did not fall himself,
but his hat did; he dropped his pistol to the
ground, and inserted both his right and his left
hand under the tails of his coat.

Mr. Brown indulged a notion, whether correctly or not I am unable to say, but one which
I believe to be not uncommon, that by pre-
senting his side instead of his front to his
adversary's fire, he exposed fewer vital parts to
danger; and if destiny intended him to be
wounded, he certainly, in the present instance,
was benefited by the above arrangement, for he
received the bullet in perhaps the least dangerous part of his body.

Mr. Brown was a stout, compact man, well
developed and rounded in the fuller parts of
his body; he piqued himself somewhat on the
fair proportions of his nether man; he was also
somewhat of a dandy; and had come out this
morning, as, I believe, was the custom on such
occasions, nearly full dressed; he had on a
black dress coat, black waistcoat, and black
well fitting trousers; and as he turned his side

to the Counsellor, he displayed to advantage the whole of his comely figure.

But, alas! its comeliness was destined for a time to be destroyed. Mr. Webb's fire passed directly under the tails of his coat; the ball just traversed along his trousers about a foot beneath the waistband, cutting them and his drawers and shirt, as it were, with a knife, and wounding the flesh in its course to the depth of perhaps the eighth part of an inch.

Directly Major Longsword perceived that his man was hit, he vociferously called for Blake.

From the position which Mr. Brown assumed on receiving the fire, it was the general opinion of all the party that he was not mortally wounded. Blake was immediately on the spot, and lost no time in supporting him.

"Where is it, Mr. Brown, where is it? Can you stand? Can you walk? Allow me to support you to the bank. You can get a seat there; we must sit down at once. My dear sir, the first thing is to get you to a comfortable seat."

"Comfortable seat, and be d—d to you!" was the patient's uncivil reply. "Go to hell, I tell you!" as Blake continued to lift him. "I'm well enough; I can walk to the carriage?"

"My dear sir," continued the doctor, "the ball must be in your side; at any rate, allow me to discover where it is."

"Ball be d—d, I tell you!" and he hobbled a little way off from his tormentor; the portion of his trousers on the part affected annoyed him sorely when he attempted to walk.

"Permit me to hope," said the Counsellor, coming up—"permit me to hope, now that this affair seems to be over, that you are not seriously hurt. Had you not better allow Doctor Blake to ascertain whether the bullet still remains in you? had you not better sit down?"

"Bother Doctor Blake, sir," said Mr. Brown, with his hands still under his coat tails.

"Ah! I see now," said the Doctor, stooping down; "I see the wound, I think. It's bleeding now—and I think I may guarantee that there's no danger; allow me one minute, for the ball may be lodged," and he proceeded to lift up the tails of the coat.

"Doctor Blake, if you touch me again, by heavens I'll kick you! when I want you, I'll send for you. Major Longsword, will you do me the honour to accompany me to my carriage—ugh, d—n it!"

This last exclamation was occasioned by his renewed attempt to walk. He managed, however, at last, to get to his carriage, and in that to Brown Hall. Major Longsword, who accompanied him, declared afterwards to his brother officers at Boyle, that Mr. Brown's efforts to support himself by the arm-straps in the carriage were really disagreeable to witness. He got home safely, however; and though he was not competent to attend to his public duties for some considerable time, it is believed he was not a great sufferer. The Brown Hall livery servant was seen in the chemist's shop the same morning, asking for a yard and a half of diaculum,* which was supplied to him; and a new pair of dress trousers, somewhat fuller than the last, was ordered from the tailor. Doctor Blake was not called in, for Mr. Brown found himself, with his son's assistance, equal to the cure of the wound he had received.

CHAPTER XXVII

FEEMY RETURNS TO BALLYCLORAN

IT will be remembered that Father John had promised to take upon himself all the trouble attendant upon the preparation for Thady's trial ; and with the view of redeeming this promise he went up to Dublin and spent a week among the lawyers who were to be engaged for the young man's defence. The chief among these was one Mr. O'Malley, and the priest strove hard to imbue that gentleman with his own views of the whole matter. The day after that on which Father John returned, he saw both Mr. McKeon and the Counsellor, and explained to them as nearly as he could all that had passed between himself and O'Malley. Though they were both greatly interested on Thady's account, they did not feel the same intense, constant anxiety, which now quite oppressed the priest; and, moreover, trusting more to their own judgment than he did, they were not so inclined to alter their pre-conceived opinion. They both, therefore, assured Father John that they were still quite sanguine as to Thady's acquittal. This raised his hopes again a little, but nevertheless, from that time till the trial, he was so absorbed by his strong feeling on the subject, that he was almost totally unable to attend to the usual duties and employment of his life. It was decided that Mr. Webb should use all his endeavours to obtain tidings of Corney Dolan, and ascertain whether, in the event of his being summoned, he would be able to give any evidence respecting the meeting at Mrs. Mehan's, which would be of use to Thady at the trial. In this he was successful, and he learnt from that respectable individual that he could swear that Ussher's name was not mentioned at all.

It must be owned that Mr. Dolan's manner was not such as to inspire the Counsellor with any great admiration for his veracity, and his opinion in this respect was strengthened when the witness added " that by Garra,* av his honor thought it'd be any use in life to Mr. Thady, he'd swear as how he was asleep all the time ; or for the matther of that, that he was out along wid de gals dancing the livelong night." It was with difficulty that Mr. Webb made him understand that he was only to swear to what he believed to be the truth, and that if he told a single lie in answer to the numerous questions which would be asked him, he would only be endangering Mr. Macdermot's life.

Father John undertook the more difficult task of explaining to Feemy what it was she was expected to do at the trial, and of making her understand that her brother's life depended on her making an effort to give her evidence in the court clearly and firmly. On reaching Drumsna

he was much distressed to find that she was no
longer at Mrs. McKeon's. For two days after
the conversation which had passed between that
lady and her charge, in which she declared her
suspicions that Feemy was *enceinte*, the latter
had made a great effort to recover her health,
or at any rate the appearance of health. She
left her bed earlier in the morning than she had
ever done for the last five months ; she dressed
herself with great care, and—for, alas! Mrs.
McKeon's suspicion was but too true—fastened
her dress with a most dangerous determination to prove that the charge was unfounded.
Patiently she endured all the agonies which this
occasioned her during the first day and during
the whole evening, till the house was at rest
and she was secure from being again visited.
On the next morning she went so far as to
come down to breakfast, and to undergo Tony's
somewhat rough congratulation as to her con-
valescence, without betraying her sufferings.
After breakfast, when he was gone out, she
again opened the subject of her return home,
and begged Mrs. McKeon to allow her to
have the car to return to Ballycloran. Mrs.
McKeon again put her off, telling her that it
would be necessary first to consult the doctor,
and that he would not be likely to call till the
following day. In the afternoon Mrs. McKeon,
with Lyddy and Louey, went out for a drive,
and as Feemy was apparently so much better,
they asked her to accompany them, but this she
declined.

"It's as well for her not to go out before the
trial," whispered Mrs. McKeon to her daughters.

" Poor girl; she has a great deal, a great deal, indeed, to go through yet." Indeed she had a very great deal to go through; a very heavy atonement to pay for her folly and her crime.

As soon as the car was gone from the door, she hurried upstairs, put on her bonnet and cloak, took a letter which she had already prepared, and opening the door of Mrs. McKeon's own room, put it on the table. She then crept noiselessly downstairs, opened the front door, and passed into the street, without having been seen or heard by either of the servants, who were alone left with her in the house. The following is the letter, which, to her great grief and surprise, Mrs. McKeon found on her table when she returned :—

" DEAR MRS. McKEON,
        " It is because I know you'd never let me go back to Ballycloran, that I've now gone away without telling you what I was going to do. Pray don't be angry with me. Indeed I'm very unhappy; but I should be worse if you were to be angry with me. I'm only a bother and a throuble to you here, and I hav'n't spirits left even to let you see how very much obliged I am to you for all your throuble; but indeed I am in my heart, my dear Mrs. McKeon, both to you and to dear Lyddy and Louey, who have been so very kind to me. It is a deal better for me to be at home with my father; my heart's nearly broken with all I've gone through; but he'll bear with me, for he's used to me. Give my compliments to Doctor Blake. Pray beg him not to come to Ballycloran. I am in his

debt a great deal already, and how will I ever
pay him ? Besides, I'm a deal better now, as you
see, in health ; it's only the heart now that ails
me. Give my kind love to Lyddy and Louey.
I felt their kindness when the sorrow within
me wouldn't let me tell them so. Now good
bye, dear Mrs. McKeon ; don't be throubling
yourself to come to Ballycloran ; it'll be a poor
place now. I'll send Katty for the things.

> "I remain, dear Mrs. McKeon,
>> "Very, very faithfully yours,
>>> "FEEMY.

"P.S.—Indeed—indeed—it isn't the case,
what you were saying."

When Mrs. McKeon found the letter on her
return, she was greatly vexed ; but she could do
nothing ; she couldn't go to Ballycloran and
fetch Feemy by force. The falsehood with
which the letter concluded was not altogether
disbelieved ; but still she felt by no means
certain that her former suspicions were not true,
and if so, perhaps it was better for all parties
that Feemy should be at home. She determined to call at Ballycloran when Feemy might
be supposed to have settled herself, and content
herself for the present with hearing from the
girl who came for the clothes that she had got
home safe.

When Father John called on the Saturday,
she talked over the subject as fully with him as
she could without alluding to the matter respecting which she was so much in doubt. He
declared his intention of seeing Feemy on the

following Monday, and of speaking to her strongly on the subject of the trial which was so soon coming on; and he begged Mrs. McKeon to do the same afterwards—as perhaps having become latterly used to her interference, Feemy might bear from her what she had to be told, with more patience than she would from himself.

"Indeed I will, Father John, but do you be gentle with her. She's broken-hearted now; you'll find her very different from the hot-headed creature she was before her sorrows began."

"I fear she is—I fear she is; but, Mrs. McKeon, has she ever shown a feeling of regard —a spark of interest, for her noble brother?— it's that so annoys me in Feemy; I could feel for her—weep for her—and forgive her with all my heart—all but that."

"Ah, Father John," answered the lady; "it's not for me to preach to you; but where would we all be at the last, if our Judge should say to us, 'I can forgive you all but that'?"

"God forbid I should judge her; God forbid I should limit that to her, which I so much need myself. But isn't her heart hardened against her brother? Oh, if you could have seen him as I have done this morning—if you could believe how softened is his heart! He had never much false pride in it—it is nearly all gone now! If you could have heard how warmly, how affectionately he asks after the sister that won't mention his name; if you could know how much more anxious he is on her account and his father's, than on his own, Feemy's coldness and repugnance would strike you as it does me. I'm afraid her chief sorrow is still for the robber that would have destroyed her, and has destroyed her brother."

"Of course it is, Father John—and so it should be. I'm a woman and a mother, and you may take my word respecting a woman's heart. No wife could love her husband more truly than Feemy loved that man : unworthy as he was, he was all in all to her. Would it not, therefore, show more heartlessness in her to forget him that is now dead, than the brother who killed him? Of course she loved him better than her brother, as every woman loves the man she does love better than all the world. How can she forget him? Be gentle to her, Father John, and I think she will do what you desire."

Father John promised that he would comply with Mrs. McKeon's advice, and he was as good as his word.

On reaching the hall door of Mrs. McKeon's house Feemy looked cautiously about her, but seeing that no one belonging to the house was in sight, she passed on through the little garden into the street. She pulled her old veil down over her face, and walked on through the village as quickly as she could. She felt that every one's eye was on her ; that all the country was looking at her ; but she had made up her mind to go through it all, and she persevered. The last time she had been out of the house was the day she had been taken from Ballycloran to the inquest. That was a horrid day, but the present seemed worse ; she had now a greater sorrow than any of which she was then conscious, and she had to bear it alone, unpitied and uncomforted. Indeed, her only rest, her only respite from absolute torture was now to consist in being alone; and yet bad as the present was, there was a worse,—she felt that there was a worse in store for her. She already anticipated the tortures of that day, when she would again be dragged out from her resting-place before the eyes of all mankind, and placed in the very middle of the crowd, conspicuous above the rest, to be stared at, bullied, and questioned horridly about that dread subject, which it even racked her mind to remember. Would she be able on that long, long day— days, for what she knew—to conceal her shame from all who would be looking at her, and to bear in patience the agonies which it would be necessary for her to endure? She walked on quickly, and was soon out of Drumsna, and in the lane leading by the cottage to Ballycloran. By the time she had walked half a mile she was in a dreadful heat, although it was still in March, for she was so weak and ill that her exertion, in proportion to her strength, had been immense. She sat down by the side of the road for a time, and then continued; and then again sat down. Her sufferings were soon so great that she was unable to walk above two hundred yards at a time, and she began to fear that she would be utterly unable to get to the house. Once when she was sitting, panting on the bank by the road-side, one of the labouring peasants recog-nised her—saw she was ill—and offered to get her a country car. Oh, what an agonising struggle she made to answer the man cheerfully, when she assured him that she was quite well—

that she was only sitting there for her pleasure
—that she required no assistance, and that she
should walk home directly. The man well
knew that she was not there for her pleasure—
that her brother was in gaol, her father on the
point of losing his property, and that she was
weak and in need of rest; but he saw that she
would sooner be alone, and he had the good
tact to leave her, without pressing his offer for
her accommodation.

At length she reached the avenue, and had
to pass the spot where she had sat so long on
that fatal night listening for the sound of her
lover's horse, and watching her brother as he
stood swinging his stick before the house. She
shuddered as she did so, but she did walk by
the tree where she had then sat shivering, and
at last once more stood on the steps of her
father's house.

The door was fastened inside, and she had
to knock for admittance. This she did three
times, till she thought she should have fainted
on the flags, and at last the window of her own
sitting-room was raised, and Mary McGovery's
head was slowly protruded. Feemy was sitting
on the low stone wall, which guarded the side
of the flags, as she heard Mary say in a sharp
voice—

"Who's that? — and what are ye wanting
here? Oh! by the mortials, but av it ain't Miss
Feemy herself come back, I declare!"

And Mary ran round, and began to draw the
bolts of the front door. Up jumped Larry at
the unwelcome sound, from his accustomed seat
by the fire.

"What in the divil's name are ye afther? What are ye doing? Ye owld hag, will ye be letting the ruffians in on me?" And he caught violently hold of Mary's gown to drag her back, before she had accomplished the liberation of the rusty bolts.

"Now go in, sir, and sit down," said Mary. "Go in, sir, will you; I tell you it's yer own daughter, and no ruffian whatever. Dra— the owld man, but he'll have every rag off the back of me! Don't I tell you, it's Miss Feemy. Will you be asy now?—do you want to have me stark naked?"

"Come away, woman, I tell you; don't I know Feemy's gone off, away from me; she'll niver, niver come back; it's Keegan and his hell-hounds you're letting in on me."

By this time Mary had accomplished her object of undoing the door in spite of the old man's exertions, and Feemy entered weary and worn, soiled with the road, and pale and wan in spite of the hectic flush which reddened a portion of her cheek.

"Father," she said, when she saw the old man standing astonished and stupefied in the hall, "father, don't ye know me—won't ye spake to me?"

"Why, thin, Feemy, is it yer own self in arnest come back again? And where's yer lover? the man ye married, ye know—what war his name? —why don't ye tell me? Mary, what's the name of the Captain Feemy married?"

"Asy, sir, asy; come in, thin," and Mary led him into his own room, and Feemy followed in silence with her eyes already filled with tears.

"Where's yer own husband, thin, Feemy dear? Ussher, I main—Captain Ussher—it's he'd be welcome with you now, my pet," and he began stroking his daughter's shoulders and back, for she had still her bonnet on her head. "Thady's not here now to be brow-beating and teasing him; it's we'll be comfortable now the cowld long nights—for the Captain 'll be bringing the whiskey and the groceries with him, won't he, darling? and Thady the blackguard's out along wid Keegan, and they can't get in through the door, for it's always locked;" and then turning to Mary, he said, "why don't you put the locks back, you d—d jade? do you want them to be catching me the first moment I'm seeing my own darling girl here?"

Feemy could not say a word to her father: his absolute idiotcy, and the manner in which he referred to Ussher, quite upset her, and she sat down and wept bitterly.

"What ails you, pet?" continued the old man, "what ails you, alanna? they shan't touch him, dear—there, you see the big lock's closed now; he'll be safe from Thady now, darling."

"Oh, Miss Feemy," said Mary, "he's quite beside himself; asy now, sir, asy, and don't be talking such nonsense; don't ye know the Captain got kilt—months ago—last October?"

"Killed—and who dared to kill my darling's husband? who'd dare to touch him? why wasn't he here? why wasn't he inside the big lock?"

"Why, don't you know," and Mary gave the old man a violent shake to refresh his memory; "don't you know Mr. Thady kilt him in the avenue?"

"May his father's curse blisther him, then! May—but I think they wor telling me about that before. Eh, Feemy?" he continued, with a sigh; "it's a bad time I've been having of it with this tipsy woman since you were gone; she don't lave me a moment's pace from morning to night; bad 'cess to her, but I wish she wor well out of the house. I'll have you to mind me now—and you'll not be bawling and shaking me as she does; but she's always dhrunk," he added in a whisper.

Feemy could bear this no longer; she was obliged to make her escape from the room into her own, in which she found that Mary had taken up her temporary residence during so much of the day as she could spare from bawling at, and shaking, poor Larry. At dinner time, she again went into her father's room, but he took no farther notice of her than if she had been there continually for the last four months. He grumbled at his dinner, which consisted of nothing but potatoes, some milk, and an egg, and he scolded Feemy for having no meat; after dinner she mixed him a tumbler of punch, for there was still a little of Tony's whiskey in the house; and whether it was that she made it stronger for him and better than that which Mary McGovery was in the habit of mixing, or that the action to which he had been for so many years accustomed roused some pleasant memory within him, when he tasted it, he said—

"Heaven's blessing on you, Feemy, my daughter; may you live many happy years with the man you love."

Feemy soon left him, and went to bed, and Katty, who had been dispatched to Drumsna, returned with her mistress's small box, and a kind message from Mrs. McKeon :—" Her kind love to Miss Macdermot; she hoped she had felt the walk of service to her, and she would call some time during the next week." She had asked no questions of the girl which could lead her to imagine that her mistress's departure from Drumsna had been unexpected, nor had she said a word to her own servants which could let them suppose that she was surprised at the circumstance.

For five or six days Feemy remained quiet at Ballycloran—spending the greater part of her time in her own room, but taking her meals, such as they were, with her father; she had no books to read, and she was unable to undertake needlework, and she passed the long days much as her father did—sitting from breakfast till dinner over the fire, meditating on the miseries of her condition. There was this difference, however, between them—that the old man felt a degree of triumph at his successful attempt to keep out his foes, whereas Feemy's thoughts were those of unmixed sorrow. She had great difficulty too in inducing Mary to leave her alone to herself. Had that woman the slightest particle of softness in her composition, anything of the tenderness of a woman about her, Feemy would have made a confidant of her, and her present sufferings would have been immeasurably decreased; but Mary was such an iron creature—so loud, so hard, so equable in her temper, so impenetrable, that Feemy could not bring herself to tell her tale of woe, which otherwise she would have been tempted to disclose. She had, therefore, the additional labour of keeping her secret from Mary's prying eyes, and Mary was nearly as acute as Mrs. McKeon.

About noon, on Monday, Feemy was horrorstruck at being told by Katty that Father John was at the back door asking for her.

"Oh, Katty, tell him to wait awhile; say I'm ill, can't you—do, dear."

"Why, Miss, I towld him as how you war up, and betther, thank God, since you war home."

It was clearly necessary that she should see the priest; but she insisted on his not being shown in till she had dressed herself; and she again submitted herself to those agonies which she trusted, for a time, would hide her disgrace, which at last must become known to all. When this was done, she seated herself on the sofa, and plucked up all her courage to go through the painful conversation which she knew she was to endure. She did not rise as he entered, but remained on the sofa with the hectic tint on her face almost suffused into a blush, and her hands clasping the calico covering of the cushion, as if from that she could get more strength for endurance.

Father John shook hands with her as he seated himself by her: the tears came into his eyes as he observed the sad change which so short a time had made in her. The flesh had fallen from her face, and the skin now hung loose upon her cheek and jaw bones, falling in towards the mouth, giving her that lean and care-worn look which misery so soon produces.

Her healthy colour, too, had all fled; part of her face was of a dull leaden paleness, and though there was a bright colour round her eyes, it gave her no appearance of health. She looked ten years older than when he had seen her last. No wonder Mrs. McKeon pitied her so deeply; she appeared even more pitiable than her brother, who was awaiting his doubtful fate in gaol—though with nervous anxiety, still with unflinching courage.

"I am glad to hear you're better, Feemy. Mrs. McKeon thinks you a great deal better."

"Thank ye, Father John; I believe I'm well enough now."

"That's well, then; but you must take care of yourself, Feemy; no more long walks; you should have waited for the car to come home that day. Mrs. McKeon's not the least angry; if you are more at ease here than at Drumsna, she's glad for your sake you're here now, and she bids me tell you how sorry she is she didn't give you the car the day you asked for it."

"Oh, Father John, Mrs. McKeon's been too kind to me. Indeed I love her dearly, though I could never tell her so. Give her my kind love. I never thought she was so kind a woman."

"I will, Feemy; indeed I will. She is a kind woman; and it will please her to the heart to hear how you speak of her. She sends you all manner of loves, and Lyddy and Louey too. She is sending up a few things for you too. Patsey'll bring them, just till affairs are settled a little. She wishes me to tell you she'll be up herself on Thursday; she wouldn't come before, for she thought you'd be better pleased to be alone a few days."

"Tell her not to come here. This is no place for her now. They never open the front door now. This is no place for any one now, but just father and me. But tell her how I love her. I'll never forget her; no, not in my grave!"

"But I've another message for you, Feemy."

"Is it from her?"

"No, not from her, well as she loves you; it's from one who loves you better than she does; it is from one who loves you better than any ever did, since your poor mother died."

Feemy raised her eyes, and clasped her hands, as she listened to Father John's words, and marked his solemn tones. No thought of Thady entered her mind; but some indefinite, half-conceived idea respecting Ussher—that he had not been killed—that he had come to life again—that some mysterious miracle, such as she had read of in novels, had taken place; and that Father John had come with some blessed news, which might yet restore her to happiness and tranquillity. The illusion was but for a moment, though during that moment it completely took possession of her. It was as speedily dispelled by Father John's concluding words—

"I mean from your brother."

Feemy gave a long, long sigh as she heard the word. She wished for no message from her brother; he had robbed her of everything; she could not think of him without horror and shuddering.

"He sends his kindest love to you. I told

him you were better, and he was very glad to hear it. Though he has many heavy cares of his own to bear, I have never seen him but he asks after your health with more anxiety than he thinks of his own prospects. Now you are better, Feemy, won't you send him some message by me?—some kind word, which may comfort him in his sorrow?"

Feemy was no hypocrite; hypocrisy, though she did not know it herself, was distasteful to her. She had no kind feelings for her brother, and she did not know how to make the pretence which might produce kind words; so she remained silent.

"What! not a word, Feemy? you who spoke so well, so properly, so affectionately, but now of that good friend of yours—have you not a word of kindness for a most affectionate brother?"

Feemy still remained silent.

"Why, Feemy, what is this? Don't you love your own brother?"

She said nothing in reply for a moment or two; and then, bursting into tears, she exclaimed—

"Don't scold me, Father John!—don't scold me now, or I shall die! I try to forgive him—I am always trying! But why did he—why did he—why did he—— " She was unable to finish her sentence from the violence of her sobs and the difficulty of uttering the words which should have concluded it. She meant to say, "Why did he kill my lover?"

"Don't agitate yourself, Feemy. I don't mean to scold you; I don't mean even to vex you more than I can possibly help; but I must speak to you about your brother. I see the feeling that is in your mind, and I will not blame you for it, for I believe it is natural ; but I beseech you to pray that your heart may be softened towards your brother, who instead of repugnance, deserves from you the warmest affection. But though I will not attempt to control your feelings, I must tell you that you will be most wicked if you allow them to interfere with the performance of your duties. You know your brother's trial is coming on, do you not ? "

" Yes."

" Wednesday fortnight next is the day fixed, I believe. You know you will have to be a witness ? "

" I believe so, Father John."

" Certainly you will ; and I wish you now to listen to me, that you may know what it is that you will then have to do. In the first place you will be asked, I presume, by one gentleman whether you were willingly eloping with Captain Ussher ? " Feemy shuddered as the name was pronounced. " And of course you must answer that truly—that you were doing so. Then another gentleman will ask you whether you were absolutely walking off with him when the blow was struck which killed Captain Ussher ; and, Feemy, you must also answer that truly. Now the question is, can you remember what you were doing when the blow was struck ? Tell me now, Feemy, can you remember ? "

" No, Father John, I remember nothing ; from the time when he took me by the arm, as I sat upon the tree, till Thady told me he was dead, I remember nothing. If they kill me, I can tell them nothing."

"Feemy, dear, don't sob so! That's all you'll have to say. Merely say that—merely say that you were sitting on a tree. Were you waiting for Captain Ussher there?"

"Yes."

"And that whilst you were there you saw Thady; isn't that so?"

"Yes."

"And Ussher then raised you by the arm, and then you fainted?"

"I don't know what happened to me; but I heard nothing, and saw nothing, till Thady lifted me from the ground, and told me he was dead."

"That's all Feemy. Surely there's no great difficulty in saying that—when it'll save your own brother's life to say so; and it's only the truth. You can say as much in court as you've just said to me, can't you? Mrs. McKeon'll be there with you—and I'll be there with you. You'll only have to say in court what you've just said to me."

"I'll try, Father John. But you don't know what it is for one like me to be talking with so many horrid faces round one—with the heart dead within—to be asked such horrid questions, and everybody listening. I'll do as you bid me; I'll go with them when they fetch me—but I know I'll die before I've said all they want me to say."

Father John tried to comfort and strengthen her, but she was in great bodily pain, and he soon saw that he had better leave her; she had, at any rate, shown him by her answers to his questions, that the evidence she could give would be such as would most tend to Thady's acquittal; and, moreover, he perceived from her manner, that though the feelings which she entertained towards her brother were of a most painful description, she would, nevertheless, not be actuated by them in any of the answers she might give.

On the Thursday following Mrs. McKeon and one of her daughters called at Ballycloran, and in spite of the bars and bolts with which the front door was barricaded, they contrived to make their way into Feemy's room. She remembered that Father John had told her that they would call on that day, and she was therefore prepared to receive them. Mrs. McKeon brought her some little comforts from Drumsna, of which she was sadly in want; for there was literally nothing at Ballycloran but what was supplied by the charity of those who pitied them in their misfortunes; and among other things she brought two or three volumes from the library. She was very kind to her, and did and said all in her power that could in any way console the poor girl. Though Father John had been gentle in his manners and had endeavoured to abstain from saying anything hard, still Mrs. McKeon was more successful in her way of explaining to Feemy what it was that she would have to do. She promised, moreover, to come to Ballycloran and fetch her, and to remain with her and support her during the whole of the painful time that she would either be in the court itself, or waiting in the neighbourhood till she should be called on to give her evidence. She did not allude either to the manner in which Feemy had left Drumsna, or to the suspicions which she had formerly expressed. Her whole object now was to relieve as much as possible the despondency and misery so plainly pictured in the poor girl's face. As she put her arm round her neck and kissed her lips, Feemy's heart yearned towards her new-found friend with a kind of tenderness she had never before felt. It was as though she for once experienced a mother's solicitude for her in her sorrows, and she longed to throw herself on her knees, hide her face in her friend's lap, and confess it all. Had she been alone with her she would have done so; but there sat Louey in the same room, and though her conduct to Feemy had been everything that was kind, she felt that it was not as if she had been absolutely alone with her mother. She could not at the same time confess her disgrace to two.

Mrs. McKeon went away, after having strongly implored Feemy to return with her to Drumsna, and remain there till the trial was over. But this she absolutely refused to do—and at last it was settled that Mrs. McKeon should come for her on the morning on which the trial was to come on, and that she should hold herself ready to attend on any day that she might be called for after the commencement of the assizes.

The time now wore quickly on. When Mrs. McKeon called it had only wanted a fortnight to the first day on which the trial could take place; and as it quickly slipped away, day by day, to that bourn from which no day returns, poor Feemy's sorrow and agonies became in every way more acute. At last, on the Wednesday,—the day before that on which she was to be, or at any rate, might be fetched,—she was in such a state that she was unable to support herself in a chair. Mary McGovery would not leave her for a moment. The woman meant kindly, but her presence was only an additional torment. She worried and tortured Feemy the whole day; she talked to her, intending to comfort her, till she was so bewildered, that she could not understand a word that was said; and she kept bringing her food and slops,* declaring that there was nothing like eating for a sore heart, — that if Ussher was gone, there were still as good fish in the sea as ever were caught, —and that even if Thady were condemned, the judge couldn't do more than transport him, which would only be sending him out to a better country, and "faix the one he'd lave's bad enough for man and baste."

About seven in the evening Feemy was so weak that she fainted. Mary, who was in the room at the time, lifted her on the sofa, and when she found that her mistress did not immediately come to herself, she began stripping her for the sake of unlacing her stays, and thus learnt to a certainty poor Feemy's secret.

Mary had a great deal of shrewd common sense of the coarser kind; she felt that however well inclined she might be to her mistress, she should not keep to herself the circumstance that she had just learnt; she knew it was her duty as a woman to make it known to some one, and she at once determined to go that

evening to Mrs. McKeon and tell her what it
was she had discovered.

As soon as Feemy had come to herself, she
got her into bed, and having performed the
same friendly office for the old man, she started
off for Drumsna ; and having procured a private
audience with Mrs. McKeon, told her what had
occurred.

Mrs. McKeon was not at all surprised, though
she was greatly grieved.   She merely said,—
" You have done quite right, Mary, to tell
me ; but don't mention it yet to any one else ;
after all this affair is over we'll see what will be
best to do. God help her, poor girl ; it were
almost better she should die," and as Mary
went downstairs she called her back to her.
" Take my silk cloak with you, Mary. Tell
Miss Macdermot I've sent it, because she'll be
so cold to-morrow—and, Mary," and here she
whispered some instruction on the stairs, " and
mind I shall come myself for her—but let her
be ready, as may be there mayn't be a minute
to spare."

Father John was certainly right when he said
that Mrs. McKeon had a kind heart.

CHAPTER XXVIII

ASSIZES AT CARRICK-ON-SHANNON

AND now the assize week in Carrick-on-Shannon
had commenced, and all was bustle and confusion, noise, dirt, and distraction. I have
observed that a strong, determined, regularly

set-in week of bad weather usually goes the circuit in Ireland in company with the judges and barristers, making the business of those who are obliged to attend even more intolerable than from its own nature it is always sure to be. And so it was in this case.

On Tuesday afternoon Mr. Baron Hamilton and Justice Kilpatrick entered Carrick-on-Shannon, one after the other, in the company of the high sheriff, and a tremendous shower of rain, which drenched the tawdry liveries of the servants, and gave a most uncomfortable appearance to the whole affair.

The grand jury had been in the town since Monday morning — settling fiscal business — wrangling about roads—talking of tolls—checking county cesses—and performing those various patriotic offices, which they would fain make the uninitiated believe, require so much talent, industry, and energy; and as they were seen stepping over the running gutters, and making the best of their way through the splashing streets, their physiognomies appeared ominous of nothing good to the criminals, whose cases had in the first instance to come before them.

Every lodging in the town was engaged, beds being let, sometimes three in a room, for the moderate sum of a guinea each for the week. The hotels, for there are two, were crowded from the garrets to the cellars. Happy the man at such a period, who enjoys a bed-room which he can secure with a key—for without such precaution the rightful possessor is not at all unlikely, on entering his own premises, to find three or four somewhat rough-looking strangers, perhaps liberated jurors, or witnesses just escaped from the fangs of a counsel, sitting in most undisturbed ease on his bed, eating bread and butter, and drinking bottled porter. Some huge farmer with dripping frieze coat will be squatted on his pillow, his towel spread as table-cloth on the little deal table which has been allotted to him as the only receptacle for his jug, basin, looking-glass, brushes, and every other article of the toilet, and his carpet-bag, dressing-gown, and pantaloons chucked unceremoniously into a corner, off the chairs which they had occupied, to make way for the damp friends of the big farmer, who is seated on the bed. This man is now drawing a cork from a bottle of porter, the froth of which you are quite sure, from the manner in which the bottle is held, will chiefly fall upon the sheets between which you are destined to sleep,—unless some half-drunken ruffian, regardless of rights of possession, and negligent of etiquette, deposits himself there before the hour at which you may think good to retire to rest.

Fruitless and vain would it be for you to endeavour to disturb that convivial party. Better lock up your bag, above all things not forgetting your brushes; and, as you are a witness yourself, go down to the court and admire the ingenious manner in which the great barrister, Mr. Allewinde, is endeavouring to make that unfortunate and thoroughly disconcerted young man in the witness box, swear to a point diametrically opposite to another point to which he has already sworn at the instigation of counsel on the other side,—and thereby perjure himself.

Never mind the bustling of eager, curious countrymen ; never mind those noisy numerous policemen with their Sunday brass-chained caps ; push
on through them all, make your way into the
centre of the court—go down there right on
to the lawyers' benches ; never mind the seats
being full — plunge in ; if you hesitate, look
timid—ask question, or hang back—you are
lost, thrust out, expelled, and finally banished
with ignominy into the tumultuous sea of damp
frieze coats, which æstuates* in the outer court.
But go on with noise, impudence, and a full
face ; tread on people's toes, and thrust them
back with "by your leave," and you will find
yourself soon seated in direct view of the judge,
counsel, witness and prisoner. You will be
taken for an attorney, or, at any rate, for an
influential court witness. If you talk somewhat
loud, and frown very angrily in the face of the
tallest policeman, you may by the ignorant even
be taken for a barrister.

In fact, into court you must come, there is no
other place open to receive you. The big room
at the hotel, in which we have been three times
on such different occasions, the long big room
where McKeon presided over so many drunken
spirits — where poor Feemy made her last
arrangements with her lover at the ball—and
where so soon afterwards she was brought forward to give her evidence touching his death,
while his cold body was lying dead on the table
before her, — this long big room is now set
apart for yet another purpose. The grand jury
are to dine there, and already the knives and
forks are laid out upon the long deal table.

The little coffee-room — so called, though whiskey-room, or punch-room, or porter-room would be much the more appropriate name, unless indeed there is a kind of "*lucus a non lucendo*" propriety* in the appellation — is full nearly to suffocation. There is not an unoccupied chair or corner of a table to be found.

Large men half wet through—reeking, smelling most unwholesomely as the rain steams up from their clothes—are keeping the cold out of their stomachs by various spirituous appliances. The room is half covered with damp straw, which has been kicked in from the passage; the windows are closed, and there is a huge fire burning on the other side of that moist mass of humanity. On entering the room you feel that you breathe nothing but second-hand rain; a sojourn there you find to be impossible; the porter drinkers are still in your bed-room, even on your bed upstairs. What are you to do? where are you to go? Back home you cannot. You have a summons in your pocket; you have been unfortunately present when Mr. Terence O'Flanagan squeezed the fair hand of Miss Letitia Murphy; false Mr. Terence O'Flanagan would not come to the matrimonial altar when required; fair Miss Letitia Murphy demands damages, and you must swear to the fact of the hand having been squeezed as aforesaid. Who can tell when the case may come on? Rumour comes from the clerk of the peace, town clerk, or some other clerk who sits there in pride of place, always conspicuous under the judge's feet, and whispers that Letitia Murphy, spinster, is coming on next. Attorneys' clerks have been round diligently to all witnesses, especially, as it seems, to yourself, warning you that the important hour is at hand—that on no account may you be absent, so much as ten minutes' walk from the court. Vainly you think to yourself that it can hardly be of such vital import that you, her father's friend, saw little Letty Murphy's hand ensconced one evening in the brawny palm of that false Lothario* O'Flanagan; yes, of serious import is it—if not to Letty, or to Terence— yet to that facetious barrister, Mr. O'Laugher, who, at your expense, is going to amuse the dull court for a brief half-hour,—and of importance to yourself, who are about to become the laughing-stock of your county for the next twelve months. It is, therefore, evident that you cannot leave the filthy town with its running gutters— the filthy inn with its steamy stinking atmosphere, and bed-room porter drinkers, for good and all, and let Lothario O'Flanagan, Spinster Letty, Lawyers Allewinde and O'Laugher, with Justice Kilpatrick, settle the matter by themselves their own way; but that you must, willy nilly, in spite of rain, crowd, and offensive smell, stay and help to settle it with them. Into court therefore return, unfortunate witness; other shelter have you none; and now being a man of strong nerves,—except when put into a chair to be stared at by judge, bar, grand jury, little jury, attorney, galleries, etc., etc., — you can push your way into a seat, and listen with attention to the quiddities of the legally erudite Mr. Allewinde, as on behalf of his client he ingeniously attempts—nay, as he himself afterwards boasts to the jury, succeeds in making that disconcerted young gentleman in the witness chair commit perjury.

Mr. Allewinde is a most erudite lawyer. He has been for many years employed by the crown in its prosecutions, and with great success. He knows well the art of luring on an approver,* or crown witness, to give the information he wants wlthout asking absolutely leading questions; he knows well how to bully a witness brought up on the defence out of his senses, and make him give evidence rather against than for the prisoner; and it is not only witnesses that he bullies, but his very brethren of the gown. The barristers themselves who are opposed to him, at any rate, the juniors, are doomed to bear the withering force of his caustic remarks.

" No, really, I cannot suffer this; witness, don't answer that question. The learned gentleman must be aware that this is irregular; my lord, I must appeal to you. Stop, stop; that can never be evidence," and so on :—the unfortunate junior, who fondly thought that, with the pet witness now in the chair, he would be surely able to acquit his client, finds that he can hardly frame a question which his knowing foe will allow him to ask, and the great Mr. Allewinde convicts the prisoner not from the strength of his own case, but from his vastly superior legal acquirements.

How masterly is he in all the points of his profession as evinced in a criminal court. With what " becks, and smiles, and wreathed nods," he passes by his brethren on the prosecuting side, and takes his seat of honour. How charmingly he nods to the judge when his lordship lays down the law on some point in conformity with the opinion expressed by himself. How rapidly he throws to the wind the frivolous excuses of some juror wishing to escape the foreseen long night's confinement. How great is he on all points of panels—admissible and inadmissible evidence—replying and not replying. How thoroughly he knows the minute practice of the place; how he withers any attorney who may dare to speak a word on his own behalf, whilst asking questions of a witness on behalf of an otherwise undefended prisoner. How unceremoniously he takes the word out of the mouth of the, in his opinion, hardly competent junior barrister who is with him. How Demosthenic*is his language when addressing the jury on the enormity of all agrarian offences; with what frightful, fearful eloquence does he depict the miseries of anarchy, which are to follow non-payment of tithes, rents, and taxes; and with what energy does he point out to a jury that their own hearths, homes, and very existence depend on their vindicating justice in the instance before them.

Mr. Allewinde was never greater than in the case now before the court. A young farmer of the better class had been served with some disagreeably legal document on account of his non-payment of an arrear of rent; he had at the time about twenty acres of unripe oats on the ground for which the arrear was due; and he also held other ground for which he owed no arrear. On ascertaining that a distraint was to be put on the ground which owed the rent, he attended there with a crowd of countrymen, and would not allow the bailiff to put his foot upon the lands; the next day the bailiff came again with police in numbers at his heels, and found the twenty acres which had yesterday been waving with green crops, utterly denuded. Every blade had been cut and carried in the night, and was then stacked on the ground on which no distraint could be levied. In twelve hours, and those mostly hours of darkness, twenty acres had been reaped, bound, carted, carried, uncarted, and stacked, and the bailiff and the policemen had nothing to seize but the long, green, uneven stubble.

The whole country must have been there— the field must have been like a fair-green the whole night—each acre must have taken at least six men to reap—there must have been thirty head of cattle, of one sort or other, dragging it home; and there must have been upwards of a hundred women and children binding and loading. There could, at any rate, be no want of evidence to prove the fact. One would think so, with two or three hundred people with their tools, horses, and carts. But yet, when the landlord determined on prosecuting the tenant, there was not a person to be found who had seen the corn removed;—not one. In fact, people who had not seen, as the bailiff had, the corn covering the broad field one day, and the same field bare the next, began to think that the fact was not so; and that the miraculous night's work was a fable. It was certain that the bailiff had been deterred from entering on the ground, but it was also certain that nothing but words had been used to deter him; he had not been struck or even pushed; he had only been frightened; and it seemed somewhat plain that his faint heart only had prevented him from completing his seizure—either that or some pecuniary inducement. Things were going badly with the bailiff, particularly when, in answer to Mr. O'Laugher, he had been obliged to confess that on the morning on which the seizure should have been made he had taken—a thrifle of sperrits! a glass, perhaps—yes, maybe, two—yes, he had taken two; three, suggested Mr. O'Laugher, with a merely raised eyebrow; he couldn't say that he had not taken three; four? again inquired Mr. O'Laugher; he didn't think he had taken four. Could he swear he had not taken four? He would not swear he hadn't. He would not even swear he had not taken five; nor even six, so conscientious a bailiff was he; but he was nearly sure he hadn't, and would swear positively he had not swallowed seven. Where-upon Mr. O'Laugher most ill-naturedly put down his morning dram at three quarters of a pint, and asked the unhappy bailiff whether that quantity was not sufficient to make him see a crop of oats in an empty field. It was going badly with the landlord and bailiff, and well with the energetic, night-working, fraudulent tenant; —and would have gone well with him, had he not determined to make assurance doubly sure.

A young man had been dining out, and had returned home at twelve o'clock on the night of the supposed miraculous reaping; he had at that hour walked home along the lane which skirted the field, and had seen no men—heard no noise—nor perceived either reapers, cars, horses, or any signs of work; yet he had passed the very gate of the field through which the corn must have come out, had it come out at all. Such was the effect of this young gentleman's evidence, when he was handed over to Mr. Allewinde by Mr. O'Laugher, with a courteous inquiry of his brother whether he wished to ask that gentleman any questions. Mr. Allewinde said that he would ask him a few questions, and the young gentleman began to tremble.

"Mr. Green, I think your name is," began Mr. Allewinde.

"Yes, sir."

And then it appeared that Mr. Green absolutely remembered the night of the 12th September; had heard the rumour of the corn having been removed, but had not observed it growing there when he went to dinner; had dined at the house of the prisoner's father, about a mile beyond the field; had certainly passed the very field; could positively swear he was perfectly sober; was certainly not carried by drunk; had not observed the field especially; could not say he had looked at the field as he passed; had heard of the bailiff's retreat that morning; did not think to look at the ground where the mob had been; did not observe the place; will positively swear he heard nothing; was not walking in his sleep; could not swear whether the oats were standing at the time or not—whether the gate was open or shut—whether or no men were in the field; only he saw none; he believed it was moonlight.

"Why, man! what did you see?" asked Mr. Allewinde.

" Nothing particular."

" Had you your eyes open ? "

No answer.

" Now, by virtue of your oath, were your eyes open ? "

No answer.

" Come, sir, I must and will have an answer ; on your solemn oath, were your eyes open when you walked by that field ? "

At last, after various renewed questions, the witness says, " No."

" Did you shut them by accident ? "

After that question had been sufficiently often repeated, the witness again said, " No ; he had been blinded ; " and in the same way it was at last extracted from him that his ears had been stopped also, and that he had been led along the road by the field, that he might be able to swear that he had passed the place during the night without either seeing or hearing what was at the moment taking place there.

Oh that miserable witness ! One could swear from the glassy look of his eyes that then also, during those awful questions, he could see nothing. The sweat rolled down his miserable face. That savage barrister appeared to him as a devil sent direct from the infernals, for his express behoof ; so unmercifully did he tear him, and lacerate him ; twenty times did he make him declare his own shame in twenty different ways. Oh ! what a prize for a clever, sharp, ingenious, triumphant Counsellor Allewinde, that wicked false witness, with his shallow, detected device. He played with him like a cat does with a mouse—now letting him go for a moment, with the vain hope that he was to escape—then again pouncing on him, and giving him a fresh tear; till at last, when the young man was desired to leave the chair, one was almost inclined to detest the ingenuity of the ferocious lawyer more than the iniquity of the false witness.

This case was now over; the bailiff again held up his head; the landlord gained his cause; the farmer was sent to prison, and the blind and deaf witness sneaked out of town in shame and disgrace. This came of not letting well alone.

The Wednesday was now advanced, and it was settled that there would not be time for the great murder case, as poor Thady's affair was called. Besides, Mr. Allewinde was also to conduct that, and he wanted some rest after his exertions; and as he walked out with triumph, some minor cases were brought forward for disposal, and Mr. O'Laugher rushed into the other court to defend Terence O'Flanagan before Mr. Justice Kilpatrick, against the assaults made upon his pocket by that willow-wearing spinster,* Letitia Murphy.

In rushed also all the loungers from the other court. In such a place as Carrick-on-Shannon, a breach of promise of marriage case is not an every-day treat, and, consequently, men are determined to make the most of it. Counsellor O'Laugher runs his hands through his dark-grey hair, opens wide his light-blue eye, pulls out the needful papers from that bottomless bag, and though but the other moment so signally defeated in the other court, with sure trust in his own resources prepares for victory.

The case is soon stated. Mr. Terence O'Flanagan, with five hundred a-year, profit rents, out of the town and neighbourhood of Mannhamilton, has, to the palpable evidence of the whole and next baronies, been making up, as the phrase goes, to Letty Murphy, for the last six months. This has been no case of Bardell *v.* Pickwick,* but a real downright matter of love-making on the one side, and love made on the other. Letters, too, have been written, and are now to be read in court, to the great edification of the unmarried jury, and amusement of the whole assemblage; and the deceitful culprit has gone so far as to inform the father, Murphy, that he has a thousand pounds saved to settle, if he, the father, has another to add to it. All these things Mr. O'Malley puts forward on behalf of the injured Letty, in his opening speech, and then proceeds to bring evidence to prove them.

In the first place the father gives his evidence, and is cross-examined with great effect by Mr. O'Laugher; then the letters are read, and are agreed by all to be very affectionate, proper, agreeable love-letters; there is no cross-questioning them, for though answered, they will not answer; and our friend, who escaped but just now melancholy from the porter drinkers in his bed-room, is brought forward to prove the love-makings of the delinquent.

All Mr. O'Malley's questions he answers with great readiness and fluency, for it was for the purpose of answering them that he came forward. He states without hesitation that love-making to a considerable extent has been going on;

that to his knowledge, and in his presence, most particular attentions have been paid by Mr. Terence to Miss Letty; that they have sat together, talked together, walked together, and whispered together to such an extent, that in his, the witness's, mind, they had for some time past been considered to be a regularly engaged couple; and that, moreover, he had himself seen Mr. Terence O'Flanagan squeezing the hand of Miss Letty. Having declared so much on behalf of the lady, he also was handed over to Mr. O'Laugher to be made to say what he could on behalf of the gentleman.

In answer to different questions, he stated that he himself was a middle-aged gentleman, about forty—a bachelor, moving in good society—sufficiently so to be acquainted with its usages; that he was in the habit of finding himself in company with ladies—married ladies and single; he confessed, after some interlocutions, that he did prefer the company of the latter, and that he preferred the good-looking to the plain—the young to the old; he would not state whether he had made up his own mind on the subject of matrimony, and had a very strong objection to inform the jury whether he was engaged. Was his objection insurmountable? Yes, it was; whereupon it was decided by the court that the witness need not answer the question, as he could not be called on to criminate himself. He had, probably, however, been in love? suggested Mr. O'Laugher; but he wouldn't say that he had. A little smitten, perhaps? Perhaps he had. Was, perhaps, of a susceptible heart? No answer. And accustomed to Cupid's gentler

wounds? No answer. Hadn't he usually in his
heart a prepossession for some young lady?
Mr. O'Laugher must insist on having an answer
to this question; as it was absolutely necessary
the jury should know the nature of a witness's
temperament, whose evidence was chiefly one
of opinion, and not of facts; how could they
otherwise know what weight to give to his
testimony? Hadn't he usually a prepossession
in his heart for some young lady? There was
a great deal of hesitation about this question,
but at last he was got to inform the jury on
his oath that he usually—in fact, always—did
entertain such a prepossession. Was he not
fond of conversing with the lady who for the
time might be the object of this feeling? He
supposed he was. Of walking with her? No,
not particularly of walking with her. Did he
never walk with his loved one? He didn't
think he ever did, except by accident. Weren't
such happy accidents of frequent occurrence?
They might be. Weren't they gratifying accidents when they did occur? Why, yes; he
supposed they were. Then he *was* fond of
walking with his loved one? Why, taking it in
that way, he supposed he was. Mr. O'Laugher
supposed so too. Did he never whisper to
this loved object? No, never. What, never?
Never. What! could he swear that he had
never whispered to the present object of his
adoration? He had no object of adoration.
Well, then, object of love? He had no object
of love; that is, he wouldn't say whether he
had or not. He thought it very hard that he
should be asked all these questions. Well,

then, object of prepossession. Could he swear
that he had never whispered with the present
object of his prepossession? Never—except
in church; that was to say, he couldn't tell.
Never except in church—never walk with her
except by accident! Mr. O'Laugher surmised
that the witness was a very cautious fellow—quite
an old bird—not to be caught with chaff. Did
he never sit by her? Sit by who? By the object
of his prepossession? He supposed he might,
at dinner, or at a party, or a concert, or a ball.

"What! sit by the object you love best at
a concert, and not whisper to her between the
tunes—and you a Connaught man!" said Mr.
O'Laugher. "Come, mend your reputation a
little; wasn't that a slip you made, when you
said now you'd never whispered to her at a concert?" Perhaps he had at a concert. "Well,
now, I thought so. I thought by your complexion you wouldn't sit by a pretty girl, and
take no notice of her. Did you never squeeze
a girl's hand while you were whispering to her?"
He couldn't remember. "Now, on your oath
did you never squeeze a girl's hand?" He
might have done so. "Did you never put your
arm round a girl's waist?" At last the witness
owned he might have done even that. "And
now, one question, and I've done. Did you
never kiss a girl?" No answer. "Come, that's
the last. After all you've owned you needn't
haggle at that; out with it, man, it must come
at last. Did you never kiss a girl?" Alas for
the sake of morality, the witness was at length
obliged to own that he had perpetrated the
enormity. "And," asked Mr. O'Laugher, with

a look of great surprise, "were you never proceeded against for damages? Was an action for breach of promise of marriage never brought against you?"

No, never; the witness had never been in such a predicament.

"What, never? You who have declared, I won't say unblushingly, for heaven knows you have blushed enough about it, but openly and on your oath, that you have always some different object of affection, with whom you walk, sit, talk, and whisper; whose hand you squeeze, round whose waist you put your arm (a crime, by-the-by, never imputed to my client), whom you even confess that you kiss; and yet you sit here secure, unassailed, unsolicited for damages, unengaged, as you lead us to suppose. What are the fathers and brothers of Connaught doing to let such a hydra-headed monster as thou near their doors—such a wolf into their sheep-pens? Go down, thou false Lothario. Go down, thou amorous Turk, and remember that a day of retribution may yet come for yourself."

The unfortunate witness hurried out of court—ran through the pelting rain to the inn—crammed his brushes and pantaloons into the carpet-bag in spite of damp, farmers, and burly porter drinkers—paid a guinea for the bed in which he had never slept, and hiring a post-car, hurried from the scene of his disgrace, regardless of the torrents which were falling.

On the Wednesday morning, for it had been forgotten till then, a summons was served on Hyacinth Keegan to attend as a witness at Thady's trial, on the prisoner's behalf; and as

he was living in the town the service was quite
in sufficient time, and there was no possible
means by which he could avoid the disagreeable
duty which was thus imposed upon him. He
was much annoyed, however, for he felt that
there were no questions, which he could be
asked on the subject, which it would not annoy
him to answer. He had been out but little
since the day on which he had been so savagely
treated at Drumleesh—indeed he had not been
able to go out till quite lately ; and he now most
thoroughly wished that he was bad enough to
obtain a medical certificate, which would prevent
the necessity of his attending in court. That,
however, was impossible, and he, therefore, set
himself to consider what answers he would give
to the questions they would be most likely to
ask him. Regard for his oath he had none ;
but there were some most disagreeable questions
which, if asked him, he would be obliged to
answer with the truth, for on those subjects he
would be unable to lie without detection. His
rancour against Thady was unabated. Unless
young Macdermot were hung he would be
unable to avenge the mutilated stump which
crippled all his exertions, and now rendered his
existence miserable.

He flattered himself, however, that Brady's
evidence would render that event certain ; and
whatever annoying questions might be put to
himself on the defence, he was determined that
Brady should swear to enough on the direct
examination to insure his purpose.

On the Wednesday evening it was decided
that Thady's case was to come on first in the

criminal court on Thursday morning, and on the same Wednesday evening Keegan sent for Brady into his office.

Pat was now regularly installed as the attorney's managing man on the property, and there was therefore nothing very remarkable in his sending for him, although he was going to be a witness on the morrow.

"Did you hear, Brady," said the master, "that they've summoned me for the trial to-morrow?"

"Iss,* yer honour; they war telling me so up at the court; there's Dolan is summoned too."

"Who's Dolan?"

"He's one of the boys, Mr. Keegan, as war in it that night at Mrs. Mehan's."

"Well, and what can he say? he can't say Macdermot wasn't there. He can't do any harm, Pat; for if he was to swear that he wasn't there, there's enough to prove that he was."

"No, yer honour, it isn't that he'll be saying, but he'll be saying Captain Ussher's name wasn't mentioned, or may be that the boys were merely taking their drink, innocent like; that's what I be afeared—and that's what Corney'll say; you'll see av he don't; he's the biggest liar in Drumleesh."

"Oh, they'd soon knock all that out of him; besides, isn't he one of these potheen boys?"

"Faix he is so, Mr. Keegan."

"Then they'll not believe him—they'll believe you a deal sooner than him that way; but you must be plain about this, Brady, that they were talking about Ussher that night—d'ye hear?

Be d—d but if you let them shake you about that you're lost. D'ye hear? Why don't you answer me, eh?"

"Oh! shure, your honour, I'll be plain enough; certain sure the Captain's name war mentioned."

"Mentioned! yes, and how was it mentioned? Didn't you tell me that Reynolds and young Macdermot were talking broadly about mur- dhering him? Didn't they agree to kill him— to choke him in a bog hole—or blow his brains out?"

"It war your honour they war to put in a bog hole."

"D—n them! I'll have 'em before I've done. But don't you know that Macdermot, Reynolds, and the other fellow agreed to put an end to Ussher? Why, you told me so twenty times."

"I b'lieve they did; but faix, I ain't shure I heard it all rightly myself, yer honour; I warn't exactly one of the party."

"That won't do, Brady; you told me dis- tinctly that Reynolds and Macdermot swore together to kill the man; and you must swear to that in court. Why, the barrister has been told that you can prove it."

"But, Mr. Keegan, do you wish me now to go and hang myself? You would not wish a poor boy to say anything as'd ruin hisself?"

"Be d—d, but some one has been tampering with you. You know you'll be in no danger, as well as I do; and by heavens if you flinch now it'll be worse for you. Mind, I want you to say nothing but the truth. But you know Ussher's

death was settled among them; and you must
say it out plainly—d'ye hear? And I tell you
what, Brady, if you give your evidence like a
man you'll never be the worse of those evenings
you spent at Mohill at Mrs. Mulready's, you
know. But if you hesitate or falter, as sure as
you stand there, they'll come against you; and
then I'll not be the man to help you out of the
scrape."

"But, Mr. Keegan, yer honour, they do be
saying that iv I brings out all that, it'll hang the
young masther out and out, and then I'll have
his blood upon my conscience."

"Have the divil on your conscience. Isn't
he a murderer out and out? and, if so, shouldn't
you tell the truth about it? Why, you fool,
it's only the truth. What are you afraid of?
after telling me so often that you would go
through with it without caring a flash* for any
one!"

"But, you see, there's so much more of a
ruction about it now through the counthry than
there war. Counsellor Webb and all thim has
made Mr. Thady's name so great, that there'd be
no pace for a boy at all av he war to say a word
agin him."

"Then it's a coward you are afther all,
Brady?"

"No, yer honour, I'm no coward; but it's a
bad thing living in a counthry, where all the
boys is sworn to stretch you."

"Nonsense, Pat; did they ever stretch me?
and haven't I done as bad and worse to them
twenty times? They're trying to frighten you
out of your duty, and you're going to let them.

Any way, I see you are not the man for me. I thought you had more pluck in you."

"Why, thin, Mr. Keegan, I've pluck enough; but faix, I don't like hanging the young man, thin—and now it's out."

"Very well—then you'll be transported for perjury, that's all; all the things you've to swear to have been sent written out to the Counsellor; and when you contradict in court what you have already declared to be the truth they'll prosecute you for perjury, and a deal of good you'll do young Macdermot afther all!"

After a few more arguments of a similar nature, Brady was again reduced to his allegiance, and at last was dismissed, having promised to swear stiffly both that Ussher's death had been agreed on at the meeting at Mrs. Mehan's, and also that in private conversation with him (Pat Brady) Macdermot had frequently expressed his determination of being revenged on Ussher for the injury he was doing to his sister. And Hyacinth Keegan betook himself to the company of the fair partner of his prosperity and misfortunes, comforting himself with the idea that he was sure of success in his attempts to secure Thady's conviction, and flattering himself that Mr. O'Malley could at the worst only ask him some few teasing questions about the property.

CHAPTER XXIX

THADY'S TRIAL IS COMMENCED

ON the same evening, namely that immediately before the trial, Father John visited Thady in prison, and it was the last time that they were to meet before the fate of the latter was decided. The priest had constantly visited the young man in his confinement, and had done all in his power to support and cheer his spirits under the horrible circumstances in which he was placed, and not without success. Thady had borne his incarceration and distress with the greatest courage. When remaining at Augha-cashel among the lawless associates with whom he had so foolishly looked for safety, he had completely lost his fortitude and power of endurance; he was aware that he was doing what was in every sense culpable, and he then could not but look on himself as a murderer flying from justice; but now he had learned to see what was really criminal in what he had done, and what was venial; and though the last five months had been spent in prison, and though he felt by no means sanguine of his acquittal, he had, nevertheless, never regretted that he had given himself up.

Father John had again to-day seen Mr. O'Malley, who now that he had the affair thoroughly at his fingers' ends, seemed to be almost sanguine of success, and consequently the good priest himself was correspondingly elated.

"I trust in God, Thady," said he, "I confidently trust you will be with me at the Cottage to-morrow night, or at any rate the next. The Cottage shall be your home for some time, my boy, if they allow you any home in the country. I don't want to give you false hopes, but I don't think any jury can convict you. I'm sure Mr. O'Malley thinks so too."

"I don't think so, Father John; it may be so, but I don't think so; it's a comfort to me to know I never meant his death, although he was doing what might have tempted me to shoot him, av I'd had a pistol in my hand; for as I sit here he was dragging her down the avenue by the waist. But I never thought to kill him, and though I think they will hang me, I feel that I haven't the weight of murdher on my hands."

"You haven't, Thady; indeed you may say you haven't. I that should teach you to repent your sins, not to hide them from your own heart, tell you that you haven't. But should they condemn you, there are those that will have. But God forbid—may God in his great mercy forbid it."

"But, Father John, what'll Feemy do? what will the owld man do when I am—when I'm gone? Keegan 'll have all now. She'll be turned out to beg across the world; and what'll ever become of her?"

"Your father'll be cared for, Thady. Though no one else should see to him, I will, for your sake. He's very infirm; you'll be astonished when you see him; but while he lives and while I have a bit of bread to share with him, or a roof to shelter him, for your sake, he shall never want it."

Thady pressed the priest's hand between his own.

"What a thing it is to have a friend like you! but Feemy—who'll provide for Feemy? she'll be the only one left of the name* when I'm gone; there'll be nothing left but her; house and family'll be gone then, and except for poor Feemy, there'd be an end of the whole concern."

"Don't go on that way," said Father John, with tears in his eyes. "You'll be able to see after and live with your own sister yet; and who knows but you may yet beat Keegan out of Ballycloran?"

"Oh no, Father John! av they don't hang me out and out—av they don't put an end to me altogether, I'll be transported, or sent back here to gaol. I'll never be at Ballycloran again. Bad as the place is, I loved it. I think it's all the throuble I had with it, and with the tinants, that made me love it so. God forgive me—I was hard enough to some of them!"

Father John remained with him till the evening was far advanced, and then left him, promising to be in court on the morrow.

"Let me see you there, Father John," said he. "Stand near me whilst it's going on; it'll be a comfort to me to have one friend near me among so many strangers, and at such a time."

"I will, my boy. I must leave the court when Feemy is to come, for I've promised to be with Mrs. McKeon when she brings her in; but excepting that, I'll stand as near you as they'll let me."

The priest then left his friend, and Thady was once more alone in his cell, about to pass the last of many long, tedious nights of suspense. There he sat, on his iron bedstead in his gloomy cell, with his eyes fixed upon vacancy, thinking over the different events of his past life, and trying to nerve himself for the fate which, he too truly believed, was in store for him. Thady's disposition had not been prone to hope; he had never been too sanguine—never sanguine enough. From the years to which his earliest memory could fall back, he had been fighting an earnest, hard battle with the world's cares, and though not thoroughly vanquished, he had always been worsted. He had never experienced what men called luck, and he therefore never expected it. Few men in any rank of life had known so little joy as he had done, or had so little pleasure; his only object in life had been to drive the wolf from his father's door and to keep a roof over him and his sister.

Had patient industry and constant toil been able to have effected this, he would have been, perhaps not happy, but yet not discontented; this, however, circumstances had put out of his power, and he felt that the same uncontrollable circumstances had now brought him into his present position. He knew little of the Grecian's doctrine of necessity*; but he had it in his heart that night, when he felt himself innocent, and was at the same time assured that all the kind efforts of his friends would not save him from his fate—a hangman's rope and the county gallows.

There he sat the greater part of that night alone on his cold bedside, not knowing whether he was warm or cold—not perceiving whether it was light or dark; and no one but God might know the thoughts that passed through his untutored brain, or the feelings which kindled his warm, though rugged heart. Did he complain that though honest, industrious, and patient, ignominy and death should be his probable doom? Had he bitter hatred in his heart for those who had driven him to his fate? Did he still love those who had evinced so little sympathy with him? Sympathy! Ah! how could he miss that which he had never felt, till Father John had blessed him with his kind words! His love had not been that conscious love which requires kindness to nurture it, and love again to keep it warm. He was not aware himself how well he loved his father and his sister. His lot had been thrown with them; he had passed his life with them, and the feelings, which in a selfish man are given up to self, had with him been turned on those to whose care it had seemed that his life should be dedicated.

I do not say that he looked forward to a probable death without a shudder, or to so speedy a termination of his career, without a wish that, unfortunate as it had been, it might be prolonged; but it was the disgrace, and the circumstances of his fate, which made by far the greater portion of his misery. Could he be but once quiet in his grave, and have done with it all—be rid of the care, turmoil, and

uneasiness, he would have been content.
Could he have been again unborn—uncreated!
He had once repined to Father John, that
existence had been for him a necessary evil;
and though checked by the priest for the
impiety of the thought, was it odd if he often
thought, that he was one of those for whom it
would have been better had they never been
born?

About three or four in the morning, he fell
asleep, and was awakened by Father John about
eight; he dressed himself in his best clothes—
those in which he had been accustomed to
go to mass—ate his breakfast, and about ten
o'clock was led out of gaol, handcuffed, into
the court-house. The gaol at Carrick-on-
Shannon is not far from the court-house, and
as they are both built on a neck of land running
into the river, no portion of the town has to be
traversed; but yet there was a great crowd collected to see the poor fellow pass by. This was
the first of the bitter moments to which he had
so constantly looked forward for the last few
months. At length, however, he was in the
dock, and here the high wooden palings, twelve
feet above the ground on which he had to stand,
would screen him from the view of all, save the
miserable prisoners beside him and the policemen who had brought him in,—until he should
be called on to take his place at the bar.

After waiting there for about half an hour,
sitting on the rude benches which surrounded
the interior of the dock, with his eyes fixed on
the red lappets of the gaoler's coat which hung
over the palings as he sat upon the bar, he

heard the noise of steps in the court suddenly
increased, and the sound of voices hushed ; the
judge was taking his seat. Mr. Baron Hamilton,
accompanied by a fashionably dressed young
gentleman with a white wand, entered the court
at a side-door, passed behind the jury-box, and
sat down on the seat of judgment, under the
dusty red canopy which for many years had
nodded over the wisdom of Ireland's soundest
lawyers.

Had that piece of red moreen been gifted
with an ear to hear, and a tongue to tell, what
an indifferent account would it give of the
veracity of judges and of the consciences of
lawyers ! How many offences had it heard
stigmatised by his lordship as the most heinous
that had ever been brought before him in his
judicial capacity ! How many murderers, felons,
and robbers, described as poor harmless, innocent, foolish boys, brought into trouble by a
love of frolic ! How many witnesses, vainly
endeavouring to tell the truth, forced by the
ingenuity of lawyers into falsehood and perjury !
What awful denunciations and what light wit,
almost in the same breath ! Of what laughter
hardly suppressed by judicial authority would it
tell—what agonizing sobs altogether unsup-
pressable would it describe—how many a clever,
smiling, self-sufficient barrister would it, from
long knowledge, have learnt to laugh to scorn—
of how many a sharp attorney would it declare
the hidden ways ! But yards of red moreen are
fitting witnesses for judicial gravities and legal
exercises. They hang profoundly, gravely—
nay, all but solemnly—over the exposition of

the criminal. They lend authority to the wrath, and protection to the wit of the wigged.* They awe the criminal, repress the witnesses, inspire the juror, silence the spectator, absorb the dust, and tell no tales.

And now the judge having taken his place, the lesser men in office being duly seated beneath him, and the contending barristers having sufficiently dived into their blue bags, the prisoner is summoned, under various indictments, to take his trial for the murder of Myles Ussher; whereupon Thady is called upon by the gaoler, and, rising from his seat, takes his stand at the bar. In his position there, he is just enabled to raise his arm to the railing of the dock, and to rest his hand upon it during the ten long, horrid, wasting hours which he is destined to pass in his present painful position. His face is pale, and—always thin and sad— now thinner and sadder than ever; his eyes wander round the court, and as they at length alight on Father John, who is seated next to Mr. McKeon on the attorneys' benches, a kind of gentle smile softens his features, and shows how great a relief he feels the presence of a friend to be. In answer to the clerk of the crown, he declares himself not guilty, professes himself ready for his trial, and the business of the day commences.

The first thing that has to be done is to call over the long panel, and the names of all competent persons in the county, from whom the jury is to be selected. But even preparatory to this, the counsel for the defence commence their fight. Mr. O'Laugher, who, as the phrase goes,

is with Mr. O'Malley,* begins by declaring that
the list from which the names are read is an
illegal list—a foolish, useless, unauthoritative list
—nothing but balderdash, moonshine, and waste
paper—all empty sounds, and consisting of a
string of names as little to the purpose in the
present case as a regimental roll-call. The
sub-sheriff, who with infinite clerkly care, and
much sub-shrieval experience, has made out the
list, opens wide his disturbed ears, and begins to
feel somewhat uncomfortable. Mr. O'Laugher
goes on to declare that the present list, instead
of being one properly, legally, and expressly
drawn out for March, 183—, is only a copy of
the one in use during the summer assizes in the
last year, and assures the judge with much indignant emphasis, that he cannot allow his client
to submit to the injustice of receiving a verdict
from a jury composed under such atrocious
circumstances.

The objection is listened to with as much
gravity as though a statement had been made
that the prisoner had been in Newfoundland at
the time of Ussher's death, and Mr. Allewinde's
assistant begins to argue the case. The sub-
sheriff and his two clerks are put into the chair,
and have to swear one thing and another.
Books are lugged into court—dirty papers over-
hauled—thick volumes quoted and consulted—
precedents urged—objections answered—a great
deal of self-confidence shown. At last, after a
weary hour's talk, it seems somehow decided
that the sub-sheriff was in the right of it—that
the list is correct, and that the prisoner may be
tried. But Mr. O'Laugher is not in the least

chagrined at the victory of his adversary; one would say, from his countenance, that his only object had been to delay the business for an hour, and that he triumphed in his success.

The list is accordingly read over, and the householders of County Leitrim are summoned to appear and answer to their names under a penalty of two pounds. A lamentable deficiency, however, is apparent; one only here and there answers to his name as it is called out in the sonorous and practised voice of the clerk of the crown. A notice is then given that they will be again invoked under a penalty of ten pounds, which, in spite of the fear which pervades the minds of jurymen that this will be a lock-up affair, entailing a bedless night and a meagre supper, surreptitiously supplied through the windows of the court-house, has the desired effect, and Cornelius O'Reilly, Patrick Tierney, Anthony Reynolds, etc., etc., reply to the call, and the court becomes sufficiently full of strong, thick-set, comfortable men.

This is only the long panel. Now the jury has to be formed. To twenty names the prisoner is entitled to object from caprice, and Mr. O'Laugher is not the man to give up one of the twenty. Then he can object to as many more as he chooses, on showing cause, and you may be sure Mr. O'Laugher has a great many causes to show. One man has lived near young Macdermot all his life, has been a friend of his, must have formed an opinion on the case, and is therefore not fit; another man has been his enemy, and is therefore not fit; a third man used to drive with Captain Ussher twice a

week; a fourth lived in Mohill; a fifth at
Drumsna; a sixth did not live in the county at
all; a seventh had not a house of his own, and
so on. Why, it appeared there was not a proper
juror in the county! On all these objections
Mr. O'Laugher was beaten; and as he was
beaten on each, he indefatigably prepared for
the next.

Then the jurors themselves objected. They
unblushingly declared themselves unfit;—as-
serted that they could not depend upon themselves to give a true verdict, and assured the
judge that their minds would be improperly
biassed by circumstances on one side or the
other. What atrocious characters!—what self-
condemned miscreants! Why does not the judge
instantly, with that stern look he knows so well
how to assume, turn them out of court, bid
them make way for honest men, and send them
home, disgraced for ever, to their sorrowing
families? Does he do so? No, indeed! he
picks his teeth while Mr. Allewinde assures this
recusant*or the other that he has no doubt but
that he will make a most eligible juror; and at
last, with considerable delay, a little trial takes
place in each case, and two other jurymen have
to decide on their oaths, whether Terence
Murphy stands indifferent between our Lord
and Sovereign the King and the prisoner at
the bar; and to enable them to decide, they
have to hear all the evidence in the case.

The twelve are at last sworn—the proper
officer repeating in each case those awful words,
"Juror, look upon the prisoner. Prisoner,
look upon the juror. You shall well and truly

try, and true deliverance make,* between our
Lord and Sovereign the King and the prisoner
at the bar—so help you God!"

As this injunction in each case reached
Thady's ear, he moved his eyes upon the man
who was then being sworn, as if demanding
from him that true deliverance to which he felt
himself entitled. And now the prisoner having
pleaded, the indictments read, and the jury
armed with pen, ink, and paper, Mr. Allewinde,
full of legal dignity and intellectual warmth,
rises to his subject. We will not follow him
through the whole of the long narrative which
he, with great practised perspicuity, and in the
clearest language, laid before the jury, for we
already know the facts which he had to detail.
He first of all described the death of Ussher;
then stated that he could prove that the prisoner
had killed him, and having informed the jury
that doubtless the prisoner's sister was in the
act of eloping with the deceased when he met
his death, launched out into a powerful description of the present dreadful state of the country.
He told the jury that it was in his power to
prove to them that the prisoner was one of an
illegal society who had often threatened Ussher,
and that he had but a day or two previous to
the affray met a sworn portion of his own
tenants for the purpose of planning the murder.
He went on to tell the jury that they were not
to allow themselves to be deceived by the idea
that the murder could not have been premeditated, because there existed a presumption that
the prisoner was not aware of Ussher's expected
presence in the avenue; for that the fact of the

murder having been talked over deliberately, and then executed, afforded the strongest evidence that the prisoner was at the time lying in wait for the deceased; and that, through the servants, or from other means, he had made himself cognisant of the projected elopement. He then, preparatory to examining the witnesses, concluded in the following words :—

"Gentlemen of the jury,—You are probably all aware that the prisoner is from that rank in life to which the greatest number of yourselves belong; and you cannot but see that the fact of his being so, greatly increases the magnitude of his presumed crime. Far be it from me to urge you on this account to come to a conviction, should the evidence prove in any way deficient; but I do implore you, if you value the peace of your country—the comfort of your hearths—the safety of your houses—and the protection of your property, not to allow yourselves to be led away by a feeling of false sympathy, or to be improperly actuated by the idea that the deed was done in legitimate defence of the prisoner's sister, if the evidence do not prove that such was the case. I do implore you to divest yourselves of any such preconceived notions. Did the evidence merely go to show that Mr. Ussher was killed by the brother whilst eloping with the sister, it would doubtless be fair that the circumstance should be taken into your consideration; but when you shall have heard it proved that the death of this unfortunate man was deliberately talked over, canvassed, and decided on by the very man by whom it was executed, you will only fall into the shallow device by which the prisoner has endeavoured to deceive you, did you not clearly perceive that he has merely used the fact of his sister's elopement as a favourable opportunity for the completion of his project. Gentlemen, I shall now proceed to call the different witnesses, satisfied that when you shall have heard their evidence, you will have no difficulty in coming to a verdict in the case."

The first witness called was Dr. Blake. He stated that he had examined the body the day after Ussher had met his death; that he had no doubt death had been occasioned by two heavy blows, one of which had fractured the skull immediately over the temple, and which was of itself quite sufficient to cause instantaneous death; that he should presume these blows to have been inflicted with some heavy blunt instrument, and that he considered the stick then produced in court and shown to him was such as had probably been used on the occasion.

This witness was not cross-examined.

Biddy was next called and took her seat in the chair with much trepidation; but her usual womanly volubility soon returned to her, and she gave her evidence fluently enough. She stated that her mistress had confided to her her intention of eloping with Ussher on the morning of the evening on which he had been killed; that in obedience to her mistress's commands, she had walked down the road towards Mohill, and had met Ussher in a gig, and had put a parcel for her mistress into it; that when she returned to the house, she believed her master—that was the prisoner—was in the house, in her mistress's sitting-room; that shortly after her return she saw him come into the hall; that he then told her to go in to his sister, and that Captain Ussher was dead. She did not know what became of him after that, and that she had not seen him from that moment till the present one.

Mr. O'Laugher then asked her, whether she had told any one of her mistress's intention of eloping with Ussher, and she replied that she had not—that she had never opened her lips on the subject to any one before she heard the prisoner say that Captain Ussher was dead. She also stated that it was her young master's habit to go out to the stables every night.

She also was then allowed to go down, and Frederick Brown was called. He proved that Ussher had revealed to him his plan of running off with Feemy, and he stated, that not thinking much about it, he had told three or four friends of the circumstance, and that he could not tell whether or not it might in that manner have got round to the ears of the prisoner.

Mr. O'Laugher in his cross-examination bothered this young gentleman considerably, but as neither the questions nor the answers are material to the story, it would be useless to repeat them.

The next witness was Pat Brady, and as the verdict to which the jury came, depended in a great degree on his evidence, it will be given as nearly as possible in detail.

Having given his name, he stated that at the time of Ussher's death he was in the employment

of the prisoner; that he had been his confidential
servant, and was intimate with all his habits;
that on the night when the deceased was killed,
at some time, he supposed, about half-past nine
o'clock, his master had entered the kitchen at
Ballycloran, and had desired him, Brady, to
follow him out into the avenue; that his master,
when in the avenue, had told him that he had
killed Captain Ussher.

By this time the counsel had ceased asking
questions, and as the witness was telling his
own story, we will leave it in his words.

"I thought it war poking his fun at me, yer
honours—for I knowed the Captain hadn't been
at Ballycloran that night, and that the masther
had been ating his dinner at home, so I didn't
be taking much notice of what he war saying,
till we war mostly half down the avenue, when
Mr. Thady told me the body war there. Well,
yer honours—what with the night, and what
wid the trees, it was a'most too dark to see; but
I felt the man's body with my foot, and then I
know'd it war thrue enough what the masther
was afther saying. I axed no questions thin,
for I knew there'd been ill blood betwixt them,
and when I comed to remember myself, I wasn't
that much surprised. But Mr. Thady axed me
what we'd be doing wid the body, and I can't
exactly take upon myself to say what I answered;
but, at last, he said as how we would take it
down to Mrs. Mehan's as keeps the shebeen
shop beyond Ballycloran. He then told me
something about Miss Feemy and the Captain—
as how he was carrying her off by force like, and
that war why he'd stretched him. Well, yer

honours, at the bottom of the avenue, at the
gate like,—though for the matter of that there
ain't no gate there,—we discovered the Brown
Hall gig, and Mr. Fred's crop-tailed bay pony
horse standing in the middle of the road—and
the masther bid me take the body away to the
police at Carrick, saying he would be off at
oncet to the mountains in Aughacashel. Well,
yer honours, this I did—I left the Captain's
body with the police—I took the gig to Brown
Hall—and I brought home Miss Feemy's bundle
as had been left there in the gig, when the
Captain came out into the avenue—and that's
the long and the short of what I knows about
it, yer honours—at laste, all I knows about the
murder."

" The prisoner then owned to you," continued
Mr. Allewinde, "that it was he who killed
Captain Ussher ? "

" Shure he made no bones about it*all—but
told me straight out that he'd killed him in the
avenue."

" Did he say why he had done so ? "

" Faix I don't remember his saying thin why
he'd done it—and I didn't think to ask him.
He was in a flurry like, as war nathural, and he
and I carrying the dead man that'd been hearty
only a few minutes afore ! But shure, yer
honour knows the thing had been talked over."

" What thing had been talked over ? "

" Why, the Captain's death."

" You mean to say by that, that arrangements
had been made by certain persons to kill Captain
Ussher ? "

" I don't know about arrangements ; but

there war boys through the counthry determined to have a fling at him."

"Now I am going to ask you a question particularly affecting the prisoner, and one to which you must give me a direct answer. Have you ever been in the prisoner's company when he and others have expressed their determination to murder Captain Ussher?"

"Faix, I don't know about dethermination and murder, but I've heard him threatened."

"Have you heard him threatened with murder?"

"I've heard the boys say that he would be undher the sod that day six months."

"Have you heard Captain Ussher threatened with death in the prisoner's presence?"

"I don't know that they ever said death or murder; they don't spake out that way; av they war going to hole a chap, it's giving him his *quiatis* or his *gruel* they'd be talking about."

"Well, now, on your oath, have you ever, in the prisoner's presence, heard such language used respecting Captain Ussher as made you think that he was to be killed?"

"Didn't I tell yer honour I thought all along how he'd be killed."

"Were you ever at Mrs. Mulready's in Mohill?"

"I war."

"Did you ever hear Captain Ussher's name mentioned there?"

"I did."

"Now tell the jury as nearly as you can what was said respecting him there."

"Why, a lot of boys swore together over a

noggin or two of sperrits, to put him undher the sod—that's all; but shure, yer honour, Mr. Thady, that's him there," and he pointed to the dock, "was niver at Mother Mulready's."

"Well, but when the boys swore to put the Captain under the sod was the prisoner's name mentioned?"

"Oh, it war ofthen."

"And what was said about him?"

"Why, yer honour it was this way—and I'll tell you all I know about it off hand—and thin you'll not be throubling yer honour's self wid all these questions. The boys war mostly tenants to Mr. Thady here—and they did be saying that av so—av Mr. Thady would jine them in putting down the peelers and the Captain—they'd undhertake Mr. Keegan 'd never put a second foot on the lands of Ballycloran; and they war the more hot about this, as they knew Mr. Thady war agin the Captain about his sisther, for he thought thim two were too thick like; and he used to be saying as how Ussher war playing his thricks with Miss Feemy. Well, along of this—and knowing as how the masther were agin Mr. Keegan too, they thought he'd jine in; and to bring him round, they swore niver to pay the rint afore he did. Well, yer honour, I was one night at the Widdy's, that's Mother Mulready's, for I'd gone there knowing as how the tenants 'd be in it, and I war noticing them to be up with the masther on Friday next about the rint. Afther I'd been telling 'em all to be up at Ballycloran, they got swearing that divil a foot they'd stir to the place, or divil a penny they'd pay any more, because Mr. Thady here war so thick with the Captain. This war jist afther the row up to Loch Sheen, when three boys war locked up about some squall—and this made the rest more bitter agin the Captain. Well, when they got swearing this way, I axed 'em, why not go to the masther like a man, and tell him what they thought. Wid that they agreed to come up to Mary's wedding—that's Mary McGovery, yer honour, as is my sisther, and who war to be married the Thursday; and so they parted, and a lot on 'em swore that blessed night that the Captain should be under the sod that day six months. Well, yer honour, the next morning Mr. Keegan called down to Ballycloran about law business, and somehow there war words atwixt him and Mr. Thady, and from that they got to blows, and I b'lieve somehow Mr. Keegan got the best of it, and Mr. Thady was a little hurted, and this made him bittherer nor iver."

"But that did not make him bitterer against Captain Ussher, did it?" asked a juror.

"Faix thin, I think it did, yer honour," answered Pat. "It seemed to make him bitther altogether agin everybody; when I war talking to him aftherwards about coming down to the wedding, he seemed to be trating all the world alike. But the Captain and Mr. Keegan especial. Well, when the supper war over, and the boys were begun dancing, Mr. Thady come down and immediately comed into the inside room, where the men war sitting dhrinking, and I war wid them : thin one of the men, a tinent to Mr. Thady, up and tould the masther all as I've tould yer honours, of what took place at

the Widdy's in Mohill, and how av Mr. Thady
would jine them to rid the counthry of the
Captain, they'd stand to him, and wouldn't let
Mr. Keegan on the lands on Ballycloran, right
or wrong. Wid that there war a dale of shilly-
shallying*—but at last the masther said as how
he would jine the boys in ridding the counthry
of the Captain, and he thin agreed to come
down to the Widdy's the next night, or that
afther, to get the secret signs and the pass-words,
and to take the oaths they war to swear him to.
Wid that he tuk an oath thin niver to tell nothin'
of what had passed that night. After that, I
don't remember rightly how it war, but he got
up to look for Miss Feemy, and she war out
walking in the road wid the Captain. Well,
Mr. Thady went down the road afther thim—
and there war a ruction in the road betwixt thim
two; but as I warn't there I can't say exactly
what was said one side or the other. By the
time they come agin to Mrs. Mehan's door,
Father John, that's Father Magrath, you know,
war there, and made the pace betwixt 'em; and
that's all I can tell yer honours about it av I war
to sit here till doomsday."

"You said just now," said Mr. Allewinde,
"that the prisoner agreed to join the men
assembled at Mrs. Mehan's in ridding the
country of Captain Ussher; now what was
meant by ridding the country of him?"

"Why, isn't it ridding the counthry of him?
yer honour knows what that means as well as
ere a boy in the barony."

"Perhaps I do; but you must tell the jury
what you mean by it."

"Is it I? I didn't mane nothin' at all : it warn't I as said it—or as war ever a going to do it."

"What did you suppose was the meaning of those who did make use of the phrase?"

"I 'sposed the boys did mane to get rid of the Captain out of the counthry ; jist that, yer honour."

"But how did you suppose they were to get rid of him?"

"Oh, yer honour, I niver heard the particklars ; I niver knew nothin' of the plan. I warn't one of them, you know."

"But the prisoner agreed to join them in any plan, or in some plan for ridding the country of Captain Ussher?"

"He did, yer honour ; shure I said that before."

"Now, you said some time ago, that when you first discovered that Captain Ussher had been killed by the prisoner, and that when you came to remember yourself, you weren't much surprised. Now, thank God! it is, at any rate in this county, a very uncommon thing to find that one man has killed another. Can you tell the jury why you were not surprised at such an event as that?"

"Becase I knowed there war ill-blood betwixt the two."

"But men do not kill one another whenever they quarrel, do they?"

"Faix, they do sometimes."

"Did you ever, of your own knowledge, know a man before who killed another?"

"Oh dear ! yes ; sure I did."

"Well, tell us an instance."

"Why, there war ould Paddy Rafferty, who war in the Cavan Militia in the Rabellion—av he didn't kill scores of the French at Ballina-muck,* he's the biggest liar I ever heard; but he's dead now, yer honour."

"Supposing that the death of Captain Ussher had happened a fortnight before—that the prisoner had killed him a fortnight before the day on which he did kill him, would you not have been surprised then?"

"Why, I don't know that a fortnight makes much difference."

"Answer my question. In such a case as that, would you not have felt more surprise than you did when the affair did occur?"

"Why, yer honour, I can't answer that—becase, you see, it didn't happen then, and I couldn't exactly be saying what my feelings might be."

"At any rate, you were not surprised?"

"Oh yes, I war surprised; in course it war a surprise to me when I kicked the dead body; but when I come to think over all about the Captain, I warn't that much surprised."

"After what had taken place at Mrs. Mehan's, you did not expect Captain Ussher would be very long lived?"

"Faix, he lived longer than I expected—see-ing the way he war going on through the counthry."

"Do you remember telling me some time ago, speaking of Captain Ussher's death, that the thing had been talked over?"

"I b'lieve I said as much."

"What did you mean by that ? "

"Why, just that the job had been talked about."

"What job ? "

"Why, this job."

"What job ?   Tell the jury what job."

" Faix, they all know well enough by this time," and the witness looked up to the jury, " —or else they oughtn't to be there, any way."

"Tell them what job you mean—never mind what they know."

" 'Deed thin, you're bothering me so entirely* with yer jobs, I don't rightly know myself which I'm maning."

" Think a little, then, for you must tell them ; you said the job had been talked over ; what was it that had been talked over ? "

The witness gave a stolid look at the counsel, but answered nothing.

" Come," continued Mr. Allewinde, " what was the job that had been talked over ? "

" Bad manners to the likes of me ; but I war niver cute,* and now I'm bothered intirely."

" You mean to tell the jury, then, that you don't know what you meant when you said the thing had been talked over, do you ? "

" Why, I s'pose it was this thing about Captain Ussher. Weren't we talking of that, then ? "

" That's for you to say. Was it Captain Ussher's death that had been talked over ? "

" Witness, don't answer that question," said Mr. O'Malley. " I'm sure my learned friend will not press it ; it's very seldom he makes such a slip as that."

Mr. Allewinde had asked a leading, and therefore an unallowable question.

" Why, the witness had just said that he supposed it was this thing about Captain Ussher," said Mr. Allewinde.

" I'll say no more about it," continued Mr. O'Malley, " feeling perfectly certain that you will not press the question."

" Well," said Mr. Allewinde to the witness, " tell the jury at once what was the thing that had been talked over."

" Why, yer honour knows well enough. Shure weren't you saying it yourself, only the gentleman here wouldn't let you."

" Well, now do you say it."

" Say what ? "

" Say what was the thing that had been talked over."

" Talked over when, yer honour ? "

" You told the jury some time since that the prisoner owned to you in the avenue that he had killed Captain Ussher, did you not ? "

" Faix, I did—and it was thrue for me—he made no bones about it at all."

" And you then added that the thing had been talked over; what thing was it that had been talked over ? "

" Ah, that's what you're wanting, is it ? 'Deed thin I'm axing yer pardon for keeping yer honours all this time in suspinse. Faix thin, Captain Ussher war the thing what war talked over ; and divil a lie in it, for he war talked over ofthen enough."

" Captain Ussher had been talked over in

such a manner as to prevent your feeling much surprise, when you found that the prisoner had killed him, isn't that it?"

"Jist so—faix, I'd have no difficulty in discoursing wid yer honour, av the other gentleman wouldn't put in his say."

"You'll find by and by he'll have a great deal more to say."

"In course; and no objection on arth on my part so long as it's one at a time."

"Now I think I have only two more questions to ask you, if you will give me direct answers to them."

"Twenty, av you plaze, yer honour."

"You have said that the tenants of the prisoner had sworn together to put Captain Ussher under the sod, and also that the prisoner had agreed to join the tenants in ridding the country of him; was the former phrase, that of putting the Captain under the sod, used in the prisoner's presence on the evening of the wedding?"

"There war a lot of thim phrases used—ridding the counthry—sodding him*—and all thim sort of disagreeable sayings; but I can't swear to any one exactly at Mrs. Mehan's—thim's the sort of words."

"Very well. Now, I think you told us that when the prisoner desired you to take the dead body to the police at Carrick, he told you he was going to some place: where did he say he was going to?"

"To Aughacashel."

"Where's Aughacashel?"

"It's a mountain behind Drumshmabo."

"And did he tell you why he was going to Aughacashel?"

"That he mightn't be tuk, I s'pose."

"I don't want your supposition. Did the prisoner tell you why he was going to Augha-cashel?"

"There war some of the tinants there, I b'lieve, and he thought he'd be safe may be."

"Did the prisoner tell you that he was going to Aughacashel because he thought he'd be safe there?"

"I'll tell you how it war, thin. We were jist talking together about what he'd betther be doing, which was nathural, and he with the dead body there, he'd been jist afther killing. Wid that, says he, 'Pat,' says he, 'where's the stills mostly at work now?' 'Faith,' says I, 'I don't exactly be knowing;' for, yer honour, I niver turned a penny that way myself—'but,' says I, 'sich a one'll tell you,' and I mintioned one of the tinants; 'and where's he?' said the masther; 'why, I heard tell,' says I, 'that he's in Aughacashel, but av you'll go down to Drum-leesh, you'll find out,' and wid that he went down the road to Drumleesh, and I druv the body off to Carrick."

"That'll do," said Mr. Allewinde. "I've done with this witness, my lord."

CHAPTER XXX

THE PRISONER'S DEFENCE

MR. O'MALLEY then rose, but before he began to cross-examine the witness, he addressed the judge.

"There's a witness in court, my lord, whom I shall have to examine by and by on the defence, and I must request that he may be directed to absent himself during my examination of the witness now in the chair. It is material that he should not hear the answers which this witness may give. I mean Mr. Hyacinth Keegan, my lord, who is sitting beneath me."

Keegan was sitting on the bench immediately under that of the barrister, among the attorneys employed in court. When he heard Mr. O'Malley's request to the judge, he rose up on his one leg, and the judge having ordered him to leave the court, he hobbled out with the assistance of his crutch.

"Your name is Pat Brady, I think," commenced Mr. O'Malley.

Pat did not reply.

"Why don't you answer my question, sir?" said the counsellor angrily.

"Why, I towld what my name war afore. Thim gintlemen up there knows it well enough, and yourself knows it; why'd I be saying it agin?"

"Well, my friend, I tell you to begin with, I

shall ask you many questions you'll find considerably more difficult to answer than that, and you'd better make up your mind to answer them ; for I mean to get an answer to the questions I shall ask, and you'll sit in that chair till you do answer them, unless you're moved from it into gaol."

"Fire away, sir; I'm very well where I am, and I'm thinking I can howld out agin the hunger longer nor yer honer."

"Your name is Pat Brady ?"

"It is."

"Whose servant are you ?"

"Whose servant ?"

"Don't you understand what I say? whose servant are you?"

"Faix thin, I don't call myself a servant at all."

"Who's your master, then ?"

"Mr. Macdermot here was my masther afore this affair."

"I didn't ask who was your master ; who is your master now ?"

"Why, Mr. Keegan."

"Mr. Hyacinth Keegan, that's just gone out of court ; he's your master, eh ?"

"He is."

"And a very good master—isn't he ?"

"Betther, maybe, than yer honour'd be, and yet perhaps none of the best."

"Answer my questions, sir ; isn't he a good master ?"

"Faix, he is so."

"How long have you been in his employment ?"

" How long ! "

" Yes, how long ? "

" Why, I can't jist say how long."

" Have you been a year ? "

" No."

" Six months ? "

" No."

" Will you swear that you never were in Mr. Keegan's pay before six months ago ? "

" I will."

" You never received any money from Mr. Keegan before six months ago ? "

" I did not say that."

" Why, if you received his money weren't you in his pay ? "

" No ; maybe he gave me a Christmas-box or so ; he's very good to a poor boy like me in that way, is Mr. Keegan."

" In whose employment were you six months ago ? "

" In Mr. Macdermot's ; yourself knows that well enough."

" And Mr. Macdermot and Mr. Keegan were great friends at that time ; weren't they ? "

" Faix they were not ; I never seed much frindship betwixt 'em."

" Did you ever see any enmity between them —any quarrelling—or what you very properly call bad blood ? "

" Indeed I did, then."

" I b'lieve Mr. Macdermot—that's the prisoner—had great trust in you ; hadn't he ? "

" I believe he had."

" You knew all the affairs about the estate ? "

" I b'lieve I did."

" He told you all his troubles—all his money difficulties, didn't he ? "

" One way or other, I b'lieve I knew the most on 'em."

" Particularly as to the money due on his father's property, which Keegan had to receive ; he used to talk to you confidentially about those things ? "

" Well, and av he did ? "

" But he did so ; didn't he ? "

" Faix, but I don't know what you're afther ; I b'lieve he towld me all about everything."

" I believe he did indeed ; and now I'll tell you what I'm after. Mr. Macdermot, unfortunately believing you to be an honest man, told you all his plans and secrets, which you, in consideration of certain pay, which you call Christmas-boxes, sold to the man whom you knew to be your master's enemy ; isn't that the fact, now ? "

" No, it an't."

" Ah, but I say it is the fact ; and now do you suppose any jury will believe a word you've said, after having shown yourself guilty of such treachery as that. Do you expect the jury to believe you ? "

" 'Deed I do—every word ; Lord bless you, they knows me."

" Now, then, tell me. Can you recall any conversation between yourself and Mr. Keegan since the death of Captain Ussher, relative to this trial ? "

" I can."

" More than one, perhaps ? "

" Oh, lor yes ; twenty maybe."

"Will you tell us any particulars you may remember of the last?"

A long conversation then ensued, but Mr. O'Malley could only elicit that Brady had, of his own accord, informed his master of all he knew on the subject, and that he had done so because he thought it right. He admitted, however, that Mr. Keegan had expressed a desire that the prisoner might be hung. A great many questions were then asked as to the present holding of Ballycloran, to which Brady answered, stating with tolerable accuracy the manner in which Larry at present lived on the property, and the hold which Keegan had upon it. He, moreover, stated that the house was in a very bad state of repair, and that most of the tenants who were left on the property were unable to pay their rent. He then, after much hesitation, owned that he had overheard what had taken place between Keegan and Thady in the avenue, on the day when the attorney had called at Ballycloran—that he had heard the name which Keegan had applied to Feemy, and that he had seen the manner in which Thady had been struck.

He was then asked whether he himself had not cautioned Thady against Ussher, telling him the reports that were going through the country as to Ussher's treatment of his sister. This he denied, stating that it wasn't probable that "the likes of him should go to speak to his masther about such things as that." He was repeatedly questioned on this point, but Mr. O'Malley could not shake his evidence. Brady, however, owned that in talking to Thady about Ussher,

he had called the latter "a black Protestant,"
and that he had always spoken ill of him;
"and now," continued Mr. O'Malley, "I don't
wish to ask you any questions by answering
which you will criminate yourself; but you have
already said that you have been a visitor at Mrs.
Mulready's shop?"

"Oh yes, I've been there."

"And you have been there when certain
persons swore that before twelve months were
passed, Captain Ussher should be under the
sod?"

"Yes; I swear I heard thim words, and saw
the boys take the oath."

"But to the best of your belief the prisoner
was never at this house when such an oath was
taken?"

"Is it Mr. Thady? He was niver at mother
Mulready's at all."

"But he met the party who had taken this
oath at your sister's wedding?"

"He did."

"And the same subject was spoken of there;
was it?"

"What subject?"

"The propriety of sodding Captain Ussher?"

"I don't know about propriety."

"Well, then, the advisability of doing
so?"

"Oh, yer honer, I ain't no scollard.* I can't
make nothin' of thim long words."

"At any rate, they talked of sodding Captain
Ussher at the wedding—didn't they?"

"I niver said so."

"Well, but did they?"

" Talk of sodding him !   Faix I don't know ;
I don't think they said sodding."

" Did they say killing ? "

" I won't say they did."

" Or murdering ? "

" No ; they did not say nothin' about
murdher."

" Oh ; they did not say anything about murder,—or doing for him ? perhaps the prisoner
and the other boys agreed to do for him ? "

" Maybe they did—maybe you were there ;
only if so I disremember you ; but thim's not
the words I swore to."

" Well, they didn't agree to sod him, or kill
him, or murder him, or do for him ; what was
it they were to do for him ? "

" They were to rid the counthry of him."

" What—make the country too hot to hold
him ? eh, is that what you mean ? "

" It don't matter what I mean ; that warn't
what they meant."

" And how do you know what they meant ? "

" Why, they meant to kill the man ; you
know that as well as I."

" But I don't know it—nor do I think it ;
nor, what is more, do you think it ; for you are
sharp enough to know that where there are so
many figurative terms in use to signify murder,
it is not probable that had they, on this occasion, wished to signify murder, they would have
used a phrase which every one knows expresses
an intention to drive a man out of the country.
Yes, sir, you know that not one of the party
would have dared to propose to Mr. Macdermot
to have a share in murder. You and they talked

of murder at Mrs. Mulready's, but you know that for your life you would not have dared to mention it before Mr. Macdermot. Now tell me, how long was the prisoner at the wedding party?"

"Maybe three hours."

"Was he sober when he came in?"

"He war."

"Was he sober when he went out?"

"Sober when he went out?"

"Yes, sir; was he sober when he went out?"

"I don't think he war—not to say sober."

"Wasn't he mad drunk?"

"Mad dhrunk?"

"Don't repeat my words, sir; wasn't he mad drunk?"

"Faix, that's thrue for you, sir—they're not worth repeating; no, he war not mad dhrunk."

"Was he drunk? and mind, sir, you are on your oath—and there were many others present there who will prove whether you answer this question truly or falsely; was he drunk when he left the wedding party?"

"'Deed then I don't know; you can ask thim as war there besides me."

"But I choose to ask you, and I choose that you should answer me; was he drunk?"

"Don't I tell you that I don't know?"

"On your oath you don't know whether he was drunk or not?"

"He war screwed; divil a doubt of that; but thin, he could walk—I wouldn't call him dhrunk."

"Wasn't he nearer being so than you'd seen him for many months?"

"Faix, he war. I didn't see him so bad since Leitrim fair, two years back."

"And now you say, that at the wedding, the prisoner promised in a day or two to meet the same boys at Mrs. Mulready's, to settle their plans of ridding the country of Ussher?"

"Yes; about that and other things."

"And the prisoner never kept that appointment?"

"No, Mr. Thady niver went there."

"Did you ever say anything to him about not going there?"

"Oh, I did; we were discoursing about it."

"And what did you say to him on the subject?"

"Why, I towld him av he guv the boys a promise, he ought never to go back from his word."

"That is to say, you endeavoured to persuade him to go?"

"By-dad, I don't know about persuading; it warn't for the likes of me to persuade him."

"On your oath, sir, didn't you endeavour to induce the prisoner to go to Mrs. Mulready's?"

"I towld him he ought to be as good as his word."

"Yes, you did; and you think he ought to have gone?"

"May be av he'd gone there, he'd never have stood here this day."

"You wanted him to go to Mrs. Mulready's, then?"

"Wanted! No, I didn't want nothing about it."

"You only asked him to go?"

"Jist as I towld you; I said av he guv the

boys his word, as a man he shouldn't go from it."

"Did you say anything to him about Mr. Jonas Brown ? "

"Jonas Brown ? "

"Yes, Mr. Jonas Brown, the magistrate ? "

"Faix, I don't know. I can't rightly say."

"Think now, my man ; when you were trying to persuade your master to go to the widow Mulready's, did you mention Mr. Jonas Brown's name ? "

"D'ye think I do be counting my words that way ; how am I to say all the names I mintioned four or five months back ? "

"On your solemn oath don't you remember mentioning that gentleman's name to the prisoner with reference to his visit to Mrs. Mulready's ? "

"What, Jonas Brown's name ? "

"Yes."

"Faix I may."

"Don't you know you did ? "

"Faix I don't."

"Didn't you threaten your master, that if he did not attend the meeting, some of the boys would swear against him, before Mr. Brown, for having joined the party and taken the oath at the wedding ? "

"What av I did ? "

"But did you ? "

"Maybe I did—maybe I didn't; I disremember thim little things."

The cross-examination continued for a considerable time ; but nothing further that was material could be drawn from Brady. He seemed even more unwilling to answer Mr.

O'Malley, than he had been in replying to Mr.
Allewinde, and at last he was sent off the table.

The next witness called was McGovery, who
had been summoned on behalf of the prosecution. He was asked whether he had not suspected that some foul play was intended against
Ussher, and he stated in what manner he had,
in the first place, cautioned Ussher himself—
then that he had told the same thing to Father
John—and that after overhearing a portion of
the conversation at Mrs. Mehan's he had gone
to Father Cullen, for the purpose of informing
him that he feared there was a conspiracy
against Mr. Keegan. Little, however, could
be learnt from him, for he owned that he had
no substantial grounds for his suspicions in the
first case, and that he had chiefly been led to
fear an attack upon Ussher, from knowing his
unpopularity and the bad character of many
of the guests expected at the wedding. Mr.
O'Laugher tried to make him say that the conversation at Mrs. Mehan's had been confined
to Keegan, and the threats which he had heard
uttered against him; but McGovery would not
say as much as this; he stated positively that
he had never heard Ussher's name mentioned,
but that during a considerable portion of the
evening he had been entirely unable to hear a
word that the men said; he declared, however,
positively that Thady was drunk when he left
the room, and that it appeared to him that he,
Thady, had taken very little part in the conversation before he was drunk.

When this witness went off the table, Mr. Allewinde declared that the case for the prosecution

was finished—stating at the same time that he abstained from feelings of delicacy and respect from putting the prisoner's sister into the witness box; and that he should trouble her with no questions unless she were placed there by the counsel for the defence.

Mr. O'Malley then rose to address the jury on behalf of the prisoner, and spoke to the following effect :—

"Gentlemen of the jury, it now becomes my duty to address to you such words as may best suit to point out to you the weakness of the evidence against the prisoner—to explain to you the different objects we had in our lengthened cross-examination of the witnesses—to inform you what we intend to prove on behalf of the prisoner from further witnesses—and, in fact, to put the case before you in a light, and point of view, differing as widely as I can make it do from that in which my learned friend has presented it to you. This you are aware is the general duty and constant object of a counsel endeavouring to obtain a verdict of acquittal from a jury. It is a duty in which long practice has made me familiar, if not skilful; and I never undertook that duty with the same assurance of its facility, as that which I now feel, after having heard the evidence which has been brought forward on the prosecution. I knew beforehand, as surely as one can trust to human knowledge, that the evidence would fail; but knowing the acute legal abilities of my learned friend, and the extraordinary avidity which exists among a large class of men for a verdict against the prisoner in this case,—

remembering, I say, these things, I did not expect such a total break down, such an exposure of weakness as that which has been just made before you. Were my object merely to rescue the prisoner from an ignominious death —had it been my mere duty on this occasion to obtain an acquittal, I should feel no hesitation in requesting his lordship at once to send the case before you, with such remarks as the evidence would call forth from him; and I should consider that I was only wasting the time of the court in pointing out to you the insufficiency of the evidence, in which each of you must perceive that nothing whatever is proved against the prisoner; but I have been employed with another object; and I must own to you that so great is my own personal anxiety —so terrible and so undeserved the present position of that unfortunate young man, and so essentially necessary is it for his future happiness, that I should effect my present object;— I must own to you, I say, for these reasons, that from the time when I first found myself standing in a crowded court to address a jury, up to the present moment, I have never felt so little self-confidence, or experienced so total a prostration of that assurance, which is a lawyer's first requisite, as I do at present.

"I have said my object in addressing you is not merely that of obtaining an acquittal; and I said so because a mere acquittal will serve that unfortunate young man but little. Unless he can walk out of this court with such a verdict as, damning as it may be to others, will altogether cleanse his name from the stain of guilt in this matter; unless he can, not only save his neck from the halter, but also entirely clear his character from the gross charges which have been brought against him,—he would as lief go back to the cell whence he has come, as return to his father's house acquitted by the voice of law, but condemned by that of opinion.

"On this account I am debarred from many of the usual resources of counsel pleading for a prisoner; I am forbidden to make use of legal points in his favour; I am forbidden to effect an escape by the numerous weak points in the enemy's plan of attack; I am desired to meet him face to face in the open field—to fight under no banner but that of truth, and not to strike my adversary below the belt. You are aware that this is a line of conduct as rare as it is difficult in a criminal court—when an advocate has to contend for his client against the law—where every possible means of success which legal ingenuity can devise is taken in the prosecution, and where you are accustomed to hear every legal technicality used in the defence.

"Had I not received instructions of so peculiar a nature, I should point out to the jury that no proof has been given direct or circumstantial, that the prisoner was the person by whose hands Ussher fell; instead of doing so I am to declare that he did, as he is supposed to have done, kill the deceased in the avenue of Ballycloran, by striking him twice with his stick. I am to justify that deed, and disprove the charge of his having entered into a conspiracy to murder the man, whom he did kill.

"The prisoner, you have been told, and are probably all aware, is above the rank of men whom you are mostly accustomed to see placed in that dock. He is the only son of a gentleman, living on his own small estate, and has for some years past acted as his father's sole agent and manager.

"I must now tell you a few particulars respecting that estate; and though, of course, you cannot receive as evidence what I tell you, still this course will be necessary, as I shall thereby be enabled to explain to you my object in obtaining answers to certain questions which I have asked, or shall ask, the answers to which you will take as evidence.

"In the time of the prisoner's grandfather, a house was built on this estate by a Mr. Flannelly, of this town, and the price of the building not having been paid, this man, the builder, obtained a mortgage on the estate for the amount of the debt. This is still due, though the house, as you have heard, is falling to the ground; and it has so been increased by interest not paid up and by legal charges, that it has completely embarrassed the present proprietor, who is even now unable to leave his house for fear of arrest. Mr. Keegan, whose name has often come before you in the evidence, and who, by-and-by, will be examined himself, is the son-in-law of this Mr. Flannelly, and owns, as I have no doubt I shall be able to prove to you, the whole interest in the estate of Ballycloran arising from this mortgage.

"The prisoner's time, since he ceased to be a boy, has been employed in futile endeavours to satisfy the legal claims of this man; and I shall prove to you by most undoubtable evidence that his industry in this object has been unceasing, and that his conduct as a son and a brother has been beyond all praise. But he has failed—times have been against him—legal costs have so swelled the legal interest as to consume the whole rents—those rents he had been unable to collect, and his life has been one manful struggle against poverty and Mr. Keegan;—and I could not wish my worst foe two more inveterate enemies.

"Some few days before Ussher's death—and now I am going to confine myself to that which I am in a position to prove—Mr. Keegan called on the Macdermots for the purpose of proposing certain terms for the adjustment of the debt, which were neither more nor less than that he should have the whole estate, paying a small weekly stipend for life to the prisoner's father. The prisoner was willing to agree, providing some provision should be made for his sister; but the father indignantly spurned the offer, and turned Mr. Keegan out of the house in no very gentle manner. The prisoner followed him into the avenue— still wishing to come to some arrangement; but the attorney was so enraged at the conduct of the father, that instead of listening to the son, he began abusing the whole family, and, as you have heard, applied the most shameful epithet to the sister with which the tongue of a man can defile the name of a woman. He afterwards struck the prisoner, who was unarmed, heavily with his stick; and I have no hesitation in telling you, that that quarrel, in which no blame appears to have been attributable to the young man, placed him in that dock.

" Brady, the confidential servant of the prisoner, both saw and overheard what took place at this interview, as he has told you, and he afterwards,—as he will not deny, though he will not confess it,—incited his master, during the period of his natural irritation, to go down to the wedding party, to meet a number of his tenants who would be willing to assist him in revenging himself against his enemy Keegan, the attorney, if he would assist them against their enemy, Ussher, the Revenue officer. And here my client made the one false step—and the only one which I can trace to him—and committed that folly from which this bitter foe has thought to ruin him. Irritated by the blow —his ear still ringing with the infamous name applied to his loved sister—full of his father's wrong, and his own hard conditions, he consented to meet men whose object he knew was illegal; though what their plans were he was entirely ignorant.

" With reference to what took place at the wedding, I have, in the first place, to remark that from the character of this man Brady, I could confidently call upon you to reject every word of his evidence; and I shall presently show you in what respects and why you are bound to do so. But, in the present instance, I am satisfied to tell you that my client did attend that meeting. But mind, that was no illegal meeting—it was not secret; the door was not locked, nor even closed; it was a party of men met at the wedding of one of their own station. The woman to be married was a sister of the prisoner's servant, and it was natural that he should be present. He directs me positively to tell you that he did attend that meeting; though I also tell you, with confidence, that he committed no crime in doing so, and his lordship will corroborate what I tell you.

" It was, however, a part of the plan organised against the prisoner that he should be induced to commit an illegal act, and he was, as you have heard, brought when drunk to promise that he would go down to Mrs. Mulready's, to take upon himself illegal oaths and obligations.

"On the following day he was invited by this same Brady to come on a certain evening; but Macdermot was no longer drunk; he was no longer infuriated by the gross outrages he had received; and what did he do then? Did he go to Mrs. Mulready's to settle the particulars of this murder which he is said to have premeditated? Did he join these outlaws of whom he is represented to have been the leader? Did he even send them an encouraging message—a word of fellowship? No! Even by the testimony of this man, now so anxious to hang his benefactor—this man, who by his own showing was at the same time in the pay of the prisoner and of his enemy Keegan—he indignantly repudiated the idea; he at once informed this wretch—equally a traitor to his confederates and to his master—that he would have nothing in common with them or their schemes; and although threatened with the vengeance of the party, and with the authority of a magistrate, steadily refused even to enter the house in which they were accustomed to assemble. Why, from what I can learn of the young man and of his daily habits, I do not conceive that there is one of yourselves who would not be as likely to join an illegal society as he would. Patient under poverty—industrious under accumulated sufferings—he has led a life which would not have disgraced a priest; he has been ever found sincere in his thoughts, moral in his conduct, and most unselfish in his actions. Is this the man to join a set of senseless rioters, furious at the imprisonment of their relatives, and anxious only to protect their illicit stills? And this is no empty praise. That what I have said of the prisoner is no more than is his due, will be proved to you by evidence which I defy you to doubt. Well, he did not go to Mrs. Mulready's; but he did go to his friend and priest, Mr. McGrath; and not as a penitent to his confessor, but as a friend to a friend, told him exactly what had passed, lamented his indiscretion, and declared his determination never to put himself in the way of repeating it.

"Up to this time my chief object has been to show to you the enmity existing between Keegan and the prisoner,—the object which the former had in view in ruining the prisoner, and that Brady was a paid spy employed to entrap him.

"I shall now come to the deed itself, and I shall afterwards refer to what absolutely did take place at the meeting at the wedding. I have told you that young Macdermot did kill the deceased. He struck him with the stick which has been shown to you in court, and as he was rising from the blow he struck him again ; and no doubt the medical witness was right in his opinion that the second blow occasioned instant death.

" You are, however, aware that circumstances might exist which would justify any man in taking the life of another. If a man were violently to attack you, and you were to strike him on the head and kill him, you would be justified. If you were to kill a man in a fray, in fair defence of a third party, you would be justified. If you were to kill a man by a blow in the quarrel of a moment, you would not be guilty of murder. But I can fancy no case in which death, however much it may be lamented, can lay less of the murderer's stain upon the hand that inflicts it, than one in which a brother interferes to rescue a sister from the violent grasp of a seducer. Such was precisely the case in the instance now before us. My learned friend on the other side has truly told you that Miss Macdermot, the prisoner's sister, had consented to elope with Captain Ussher on the evening on which that man was killed. You have learnt, from evidence which you have no reason to doubt, that she had prepared to do so. In fact, you cannot doubt that she left the house of Ballycloran for that purpose ; this has been proved—but there are circumstances beyond this on which it is essentially necessary that you should have evidence, and this evidence can only be given by the young lady herself. I shall therefore have to bring her before you.

When my learned friend told you that he would not call upon her, nor question her unless placed in that chair by me, he forgot his usual candour, and assumed to himself credit for humanity to which he has no title. He himself has nothing to learn from her, as he will prove to you if he attempts to cross-examine her. Moreover, he was as fully aware as I am myself, that the prisoner must rely on her alone for anything like a true account of the affray.

"The brother and the sister are the only living witnesses of that scene. He has within him that high consciousness of innocence and rectitude of intention which has enabled him to bear his sufferings, his imprisonment, and the misery of his position, with a fortitude which I not only admire, but envy. But that can avail nothing with you; from the sister's lips you must hear the only account which you can receive, and if we find that she has been unable to recall the dreadful circumstances of that night, that fact will bear me out in the history of the occurrence which I am now going to give you."

Mr. O'Malley then gave as exact an account of the occurrence as he had been able to collect from Thady, from Feemy's evidence before the coroner, and from such words as Mrs. McKeon had been able to extract from Feemy on the subject. He then continued—

"When the prisoner struck Ussher, he had come to the knowledge of what the burden was which this man was dragging, solely from the words which the man had used. Miss Macdermot was lying senseless in his arms, and,

supporting her by her waist, he was forcing her
down the avenue. The words he used were,
'This is damned nonsense,—you must come
now.' Then the brother perceived the fate to
which this man was—not alluring—but forcing
his sister. At that moment—and it was the only
one in which the prisoner had to judge of the
circumstances of the case—she was not in the
act of eloping willingly; she had seen her
brother's form, and had refused, or been unable,
to rise from the timber on which she was seated.
She was forced from thence by this man, whose
death protects him from the language in which
his name would otherwise be mentioned. She
fainted in his arms, and only came to her senses
to find her lover dead, and her brother standing
beside her, red with his blood. Yes; he had
avenged her !—he had punished the ruffian for
his barbarity towards her, and saved his sister
from the ignominy to which Mr. Frederick
Brown told you with so much flippancy that
she had been doomed.

"If this was the young man's conduct, was
there anything in it that you can even blame?
Which of you would have done otherwise?
Which of you will tell me that in avenging the
wrongs of a sister, or of a daughter, he would
pause to measure the weight of his stick, or the
number of his blows? Fancy each of you that
you see the form of her you love best in the
rough grasp of a violent seducer ! Endeavour
to bring home to yourselves the feelings to
which such a sight would give rise within you !
and then, if you can, find that young man guilty
of murder, because his heart was warm to feel

his sister's wrongs and his hand was strong to avenge them.

"But you have been told that as the prisoner had met certain persons for the purpose of entering into a conspiracy of murdering Ussher —and that that fact would be proved to you— you are bound to consider that his coming across Ussher was not accidental, and that the manner in which he attacked that man whilst carrying off his sister was a part of his preconcerted plan. I first of all deny that any credible evidence, any evidence worthy of the slightest belief, has been brought before you to induce you to suppose that the prisoner had even joined any such conspiracy ; instead of which you have strong circumstantial evidence that he had never done so.

"You have most of you, no doubt, heard, on various occasions, from different learned judges seated on that bench, that a crown approver's evidence is to be taken with the greatest caution, and only to be believed in detail, when corroborated by other evidence or by circumstances. Now this man, Brady, on whose sole evidence you are desired to convict the prisoner, has shown himself an approver of the very worst description. You are aware that he was the prisoner's servant ; that he is now Mr. Keegan's ; that there has been long enmity between these men ; that the former has been an oppressed debtor—the latter a most oppressive creditor. Mr. Keegan's spirit towards the prisoner's family you may learn from the scandalous and unwarrantable language which has been proved to you to have been used by him towards them. Mr. Keegan's acerbity has been increased by the mutilation he has undergone, and which he conceives he owes to his interference with the Ballycloran property. This man and the witness Brady have, as you have heard, constantly been talking over this trial, and the attorney, it seems, has repeatedly expressed to his servant his ardent wish that the prisoner might be hung. This is his expressed eager desire; and then this new servant, but long-used spy, comes forward boldly to swear away the prisoner's life! Why, it would be ridiculing you to suppose you could believe him. Then look at the man's character. He was a constant attendant at that scene of villany into which he vainly endeavoured to seduce the prisoner at Mrs. Mulready's. It is plain enough that Ussher's death was a constant theme of discourse at that haunt; it is plain enough that a project did exist there to accomplish his murder; and is it not plain enough that this man was one of the conspirators— one of the murderers? Would he have been admitted to their counsels—to their dangerous secrets—unless he had been an active participator in their plans? Would they have taken in his presence a solemn oath to put this unfortunate Revenue officer under the sod, unless he had joined in that oath? Of course they would not! And this is the man whom they expect you to believe with such confidence, that on his unsupported evidence you should condemn the prisoner! What I have said to you respecting this respectable witness, and his not less respectable master, will perhaps be made somewhat plainer to you when you shall have heard the evidence which I hope to extract from the latter. Now, as to the meeting at Mrs. Mehan's, even were you to believe Brady, I maintain that nothing whatever has been proved against the prisoner. Brady states that at Mrs. Mulready's certain men swore together that at a certain period Captain Ussher should be under the sod. This phrase brings to the mind of every one the conviction that they meant to express murder, The man could not be under the sod unless he were dead.

" But at the wedding, when young Macdermot was present, even by the showing of Brady himself, the men were afraid to use any such phrase. They implored their landlord's assistance to help them to rid the country of him; to frighten him off; to make the place too hot to hold him. As I told that wretched reptile, whilst in the chair, they would have no more dared to propose a scheme of murder to young Macdermot, even in his drunkenness, than they would have to you or to me.

" Now as to the probability of the prisoner's having been aware of his sister's project for eloping, and having made use of that opportunity for the safe execution of a scheme of murder,— and this perhaps is the most material point of all; for were there good grounds to suppose that he knew that this elopement was to take place—that he took no precautionary steps to prevent it—but that having this previous knowledge, he rushed out at the time, and killed the man, I should be very far from telling you that he was perfectly justified, as I do now. But I must positively maintain that you cannot come to such a conclusion. It has, to a degree, been proved to you, and will be so more clearly, that the prisoner had all along shown himself averse to the intimacy which existed between Ussher and his sister; it is therefore to be presumed that both of them took every means in their power to prevent the prisoner from learning their intention; and there is every reason to suppose they were successful.

"Two persons appear to have been told, as their services were required, both of whom have been examined before you—the servant girl and Mr. Frederick Brown. The former has sworn that she mentioned it to no one, and there is no reason to disbelieve her. The latter proved himself not so trustworthy. It seems that with that foolish flippancy which distinguishes him he told his friend's secret to other friends of his as a good joke. But you must remember that Mr. Brown's friends were not the prisoner's friends—that they rather were in such different circles, that what was said in one, would be very little likely to find its way into the other; and above all, that those to whom Mr. Brown or his friends communicated it, would think that the brother was the last person who should be told of it. Again, had the prisoner known the projected elopement, and intended to make use of it for the perpetration of a preconcerted murder, would he—could he have acted as he did? Could he have waited for such an unexpected accident as his sister's fainting before he drew near to his victim. His sister had walked down the avenue, and after waiting some time in the road, returned and sat down upon a fallen tree; it was whilst so seated that she heard the brother open the hall door; had she, as she expected, met her lover at the hour appointed, they would have been far beyond the prisoner's reach before he had left the house;—would he have allowed this to be the case, had it been his intention to take advantage of the opportunity? It is absurd to argue on such a point. It is unnecessary almost to call your attention to things which must so manifestly present themselves to you. The whole of this case has received additional weight and importance from official authority. It has been considered worthy of especial government interference. My learned friend has come express from the metropolis for the purpose of conducting it;—a rumour has been spread abroad that most conclusive evidence would be produced to prove that a prisoner from the better orders of society had joined, and headed one of those illegal bodies of men whose existence is supposed to be the cause of the troubles of this distracted country; and that he had, in unison with these schemes, committed a foul and deliberate murder; and my learned friend has not hesitated to tell you that it is essentially necessary to use the utmost extent of legal severity, that an end may be put to the agrarian outrages which are now becoming so frightfully prevalent in the country. Has anything been proved to warrant this official zeal—this government interference? No, nothing; not one iota; but still these paraphernalia of office, this more than ordinary anxiety to obtain a verdict, may have an effect upon your minds most prejudicial to my client. I have no doubt as to your actual verdict. I have no doubt that you will—nay, I know that you must—acquit that young man of murder. But I beseech you to remember that, though in the indictment he has been charged with murder only, he has been by the servant of government, by my learned friend on the other side, accused of other grievous crimes; and I implore you by your verdict, to purge his character of the stain which has been so unjustly attached to it, if you find, on examination of the evidence, no cause to suppose that he had been a participator in the councils of such societies. I beseech you to do him that justice, which can now only be done by the strong expression of your unanimous assurance of absolute innocence. I beseech you to reject from your minds those preconceived opinions so injurious to the prisoner, with which the present unfortunate state of your country may so naturally have influenced you, and to remember that it is your duty, as jurors, to confine yourself to the individual case before you; and that the doctrine laid down by my learned friend, that you should make an example in one case for the sake of prevention of crimes in others, is most unconstitutional, and would imply, that whilst the solemn oath you have taken is still vibrating in your ears, your object should be far wide from that for which you have been assembled—that of making a fair and true trial between your sovereign and the prisoner. I shall now call a few witnesses, and then leave the case, with confidence, in your hands."

CHAPTER XXXI

THE LAST WITNESS

WHEN Mr. O'Malley had finished his address to the jury, it was past seven o'clock, and the judge suggested that as it would be evidently impracticable to finish the case that night, so as to release the jury, they might as well at this point adjourn it till the morrow. To this Mr. Allewinde readily assented; but Mr. O'Malley declared that though he was most unwilling to detain his lordship and the court at that late hour, he must request permission to be allowed to examine one of his witnesses, as otherwise his caution in having had him ordered out of court would have been in vain. It was most essential, he said, that his examination of Mr. Keegan should take place before that man could have an opportunity of conversing with his servant, Brady; whereupon the judge consented to hearing Keegan's evidence that evening, and forthwith the name of Hyacinth Keegan was called out in a loud voice by the crier, and was repeated by every policeman in court, till a stranger to the proceedings would have thought that Hyacinth Keegan's society was the one thing desirable in Carrick-on-Shannon.

It would be drawing this trial out to a weary length to give the whole of his evidence; but Mr. O'Malley's questions were such as the attorney found it almost impossible to answer. He was asked in the first place whether he at present received the rents from Ballycloran, and then whether he received them on his own behalf; the latter he denied, but when told that if he denied the fact Mr. Flannelly would be brought forward to prove it, he at last owned that Mr. Flannelly had promised to make over that property to him; he then denied that any conversation had passed between him and Brady as to the nature of the evidence the latter was to give at the trial, or that he had expressed any anxiety on any occasion that a verdict might be given against the prisoner; he confessed that he might, in conversation, have attributed the loss of his foot to the influence of the prisoner; but he could not remember that he had ever said that Macdermot should pay for it with his life. In answering the different questions put to him, he hesitated and blundered so much—stammered so often, and spoke so low, that every one in court was convinced that he was perjuring himself; but still he persisted in denying everything. The only good effect Mr. O'Malley could get from his evidence was, that the master frequently contradicted what had been said by the servant. But then Brady had shown so much confidence and self-assurance in his replies, and Keegan so much hesitation and confusion, that it was much more probable that the jury would believe the former, than the latter; and if so, Keegan's contradicting the statements made by Brady, would not serve to invalidate the material evidence given by that man.

When Mr. Keegan came down from the chair, the court broke up for the night, and the jury were informed that the sheriff would afford them all the accommodation in his power;—and with long faces they were marched away to durance vile.

The court, which, during the trial, had been so densely crowded, again became desolate and silent. Baron Hamilton, with his brother Kilpatrick,* retired to their dinner, which they had well earned; and the coffee-rooms at the hotels again became crammed with hungry guests, clamorous for food; and the evening was passed in speculations as to what would be the verdict in the case to which they had all been listening.

In the barristers' mess-room all the feuds of the day were forgotten, and a most jovial party was assembled. As each bottle of claret succeeded the other, fresh anecdotes were told, and innumerable puns were made. Mr. Allewinde was quite great; his forensic dignity was all laid aside, and he chatted to the juniors with most condescending familiarity.

Mr. O'Laugher became the originator of incessant peals of laughter; all that had taken place during the day he turned into food for merriment; not for one moment did he hold his tongue, nor once did he say a foolish thing. He was the pet of the bar-room. The Connaught bar*was famous for Mr. O'Laugher; and they knew it, and were proud of him.

Of all of them assembled there but one seemed to have any memory of the sadness of the scene that they had that day witnessed. How should they? Or rather how miserable would be a barrister's life, were he to be affected by the misery which he is so constantly obliged to witness in a criminal court. On this occasion, however, the anxiety which Mr. O'Malley had expressed when addressing the jury had not been feigned, and the doubt which he felt as to the fate of his client lay heavy on him. He was aware that he had failed in shaking Brady's testimony, and he feared that in spite of all he had done to prove the depravity of that man's character, the jury would be too much inclined to believe him.

It had been decided that Feemy was not to be brought into Carrick from Drumsna till such time as Mr. O'Malley sent out word that she would be required; and when he found how late it was before he began his speech, he had told Father John in court that she would not be wanted on that day. She had, therefore, been left tranquilly at Mrs. McKeon's, who had fetched her to her own house from Ballycloran on the morning of the trial.

When Larry Macdermot saw the car at the door, in which Feemy was to go away, he was dreadfully wrath. He first of all declared that his daughter should not be taken away to Mr. Keegan's—that his own son had deserted him and tried to sell the estate, and that now they meant to rob him of his daughter! And he wept like a child, when he was told that unless she went of her own accord, the house would be broken open, and she would be taken away by force. It was in vain that Mary McGovery endeavoured to make him understand that Feemy's presence was necessary in Carrick, and that she had to appear as a witness at her brother's trial.

Whenever Thady's trial was spoken of;—and

Mary, by continually recurring to the subject, had made the old man at last comprehend that his son was to be tried;—but whenever it was spoken of now, he merely expressed his approbation, and a wish that Thady might be punished, for making friends with such a reptile as Keegan —for deserting his father, and planning to cheat him out of his house and his property. Mary took great pains to set him right, and bellowed into his ear as if he were deaf instead of stupid, twenty times a day, that Thady was to be tried for Ussher's death; but Larry couldn't be got to remember that Ussher was dead, and would continually ask his daughter when her lover was coming back to live with them, and defend them and the property against the machinations of Keegan and her brother.

All the Thursday Feemy remained at Drumsna, every moment expecting that she would be immediately called on to go to Carrick. She sat the whole day in the drawing-room, close by the fire, with her friend's cloak around her, without speaking to any one. The girls had come and spoken kindly to her when she first arrived; but their mother had told them that they had better not attempt to converse with her. Mrs. McKeon herself sat with her the whole day, and spoke to her a gentle word now and again; but she purposely abstained from troubling her, and she made no allusion whatever to the subject on which she had thought so much, and on which her own suspicions had been corroborated by Mary's information. Necessary as it was that the poor girl should tell some one, this was not the time to press her.

There sat Feemy. Ah! how different from the girl described in the opening of this tale. Her cheek was pale and wan, and the flesh had gone, and the yellow skin fell in from her cheekbone to her mouth, giving her almost a ghastly appearance; her eyes appeared larger than ever, but they were quenched with weeping, and dull with grief; her hair was drawn back carelessly behind her ears, and her lips were thin and bloodless. Two or three times during the day Mrs. McKeon had given her half a glass of wine, which she had drank on being told to do so, and she had once tried to eat a bit of bread. But she had soon put it down again, for it seemed to choke her.

About five o'clock Mrs. McKeon learnt that Feemy would not be called for that day, and the poor girl was then induced to go to bed; but nothing could persuade her to allow any one to assist her. It was wonderful how she could have undressed herself, and dressed herself the next morning, she seemed so weak and powerless!

Tony and Father John got home to dinner about eight. They were both in good spirits, for Mr. O'Malley's speech had been so convincing to them, that they conceived it could not but be equally so to the jury. They forgot that they had previously assured themselves of Thady's evidence, and that therefore they were prepared to believe every word said on his behalf; but that this would by no means be the case with the jury. They were very sanguine, and Tony insisted that Counsellor O'Malley's health should be drunk with all the honours.

On the morning they went early into town; they had obtained from the clerk of the peace permission to make use of a small room within the court, and here Feemy and Mrs. McKeon were to remain undisturbed till the former was called for; then that lady was to bring her into court, and even undertook to go upon the table with her, and repeat to the jury, if she would be allowed to do so, the evidence, which they were all sure Feemy herself would not be able to give in a voice loud enough to be heard by any one. When the car stopped at the court-house in Carrick-on-Shannon, it was found absolutely necessary to carry her into the room, for she had apparently lost all power of action. She neither cried nor sobbed now; but gazed list-lessly before her, with her eyes fixed upon vacancy, as the two strong men lifted her from the car, and supported her between them by her arms up the steps into the court-house.

" This will never do," said Tony to his friend after leaving her in the room; " this will never do; she'll never be able to say a word on the table; it's only cruelty, Father John, bringing her here."

" But O'Malley says she must come," said Father John; " he says, if she can take the oath, and speak but three or four words to Mrs. McKeon, that will do."

"She'll never do it; she'll never be able to take the oath; she'll have to be carried on the table, and when there, she'll faint. Poor Thady! if he's acquitted, the first thing he'll have to learn will be her disgrace. You must tell him of that, Father John; no one else can."

"Poor fellow; it will be worse to him than all. But she brought him to this, and she must save him if she can."

"I tell you," said Tony, "she'll never speak a word upon that table; we'd better tell O'Malley at once; 't would be only cruelty to put her there."

They both accordingly went to O'Malley, who was now in court, and told him that they thought Feemy Macdermot could not be safely brought there. He, however, still declared that it was imperative for her brother's safety that she should appear, even if it were utterly impossible to get her to speak; and that as she had been the person in fault, and as he had had all the suffering, the cruelty would be to him, if she were not brought forward.

Father John returned to the private room, and tried to make her speak. He kneeled down before her, and again began explaining to her the purpose for which she was there, and implored her to exert herself to save her brother. She once or twice opened her mouth, as if speaking, but uttered no sound. She understood, however, what the priest said to her, for she gently pressed his hand when he took hold of hers, and nodded her head to him, when he begged her to exert herself.

In the mean time Mr. O'Malley was continuing the examination of his witnesses. The first who appeared on this the second morning of the trial was Corney Dolan, who unfortunately came prepared to swear anything which he thought might benefit the prisoner. He said he remembered the evening of the wedding, he remembered the conversation at which the prisoner had been present, that he was quite sure Ussher's name wasn't mentioned—or at any rate that if mentioned, it was not accompanied by any threat—that the only plan of violence alluded to during the evening was that one or two of the boys said that they would duck Keegan in a bog hole if he came to receive rents at Ballycloran.

This was all very well, as long as the questions were put to him by Mr. O'Malley; but he was forced to tell a somewhat different tale when examined by Mr. Allewinde, by whom he was made to own that there had been projects abroad for murdering Ussher, though he still maintained that none of them had been alluded to by the party at Mrs. Mehan's. He was also made to give himself so bad a character that it was more than probable that the jury would not believe a word he had said.

Father John was the next; he was only called on to prove that Thady had been intoxicated when he left the party at Mrs. Mehan's, and to speak as to character. With tears in his eyes he corroborated all that the barrister had said in his speech in praise of his poor young friend; he described him as honest, industrious, and manly—patient under his own wrongs, but unable to endure quietly those inflicted on his family.

Tony McKeon was the next and, with the exception of Feemy, the last; and he too had only to speak as to character.

Just as Father John had been getting into the chair, a policeman had come into court and whispered to Doctor Blake, who was sitting in one of the lower benches; and the Doctor immediately got up from his seat and went away with the man.

Father John had not observed the occurrence; but when he was leaving the table, and as Tony was getting up, the latter whispered to him—

" Blake has been called out. Just look to Feemy."

And at the same moment Mr. O'Malley said out aloud—

" Mr. McGrath, if I might trouble you so far, would you have the kindness to bring Miss Macdermot into court? I do not anticipate that we shall have much delay with Mr. McKeon's evidence."

Father John immediately hurried into the room where Mrs. McKeon had been left with her charge; and his heart trembled within him as he remembered the death-like look the poor girl had when he left her but an hour since, and reflected that it was too probably to her aid that Doctor Blake had been called.

And so it was. When he entered the room, round the door of which a lot of frieze coats had crowded, but which was kept shut, he found Feemy on the ground, with her head supported on Mrs. McKeon's lap, and Blake kneeling beside her, endeavouring to pour something into her mouth. There was another woman standing in the room, and an apothecary, whom the doctor had sent for; but Father John was soon made to understand that medical skill could avail but little, and that all the aid which

Feemy could now receive from her fellow-creatures was to come from him.*

To describe the scene which immediately followed would be to treat so sacred a subject much too lightly. The priest, however, found that neither life nor reason was extinct; she acknowledged the symbol of salvation in which she trusted, and received that absolution for her sins which her church considers necessary. Who can say how deeply she had repented of her misdeeds during the many hours of silent agony which she had endured !

Her arm was stretched out from her body, and her hand was clasped tightly in that of Mrs. McKeon's. The moment before she drew her final breath, she felt and tried to return the pressure; she made one great struggle to speak. "Myles" was the single word which her lips had strength to form; and with that last effort poor Feemy died.

In the mean time McKeon had given his evidence in the court and had left the table— Mr. Allewinde having declined to cross-examine either him or Father John. There was then a pause of some little duration in court, during which Mr. O'Malley, addressing the judge, said that Miss Macdermot, the witness now about to be brought forward, was unfortunately in a very weak state of health, so much so, that had her evidence not been essential to her brother, he should be most unwilling to have troubled her ; he then apologised for the delay, and asked for and obtained permission for Mrs. McKeon to be on the table and repeat the answers of the witness to the jury : the judge merely premising that it would be necessary that that lady should be sworn to repeat the true answers.

There was still some further delay after Mr. O'Malley had sat down. Mr. McKeon got up to go and help to bring her into court, but just in the doorway he met a man who whispered to him ; he did not return, however, but hurried on to the room where he had left his wife, and reached it just as the breath left the poor girl's body. In spite of their distress it was apparent to all that the truth must be immediately made known in the court, and Mr. McKeon was leaving for the purpose of telling Mr. O'Malley, when Father John laid his hand upon his friend's shoulder, and said—

"Poor Thady, it will break his heart to hear it. It must be kept from him. But heaven only knows what's best ; he must hear it at last. Go, McKeon, and tell O'Malley ; he'll know what's best to do."

McKeon returned into court, and making his way with difficulty close up to the barrister, whispered in his ear that his witness was no more.

Mr. O'Malley, who had been standing, instantly sat down, as if appalled by the suddenness of the event. Every one in the court who had seen McKeon's face as he entered, felt aware that something had happened to Feemy.

The judge leaned forward over his desk, addressing himself particularly to Mr. O'Malley, and said—

"Is Miss Macdermot too unwell, Mr. O'Malley, to be brought into court?"

"My lord," said he again, rising from his seat, "she has already gone before another judgment-seat. Macdermot," and he turned round to the prisoner in the dock, "you have borne your sorrows hitherto like a man; you must try and bear this also—your sister is dead. She has fallen the first victim—God forbid that another should be sacrificed. My lord, my cause is now done; there is now no living witness, but the prisoner, of that scene which I described to you. The case must go to the jury as it is."

During the time of the whole trial, Thady had stood upright at the bar, with his elbow leaning on the wooden rail, and his face resting on his arm. He had almost constantly kept his eye upon the speakers, occasionally turning his gaze to the place where Father John had sat during the trial, to see that he had not deserted him. During the speech which Mr. O'Malley had made on his behalf, he had brightened up, and looked more cheerful than he had done for many months. When that was finished he had felt more sanguine as to his acquittal than he had done at any time since he had first given himself up as a prisoner. During the short pause which occurred in court immediately after McKeon left the table, he had once or twice looked round to learn if Feemy were coming, though the high woodwork of the dock would effectually prevent him from seeing her till she was at the table.

It will be remembered that Feemy's extreme illness had never been made known to her brother,—much less her lamentable situation.

Father John had told him that she was unwell, but he had not thought it necessary to frighten him at the present time by letting him know how very ill she was. The doctor's departure from court he did not notice at all. Father John was sent for to his sister in a manner which caused him no apprehension,—and even when McKeon went out to see whether she was coming, it never occurred to Thady that the delay in his sister's appearance was occasioned by ill health. It was only when he saw O'Malley sit down, after hearing some whispered tidings from McKeon, that he felt alarmed. When the barrister told the judge that his witness had gone before another judgment-seat, it was still evident from his face that he did not perfectly comprehend what had happened; but there was no misunderstanding the language in which the tidings were immediately afterwards communicated to himself. He seemed to make one attempt as if to say something; but the feeling of his situation and the paraphernalia of the court awed him into silence, and he sank down within the dock to hide his sorrow from the crowd that were gazing at him.

There was some considerable delay in the court after this, as though all the parties concerned felt unwilling to commence business after the shock which Feemy's death had occasioned. The judge sat back in his chair, silent and abstracted, as if, valuable as he must know his own and the public time to be, he felt unable to call on any one to proceed with the case immediately after so sad an event.

At last Mr. Allewinde rose and said that no

one could regret more than himself the dreadfully tragical manner in which the prisoner had lost the benefit of the evidence, which it was expected his sister would have been able to give on his behalf; that he conceived that it would be anything but mercy to the prisoner to delay the proceedings in their present stage on account of what had happened; moreover, he considered that doing so would be illegal. He would suggest to the judge, to his learned friend on the other side, and to the jury, whether any legal and available use could be made of the evidence which had been given by the prisoner's sister before the coroner.

This, however, Mr. O'Malley declined, alleging that the questions put to Miss Macdermot by the coroner, were merely intended to elicit evidence that Captain Ussher had been killed by her brother, and that the answers she then gave were of course not such as would be favourable to the prisoner; nor were such as could prove those facts which Mr. O'Malley had intended to prove. Mr. O'Malley finished by stating that as far as he was concerned the case was ready to be submitted by his lordship to the jury.

Mr. Allewinde, however, still had the right of reply, and he was not the man to allow any chance circumstance to prevent him making use of it. He accordingly again got up to address the jury. He told them that what he had to say would not keep them long, and considering that he was a lawyer and a barrister, he kept his word with tolerable fidelity. He remarked that the evidence of Brady had in no degree been shaken. That the subjects in which Keegan had been examined had had no reference to the case; and that it was quite plain that Dolan had come forward to swear to anything which he thought might tend to the prisoner's acquittal. He made no allusion whatever to Father John and Tony McKeon, and then ended by saying, that "the unexpected and melancholy death of Miss Macdermot was an occurrence which could not but fill the breast of every one present with most profound sympathy for the prisoner,—that he should abstain from saying a word which might be unnecessarily disagreeable or painful to the feelings of any one—but that the jury must feel that the prisoner would lose nothing from the loss of her evidence. Of course," he continued, " in a point of law you are bound to look on the case as if Miss Macdermot had died at the same moment with her betrothed husband, for you are aware that you cannot allow anything which my learned friend has told you to be taken into consideration by you in finding your verdict. But it will lessen the pain which more or less you must suffer in this sad case, to reflect what strong grounds you have for supposing that the sister, had she lived, could have proved nothing favourable to the brother; for had she been able to do so, she would have done it when examined before the coroner. I shall now trouble you no further. His lordship in submitting the case to you will give you doubt-less the necessary caution against allowing excited feelings to have any influence over the verdict to which you shall come."

Mr. Allewinde then sat down, and after the lapse of one or two minutes the judge turned to the jury, and spoke his charge to them upon the question. He went deliberately through the whole evidence—dwelt upon various minor points in the prisoner's favour—told them that the prisoner could not be considered as guilty of murder, if there was ground to believe that he had committed the act whilst the deceased was forcibly carrying off his sister; and that if they believed that the prisoner had never before premeditated the death of the man he killed, he could not be considered to have been guilty of the crime for which he was now tried. He then went at length into all the points; he showed the jury that no evidence whatever had been brought up to prove that the girl was in a senseless state when Ussher was attacked; and that for anything they had heard proved, she might have been walking quietly with him. He then went into the evidence given by Brady, and he stated it as his own opinion, that the man was in the main to be believed; he argued that his whole evidence, both on direct and cross examination, had been given in a manner which seemed to him to show an unwillingness to give more information than he could possibly help on either side—but still with a determination not to forswear himself. But at the same time he told them that this was a question on which each juror should form his own opinion; in fact, that it was to judge of the value and credibility of evidence that they were summoned. It was, also, he said, for them to decide whether the death of the revenue officer was premeditated by the party at Mrs. Mehan's when they talked of ridding the country of him. He passed very slightly over the remaining evidence, merely saying that this was a case in which character could not weigh with them, as, if the prisoner were guilty, his former apparent good character only aggravated his sin. He then concluded by telling the jurors that they were bound by solemn oaths to allow nothing to interfere with the truth of their verdict—that they must all deplore the untimely death of the young woman who was to have appeared before them, and sympathise with the brother for the loss of his sister—but that his misfortune in this respect could not lighten his guilt if he were guilty, or diminish the sacredness of the duty which each juror owed to his country.

When the judge had finished, the jury retired to consider their verdict; and the other business of the assizes was proceeded with, as if nothing peculiar had happened to check the regular routine duties of the court.

CHAPTER XXXII

THE VERDICT

IT was not very late in the day when the jury retired, and it was generally thought that they would come to a verdict in time to escape being immured for a second night; but they did not.

Immediately after hearing the judge's charge, Father John, McKeon, and Webb agreed among them that it was absolutely necessary that old Macdermot should be acquainted with his daughter's death; but who was to take upon himself the sad errand! Father John had for the last few days been so harassed, so worn down by anxiety, and was now so depressed by, as he conceived, the unfavourable tone of the judge's charge, that he looked like the ghost of himself; and yet the duty of seeing old Macdermot could fall on no one but himself. Neither Webb nor McKeon knew the ways of the old man, and it was more than probable that neither of them would be admitted into the house. Father John therefore put himself on a car and hurried off to Ballycloran, making his friend promise that he would wait in Carrick for him till his return.

Father John soon found himself in the presence of Larry; but he could with difficulty find words to tell him of his bereavement. The old man was seated on his bed—he always slept now in the parlour—he had his legs thrust into a tattered pair of breeches, and had worn-out slippers on his feet; and an old and ragged coat, into which he had been unable or unwilling to thrust his arms, hung over his shoulder; but he had no stockings on—no cravat round his throat; his long-worn shirt was unbuttoned over his breast; and his face was not only unshorn, but was also, as well as his hands and feet, unwashed and filthy. When Father John entered the room he was seated on his bed, which had not been made since he rose from it. He had a pipe in his mouth, and a glass of grog in his hand. The smell of the room was most offensive, and it seemed from the dreadfully close atmosphere, that no window had been opened in it for weeks past. Mary McGovery followed the priest's steps into the room, running through numerous apologies as to the state in which the old man was found, and assuring him that Macdermot was so stupid and so obstinate that it was impossible to get him to do or to understand anything; and she forthwith took hold of his shoulders, and began shaking him, and scolding him—bawling into his ear, till the poor idiot shook in her grasp.

Father John at last succeeded in rescuing him from her hands, and, seating himself in a chair immediately opposite to him, he began his sad tale. He told him by degrees that his daughter had been taken very ill—that she had got worse and worse—that Doctor Blake had been sent for—that she was found to be in imminent danger. But it had no effect on Larry; he kept on continually thanking Father John for his friendly visit, saying how kind it was of him, to come and sit with an old man like him—how hard it was to be shut up alone with such a d—d old jade as Mary; and then he began telling Father John a history of the ill-treatment and cruelty he received from her, —which, to do Mary justice, was in the main false; for, excepting that she shook him and bawled to him, by way of rousing his dormant intellect, she had always endeavoured to be as kind to him as the nature of her disposition would allow. He begged of Father John to tell him when Ussher and Feemy would come back to take care of him; asked if Feemy hadn't gone away to marry her lover; and complained that it was cruel in his own dear girl not to let her old father be present at her wedding.

At last the priest saw it was no good trying to break this bad news, by degrees, to such a man as Larry; and he told him that his daughter was dead. The old man remained silent for a few minutes staring him in the face, and Father John continued—

"Yes, Mr. Macdermot, your poor daughter died in Mrs. McKeon's arms."

"Is it Feemy?" said Larry. "My own Feemy?"

"It is too true, Mr. Macdermot; and indeed, indeed, I feel for you."

"But it ain't true, Father John," said the idiot, grinning. "Shure didn't I see her myself, when she went away on the car to the wedding?" And then the old man paused as if thinking, and the stupid smile passed off from his face, and the saddest cloud one could conceive came over it, and he said, "Ah, they're gone away from me; they're gone away to Thady, and now I'll never see them agin." He then paused for a moment, but after a while a fire came into his eyes and he began again, " but curse her— curse——"

This was too horrid; Father John got up and held his hand before the father's face, as if to forbid him to finish the curse which he was about to utter; and the old man trembled like a frightened child upon his seat, and sat silent with his eye fixed on the priest.

Mary had not been present at this interview; Father John, however, now found it necessary to call her, and to commission her if possible to make the father understand that he had been bereaved of his daughter. Poor Mary was dreadfully distressed herself, and for a long time sat sobbing and weeping. But by degrees she recovered her tone, and commenced the duty which Father John had enjoined her to perform; but nothing could convince Larry of Feemy's death; he felt assured that they were all trying to deceive him, and that Feemy and her lover had now deserted him as well as Thady.

When Father John returned to Carrick, anxious, yet fearing to hear the verdict, he found that the jury had not yet agreed. Even this was some comfort, for it made it evident that there was doubt on the subject; and surely, thought he, if a man doubts on such a subject as this, he must ultimately lean to the side of mercy. He remained with Tony McKeon in court till about eight, when they went to the hotel and got their dinner—for they would not leave the town till the jury were locked up for the night.

Soon afterwards Webb joined them, and the three sat together till eleven o'clock, when it was signified to them that the judge would not receive the verdict that night; and that the jury were, therefore, again to be locked up. Webb then went home, and the priest and his friend both returned to Drumsna to sleep.

Thady had remained in the dock that he might be ready to hear the verdict, till the judge left the bench. He was then conducted

back into the prison, and it was so late that the
prison regulations did not allow him to see any
friend or visitor; he was, therefore, debarred
from the comfort which a few kind words from
Father John would have afforded him. After
he had heard the news of his sister's death he
never once raised himself from the position into
which he almost fell rather than sunk. During
the whole of the long afternoon he remained
crouched down in one corner of the benches
within the dock. When the judge commenced
his charge to the jury, he had once attempted to
rise; but he felt that he could no longer endure
the gaze of those around him, and he remained
on his seat till he was taken back to gaol.

Father John and McKeon agreed that the
cause of Feemy's death should not be told to
Thady—at any rate, till after the verdict had
been given. If he should be condemned it
would only be a useless cruelty to increase his
sufferings by telling him of his sister's disgrace.
Should he be acquitted, it would then become
a question whether or no he might still be
suffered to live in ignorance of that which, if
known, would so deeply embitter the remainder
of his life.

On the Friday morning the two friends again
took their seat in court, waiting anxiously till
the jury should send in word that they had
come to a unanimous decision.

Thady was again in the dock, and Father
John was just enabled to say one word to him
over the wooden paling;—to bid him still keep
up his courage, and to press his hand closely
within his own.

Hour after hour passed on, and the dull stupid work of the week went on. Mr. Allewinde's eloquence, Mr. O'Malley's energy, and Mr. O'Laugher's wit, sounded equally monotonous to the anxious priest and his good-natured friend. Though they seemed to listen, and indeed endeavoured to do so, yet at the close of each trivial case that was tried, they had no idea impressed upon them of what had just been going on. One o'clock struck—two—three—four—five—and yet they remained in the same position; and still the jury who had been considering the subject remained undecided.

The business in the Record Court*had been closed on the Thursday, and therefore both the judges heard criminal cases during the whole of Friday; and by six o'clock the business of the assizes was finished, and the prisoners are all disposed of with the exception of poor Thady. It was absolutely necessary that the judges should commence their business at Sligo on the following Saturday, and if the jury did not agree to a verdict before eleven on that morning, they would have to be discharged, and the case must stand over for a fresh trial at the summer assizes. This now seemed almost desirable to Father John and McKeon. Immediately after hearing Mr. O'Malley's defence they had felt sure of success; but the judge's charge had dreadfully robbed them of their hopes, and they began to fear the arrival of the foreman.

At six Baron Hamilton left the court, saying that either he or his brother would be within call till twelve o'clock to receive the verdict, and that he would remain in town till eleven the next morning, should the jury not have decided before then. Thady was yet once more taken back to prison in doubt, and whilst McKeon went to the inn again to get some dinner ready, Father John went up to the prison to visit the prisoner in his cell.

The young man had to a great degree recovered his self-possession. He told Father John that he had given up all hope for himself—that he believed he had made up his mind perfectly to face death like a brave man. He then talked about his sister, and lamented grievously that she, ill as she was, should have been dragged into court with the vain object of saving his life. He asked many questions about the manner of her death—her disease—the state of her feelings towards himself—all which Father John found it most difficult to answer; and he was just beginning to inquire how his father had borne all the griefs which had accumulated themselves upon him, when one of the turnkeys opened the door of the cell, and told him that he was to return immediately into court—that the jury had agreed—and that the judge was now going into court to receive the verdict.

Father John turned deadly pale, and leant against the wall for support. A hectic red partially suffused the prisoner's face, and his eyes became somewhat brighter than before. A slight shudder passed over his whole frame; in spite of all that he had suffered—all that he made up his mind to suffer—it was evident that there was a fearful degree of anxiety in his bosom, a painful hope still clinging to his heart.

The fetters were again fixed on to his legs, and he was led away in the midst of a body of policemen into court. Father John hurried to the same place, where he found Mr. McKeon already seated on one of the dark benches. There were but very few there, as every one had left it after the business of the day had been concluded; some of those who were in town and had heard that the jury were at last unanimous, had hurried down; but the generality of the strangers who were still remaining in Carrick, preferred the warmth of the hotel fires to paddling down through the rain, dirt, and dark, even to hear the verdict in a case in which every one was so much interested.

The barristers' and attorneys' seats were wholly deserted by their customary learned occupants; there was but one lawyer present, and he, probably thinking it unprofessional to appear to take more than a lawyer's interest in any case, was standing by himself in the dark obscurity between the dock and the bottom of one of the galleries. This was Mr. O'Malley—and though he would not be seen in court after his business there was really over, he felt so truly anxious in the matter that he could not wait to hear the verdict from a third party.

At length the judge took his seat, and the clerk of the crown sat beneath him ready to record the decision of the jury. A few lighted candles were stuck about in different parts of the court; but they were lost in the obscurity of the large, dark, dismal building. The foreman stood ready with a written and signed paper. The judge asked him if they had all

come to a unanimous verdict, and he answered
in the affirmative ; and handed the paper to the
clerk of the peace, who glancing his eye upon
it, and half turning round to the judge said in
his peculiar, sonorous voice—

"My lord, the prisoner has been found guilty."

"Gentlemen, is that your verdict?" said the
judge ; and they said it was.

The prisoner stood up at the bar erect without
moving. He neither shook nor trembled now.
If it were not that his lips were pressed quite
close together, he would have appeared to have
heard the verdict without emotion. Not so
Father John ; he had been leaning back,
anxiously waiting till the one fatal word met
his ear ; and then his head fell forward on the
desk, and he sobbed like a woman.

Baron Hamilton immediately placed the
black cap on his head, and proceeded to pronounce the dreadful sentence of death. As
he did so, his voice seemed like some awful,
measured tone proceeding from an immovable
figure or statue placed beneath the dusky
canopy ; so dark was it—and so cold and stern ;
so slow and clear were his words and manner ;
he must have felt, and felt strongly, as he
doomed that young man to a sudden and
ignominious death, for he was no heartless man ;
but so powerfully had he schooled his emotions,
so entirely had he learnt to lay aside the man
in assuming the judge, that had he been the
stone he looked like, he could not have betrayed
less of the heart within him.

He dwelt at considerable length on the
enormity of the offence of which the prisoner

had been found guilty; he stated his own conviction that the verdict was a just and true one; alluded to the irreparable injury such illegal societies as that to which the prisoner too evidently belonged, must do in the country; assured him that he had no hope for mercy to look for in this world, and recommended him to seek it from Him who could always reconcile it with his justice to extend it to the repentant sinner. He concluded by ordering that he should be taken back to the place from whence he came, and be brought from thence to the place of execution on the Monday week following, and then and there be hung by his neck till he should be dead.

The assizes were then finished—the judge immediately left the court—the prisoner was taken back to his cell—the lights were extinguished—and when the servants of the sheriff came to lock the door, they found Mr. McKeon still vainly endeavouring to arouse the broken-hearted priest from his ecstasy of sorrow.

CHAPTER XXXIII

THE END

On Saturday morning the little town of Carrick-on-Shannon again became quiet and, comparatively speaking, empty. The judges left it very early; most of the lawyers had taken wing and flown towards Sligo, seeking fresh quarries, on the previous evening. The jury were released, and had returned weary to their homes; the crowds of litigants and witnesses who had filled the Record Court had also left on the Thursday evening; and now those who had been wanted in the criminal court were gone, and peace and quiet were restored. At eleven o'clock neither of the hotels were open; the waiters and servants who, during the last week, had literally not known what a bed was, and who, during that week, had snatched their only disturbed naps before the kitchen fires, or under the kitchen dressers, were taking their sleep out for the past week. It was still raining hard, and the long, narrow, untidy street was still as dirty and disagreeable as ever; otherwise there was no resemblance in it to the street of the last few days. There was no crowd around the court house, nor policemen with cross chains on their caps, nor sheriff's servants with dirty, tawdry liveries. The assizes were over; and till next July—when the judges, barristers, jury, etc., would all return, Carrick was doomed to fall back to its usual insignificance as a most uninteresting county town.

As Father John left the town on the previous evening, he sent word up to the governor of the gaol that he would see young Macdermot early on the following morning. He did not go home to the Cottage, but again passed the night at Mr. McKeon's, at Drumsna; and a most sad and melancholy night it was. After witnessing Feemy's death, and seeing that the body had been decently and properly disposed, Mrs. McKeon had returned home, and her husband had found her quite ill from the effects of the scene she had gone through.

Soon after the two men had made their apology for a dinner, Mr. Webb, who had had the verdict brought to his own house, called, and the three sat for some time talking over what possible means there might be still left for saving the young man's life. It was at last agreed that Webb should go up to Dublin on the morrow, and make what interest he could to see the Lord-Lieutenant himself, as well as the Under Secretary; and endeavour, by every means in his power, to obtain a pardon.

After what had been said by the judge whilst pronouncing the sentence, they all felt that there could be no reasonable ground for hope; but still they would leave no chance untried, and it was therefore settled that the counsellor should start by the morning coach.

Early the next morning the priest left Drumsna for Carrick, to see Thady for the first time since his condemnation. McKeon offered to go with him; but he declined the offer, saying that this morning he would sooner be left alone with his doomed friend. He refused, too, the loan of McKeon's car. He wanted to collect his thoughts and his energy by the walk, for he felt that he had much to do to school his own feelings before he could make his visit a comfort instead of a cause of additional distress to Macdermot.

About ten o'clock he passed through the town, and rang the governor's bell at the gaol door. He was a well-known visitor there now, and when the door was opened he expected at once, as usual, to be shown the prisoner's cell; but instead of that he was taken into the governor's house.

This officer had always been extremely civil to Father John; and had shown all the kindness in his power, and that was no little, to the prisoner. He expressed himself to the priest greatly distressed at the verdict, and the consequent fate of Macdermot.

"It's four years, Father John," said he, "since I had a prisoner in my charge condemned to die. It's four years since there was an execution here, and then the victim was a criminal of the blackest dye—a man who had undoubtedly committed a cold-blooded, long-premeditated murder. And then his death weighed heavy on me; but I cannot but believe that this young man is innocent,—at any rate, so much more innocent than he was,—my heart has failed me since he was brought back last night condemned."

"More innocent than he was!" said Father John. "Ah, indeed he is! If we were all as innocent of guilt as this poor fellow is, it would be well for most of us. I promised to see him early this morning. Will you let me go up to him now? though God knows I know not what to say to him!"

"Yes, of course. You shall go up now immediately; and God grant you may be able to comfort him! But you know you cannot see him as you have done always. That is, you may see him as often as you please, but you cannot see him alone."

"Not alone!" said Father John.

"Not now," said the governor. "When brought back capitally condemned, he was of necessity put into the condemned cell; and when once there, no visitor may be left alone with him."

"How is he to receive—how am I to perform the sacred duties*of my profession?"

"When the prisoner is about to confess, the turnkey will step outside the door, which you can close. You know, Father John," continued the governor, "it is not from my own heart I give these orders; you know I would give him every indulgence I could; but you also know that I must obey the rules of my office, and they imperatively forbid that any visitor shall be left alone with a condemned prisoner."

"I know it isn't your fault; and if it must be so, it must. But will you desire the man to be sent for, for Macdermot will be expecting me?"

In a minute or two the gaoler arrived with his huge keys, and, with a palpitating heart, Father John followed him to the condemned cell.

The priest, during his walk from Drumsna, had made up his mind exactly as to what he would say on seeing Thady; how he would mix pity with condolence; how he would use such words as might strengthen him in his determination to bear his sufferings with resignation; how he would teach him to forget the present in the thoughts of his future prospects. But when the iron door was opened, and he saw Macdermot seated on the one small stone seat in the wall beneath the high, iron-barred window; when his eye rested on the young

man's pale and worn face, he forgot all his
studied phrases and premeditated conduct, his
acute grief overcame his ideas of duty, and falling on the prisoner's bosom, he sobbed out,
" My boy—my boy—my poor murdered boy !"

It would be useless to attempt to describe at
length the scene between them. Father John
remained with him nearly the whole of that day,
—the patient, silent turnkey leaning up against
the corner of the cell during the whole time. For
a long time Thady was the most tranquil of the
two ; but at length the priest regained his com-
posure, and was able to listen to the various
requests of his friend, and to say all that could
be said to comfort and strengthen him.

Thady's first request was that he might see
his father. This, Father John felt, would be
impracticable, and if accomplished would only
be in the highest degree painful. Larry was
now so perfectly a lunatic, and at the same time
so resolute in his determination not to put himself in the way of being arrested by Keegan,
that it would be impossible either to make him
understand the fate which awaited his son, or
to induce him, by any means short of force, to
leave his own room. Besides, were a meeting
to be effected, the idiotical father would probably
not cease to abuse his son, and would certainly
not comprehend his tenderness and affection.
It was difficult to tell the son that his father
had so utterly lost his intellects as to be unable
to be brought to see him ; but even this was
better than allowing him to think that he was to
see him, and then deceive him.

Thady bore this blow even worse than Father

John had expected that he would do; it made him feel so desolate—so alone in the world! Stupid and cross as his father had been for years past—cruel and unjust as he had been on the last time they met,—still, the long time which had passed since that meeting, and the manner in which the interval had been passed by Thady, made him forget his father's treatment, and only remember that he was his last surviving relative. He submitted, however, to Father John's advice, and consented not to urge his request.

He then talked of his sister, and began to speak more feelingly of Ussher, and to allude to the deed which had brought him to his dreadful doom, with more freedom than he had ever done before. The facts of his last month's residence at Ballycloran seemed to be made less obscure than they had been, to his mind's eye, by the distance through which he looked at them. He appeared to comprehend more clearly both Feemy's conduct and that of her lover, and he spoke with the greatest affection of the former, and with justice to the latter.

"Oh! Father John," he continued, after they had been talking together for hours, and when they had become so habituated to the presence of the turnkey as almost to forget it, "no one but yourself can ever know how far murder was from my thoughts that day!—nor all that I had suffered for having listened for one moment to the plots which them boys were making for his death. But who can wonder that I hated him! God knows I have forgiven him for all that he

has brought on us—both me and Feemy; but
who can wonder that I didn't love him then?
I knew in my heart he never meant to marry
her. And oh! Father John, av I hadn't seen
her that night, what would she have been now?
I did hate him then;—and hadn't I cause? And
for that one night at the wedding, when I was
mad with the name they had called my sisther;
I did think I'd be glad av the boys that hated
him so should murther him at last. But when
I woke in the morning and remembered that
the sounds of murther had been in my ears, I
felt as though I could never more be quiet or
at ase in this world. And I never was; every
man's hand was against me since then, Father
John, except yours. I felt, as I walked through
the fields that morning, that it was here I should
spend my last days, and here I am. And I was
warned of it too; I was warned of what would
come of it, av I meddled with them boys that
night at Mrs. Mehan's. He himself called me
out that night when I first got there, and tould
me what it was Brady was afther. And I believed
him, and yet I went; for my heart was full of
hatred for the man who warned me. Oh! why,
Father John, could he not let us alone? We
were poor, but we were no worse; but there's
an end of us now altogether, and perhaps it's
for the betther as it is!"

He then earnestly begged Father John to
attend to his sister's burial, and to take some
little heed of his father during his few remaining
years; and all this the priest promised. He
spoke of the property, and of the chance there
might be of saving something out of it for the

old man's support. Father John, however, told him that for his, Thady's sake, and for the love he bore him, his father should never want till he wanted himself; and though this promise, for many long months, entailed a heavy burden on the priest, he most religiously kept his word.

Thady then spoke of his own coming death; and though he had made up his mind to die, and could think, without regret, of leaving the world where he had known so many sorrows and so few joys, still he shuddered when he remembered the gaping crowd which would be assembled to see his expiring convulsions, and the horror which he could not but feel, when the executioner's hands should touch his neck, and the dreadful cap should be drawn over his eyes. Oh! that that horrid moment might be over—when he would still be alive—still sensible to the thoughts of life—but when the light of the sun would have been for ever excluded, and his last thoughts would be wandering between doubtful hopes of Heaven's mercy, and awful fears of his coming agony.

The cold sweat stood upon his brow as he endeavoured to explain his feelings to the priest. And assiduously, patiently, warmly, and kindly, did that friend endeavour to allay his sufferings, and make him feel as confident of God's pardon for his sins as he was of the executioner's doom. He told him also that, if possible, no crowd should be assembled to gaze at his death; and he promised himself to stand by him, and hold his hand to the last moment of his life.

At six the priest left him, promising to see him again on the Sunday, and on every day till it was all over. He then returned to McKeon's, where he dined.

At about ten they were sitting together with Mrs. McKeon by the fire talking over the affairs of Ballycloran, and consulting as to what had better be done with Larry after the execution, when the girl entered and said a man was waiting outside wishing to speak to Mr. McKeon. Tony accordingly went out; and standing at the back door, for he would not enter the kitchen, with his hat slouched over his face, he found Pat Brady. He was very much astonished at seeing this man; more especially so, as since the trial Brady's name had been mentioned with execration by almost every one, and particularly by those who, like McKeon, had taken every opportunity of showing themselves Macdermot's friends; and it would have been thought therefore that McKeon's house was one of the last places to which he would be likely to come.

Pat was the first to speak.

"There's a word or two I want to spake to you, Mr. McKeon."

"To speak to me," said Mr. McKeon; "well, what is it?"

"I couldn't just be telling you here; av you wouldn't mind stepping out, a minute or so—it's not five minutes I'd be keeping you."

McKeon accordingly went out into the dark yard, about thirty paces from the house, and Brady continued—

"It's about the young masther, yer honor."

"You've said enough about him; you've hanged him; now, what more have you?"

"May I niver see the Blessed Virgin in glory

av I towld a word of a lie agin the masther.
Av I iver towld the truth it was that day ; an'
worse luck—av I'd lied then maybe it'd been
betther for Mr. Thady."

"It wasn't to tell me that, you came here ;—
if you've anything to say, let me hear what it is."

"Why, then, yer honor, is Mr. Larry, the owld
man, a going to see the young masther?"

"And what if he is?"

"Why jist this thin ; av he do, Keegan's boys
is to saze him as he comes out on the road from
Ballycloran."

"Gracious God! would he arrest the man
coming to see his own son for the last time!"

"Faix, he will, Mr. McKeon ; so don't let
him do it ; I heard him telling the bailiff."

McKeon seemed lost in astonishment, at this
fresh instance of the attorney's relentless barbarity, and Brady turned round to go away.
But after having walked a few yards, he came
back, and said, in a hesitating whisper—

"You'll be seeing Mr. Thady afore it's all
over, Mr. McKeon?"

"Well ; I shall see him."

"Would you mind axing him to pardon a
poor boy, Mr. McKeon?"

"May God pardon you, Brady. Your master
that was, has been taught before this to forgive
all his enemies ; but I wouldn't dirty my mouth
with your name the last time I see him."

"Sorrow a word of a lie thin I towld, Mr.
McKeon."

"Never mind ; truth or lies it's much the
same." And McKeon returned to the house,
and told Father John what he had heard from

Brady; and the priest and he agreed together that it would be by far the best course to make Thady understand that his father could not leave his home to see him, for fear of falling into the hands of the attorney.

On the next day, Sunday, Father John performed mass and preached as usual in the parish chapel. When the service was over, he addressed his congregation from the altar on the subject of Thady's approaching execution, and he begged them all, as they valued his good opinion, not only not to be present at it themselves, but also to do all in their power to prevent others from being so. The same thing was done in Carrick, where the priest, moreover, begged his parishioners not to open their shops on that morning until the execution should be over.

The ensuing week passed slowly away. Father John was with the doomed man constantly, and McKeon saw him two or three times. On the Wednesday Mr. Webb returned from Dublin, but his journey had been a fruitless one; he had seen the Lord-Lieutenant, and had been kindly received by him; but at the same time he was informed that he could not exercise his privilege of mercy in this case, as he had been strongly advised not to do so, both by those in office under him and by the judge.

Macdermot kept up his heart wonderfully through the whole week. He never repined, nor once even alluded to Keegan. Father John spent the whole of Sunday with him. It was to be his last in this world; the last time he was to watch the light growing out of the darkness—and the darkness following the light. As the minutes flew by, his face became gradually paler, and his hand occasionally trembled. The brave soldier goes to meet Death, and meets him without a shudder when he comes. The suffering woman patiently awaits him on her bed of sickness, and conscious of her malady dies slowly without a struggle. A not uncommon fortitude enables men and women to leave their mortal coil, and take the dread leap in the dark with apparent readiness and ease. But to wait in full health and strength for the arrival of the fixed hour of certain death—to feel the moments sink from under you which are fast bringing you to the executioner's hand;—to know that in twelve—ten—eight—six hours by the clock, which hurries through the rapid minutes, you are to become —not by God's accomplished visitation—not in any gallant struggle of your own—but through the stern will of certain powerful men—a hideous, foul, and dislocated corse;—to know that at one certain ordained moment you are to be made extinct—to be violently put an end to;—to be fully aware that this is your fixed fate, and that though strong as a lion, you must at that moment die like a dog;—to await the doom without fear—without feeling the blood grow cold round the heart,—without a quickened pulse and shaking muscles, exceeds the bounds of mortal courage, and requires either the ignorant unimaginative indifference of a brute, or the superhuman endurance of an enthusiastic martyr.

Thady was neither the one nor the other;

and the blood did grow cold round his heart
—his pulse quickened, and his nerves shook
within him; but these were involuntary signs
of his human nature. He spent the day in the
performance of his religious duties, and made
continual efforts to fix his mind on those subjects to which it was directed by the priest;
and at last he received from him final absolution
for his sins, with a full assurance in its efficacy.
And if true and deep repentance can make
absolution available, the priest's assurance was
not ill grounded.

Father Cullen, at Drumsna, and different
priests in the neighbouring parishes again desired their congregations to absent themselves
from the execution, and on the Sunday evening
before the fatal day it was thoroughly understood through the country, that it was the wish
of the priest that no one should be present.

The Monday morning came. Though Father
John had not been allowed to remain all night
in the prisoner's cell, he did not leave it till
eleven, and was with him again at six. When
the gaoler turned the key in the door, Father
John found the prisoner still sleeping on his
pallet. Even the loud noise of the key in the
lock and the dropping back of the heavy bolt
had failed to awaken him. Before he left him
on the previous evening he had insisted on his
partially undressing, and he now found him
exactly in the position in which he had left
him.

Eight*was the hour fixed for the execution,
and though it seemed cruel to rob him of his
last human comfort, still as so few minutes of

life remained, the priest thought it better to rouse him. He laid his hand on his shoulder, and calling out his christian name, gently shook him. It was wonderful how soundly the poor fellow slept; and at last he jumped up with a smile on his wan face, uttering those confused words of acknowledgment which so readily come to the lips of any one conscious of being caught sleeping too late, to the neglect of his worldly duties. He had been dreaming —and in his dreams he was again at Bally-cloran—again sitting over the warm turf fire, talking with his father, after his hard day's work, of their lands, and their rents, and their difficulties. Father John's presence—the cold close white wall and his own memory soon made him again conscious of the truth; and as he pressed his hands to his forehead, re-membering that he should never again feel the luxury of sleep, the expression of his face was dreadful to be seen.

There is nothing further to relate respecting him. As the clock struck eight he was standing on the iron grate over the front entrance into Carrick gaol. He had supported himself firmly —though evidently with difficulty. The cap was over his face—his hands were tied behind his back—and the rope was round his neck. The last sound that met his ear was the final prayer which Father John sobbed forth that God would receive him into his mercy; the bolt was drawn—and Thady Macdermot was soon no more.

Not one human form appeared before the gaol that morning. Not even a passenger

crossed over the bridge from half-past seven
till after eight, as from thence one might just
catch a glimpse of the front of the prison. At
the end of the bridge stood three or four men
guarding the street, and cautioning those who
came, that they could not pass by; and as
their behests were quietly obeyed the police
did not interfere with them. Among them
were Joe Reynolds and Corney Dolan, and
they did not leave their post till they were
aware that the body of him to whom they
showed this last respect had been removed.
The shops were closed during the whole day;
but it was many days before the sad melancholy which attended the execution of Thady
Macdermot wore away from the little town of
Carrick-on-Shannon.*

THE END

APPENDIX

The Three Omitted Chapters

The 1860 revised text of *The Macdermots* omits three chapters, all from Volume III of the original text: Volume III, chapters II, III, and XII. Chapters II and III intervened between chapter XXV and XXVI of the present text. Chapter XII was originally the final chapter. They are here reprinted as they appeared in 1847.

CHAPTER II

ON the same day that Mrs. McKeon had had her painful interview with Feemy, father John had come to dine with her husband for the purpose of canvassing with him some of the steps necessary to be taken before the time of Thady's trial, which was now fast approaching.

The Judges were to come into Carrick in the first week in April, and it now did not want a full month to that time. They had long since determined to employ Mr. O'Malley for the defence. Mr. O'Malley was a barrister who had for some years gone the Connaught Circuit, and was not only the most talented man upon it, but in many respects was considered one of the most able lawyers in Ireland. Counsellor Webb had advised above all things the services of Mr. O'Malley should be secured, as it was a case in which his power of argument, and passionate eloquence would be peculiarly likely to make an impression on a jury; and he had consequently been retained. Mr. Webb, however, had explained to father John that to ensure the full services of this able advocate more than a fee was necessary. It was necessary, if possible, to enlist his feelings and his sympathy with the side he was to take, and induce him to believe that his abilities were required to protect innocence and not to shelter guilt. For this purpose it was decided that father John should himself proceed to Dublin—see Mr. O'Malley—give him as accurate an account as possible of all the facts of the case—make him understand the strength of all the evidence which would be brought against the prisoner, both as to the absolute fact of the deed, which admitted of no doubt, and as to his previous conduct at Mrs. Meehan's, and also to explain exactly the circumstances under which the deed had been perpetrated, and the truth as far as it could be learnt and proved, as to what had taken place at the meeting alluded to.

The two were now sitting over the fire after dinner. Tony's daughter had left the dining-room, but the mother remained to hear the wisdom which should fall from the mouths of the two men, whom she most loved and respected, and perhaps, also, occasionally to take a sip from the tumbler of her own temporal lord and master.

"Well, father John," said Tony, "indeed I'd go with you willingly—I'd think nothing of the time or expense, and I'd like the fun, only I know you'd be better without me—I'd never the gift of the gab* like you—you'd make the chap understand more in half an hour, than I could in a week of Sundays."

"I don't know much about that," replied the priest, "it's a plain story we have to tell I take it, and any plain man might tell it; but perhaps there's but little use in the two of us going, and as I want to see my brother, and have the most time to spare, it's fittest for me to undertake it."

"Of course it is, father John," said Mr. M'Keon's helpmate, "who could think of Tony's leaving home at such a time as this, and he with above twenty horses at work about, at one place or other."

"Well then, I'll go myself—I've no horses on the ground, and I must trust Cullen to look after the flock I have got by himself for a day or two; to-morrow is only Tuesday, if I start to-morrow I'll be down again on Friday or Saturday at latest."

"You know you'd have to make an appointment with Mr. O'Malley, perhaps a day or two before you saw him, still I should think you might be back by Saturday; but what harm—sure Cullen could say mass by himself one Sunday in the year."

"So he could for the matter of that; but it's not so easy

as you think to be saying mass at eight in the morning, and again at twelve, and both without eating a bit* in the world; however, he's not the man to grumble if he had to do it every week in the year."

"Is it Cullen?" said Tony, "faith I think he'd say mass all the morning, and talk politics all the evening, if he'd be let, only he should get a drop to wet his whistle between the whiles; be dad for a talker Cullen beats all the world, if he's once set a-going; I would any horse in my stable had so good a wind, only the pace is slow, and the motion so d—d awkward; but come, father John, you've been sipping that glass of sherry till my heart's cold to see you; make yourself a tumbler of punch, man."

"Come father John, do," said the lady, "the water's hot, and you see I'm drinking myself."

Father John, unable to withstand the force of so good an example, did as he was bid, and then continued—

"But what did the Counsellor say about the expense, Mr. McKeon? It'll be a heavy penny before it's all paid, and I shouldn't like to go too far in Dublin before we know whence the cash'll come from."

"He acted like a trump then, as he always does; no shilly shallying, or anything of the kind. He said he was rather short of the mopusses* himself at the moment; but he told me he'd put down twenty pounds with a heart and a half, if I'd advance it for him till May, when his rents come round, and I could pay myself, and he desired me particularly, father John, to tell you he wouldn't allow you to be at any expense in the matter, and that if a further sum were necessary, he would supply it wherever it came from."

"No," said father John, "Mr. Webb has proved himself a kind hearted man, and a good Christian; but I'll not be so bad as that either; I'll not let all the expense, or the greater portion of it fall on him. I pledged myself to the poor fellow, when I first left him in the prison, where he now is, that, if I sold every chair and table that I had, he shouldn't want all the assistance which money could procure him, and I'll not now put the whole weight on another man's shoulders, though God knows I'm poor enough myself; but

I'm not quite so bad as that; there's my brother in Dublin, he's as rich as a Jew; I've never yet asked a penny from him, and I don't .think he'll refuse me now the loan of twenty pounds—or for the matter of that the gift all out—when I tell him what it's for. I shouldn't be happy if I didn't somehow or other take my own share of the burden when I promised so much.''

''I don't doubt but you're right, father John, and if the butter-merchant in Capel-street will come down with the dust, so much the better—a man who has sold so much butter ought to be soft hearted; he ought to melt at a tale of sorrow like a firkin of his own goods on an August afternoon, and the milk of human kindness in his bosom should be churned into the butter of charity, and melt out now that it is required, in the shape of hard cash and good notes.''

''Never mind Mr. Keon, I don't see but what butter-selling in Dublin is as good as farming at Drumsna, if a man can make the money by it.''

''And a deal better,'' said the lady, ''for there's no rent to come and eat up all the profit, and no temptation besides to waste your money when it is made with horses and races, and all such nonsense as that.''

''That's well,'' said Tony, ''coming from her, when every farthing that the mare won at Carrick the other day went to buy a new car and harness for her and the girls; if it hadn't been for Bob Gayner and Playful, Heaven knows when they would have had either.''

''Oh they'd been promised long ago—long before Playful was bought—for the matter of that before she was born I should think—I believe the old car was the one your mother went to Chapel on, the Sunday after you were christened.''

''Only listen to what she says, father John; would you think now to hear her talk that she's had as many as three or four different cars, if not new as good as new, since she was married?''

''Yes, and they went as they came, in some horrid handicap or other, and now the one I've got is decent and proper to take the girls out on; I expect some fine morning to hear 'there's a servant in the yard with Mr. Somebody's compliments, and wanting the car that Mr. McKeon parted to his master last night, and probably bearing some broken-down raw-boned, horrid looking animal in its place.''

''There you wrong me; my worst enemy can't say I ever parted with a good article, after paying ready money for it. However, to return to business, father John, Counsellor Webb will give twenty pounds, and you and the tender-hearted butter dealer will do as much. Well, in spite of what Maria says about the bad times we farmers have of it, I'll do the same—that'll be sixty—that'll go near the mark, I should think, father John.''

''Why, yes; I should think that ought to be enough; but it must be all ready money; if you pay down twenty pounds out of your own pocket, will you be able to advance the other twenty for Mr. Webb?''

''I think I'll manage both,'' said McKeon.

''Is it Tony?'' said his wife. ''He's as rich as the bank, father John, if one only knew where he kept it.''

It was then agreed that father John should start on his journey to Dublin on the morrow, and wherever the secret cofters in which Tony kept the unlimited wealth of which his wife accused him, he managed at any rate to put into the priest's hands, before he left him, forty pounds, composed chiefly of dirty, greasy, well worn one pound and thirty-shilling notes, which had been cut and joined, re-cut and re-joined, till it was impossible to decipher more on the face of them than the large round letters which denoted their value. They, however would be as good in Dublin, and a great deal more convenient than the cleanest paper that ever left the bank of England, and were received by father John with gratitude and thankfulness. McKeon followed his guest to the door, and when they were out in the little garden said—

''I didn't chose to mention it in there before the mistress, but as sure as I'm standing here, this affair of poor Thady's 'll lead to more than we were thinking of.''

''Why, what do you mean?''

''As sure as I'm alive there'll be some quarrel between Webb and old Brown.''

''You don't mean they'll be fighting or duelling with one another.''

"Faith I don't know; you know that Jonas Brown, and be d—d to him, begging your pardon for cursing, father John; but that fellow's enough to make a cat curse; you know how inveterate he's been all along against young Macdermot, saying he wished to see him hanged, and all that. Well, there was a meeting on Saturday, at Carrick, and it appears, for I wasn't at it myself, that Webb gave him a tremendous cut about what he'd said, before Sir Michael and all of them, and serve him right too. Now, it seems that old Jonas is terribly angry, and they were telling me at Carrick that he had declared, that if Counsellor Webb wouldn't give it to him in writing that he didn't allude to the Brown Hall family, he'd have him out on the sod. Now, the Counsellor would sooner cut his hand off, than write a lie for any man—much less for Jonas Brown—and he'll think as little of going out with him as you do of saying your prayers, and by the lord he'll shoot him too, for he's able, and when Webb's in earnest he's not the man to be trifled with."

"Pray God we may not have any more bloodshed; isn't that young man's death enough to rise out of a vain girl's folly without old men and magistrates falling out and fighting."

"Come now, father John, don't talk nonsense. As for old men, Webb isn't much older than I am, and I hope I'm not too old to fight if a man asks me, and as for being a magistrate, I can't for the life of me see why a magistrate's to be insulted with impunity more than any other man—not that I want to see the two men fighting—though if Jonas did get an ounce of lead in his arm or his leg, I can't say if I'd grieve much; but good bye, father John, I won't keep you any longer; let us see you as soon as you get back, and don't let the attorneys be too hard upon you, and mind, father John—mind you pitch the blarney well into the tender-hearted butter-merchant." With these last words McKeon returned into his house, and father John walked briskly home to his cottage.

The next morning, at about seven o'clock, he was to be seen standing at the Cross-road, where the lane from his house joins the mail coach road, about a mile on the Dublin side of Drumsna, waiting for the coach from Boyle, and Patsey was also there with his carpet bag. Father John was muffled up with coats, handkerchiefs, and leggings, till he seemed as broad as he was long. The air was very sharp; there had been a hard frost for a morning in March, and the pools of water in the ruts and on the road were covered with thin ice. In spite of his walk there, he was very cold, and yet he was so muffled he could hardly move. He began clapping his hands, stamping his feet, taking short turns on the road, and in a very little time got rather impatient at the delay.

"Why, Patsey, the coach must have passed."

"Ah no, yer riverence, it aint."

"Then it's very late."

"No it aint, yer riverence, it won't be here this long time."

This put father John a little more out of temper, for in his anxiety he had been up and dressed some time before Patsey had been ready to take charge of his bag, and he had rated the boy, declared that he should be too late, and that it would all be his fault. Patsey, however, who knew well from experience the exact time the coach usually passed the spot where they were standing, was now enjoying his revenge at having been drawn out of his bed, by seeing his pastor and master vainly endeavouring to keep himself warm, and splashing himself all the time, by stamping on the crackling ice beneath his feet.

"Why what do you mean boy, not being here for a long time?" said father John, pulling out his watch, "why they told me in Drumsna, at the agent's, that half-past seven was the time, and it's ten minutes past that now. I think the coach must have passed."

"They always do be telling people twenty minutes before the time, yer riverence, for fear the coach 'ud be too sharp upon 'em, and then, what with stopping there and coming to this, it's mostly past eight when it's here."

Father John began walking backwards and forwards strenuously, up the lane and down the lane, kicking his feet, and rapping his hands, and in three minutes more, he looked at his watch; then he stood still for two minutes, and

again applied to the watch, walked about for a minute and
a half, and again did the same thing, each time having to
unbutton his great coat and under coat, and with much exertion lug the watch out of his fob, replace it, and button up
again.

"Patsey, I'm sure it's passed."

"Not at all yer riverence; you've ten minutes good* yet."

"Good, you fool, what do you mean by good? it's
anything but good."

Patsey, however, with his bare feet, uncovered head, thin,
ragged trowsers, and tattered jacket, seemed to think it very
good fun, and apparently kept himself quite warm, by jumping from one foot to the other, as though he were diligently
working at an imaginary treadmill. However even when a
man is waiting by the road side in winter for a coach, time
will at last pass away, and just as father John was beginning
to make up his mind positively that the coach had passed
by—that Patsey was deceiving him—and that he might as
well go back to the cottage to breakfast, he heard the sound
of the horses' feet and the rattle of the wheels on the road,
and at length it pulled up at the Cross-road, and father John
prepared to mount.

Down jumped the guard, an old friend of father John's,
and having succeeded in cramming the bag into the already
crowded boot, politely begged his reverence to mount.

"But where am I to go John—there's no room behind?"

Indeed at the first glance any body would have said father
John was in the right of it, for on the guard's seat there were
two besides himself—both burley-looking men—not of the
soft, compressible flabby genus, but large, strong, bony
men; you would sooner get an inch by pressing against a
stone wall, than by squeezing against the sides of such rocky-
looking individuals; on the opposite seat there were also
three people; on the outside there was a dirty-looking
traveller—a pig-jobber by trade—apparently as sullen and
as obstinate as any of the swine whom it was his business to
buy and sell; then a goodnatured, fat gentleman, in a vast
blue cloak; from his face, you might have sworn he would
have done anything to accommodate a fellow-traveller, he

looked so soft—so yielding, and so modest; but what could he do? He was eighteen stone weight, and might have almost acted Falstaff without stuffing; the third was a female, with a sharp, red nose, a cotton umbrella, a basket-full of buns, and a child about five years old, who, for the sake of the free seat, she had converted into a baby, and purposed carrying in her lap, though between Boyle and Drumsna, she had contrived pretty nearly to wrap the boy in the goodnatured man's cloak, and to transfer at any rate half his weight, on his unresisting knees.

The front of the coach was also quite full; on the box was the Captain from Boyle—the owner of the Kickie Wickie, going up to the steeple chase, smoking cigars furiously, and detailing to the coachman the certainty with which he should have won the Carrick race last October, if the gentleman from Galway hadn't disappointed him. Behind him were two gents talking loud, with flash great coats, newish silk hats, vast chokers,* and most complete assortment of all travelling appurtenances, mackintosh capes, oil-skin caps, and hairy galoshes; any one at all used to the road could have sworn to their genus, without looking at the tin boxes with leathern straps which were loaded on the coach behind them; they were commercial travellers—knowing fellows—first rate judges of whiskey—chaps determined to make themselves at home, and men on the whole, whose soft side it would be rather difficult to find. The remaining seats were filled by two young gentlemen going up to Trinity*—the elder, an old stager, who flattered himself he knew Dublin well—one well known at Burton Bindon's—a great drinker of bottled porter* at Judes—a dab at billiards and rackets—a giver of loo-parties—a reputed favourite with the girl behind the counter at the cigar-shop in Nassau-street, altogether a second Frank Webber* in his own opinion, was successfully endeavouring to eradicate from the mind of his younger cousin the excellent precept with which his parents had crammed him, previously to sending him up to college for the first time.

Well might father John ask where was he to go?—but John the guard was a man above trifling difficulties—a man not to be disconcerted by any red nose, umbrella, or precocious baby—a man whom a brace of Falstaffs or a legion of pig-jobbers would not frighten—one who, to oblige such a friend as Mr. Magrath, would have attempted the impracticability of compressing the sterner materials of which the two big, burley, boney Sligo traders,* who sat on the same seat with himself, were composed.

"Get up Mr. Magrath—we'll find room," he whispered, "get into my seat till I pack some of that live lumber a little closer—it's astonishing how much flesh and blood can be put into a small compass if its well packed. All right, Harry—go on." And father John sat down in the Guard's seat while he began his arrangement, thrusting himself in among their unwilling legs.

"Come, my friend," said he, addressing the pig-jobber, "that iron bar won't hurt you—make a little room—by the way you're sitting, you want as big a seat as the Lord Mayor's chair."

"I can't go no furder—I'm up to the rail."

'Oh, but you must go furder."

"I didn't pay for my seat to set a top of a iron bar like that—and be pitched on my head the first time the coach sways."

Then to the fat gentleman.

"Might I trouble you, sir—a little further to make room for this gentleman?"

"Why really if I could—but I'll try," and the fat gentleman made himself a little more uncomfortable, though he seemed greatly averse to harass his neighbour the pig-jobber.

"If you'd just try the weight of your character against that rather unmoveable gentleman to your left, you can't conceive how amenable to reason he'd become. Just, sir, lean slightly on his shoulder—he'll not take it amiss—a few stone of humanity well applied has a beautiful effect in convincing a man of his temperament."

The fat gentleman did partially as he was bid, and obtained a few inches from the vender of swine.

"Now, madam, if you and your pretty little babe could

contrive to squeeze a trifle nearer to this gentleman, I'm sure you'd find him a very pleasant neighbour.''

The lady's nose grew redder—her face uglier—and she only answered by rattling the cotton umbrella—taking a fresh hold of the provision basket—shoving a bit more of the free baby into the fat gentleman's cloak, and preparing for dire war with her new neighbour the priest.

''Thank you, ma'am, that's very kind; if all travellers were as gracious and accommodating as the ladies, we guards should have no trouble. Now, Mr. Magrath, as the lady with the little infant is so good as to make room for you next to her pretty self, you'll have the most comfortable seat on the coach.''

And father John, relinquishing the guard's post, endeavoured to place himself in an interval of about three inches between the rednosed woman and the iron bar.

''It's all nonsense, John; you know I can't sit here—I'm not one of the lean kind myself. Heavens and earth,'' he exclaimed, as the coach gave a jolt over a stone. ''I'll be off in a minute—have you any room inside.''

''Not enough for this pretty little babby in arms. There's Minor Biddulph and his three daughters from beyond Ballina going up to Dublin to look for husbands; there's none at all, I'm told, to be got in Co. Mayo since the Clare Militia went out of Castlebar.''*

''Well, any how, I can't sit here.''

''You don't try, sir; you're afraid of being too close to this pretty lady—only try—allow the centre of gravity to have its due weight and preponderance, and you'll soon find you are very comfortable.''

The absolute necessity of the case had its effect on our reverend friend; he had paid for his seat, and he must go on; and what was more important still, he mustn't fall off, if he could help it; so setting himself somewhat sturdily to work with his left shoulder, elbow, and hip bone, he, at last managed to drive her of the cotton umbrella still further into the fat side of the gentleman in the cloak, who was thus forced to employ the enormous visinertiæ of his own mass against the pig-jobber, and compel that respectable but somewhat unaccommodating member of society to reduce himself to a compass more befitting his humble appearance.

"Laws, sir—them's not manners as I understand at all," said the lady; "the poor child 'll be killed between you."

"I hope not, ma'am," said the guard, "I trust not—thank God he looks pretty strong—is he weaned yet—the pretty little fellow."

The lady gave a look of unutterable scorn—and the red-nose scintillated with wrath—she was a maiden, and the presumption that she should perform the offices of maternity to a lump of a boy of five years old was enough to disturb her virgin peace of mind, and ruffle her usual tranquillity.

"The child's not my own, sir—you knew that before—it's a brother's wife's child as I'm taking back to its parents. I wish I'd never see'd the coach to sit here upon nothing and be squeeged this way."

"I beg ten thousand pardons," continued the guard. "I really thought the lovely boy had been your own; and so you haven't yet experienced the comforts of matrimony; but you'll not be long so."

"There's very little comforts here any way, married or single. I wish you wouldn't crush my bonnet, sir. Can't you put your arm no where but round my neck?"

This was addressed to father John, who, by way of getting rid of his arm, had put it behind the lady's shoulders on the luggage.

"Gentlemen," she continued, "in public conveyances ought to keep their arms to themselves."

"I beg your pardon, ma'am; I really don't intend to inconvenience you," replied the priest, "but you see I must put my arm some where."

The guard could not help laughing at the accusation against father John, when she added, still more irritated by his merriment.

"That's all very well, sir; but I don't choose to have no embraces from no strange gentleman—whether he's a gentleman or not—so take your arm out of that." And she accompanied the declaration with a punch at the priest's ribs with her elbow, which nearly sent him off the coach.

This put all the party, except the pig-jobber and the lady herself, into a roar of laughter, in which father John, though blushing scarlet at the scandalous insinuation, could not but join.

"Well, Mr. Magrath," said the guard, "after that you'll never be able to show your face in Drumsna again. Do you really mean to say, ma'am, that his gentleman was embracing you? Well, Mr. Magrath, who'd have thought it of a man of your profession?"

They had now reached Dromod, where they changed horses; and where the red-nosed lady asked the ostler, (she was too much offended to speak to the guard,) for a glass of water. This was given to her; and she then lugged from her basket a very suspicious looking bottle, and having carefully emptied about half the water on father John's trowsers, poured into the remainder a very considerable quantity of some light-coloured fluid out of the bottle, observing that the water was so bad in these country parts, that one ought not to drink it pure.

Whether in its purity it might be objectionable or not, she evidently thought it very fair tipple, when mixed, for she swallowed the whole with very little difficulty, and restored the bottle to the provision basket.

"Ah," said the guard to father John, as they were preparing to resume their seat. "I thought there was stronger colouring in that nose than what the wind put there. You may take my word for it, there was a pint of whiskey in that bottle when she got on the coach at Boyle; and I wouldn't give much for what she'll have left of it, when she gets to Dublin."

On they started again through one of the ugliest, if not the very ugliest part of Ireland, in fact, a more uninteresting road than that from Boyle to Dublin it would be impossible to find. The country is mostly flat and unproductive—the bogs numerous—the villages poor—the gentlemen's residences few and far between—the towns dirty—and the prospects barren. The first idea that strikes a stranger on passing through this portion of Ireland is astonishment that Erin should have had the epithet green applied to it—for certainly in most of the central counties, it is, generally speaking, as brown a country as ever the eye rested on. On, however, the Boyle coach rattled, and the passengers, just at present, thought but little of the want of agreeable objects to the eye, for at Longford, the next stage, they were to breakfast, and after travelling for four hours on a frosty morning visions of eggs and beefsteaks, tea and toast afforded the view to which the attention of most was exclusively turned. They passed by Rooskey, then a quiet little village, with an old bridge over the Shannon, but now bustling with Shannon commissioners* and their servants—young engineers, carpenters, bricklayers and labourers, busy at their work, disturbing the sleeping river with their piles, coffer dams and masonry—through Newtown Forbes,* with its beautiful and deserted demesne—by the Longford Artillery barracks —and at last. the horses stopped at their well-known appointed spot before Sutcliff's hotel.

Such a rush as there was then into the coffee-room; the Sligo traders were on the ground as soon as the coach had stopped, determined that on leaving Longford they would not have to regret the expenditure of the eighteen-pence, which their breakfast would cost them; but quick as they were the commercial gents beat them in the race, and had their backs to the fire and their coat tails over their arms before any one else was in the room. The Sligo traders were, however, first at the table—it was food and not warmth they had to pay for, and in an incredible short space of time each of them had about a pound and a half of ham on his plate before him. The University gentlemen were not backwards either, and called for their food with such voracity that the waiter rushed into the kitchen demanding furlongs of toast, acres of beefsteaks, and pyramids of eggs.

"Waiter," said the gallant owner of Kickie Wickie, when the six above-mentioned travellers had about half cleared the table, "what is there for breakfast, waiter—damn it—I see nothing—do you call this breakfast?"

"Tea—steaks—chops—ham—beef—and eggs, sir," said the rapid waiter in a breath. "Hot steaks in half a minute— better sit down, sir—only twenty minutes—take tea, sir?"

And the sporting Captain was absolutely obliged to sit down and drink tea out of the same pot which had supplied the Sligo trader.

Father John and Mr. Biddulph, the Ballina Squire, were also warmly at work—not being so fastidious as the Captain—they found tea—steaks—chops—ham—beef and eggs, sufficient, and not so greedy as the others, they saw no necessity in choking themselves.

The four females now came in, and clustered round the fire; females travelling in stage coaches never eat breakfast—men always do if they have eighteen-pence to pay for it—sometimes even when they have not—from this I am led to believe that females generally are more powerful than the nobler sex in resisting strong temptation, and I know none stronger than that of a good breakfast after travelling four hours on a cold March morning. Our friend, however, with the cotton umbrella, which, with her basket, she still pertinaciously kept with her, evidently did not despise the comfort which suitable refreshment affords to the inward man or woman; for having obtained the cheap luxury of a glass of water, and having again had recurrence to the calumniated bottle, she, together with her charge, set to work at the buns. The urchin bellowed lustily for tea; but his aunt instead of gratifying so mawkish* a taste, dosed him with grog—no doubt remembering that if you train up a child in the way he should go, he will not depart from it in his old age.

During all this time the fat gentleman had been endeavouring to warm his fingers without disturbing any body, and failing in that had regaled himself with sundry cups of tea and slices of buttered toast, under the influence of which his face had become a little less purple than it had heretofore been; and he was just giving father John some of his impressions on Ireland, for he was a touring Londoner, when the guard announced that the horses were putting to; out rushed the collegians in a trepidation lest the horses that were out should be off without them. Slowly and deliberately began the commercial gents to button their coats, and arrange their leggings.

The Sligo traders took a last, large desperate cut at the half consumed loaves of bread to make up the last pennyworth of the value of the money. The three rather ancient Miss Biddulphs bundled into the interior, followed by their father; father John and his fat friend toddled off together, and the red-nosed lady, eagerly swallowing the last drop of her precious grog, and hastily repacking the buns and the bottle, seized hold of the basket, the boy, and the umbrella, and hurried out to see what favourable arrangement she might make in obtaining a more comfortable seat for herself and her possessions.

"And have you got no ladder, young man, for ladies?"

"A ladder, marm, is it—why thin there is a ladder, but it's shuk mostly."

"And how am I to get up? do you think I'm going to step up on that wheel there—no such thing—you must get me a chair."

"John," said the ostler to the guard, who now came out, "here's a lady what wants a chair, she's afeard the wheel an't sthrong enough to bear her weight."

"I'm very sorry, marm, we haven't a ladder, but if you'll allow me, you'll be up in half a moment."

And the guard proceeded to lift her up bodily by the waist; unfortunately at this moment father John came round to get his seat; and the modest maiden now suspended mid-way between the coach top and the ground screamed out—

"Now, sir, if you'll go away, I'll be obliged, for I don't want none of your attentions—it's very hard a young woman can't keep her own legs to herself in public—but the likes of you must come spying at them."

Her modesty nearly occasioned her total discomfiture; for the guard was so overwhelmed with laughter that he all but dropped her—however, she was landed at last, and deliberately seated herself in the middle seat, which had been occupied by one of the Sligo traders. Then there was her dear duck of a darling to be handed up, and her precious basket, and her cotton umbrella.

"You might have left that on the coach, marm, with perfect safety," said John, as he handed up the rattling antiquity.

"I don't know," rejoined the lady, "these light fingered gentry as manages the osses is too fond of making off with what ain't their own, when they find anything of value about on coaches. I knows their ways."

By this time father John, the fat gentleman, and the pig-jobber were up, and the two traders, with their jaws still at full work, began to ascend the wheels.

"I'll throuble you, misthress, to get out of that, av' you plaze—that's my place."

"Is it me, sir? I thought any gentleman as was a gentleman would give up his place to a lady on a coach."

"Faith—I don't know much about that—the ladies go inside mostly, I believe—so, av' you plaze, I'll throuble you to move."

The lady clutched her umbrella, but didn't move—and the Sligo man of muscle put his brawny hand on her shoulders to lift her out of the place.

"Guard—guard," shrieked she, "I looks to you for protection—I look to you to protect me from this ruffian—take your hands off me, sir—I'm not accustomed, sir, to be pulled about by any common fellow like you."

"Nonsense owld girl; out of that, and take yer own place—it'll be long enough before I touch you there."

"Guard, I look to you for protection, if I sit over there—I beg your pardin, gentlemen, for mentioning it—but if I sit over there, I know I'll be sick—I always womits with my back to the osses."

"Perhaps sir," interposed John, "as the lady's stomach seems to be a little delicate, you'll give way this once; maybe she's not quite in health this morning, and you'd find it a little inconvenient if she was overtaken with one of those disagreeable fits."

"Dilicate be d—d," answered the Sligoman, "av she's afeard of being sick, and don't want to 'womit' as she calls it, she'd better lave the sperrits alone—out of this, I say—I mane to have my place, I tell ye—so toddle."

This allusion to the innocent bottle in her private basket utterly exasperated the lady; she jumped out of the seat, and flounced into the fat gentleman's lap, throwing her nephew into father John's arms.

"You nasty, vile, low-born ruffian, to offer to put your nasty, filthy hands on me, you main debased creture. You to talk of sperrits, that is drunk morning, noon, and night, when you gets it for nothing; you think I don't know you, Mr. Mooney—do you?—can you tell me the price of red herrings* in Sligo—eh? you vile, filthy creture you."

"It's you that are a lady, a'nt it?" said her adversary somewhat irritated by the allusion to red herrings, "it's you that have a dilicate stomach!—faix the gintleman you're sitting on is a dale more good-natured than I'd be, av such a rantipole jade* as you stuck herself down on my knees."

The war continued for three or four miles, till by degrees the Guard quieted the contending parties, by persuading the man to hold his tongue, and by allowing the woman to scold till she was tired, which soon occurred when she was no longer answered. The latter by degrees resumed her old place next to father John, transferring the boy alternately to him and to her fat neighbour on the other side. She did not, however, fail to turn a cautious eye from time to time to the priest, to counteract any of the amatory intentions on his part of which she seemed to be in such continual awe.

They now reached Edgeworth's Town, and the guard pointed out to the Englishman the residence of the authoress* of whom Ireland may well be so proud; I doubt if any travel that road, however poor or uneducated they may be, without looking with some degree of interest to the house where Maria Edgeworth is still living, and where she has passed the greatest part of so long and so valuable a life. Then they passed through Rathowen, Mullingar, and Kinnegad, places conspicuous for their dirt, remembered only for the number of beggars by which they are inhabited, across the Boyne so celebrated* in Irish history, though in this spot only a murky stream, very different from the magnificent river which at a few miles distance across the same county is able to bear the wealth of nations into the town of Drogheda, through Enfield and Kilcock—miserable specimens of the poverty of Irish towns—and within a few yards of the College of Maynooth.

To what wrath and sorrow—to what indignation and vexation has that word lately given* rise in the minds of the truly orthodox members of the Church of England. In that college is to be implanted the seeds, all the piety which is to foster and instruct the religious feeling of Ireland—which is to restrain the vice and animate the virtue of thirty-two counties, and which not only is to do it, but which does it; whatever religious instruction the people of those counties do get, is from Maynooth; but yet how horrid is it that its students should be fattened by the contributions of Protestants, and that the wealth of the orthodox should be squandered in enabling them to sleep in separate beds.

It is now pretty generally admitted that we cannot convert these staunch Romanists* to Protestantism—that they will adhere to their old tenets and principles, and that they are likely to remain in the errors which they love so well—nay more, it is pretended by many that they are re-converting us*—that if any essential movement is being made by either party, that it is the Church of Rome, which is advancing. Priests, therefore, of the Roman persuasion are, it is to be presumed, necessary, and yet it is considered better to have untaught, or poorly taught clergymen among the poor, than men, who, by having their minds opened by the process of a more liberal education, will enter on their duties with abated prejudices, and enlightened feelings. It is alleged that the priests of the present day are dangerous men— enthusiasts—political fanatics and bigots; if it is so are these faults most likely to be found in an imperfectly, or in a highly educated character? if in the former, sure the more that is done for the priests of the next generation, the less likely are they to be imbued with the crimes which are now attributed to their predecessors.

After leaving Maynooth, our travellers passed under the walls of Carton, the magnificent seat of Ireland's only Duke,* through the pretty village of Leixlip, pretty enough to give the lie direct to my former declaration that the road from Boyle to Dublin would be found all barren. The Liffey at Leixlip is a beautiful river and the salmon-leap above the town is fully worthy of all the picnic parties which Dublin sends forth to fish, eat cold lamb, and drink cold punch on

its margin; but now when the coach rattled over the bridge
it was dark; it was past six o'clock, and in spite of the work
they had performed at Longford, the whole party were looking forward with impatience to reaching the gas-lamps of the
metropolis,* and encountering the pleasures of dinner.

The Lady had by no means discontinued her visits to the
bottle in consequence of the ill-natured remark made by
the herring-merchant; she evidently scorned any such
pusillanimity. At Mullingar she had refreshed herself, and
again at Kinnegad, at each of those places obtaining, as she
had done before, the loan of a glass of water; but after that,
actuated, no doubt, by a dislike to give unrequited trouble
to the waiters and ostlers along the road, she lifted the bottle
to her lips as occasion required, and took the liquor neat,
and by the time that the coach had passed Leixlip, it seemed
highly improbable from her situation, that she would soon
commence carrying into execution the threat which she
made at Longford, whilst battling for the seat which her
uncourteous adversary would not give her.

The care of the child she had entirely relinquished to the
fat gentleman, who had been too good-natured to repulse
the unwelcome urchin, and who had in consequence subjected himself to a degree of martyrdom, not to be conceived
by the hard hearted, in allowing the boy to stand wedged in
between his own legs. She had long since ceased to shew fear
at the prospect of father John's embraces, and was continually making efforts to lay her head lovingly on his
shoulders, which he, less humane than the other neighbour,
as often declined. Still, however, she retained the umbrella,
and every time he hoisted the brown straw bonnet from his
arm, she rattled the loose whalebones,* and gave the guard
an angry, drunken stare, as much as to say, she knew what
she was doing as well as any one, and that she "didn't mean
to bear no insinuations from nobody."

They passed through Lucan, Palmerstown, and
Chapelizod by the Phœnix park, and under the huge mile-
stone which bad taste and ten thousand pounds, some five
and twenty years since erected, in honour of the Duke of
Wellington,* affording, probably, the instance in which the

largest sum of money and the worst taste, were allied together in constructing the ugliest and most unmeaning record of illustrious deeds.

"You go along the quays, don't you, John?"

"Yes, Mr. Magrath," answered the guard, "will you get down there?"

"Yes, if you please—at the end of Capel-street; you can give me the bag out, can't you, without going to the office?"

"Certainly I will; will you be wanting a cab?"

"Oh no—it's only a few doors I have to walk—I'll carry the bag myself."

And now they were on the quays, passed by the Four Courts,* that busy scene of Irish wit and Irish love of law, and soon reached the point where father John was to leave his fellow-travellers. He got down gladly from the seat, where he had been long enough to become throughly tired of his companions, gave his shilling to the guard, and started off for his brother's the butter-seller, with his bag under his arm and a good appetite.

We have not space to follow the coach to Dawson-street, to see what was the fate of the red-nosed lady and her possessions, or how the coachman failed in his attempts on the pockets of the Sligo traders, nor to hear the gratitude he expressed, when the Captain rewarded with a treble fee the attention he had paid to all the circumstances connected with the birth, breeding, qualities, and performances of Kickie Wickie, as we must return to father John, and ascertain what success he had in opening the heart and the purse-strings of his brother in Capel-street.

CHAPTER III

WHEN father John left the coach he walked on, surrounded by applicants for the carpet bag and a gratuity.

"Will I be getting it thin yer honor.?"

"Thin I'll carry it to the other side of the city for yer riverence for two-pence."

"Shure thin I'll take it all round the county for a penny."

"The likes of yer riverence thin wouldn't be demaining yerself by carrying yer own porkmanty* through the town."

"Musha thin yer honer's riverence, I'm the poor boy that all the jintlemen knows, 'ticklerly the clargy—won't I be getting it?"

By the time, however, that the lot had nearly succeeded in wrenching the bag from his hand, father John had reached his brother's house, and disappointed them all by rushing from their clutches, bag and all, into the shop.

His brother had been acquainted with his intention, and consequently the family were not surprised at his arrival; out came the butter-man himself from behind one of the counters, with his greasy apron still about his loins; out came the butter-man's wife from behind the other, with a huge pinafore covering her extended bosom and capacious front, and out rushed, from the inner parlour, the butter-man's young fry to welcome their uncle with greasy fingers and unctuous kisses.

There was certainly a great savour of the trade about father John's relations; but still they were not only his nearest, but as far as he knew, his only relations, and they were very dear to him. The name of father, brother, and uncle were pleasant in his ear, and although the family, such as they were, very probably were not such as he would have chosen as his friends, they still had sufficient sterling qualities among them, to make him fully satisfied with them as his kindred.

His brother loved him and always made him welcome; his sister-in-law was as warmly attached to him, and was continually scolding him for not coming up to Dublin, and scolded him when he was there for going away again, and the caresses of his little nephews and nieces were so far different from anything he could ever enjoy in his own cold, desolate home, that in spite of the reminiscences of the stress which their fingers were sure to leave on his new black coat, he always entered his brother's house with pleasure and left it with regret. He was soon seated at his dinner, with his brother on one side, mixing hot brandy and water for him, and the wife on the other, pouring out tea, for it was eight o'clock before he had washed his hands and face, got the cold out of his toes, and shaken hands and kissed the party often enough to be able to sit down in comfort.

"Now, John take that—that's the stuff'll drive the cowld out of you—never mind the tay till by and bye," said the brother.

"A cup of tea's the best thing in life after a journey—take my advice, John, a cup of tea's the surest thing in life to warm you," said the sister-in-law.

"Will I give you another tatoe, uncle John?" said one brat, "Won't I be helping you to some gravy?" bawled a second, and suiting the action to the word nearly capsized a spoonful of grease into the priest's lap. "Doesn't uncle John want a bit more bread?" suggested a third, who on the spur of the moment nearly cut his finger off in his hospitable intentions to supply the wants of his revered kinsman.

As soon as his more pressing wants were supplied, and the children had been, after many solicitations, at length somewhat sternly dismissed to bed by their mother, with a kind blessing and warm kiss from their uncle, father John at once began to open to his brother the chief purpose which had brought him up to Dublin.

"Tom," said he, "I'm going to do what I never did before to you or to any man, and what, I hope, I shan't soon have to do again—I'm going to ask you to lend me some money."

Tom was a man who loved his money—much butter had he to sell monthly before he could add to the stock which he was lying by as a provision for his age, and that of Sarah, the wife of his bosom, and for the maintenance of the little Tomlings and Sallys, who would have at some future time to be turned out from the parents' nest; selling butter by the pound, half pound, quarter pound, and pennyworth, he had found no very easy labour, and that which a man wins with the sweat of his brow is dear to him—his face therefore became rather elongated at the intelligence, and he assumed somewhat a look of woe.

"I hope it a'nt much John, for times is very bad, and butter is fell a'most to nothing at all."

"To tell the truth I'm so little accustomed to borrowing, that I don't know whether you'll call it much or little; but the worst is I don't know when I shall, or if ever I shall, be able to pay it back again."

"That's a bad way of borrowing, John."

"May be it is so—may be it sounds too much like begging; but at any rate you shan't say I deceived you about it."

"That's thrue any way—but still lending on them terms won't feed a man's family."

"Come, Tom, I don't think you're so badly off as that—If you were, I wouldn't ask you for the sum I want. Indeed, pressing as is the necessity for which it is required I wouldn't ask it if I thought you'd ever feel the loss."

Tom, the butterman, knew well that his brother had built himself a somewhat more than ordinarily nice cottage in his own parish—and he was not aware whether the said cottage had yet been paid for—when his brother told him that he was wanting to borrow money, it very naturally occurred to him that the sum he was to advance, and which it seemed he was expected to lend without any chance of being repaid, was to pay the builder—and the idea that he was either to rob his estate at one blow of three or four hundred pounds—or else to refuse to accommodate his loved and venerated brother, seriously disturbed his equanimity, he scratched his head, and stirred his punch, fidgetted in his chair, and began to look very hot and oily.

"Ah, as for that, John, a man with a family like me can't have a loss, and not feel it—and pretty sharply too. I'm sure I thought we'd never get over it, when Stiggins, as used to keep the Waterloo, failed, and let us in for two hundred and forty—but, come, out with it—let us hear how much it is—and we'll see how far we can go."

"Why then, the sum I want is twenty pounds."

Tom was greatly relieved—if his brother had asked him for half-a-crown before the horrible idea of the cottage had got into his head, he would have thought as little about it.

"Twenty pounds! why man alive, you frightened me out of my life the way you began. I thought it was to be five hundred at least, you pulled such a long face about it, and that you know would be very serious with a baby coming every year.''

"Now, Mr. Mag.," for by this tender appellative did Mrs. Magrath always address her husband. 'Now, Mr. Mag., how can you say any such scandal—wasn't Minney fourteen months when baby was born—and isn't Jack the full thirteen months older than Minney—and I'm sure baby'll be above the year, when the next comes—that's if I'm right—and I believe you'll own I'm seldom much out in my calculations.''

"They come quick enough anyhow to make a man look sharp about him—if he don't wish them to run about with naked backs and empty bellies. Ah, John, you happy fellows escape a deal of cares, which we married men has to go through.''

"I don't think you'd change with me—and I'm sure you'd be wrong if you would—it was only just now, when I saw the children all round you, I was thinking what a happy man you were. Sarah must be giving me one of the boys some of these days, to make a priest of—and I long promised one of the girls to keep my house.''

"You shall pick and choose, John—when they're old enough—you shall pick and choose—they're decent good children—though they are so troublesome—I don't know well what I'd do without them.''

"Do without them indeed, Mr. Mag.—a precious father of a family you'd be without any children.''

"That's thrue, my dear," answered the butterman, "but enough's as good as a feast, they say.''

"Well, Mr. Mag., and whose fault is it if you've got too many, I'd like to know if it's not your own.''

"Faith then, Sarah, I can't say, unless it's yours.''

"But to return to business," said the priest, "can you let me have the twenty pound, I'm wanting? for I must settle that at once.''

"Twenty pound," said the butterman, now in the height of good humour, "of course I can in a jiffey,* or forty either, if you wanted it, John," and he put his hand affectionately on his brother's knee, "it was only when you put it into my head that it was hundreds you were wanting, that I began thinking of the brats, that are fast asleep in their beds by this time, God bless them—so that's settled—at least, it will be when you've got the rhino,* and you shall have that to-morrow morning, if that'll do you—and now let's be cosy—it's nigh two years since you put your feet under the table, and now you are here, we'll try and make you comfortable.''

''What in spite of times being so very bad, and butter down almost to nothing!''

''Oh, bother butter now—and as for the times—there's no time like the present, they say—so, Sarah, let's have something hot for supper—what with the children playing, and what with the cowld, and your wishy washy tay slop, John didn't get a bit at all yet, at laste, not a bit that'd do him any good.''

And now, the question of the money being so satisfactorily settled, the three proceeded as Tom said, to make themselves cosy—and very cosy and comfortable they were—from the supper which Mrs. Magrath provided—and the quality of the brandy and whiskey, which were on the table, one would have said that the depreciated state of trade in the Irish metropolis, respecting which the patriots made so many, and such grievous moans, had not at any rate yet affected the butter business; for there appeared neither stinginess—nor yet very close economy in any of Mrs. Magrath's family arrangements; and though, doubtless, the worthy master of the house had, as he had said, lost two hundred and fifty pounds by that villain Stiggins of the Waterloo, no one would have said, from his appearance that night, that he had any immediate prospect of the horrors of bankruptcy himself.

After supper, father John told them the purpose for which he wanted the twenty pounds, and they both expressed great sympathy for the unfortunate young man and his sister, and yet the good citizen would not approve of his brother's expending twenty pounds on Thady's defence.

''It ain't that I begrudge the money, John, that I'm lending you for your own pleasure; as long as you were pleased I didn't care if you pitched it into the Liffey—but it do seem a pity to be giving so much money to them scoundrelly lawyers. If the young man didn't murder the other young man—why he didn't—and surely the jury wouldn't hang him if he's innocent, because you don't pay twenty pounds to a man in a wig to tell them so.''

''But you see the government will pay another man in a wig to get up and tell the jury that he is guilty—and, therefore, if we can't get some one to tell them he is not, may be they'll believe the first fellow they hear.''

''What, and hang a man because he was protecting his sister, and killed another fellow by a rap on the head—not if I was on the jury they wouldn't—but haven't the young man property of his own—or his father—it's very hard any way you should have to pay twenty pounds to protect an innocent man.''

Father John did not tell him that not only he, but two others likewise, were giving similar sums for the same purpose, as that would have made the matter less comprehensible to his brother, so he dropped the subject, and contented himself with reflecting that he had not had his journey to Dublin for nothing.

On the next morning he started at about ten o'clock to call on Mr. O'Malley, the barrister—that gentleman lived in Clare-street—and on knocking, father John was informed by the servant that his master would not be disengaged before two; he had, therefore, the whole morning to kill, but in a town such as Dublin, which he visited but once in every two or three years, that could not be difficult. It was a holy-day, and there would be mass at twelve o'clock in Marlbro' Street,* he would go there. So he returned along Leinster-street, and Nassau-street—not the Nassau-street of the present day, since it has been thrown open to the gardens of Trinity* College, and made one of the handsomest streets in Europe—but the Nassau-street of ten years since, when it was as narrow, dirty, crowded and disagreeable as any large and thronged thoroughfare need be, through the bottom of Grafton-street, between the gates of Trinity and the famous statue of *pious, glorious and immortal* Willy*—under the splendid portico of the bank,* by far the finest building in Ireland—down Westmoreland street, over Carlisle Bridge, and up Sackville-street* till he reached the foot of the splendid pillar,* with which Ireland has testified her admiration of England's naval hero. The taste which has been displayed in erecting the pillar in this magnificent street to Nelson's honor, must, it is presumed, be taken in atonement for the atrocious pile of gigantic stones with which the Duke of Wellington had been disgraced in the Phœnix Park.

It was now nearly twelve, and he turned down Earle-street into Marlbro'-street, and entered the chapel. The square cold look of this building always failed to inspire him with that religious awe, which the long aisles, pointed cross, and beautiful arches of the continental churches had long years since so frequently and so strongly generated in his bosom—and before the service began he could not but regret that they had not a St. Peter's, a Notre Dame, or a St. Gudule's in Ireland, where the zeal and faith of the multitude so richly merited such a prize; but when the service was being performed, and when he observed the devout submission with which the enormous congregation of poor there assembled, attended to their religious duties, he could not but reflect that what they wanted in edifices they made up in faith, and that they gained more in sincerity than they lacked in wealth.

In Europe there is no country where the religion of Rome is so sincerely trusted to, and acted on as in Ireland. In France it now, where it exists, serves for little better than amusement. In Spain so long its strong hold—its enthusiasm has all but perished, and the church even now is fighting against itself. In Italy, even in the Papal States, it is considered rather as a gorgeous pageantry than as a religion sent from God for the guidance of mankind. In Flanders it bears the nearest resemblance to the warm fidelity of Ireland—but even there it is among the women that its strong influence is to be found. Rarely in either of these countries one finds men of education believing in, submitting to, and guided by the religion which they possess, and allowing that by that only can they regulate their conduct in this world, and hope to meet salvation in the next.

Such is the case though in Ireland—the people have a real though sincere belief in their creed—whether they act according to its tenets or no—whether they are good or bad they no more doubt the truth of the doctrines they have learnt than they doubt their own existence. I have met no Romanist Irishman who would express the remotest doubt as to any portion of the doctrines of the creed of his church—miraculous and difficult to believe as they are—and it is this unshaken belief—this firm sincerity of trust which has kept Ireland so faithful to her church, through all the frightful means which have been taken to convert her.*

When mass was over, father John retraced his steps to the lawyer's, and was lucky enough after kicking his heels for about an hour in an ante-room to obtain an audience of the man of business.

Mr. O'Malley was sitting behind a huge table covered with papers in a back parlour of the house. He was a small, dark, swarthy man, with small bright eyes, large black eyebrows, and a quantity of very black hair. The upper part of his countenance would have given him an austere stern look, had it not been for the good-humoured smile which continually played around the corner of his mouth.

"The Reverend Mr. Magrath, I believe," said the lawyer; "I presume you have done me the honor of calling respecting that lamentable case at Carrick."

"Exactly so," said the priest, astonished to find that the lawyer knew his business so well.

"Yes—Messrs. Hall and Tomkins mentioned your name when they handed me the first instructions—and my friend Mr. Webb, of Ardmore, has written, explaining some of the circumstances of the case somewhat cursorily—and informing me that I should have the pleasure of seeing you—you are interested, I believe, Mr. Magrath, in the matter, and Webb tells me that you are very sanguine in the hope of an acquittal."

"Indeed I am, Mr. O'Malley—and it is on that account alone that I have come up to Dublin at present—my object is to learn from you whether I have good grounds for being sanguine in that hope—or whether the circumstances connected with this unfortunate event are such as to endanger the life of my poor young friend, who is at present in Carrick gaol."

"That is a question I may be better able to answer after I have heard from you the full particulars of the case—but I should surmise from the fact of a man of your character and profession, feeling so warm an interest on behalf of the prisoner, that there must be features in the case greatly to palliate the deed which, I fear, there is no doubt the young man committed.

"Not the slightest doubt, Mr. O'Malley—not the slightest doubt on earth—and Mr. Macdermot, the young man himself, I mean, has particularly begged that no attempt may be made to give rise to such a doubt—that his defence may not at all rest on the point whether it was he that absolutely killed Captain Ussher—for he openly avows that it was—but on this—that from the manner in which the deed was done, it was evidently not his premeditated intention to cause death—and that the circumstances and provocation which led to the attack, were fully sufficient to justify him in inflicting such punishment on the man now dead, as he would probably be able to inflict on a man with a stout stick, the instrument which, as you are aware, was used."

"I see—in fact, I nearly heard as much from Hall, the attorney, though not exactly as you put it. I understood from Hall that Macdermot wished to justify the deed, under the plea that he was avenging, or preventing a presumed rape— a violent attack on his sister."

"Not at all, Mr. O'Malley, not in the least to justify the deed—but to justify that which accidentally caused the deed."

"Exactly—exactly—as you're a Connaught man, Mr. Macgrath—I'm very glad you're in the church, and not in the law—if you were a barrister, no one on the circuit would have a chance against you. But now before I go into circumstances of the fact itself, I must get you to answer me one or two questions—and in the first place I must earnestly beg you—as I should desire the young man himself were I talking with him—not to conceal from me any portion of his real conduct, however criminal it may have been. As I believe Mr. Macdermot's position in life was respectable—and especially as he seems to have been, nay, I may add, to be personally a friend of your own, I am sorry to say anything which, on his account, may hurt your feelings—but there may have been much that was very wrong—in the eye of the law very criminal—in his conduct—and yet he may not in intention have been guilty of the crime for which he is to be tried—but you must remember that I cannot hope to conceal that from the jury, which my client conceals from myself. I cannot expect to influence their minds on a subject, with the whole circumstances of which I am not myself thoroughly acquainted.''

''Certainly not—but there is nothing to conceal. Thady, that is Mr. Macdermot, wishes to conceal nothing—all he wants is to have the very truth—the very bottom of the truth laid open—the influence he wishes you to use on the minds of judge, jury, and all, is to show them from absolute facts that he is no murderer. It is not only to save his neck from the rope—but also to shelter his character and name from the ignominy, with which too many are already willing to defile it, that my friend is desirous to acquire the full weight of your energies and ability. You said just now that he was once my friend—that perhaps he might still be so. If I were not more warmly his friend now, than I ever have been before, I should be ashamed of myself—for I am surely convinced that no crime has placed him in the situation, in which he now is—and whether acquitted or convicted— whether disgracefully hung, or restored to his afflicted family, I shall always be equally certain of his innocence.''

''I am glad to have to endeavour to defend a client of whom you think so well; but do not allow your kind feelings to blind you, or to blind me to, we will say—any follies he may have committed, or our blindness may occasion him to pay a heavy penalty for them. If, as you say, there is nothing to conceal, his is, comparatively speaking, an easy case to conduct; but I was afraid that there was much which we ought, if not to conceal, at any rate to endeavour to render doubtful. In the first place is he not, or was he not a ribbon-man?''

''Decidedly not.''

''Had he not joined some secret society?''

"Never. I'll tell you, if you'll let me, the whole and absolute truth about that."

"I'll not only let you, but I'll particularly beg you to do so; but I think it fair to tell you, in the first place, that the crown solicitor is prepared not only to prove, that the young man had joined some such society—but also that in one of the meetings of that society, Ussher's death was canvassed and decided on; and, moreover, that the prisoner was present at that meeting, took a strong part in that discussion, and warmly concurred in that decision."

"Impossible, Mr. O'Malley! it is perfectly impossible that anything can be proved which is so absolutely false."

"Well, I have told you what the other side is prepared to prove; whether they will succeed in doing so is another question and now will you tell me what means we have of disproving any of these things—that is, getting more credible witnesses, or witnesses equally so, to disprove that, to which the Government witnesses will, as I tell you, most assuredly be prepared to swear."

"He never joined any such society, Mr. O'Malley, on my word, as a man and a servant of God."

"Now, Mr. Magrath, you're losing the character I gave you as a lawyer. I am ready to admit that he did not do so— at any rate I am sure you feel confident that he didn't; but tell me now, were you in a jury box, what weight would you give to an unsupported assertion, such as that you just made—why it would not have the slightest influence on your verdict. It is proof we must have. He is innocent till proved guilty; but when proved guilty, he will be held to be so, unless we again can prove him innocent."

"Must his life then be sworn away by villains and perjurers—men whose reckless malice will, I fear, induce them to swear anything."

"I hope not—if the motives which bring the crown witnesses into the box are such as you state them to be, we may, by adducing proofs of certain concurrent circumstances, invalidate their evidence, even though we may not be able to bring up other witnesses to swear directly that the testimony against the prisoner is false—we may know that the man or men giving that evidence is or are unworthy of that belief, that they were themselves guilty parties now endeavouring to screen themselves, or we may prove from their own mouths a portion of their own words to be false; but at present I am talking on a subject with which I am but imperfectly acquainted, and with the whole details of which I should be intimate.''

Mr. O'Malley then searched among the papers on the table till he found the one he required, and continued looking rapidly over the pages of the document he held.

"Wasn't this young man present at a country wedding on Thursday the 16th of October last.''

"He was at the wedding party certainly.''

"Well, now will you tell me exactly your version of what occurred there as far as your friend is concerned?''

Father John then told him as concisely as he could the exact facts of that evening, as he had since learnt them from Thady: he told him that Thady had certainly spoken, previously to that evening, of joining some illegal meeting which certain of the men in the country were in the habit of holding at Mohill; and he explained how he had been tempted to do this by Brady, after the insult which he had undergone from Keegan.

That he had consequently met some of the party at Mrs. Meehan's on the night of the wedding—that he had there got drunk—and had now no exact recollection of what had taken place—but that McGovery had overheard a portion of what did take place at that meeting—and that it was according to him that Keegan was threatened and not Ussher.

"Well now,'' said the barrister, at this point, "that's something like; was this McGovery one of the party?''

"No, he was not—he was endeavouring to overhear what these men were talking of—as he suspected them of plotting something.''

"But can he swear that he overheard all that was said?''

"He cannot do that.''

"But he can swear that Keegan was threatened.''

"He can swear that he overheard something about Keegan and a bog hole.''

"That's very vague—and would tell more against us than for us—for this Keegan, who it appears was threatened with some injury at that very meeting, has since been mutilated on Macdermot's property. I am afraid we must leave him alone—it wouldn't be safe to put him in the witness box."

"But Mr. O'Malley, although I believe there were some senseless threats uttered; surely the fact, which this man—and indeed which I could prove, that Thady Macdermot was drunk at the time—would show that Ussher's death could not have been owing to those threats."

"In the first place I tell you it wouldn't be safe to put McGovery in the box at all—in the second place, I fear you could only prove he was drunk after the meeting, and not at it; thirdly, his being drunk at it could be no excuse for his voluntarily going to it, as that man Brady will prove that he did—for he promised to do so; and lastly, if the jury believe that he did go to that meeting with the intention of plotting the murder of the man, whom he afterwards killed, they could not—no jury could look on the fact of his being intoxicated while there as any point, not if it were proved beyond doubt that he were as drunk as Bacchus. Now, Mr. Magrath, who were the other parties at that meeting. Do you know any of the other men? the men concerned, I mean?"

"I know who two of them were."

"Very bad characters, I suppose?"

"Why certainly none of the best."

"Whose tenants?"

"Both tenants of old Mr. Macdermot."

"That's bad; but this Brady was a tenant of theirs too. What are these men's names?"

"Joseph Reynolds, and Corney Dolan."

And Mr. O'Malley wrote the two names down.

"Now Mr. Magrath, suppose without any reference to this affair—a month, we'll say, before the wedding had you been asked which bore the best character, this Brady, or either of these men, which should you have said?"

"Oh, Brady decidedly."

"Then you think that you would have sooner believed,

and consequently that a jury would sooner believe him than either of these men.''

"I'd as soon believe the devil now as I would Brady. I know he's prepared to perjure himself.''

"Ah, my dear sir; but the jury won't know it; they'll go upon character, you should endeavour to judge as they will be likely to do; both these men are desperate characters, I suppose; which now is the better of the two?''

"Why, really I hardly know which to say is the better—I think Reynolds is perhaps the worse.''

"Well, that's arriving at the same conclusion by different means; do you think we could get this Dolan into a witness box, and get him, when there, to contradict Brady's story?''

"Really I don't know—but we can try. I think that before that he'll most likely be in jail himself.''

"However, if we get him we may very probably be able to invalidate this Brady's evidence—at any rate he will be a safer card to play than McGovery—those sort of witnesses always stick to the prisoners, and though he mayn't be believed, and probably won't be, he'll serve to shew at any rate that there are two sides to a story; but now Mr. Magrath, didn't Macdermot receive secret signs or pass words at this meeting, or take an illegal oath, or in short do some of those things which in the eye of the law constitute joining an illegal Society.''

"He received no secret signs or pass-words; he took an oath not to betray the men who were with him; but as the meeting was not held in the usual place, they refused to give him the secret signs. He was to have met them at their usual rendezvous, and then have been initiated. Had he done this—had he kept the promise which he made in the moment of his anger, or in the madness of his intoxication, they might have brought it up against him now; but when he did not do this—but, instead of doing so, refused to have any further communication with these men, I cannot see how any Jury could consider that he was one of their party, or that he could have been leagued with them to perpetrate any such act as Ussher's murder.''

"It's a bad business I'm afraid—a most unlucky

business—for I have no doubt that there was no real connection between his joining that meeting, an illegal act in itself, and the death of the young man; there can be no doubt that his joining in that meeting was an illegal act, and in the state in which the County Leitrim now is, it is one which a jury will not be likely to overlook; didn't he join these very same men after he had done the act? Didn't he immediately go to their haunts and remain with them for some days?"

"He went to the house of that Dolan we were speaking of, and remained with him, or at some hiding-place to which he took him for two days—then he gave himself up."

"It was a most unlucky folly, both his joining the meeting before Ussher's death, and his associating with these men after it. The way in which it will be put before the jury will be fatal, with the Country in such a disturbed state—his killing the man was nothing. It is the man's death, which I firmly believe to have been accidental, joined to his own criminal conduct, in which he was, doubtless, guilty—guilty as a man; but doubly guilty as a landlord; it is the two combined together which will render the fight so desperate."

"But do you mean to say there's no hope, Mr. O'Malley?"

"No, I don't say that; but I do say there is great danger. I'll tell you what we must do; I fear we must give up the question of the illegal meeting; it is useless to attempt to disprove that he was at such a meeting; but we must shew that nothing which could have taken place at that meeting could have influenced his conduct, or have had any connection with the man he had killed—we must separate the two circumstances, which the other party will use all their efforts to unite—we must shew that at any rate no definite preconcerted plan has been proved to have been arranged, and put it to the jury that his guilty participation in one crime cannot afford any grounds for presuming him to be guilty on another; and now, Mr. Magrath, with reference to the deed itself, I must beg you to answer me a few questions with the same sincerity, as those I have already put to you."

"Indeed I will, were he my brother, and if he were, I couldn't love him better; but if he were, I would falsify nothing to screen him."

"We shall then be all right, for if I know the whole truth on the principal subject, we can at any rate make the best fight the matter admits of—now I believe there is no doubt the sister had agreed to elope with Ussher."

"None at all, I'm sorry to say."

"Nor that her father had altogether approved of their acquaintance."

"So he had; but then you must remember the state of the old man's mind. He is a complete idiot; the coroner considered him so completely so, that he would not take his evidence. Indeed he wouldn't have given any; he put the prayer book in his pocket when they offered to swear him."

"That's very true; but they say that his senses were unimpaired till he received the double shock of hearing of Ussher's death and his son's guilt."

"But you should remember, Mr. O'Malley, that though the father approved of the acquaintance as far as an idiot could approve of anything, the son did not; there is plenty of evidence that Thady entirely disapproved of it."

"So much the worse; don't you see that would be only proving the premeditated cause of the deed—would shew that there was a dislike between the two men, and give a colouring to the story of the affair having been planned; now a great matter—I may say the chief matter—hangs on this point; what was Miss Macdermot doing—in what position was she—and in what situation, both as to the body and mind, at the moment that Ussher was struck?"

"That is very difficult to ascertain accurately; there is no one able to give any evidence on the subject except the young lady herself, and you may easily suppose that her memory of the moment is too confused to enable her to give a correct account of it, besides it is all but impossible to get her to speak on the subject."

"I suppose she won't hesitate to speak when the object is to save her brother's life by telling the truth."

"You'll find her a very difficult witness; she is, and has been so ill ever since the occurrence, that it has been all but impossible to speak to her."

"She must come forward at the trial, Mr. Magrath . . .

she must speak there, or we shall be lost; what she said at the coroner's inquest was worse than nothing for our side. The question is, was she fainting or in a fit, when her brother first saw her, and was Ussher in that state dragging her off?''

"I am sure he was; whether at the moment she had repented or hesitated, or had for any reason refused to go with Ussher, or whether she had, from apprehension on seeing her brother, fainted, it is impossible to say, unless she can tell herself; but when Macdermot first saw her, Ussher was apparently in the act of raising her bodily from the side of the road, not by the hand, or by the arm, but by the body, so that Macdermot at first thought that the man he saw was dragging some inanimate object; it was only when Ussher spoke that he recognised him or his sister.''

"That is young Macdermot's own version?''

"And the true one I'm sure," replied father John.

"I dare say . . . I dare say . . . but then you know a prisoner can prove nothing for himself; if we could get that proved . . . if we could merely get it proved that the girl was fainting, or insensible at the moment, I think we could justify the deed, and bring him off still.''

"There is no one but his sister Feemy could prove it, but as certain as I stand here so it was.''

"She must prove it, sir . . . she must prove it. Good God, do you mean to tell me, with her brother's life at stake, that she'll hesitate, and that, when the original fault was all her own. If he is hung . . . and he will be unless she saves him . . . his death will be at her door; tell her this; if it is necessary, tell her that the world will say so . . . tell her that she must come into court and tell the truth.''

"Indeed I will; all that persuasion . . . all that commands can do, shall be done; but I fear at the moment she'll fail you, should she faint in the court . . . that's what will happen.''

"I'd not mind that; we'd wait if it was from day to day, till the judges left the court, though she fainted fifty times, if we could at last or at first but get it from her on her oath that she had refused to go with the man, or had hesitated, or that violence was used to her, or that she had fainted, no jury could convict him; but if they are left to suppose that Ussher and the girl were going quietly together down the avenue, and that Macdermot, whom they will presume to have been there designedly, in this state of things knocked the man down with a bludgeon, and when down, despatched him with the same instrument; there is not a jury in Ireland but would find him guilty.''

"But Mr. O'Malley, it is evident that he was not there designedly, and that he had no previous knowledge that Ussher was expected to be in the avenue at the time?''

"How is it evident? If it is really evident, it can be proved in evidence.''

"He had gone out to look at the horses, and on returning to the house heard the sound of gig wheels; he merely then remained before the house smoking till he heard the wheels stop at the end of the avenue.''

"Mere assertion, Mr. Magrath; very good between man and man, but mere breath in a court of law, less even than that, for it would be idle breath, and when a counsel has recourse to idle stories, it's all up with his client.''

"But surely the *onus probandi** should be with the other side; they should prove that he was there by design . . . not we that he was not.''

"Sure enough if they had to prove the deed; but that is already done to their hands; if the deed were one which is usually or not uncommonly a justifiable one, then they should prove that circumstances rendered it in this instance unjustifiable; but in such an act as causing death, and that by a violent attack, the presumption is, that the deed is unjustifiable, and it is then for the actor to prove that in his peculiar case circumstances existed, which render his case different from others of the kind; for instance, were I to brain you in this room with the poker, if I could prove that at the time I did so, you were strangling my child, I should be justified; but if I could not prove it, of course I should be held as a murderer. It would not be for the crown solicitor prosecuting me to prove that you were not strangling the child. If I made up the story that you were doing so, it would be for him or his counsel to shew that I had not brought reasonable evidence to convince the jury that you were committing such an act. This may be a stronger case than ours at present, but the reasoning is the same; our client has killed this man by, as it appears, two violent blows on the head; it also appears that he struck an unresisting man who was not conscious of his presence; this, unaccompanied by other circumstances, would be murder; we ought now to endeavour to find, and moreover to prove, that circumstances do exist, which give the affair another complexion. If we could shew that he was in the avenue by accident only, it would prove that he could not have premeditated the deed; but this I take it we cannot do. It seems that at any rate his sister had told a servant that she meant to elope, and that Ussher had told a friend of his that he was going to take the girl off; both these facts will come out at the trial, and it will therefore be difficult to convince a jury that the young man could not have heard of their plan. We cannot, therefore, prove what seems to you to be so very evident; we must rest on the fact that Ussher was violently carrying off a fainting girl, and the girl must prove—must be made to prove—that she was either insensible, or that she was being dragged away by violence— that is," he added, "if the fact be so—and it must be your business to prepare her to come into court with a determination to save her brother's life—if she can do so by swearing to the truth."

"But if she should die—suppose she were to die before the trial came on, must her brother therefore be found guilty and be hung?"

"Her evidence might be taken in the shape of an attested information, if she were thought to be in imminent danger; but such a document would only be admitted in evidence in case of her death, or on the sworn certificate of a medical man that it would be impracticable to bring her into court."

"Would it not be best, in any event to get her evidence in that way. I am sure she would break down under a cross-examination."

"Never mind the cross-examination, if she doesn't break down under the direct; the more confusion she shews as to the event, the more likely will a jury be to be convinced that she was insensible at the time. If I can once get her to say that she had fainted before the blow was given—that she was insensible when her brother came up, I can make enough of that I think, to acquit him. No, she had better, if possible, come into court. The Judge will be very unwilling to admit the evidence of such a witness, except coming from her own mouth; you must bring her into court, Mr. Magrath, if you wish to save your friend's life.''

"With God's blessing—I will do what I am able; but I fear she will be difficult to manage; she is thinking more of her lover that is dead, than her brother that has so deeply perilled himself to save her from dishonour.''

"If that is the case—if it's ill-will towards her brother that you're afraid of, she shall come into court, and the truth shall be dragged from her, though she fainted fifty times; make her thoroughly understand that if she hopes to be treated with lenity, she must give her evidence cheerfully, or at any rate firmly. Talking of that, my examination of her will be the cross-examination; you may be sure the other side will bring her forward to prove that she had left the house for the purpose of eloping; now can you tell me, Mr. Magrath, whether Ussher had made any arrangements for his marriage with Miss Macdermot, or whether it was expected in the country that he intended to marry her? my reason for asking is this, that the case will seem strong against our client if his sister were on the point of marrying, whereas if he were carrying her off without any such intention, the jury will be more apt to look on the act as one done in the justifiable protection of the sister. As far as the real guilt or innocence goes, Ussher's intention can make no difference, but nevertheless if I could say without probability of contradiction that there was no intention of marriage, the Jury, who will all have sisters or daughters, will listen to what I say, and though the Judge will expose the fallacy of the argument, it will still have its weight with them.''

"As God is my judge I believe he had no thought of ever marrying her; they say he told his friend Mr. Brown as much.''

"Which Mr. Brown?"

"Mr. Fred. Brown. It was he who lent him the gig to carry Feemy off."

"Very well, then I'll know what to say to Mr. Fred. when I see him. Is he a witness, I wonder, on the other side—I suppose he is, for they'll want to prove that Ussher had talked about the elopement, and it appears he told him—at any rate we'll summon him, he'll prove that there was no intention of marriage—this will be clap-trap—but I fear this is a case in which we must use clap-trap. Now I've one more question to ask, and then I've done: you said some time since that Macdermot's life was to be sworn away by villains and perjurers. It was too strong an expression to be used anywhere, except among friends; but, nevertheless, though your energy and benevolent feelings towards your parishioner may make you look on things with coloured eyes, I still fear that there may be some ground for the charge; what is the interest or what the vindictive feelings which will adduce false evidence against our client? and what false evidence will they bring up? Just give me the *carte du pays*,* Mr. Magrath, that I may know how to shape my questions in court; who is Mr. Macdermot's enemy?"

"The attorney in Carrick, Mr. Keegan."

"What Hyacinth Keegan, as big a schemer as ever stood upright in Connaught, which he never did, for he never did anything upright yet. But tell me what's the quarrel between them?"

Father John then described the exact relation in which Mr. Keegan stood to the Ballycloran property, that whilst taking temporary possession of that property he had been mutilated, and that attributing his misfortune to the Macdermots' influence on the property, he had been using every effort to secure Thady's conviction. He also explained that Pat Brady had been Thady's confidential servant, and that it was he who had lured him on to talk of Ussher and Keegan, and had prompted him to join Reynolds and the others with the prospect of avenging himself upon them by the aid of these men; that this Pat Brady was now Keegan's servant, and that he was the witness who was to prove that his former master had been at one of the illegal meetings at Mrs. Meehan's, and had there and at other times uttered, or at any rate listened to, threats against Ussher.

"Then this Brady," said Mr. O'Malley, "is himself a ribbonman or a terryalt, or a white-boy,* or a boy of some denomination, he must be a member of these secret societies."

"Oh, there is no doubt on earth of that."

"Well, I think I'll make something of him, and Mr. Keegan too; of course we must summon him, as he will not probably be wanted on the other side. I think I understand the general bearings of the case now; any other particulars I want, the attorney will ferret out for me on the spot; at any rate, Mr. Magrath, you may be sure we will do our best, and I trust in God we may bring him through. I perfectly agree with you, that he contemplated no murder; in fact, that he is not a murderer."

"Indeed he is not; if there is a man with a kind heart in County Leitrim it is Thady Macdermot; great sorrows, and almost unendurable calamities at last drove him into one folly; he immediately repented of it; if he is to fall a victim for that, he will indeed be to be pitied."

"I trust he will not—I trust he will not—if at the last we find every thing else fails us, we must go back to what you said at first; if we cannot justify the deed—we must not exactly justify the accident which led to the deed—but attribute the deed to accident; we might at any rate bring it to manslaughter, and it would then depend on the judge to name the punishment. Let me see, the circuit goes to Roscommon first. It will come on before Baron Hamilton— a bad judge for a cause like this—a stern, cold man—there's no reaching his feelings—but as clear-headed as Solon, and as just as Aristides."*

"It distresses me much, Mr. O'Malley, to see you think so badly of it; I see you think it will go very hard with him— you have no hopes."

"Don't say so, for indeed I have; it isn't the judge but the jury that we've to look at; we must have no Tories on the jury—they'd think the death of a revenue officer high treason at least—we'll have twenty objections you know

without cause—and as many as we please with—it'll be a
great thing to get a favourable jury—and don't say that I'm
without hope; you know a doctor always makes the worse of
a patient's disease, to magnify his own skill in the case—you
may be sure we lawyers do the same. But in truth I've strong
hope; but at the same time I wouldn't have you or the young
man's friends in general to be too confident, for though I
have hope of success; I cannot but feel that there is great
danger of failure.''

"One word more, Mr. O'Malley, and I'll not take up
more of your valuable time. If my friend should be convicted, and condemned, would there be any chance in an
appeal to the lord-lieutenant?''*

"Of that, in the ordinary course of things, you must be
as good a judge as myself—but I should say there would be
none—the country is in so deplorable a state—and the
offences in it during the last few months have been of so
black a die, that, although it is known that his lordship is
inclined to the side of mercy, where he dares to exercise it,
I fear that were young Macdermot condemned, he would be
obliged to let the law take its course. The public press would
be so against him, and the opposition would make such a
handle of it on the other side of the water,* that I don't think
at present he could venture to respite a criminal, whose conviction was obtained on such evidences as that which we
brought forward in the present case; you see the state of the
country is entirely attributed to those secret societies—and
the strongest point against Macdermot is that he, in the position of a landlord, had joined them. No, we must get a verdict, if possible, and not a pardon; and now good morning,
Mr. Magrath; of course you are aware we shall want you at
the trial as to character and all that? but you'll receive a
summons in regular course. Good bye, till the trial, and my
last words to you are, do not be too sanguine; but yet do not
despair.''

Mr. O'Malley intended his last words to be words of comfort; but they were not confident enough to do away with the
impression which the whole of the conversation had made on
the priest's mind; that Thady's danger was much more

imminent than he had thought it to be. Although father John had been anxious in the extreme before, it was the anxiety of excitement which he had felt; till he had entered the lawyer's house he had in fact felt confident of Thady's acquittal; he now not only doubted it, but all but despaired of it.

Mr. O'Malley had shewn him so many things which had not struck him in the same light before, and which seemed to shew too plainly that there was hardly ground for hope.

He walked about Dublin till it was dinner-time endeavouring to rally his own spirits—but it was in vain—and when he returned to Capel-street he was unable to join the children's play, or to converse in his usual manner with his brother or sister-in-law. He had promised to remain at any rate the next day with them—which he did; but he was as melancholy and unreasonable as he had been on the previous evening; at length, after dinner on the Thursday, his brother began to upbraid him.

"Why, John," said he, "this Macdermot is nothing to you; and though, if he's innocent, as you say, it's all very well you're trying to get him off, and all that; it ain't no great compliment to your own flesh and blood, whom you didn't see for so long, thinking so little of them, and so much of him as is, as I say, nothing to you. I wonder if I was going to be hanged, whether you'd take on so for me?"

"Ah, Tom," answered his brother, "you've your wife—you've your children—I have no nearer ties round my hearth, and in my home, than those of my flock, and of them all he is the dearest to me. His miseries have made him dear to me, his sorrows have made him as my son to me; do not begrudge me my love for him, or the tears I must shed at a fate so horrid and undeserved as that which awaits him."

On the next day, Friday, father John returned home by the same coach; but he saw no one that evening, to whom he could communicate his bad news.

CHAPTER XII

IT now only remains for the narrative of this sad story to tell in as few words as he can the fate of one or two of the principal actors, whose names have become familiar to the reader, as connected with the fortunes of the Macdermots of Ballycloran.

Larry was the only surviving member of the family, and at the time of his son's death was still the holder, and nominal possessor of Ballycloran. He was however then, and always afterwards a confirmed idiot. By some legal process he was formally declared to be so, and as such was removed from his house, though to the last he maintained his determination not to quit it, and when the men employed, had made their way through the kitchen into the hall, he barricaded the door of his room against them, and they were obliged to knock it off the hinges before they could get in. Keegan foreclosed on the property but he was unable to get possession of it, as he expected to have done. Counsellor Webb and Mr. McKeon put the affairs into proper hands, and the Chancellor appointed trustees for the property whose duty it was to guard the interests of the lunatic—after much litigation the estate was sold, but Keegan was not the purchaser. He still merely received a portion of the interest of the debt, out of which he had to pay sundry very heavy legal costs. The property was bought by an opulent land-holder—member for one of the adjoining counties—but the title is not even made good, and therefore, though he receives the rents, and has paid the purchase money into court, that purchase money cannot be appropriated to the payment of the debts; but has been invested in the funds, and Keegan receives the interest.

This being the case the new proprietor can neither pull down nor repair the house, and it therefore stands in the state, which I have endeavoured to describe at the commencement of my tale, a sad monument to the memory of the Macdermot family.

Father John never forgot his promise to Thady respecting his father. A home had to be found for the old man when he was removed from Ballycloran, and as from habit he had become somewhat more obedient to Mary MacGovery than any one else; he was taken to her husband's house for a while—and he has continued with them ever since. Father John undertook to pay such a small weekly stipend as would enable them to keep him in health and tolerable comfort—and in this he has been aided by many—but chiefly by Tony McKeon, who had he been allowed to do so, would have taken the whole expenses on himself. Larry is still alive—he may be seen of a warm summer day basking in the sun before MacGovery's forge, and in the winter, he will seat himself on the raised hearth, close to the smithy fire and remain there till it is extinguished—warmth and whiskey seem to be his only remaining comforts—the latter he will steal as a child will fruit, if it is left anywhere within his reach. Mr. McKeon takes care that he shall always have as much as may be really serviceable to him—and as MacGovery and Mary have both gone with the prevalent fashion in Ireland, and taken the pledge,* he gets the whole of what his kind neighbours intend for him. He often asks after Feemy and Ussher, wondering when they will come back, and seeming to expect that he is only waiting for their return to take possession of Ballycloran again—Thady's name he never mentions. He has by some means or other been made to understand that he must not speak ill of him—and he now never alludes to him.

Mary and her husband still live at Drumsna. When it became a settled thing that Larry was to be a lodger with them, Denis took a somewhat more fitting abode—and he now prospers as a skilful man in his trade. Industry and frugality were always his virtues, and he has now added to them that of being a careful, though perhaps not a tender husband.

Mary has not been blessed with the family, for whose sake, as she told Feemy, she was chiefly induced to commit matrimony—she is childless—and she is therefore enabled to lavish on poor Larry, the care which otherwise would have been bestowed on her own offspring—she still shakes him, and bawls to him, as though deafness were his malady—but he is used to that, and in other respects she is kind to him—were the truth known it is probable that the last years have been the least painful of Larry's life since he came to man's estate.

Tony and his wife go on as they always did, kindly together, and kindly with the world. Liddy and Louy are both married, and somewhat too well married for Mary Cassedy's peace of mind—for some three or four years since it became known that Tony had three thousand for each of them—ready cash—and after that they were not long hanging on his hands. Louy married Bob Gayner, who undertook as one of the marriage articles to give up steeple chase riding—I grieve to say that he has not strictly kept the compact.

Tony still drinks more punch than any man in the barony, and is open to a challenge for any article he possesses, these are his failings, and he does not try to hide them—he still works hard at his various vocations; and not unfrequently owns the winning horse at some neighbouring race. Playful has been gathered to his high bred sires; but not without leaving sundry offspring strongly impregnated with his virtues and vices.

The Browns, of Brown Hall, are as unpopular and useless as ever; Jonas by the aid of diaculum was soon enabled to resume his seat on the bench; Fred still waits impatiently for his father's death; George still rides boldly—but badly; some singular accident, or series of accidents, has preserved his life; but he is dreadfully in debt, and has taken to hard drinking; and it is not often that he has a horse to mount.

Counsellor Webb still flourishes like a green bay tree. He and Jonas were partially reconciled, and can therefore again quarrel amicably at the petty sessions respecting every case that comes before them. Webb is one of the contributors to Larry's support, and is still the object of McKeon's idolatry.

Major Longsword is now a Colonel; it is to be hoped that the owner of Kickie Wickie is a Captain, but on this head I can say nothing certain.

Of Joe Reynolds' present state I am not informed. He was tried some time since for administering illegal oaths,* but he was acquitted; he was since tried for murder and escaped;

he has, there is too much reason to believe, spent the greater portion of his time in gaol; were I bound to find his whereabouts at present, I fear I should have to search for him in Botany Bay.* Wherever Joe Reynolds is, there also is Corney Dolan.

And now I must say a word or two of Keegan and Brady. For a long time Keegan determined to stand against the hatred of his neighbours, to endure the odium of public opinion, but he was beaten at last; he was unable, as has been told, to obtain possession of Ballycloran, he lost his agencies, he lost his custom—he gradually lost everything but his wife; and after remaining three years in Carrick— three years fatal to his prosperity—during which the death of Flannelly was his only hope, he was forced to leave the town, and he vanished no man knoweth whither.

Flannelly is now dead; and it is to be feared that his hateful son-in-law still has more of this world's comforts than should fall to his lot. Those in Carrick who now ever allude to him and his deserts, look forward to the next world for the punishment, which no one has sufficient charity to wish he may escape.

After Thady's death, Brady soon quarrelled with his master. Whether Pat really lamented what he had done, and found, when it was too late, that he had something in his hard heart like affection for his old master, or whether he found from the aspect of Keegan's affairs that that man was no longer likely to be a profitable master to him, I cannot say, but soon after the execution he began to show manifest disrespect to the attorney, and it was not long before they finally quarrelled and parted.

Some time after that, Pat was seen in County Sligo. He contrived to get into the pay of one of the revenue police there; and also to learn where the stills were at work. For a couple of years he carried on his trade as a successful spy; but at the end of that time he was detected, and at last murdered in the cabin in which he lodged, half-way between Tubbercurry and Aclare. Two men were tried for his murder—and they were evidently the guilty men; they were condemned and sentenced; but a point of law was raised, and they escaped. Joe Reynolds was one of the men.

Father John alone remains. For a considerable time after the execution of the young friend he loved so well, he was too ill to take any part in the duties of his parish. A low, nervous fever came on him, during which the McKeons wouldn't allow him to leave their house. She nursed him through his illness with as much tenderness as if he had belonged to her—and so he did, for he was her friend, her guide, and her priest. During this time Cullen manfully struggled through the hard duties of the parish—usually grumbling, and always working; when father John recovered, he still felt unequal to the duties of the parish where he had suffered so much, and he applied to the bishop for permission again to travel for the purpose of raising money by preaching for the building of chapels in Ireland; this he did for some years most successfully both in France, Italy, and America, during which time another curate was appointed to assist Cullen; he is now again in Ireland, and is one of the most popular preachers at the crowded chapels in Dublin . . . but neither when in Dublin, or whilst he was abroad, did he forget his promise, or neglect the old man who was confided to his charge; his income is now more than sufficient for his wants; but not even when he was poor—and he was very very poor for some time after Thady's death—would he allow any one to contribute more than himself towards the stipend which McGovery received.

He now has a comfortable residence in Dublin—sufficiently stocked with crockery and with glasses—nor are handsome shelves for his numerous books wanting. The comfort of the whole house shews that a woman's hand has been there—a nephew and a niece—children of his brother the butter merchant live with him, and though he is a welcome guest in many a handsome house, though he is valued by the learned, and courted by the elegant, he is often to be found in the little back parlour in Capel Street, scrambling and romping with the children of every age, and though his brother has been married now twenty years there is always a new baby to play with.

He rarely mentions Thady's name; but sometimes as he sits over his own fire of a winter evening with one single friend, he will do so, and when once he begins, no other subject will be mentioned that night—he has utterly forgotten all his faults, and all his follies—he speaks of him as a martyr to the villainy of his enemies—as a man whose life and death were such as could only inspire love and pity; but as one who to a certainty would receive in the glories of heaven full compensation for the miseries of his human existence.

Once a year he spends a week with Mr. McKeon, when he personally inspects the comforts of his old pensioner, and charges Mary to make him as comfortable as she can— and every one in Drumsna looks forward to that week. It must be no slight pleasure to such a heart as his to see the true delight with which all his old parishioners come to see him. He was always a man loved—rarely feared—never despised—and thoroughly respected, and he is now rewarded for the exercise of those qualities which gained him such a character.

My story is finished, and I fear it will be thought to be too sad a history; but fearful as it is, I do but—

'Tell the tale as 'twas told to me.'

THE END

EXPLANATORY NOTES

IE: Irish- or Hiberno-English; Ir.: Irish.

1 *Drumsna . . . mail coach road*: Drumsna (Ir. *Droim na Snamh*, the ridge at the pool), is on the east bank of the Shannon, which separates Leitrim from Roscommon. Population (1841): 516. Connaught is roughly the western quarter of Ireland. Trollope gives distances in Irish miles; 1 Irish mile = 1¼ statutory English miles. A mail-coach road was a highway maintained for passenger coaches carrying the royal mails.

2 *Sir G— K—*: Sir Gilbert King (1812–95), third baronet, of Charlestown, County Roscommon, just across the Shannon from Drumsna.

agremens: *les agrémens*, agreeable features.

turf . . . double kishes: turf is compressed vegetation, dug from bogs, dried, and used for fuel. A kish (Ir. *cis*) is a wicker basket.

6 *rints . . . two pounds tin*: £2 10 shillings seems a bit high; Tocqueville reports £1 an acre as average around Galway in 1835. Alexis de Tocqueville, *Journeys to England and Ireland*, tr. George Lawrence and K. P. Mayer (New Haven: Yale UP, 1958), 176.

praties: potatoes (Ir. *práta*, plural *prátaí*).

Carrick: Carrick-on-Shannon, the county town of County Leitrim.

7 *Mr. Hartley's servants*: the firm of Bourne and Hartley built and operated mail coaches under government contract. They were bought out by Charles Bianconi (1785–1875), Trollope's friend, in the mid-forties.

McC—, the guard: McCluskie, a Bianconi guard, was famous for his wit and general knowledge. Travelling with him, Trollope once praised the virtues of donkeys; 'Ah well, sir, a fellow feeling makes us wondrous kind', McCluskie replied. McCluskie was not on the Boyle coach, but worked out of Clonmel; Trollope probably rode with him often after moving there in March 1845.

Milesian: the Irish are traditionally descended from the sons of Mil or Milesius, a legendary King of Spain.

king somebody: The Macdermots claim descent from a seventh-century King of Connaught. As Princes or Kings of Moylurgh (Ir. *Moy luig*), they ruled parts of Sligo, Mayo, and Roscommon from about AD 1000 until the Cromwellian confiscations.

8 *no legal will*: under the Penal Laws (1704), a Catholic land-owner could not dispose of property by will, nor would it automatically pass to his eldest son; instead it was divided among all his sons on his death. Catholics could not purchase land, only lease it for a maximum of 31 years. These laws were abrogated in 1778.

long bills: loans for which the principal need not be repaid for a long period, provided the interest is paid.

9 *thirty shillings an acre*: £1 10s. an acre. Note the rental increase between the time of the story and the narrator's visit to Ballycloran (6); Trollope knew that the new purchasers of 'Encumbered' (with debts) Estates were more ruthlessly determined to profit than the old gentry.

potheen: (Ir. *poitín*) illicitly distilled whiskey.

Longford: the county town of County Longford, on the main Sligo–Dublin road.

writs: warrants to arrest for debt.

10 *Mohill*: a village about 6 (statutory) miles east of Drumsna. In 1841 the village population was 1,626, the civil parish of Mohill 17,918.

head driver and ejector: Thady himself seized the pigs or cattle of tenants in arrears, and carried out evictions.

11 *dhudheen*: (Ir. *dúidín*), a short-stemmed clay pipe.

12 *summer of 183–*: 1837 or earlier, since Thady is tried in the King's name at the April assizes. Victoria succeeded William IV in June 1837.

stirabout: (IE) porridge made by stirring oatmeal into boiling milk or water.

bad cess: (IE) bad luck, from 'cess', a tax or assessment.

13 *"Mysterious Assassin"*: there is no such Gothic novel, but Trollope may be remembering Isaac Crookenden's *The Mysterious Murderer, or, the Usurper of Naples, to which is prefaced The Nocturnal Assassin, or Spanish Jealousy* (London: 1806).

what he can do: what he can seize in lieu of rent.

cozened: tricked, beguiled.

crayturs: creatures; the term is often used for an untrustworthy or unpredictable person or animal.

14 *incubus*: an evil spirit that takes possession of someone, an oppressive nightmare.

17 *fair*: a regularly scheduled gathering of buyers and sellers at a specific place. There were fourteen fairs at Mohill each year, among them one on the second Thursday in September and one on 19 October. Since this conversation takes place on Wednesday, 15 October, Trollope has made a rare slip.

boys in it: Thady is asking if his tenants were actively buying or selling.

18 *gale*: rent-day.

gammoning: pretending, stalling.

car: a carriage, Mr. Tierney's device to establish his gentility.

hay all saved . . . bottoms: the hay has been cut and gathered into cocks or bundles, thus saving it from possible rain. Bottoms are low-lying meadows.

19 *Drumleesh*: (Ir. *Druim lis*, the ridge of the fort). There is no such place near Drumsna, but Trollope may have remembered Drumlease, in North Leitrim, or Drumlish, a village in County Longford, on the Mohill-Edgeworthstown road.

Hibernice: Latin: the Irish term for ——.

20 *will out of that*: will go out, will be evicted.

21 *recates*: receipts.

ceade mille faltha: Ir. *céad míle fáilte*, a hundred thousand welcomes.

22 *blagguards*: blackguards, rascals.

Ballinamore Bridewell: Ballinamore is north-east of Mohill on the road to Enniskillen. Population (1841): 946. A bridewell was a jail for those convicted of minor offences, or those being held for trial.

23 *peelers*: policemen, so called after Sir Robert Peel, who established an Irish constabulary in 1814.

hole him: stab or shoot him.

thrawneen: a wisp of straw or grass (Ir. *tráithnín*).

Master Myles: Ussher.

gauger: a revenue officer. They were responsible for gauging or measuring the capacity of a cask or barrel.

24 *a black Protestant*: (IE) here *black* is an intensive, implying bigotry against Catholics, and probably a Protestant from the north-eastern counties of Ireland; Ussher is in fact from Co. Antrim.

27 *Father Mathew's pledge*: in 1838, Father [Theobald] Mathew, a Capuchin, organized a total abstinence association in Ireland, inducing thousands to 'take the pledge' that they would abstain from alcohol.

29 *Patsy*: a diminutive of Patrick.

30 *Cashcarrigan*: Keshcarrigan, a village on Lough Scur, north of Drumsna on the Carrick–Ballinamore road.

32 *Dat*: that.

spalpeen: a seasonal labourer, hence a rude person, a rascal (Ir. *spailpín*).

33 *Cash*: Cashcarrigan.

Ochone, ochone: Alas! woe is me! (Ir. *ochón*).

36 *gossoon*: a boy (Ir. *garsún*, from French *garçon*).

town-land: (IE) a subdivision of a parish, the smallest Irish unit of territory short of the individual farm. The term literally translates Ir. *baile fearainn*, home land, stead land, but *baile* also means town or settlement.

37 *Ribbonism*: in the early nineteenth century, a secret society made up of tenant farmers and landless labourers. There were usually oaths, passwords, and signs by which members could identify one another. Though allegedly part of a national conspiracy against English rule, Ribbonmen were in fact independent local groups, sometimes struggling against unjust landlords, as often organized for extortion, illicit distilling, or private revenge. Ir. *Ribíneach* (Ribbonmen), either from wearing a ribbon (*ribín*) or perhaps from *ribíní*, rags, tatters.

40 *demesne*: land immediately surrounding a landlord's house, which he farmed himself or used as a pleasure ground.

chapel: the term *church* was legally reserved for places of worship belonging to the Established (Protestant) Church of Ireland; Catholic places of worship were called chapels.

St. Omer: under the Penal Laws, seminaries or colleges for the training of Catholic priests were not permitted in Ireland.

Irish candidates for the priesthood studied in France or Spain, many of them at the college of St Omer, in north-east France near the Belgian border. The French Revolutionary government closed the college in 1793. See Maynooth (44).

curé: French: a parish priest.

43 *cob*: a thickset short-legged horse.

St. Chrysostom . . . Charles O'Malleys: St John Chrysostom (*c*.345–407), theologian and scriptural commentator, is one of the Fathers of the Church. Charles Dickens's *Nicholas Nickleby* appeared serially in 1838–9, and in three volumes in 1839. Charles Lever's *Charles O'Malley, the Irish Dragoon* was a serial in the *Dublin University Magazine* (1840–1) and a book in 1841. Father John was privileged indeed to own both novels by 1837.

44 *Maynooth*: after the Revolution closed seminaries in France, the Irish Parliament, persuaded that priests would oppose revolutionary ideas, established (1795) a seminary at Maynooth in County Kildare. Maynooth is still the chief seminary in Ireland. Because it was more accessible, Maynooth attracted farmers' and merchants' sons to what had often formerly been a gentleman's profession.

Catholic Emancipation: the most important remaining civil disabilities were removed from Catholics in 1829, after agitation skilfully led by Daniel O'Connell (1775–1847), the 'Liberator'.

Repeal of the Union: the Irish Parliament voted its own extinction in 1800, and by the Act of Union merged or united with the British Parliament in London, where Irish members would be a permanent minority. In 1840 O'Connell began a campaign for Repeal of the Union and re-establishment of an Irish Parliament in Dublin.

52 *scrimmage*: a noisy, confused struggle.

53 *sorrow a foot*: an emphatic (not a single foot will I stir to invite Ginty!; Ir. *shoraidh*, a mild expletive on the order of *drat it! darn it!*).

shake her feet: dance.

the stuff: whiskey.

By dad . . . on the point: like *Begad* and *Egad*, *By dad* is a euphemism for *By God*. Irish families too poor to eat salt or meat were said to point their potatoes at these things and imagine the added taste. Compare Winston Churchill's belief that the mixer of martinis ought only to glance at the vermouth bottle while mixing.

54 *two thirties*: two thirty-shilling notes, or £3.

56 *quizzing*: teasing or ridiculing.

half-crown: two shillings and sixpence, the sum Ussher would probably contribute.

57 *she's no mother*: she has no mother.

59 *Whisht . . . whisht!*: hush, be silent! (Ir. *fuist*).

62 *trash*: anything worthless.

69 *harriers*: a pack of hunting hounds, originally bred to hunt hares.

Lord Lorton's new farms: Viscount Lorton, of Rockingham House, on the Carrick–Boyle road, was a capable landlord.

70 *messages*: (IE) errands.

82 *fooling*: deceiving.

89 *gutther*: gutter, here meaning mud or filth.

meerings: usually merings or mearings; boundaries.

92 *ex pede Herculem*: (You may know) Hercules from the foot. According to Aulus Gellius (*Noctes Atticae* I.1), Pythagoras was able to calculate Hercules's height after learning that the length of the stadium at Olympia equalled the length of Hercules's foot multiplied by 600. Proverbially, therefore, one can deduce a whole from a part. Father John plays with the phrase more literally.

93 *once a week*: Blake is the dispensary or public doctor; Father John has tried to arrange weekly clinic hours at Drumsna.

95 *optat ephippia bos piger*: The lazy ox wants the horse's saddle (Horace, *Epistles* I. 14. 43). Horace observes that each creature envies another. Father John plays with the subtext: the ox could not use the saddle properly, and the girl misused the inappropriate and unfamiliar decanter.

Fumum bibere institutae: placed to drink smoke (Horace, *Odes* III. 8. 11). Horace refers to a Roman method of ageing wine by storing it in sealed jars placed in the path of furnace smoke. The priest neatly adapts the phrase both to the steam rising from the punch—a mixture of hot water and whiskey—and the odour of turf smoke that clings to good Irish whiskey.

96 *drinking parliament*: drinking licitly distilled whiskey, on which the tax has been paid.

103 *tippet*: a loose scarf-like garment covering neck and shoulders, and hanging down in front.

mangle: a machine for rolling and pressing linen and cotton clothing.

106 *laste taste*: least taste. A taste (IE) is a tiny amount of anything.

107 *Shamus na Pe'bria*: Seamus (James) the Piper (Ir. *an píobaire*), *O'Connell*: Daniel O'Connell, the subject of many patriotic songs.

109 *alanna*: my child, my dear (Ir. *a leanbh*).

110 *have their gag*: have their idle talk. Possibly a misprint for gab (Ir. *geab*, talk, chatter).

122 *cocking*: crowing, exulting, acting superior.

125 *scraughs*: scraws, strips of sod used for roofing (Ir. *scraith*). They were commonly covered with thatch, but these houses are in extreme disrepair.

128 *Lord Birmingham*: there was no such peer, but Robert Bermingham Clements, Viscount Clements (1805–39), lived near Mohill at Lough Rynn, and represented Leitrim in Parliament (1826–30, 1832–9), where he sat as a Whig. He was the son and heir of the second Earl of Leitrim (1768–1854), who owned most of Mohill. Unlike 'Lord Birmingham', Lord Clements lived in Ireland for part of each year, and actively encouraged local agriculture. He was the author of *The Present Poverty of Ireland convertible into the Means of her Improvement under a well-administered Poor Law* (London, 1838).

relieving the Poles . . . giving . . . Blacks their liberty: after an unsuccessful revolt against Russian rule (1830–1), many Polish patriots took refuge in England. The Lock Hospital treated venereal diseases. The Anti-Slavery Society was formed in London in 1823, and slavery was abolished in all areas under British rule by the Emancipation Bill of 1833.

distribution of meal: the method of feeding the poor in time of famine.

129 *grand new . . . poor-house*: in 1834 Parliament reformed the English Poor Law, establishing the poor-house or workhouse system in place of outdoor relief. These houses were economically efficient and uncomfortable, to discourage idleness (see Dickens, *Oliver Twist*, chaps. 1–4). The poor-

house system was extended to Ireland in 1838. The poor-house at Mohill opened in 1842.

shebeen: an unlicensed drinking establishment (Ir. *síbín*).

130 *Hebe*: the beautiful daughter of Jupiter and Juno; she served the wine at the gods' banquets.

131 *agra*: my love, my dear (Ir. *a ghrá*).

132 *brads*: money.

frieze: coarse woollen cloth, so commonly used for coats by the Irish poor that frieze came to mean coat.

133 *thief of the world*: devil (IE).

jawed it out: talked it out.

138 *Tear and ages!*: a euphemistic oath, by Christ's tears and agony (IE).

144 *reskey*: rescue.

shilelahs . . . pailers: shilelahs are knobbed blackthorn, oak, or willow sticks (Ir. *sail éille*, a wooden or willow stick). Pailers: Peelers, or police.

146 *Drumshambo*: a village north of Drumsna, near the south end of Lough Allen.

148 *the Curragh*: a grassy plain in County Kildare, a centre for horse-breeding and site of the race-course where the Irish Derby is run.

151 *latitats, and distraining*: latitats are writs (*latitat*, Law Latin: he lies concealed) against someone assumed to be in concealment, summoning him to appear in court. Distraining is seizing property to satisfy or secure a debt.

158 *strip their roofs*: the tenants would be evicted by removing the roofs from their cabins, making them uninhabitable.

162 *compos*: not of sound mind (Law Latin, *non compos mentis*).

164 *'list*: enlist in the army.

172 *obtain the sub-shrievalty*: become sub-sheriff of the county.

173 *informer*: spy.

176 *faix*: faith.

braich of the pace: breach of the peace.

179 *tunder and ages!*: thunder and aches or agonies; cf. tear and ages (138).

right side of the door: Larry cannot be arrested unless he goes out-side his house.

180 *resavers*: receivers, who will collect the Ballycloran rents for Flannelly.

sthrick: struck. Trollope should have written sthruck.

thick with him . . . inimy: close to, friendly with (IE) . . . their enemy.

183 *axing*: asking.

walked him off: saw him off the premises.

184 *taken*: arrested for debt.

185 *rapparees*: outlaws (probably from Ir. *ropaire*, a robber).

195 *salute nostrâ . . . kiss the bride*: by or through our salvation. According to custom, all male guests, and sometimes the priest, struggled to be the first to kiss the bride at the conclu-sion of the service. See William Carleton, 'Shane Fadh's Wed-ding', in *Traits and Stories of the Irish Peasantry* (1830). I have not been able to find the Latin phrase in any printed text of the marriage ritual.

shiners: coins.

avick: my son, my boy (Ir. *a mhac* or *a mhic*).

200 *Go on . . . do be saying*: to go on is to tease or make fun; the *do be* construction follows Irish syntax and implies a frequent or habitual action.

201 *copper harp*: the Irish penny had a harp on the reverse.

203 *folly on*: follow on, that is, keep the joke going (IE).

210 *"Paddy Carey"*: a traditional march, No. 1820 in Francis O'Neill, *Music of Ireland* (1903). I am indebted to Prof. Seoirse Bodley of University College, Dublin, for this citation.

before they're down: too exhausted to dance any more.

bait: beaten, worn out.

217 *intirely*; completely (IE).

218 *tithes, or county cesses*: tithes were taxes on farm produce and animals, levied and collected by the state to support the [Protestant] Church of Ireland. Catholic resentment at tithes often led to Ribbon activity, and eventually to the Tithe War (1830–8) between tenants and tithe collectors. Parliament con-verted the tithe to a charge on rent in 1838. A cess is a tax or assessment.

221 *the fiddle in the German tale*: there are several tales of magical instruments which compel those who hear them to dance. Trollope is probably thinking of No. 110, 'The Jew in the Brambles', in the Grimm brothers' *Kinder – und Hausmärchen*.

222 *'the wind that shakes the barley'*: a lively reel (O'Neill 1518). There is a well-known song of the same name, but sung to a different, slower air.

223 *asy*: easy, in the sense of easy-going.

224 *iron throttle*: an iron throat.

228 *taken the oath*: become a sworn member of the gang.

231 *foranenst her*: opposite her (IE, formerly standard English).

at all at all: repeated for emphasis (IE).

232 *slating*: quarrelling, fighting.

ruction: fight (IE, a corruption of *insurrection*).

235 *blarney*: smooth, coaxing talk.

238 *stretch you*: strike you dead.

239 *alpine*: a heavy knobbed stick (Ir. *ailpín*).

247 *baulking*: avoiding.

249 *gagging at me*: making fun of me.

251 *ears cut off*: the traditional punishment for an informer, for betraying what he had heard.

253 *underlet . . . corn-acre*: McKeon leased land, then sub-leased some of it to under-tenants. Conacre was a system by which a farmer prepared land for planting, then let it in small portions at high rent for a single season and a single crop (probably from Ir. *cion*, share, and English *acre*).

254 *a handicap . . . "knocking"*: to handicap is to calculate and bet on the odds on a horse race. Trollope explains and describes 'knocking' on page 306.

256 *lave off*: stop, cease.

257 *arrah*: look here, listen, pay attention (Ir. *aire*).

259 *at all hours*: at any time, with no regard for conventional visiting hours, implying that the Captain sometimes stays until nearly dawn.

261 *fix him*: insist that he declare his intentions towards Feemy.

274 *very mad*: very angry (IE).

275 *inisheated*: initiated.

noticed: summoned to a meeting.

276 *to Jonas Brown's . . . word agin you*: Brown is a magistrate. Some of the boys would accuse Thady of criminal conspiracy, to forestall Thady accusing them.

'peach: inform (from *impeach*).

280 *Cashel*: the county town of Tipperary.

292 *Terryalts*: another term for an agrarian secret society.

293 *death or transportation*: execution or exile to the penal settlements in Australia.

294 *know their signs*: the insignia or gestures by which they recognize one another.

298 *assize town*: the town where the circuit court met.

299 *long panel*: those summoned as eligible for jury duty.

Terpsichore: the Muse of the dance.

an ordinary: a meal served at a fixed price.

300 *crossed a horse*: sat astride.

301 *gentlemen riders*: skilled but amateur riders.

304 *petard*: an explosive device.

land of the Blakes, Burkes, and Bodkins: County Galway; the families named are among the 'Tribes' or prominent and numerous families of Galway.

garron: a small horse (Ir. *gearrán*).

308 *a hedge*: to hedge a bet is to guarantee winning by betting on one horse, then taking odds on another.

Crom-a-boo: the name means 'Crom for ever' (Ir. *abú*).

310 *the pick up*: the winnings.

311 *the Galway dogs*: probably the Galway Blazers, a pack of fox-hounds.

313 *down through the rack to be cleaning her*: because it is dangerous to enter her stall.

under his gig: harnessed to his light carriage.

334 *"Nimrod upon Horses"*: Remarks on the Condition of Hunters, the Choice of Horses, etc. (1831) by 'Nimrod', Charles James Apperley (1777–1843).

a rack rent: an excessive rent, which leaves the tenant too poor to farm properly.

strictly entailed: the elder son would inherit the entire estate.

thrush, sandcracks . . . a spavin: thrush is an inflammation of the hoof, sandcracks a disease of the hoof. Overreaches are laming injuries, caused when the point of a hind-foot shoe strikes and cuts the heel of the corresponding fore-foot. A splint is a callous tumour on a horse's leg bone, a spavin a hard bony tumour in the leg joint.

tabbies: cats; here gossiping women.

335 *squireen*: a gentleman of small rank and fortune.

Di Vernon: the beautiful, hard-riding, and learned heroine of Walter Scott's *Rob Roy* (1817). Wishing to talk with the hero, Die (Diana) invites him to assist her with ' "a difficult passage in the Divina Commédia of Dante" ' (chap. 12).

337 *the Marshalsea*: debtors' prison.

344 *musha*: Indeed! Well! (Ir. *muise, mhuise*).

be quiet: stand still (IE).

354 *Almack's*: a fashionable London ballroom (1765–1863).

tallow candles: cheaper—and smokier—than wax candles.

355 *the "Widow Machree"*: 'Machree' is not a name, but an affectionate mode of address (Ir. *mo chroí*, my dear; literally, my heart). Trollope seems to have confused the rather sentimental and lugubrious 'Mother Machree' by John Philpot Curran (1750–1817) with a much livelier song, 'Widow McGrath', in which the widow's son enlists. When he returns legless, the widow is angry, but he replies,

> 'Arrah, mother, ma'am, don't take on so,
> I got fifty pounds for every toe,
> And if I had another pair
> I'd be off to the wars and lave 'em there.'

a game at loo: a card game.

375 *sitting on the body*: a coroner's jury will sit 'on the body', that is, hear evidence as to how the deceased met death.

376 *as it's a public*: a licensed public house, obligated to admit the corpse and provide accommodation for the coroner's jury.

389 *an outside vehicle*: a carriage with no covering to protect/conceal the passengers.

390 *hack chaise*: a carriage for public hire.

399 *Irish miles*: see note, p. 1. Thady has travelled about 6¼ miles.

400 *between the hearth and the wall*: there is no chimney, only an open hearth in the middle of the floor, with a smoke hole above.

401 *skirring*: running, scurrying.

403 *barony*: a subdivision of a county, intermediary between county and parish.

404 *av*: if.

406 *Aughacashel*: a local name for Slieve Anierin, from a town-land, house, and rivulet on the mountain's southern slope.

407 *Loch Allen*: a large lake (8 miles by 3) north of Drumsna, formed by the River Shannon (Ir. *loch*, lake).

   Cash: see notes, pp. 30, 33.

411 *beneath the sod*: buried in his grave.

   aguy: ague.

   shingles: stony waste land.

412 *boreen*: a lane or path (Ir. *bóithrín*, diminutive of *bóthar*, road).

414 *cotton tick*: a cotton bag or casing containing straw or feathers, used as a pillow or mattress.

422 *lumpers*: large coarse potatoes.

424 *my lad of wax*: a weak, poor sort of fellow.

432 *gay man*: an amorous or immoral man.

439 *assizes*: sittings of the circuit court, usually held at Carrick four times each year.

443 *ould blood*: the old family.

456 *many a good man's case*: a common failing (IE).

457 *philippic*: a denunciatory speech, so called from the Greek orator Demosthenes's speeches denouncing King Philip of Macedon.

460 *barrack*: an unfinished room or building (IE).

461 *herself*: in 1847 chapters 2 and 3 of Volume III came next, followed by the present chapter 26.

468 *go out with my own son*: appear as a duellist with my own son as my second.

   on his keeping: a fugitive, in danger of arrest (IE from Ir. *ar a choimeád*, on his guard, in hiding).

his back to the sun: an advantageous position, since the sun would shine in the other duellist's eyes.

469 *stepping the ground*: pacing to measure the distance to separate the two duellists, one of the seconds' duties.

470 *men in broad cloth*: gentlemen.

472 *première jeunesse*: first youth.

475 *a blast*: a puff on his pipe.

whisper now: listen (IE); no lowering of the voice is implied.

wirrasthrue: alas! (Ir. *A Mhuire, is trua*, O Mary, it is pitiful).

476 *a dail*: a [great] deal, a lot.

480 *diaculum*: a sticking plaster containing soothing ointment (more commonly *diachylon* or *diachylum*).

482 *by Garra*: euphemism for an oath 'by God' (Ir. *Ba ghairid Dia*, a godsend).

502 *slops*: invalids' food, weak and tasteless.

506 *aestuates*: spreads out, like a river's estuary.

507 *a kind of "lucus a non lucendo" propriety*: Quintilian (*Institutiones* 1. 6. 34) suggested that *lucus*, a grove, derived from a grove's absence of light shining (*non lucendo*). The phrase became proverbial for a place or thing named for something obviously lacking: 'As by the way of innuendo / Lucus is made *non lucendo*' (Charles Churchill, *The Ghost*, II. 257).

508 *Lothario*: a seducer of women, from a character in Nicholas Rowe's *The Fair Penitent* (1703).

509 *approver*: one who proves another guilty, often a criminal who testifies against associates.

510 *Demosthenic*: denunciatory, like that of the Greek orator Demosthenes. See note to 457.

515 *willow-wearing spinster*: the willow signifies sorrow over unrequited or betrayed love. Cf. Desdemona's 'Willow' song in *Othello* IV. iii. 27–55.

516 *Bardell v. Pickwick*: in Dickens's *Pickwick Papers* (1836–7), Pickwick's landlady, Mrs Bardell, thinks he is proposing to her when he speaks of engaging a servant. Unscrupulous lawyers later persuade her to sue him for breach of promise. The court's proceedings, and Pickwick's friends' sufferings under cross-examination, are described in chapter 34.

522 *Iss*: yes (IE). Irish has no word for yes, so a question is

answered by an assertion: 'Is it raining?' 'It is.' *Iss* thus partakes of both languages.

524 *caring a flash*: a flash is a tiny portion of anything.

528 *left of the name*: left of the family.

529 *doctrine of necessity*: Democritus (fifth century BC) taught that all was of necessity predetermined.

533 *the wigged*: judges and lawyers, who wore wigs in court.

534 *is with Mr. O'Malley*: is associate counsel for the defence.

536 *recusant*: one who refuses a duty or obligation.

537 *true deliverance make*: will truly determine the question at issue.

542 *made no bones about it*: did not hesitate.

543 *his quiatis or his gruel*: his death. *Quiatis* is *quietus*, a discharge from life; *gruel* is slang for killing.

546 *shilly-shallying*: vacillating.

548 *Cavan Militia in the Rabellion . . . French at Ballinamuck*: in 1793–1816 Ireland maintained a peasant and artisan militia, organized by counties but always stationed outside their own county. In August 1798 a French force led by General Humbert landed at Killala, Co. Mayo. Many Irishmen joined it. After several victories. Humbert marched towards Dublin, passing close to Drumsna. Government forces, composed of regulars and militia, surrounded Humbert's small army near Ballinamuck, Co. Longford. The French were allowed to surrender, but their Irish allies were slaughtered.

549 *bothering me so entirely*: thoroughly annoying or confusing me (IE from Ir. *bodhar*, deaf, no longer able to hear because there has been so much talk).

cute: acute, sharp (IE).

551 *sodding him*: putting him under the sod, killing him.

558 *scollard*: an ignorant version of *scholar*.

583 *Baron Hamilton . . . his brother Kilpatrick*: Hamilton is a Baron of the Exchequer, a title reserved for certain judges. British judges refer to one another as 'my learned brother'.

The Connaught bar: the lawyers of the Connaught circuit.

587 *on the table*: on the witness stand.

591 *come from him*: the 1847 text adds another sentence here: 'Her

many griefs and inward struggles had brought on premature parturition, and she was now dying from its effects.'

604 *the Record Court*: civil, as opposed to criminal, proceedings.

612 *sacred duties*: hearing Thady's last confession and preparing him spiritually to face death.

621 *eight*: Thady's execution was at 9 a.m. in the 1847 text.

623 *Carrick-on-Shannon*: the 1847 text contained one more chapter; see volume III, chapter XII, reprinted below.

APPENDIX

CHAPTER II

626 *the gift of the gab*: the ability to speak easily and eloquently (Ir. *geab*, talk, chatter).

627 *without eating a bit*: a priest who is to say Mass must fast from the preceding midnight.

the mopusses: money.

632 *ten minutes good*: ten minutes extra.

633 *flash great coats . . . vast chokers*: showy great coats and vast cravats.

up to Trinity: to Trinity College, Dublin, then the only university in Ireland.

bottled porter: costlier than draught porter.

Frank Webber: the hero's Trinity College roommate in Lever's *Charles O'Malley*, an exuberant prankster, drinker, and gambler.

634 *Sligo traders*: traders from Sligo, county town of County Sligo, the western terminus of the coach route.

635 *since the Clare Militia went out of Castlebar*: see note to 548. This may be a sardonic reference to the 'Castlebar Races', General Humbert's rout of forces composed chiefly of militia at Castlebar, County Mayo, on 27 August 1798.

638 *Rooskey . . . Shannon Commissioners*: Parliament established a commission to improve the navigation of the Shannon in 1839; one improvement was a canal around the rapids at Roosky, County Leitrim.

692   EXPLANATORY NOTES

Newtown Forbes: site of Castle Forbes, seat of the Earls of Granard.

639 *mawkish*: weak, sickly.

642 *price of red herrings*: smoked herrings, sometimes eaten to mask the smell of alcohol on the breath.

rantipole jade: a noisy boisterous woman.

the authoress: Maria Edgeworth (1767–1849).

the Boyne so celebrated: William of Orange (William III defeated the Catholic James II at the Battle of the Boyne (1690), establishing Protestant domination of Ireland for more than a century.

643 *that word lately given*: see note to 44. In 1845, Sir Robert Peel, then Conservative Prime Minister, persuaded Parliament to guarantee Maynooth an annual grant and to raise that grant from £9,000 to £26,000. Protestant resentment at the measure almost split the Conservative Party.

Romanists: Catholics.

they are re-converting us: the Oxford Movement (1833–45), led by Edward Pusey and John Henry Newman, re-examined the Church of England's Catholic origins and elements, and was seen as subversive by many Protestants.

Carton . . . Ireland's only Duke: Carton House, seat of the Dukes of Leinster.

644 *gas-lamps of the metropolis*: Dublin's streets were illuminated with gas by the end of the 1820s.

whalebones: the ribs of the umbrella.

huge mile-stone . . . in honour of the Duke of Wellington: the Wellington Monument (1817) in Phoenix Park, a 200-foot obelisk designed by Sir Robert Smirke.

the Four Courts: the building housing Ireland's chief law courts, originally Exchequer, Common Pleas, King's Bench, and Chancery.

CHAPTER III

646 *porkmanty*: portmanteau.

649 *in a jiffey*: right away.

650 *the rhino*: the money.

651 *a holyday . . . Marlbro' Street*: a day when Catholics would be

obliged to attend Mass. Since Father John visits Dublin in March, he is perhaps there for St Patrick's Day (17 March) or the Feast of the Annunciation (25 March), both then holy days in Ireland, or for St Joseph's Day (19 March), a holy day until 1778. The Catholic pro-cathedral (1816) is in Marlborough Street.

thrown open to the gardens of Trinity: Nassau Street, beside Trinity College park, was widened and improved in 1842. The college park wall was replaced with iron railings.

pious, glorious and immortal Willy: an equestrian statue (1701) of William III (William of Orange) stood in College Green until 1929, when it was blown up. Trollope quotes part of the 'Orange' toast: 'To the glorious, pious, and immortal memory of the great and good King William, who saved us from Popery, brass money, and wooden shoes.'

the bank: the Bank of Ireland; until 1800 the building housed the Irish Parliament.

Carlisle Bridge . . . Sackville Street: Carlisle Bridge (1794) was rebuilt and renamed O'Connell Bridge in 1880; Sackville Street was renamed O'Connell Street in 1925.

652 *splendid pillar*: Nelson's Pillar (1808–9; 134 feet) commemorated Admiral Lord Nelson's victory at Trafalgar; it was blown up in 1966.

653 *frightful means . . . taken to convert her*: the Penal Laws, with their numerous penalties against Catholics.

663 *onus probandi*: the burden of proof (Law Latin).

666 *the carte du pays*: literally, a map of the country, i.e. a description of the situation.

667 *a white-boy*: like Ribbonman and Terry Alt, a member of an agrarian secret society.

Solon . . . Aristides: Athenian statesmen.

668 *an appeal to the lord-lieutenant*: the official representative of the British Crown in Ireland. He could pardon or commute sentences.

the opposition . . . on the other side of the water: the Lord Lieutenant had no fixed term, but was appointed by the party holding a majority in the British Parliament. The opposition party would rouse public opinion against any act of leniency.

CHAPTER XII

671 *taken the pledge*: Father Mathew's pledge, to abstain from alcohol. See note to 27.

672 *illegal oaths*: swearing men into a secret society.

673 *Botany Bay*: a penal settlement in Australia.